DRAGONHEART

By Todd McCaffrey

Dragonsblood

By Anne McCaffrey and Todd McCaffrey

Dragon's Kin
Dragon's Fire
Dragon Harper

For more information on Todd McCaffrey and his books, see his
website at www.toddmccaffrey.org

DRAGONHEART

TODD McCAFFREY

BANTAM PRESS

LONDON · TORONTO · SYDNEY · AUCKLAND · JOHANNESBURG

TRANSWORLD PUBLISHERS
61–63 Uxbridge Road, London W5 5SA
A Random House Group Company
www.rbooks.co.uk

First published in Great Britain
in 2008 by Bantam Press
an imprint of Transworld Publishers

A CIP catalogue record for this book
is available from the British Library.

ISBN 9780593058671

Addresses for Random House Group Ltd companies outside the UK
can be found at: www.randomhouse.co.uk
The Random House Group Ltd Reg. No. 954009

The Random House Group Limited supports The Forest Stewardship
Council (FSC), the leading international forest-certification organization.
All our titles that are printed on Greenpeace-approved FSC-certified paper
carry the FSC logo. Our paper procurement policy can be found at
www.rbooks.co.uk/environment

Typeset in 11/14 pt Palatino
Printed and bound in Great Britain by
CPI Mackays, Chatham, ME5 8TD

2 4 6 8 10 9 7 5 3 1

Mixed Sources
Product group from well-managed
forests and other controlled sources
www.fsc.org Cert no. TT-COC-2139
© 1996 Forest Stewardship Council
FSC

This book is lovingly dedicated
to Steve and Natalie.

FOR READERS NEW TO PERN

Thousands of years after man first developed interstellar travel, colonists from Earth, Tau Ceti III, and many other worlds settled upon Pern, the third planet of the star Rukbat in the Sagittarius sector.

They found Pern idyllic for their purposes: a pastoral world far off the standard trade routes and perfect for those recovering from the horrors of the Nathi Wars.

Led by hero Admiral Paul Benden and Governor Emily Boll of war-torn Tau Ceti, the colonists quickly abandoned their advanced technology in favor of a simpler life. For eight years—"Turns" as they called them on Pern—the settlers spread and multiplied on Pern's lush Southern Continent, unaware that a menace was fast approaching: the Red Star.

The Red Star was actually a wandering planetoid that had been captured by Rukbat millennia before. It had a highly elliptical, cometary orbit, passing through the fringes of the system's Oort Cloud before hurtling back inward toward the warmth of the sun, a cycle that took two hundred and fifty Turns.

For fifty of those Turns, the Red Star was visible in the night sky of Pern. Visible and deadly, for when the Red Star was close enough, as it was for those fifty long Turns, a space-traveling spore could cross the void from it to Pern. Once the spore entered the thin, tenuous upper atmosphere, it would thin out into a long, thin, streamer shape and float down to the ground below, as seemingly harmless "Threads."

Like all living things, however, Thread needed sustenance, and it ate anything organic: wood or flesh, it was all the same to Thread. The first deadly Fall of Thread caught the colonists completely unawares. They barely survived. In the aftermath they came up with a desperate plan: having abandoned their high technology, they turned to their knowledge of genetic engineering to modify fire-lizards—six-limbed, winged life-forms indigenous to Pern—into huge, rideable, fire-breathing dragons. These dragons, telepathically linked at birth to their riders, formed the mainstay of the protection of Pern. Other solutions were tried, as well, but none proved to be as effective as dragons.

The approach of the Red Star caused further difficulties in the form of violent tectonic activity throughout the Southern Continent. Overwhelmed by the sudden proliferation of volcanic eruptions and earthquakes, the colonists abandoned their original settlements in favor of the smaller, stabler, northern continent. In their haste, much was lost and much was forgotten.

Huddled in one settlement, called Fort Hold, the colonists soon found themselves overcrowded, particularly with the growing dragon population. The dragons—with their riders—moved into their own high mountain space, called Fort Weyr. As time progressed and the population spread across Pern, more Holds were formed and more Weyrs were created by the dragonriders.

Given their great losses, particularly in able-bodied older folk, the people of Fort and the other Holds soon found themselves resorting to an authoritarian system where one Lord Holder became the ultimate authority of each Hold. The Weyrs developed differently. Unable to both provide for themselves and protect the planet, the dragonriders relied upon a tithe from the Holds for their maintenance. Instead of a Lord Holder, they had a Weyrleader—the rider of whichever dragon flew the Weyr's senior queen dragon.

And so the two populations grew separate, distant, and too often intolerant of each other.

As the Red Star moved away again, Thread stopped falling. Then, after a two-hundred-Turn "Interval," it returned to rain death and destruction from the skies for another fifty-Turn "Pass." Again, Pern relied on the dragons and their riders to keep it Thread free. And, again, the Pass ended, and a second Interval began.

Twelve Turns before the start of the Third Pass, a strange plague spread across Pern, decimating the holder population.

Even now, as the Red Star heralds the return of Thread and the beginning of the Third Pass, some smaller holds still lie fallow and deserted. The farmers of Pern struggle to provide enough food for the holders and weyrfolk. Miners work long hours to make up for fewer bodies, and few young holders are sent to the Harper Hall or Healer Hall to learn the ancient crafts.

CONTENTS

DRAMATIS PERSONAE

AT FORT WEYR, AL 507
K'lior, Weyrleader, bronze Rineth
Cisca, Weyrwoman, gold Melirth
Tannaz, Weyrwoman, gold Kelsanth
H'nez, wingleader, bronze Ginirth
T'mar, wingleader, bronze Zirenth
Melanwy, aged headwoman
Xhinna, a girl of the weyr
Terin, a girl of the weyr

TRADERS
Azeez, Master Trader
Mother Karina
Tenniz

AT FORT HOLD
Bemin, Lord Holder, bronze fire-lizard, Jokester
Fiona, his daughter, gold fire lizard, Fire

AT THE WHERHOLD
Aleesa, WherMaster, gold Aleesk
Arella, Aleesa's daughter
Jaythen, wherman

AT BENDEN WEYR
M'tal, Weyrleader of Benden Weyr, bronze dragon Gaminth
Salina, Weyrwoman, gold dragon Breth
Lorana, Weyrwoman, gold Arith
Kindan, journeyman harper, bronze fire-lizard, Valla

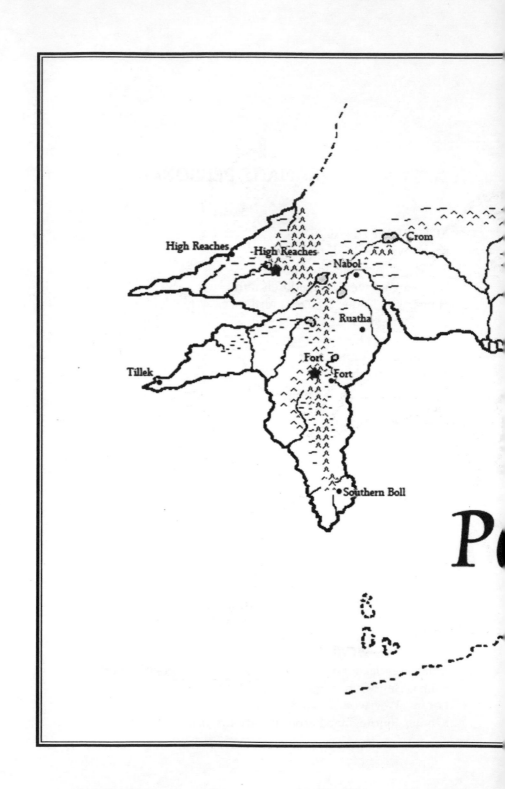

High Reaches

High Reaches

Crom

Nabol

Ruatha

Tillek

Fort

Fort

Southern Boll

P

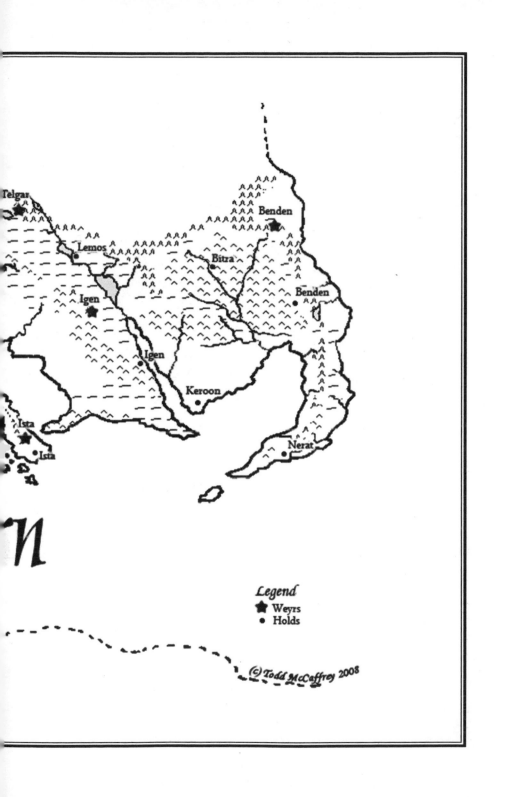

DRAGONHEART

ONE

Heart, give voice to sing
Of life on dragonwings!

Fort Weyr, AL 507.11.17, Second Interval

"... and you wouldn't believe how many holders they've saved over the last ten Turns," Benden Weyrleader M'tal said, continuing to press his case for the watch-whers.

The three remaining Weyrleaders had adjourned to Fort Weyr's Council Room to await the Hatching and confer.

C'rion of Ista Weyr snorted and shook his head. "I'm sorry, M'tal, but the time's all wrong," he said. "Threads will be falling all too soon and here you are with this radical notion of training dragons and watch-whers to fly Threads together at night."

M'tal took a slow, calming breath to stifle the hot retort he wanted to make. He looked expectantly to K'lior.

The youngest Weyrleader of Pern shifted uneasily under the gray-haired man's gaze. Well aware that M'tal had been a Weyrleader since before K'lior was born, he found it hard to refute such a length of experience. Of course, C'rion was even older still and had made *his* feelings well-known.

"Look," M'tal began again, his hands outstretched in a placating gesture, "just think—"

He broke off as his ears detected the unmistakable hum of dragons at Hatching. He smiled and gestured at K'lior. "Weyrleader?"

K'lior was already on his feet and heading for the doorway that led to the Hatching Grounds.

Kindan and Kentai, Fort Weyr's harper, were waiting on the stairs to the viewing stands in the Hatching Grounds, ready to escort the more feeble or overly-excited holders up to a good perch. Kindan nodded to M'tal as the Weyrleader passed by, still engrossed in fervent conversation with the Istan and Fort Weyrleaders.

"I see D'gan has departed," Kentai murmured to Kindan as the Weyrleaders climbed out of earshot.

Kindan shrugged. He knew that M'tal had not been counting on D'gan's support anyway. He was less pleased at the looks he'd seen on C'rion's and K'lior's faces—neither looked very thrilled with what M'tal was saying to them. Kindan, who was familiar with M'tal's plan, shook his head. Couldn't the other Weyrleaders see that watch-whers, with their night-seeing eyes, were *supposed* to fly the night Threadfalls?

"Lord Itaral, Lady Nelyssa," Kentai called as he spotted the Lord and Lady Holders of Ruatha Hold. He smiled as he spotted the third person in their party. "I see that you've convinced Lady Ilyssa to join you this time." He nodded to their young daughter and raised an elbow invitingly. "May I escort you to your seats?"

Ilyssa blushed, but, overcoming her embarrassed smile, curtsied most elegantly and took his arm.

"This is Kindan," Kentai said with a nod toward the other harper. "He's come with Lord M'tal from Benden Weyr."

Lady Nelyssa started at his name and peered at him more closely. "Aren't you the one—" She caught herself and rapidly switched her comment. "—I mean, aren't you the young man who gave up his watch-wher to Nuella, the WherMaster?"

"Among other things, I am known for that," Kindan agreed, inclining his head politely and giving her a slight smile. He knew what she'd started to say, and wondered if he would ever live down the stigma of the fire in the Harper Hall's Archive rooms. He hadn't been solely responsible, after all, and he'd fought the hardest to put the blaze out, preserving countless other Records . . .

"Kindan!"

Before he could even react to the sound of his name, the speaker pummeled into him, clutching him tightly about the waist and trying her best to squeeze the breath out of him. Brilliant sea-blue eyes looked out from behind a lock of rebellious honey-blond hair as the youngster turned her head and called back accusingly to the well-dressed Lord Holder behind her, "You didn't tell me he'd be here!"

Bemin of Fort Hold smiled indulgently at his daughter. "There are such things as surprises, Fiona," he said with a wink.

"Oh, Kindan, it's so good to see you!" Fiona exclaimed, burying her face once more in Kindan's chest.

"It's good to see you, too," Kindan replied. He held out a hand to Fort Hold's Lord Holder. The older man, face lined with age and sad memories, took it in his own and gripped it tightly.

"Good to see you again, lad," Bemin said. He looked up the stairs. "I think we'd better get up there or the dragons will all have hatched."

Fiona turned toward the steps, firmly locking her arms around Kindan's elbow. "Harper Kindan," she said, sounding every inch a Lord Holder's daughter, "would you do me the honor of escorting me?"

"It would be my pleasure, Lady Fiona," Kindan replied with equal aplomb. A bronze fire-lizard darted down from the heights, alighted for a moment on Kindan's shoulder, chirped happily to him, then rose again in the air.

Lord Bemin chuckled. "I see that Valla followed you."

"I can't keep him away from a Hatching," Kindan confessed. He craned his neck up and scanned the swarm of fire-lizards overhead. "Where are Jokester and Fire?"

"We left them behind," Bemin said. "I doubt either of them is as well-trained as yours."

"Well, they've barely two Turns out of the shell," Kindan allowed. "Give them time."

"Like all youngsters, they are impetuous and brash," Bemin agreed with a twinkle in his eyes. "Why, you would not believe where I found my daughter—"

"Father!" Fiona protested, a warm blush highlighting her freckles. Bemin laughed.

"Chasing tunnel snakes again?" Kindan asked her in a voice pitched for her ears alone.

He was not successful, as Bemin snorted, saying, "I cannot teach her any decorum at all!" He continued, "She was hours in the bath and I'm sure there's still dirt on her."

Kindan felt Fiona grab him tighter and heard her groan, but when he glanced down he saw the smile in her eyes.

"He's sounding much happier," he said quietly.

"He deserves it," Fiona replied.

Kindan nodded in agreement. Lord Holder Bemin had kept his Hold together twelve Turns before when the Plague had struck and killed nearly one in four of his Holders, including his wife and all his children, save for the youngest, Fiona.

Kindan, sent from the Harper Hall to Fort Hold in disgrace after the fire, had helped Fort's old Healer, Kilti, to do everything possible for the sick and dying. In the end, Kilti had succumbed to the Plague himself, leaving Kindan, at fourteen, in charge.

Fiona cocked her head at a change in the sound and then leapt up the steps, dragging Kindan along. "Come on, they're hatching!"

Indeed they were. Kindan, Fiona, and Bemin found seats saved for them next to Lord Itaral and his family.

"Just some greens," Ilyssa assured Fiona as she patted the empty seat she'd saved for her friend. Fiona relinquished her grip on Kindan with an apologetic look and happily took her place beside Ilyssa. The two leaned toward each other and began to speak in low voices.

The hot sands rapidly filled with white-robed candidates, flown in by Fort Weyr's bronze dragons. The rest of Fort's dragons, perched high above, hummed in welcome, the sound growing louder as the eggs began to rock and crack.

Suddenly there was a hush as the first egg cracked open. A brown dragonet flopped out, awkward and creeling. A group of candidates darted anxiously around it—some moving toward it, some away. And then—one candidate reached out to the baby dragon and Impressed. The dragons hummed approvingly.

Another dragonet burst forth from its egg, and another, and another. From the stands, it seemed as though of tide of white-robed candidates flowed and ebbed around the blue, green, brown, and bronze dragonets until, finally, one white-robed figure stood protectively beside each dragonet as the miracle of Impression was repeated.

"Look there!" Fiona called, pointing toward one of the larger eggs. "Is that a queen?"

"It could be," Kindan said. A great rent appeared in the shell, followed moments later by a golden head. "It is!"

The little queen made quick work of extricating herself from her egg while all around the bronzes crooned excitedly. Freed at last, the little gold queen walked around, looking from one candidate to another.

"What would happen if there wasn't a suitable candidate?" Fiona muttered to Kindan, who shrugged in response. The girls were trying; one bold girl just barely dodged the dragonet's awkward movements, pulled aside at the last moment by a shorter, younger, dark-haired girl.

Kentai had overheard the exchange. "There are Records," he said, looking uncomfortable.

"Well, she's coming this way," Ilyssa noted with excitement.

"We're near the exit to the Bowl," Kentai remarked. "Maybe she's looking for someone out there."

She wasn't. Still ignoring the girls clustered around her, even the bold dark-haired one that Fiona would have thought she'd like, the dragonet lurched over to the visitor stands. She looked up into the stands and creeled desperately. Kindan and Bemin exchanged alarmed looks as the little gold gazed toward Fiona. Fiona's eyes grew wide with shock and she glanced worriedly at Lord Bemin. Bemin seemed to wilt in despair—Fiona was his last surviving child—but he recovered and nodded weakly.

"What's her name?" he asked his daughter, gesturing to the gold below and forcing his lips into a smile.

The dragonet creeled again piteously and Fiona turned back to her, her face glowing in pure joy as she declared, "She says her name is Talenth!"

Kindan picked out K'lior and Cisca climbing down the stairs toward them. It was obvious from the look on her face that Cisca had taken in the full import of the event. She would handle things from here. Kindan, who, after all, was beholden to Benden not Fort Weyr, turned away for a last look at the now empty Hatching Grounds.

For a moment, a very brief moment, before the egg had proved to be a gold, Kindan had imagined what might have happened if *he* had Impressed. A chirp from above distracted him as his fire-lizard, Valla, swooped down from his perch above, pleased with himself for locating Kindan and thrilled to have seen the Hatching.

Kindan shook himself from his reverie. He had been a miner, had bonded with a watch-wher, the dragons' kin, and now he was a harper who had Impressed a fire-lizard. The Red Star was approaching, bringing the deadly Threads, and everything would change when the dragons began the fifty-Turn battle to save Pern from extinction. Vaguely Kindan wondered if he would live to see the end of the Pass and the return of the less trying times he had been born into.

The beating of a drum, the call to dinner, and a personal plea from Kentai for help in entertaining the revelers spurred Kindan up and out of the Hatching Grounds. At the entrance, he turned back once more, unable to contain his longing.

Kindan couldn't remember who waved him toward the sleeping quarters or quite how he got himself into bed. The evening had been a raucous celebration at which he had sung much, danced much, and drank much—far more than his usual. He had no idea why he'd drunk so much, nor why he'd worked so hard that evening . . . until he woke in the middle of the night in a cold sweat.

The Weyr was silent, but the silence seemed more oppressive than comforting. The sound of his labored breathing came harshly to his ears and he sat up in his cot, glancing around nervously to check if his nightmare had disturbed anyone else to whom he'd have to make a quick apology.

He heard no one.

In the distance a dragonet creeled uneasily. Then silence.

Kindan sighed and swung his legs over the side of the cot.

It wasn't as if he was the only one who had nightmares of the Plague, but he hadn't had many in the past several Turns, so he was surprised that he'd had one now. Something about the day before must have reminded him subconsciously, so that he sang so hard and drank so much to keep away the pain. Not that it had worked, obviously.

The Plague that had swept across Pern and then—just as quickly—disappeared, had struck when he had only fourteen Turns, leaving him solely in charge of Fort Hold's sick when the aged healer had himself succumbed to the disease. So many had died.

So many, including Koriana, Lord Bemin's daughter and Fiona's older sister.

"Koriana," Kindan whispered. The sound of her name brought both joy and pain, like a rose: pretty smell, prickly thorns. He shook his head. "I'm sorry."

I tried, he thought. But he wondered, as he always wondered: *Did I try hard enough?*

Resolutely, Kindan lay back in the cot and closed his eyes. Presently, his breathing eased and he relaxed, but he did not sleep. And in that space between sleeping and waking, he heard the sound of a dragon departing *between.*

Talenth's creel woke Fiona instantly.

What is it? she asked, jumping out of her bed and rushing to the young queen's lair.

He hurts, Talenth whimpered. Fiona knelt and pulled the young queen's head into her lap.

I'm sorry, she thought to her dragon, gently caressing the leathery hide.

He hurts and you feel it, Talenth said. *How is it that you feel it?*

Fiona furrowed her brow in surprise. At first she thought that Talenth was referring to her father, but then she forced herself to be honest. She had wheedled and whined her very best to convince her father to bring her to this Hatching, all because she knew that Kindan would be here.

I don't know, she confessed. *I just do. I'm sorry that it hurts you, too. Can you help him?*

Fiona bent to cradle Talenth's head with her whole body. *I'm not sure,* she said. But deep inside her, Fiona knew that was a lie. As she considered it, she heard a noise—a dragon going *between.*

*W*e've *been here long enough, let's go,* the rider thought to the dragon under her.

As you wish, the dragon responded. With a great heave of its hind legs, the dragon leapt into the air and went *between.*

TWO

*Skin stretch
Flake, peel.
Oil, scratch,
Feed, creel.*

Fort Weyr, The Next Day

"I'll be just fine, Father," Fiona assured Lord Holder Bemin as he took his leave of her the next morning. "You can send Jokester to check on me—" Catching herself, she gestured lovingly down to the gold queen beside her. "—*us*, whenever you need."

"It's just that   "

"You must get back to the Hold, Father," Fiona told him firmly. "I'll be fine—" She paused, raising her hand to stifle a yawn. "—here."

"You look exhausted," Bemin said, glancing to the Weyrleader and Weyrwoman for support.

"A late night and a stressful day," Fiona assured him, again stifling a yawn. She smiled ruefully down at Talenth. "We'll be fine."

Lord Bemin gave his daughter one final, worried look. "I'll send Jokester to check on you." The bronze fire-lizard perched on his shoulder made a cheerful noise of agreement.

"T'mar will see you back to your Hold, my Lord," Weyrwoman Cisca said, gesturing to a sturdy rider and his bronze dragon waiting nearby. She glanced at Fiona, adding, "He'll be able to guide your fire-lizard back on his return."

"Thank you," Fiona said, much relieved. She couldn't wait to see Fire's reaction to the larger gold queen.

"Wingleader," Bemin nodded absently, gesturing for the rider to precede him.

With T'mar's help, he mounted the great dragon easily enough and had time to look down once more at Fiona and her dragon. Despite another yawn, she waved merrily as the bronze leapt into the air, rose above the Weyr, and winked out *between*.

For Fiona, the next few sevendays passed in a frenzy of feeding, oiling, scratching, and tending the baby gold dragon whose only activities were eating, sleeping, and complaining.

Her fire-lizard, Fire, after hours in a state of mixed surprise, delight, and jealousy, found herself helping joyfully, often finding the itchiest spots and scratching them with her own claws.

You know, Fiona had admitted to the dragonet early on, *I'm only doing this because it's you.*

And you love me, Talenth had agreed, turning over so that Fiona could reach another offending itch. With a laugh, Fiona obliged, sweat running down her nose as she scratched the flaking skin and poured more oil on it.

As Talenth grew, the job of scratching and oiling her grew as well, until Fiona began to wonder if she'd ever done anything else. Occasionally she saw others in the Weyr. She knew she ate, but her memories of both food and sleep were truncated and foggy at best.

In fact, "foggy" was a great description of her time so far at the Weyr. She had only a foggy map of the Weyr: She had traveled only once from the Hatching Grounds into the Weyr Bowl and up the short ramp into her Weyrwoman's quarters, and had made only a few trips to the Kitchen Cavern before before figuring out how to use the Weyr's amazing conveyor system to order food for her quarters. Fiona could never remember feeling so at odds and disjointed. She envied the weyrbred riders who already knew their way around and had been more prepared for these first weeks with a new weyrling.

"She's growing well."

Fiona jerked, startled by the voice behind her. But she turned quickly enough to nod to Cisca, amazed that such a big person could move so quietly.

"That she is," Fiona agreed, giving Talenth a final pat. Fiona wasn't quite sure how to deal with Cisca. Having grown up as the only surviving child of a grieving Lord Holder, she'd never had to listen to an older woman's directions before. And the Weyrwoman was only six turns older than she was.

"Will you let me take your rider, Talenth?" Cisca asked the young gold dragon. As Talenth had curled up once more and was engaged in her favorite pastime—sleep—she made no reply. Cisca smiled at Fiona. "I think we can take that for a 'yes.' "

Fiona looked expectantly at her queen fire-lizard, but Fire glanced her way only once, then lay her head back down on her perch on the dragonet's neck and closed her eyes, clearly saying, *Go on without me.* With a smile, Cisca gestured for Fiona to follow her and led the way out of the weyr and down the corridor to her own quarters.

"I'm to teach you your duties as a Weyrwoman," Cisca said as they entered her rooms. Fiona's eyes widened as she caught sight of Melirth lounging in her weyr. Cisca caught her glance and laughed. "You think you're oiling *now*!"

Fiona's attempt to stifle a groan was noticed by Cisca, who continued sympathetically, "Really, it's not as bad as all that." She gestured to the small shapes surrounding her dragon. "The fire-lizards are an immense help . . . most of the times."

"My father has a fire-lizard," Fiona said, forgetting that Cisca had met Jokester at the Hatching.

"Maybe you can entice your father into letting him help you and your little queen," Cisca suggested, gesturing to a day table flanked by several chairs.

"No," Fiona said, shaking her head sadly, as she sat down. "With me here, Father's only got Jokester." She pursed her lips, then shook her head again. "Anyway, if Jokester came, I'm not sure he'd leave Fire alone." She met the Weyrwoman's eyes. "I think it would be best if Jokester stayed at the Hold."

"Did your father teach you much of holding?" Cisca asked, taking a chair of her own.

Fiona made a face. "That was *all* he ever talked about!"

"Well, he did you a service, then," Cisca said. "Running a Weyr is not all that different from running a hold."

The look Fiona gave her was mulish.

"You don't think so?"

"I can't imagine that you've got to spend your time sitting with old grannies while they go on and on about the good old . . ." Fiona trailed off as she noticed Cisca's expression.

"I get to listen to old dragonmen," Cisca informed her with a smile. She couldn't resist adding, "Of course, now, I've got you to help me."

Fiona turned a groan into a deep breath and let it out slowly, squaring her shoulders.

"Of course, instead of just running a hold, you've got a dragon as well," Cisca added.

Fiona thought of the sleeping Talenth and her expression softened. She nodded slowly. "Indeed, I do." She shivered in response to another thought. "And Thread is coming soon."

"Yes, it is," Cisca said. "But your Talenth will be too young to join the queen's wing for several Turns yet."

Fiona seemed not to hear her, her attention still directed inward. "I will not fail the Weyr." She sat in silence for a moment, then shook herself and looked up at Cisca. "I'm sorry, Weyrwoman, you were saying?"

"I was talking about the queen's wing," Cisca said. "There's only Tannaz and her Kalsenth now. Weyrs don't fly a queen's wing unless there are three queens."

"Oh, I'm sorry."

Cisca waved the apology aside. "There's nothing to apologize for, unless you know how to speed up time and you've been holding out on us."

Fiona shook her head.

"I thought so," Cisca said. "Now, why don't you tell me what you think a Weyrwoman's duties are, based on what you know from holding?"

"Okay," Fiona said. She thought for a moment, then continued. "A Weyrwoman is responsible for the proper running of the hold—I mean, Weyr. She has to handle the staff—" She caught Cisca's look. "Not staff?"

"Weyrfolk," Cisca supplied.

"Weyrfolk," Fiona repeated, nodding as she fixed the word in her memory. "She handles the weyrfolk in the preparation of food—" Fiona's brow furrowed. "—the food from tithe?"

"Yes," Cisca agreed. "When Thread is falling we don't have time to find food."

"Nor do we," Fiona replied tetchily. She caught herself and blushed, shaking her head. "I meant the hold. Holders."

"I'm weyrbred," Cisca responded. "I'm counting on you to remind me of what it is to be a holder."

"It's just that . . ." Fiona trailed off in embarrassment.

"Go on," Cisca said. Her tone was kind.

"It seems that dragonriders don't do that much and yet they get whatever they need, whenever they want it," Fiona said, her frank blue eyes meeting Cisca's warm brown ones. Cisca waited silently. Fiona lowered her gaze and pursed her lips. Finally, she sighed and looked up again at the Weyrwoman. "I've heard holder lads say the same thing about me."

"And is it true?"

Fiona's shoulders slumped. "I know I didn't work as hard as some of them."

"Are you lazy, then?"

Fiona's eyes flashed angrily. "I never shirked a duty, never stopped until I was told, never—oh!"

Cisca smiled at the younger girl. "Perhaps you understand being weyrfolk better than you imagined."

Fiona nodded ruefully. She started to say something but stopped abruptly, stricken.

Cisca said nothing as she too was suddenly stricken.

Outside, dragons bellowed in anguish, their voices almost drowned out by the nearer sound of Melirth's keening. Fiona could hear Talenth's anguished cry mingling with the others.

I'm here! she called to her dragon.

Talith is no more, Talenth told her sadly.

A hand covered Fiona's and she looked up as Cisca told her sadly, "That is one of the extra prices dragonriders pay."

The death of Talith and his rider J'trel left Fiona distraught for the next several days. She tried to hide it from Talenth, but the young queen was too perceptive.

What is hurting you? Talenth asked in mixed tones of confusion and protectiveness.

Talith, Fiona replied.

Who?

Never mind, Fiona assured her, her tone as bright as she could make it. *Let's get you oiled up again; you've rubbed it all off in the sand.*

Later, when Talenth was sleeping, Fiona sought out the Weyrwoman.

"You want to know why Talenth doesn't remember?" Cisca asked. She smiled. "That's one of the gifts of the dragons—their memories are short, they forget most things quickly."

"You say most things?"

"Sometimes they remember; usually the strangest things." In response to Fiona's confused look, she added, "You'll soon find out for yourself."

"How did Talith die?" Fiona asked the question she'd been dreading for days.

"J'trel was old," Cisca said. "They went *between* together."

"Do dragons die of old age?"

"No one really knows," Cisca said, shaking her head. "Usually the rider dies of old age first and the dragon goes *between*." She smiled at Fiona. "You've many Turns before that'll be a concern for you."

Fiona nodded and returned to her quarters to curl up comfortably with Talenth.

Yet it seemed that Cisca was wrong. Four days later, Fiona was startled awake in the middle of the night. Talenth was trembling in her sleep, and none of Fiona's comforting could still the hatchling, yet neither did the queen wake.

Fiona heard voices nearby and stumbled out of her quarters toward the sound. Her fire-lizard stirred on her perch atop Talenth and flitted to Fiona's shoulder. Fiona shushed her absently and strained to hear.

"Ban the fire-lizards?" K'lior was saying to Cisca.

"That's what they said," Cisca agreed. "The fire-lizards have gotten sick and three—at least—have died. They're afraid that the dragons—"

"Dragons?" K'lior broke in. He started to say more, but at that moment Fiona stumbled on a pebble and the noise distracted him. "Who's there?" he called, thrusting his head out the doorway of his quarters.

"It's me," Fiona said, coming farther down the corridor. "I heard voices."

K'lior turned back to his room and murmured something that Fiona didn't catch, then turned back to her. "I'm sorry we woke you; it's nothing to worry about."

"K'lior!" Cisca called reprovingly. "She'll know soon enough."

K'lior grimaced, then gestured for Fiona to join them. "What did you hear?" he asked as she followed him into the Weyr-woman's quarters.

"Something about fire-lizards being banned," Fiona replied, her hand going, uncontrolled, to the fire-lizard on her shoulder.

"Kindan's fire-lizard went *between*," Cisca told her softly. "They think he went *between* to die."

"Why?" On her shoulder, Fire chirped worriedly.

Cisca shook her head. "We don't know," she said. "Apparently he got ill, something in the lungs."

"Could this illness affect the dragons?" Fiona asked, glancing back toward her weyr, filled with dread that she might lose both of her only true friends one after the other.

"We don't know," K'lior said.

"But the dragons and fire-lizards are related," Cisca added.

"So maybe they *could* get sick," Fiona surmised. "And that's why you want to ban the fire-lizards."

"Yes," K'lior agreed.

"Many of our weyrfolk have fire-lizards," Cisca reminded him.

"Yes, I know," K'lior said. He turned to Fiona. "How will they react?"

On her shoulder, Fire creeled and Fiona shuddered. She thought of Kindan, of how he must feel in his loss. Then she thought of—"Father!"

"That's right," Cisca said, "your father has a fire-lizard, too."

"Father?" Fiona repeated numbly. "But he's not at the Weyr."

"It would have to be a general ban," K'lior told her.

"Wouldn't just this continent be enough?" Cisca asked, brows furrowed.

"Yes," K'lior said. "As long as the fire-lizards can't infect the dragons."

"What happens to a fire-lizard that's separated from its person?" Fiona asked.

"We don't know," K'lior said, frowning. "A fire-lizard's bond is not as strong as a dragon's. If we send them to the Southern Continent, perhaps . . ."

"Not all will go, will they?" Fiona asked.

"No," K'lior admitted.

"But without the dragons—"

"Thread comes soon," Cisca said.

Fiona turned her head in the direction of her sleeping dragon, then back to the Weyrleaders. "My father survived the Plague, he'll understand. He's strong." She turned again toward her quarters. "Come on Fire, we'd best tend to Talenth."

K'lior started to say something, but Cisca held up a restraining hand, cocking an ear and waiting until she could no longer hear Fiona's footsteps.

"What was that about?" K'lior asked incredulously.

"She's in shock, she's grieving," Cisca told him. "She needs time to say farewell."

K'lior nodded then. "I'd like to talk with the weyrfolk in the morning," he said. "And give all those who have fire-lizards a chance to say farewell."

Cisca nodded abstractedly.

"What?" K'lior said. "What are you thinking?"

"Have you noticed the way Fiona behaves?"

"I don't know how else she could behave, given the news," K'lior replied.

"Have you talked with the weyrlings recently?"

"Are you afraid they have this illness?" K'lior asked, suddenly alarmed. "Could her fire-lizard have spread it to the dragons?"

"No," Cisca replied, "although that's a horrible possibility." She frowned, mulling the notion over, then shook her head. "Have you noticed how they all seem so tired?"

"And distracted," K'lior agreed. "They seem only half here— T'jen was muttering about it just this morning."

"And you paid attention?" Cisca asked, amused. It was almost tradition that every Weyrlingmaster was convinced that the latest group of weyrlings was the worst ever.

"Yes," K'lior agreed. "Because he'd just told off the same rider twice for the same silly thing—he couldn't get his practice harness on properly."

"With the Plague, though, it was the strongest who succumbed," Cisca remarked.

"That was humans, not dragons," K'lior said. "We can't be sure of anything."

"Well, it's clear that the fire-lizards must go," Cisca said. "If things work out, perhaps we can have them return."

"That'd please a lot of our weyrfolk," K'lior agreed.

There were no signs of pleasure the next morning as dragonriders and weyrfolk collected in the Kitchen Cavern. K'lior could tell that most of the dragonriders knew what was coming: Those with fire-lizards had placed themselves near those weyrfolk who had fire-lizards.

Looking upon the sea of faces, most many Turns older than he, K'lior had never been more aware of how young he was to be a Weyrleader.

"I have grave news from Benden Weyr," he announced, his voice loud enough to fill every corner of the great room. "M'tal informs me that they have identified a sickness among the fire-lizards—"

"The fire-lizards!" several exclaimed at once.

"Yes," K'lior agreed. "Kindan's bronze Valla succumbed to it yesterday. The symptoms are a cough that doesn't get better, and green sputum—"

"Can it affect the dragons?" someone shouted from the back of the room.

"We don't know," Cisca said, stepping up beside her mate. "But—"

"We can't take the risk!" another of the weyrfolk called. " 'Dragonmen must fly when Thread is in the sky!' "

There was a chorus of assent.

"What do you want us to do, Weyrleader?" J'marin, Asoth's rider, asked. His gold fire-lizard Siaymon sat nestled on his shoulder.

"We're going to have to send the fire-lizards away," Cisca said. "We think we can send them to the Southern Continent."

J'marin stepped forward, his expression grim. He was more than twenty Turns older than either Cisca or K'lior. "Not all will make it."

"That may be so," K'lior agreed, leaving unspoken the acknowledgment that the others would go *between*. He spoke up to the rest of the Weyr. "We have to protect the dragons—it is our duty. I called you here to tell you what we must do and to give those of you with fire-lizards a chance to say farewell."

"Daddy's fire-lizard has to go away?" Janal, J'marin's sturdy lad of seven Turns, piped up.

J'marin knelt beside his son. "Yes," he said, his eyes bright with unshed tears. "Say good-bye to Siaymon."

" 'Bye Siaymon!" Janal said. He turned to his father. "Will we ever see her again?"

"I don't know," J'marin admitted, tears leaking beyond his control as he stroked the beautiful gold fire-lizard who had brought so many clutches of fire-lizard eggs to the Weyr. "But she'll be all right. She'll play in the sun of Southern."

"Can we visit her there?" Janal asked hopefully.

"No," J'marin said. "She and the others have to go so that the dragons will be safe."

"Safe?" Janal repeated, peering past his father to the Bowl and the dragon weyrs above. "The dragons can't be hurt."

"That's right," J'marin agreed. "And Siaymon will protect them by going away." He stroked his precious gold one last time. "Have you said good-bye, son?"

"Good-bye, Siaymon," Janal said. "I love you."

J'marin nodded. "That was well said," he told the youngster, ruffling his hair before turning his attention back to the gold fire-lizard. "I love you. Farewell."

Asoth, tell Siaymon she must go to the Southern Continent, J'marin said to his dragon, tears now streaming freely down his face.

She must go? Asoth asked sadly.

Yes, she must, J'marin repeated. *To protect the dragons.*

I will tell her, Asoth replied.

In front of him, Siaymon gave one horrified squawk and disappeared *between.*

As the others began to send their fire-lizards away, K'lior grabbed Cisca's hand. She squeezed back, tightly, her grip flexing every time another fire-lizard went *between* until, finally, the Kitchen Cavern was a silent mix of sad dragonriders and tearful weyrfolk.

Fiona was in her weyr, curled up tight against Talenth, her arms wrapped tightly around Fire, when the other fire-lizards left.

"Fiona?"

She recognized her father's voice. She made no reply, but clutched Fire tighter. The queen fire-lizard craned her neck around to look at her, her faceted eyes whirling red and green.

Fiona heard the sound of feet coming toward her.

"Fiona," Lord Bemin said. "I came as soon as I heard." She didn't move. She heard him bend down, saw his face come into view. Jokester rode on his shoulder. There were tears in her father's eyes. Fiona closed her own eyes tightly, not wanting to see his tears. Hadn't he cried enough?

She closed her eyes, but she couldn't close her ears.

"When we came here, to the Hatching," Bemin said softly, his voice hoarse with emotion, "I never thought that you'd Impress."

He sniffed. "My daughter, a queen rider!" She could hear the pride in his voice. She turned away from him, clutching Fire tight.

"I never hoped, never dreamed that our line would be so honored," he went on in a whisper. "I thought my heart would break, I was so proud!"

Fiona turned back to him. "You were?"

She opened her eyes to peer at his face and saw, beyond the tears, the immense pride he had in her.

"Yes," Bemin said. "You bring great honor to our Hold, and to me." He took a breath and told her gently, "I know this is hard." He reached up and stroked Jokester on his shoulder. "But you have duties now, duties to your Weyr and to Pern, just as I have mine to Fort Hold."

He reached for her with one hand and gently helped her to her feet. "You are of Fort," he said, his voice becoming firm, commanding. "You are *twice* of Fort, of Hold and Weyr." He peered down at her, the corners of his lips quivering upward. "You are my last child and I would not deprive you of anything—"

"Then I can . . . ?" But her words trailed off as Bemin shook his head gently.

"You and I have so much," he told her gently. He gestured to the sleeping queen dragonet, who was trembling in her sleep. "As you have your queen, I have Forsk, the watch-wher. Do you think it would be dutiful to risk all Pern to keep our fire-lizards, too?"

Fiona sniffed, her eyes catching his pleadingly, but he shook his head again.

"It is time, now," he told her, "to say good-bye." He turned his head to Jokester and reached up his arms, bringing the brown fire-lizard down to settle in his clasped hands. He caught Fiona's eyes. "Queen rider, ask your queen to send them to the Southern Continent."

"Father—" Fiona began, tears streaming down her face, but Bemin once again shook his head and lifted his chin slightly.

"Head high, Weyrwoman," he told her.

Fiona took in a deep breath and nodded, her tears falling unchecked.

Talenth?

What is it? the young queen asked sleepily. *You sound sad.*

Tell Fire and Jokester they must go. Fiona sobbed as she relayed the thought.

Go?

Yes, go, Fiona replied. *To the Southern Continent.* Her heart broke as she cried, *Do it now!*

She heard two surprised squawks, cut off suddenly, *between.*

"Oh, Father!"

THREE

My small fire-lizard friend
Frolic in the sun.
Our love will never end
No matter where you run.

Fort Weyr, AL 507.12.20

The next day dawned bright and sunny, though still full of winter's cold.

With effort, drained from the previous day's events, Fiona roused herself and Talenth to go out into the Weyr Bowl. She had to leave her weyr, if only for a moment. She milled with the sad, nervous, confused weyrlings who were feeding their dragonets. The youngsters, some her age, some not much older, were very interested in her and insisted upon helping her feed Talenth, even to the neglect of their own dragons.

"Let me tend to her," Fiona told them finally, with a touch of acerbity. She tried hard not to think of a cheerful chirping voice or a gold streak darting through the air.

"If you're looking for distraction, there's tack to be oiled," a voice growled from beside her.

Fiona looked up, startled, to see a grizzled older dragonrider standing beside her.

"T'jen, Salith's rider," the man said, gesturing up toward a brown dragon that was peering down at them from several levels above. "Weyrlingmaster."

He waved at the weyrlings. "They weren't disturbing you, were they, Weyrwoman?"

Fiona knew instantly that T'jen had heard her entire exchange with the weyrlings. She smiled at him, shaking her head. "They were just trying to help."

"They could help themselves more by tending to their chores," T'jen grumbled loudly enough that several weyrlings glanced worriedly in his direction and suddenly looked more energetic.

After the weyrlings were out of earshot, T'jen murmured to her, "I can understand the ones in your Hatching carrying on the way they do, but the older ones . . ." He shook his head.

"But—" Fiona began, her thoughts all jumbled. "I mean, isn't this normal?"

"What, Weyrwoman?" T'jen asked, turning to face her directly. "Tell me how you feel."

"I'm all right," Fiona said immediately. "Talenth's fine—"

"And you'd know, being a Weyrwoman for . . . ?" T'jen asked her, raising his brows in curiosity, a faint smile on his lips.

Fiona blushed in response. She thought back, her blush clearing into a smile as she remembered her amazing Impression of Talenth. How long ago had it been? It seemed forever. But how long? Her frown deepened as she realized she couldn't quite remember.

"This is the twentieth day of the twelfth month," T'jen supplied helpfully.

"Oh!" Fiona said. "Then it's been—it's been—" Angrily she chided herself, This is simple! There are twenty-eight days—four sevendays—in each month, and she'd Impressed Talenth on the seventeenth of the month before so that meant that . . .

"Thirty-one days, Weyrwoman," T'jen told her softly. Fiona looked up at him, chagrined. "You're not the only one confused. All of my weyrlings, even the steadiest of them, are acting like you."

"Is it the sickness?" Fiona asked with a feeling of dread knotting her stomach.

"I hope not," T'jen said fervently. "And there's no sign of distress among the dragonets—they're merely a bit sleepier than I'd expect at this age."

"I thought they always slept a lot when they're this young," Fiona said.

"They do, but not *this* much," T'jen told her. "It's difficult enough to wake them to eat, much less anything else."

"And that's not normal?"

"No," T'jen replied, shaking his head. "It's not."

"Have you told the Weyrwoman?"

"She pointed it out to me, actually," he admitted.

It took Fiona a moment to follow his thought through to its conclusion. "Because of me?"

The weyrlingmaster smiled. "Well, you *are* the newest Weyrwoman, she's right to keep an eye on you," he told her. "You never know . . ."

"Know what?" Fiona prompted.

"Know when you'll become Weyrwoman," T'jen said sadly. He met her eyes. "It happened quick enough for Cisca."

"How?"

"You'd have to ask her," he said. "It's her story to tell or not." Fiona yawned and T'jen laughed. "Not that you'd be awake long enough."

"I'm sorry," she apologized.

"Don't be," he told her. "Whatever it is, you need your rest, so go get it." He turned to the massed weyrlings. "You lot, on the other hand, still have work to get done before you can take a break."

A chorus of groans greeted his words.

"... **S**o I'd say that she's the same as the rest," T'jen concluded in his recounting to the Weyrleader and Weyrwoman over dinner that night. "Even the older weyrlings are acting odd."

"I'm sorry I didn't listen to you sooner," K'lior said to the old Weyrlingmaster. "You'd said this last Turn when the others Impressed, but I thought . . ."

"You thought I was just moaning," T'jen finished for him with a snort.

"I've never heard a Weyrlingmaster *praise* his charges, after all," K'lior said defensively.

"And by the First Egg, I hope you never do!" T'jen replied. Thoughtfully, he added, "And if you ever do, Weyrleader, you should let the man go. As you know: 'There's—' "

" '—always better from a weyrling,' " K'lior finished with T'jen. "Exactly."

"And what about now?" Cisca asked. "Does not 'always better' mean we should be pushing these weyrlings further? Particularly as the next Pass is nearly upon us."

"Actually," K'lior replied diffidently, "that's a good reason to go slow."

Cisca gave him a questioning look.

"The Weyrleader's right, Weyrwoman," T'jen told her. "With Thread coming, it's more important to have these youngsters trained the best we can rather than put them and their young dragons against Thread too early."

"We can expect the most losses in the first Turn of Threadfall," K'lior said in agreement. In response to Cisca's look, he explained, "It's in the Records. I think it's because it always takes time to adjust to the reality of fighting Thread."

T'jen nodded. "Any mistake fighting Thread can be the last mistake a rider or dragon makes."

"So we should go slow with these weyrlings?" Cisca asked.

"And keep an eye on them, as well," T'jen said. "We don't want them doing something foolish because they're too drowsy to think clearly."

"What does the harper say?" Cisca asked.

"He's got no better idea than I," T'jen said. "It *could* be this sickness that affected the fire-lizards, but there's been no sign of coughing from anyone." He paused, his brow furrowed, then shook his head. "No, I don't think they're related—but I don't know what is affecting the weyrlings so." A moment later, he added, "They've got good days and bad days, some more than others."

"Does anything help?" K'lior asked.

"*Klah*," T'jen said with a shrug. "The stronger, the better. For some, it's *klah* in the morning, at noon, and mid-evening. That's for the worst of them, though."

"So we just leave it at that?" Cisca asked, perturbed.

"I'd say it's all we can do, for the moment," T'jen replied.

"And I think Tannaz and I will keep a closer eye on our young Weyrwoman," Cisca said.

The next morning Cisca found Fort's second Weyrwoman in her quarters just as she finished her daily grooming of her queen, Kalsenth.

"Good morning," Cisca called brightly to Tannaz and her dragon as she entered. "Kalsenth, if you can spare her, I've got a task for your rider." And she repeated the conversation she'd had with K'lior the night before.

"I'd heard about the older weyrlings," Tannaz said when she was done, "but not the younger ones."

"And the new queen," Cisca added.

The two queen riders were a study in contrasts: Cisca was tall, broad-shouldered and muscled without appearing so, with shoulder-length brown hair and eyes to match, while Tannaz was short, thin, wiry; her eyes, so dark they looked black, were set in a stark face of dusky skin surrounded by wavy black hair that announced her Igen origins to anyone looking at her.

Their personalities were even less matched than their forms, and for a time Cisca had been concerned that the older woman— for Tannaz had been three Turns older than Cisca when she Impressed—would cause problems. She had refused to return to Igen Weyr when she Impressed, which had perhaps been the final death blow for the desert Weyr. Having met D'gan, Igen's Weyr-leader—and heard K'lior's recounting of their meeting—Cisca did not begrudge Tannaz her choice, even while she worried that she and the older woman would come to blows.

But it was not so, partly because they were both fundamentally too good and concerned for the Weyr's well-being to allow any disagreements to exist between them for long. In fact, Cisca had come to value Tannaz's fiery spirit, quick wit, and steadfast loyalty.

"So what would you like me to do?" Tannaz asked.

"I think we should both spend more time with Fiona," Cisca said. As Tannaz's eyes narrowed, Cisca added quickly, "I don't want her to feel that we're intruding or being overly cautious, so I think if we trade off, that will cause her less concern."

"Great, I'll be happy to help," Tannaz told her cheerfully. Cisca gave her an inquiring look and Tannaz shrugged, saying, "I wanted to get to know her; we'll be working together for Turns to come."

"We will, at that," Cisca agreed, surprised that she hadn't thought to introduce her two junior Weyrwomen earlier. She paused long enough to reflect on the matter: A large part of the reason she hadn't thought of it sooner was simply because she was, as Senior Weyrwoman, quite busy, but she was also honest enough to recognize that it was partly due to her concern that the other two might find they liked each other more than her. It was a silly notion really, she admitted to herself, but she sometimes forgot that *she* was the Weyrwoman now.

"Do you think there might be something in the Records?" Tannaz suggested.

Cisca frowned. She preferred to avoid the dusty Records when she could, but there were some times when there was no recourse—there were some questions that she didn't feel secure asking the Weyr harper to research for her. Her frown turned to a happier look as she realized that this was not one of them.

"I'll ask—" She caught herself, and corrected: "Would you ask Harper Kentai to investigate?"

"Certainly," Tannaz said. "Perhaps I should bring him with me to meet Fiona." She added, "We could use the excuse that he needs to know what Teaching Ballads she might need to learn for her Weyr duties to give him a chance to observe her himself."

"A good idea," Cisca agreed. "Although I suspect his contact with the weyrlings has already given him a pretty good notion of the symptoms."

Tannaz nodded in agreement. "Then I'll check in on her now myself." She patted Kalsenth's neck with a finality that indicated that her grooming was complete for the morning and, with a reassuring smile to Cisca, headed off on her task.

Fiona's weyr was next to Tannaz's, the Weyrwomen's weyrs being allocated according to rank. Tannaz found Fiona, as she'd expected, in the queen's weyr, busily oiling the new hatchling. With a grin, she found a cloth, dipped it in the pail of oil, and started in at Fiona's side. She was quite surprised at how long it took before the youngster noticed her.

"Oh!" Fiona cried when she spotted her. "Oh, my, how long have you been here?" She made a face and added hastily, "Not that I'm not grateful for the help, it's just that . . ."

"They get bigger," Tannaz said with a smile, marveling at how quickly they finished going over the young queen's skin. She extended an oily hand to the girl. "I'm Tannaz, Kelsanth's rider."

Fiona looked at her in surprise, and then her face took on the abstracted look of a rider communicating with her dragon, followed by a more natural expression of irritation as she realized that Talenth had, as usual, fallen solidly asleep during her oiling.

"Kelsanth . . ." Fiona repeated, indicating that she was unfamiliar with the name and mortified. "Oh! She's the other queen here!"

"We sleep next to you," Tannaz informed her, adding, "I'm surprised her snores haven't kept you awake at night."

Fiona shook her head, her hand rising to her mouth to stifle a yawn. "I've no trouble sleeping," she confided. "It's staying awake . . ."

"That's *always* a problem with a hatchling," Tannaz agreed passionately. She cocked her head thoughtfully at Fiona. "Though I'd say you've got it worse than most."

Belatedly, Fiona noticed Tannaz's hand and reached for it, shook it quickly, and let it go.

Tannaz frowned at the motion, wondering what had gotten into the girl that she'd gone so cold so quickly. "What?" she demanded hotly. "Is my hand not good enough for a Lady Holder?"

"No," Fiona replied, her face crumpling in despair, "It's just that *everyone* says I'm lazy." And she surprised herself by bursting into tears. The tears streamed unchecked down her face, her oily hands hanging limply at her sides as her sobs wracked her body.

Tannaz didn't deal well with tears or crying girls—her first tendency was to run away or slap them. But this girl's behavior was different and Tannaz felt strangely moved by it.

"Fiona," she said gently. When the tears continued and the girl's body started to shake more violently, she tried again. "Fiona."

In the end, much against Tannaz's inclinations, she hugged Fiona close to her, whispering the gentle shushing noises that she'd used only with her own hatchling Turns earlier. Slowly Fiona's sobs quieted and her tears dried up. Tannaz could measure the girl's recovery by the hardening of her body and the way she slowly pulled away.

"I'm sorry," Fiona said, her eyes cast to the ground. "I don't know what got into me."

"I do," Tannaz told her gently, surprised at herself. "It's not just that you're tired."

Fiona looked up at her.

"You're afraid you won't measure up, that we're all judging you." Tannaz shook her head, smiling. "And it doesn't matter." Fiona's brows furrowed in puzzlement. "No one can take your dragon away from you."

Fiona chewed her lower lip nervously before saying in a quiet voice once more close to tears, "But what if I can't keep her?" Tannaz gave her a puzzled look and Fiona replied with a wave of her hands to the pail of oil and the sleeping dragon, "What if I don't have the energy? What if—is it possible that she got the wrong person? I can't seem to—can a person be allergic to Impressing?"

"Allergic?"

Fiona's face worked through a range of emotions as she groped for the words. "I just seem so scattered, so lost. I never thought I couldn't do this." Fearfully she turned to her sleeping dragon and back again to Tannaz to whisper, "She can't hear me, can she?"

Tannaz eyed the sleeping dragonet carefully before answering. "No, she's fast asleep," she said. "But you have to watch your thoughts—they can disturb your dragon even when she's sleeping."

Fiona's eyes widened fearfully. "Now?"

"No," Tannaz assured her. "She'd be twitching."

Fiona heaved a sigh of relief but she persisted with her question, asking in a whisper, "So, could I be allergic?"

"I've never heard of such of thing," Tannaz told her. "And I don't think so in your case." She paused for a moment before confiding to Fiona, "You're not alone. All the weyrlings, even those from the last hatching, are behaving oddly."

"They are?" Fiona repeated. Tannaz saw the way the girl's whole body seemed to shift as she absorbed the news. "The ones from the Turn before, too?"

"Yes," Tannaz assured her.

"Does anyone know why?" Fiona asked after a moment. Tan-

naz shook her head. Fiona looked down to the ground thoughtfully for a moment, then looked up again, asking, "Is anyone else
acting this way?"

"That's an excellent question," Tannaz told her. Out of curiosity,
she asked, "How would you find out?"

Fiona pursed her lips thoughtfully. "Well, if this were back at
Fort Hold, I'd ask our healer if anyone had complained about feeling poorly."

Tannaz nodded in agreement, then shook her head. "But dragonriders aren't holders."

"They might not want to admit to feeling poorly," K'lior agreed
that evening when Tannaz discussed her findings with the Weyrleaders.

"Hah!" Cisca snorted. "Getting *you* to admit to a head cold
took—"

K'lior silenced her with a warning look.

"No rider wants to be grounded," J'marin growled. "Even that
silly D'lanor."

K'lior gave the Weyrlingmaster a questioning look.

"That's the one who couldn't get his harness sorted . . . *twice*,"
J'marin explained.

"Riders are a healthy lot," T'mar remarked.

Cisca snorted, looking squarely at K'lior. "Even healthy riders
get sick sometimes."

"The older weyrlings have been this way for over a Turn,"
T'mar pointed out, his tone suggesting that perhaps the issue
wasn't that important.

"It's affected their training," J'marin objected. "And they *are*
sicker than most."

" 'There's always better,' " T'mar repeated the old saw with a
sour look toward the Weyrlingmaster.

"As you've said yourself," K'lior reminded the wingleader in a
lighter tone. He turned his attention back to Tannaz. "So what do
you think of our newest Weyrwoman?"

Tannaz pursed her lips in thought, then said tersely, "She'll do."
K'lior raised an eyebrow questioningly. "Oh, she's got her plate

full with all the things bothering her—not the least that she's little more than thirteen Turns to her name—"

"And we all know how difficult *that* can be," Cisca inserted with a sympathetic wince.

"That's a harder age for girls than boys," J'marin observed.

"But it's a good age to Impress, boy *or* girl," T'mar said.

K'lior waved the conversation aside. He had his answer, not that there was much he could do—the dragon had chosen her rider and that was that. "Did Kentai have a chance to talk with her?"

"I brought her down to his quarters for lunch," Tannaz said. She smiled, adding, "We fed her a full mug of hot, strong *klah*—that woke her right up. Anyway, Kentai told me later that her knowledge of Holder duties was well advanced, and she knows more about the Weyrs than most of our weyrlings." She turned to Cisca, concluding, "I don't think she'll need much training from the harper."

"Good." Cisca gave the other Weyrwoman a firm nod. "You and I will manage her then."

K'lior smiled at his mate, then turned back to the others. "In the meanwhile, I want us all to be alert for any similar signs in our riders."

"If they're like D'lanor, you should have noticed already," J'marin noted sourly.

"So we should be looking carefully at those who are *not* like D'lanor," K'lior observed affably, rising from the table and terminating the discussion.

Afterward, in their quarters, Cisca turned to K'lior. "You know, everyone expected T'mar's Zirenth to fly Melirth."

"Yes, I know," K'lior replied, one brow quirked irritatedly, adding, as he snuggled in closer to her, "You choose an odd time to remember that."

Cisca shook her head, a gesture that was more felt than seen in the darkened room. "That was not a complaint," she told him. "It's just that before then, everyone was certain Zirenth would outfly Rineth, but not long before, T'mar started acting odd."

"And that's not usual coming up to a mating flight that will determine who is the new Weyrleader?"

"It just struck me as odd, K'lior," Cisca replied with a touch of frost.

"He's an able wingleader and he's never begrudged me my position," K'lior told her. "I wouldn't want to belabor him with unwarranted suspicions."

"Unwarranted!" Cisca repeated and, with a huff, rolled away from him.

It took the Weyrleader a solid sevenday to regain the good graces of his Weyrwoman. They neither bickered nor fought openly, but K'lior knew that Cisca was irritated with him and worked hard to repair the rift.

"It's not *all* the weyrlings," K'lior remarked to Cisca over dinner on the seventh day.

Cisca raised an eyebrow to indicate her interest.

"Some of them behave no different than any other weyrlings I've seen," K'lior said.

"And you've seen so many," Cisca snapped.

K'lior shrugged. He'd barely finished his weyrling training himself when his Rineth had flown Cisca's Melirth and he'd become Weyrleader.

"Even so," K'lior persisted. "It's not so much that I've seen so many weyrlings as that I knew some of these weyrlings particularly well—"

"You played with them not all that long ago," Cisca interjected.

"Precisely," K'lior agreed with a slight smile. "And while D'lanor was always . . ." He waved a hand, inviting Cisca to supply a word.

"Dim," Cisca said. K'lior winced and Cisca tried again, "Slow."

"Challenged," K'lior ventured. "But his heart was always in the right place."

"He follows orders, understands his place, and will make a great green rider," Cisca said.

"J'nos, on the other hand, is one of the best I've seen."

"Pilenth *is* well-formed," Cisca admitted with an understandable touch of pride in her dragon's offspring.

K'lior nodded quickly in agreement. "Mind you, neither's flown yet—"

"J'nos was holder born, wasn't he?"

"I don't think it's a question of origin," K'lior said. "F'jian was Searched and he's nearly as bad as D'lanor."

"On the whole . . . ?" Cisca prompted.

"On the whole, T'jen is right," K'lior said, his expression grim. "The same is true for the older weyrlings."

"And T'mar," Cisca muttered.

K'lior opened his mouth to protest but shut it again. After a moment he sighed, "Possibly."

"I knew you'd get there in the end," Cisca told him. "So now what do we do?"

"There's no sign of this fire-lizard illness," K'lior said.

"Certainly it doesn't sound like it would linger for over a Turn without more symptoms," Cisca observed.

"I can't figure out what it could be, though."

"You will," Cisca assured him, gesturing to his plate, "after you've had a chance to eat and sleep."

K'lior wisely chose not to argue.

The relief Fiona felt at knowing she was not alone was quickly banished by her exhaustion and dulled mental state. The *klah* helped. She returned to her daily activities of feeding Talenth, oiling Talenth, praising Talenth, catching a nap when she could, and hurriedly eating the meals that were delivered directly to her quarters. Except for the constant muzziness, this would have been a time of unalloyed joy for two reasons: first, because she got to spend every waking moment with her marvelous, brilliant, and fabulous Talenth; and, second, because her time was for once completely her own. She could be slovenly, she could forgot to bathe for a whole day, she could be angry, she could curse, and she didn't have to worry about being judged, frowned at, or silently derided because she was the Lord Holder's daughter and the sole representative of Fort Hold's future. Never mind that she was a girl and expected to marry the man who would be future Lord Holder, she was still required to "Set an example, Fiona!" "People look up to you!" "What would your father say if he saw you look that way?"

It was really only here, in the freedom of Fort Weyr, as Talenth's Weyrwoman, that Fiona would ever have realized how much her role as Fort's Lady Holder—in waiting—was a position that stifled her, that restricted her, and that caused her to wake every morning with dread. She was free! She was a queen rider, and soon, when Talenth was old enough, she could go anywhere, do anything and—

"Fiona!" a voice called from her doorway. "We've brought you some company."

Company? Fiona looked up from her perch between Talenth's legs where she was lying, still covered in the oil and muck of Talenth's morning's ablutions. I'm not ready for company!

"Fiona?" another voice, deeper, called. It was her father.

A lifetime of training had her scampering to her feet before she had a moment to think.

"My lord?"

"Well, perhaps we should not have surprised her like that," Cisca said later that evening as she and Tannaz met to discuss the day's events.

"She looked like a chicken cornered by a tunnel snake," Tannaz agreed with a sigh.

"She really didn't handle it well," Cisca continued. "Lord Bemin was clearly desperate to see her; I don't know why she insisted on keeping him waiting while she bathed first."

"Why?" Tannaz retorted hotly. "Would *you* greet a Lord Holder dressed in your worst, oil-grimed, sleep-stained clothes with your hair and face all oily from your latest dragon-grooming?"

"Sure," Cisca responded with a toss of her shoulders. "Why not? It's only a Lord Holder, after all." She noticed Tannaz's look and continued, "Oh, certainly, if I could, I'd prefer to be better dressed, but if the matter was sufficiently urgent, I'd have no problem greeting him at my worst."

Tannaz mulled Cisca's response over for a moment before admitting, "I think you could greet him sky-clad and make him feel overdressed."

Cisca felt herself blushing but could only nod in agreement, grinning. "It would *not* be my preference but, yes, if I had to, then I would certainly work to ensure that he felt overdressed."

Tannaz chortled.

"Still," Cisca continued when their moment of mirth had passed, "I'm sorry it didn't work out better. By bringing him here, I'd hoped to cheer up both Lord and rider—or at least raise Fiona from her lethargy."

"Well, you have to admit she was roused," Tannaz said with a grin.

"Right—with a screaming match that scared every dragon in the Weyr. Not exactly what I'd had in mind," Cisca said, her eyes flashing.

Tannas shrugged. "In the end, I think it worked out fine." When Cisca shook her head in disbelief, Tannaz went on, "If you weren't weyrbred, you'd understand. Weyrfolk have a different way of looking at things."

"I should hope."

"Bemin is a Lord Holder," Tannaz explained. "He has spent his entire life expecting to be heard and instantly obeyed."

"So?" Cisca demanded. "He's still a fair man."

"He's a fair man, but it's become ingrained in him that his word is law."

"Hmm," Cisca murmured, looking at the second Weyrwoman thoughtfully.

"Whereas here a Weyrleader's authority only lasts until the senior queen's next mating flight," Tannaz continued. "So no one in the Weyr is used to as much authority as Lord Bemin wields in his Hold." She paused. "And nowhere is he expected to wield that authority more than in his own Hall, over his own children."

Cisca nodded in comprehension, then frowned. "I still don't see why this shouting match can be seen as a good thing."

"It was an excellent thing," Tannaz corrected. "The worst alternative would have been for Fiona to respond with meek acquiescence to her father's every request, fawning over him like a holder drudge. Instead, she lost her temper and told her Lord off in a manner that completely severed that relationship."

"But he's still her father," Cisca said.

"He's still her father," Tannaz agreed. "And the wounds will take a while to heal. For both of them."

"I'm still not seeing the good in this," Cisca told her.

"When they meet again, it won't be as Lord Holder and dutiful daughter," Tannaz explained. "It will be as Lord Holder and tithe-bound Weyrwoman." She paused, a look of admiration crossing her face. "I'm sure she didn't plan it, but the break between them will make it much easier for the both of them to adjust to her new role—and it reaffirms in his mind his duty to the Weyr."

"How do you see that?"

"Fiona asserted herself as a Weyrwoman," Tannaz said, "and that assertion carries with it the weight of the whole Weyr. Without meaning to, Fiona reminded Lord Bemin that the safety of his Hold depends upon this Weyr and that he's beholden to us." An impish grin flashed on her face as she added, "I'll bet our tithe from Fort will be much better this year than last."

Cisca looked at the other for a long moment before shaking her head sadly. "I don't think I'll ever be able to match you for deviousness."

"Ah, so aren't you glad that I'm your junior Weyrwoman?"

Cisca reached forward and hugged her. "I certainly am!"

"Maybe it was a bad idea, sending the fire-lizards away," T'mar said to K'lior at the end of the wingleaders' meeting some twenty days after that tragic event. T'mar had waited until the other wingleaders had headed down to the Kitchen Caverns to join their wingriders for dinner.

K'lior gave him an inquisitive look.

T'mar went on. "There's been no word of further outbreaks—"

"Perhaps because the fire-lizards are all gone," K'lior suggested.

"Perhaps it was a fluke," T'mar retorted.

K'lior nodded in understanding, then looked over and caught T'mar's eyes. "Tell me, bronze rider, do you wish to stake your dragon's life on a fluke?"

T'mar's face colored.

K'lior made a calming gesture. "I don't mean to anger you,

T'mar," he said. "I don't like this any more than you." Tension had been building in the Weyr; there had been two fights, one involving a dragonrider. K'lior was no fool; he knew that both were reflections of resentment and fear.

"I've spoken with Kentai," he continued, "and he suggests that we should listen for word from Benden—"

"Benden?" the word exploded out of T'mar's lips.

"Yes, Benden," K'lior said calmly. "Because Harper Kindan was not only a witness to the death of his own fire-lizard, but he was also a firsthand witness to the Plague that struck the holders nearly twelve Turns back."

T'mar's angry look cleared slightly as he absorbed his Weyr-leader's words.

"He may not be a dragonrider," K'lior said, "but from everything I've heard, he regards all life carefully and won't take chances with the dragons."

"He'd be a fool to do so this near to the Pass," T'mar murmured, then shook his head abashedly. "As I was to suggest it," he said more loudly, meeting K'lior's eyes. "I'm sorry, Weyrleader, my previous behavior was—"

"No more than to be expected this near the Pass," K'lior assured him, clapping the older man on the shoulder. "Now come along, your riders are waiting for you."

Later that evening K'lior recounted the encounter to Cisca as they were preparing for bed.

"So?" Cisca demanded.

"Well, it *was* odd," K'lior said.

"But?"

"But," K'lior said with a sigh, "it could have been nerves."

Cisca took a dim view of this, saying, "If it's nerves, he's had it for over a Turn now—do you really want someone like that leading a wing?"

"His wing is doing well," K'lior protested. Cisca glared at him and he sighed again. "I'll keep an eye on him."

"Thread could come any day now," Cisca said.

"Thank goodness Verilan discovered those Threadfall charts," K'lior said. "Once we know the location of the first Fall, we'll be able to predict the rest."

"What if those charts were only meant for the Second Pass?" Cisca asked.

"I admit that it's possible," K'lior said. "And we'll be vigilant. But certainly with each consecutive pass matching those charts, we'll get more confidence."

"I don't see how we can fight Thread every seventy-five hours," Cisca said dubiously.

"Spread among six Weyrs?"

"Five Weyrs," Cisca corrected. "I'd be happier if it were six."

"And we're wing light," K'lior agreed, his optimism ebbing.

"*That* doesn't bother me," Cisca said, poking him playfully in the ribs and grinning impishly. "Between Tannaz's Kalsenth and my Melirth, I think we'll have the Weyr up to strength pretty soon."

But the Weyrleader shook his head. "Melirth won't rise again for months yet. And then we've got at least three Turns—"

"A Turn and a half," Cisca interjected.

"Only if we force weyrlings into fighting wings early," K'lior told her. "And the Records—"

"We'll survive," Cisca interjected.

"Of course we will!" K'lior replied. "Oh, we may have it hard for the first Turn or so, but we'll manage."

"With two hundred and eighty-five fighting dragons?" Cisca snorted. "I expect we'll do more than manage."

K'lior managed a weak smile, thinking about Cisca's concerns over T'mar and his own concerns over what had happened to Kindan's fire-lizard.

"It's been nearly three sevendays; maybe we'll be able to bring the fire-lizards back," Cisca said, much to K'lior's surprise. In response to his look, she explained, "They'll bring up morale for everyone."

K'lior gave her a doubtful smile and was about to say something but stopped suddenly, turning toward the weyr and his dragon.

Cisca felt a sudden disquiet from Melirth.

Kamenth of Ista is no more, her dragon told her, rushing out of her weyr and into the Weyr Bowl, keening sorrowfully.

"Was it the—"

Jalith of Telgar is no more, Melirth said then. The Weyr was filled with the voices of hundreds of distressed dragons.

"Two dragons!" K'lior groaned.

"Was it the illness?" Cisca wondered. Before she could repeat the question to her grieving queen, the keening of the dragons increased to a fever pitch.

Breth of Benden is no more!

FOUR

Their lungs melted,
Their breath turned green.
Sick, listless, ailing,
Dragons fled between.

Fort Weyr, AL 507.13.12

Fiona groaned when she awoke. The sun was high in the sky. Her muscles were all sore, aching from the awkward position in which she'd finally found sleep after the awful nighttime awakening that she and all the dragonriders had experienced. But the ache in her muscles was nothing to the ache in her heart. She felt hollow. So hollow that for one frantic instant, she looked around wildly for Talenth only to stop, realizing that the bulk of the young dragon lay beneath her. She pulled back and spent several long, tense moments watching her queen, searching for signs of life. She didn't realize that she'd been holding her breath until she let it out in a sigh as she saw Talenth's chest rise and fall in the steady breathing of an exhausted dragonet.

Then, to her surprise and annoyance, Fiona's stomach grumbled loudly. She nearly hissed at it in anger, afraid that it might disturb the sleeping queen. When it rumbled again, she beat a hasty retreat from the queen's lair, rushing out into the Weyr Bowl.

Out there, Fiona was struck by silence. She glanced at the sun overhead in confirmation of the late hour and frowned—usually by this time the Weyr Bowl was bustling with dragons, riders, and weyrfolk.

Had something happened to the whole Weyr, she wondered, a jolt of fear running down her spine. At a half-trot she rushed down the incline onto the Bowl proper and over to the Kitchen Cavern.

It was a moment before she spotted anyone and then her sigh of relief carried through the entire room.

Tannaz beckoned to her. Fiona closed the distance quickly, her brain teeming with questions, but when she got to Tannaz's table, she found that she could only sit numbly and stare at the small basket of rolls.

Tannaz caught the look and pushed the basket to her, sliding over a tub of butter with her other hand.

"You'll feel better when you eat," the older Weyrwoman told her. "I know I did."

"Better?" Fiona repeated, startled by the hollowness in Tannaz's voice. She was surprised at the sound of her own voice: hoarse, empty, lifeless.

"Eat." Tannaz leaned forward and grabbed a roll, setting the example.

Fiona followed suit and buttered her roll slowly. There was something reassuring, almost peaceful, in the way the cool butter spread on the roll. Normal.

She took a bite and chewed slowly. The butter and the fresh bread were wonderful! Fiona finished her first bite and took another bigger bite of her roll. She could hardly believe how good the roll was, how fresh the butter was.

"Tastes good, doesn't it?" Tannaz asked before taking another bite herself.

Fiona could only nod, her mouth full.

"That's because you're hungry," Tannaz told her. She pushed a pitcher over to her and gestured toward a mug. "The *klah*'s cold, try it."

Fiona wasn't much of a fan of *klah* at the best of times, and cold wasn't the best. But the scent wafted over to her and she found herself filling the mug without thinking.

"It's great!" she exclaimed after her first sip. She was thirsty, and at that moment the cold, spicy brew was better than the freshest stream water. She finished her mug and filled it again.

Tannaz chortled. "That's because you're thirsty."

"Where are the others?" Fiona asked. She already felt more awake.

"Grieving," Tannaz told her flatly.

"Well, they can't grieve any longer," a voice boomed from the entrance. Fiona turned and saw Cisca. Reflexively, she rose.

"Have some food," Tannaz murmured, her mouth half-full, as she got to her feet with the basket of rolls in one hand.

As Cisca crossed the distance between them her expression changed from one of anger to one of hunger. She took the proffered roll and, sitting down, slathered it with butter from the tub Fiona pushed in her direction. Two rolls later she said, "You're right, I was hungry."

"*Klah*," Tannaz said, sliding the pitcher in her direction.

"It's cold," Fiona warned.

Cisca acknowledged the warning with a nod and looked around for a mug. Tannaz offered hers, and the Weyrwoman took it gladly.

"Better, huh?" Tannaz asked as Cisca gulped down the cold liquid. Cisca nodded wordlessly. Two rolls and another mug of cold *klah* later the Weyrwoman confessed, "I didn't realize I was *that* hungry."

Tannaz rose to her feet and gestured for Fiona to follow her. "We'll rouse the weyrfolk and get a proper meal," she declared. "You stay here and rest."

Cisca nodded gratefully.

"You'll probably have to bring food to the riders," a voice declared from the entrance.

"Ah, Kentai," Tannaz called to the man garbed in harper blue, "we'll be glad of your help."

The harper's lips turned up, the nearest anyone had come to a smile so far that day.

"Is it like this across Pern?" Fiona wondered.

"Very likely," Kentai said. "Certainly at the Weyrs."

"It's not just the news—it's what it means," Tannaz elaborated.

"Well, this illness hasn't affected Fort." Fiona recognized T'jen's voice before she spotted the Weyrlingmaster striding in from the brilliance of the midday sun. He nodded briefly to the Weyrwomen and again to the harper. "The weyrlings have started to recover," he told them. "The rest of the Weyr will be back on their feet soon, I'm sure."

"It was the shock," Tannaz declared, shaking her head. "I was so *certain* that it wasn't going to happen—"

"It's yet to happen here," T'jen reiterated. "If we close the Weyr, we're not likely to be—" He broke off, alerted by a sound, and turned quickly, looking back the way he'd come. Fiona turned in the same direction, listening intently. The sound echoed around the Weyr: the deep noise of a dragon coughing.

"Salith!"

"What are you going to do?" H'nez demanded as K'lior entered the Council Room.

"Give him a chance to sit at least," M'kury snapped.

K'lior used the moment of their bickering to take a deep breath and look around the room. Before the wingleaders had settled down, he heard the rustle of cloth behind him and was not surprised when Cisca, Tannaz, and Fiona entered the room.

H'nez glared at them, but M'kury rose from his seat, gesturing politely to Cisca. "Weyrwoman."

Cisca nodded her thanks and settled herself in the chair beside K'lior.

"Well?" M'kury demanded of the rest of the room. "Are you going to leave our Weyrwomen standing?" His eyes settled challengingly on H'nez.

T'mar and P'der rose quickly and gestured to the Weyrwomen.

"I want them to sit by me," Cisca said, glancing at H'nez. The grizzled rider grimaced before relinquishing his chair to Tannaz.

A younger rider, wearing the knots of a wingleader, vacated the seat on Cisca's other side. "Sit here, little one," he said to Fiona.

"Thank you, V'ney," Cisca said as he moved to the edge of the room. The young man nodded back courteously.

Underneath the table, unseen by the others, Cisca patted

K'lior's knee reassuringly. He looked over to her and smiled, then turned his attention to the rest of the room.

"What are we going to do?" he said, repeating H'nez's words. He nodded to Kentai, the Weyr harper, who stood against one wall. "Harper, what do you say?"

"I haven't got much to say," Kentai admitted, shaking his head sadly. "You all know better than I what happened at the other Weyrs and the symptoms of this illness." He gestured with one hand vaguely in the direction of T'jen's weyr.

"And you're not a healer," H'nez added, glaring at K'lior. "When are you going to get Zist and Betrony—"

"That's a question for a later day," Cisca cut in.

"You know why we've no healer, H'nez," M'kury growled. "It's because you goaded old Sitarin into that duel."

H'nez's jaw worked angrily.

"H'nez," K'lior said with a restraining hand upraised. The older rider locked eyes with him for a moment then glanced away, letting out a long, slow breath. K'lior glanced at Cisca, asking, "Have you spoken with Benden's new Weyrwoman?"

Cisca shook her head. "But Melirth has heard from Lorana."

"Who's Lorana?" someone muttered from the back of the room.

"I thought Tullea was second Weyrwoman," someone else added.

"Lorana Impressed at Benden's latest Hatching," Cisca said. "She bespoke Melirth at M'tal's request."

"But her hatchling can't be more than—" M'kury began.

"She's younger than Talenth!" H'nez exclaimed. "How can you expect a dragonet to say anything sensible at that age?"

"Lorana spoke directly to Melirth," Cisca replied. With a slightly wistful look, she continued, "She can speak to any dragon."

"Like Torene?" Fiona blurted in surprise.

"Like Torene," Cisca agreed. "Although I got the feeling from Melirth that . . ." Her voice trailed off and she shook herself, saying, "Anyway, she told Melirth about Kindan's fire-lizard and Salina's Breth."

"And?" H'nez demanded. Cisca turned her head slowly toward him, her dark eyes simmering. The bronze rider cleared his throat hastily and bobbed his head. "My apologies, Weyrwoman."

Cisca held his gaze for a moment more, then looked away, dismissing him from her regard as she said to K'lior, "They can't be certain what is causing the illness or how long it lasts."

"Do they have a cure?" K'lior asked.

Cisca closed her eyes, linking with her dragon, then opened them again. "Lorana is not answering; she may be asleep."

"No help there, then," H'nez growled.

"When people are sick," Tannaz spoke into the ensuing silence, "we quarantine them."

"We started that with the fire-lizards," T'jen agreed. He looked down to the floor a long moment, then brought his chin up jerkily, saying, "Salith and I should be kept away from the weyrlings at the very least."

"Nonsense!" H'nez declared loudly. "Who will teach them?"

"If they are coughing," Fiona spoke up nervously, "could we put masks on them like they did in the Plague?"

A few riders nodded thoughtfully, but H'nez shattered it with a loud guffaw. "Who would put a mask on a dragon?"

"I would," Tannaz declared. "Especially if it helped prevent infection."

K'lior pursed his lips and shook his head. "Perhaps we should wait until we know more."

"How many dragons will die before then?" H'nez demanded angrily.

"Until we know what's causing it, we won't know whether we're helping or hurting," Cisca shouted. Outside, they heard a dragon bellow, and then another—closer—bellowed back.

"That's you put in your place," Tannaz murmured to herself, recognizing the sounds of bronze Ginirth and gold Melirth.

"But we should do *something*," H'nez protested.

"Yes," T'mar agreed heatedly. "We should think and not act rashly."

"As long as Salith isn't near the hatchlings," T'jen said.

K'lior glanced consideringly at the Weyrlingmaster, then nodded. "Take Salith to one of the unused weyrs at the far end of the Bowl." He glanced at T'mar. "I want you to take over the weyrlings."

T'mar looked ready to argue, then paused and finally nodded in acquiescence. "Yes, Weyrleader."

"Everyone is to keep an eye and ear out for any more signs of the illness," K'lior declared. "Report it to me or Cisca immediately." He rose decisively and, with a polite gesture for Cisca to precede him, left the room. Tannaz followed immediately after.

Their departure startled Fiona. She remained seated as the other wingleaders slowly drifted past grumbling darkly among themselves.

"He's too young," she heard H'nez mutter heatedly to himself as he bustled by her. "*You* should have flown her." The rumble of agreement in the Bowl beyond belonged to Ginirth.

Long after everyone had left, Fiona sat, trembling. It was only when she heard Talenth's plaintive, *I itch!*, that she roused herself and left the darkening Council Room.

A fter she finished oiling Talenth into contented slumber, Fiona set off in search of the other Weyrwomen. She found Tannaz first.

"Can you help?" Tannaz asked as she caught sight of her. When Fiona nodded, the older Weyrwoman slumped against the corridor wall and closed her eyes in relief. "Good."

"What do I do?"

"Oh, sorry," Tannaz said shaking herself and standing upright again. "We need to talk to the riders, check on the dragons . . . that sort of stuff."

"Deal with sick aunties?" Fiona murmured, unable to contain herself. "Old uncles?"

"Dragonriders," Tannaz corrected her firmly. Fiona felt herself burn in shame. Tannaz noticed, even in the shadows of the corridor, and relented. "Yes, they probably *are* a bit like old uncles at this moment, but they'll be *protecting* those sick aunties." She nodded forcefully. "So don't forget that."

"What do I say to them?" Fiona asked, working to keep a whining tone out of her voice.

"You know how they feel," Tannaz said, her voice turning softer, warmer. "Probably more than most, since you lost your fire-lizard."

Fiona bit her lip, then shook herself fiercely and nodded for the Weyrwoman to continue.

"So talk to them about how they feel, how you feel. Don't lie but be positive." Tannaz put a hand on her shoulder and squeezed firmly. "You are a Weyrwoman now."

Something in the other's tone made Fiona realize that Tannaz was bestowing upon her a gift, not weighing her with a burden. Tannaz must have seen it, too, for she let go of the young girl and told her brusquely, "Off you go, now!"

As Fiona started off down the corridor in the direction Tannaz had indicated, she realized that she didn't know where to start and slowed down, dithering between going back and asking the other Weyrwoman or just picking a spot and starting.

As if reading her thoughts, or recognizing her omission, Tannaz called after her, "First weyr after the stairwell."

Fiona picked up her pace again, looking anxiously in each entrance to see if it was a stairwell. After a while her pace slowed down again as she began to think about what she was going to do.

What did one say to grieving dragonriders? Fiona wondered. She mulled on this, growing more and more anxious with each step until, by the time she reached the stairwell, she was nearly trembling with fear.

I can't do this, she thought miserably, stopping one pace before the entrance to the weyr. I've only thirteen Turns!

She thought of turning back, of telling Tannaz that everyone had made a mistake, that Talenth had made a mistake in choosing her—and that thought, that horrible thought, brought her up short. She reached out and touched the sleeping queen lightly with her mind. She felt Talenth's fatigued response, realized that the queen was groping slowly toward full consciousness in response to Fiona's needs, and pulled away.

Back to sleep, little one, she thought fondly to her mate.

Kindan had no one, Fiona chided herself, and he was your age when the Plague struck. He saved you and everyone at Fort.

Well, she corrected herself, tears filling her eyes, almost everyone. He couldn't save Mother, or my brothers, or even my sister, the girl he loved.

But he saved *me,* she remembered, and thought of the tales her father had told her of Kindan's bravery. With those in mind, along with images of her own Impression, she lifted her head and stepped forward.

I can do this, she thought, and she called out, "Hello?"

"Who's there?" From the sound, Fiona guessed that the rider was calling from his dragon's weyr.

"Fiona, Talenth's rider," she replied, walking through the rider's quarters to the entrance to the dragon's weyr.

"The new Weyrwoman?" the rider muttered to himself. Then he said, "See, Danorth, that's the youngster we saw Impressing that queen at the last Hatching."

Fiona heard a dragon make an inquiring noise and stepped into view. Danorth was a green dragon. Her rider was an older man, older even that H'nez but, at least from first appearances, not nearly as irascible.

"I'm forgetting my manners!" he exclaimed, rising to his feet and bowing his head. "I am L'rian, Danorth's rider, at your service, Weyrwoman."

Fiona smiled and nodded back.

"Fiona . . ." he murmured thoughtfully, then comprehension brightened his expression. "You were Lord Bemin's child, weren't you?"

"Yes," Fiona replied, not seeing the need to state that she still *was* Bemin's child.

"She was just a baby back then," L'rian said, speaking mostly to his dragon, then caught himself. "My apologies, Weyrwoman, but I often find myself talking aloud to Danorth, just to hear my voice."

"But you get out, don't you?" Fiona asked quickly. The man appeared no older than her father, but then Fiona remembered that weyrfolk aged better than holders, so perhaps he was nearing sixty Turns or even the seventy Turns that Masterharper Zist had.

"Indeed I do!" L'rian replied, straightening up. "My bones might be old, but the mind's still able."

"You knew me as a baby?" Fiona asked uneasily.

"Indeed, I did," L'rian replied. "I was lucky enough to be on the Weyrleader's wing back then, and there was many a time when I'd attend a Gather at Fort Hold."

"Did you know my mother?" Fiona asked, curious. The only memories she had were so dim that she was never willing to put much faith in them.

"I did," L'rian told her, shaking his head sadly. "I knew her before she was Lady Holder, even." He smiled at her. "She looked a lot like you, actually.

"She came from Ruatha," he continued, pleased to see that he had such a willing audience. "At first she spent time at the Harper Hall." L'rian winked at her. "Rumor was that she was sweet on a harper, even though she was the eldest of Ruatha's daughters."

Fiona listened, entranced, for the next half hour while L'rian reminisced.

"Oh, I can go on, can't I?" he said in apology when he realized how long they'd been talking. He smiled. "But it's good to talk to fresh ears; all the stories become new again."

Fiona smiled back. "Thank you for telling me."

"Was that the purpose of your visit?" L'rian asked, somewhat bemused. "I can't think of anyone who might know that I'd met your mother, you know."

"No," Fiona said, rising to her feet and looking anxiously toward the door. "Tannaz asked me to—"

"Check on us?" L'rian guessed with a knowing look.

Fiona thought of prevaricating but realized it was futile. "The loss of the dragons—"

"That was horrible," L'rian confessed. "Even for the weyrfolk, who can only know what's been lost, not what was had."

"Some of them had fire-lizards," Fiona remarked.

"So they did," L'rian agreed. "And those would understand, even if they were still in pain. But only someone who has Impressed can really understand what it is to lose a dragon." He pursed his lips, then leaned closer to Fiona, saying conspiratorially, "If anything were to happen to Danorth, if she were to get ill, I think I'd go *between* with her."

"But what about your loved ones?" Fiona asked in dismay.

"I've seen many of the ones I've loved go *between* already," L'rian told her. "My sons and daughters are all grown, their mothers are well partnered, and my best mates are in the past. I'll have no regrets when the time comes."

"Except one," Fiona corrected. "Fighting Thread."

L'rian barked a laugh. "Fighting Thread!" He turned back to Danorth. "Did you hear that? She thinks we'll fight Thread!"

"It's coming soon," Fiona replied hotly. "And we'll need all dragonriders then."

L'rian paused then, absorbing her words. "I suppose we will at that, if only to carry firestone to the fighting wings," he allowed.

"There, you see, you've something to live for, then," Fiona told him.

L'rian smiled and gave her a tolerant look. After a moment, he grinned and wagged a finger at her. "I'll tell you better."

Fiona looked at him inquiringly.

"I'll wait around until your gold rises, and *then* we can have some serious conversations," the green rider teased.

Fiona felt herself turning bright red, and L'rian burst into a loud, long laugh. She brought herself under control enough to declare, "Heard and witnessed!" which wiped the smirk off the old man's face. She turned to his quarters, saying, "And now, if you'll excuse me, I really must check on the others."

"Go, lass!" L'rian called after her. "Go and may you bring as much joy to the others as you've done to me." As she left she heard him muttering to his dragon, "Did you hear that, Danorth? We're staying on for another three Turns if we can make it. Staying on to talk with the wee one after her dragon rises." There was a thoughtful pause and she heard, just before she moved out of hearing distance, "We might even stick around for her Hatching!"

Fiona schooled herself to spend less time with the next rider and was glad that she managed to spend no more than a quarter of an hour with each of the next six. However, she did promise herself that she would find more time in the coming months to talk with more riders. So many of them reminded her of her father's guards, sturdy men who worked hard and determinedly to provide peace and protect the Lord Holder if the need ever arose.

However, the riders were also different; a breed apart. They spoke of firestone. The older ones spoke of spicy firestone, the sort that burned the throats of their dragons. They spoke of riding straps and tack, they shared with her their horror stories of oiling patchy dragonhide, and they shared memories of past Games, and reminiscences of past mating flights.

While none seemed too overwhelmed by the death of the four dragons, Fiona had been in her father's company long enough to note those who spoke with a forced heartiness—she'd heard the same tone in prideful holders who had over-farmed their lands or were afraid to admit other shortcomings. Often the neediest Fort holder was the one least likely to ask for aid. Lord Bemin was constantly visiting the smaller holds, always on the pretext of preparing or collecting tithe, but even with only thirteen Turns to her, Fiona had noticed the times when her father had ordered some of the guards to help out with a planting or a fencing, or had sent back to the Hold for some special spices or tubers.

"I've so many tubers in our root cellars that I'll have to get rid of them or let them rot," she recalled him saying to one farmer whose entire crop had been ravaged by tunnel snakes. "Would you do me the favor of taking some?"

Or, "My men have grown soft on this trip; would you let me put them to work on that field over there?"

She knew that she still had a lot to learn, so she found it easy enough to listen to the dragonriders and sometimes surprised herself by suggesting that she was hungry—even when she wasn't—and would they have some food with her. Then she'd order down or have their dragon bespeak the watch dragon and have some food brought up to them, and that way she could be certain that the rider ate something that day.

She was genuinely sorry, hours later, to have to interrupt her latest meeting when Talenth woke.

"I've got to go oil her—her skin's itching again!" Fiona declared as she made her departure.

"Go! Give her a good oiling," the brown rider told her, waving her to the door.

"I could come back," she offered tentatively.

"No, I'll need to oil my own beast," he told her kindly. "You go on and see to the others."

Fiona nodded gratefully and rushed back down to the center stairwell and across the bowl to her weyr and itching dragon. She was pleased with her efforts; she'd managed to see everyone on her half of the level.

She oiled Talenth quickly, making sure to lavish lots of praise—using some of the new phrases she'd heard from the older riders—and then rushed off, promising to return when needed.

Go! Be Weyrwoman, Talenth replied with a mixture of pride and curiosity—she was still too young to grasp all the responsibilities of her rider, but she was pleased to know that Fiona was doing what was expected of her.

As Fiona crossed the Weyr Bowl again, she saw that there were many dragons on the ground and in the air: The activity at Fort Weyr looked more normal.

"Fiona!" Tannaz called to her from near the Kitchen Cavern. Fiona waved and rushed over.

"Cisca said we should stop what we're doing and help with the evening activities," Tannaz told her as she got closer. She smiled at the younger Weyrwoman. "Kentai is going to put on a performance and the cooks are putting on a feast."

So, with a mixture of relief and regret, Fiona turned her skills to the evening's activities, and was soon busy learning things she'd never known about Southern Boll cooking from the head cook, Zirana.

"Do you sing?" Kentai asked her at one point.

"Sing?" Fiona repeated, wrestling her attention away from the pungent smells and thinly-sliced meats and vegetables being quickly cooked in front of her. She couldn't help but make a face as she answered, "I sing when I can't avoid it."

"Hmm," Kentai murmured thoughtfully. "Would you prefer to dance?"

"I'd prefer to learn the swords, to be honest," Fiona told him. She'd grown up on the tales of Nerra of Crom, but no matter how she'd tried, she'd never managed to get her father to agree to her taking lessons.

"Ah, Nerra of Crom!" Kentai said with a knowing nod. "Weyrwomen are more often encouraged to gain skill with the bow, and tonight would not be the time for a display of such skill."

"Flaming arrows," Zirana muttered as she poured a batch of thinly-sliced vegetables into a cooking bowl.

"Not after last time!" Kentai laughed. When he caught Fiona's perplexed look, he explained, "Cisca nearly set the weyrling barracks alight."

"Strong," Zirana agreed tersely. She flicked her eyes up to Fiona for a moment. "Good for the Weyr."

"Why bows?" Fiona inquired of Kentai.

"Tradition," Kentai replied. "Besides, using a bow is similar to using a flamethrower a-dragonback, or so the Records say." Before Fiona could ask, he added, "You probably won't be taught until Talenth is old enough to mate."

"Probably?" Fiona said, seizing on the word.

Kentai shrugged. "Nothing is for certain in a Weyr."

"Food is certain," Zirana corrected him. She made a shooing gesture to Kentai. "Hungry harpers is certain."

"Harpering is hungry work," Kentai said reprovingly.

"Cooking is hungry work," Zirana retorted. She beckoned Fiona to come closer. "Come, learn to cook."

Fiona didn't say that she'd been haunting the Fort Hold kitchen since before she could remember, because Zirana's style of cooking was so completely different from Neesa's that Fiona wanted to learn all about it. For one thing, it looked like Zirana tended toward lighter fare than Neesa, working with fresh vegetables, thin-sliced meats, all cooked together quickly at high heat. Neesa's food was more the sort that stewed for half a day or was marinated days in advance. The aroma of cooking food, pungent with fresh spices, banished Fiona's fatigue.

"Weyrwomen—dragonriders and weyrfolk—must know how to cook," Zirana declared, waving a wooden spoon threateningly at Kentai, who had sidled back toward the cooking bowls. "Harpers always know how to eat."

Kentai raised his hands in defeat, saying to Fiona, "Once you've learned as much Boll wisdom as this one is willing to teach you, feel free to find me."

Tannaz, who had been helping one of the dessert cooks preparing fresh fruits, called over to Fiona, "And when you've learned from Zirana, you come to me and I'll teach you proper Igen cooking."

"Igen!" Zirana swore, tending to her pots. "Igen food is thick and heavy."

"I'll teach you how to make desserts from nothing," the cook at Tannaz's side piped up.

"You listen to Ellor, here," Tannaz agreed vehemently. "She's the best."

Ellor blushed and bent back down to her work, looking flattered.

"Keep chattering, Melanwy will hear," Zirana cautioned.

Fiona was startled by the silence that descended. "Who's Melanwy?"

"Headwoman," Zirana replied, bending back down to her

cooking. Fiona saw that Ellor had also returned intently to her work. When she caught Tannaz's eye, the older Weyrwoman shook her head quickly, in an obvious "not now" movement. Fiona sighed and turned her attention back to the amazing dishes that Zirana was preparing.

"Ginger, garlic, onions, mushrooms, pernooms, all a good start for cooking," Zirana explained as she started a fresh cooking bowl, pouring in a quick daub of oil and then throwing in many of the ingredients she'd listed. The smell of ginger, garlic, and pernooms wafted up enticingly. Zirana passed the spoon to Fiona. "You try."

Fiona gave her a startled look before taking the spoon and quickly swirling the ingredients around the bowl.

"No burning, no sticking," Zirana instructed. "Just stir fast."

As Fiona did so, Zirana started throwing in sliced onions, followed by a darkish sauce. "From soya bean," Zirana explained, smiling as she poured it on. "Now meat." And Zirana scooped in a cup of thinly sliced wherry meat.

The aroma arose mouth-wateringly from the bowl and Fiona's stomach gave a lurch, suddenly reminding her that she'd missed lunch. Zirana must have noticed, for she said, "Cooks always hungry, never eat." She patted her flat belly. "Stay thin!"

Under Zirana's guidance, Fiona constructed three more dishes, then the cook surprised her by saying, "Now you make your own."

"What?" Fiona cried in surprise.

"Make your own," Zirana repeated loudly.

"You're letting her make her own, Zirana?" Tannaz called from her cooking island. She told Fiona, "You should be honored. She wouldn't let *me* cook for a whole Turn."

"That's because you're Igen," Zirana retorted, shaking her head. "Igen only think thick food."

Fiona let the conversation wash over her as she looked at the ingredients waiting to be cooked. Garlic, lots of garlic, she decided, throwing it in the sizzling bowl and stirring it quickly. She found a pepper mill and ground it over the garlic, tossing in only a drop of the soya sauce before stirring more. The smell wafted up enticingly. Pernoom, Fiona decided, looking among the various edible Pernese fungi for the one she wanted the most. It had a special flavor, piquant, and unlike any other flavor, hearty yet fresh. There!

Sagooms. She only needed a few and that was just as well as they were always hard to find. She shredded three and poured them on. The smell changed again and she looked for some vinegar. Yes. Then she was ready for the vegetables. Broccoli, carrots, onions. She added beef and, when it was brown, more soya sauce. A bit more pepper, she decided.

"Done?" Zirana asked, intruding into Fiona's reverie. She didn't wait for Fiona's answer but spooned up a small piece of meat and tasted it. "Good," she declared. "You serve this to Weyrleader."

"Me?"

"Weyrleader and wingleaders," Tannaz called across from the hall. "It's a Fort tradition."

Fiona's eyes widened and she looked accusingly at Tannaz. Tannaz understood the look perfectly and laughed. "Not telling you is also a Fort tradition."

"Weyrwomen must cook," Zirana said in agreement.

"It smells good," Ellor added. "Save us some, will you?"

"I've written down the recipe," Kentai said from an out-of-the-way corner, holding up a slate. "You can make more later."

"It's never the same," Fiona said, surprised to hear Zirana echoing the words in unison with her. The older cook turned to her and said approvingly, "You'll do."

Fiona beamed with pride. She'd never been allowed to cook at Fort Hold, even though she'd been in the kitchens since before she could remember. And here, on her first try, she was serving the Weyrleader and Weyrwoman.

She felt awkward that evening as she helped to carry the warming plates to the Weyrleader's table. She was suddenly aware of the amount of noise in the cavern and looked around in surprise to see that most of the tables were full, many of them with women and children. Harper Kentai nodded to her as he made his way to a raised platform set between the two openings to the Bowl. He was busy directing a group of youngsters up onto the stage.

"The children often practice and perform here," Tannaz told her. "Is it different at Fort Hold with the Harper Hall so close?"

Fiona smiled and shook her head. "I suspect we have more performances than the Weyr," she said. "Not only do we host the Hold's performances, but also those of the Hall itself."

"So you get a double dose, do you?" Ellor asked. "Is that a good thing or bad?"

Fiona's eyes twinkled. "As a Lady Holder, I am required to say that it was always a good thing."

"And when you're not a Lady Holder, what would you say?" Tannaz asked.

"I would say that each performance is different," Fiona replied diplomatically.

"Some are better than others," Tannaz guessed.

"A Lady Holder would never say that," Fiona replied, pretending to be shocked. The others laughed.

"I suspect tonight will be good, even for those of us who aren't Lady Holders," Tannaz said.

"I'm not a Lady Holder, I'm a Weyrwoman," Fiona said, partly to remind herself.

"The distinctions are not all that great," a new voice chimed in from behind her. Fiona turned to greet Cisca, who waved her motion aside, saying, "I just wanted to see if Zirana and Ellor weren't overworking you." She glanced at Tannaz and added, "I heard you'd already been put in harness by this one."

"She did well," Tannaz said, not sounding at all contrite.

Cisca cocked her head to one side thoughtfully but said nothing. The gesture must have had some meaning to Tannaz, for the other Weyrwoman blushed and shook her head in silent mirth. Cisca grinned then.

"I take it you've suffered no lasting harm," she said, turning back to Fiona.

"They let me cook!" Fiona exclaimed.

Cisca looked really surprised and gave Zirana and Ellor looks. "Really?"

"Not me," Ellor said, tossing her head in Zirana's direction.

Cisca's eyes widened. "*You* let her cook?"

"She grew up in Neesa's kitchen," Zirana replied. "She learned."

"But they wouldn't ever let me—" Fiona began.

"You watched, didn't you?" Tannaz pointed out.

"Well, yes," Fiona admitted. "But—"

"You learned," Zirana told her. She pointed to the bowl of food that Fiona had prepared, still steaming on the warming trays. "She'll serve you tonight."

"Excellent!" Cisca declared. "I'm looking forward to it."

When the time came, however, Fiona found herself far more nervous than she'd ever remembered. What if no one liked it?

"Take," Zirana told her tersely, pointing to the serving bowl into which she'd heaped the greater portion of Fiona's dish. Repressing a gulp, Fiona lifted the dish by the handles and stopped abruptly as Zirana caught hold of her shoulder, pulled her around, and clapped a lid on top of the dish. "K'lior second, Cisca first," she commanded.

Swallowing nervously, Fiona nodded and started carefully toward the table at which the Weyrleader and Weyrwoman were seated. Their table was directly in front of the stage that Kentai and the youngsters had occupied.

Fiona felt as though all eyes were on her and for a moment she stumbled and felt an instant of blind panic as she envisioned falling down, the beautifully decorated serving dish shattering, and her food splattering all across the clean stone floor.

You'll do fine. Fiona blinked and swallowed hard. The voice was not Talenth's. Was she imagining things?

She took a deep breath to steady herself, raised her head again to look to the Weyrleader's table, and walked with head high and shoulders back, as befitted the daughter of Fort Hold's Lord.

Cisca smiled as Fiona approached her left shoulder and lifted the lid, allowing the steam to rise toward her.

"Ahh! What is this?" she asked theatrically, her eyes twinkling up at Fiona.

"A dish I prepared for you and the Weyrleader," Fiona replied, glancing to K'lior, who returned her look gravely. Cisca took the serving spoon and helped herself to a good portion. She took a quick bite and closed her eyes to help her savor the tastes. She opened them again and smiled at Fiona. "That's wonderful."

Fiona beamed with pleasure and, following Cisca's gesture, moved on to K'lior. The Weyrleader helped himself to a larger portion, added some rice, and took a small taste.

"Hmm, ginger beef!" He gestured to the dish and the table, saying, "Set it down and let others try it."

Fiona put the serving dish down on the warming tray that ran the length of the table and turned to go back to Zirana at the cooking fires.

"Sit here, Fiona," Tannaz said, approaching from behind her and indicating the seat next to Cisca. Taking the seat on Fiona's other side, she grinned and gestured to the serving dish. "Why don't you try the beef? I hear it's great."

Fiona sat and was surprised when the rider sitting opposite Cisca passed her the serving dish.

"Thank you, P'der," Tannaz said to the rider.

The rider nodded to both of them, saying, "Just be sure to leave me some."

"Kentai has the recipe," Fiona told him.

"It wouldn't be the same," P'der replied, retrieving the serving dish that Tannaz was passing back to him, "*This* is your first dish as a Weyrwoman."

"One day you might be the Weyrwoman, and for some reason, the dragonriders set store by how well you can cook," Tannaz murmured to her.

"Is that because Sorka was a great cook?" Fiona wondered out loud, remembering the first Weyrwoman of Pern.

Tannaz laughed. "No, I think it's because a rider thinks first of his stomach."

"Second," K'lior corrected her with an impish grin.

"First of his dragon," Cisca agreed.

"I understand," Fiona replied somberly. Tannaz looked at her in surprise and Fiona hid her discomfort by spooning up a bite of her dish.

It really is good! Fiona thought, amazed. Tannaz, who was still watching her, chuckled, saying, "What, did you think Zirana would let you serve something that wasn't good?" Fiona's look answered her and the Weyrwoman continued, "You're not at the Hold anymore. You'll be treated with respect, but no one will lie to you.

"Of course, if it had been Melanwy, you might have had to make a dish three times before she'd let you serve it to—"

"And a good thing, too," a voice hoarse with age rasped through Tannaz's words.

Tannaz's face drained of color before she could school herself and turn to the speaker.

"Headwoman Melanwy," she said formally. "I'd like you to meet Weyrwoman Fiona, Talenth's rider."

"Hmph!" Melanwy snorted. "Think I can't tell who she is for myself? What, think I'm blind?"

Fiona found herself looking up at a white-haired, stooped, aged woman whose face was lined with Turns of hard living.

"Just because I lost my dragon doesn't mean I've lost my reason, too," Melanwy continued harshly.

Suddenly Kentai was at her side, a hand close to hers. "You'll join us on the stage tonight, won't you?"

"You want me to sing?" Melanwy barked.

"Drums, if you would," Kentai replied courteously. He leaned down to her, adding, "These youngsters can only keep time with a decent drummer."

"Hmph, I can't disagree with you there!" Melanwy snorted. "In my day, they wouldn't have been allowed to entertain even D'mal—" Her voice broke off suddenly and her eyes misted.

"How I miss him." She glanced disapprovingly at K'lior, who had diplomatically engaged in an animated discussion with P'der and could pretend not to hear her.

"Come, then," Kentai said, gently guiding her away, "and show us all how it's done."

For a fleeting moment it looked as though Melanwy was going to rail at the harper's obvious distraction, but her obstinate look faded and, instead, she looked momentarily puzzled.

"Who are you?" she asked Kentai querulously, in a voice and expression that reminded Fiona of a small child looking for her mother.

"I'm Kentai, Melanwy," the harper replied courteously, his troubled eyes darting to Tannaz and Fiona. He gestured to the stage. "You were going to play with us."

"I can't sing," she said once again.

"No, drums," Kentai told her. The rest of their conversation faded away as the harper and the old woman moved toward the noise of the stage.

"I've never found out how old she really is," Tannaz murmured to Fiona. She seemed unsettled by the encounter.

"I think Kentai did wonderfully," Fiona said. When Tannaz gave her a surprised look, she added, "We've any number of older people at Fort Hold who've lost their measure of the days." She remembered all the times she'd sat in with old aunties and uncles. "One moment their thinking is clear and brilliant, the next they're like lost children." She sighed. "It's sad, really. Sometimes I think growing old is no gift at all."

"Melanwy would be the first to agree with you," Tannaz told her. "She wanted to go *between* with Nara and Hinirth and railed at her lot for Turns afterward."

"And she's the headwoman?"

"Not even I have the heart to take that away from her," Tannaz admitted. "When she's not addled, her knowledge of weyrcraft is invaluable." She glanced at Cisca. "We take turns spending time with her, hoping to learn as much as we can before her last day."

"I'll help," Fiona offered. "When Talenth is a bit older, I'm sure I'll have more time."

"I'm not sure I want you around her," Cisca chimed in, surprising Fiona. "She's a morbid thing these days, and I don't think it'd be fair to you."

"I wouldn't mind, Weyrwoman," Fiona told her. "It'd be nothing more than I've done at the Hold, as I was telling Tannaz."

Cisca smiled at her. "I know that," she said. "And that's all the more reason to let you have what few Turns there are to you before you shoulder a grown woman's burdens."

"Thread's coming," Tannaz added in agreement. "You might see the full Pass through."

"I intend to," Fiona declared. She paused for a moment, not because she didn't know what she meant to say next but because she wanted to give the two older Weyrwomen a chance to fully absorb her words. "So it seems that it would make sense for me to know everything I can about the Weyr, wouldn't you agree?"

Tannaz gave her an astonished look, then turned to Cisca, who laughed.

"You made your case." She frowned and added, "Still, I don't think it's fair to rob you so young of your youth. I have a motherly duty—"

"Pardon, Weyrwoman," Fiona interruped, her throat hard, her face hot, "but I lost my mother before my third Turn and, with her, any chance of a proper childhood."

Cisca gave her a look that was part affront, part surprise, but

Fiona met her eyes squarely. "I'm young, I know, but I've had to grow up fast and I don't think I know how to stop."

Before Cisca could respond, K'lior laid a hand on her arm in a gesture that Fiona couldn't interpret: she had never seen her mother and father together. Cisca and K'lior exchanged the briefest of looks before the Weyrwoman turned back to Fiona. "We will talk about this after we've eaten." She raised her free hand above her head to signal for dessert.

"Don't be in such a rush to grow up," Tannaz murmured as their plates were cleared.

"I can't tell you when I ever really thought I was a child," Fiona responded. But in her heart she recalled all the times when she'd been with Kindan and wondered—until the fruit dessert that Tannaz and Ellor had made was served, and she enjoyed it so much that she completely forgot the previous conversation.

As hot *klah* was being served and everyone sat back from their tables, replete, Kentai and the singers began their songs.

> *Drummer, beat, and piper, blow.*
> *Harper, strike, and soldier, go.*
> *Free the flame and sear the grasses.*
> *Till the dawning Red Star passes.*

As they finished, they moved on to a song that Fiona knew quite well and it brought tears to her eyes:

> *In early morning light I see,*
> *A distant dragon come to me.*

Kindan had written the song long before he had come to the Harper Hall, long before the Plague that had killed so many, including all of Fiona's family, except her father. She wondered now, with a thrill running down her spine, how Kindan would feel when he saw her flying *her* dragon toward him one morning.

Before the song was completed however, Fiona felt Talenth stirring.

"Talenth is waking up," she said to Tannaz, wondering what to do.

"Go feed her and see to her," Tannaz ordered with no attempt to keep her exasperation out of her voice. "Your dragon always comes first."

With an apologetic nod to the Weyrleader and Weyrwoman, Fiona rushed out of the Kitchen Cavern and into the dusky Bowl.

I'm coming, she told her dragon.

Fiona was relieved to find that Talenth had no more serious issues than a rumbling stomach and a small flaking spot under her chin. She fed her and oiled her, told her about making her first meal, and calmed the queen down until she settled back into the half-slumber that characterized the majority of her daily activity.

"I'm going back now; call me if you need me," Fiona said. Talenth said nothing in response, and Fiona could sense only the dimmest of images in the sleepy dragonet's mind.

When she went back out into the corridor, she heard voices from the Weyrwoman's quarters, so she headed that way, instead of back to the Bowl.

"Weyrwoman?" Fiona called politely at the entrance.

"Come on in, Fiona," Tannaz called back. "We're having a quick conference before we call it a night."

Inside, Fiona found Cisca, Tannaz, and K'lior grouped around the table. The room was lit by large glow baskets, two glowing green, one blue, and a fourth a dim yellow. With nightfall, the glows brought out the shadows and dark places in the room. Tannaz beckoned to Fiona to come sit on her knee.

"*Whoof!* You're heavier than I thought!" the Weyrwoman exclaimed.

"Maybe you should switch," Cisca suggested.

"What, and admit that I'm smaller than a weyrling?" Tannaz replied. "Think what that would do to my esteem."

Although Fiona knew that she was taller than the older Weyrwoman, it was still a shock to have the fact demonstrated so completely. Tannaz was just one of those people who *seemed* big, no matter what their size, because of their great presence.

"Although," Tannaz admitted after a moment, "if our conversation goes on too long, you're going to have to find a different perch." She complicated manners by tickling Fiona's side. Fiona was still young enough that she was ticklish, and she tried vainly to shift away from Tannaz's teasing fingers.

"We won't keep you long," Cisca said in a tone that silenced both Fiona's giggling and Tannaz's antics. Tannaz turned her complete attention to the Weyrwoman.

"I can't be sure, but I thought I heard two more coughs on the way up here," Tannaz said with a grimace.

"That's what I heard, too," K'lior agreed.

"Melirth says that Asoth and Panunth don't feel well," Cisca reported.

K'lior turned toward the Bowl, thoughtfully. "M'rorin and J'marin ride in H'nez's wing."

"Should we move them up to Salith?" Tannaz wondered.

"I'd say yes," Cisca replied, looking questioningly at K'lior.

"I'll check with Kentai in the morning," he said.

That made sense to Fiona. Everyone knew that harpers got some training in healing.

"I'm not sure that it won't create more tension to separate the wingriders from their wing," K'lior went on.

"When there's a cold going around Fort, the sick people either stay in their quarters or go to the infirmary," Fiona offered tentatively.

"We do that when weyrfolk get sick," Cisca said.

"They don't get sick nearly as much as holders," Tannaz added. "And the riders *never* seem to get sick."

"Why would they go to the infirmary?" K'lior asked Fiona.

"They'd go when they were so sick that they couldn't care for themselves," Fiona replied. "Father and I would visit them either way—usually we'd bring soup or fruits—but it was better for a really sick person to be near the healer at all times."

"We've no healer," Cisca said bitterly.

"I'm not sure it would help with the dragons," K'lior said.

"So who's going to patch them up when they get Thread-scored?" Cisca demanded. She gestured to Tannaz, Fiona, and herself. "We'll be flying queen's wing."

"Not for a while," K'lior reminded her. "And by then I'm sure the Healer Hall will have dispatched a journeyman to us."

Fiona chewed her lip before confessing, "Father said we didn't have enough spare hands to send them to the Halls for eight Turns of learning."

The others looked at her inquiringly.

"That's how long it takes to train a healer," Fiona told them. "Four Turns in the Harper Hall, four more in the Healer Hall."

"Why so long?" Cisca asked.

"Why not just teach healing?" Tannaz added.

"Kindan said that a harper learns a lot of healing," Fiona replied. "The extra turns at the Healer Hall are to learn even more."

"Fort was hard hit by the Plague," K'lior remembered.

"Father said it was the same with all the holds and crafts," Fiona responded. "He said it was getting better now that the holds and crafts were recovering from the Plague, but that there were still fields lying fallow and looms gathering dust."

"I could see how hard it would be to give up an able body in such times," Tannaz said. When Cisca looked ready to disagree, Tannaz explained, "The grain from the fields is needed for the cattle for the dragons, as well as for the holders who tend the cattle."

"Well, we won't solve that problem here," Cisca said, dismissing the issue. "The question is, what to do with these sick dragons?"

"The question is, how many are sick, will they recover, and when?" K'lior corrected her. When she looked at him blankly, he reminded her, "Thread will be coming soon and we'll need every dragon and rider we have."

Even though the conversation was engrossing and worrying, Fiona found herself so tired from the day's events and her own efforts that she could only poorly stifle a yawn.

"And we won't answer them tonight!" K'lior said, rising from his chair. He bowed his head to Fiona. "My apologies, I forgot that not only is your dragon young and growing but so are you."

"Both of you need your rest," Cisca agreed. She, too, found herself yawning. "We *all* need our rest."

"I'll talk with Kentai tomorrow," K'lior said.

"I'll want to listen in," Cisca told him.

"Get up," Tannaz ordered Fiona. "I'll see you to your Weyr."

The last thing Fiona remembered was the sight of Tannaz stretching on her tiptoes to reach up and turn over the last glow in her room.

FIVE

Eyes green, delight
Eyes red, fright
Eyes yellow, worry
Eyes closed, no hurry.

Fort Weyr, Next Morning, AL 507.13.15

The light of morning streaming in to her room woke her. Fiona leapt out of her bed in horror; she hadn't meant to sleep so long. One gentle touch to Talenth confirmed that the young queen was still sleeping, though Fiona got the feeling that Talenth's dreams were troubling her.

As Fiona hastened through her toilet she kept an ear out for any sound of her dragon stirring. She had just finished pulling on her day gown when she heard the unmistakable sound of a dragon coughing.

Talenth? Fiona thought nervously to her dragon. But Talenth did not respond, her mind still sleeping, though twitching with whatever dream bothered her. Fiona raced to her dragon's weyr to confirm her impression: Sure enough, she could see Talenth's flanks and wings twitching as though in some dream flight.

Another cough. Fiona spun around toward the noise. She ran out to the ledge that overlooked the Weyr Bowl and connected her weyr with the other queen's weyrs, her head cocked in the direction of the noise.

It came from her left—that was Tannaz's weyr.

Fiona raced that way, her nostrils flaring for breath. When she reached Kalsenth's weyr, Tannaz looked up at her approach, her eyes red with tears, wide with fear and worry.

"She started last night," Tannaz told her.

"Fiona!" Cisca called, coming into the dragon's lair from Tannaz's quarters. "Good, run to the Kitchen, they should have that decoction ready. Bring it back as fast as you can."

Fiona spun on her heels and took off, racing down the ledge, across the Weyr Bowl, and into the Kitchen Cavern.

"I'm to get the decoction for Kalsenth," Fiona called as she entered, looking around frantically.

"Over here," a man's voice called. She turned to it, saw that it was Kentai, and trotted over, her sides heaving from her run. "It's nearly ready."

Whatever it was smelled good, Fiona realized as she neared the steaming pot. Kentai waved her back, then pulled the pot off the coals, grabbed it with wherhide gloves, and poured its contents into a large bucket that had a ladle hanging from its side.

"Will you be able to manage?" he asked as he handed her the bucket.

Breathless, Fiona nodded and took off again, running nearly as fast as she had on the way down. Her legs complained and she caught a stitch in her side just as she started to climb the incline of the ledge to the weyrs.

"Great," Cisca called, grabbing the bucket from her and leaving Fiona to lean against the wall, panting to regain her wind. "Tannaz, they say that the Weyrwoman at Benden recommended it," Cisca said. Tannaz looked up at her, hollow-eyed. "You know, the one who Impressed that gold before Breth . . ."

Tannaz looked down, then back to her dragon. Fiona stumbled over to her, knelt beside her, and hugged her tight. Tannaz did not react. Worriedly, Fiona exchanged looks with Cisca, but the other only shook her head slightly and frowned down at the bucket, stirring it with the ladle to cool it more quickly.

"Tannaz . . ." Fiona began but was cut off by another cough

from Kalsenth. Again Fiona noticed that sickly smell. Tannaz crumpled against her dragon's side.

Fiona? Talenth called from her weyr.

Wait, Fiona replied, surprising herself. Tannaz was so strong, she couldn't give in now, so soon, she just couldn't!

Setting her jaw, Fiona leaned forward, grabbed Tannaz by the shoulders, and pulled her back.

Tannaz looked up at her, her expression one of mingled surprise and anger.

"You need to take care of your dragon," Fiona said, looking down at her. "You need to feed her this stuff that they use in Benden." A faintly puzzled look entered Tannaz's eyes. "You are her rider; you must be strong."

Fiona leaned back, getting her feet under her and urging Tannaz to rise with her.

"Come on, Tannaz," Cisca added, scooping some of the liquid into the ladle. "Fiona's right."

Tannaz looked at the ladle, looked at her dragon, and nodded.

"Kalsenth," she said aloud, "open your mouth." Before she poured the liquid down her dragon's throat, she checked the temperature against the inside of her wrist. "It's not too hot, you should like it."

"It smells good," Cisca added encouragingly.

The gold dragon waited until Tannaz retracted her arm before closing her mouth and raising her head to swallow the liquid.

"Feed it all to her," Cisca said, extending the bucket to Tannaz.

"There," Fiona said as the gold opened her mouth once more and Tannaz ladled in another dollop, "that's better, isn't it?"

The bucket was empty in no time. Kalsenth lay her head back down and closed her eyes. In a short while she was asleep again.

"You should get some sleep, too," Cisca said to Tannaz. Fiona darted into Tannaz's quarters and returned with pillows and blankets. Tannaz took them gratefully and curled up against her gold.

"We'll check on you later," Cisca promised, passing the empty bucket and ladle over to Fiona and gesturing for her to leave through the weyr entrance.

As Fiona followed the Weyrwoman down the ramp toward the Kitchen Cavern, she spotted Talenth peering timidly out of her weyr. Cisca noticed and nodded to Fiona, "See to her and meet me when you can."

Fiona insisted upon oiling Talenth before feeding her, and between the two tasks it was over an hour before she had the dragonet back in her weyr, sated, scrubbed, and somnolent. Fiona failed to stifle a yawn herself as she headed down the incline toward the Kitchen Cavern, wishing that times were such that she could curl up with her dragon.

Cisca wasn't in the Kitchen Cavern when Fiona arrived. Zirana directed her to a doorway at the back of the cavern and Fiona found herself in a corridor she'd never been in before.

As with all of Fort Weyr, the walls were just as smooth as those at Fort Hold. Fiona ran her hands along them, delighting in the cold smoothness. She knew from her times at other holds and at the Harper Hall that whatever the Oldtimers had used to create such smoothness had failed before all the holds or Weyrs were finished, and she was glad that, having left Fort Hold, she'd been lucky enough to come to Fort Weyr with its reassuring similarities.

I wonder if the layouts are the same? Fiona thought, turning to the right to follow her hunch. She'd been told that Cisca was in the storerooms, and at Fort Hold, the storerooms had been set to the right of the lower corridors.

A faint smell of herbs came to her, and Fiona smiled to herself: She'd guessed right.

"I don't care if we don't have enough," Cisca was saying impatiently as Fiona entered the room. "We'll send for more. Just get all the dried echinacea and bring it to the cooks—we've got to make more of that potion!"

"Just where will you get it?" an older woman's voice asked tetchily.

"It doesn't matter," Cisca said. "Our first need is the sick dragons."

"Dragons don't get sick!" the woman replied. "And who do you think you are, the Weyrwoman?"

Fiona entered the doorway in time to identify the irritable woman as Melanwy.

"But she *is* the Weyrwoman," Fiona declared, only to be surprised by the shushing motions Cisca was making behind the old woman's back. The room was filled with cabinets, except for the far end where there was a work desk and some chairs. Glowbaskets hung from hooks on the walls.

Melanwy's eyes widened in surprise and she said to Fiona, "Who are you?"

"She's Fiona, Melanwy," Cisca said. "She cooked for us last night."

Melanwy's face drained of expression and she tottered to the table and sat down, hard. She dropped her head into her hands. Finally she looked up at Cisca. "But what happened to Nara?"

"She went *between*, Melanwy," Cisca told her softly.

"She did?" the old woman asked, straining to find the memory. "Oh, now I remember." There was a long silence as Melanwy absorbed her loss once again and then, with a sigh, the old woman pushed back the chair and stood up again. "What are we doing here?"

"We're looking for herbs, Melanwy," Cisca said. "We need echinacea and ginger and—"

"Why?"

"Because the dragons are getting sick," Cisca said, trying to keep the weariness out of her voice.

"Dragons don't get sick," Melanwy insisted again. Cisca glanced over at Fiona in exasperation.

"What do we need, Weyrwoman?" Fiona asked, stepping into the room and glancing around. "Besides ginger and echinacea?"

With a relieved look, Cisca passed a slate to Fiona. "Here's the list."

"Melanwy and I can find them," Fiona said, and was instantly gratified to see relief on Cisca's face. "Can't we, Melanwy?"

"Who are you?" Melanwy asked.

"Fiona," she replied quickly. "I'm from Fort Hold, Lord Bemin's daughter."

"What are you doing here?" Melanwy asked, then remembered her manners. "How delightful to meet you; how is your mother?"

"Perhaps Melanwy can help *me*," Fiona said with a significant glance to Cisca.

Cisca brightened. "I'll send some folk to help," she promised, clapping Fiona on the shoulder in thanks as she passed around her and through the doorway.

Fiona turned back to Melanwy. "The Weyrwoman's offered us some of your stores; we'll pay them back as soon as we can, but we've got a sickness and need some herbs—"

"What do you need?" Melanwy asked briskly, gesturing for Fiona to hand her the list.

Melanwy was tired when they had finished locating the last of the herbs, so Fiona escorted her back to her quarters before returning to the Kitchen Cavern.

"Take this up to T'jen," Cisca was saying to one of the kitchenfolk as Fiona entered. She turned to a young rider standing attentively beside her and continued, "Take this to the Harper Hall and see if they can help."

The rider nodded and left, moving briskly. It was then that Cisca noticed Fiona.

"Melanwy was tired, so I brought her back to her quarters to rest," Fiona told her.

Cisca gestured her to a table on which were laid out some rolls, butter, mugs, and a pitcher of *klah*.

"Right now there are five sick dragons," Cisca told her once as they were seated. "Salith, Asoth, Danorth, Panunth, and Kalsenth."

Fiona was confused. "Salith is T'jen's brown, right?"

"Oh, sorry, I forgot that you've only been here—how long has it been?" Cisca said, then waved the question away. "Asoth is J'marin's blue—he's the one who had the gold fire-lizard, Siaymon—Danorth is L'rian's green, and Panunth is M'rorin's blue."

Fiona tried to fix the names of the riders, the dragons, and their colors in her head but found, to her annoyance, that she couldn't.

"I used to be good with names," she said, frowning. "I know all the names of every holder in Fort Hold and all the heads of every hold minor or craft—"

"Don't worry," Cisca assured her. "You'll learn them all in time."

Fiona contented herself with a sip from her mug and another bite of her roll. She was surprised that she was so hungry until she remembered that she hadn't eaten at all that morning . . . which brought her back to the issue she'd been avoiding. "I seem to be in such a muddle all the time," she confessed to Cisca. She met the Weyrwoman's eyes. "I didn't use to be like this."

Cisca picked up on Fiona's unspoken plea. "I don't think it's the illness," she told her.

"But you've noticed?" Fiona persisted. "Is there something wrong with me?"

"If there is, you're not alone." The speaker was K'lior, who was striding up to them. He smiled at Fiona, kissed Cisca on the cheek, and, hooking a chair with his foot, dragged himself up a seat. He looked Fiona over intently. "How are you feeling?"

"I'm tired all the time," Fiona said. "But isn't that normal after an Impression? And I've thirteen Turns, and all the old ones said that being a teen was tiring."

K'lior smiled reassuringly at her. "It is normal to be tired for the first few months or more after Impressing a dragonet—it takes time for them to reach their growth!" His eyes twinkled as he added, "And I recall being tired for much of my teens, too." He looked over at Cisca, questioningly.

Fort's Weyrwoman spent some time choosing her words. "Both are very tiring," Cisca began.

"But Kindan had only fourteen Turns when he fought the Plague," Fiona remarked. She pushed herself up straighter. "If he can do that, I don't know why I can't manage a dragon while being a teen."

"Of course you'll manage your dragon," Cisca told her emphatically. With a nod toward the Weyrleader, she added, "Neither K'lior nor I have any doubt about *that*."

"But . . ." Fiona prompted then blushed as she remembered to whom she was speaking. Before she could apologize, K'lior responded, "But we have noticed that you and many others seem more tired than usual, even for those who have newly Impressed."

"There are even some who Impressed many Turns ago," Cisca added, thinking of T'mar.

Fiona was only half relieved by the news. "No one knows why we're feeling this way?"

K'lior shook his head. "No, but we're keeping an eye on it."

"So far it hasn't affected the dragons," Cisca assured her, "just the riders."

"And they're able to do their duty," K'lior added. Fiona noted the way Cisca glanced at the Weyrleader when he made this pronouncement.

"You don't agree, do you?" Fiona asked her.

Cisca chewed her lip thoughtfully before saying, to K'lior's evident irritation, "I have some reservations."

"We've more important matters at the moment," K'lior said, changing the topic. He turned to Cisca. "How are our stores for that herbal recipe Benden sent?"

Cisca shook her head and grimaced. "We'll be out before the end of the day, with just these five."

"We can send riders to the Holds," K'lior decided. He took on the abstracted look of a rider talking to his dragon, smiled briefly, then said, "I've asked T'mar to go to Fort, P'der to go to Southern Boll, and M'kury will go to Ruatha."

"And V'ney and H'nez?" Cisca wondered.

"They'll be handling drill today," K'lior told her.

"Mixed wings?" Cisca asked.

"Of course," K'lior replied, smiling.

Fiona looked confused, so Cisca explained, "K'lior likes to mix up wings to be sure that every rider can work with every wingleader."

"Oh."

"It keeps them on their toes," K'lior told her with a wink.

"It stops them from being bored," Cisca allowed.

"Bored?" Fiona asked, surprised that dragonriders could be bored.

"You must remember that some of them have been drilling all their lives," K'lior said.

"But the Red Star," Fiona protested. "Thread is coming soon!"

"Which is why we drill with mixed wings," K'lior agreed.

Fiona thought on that for a moment and nodded. "Father often makes his guards change posts."

"Probably for the same reason," Cisca said.

A sudden thought caused Fiona to perk up. "Do you suppose, perhaps, that is, if it wouldn't be too much of a burden—"

"Spit it out," Cisca said, gesturing with one hand. She pointed at K'lior. "He won't bite."

K'lior gave them a look of feigned indignation.

"If Talenth doesn't wake, would it be possible for me to go to Fort?"

Cisca and K'lior exchanged a look.

"I told you that she wasn't all addled," Cisca said to the Weyrleader.

"I never said she was," K'lior responded.

"But,"—Fiona shook her head sadly—"I don't know how long Talenth will stay asleep."

"I'm sure you've got at least an hour yet," Cisca assured her.

"And if not," K'lior added, "we'll send word to P'der; he can bring you back and return to Fort Hold for the supplies."

"I'm sure it would help to have you there," Cisca told her.

"You could stop at the Hold while P'der goes to the Healer Hall," K'lior observed. "That would save time." He looked inward for a moment and then back up at Fiona. "T'mar and Zirenth are waiting for you." He gestured to the Bowl outside. "You'd best get going."

"Thank you!" Fiona said, jumping up from her chair and rushing out.

Cisca and K'lior watched her go. Then Cisca turned to the Weyrleader and said, "You know, if this is what she's like when she's tired . . ."

K'lior laughed. "She'll be like you when she's recovered!"

Cisca gave him a fierce look and poked at him. "Enough of that!"

Compared to her dragonet, the bronze dragon waiting for her in the Weyr Bowl was immense. Zirenth craned his long neck around to peer at her as she came running over, and Fiona waved at him, feeling for the first time in a long while like a young girl again.

T'mar waited for her beside Zirenth's huge forefoot and helped her climb up onto the dragon's neck.

"Hold on to the strap, Weyrwoman," T'mar said as he climbed up behind her. He wrapped one arm around her waist and grabbed the fighting strap with the other.

"I'm used to riding behind," Fiona warned him just as Zirenth flexed his huge hind legs and leapt into the air.

"I know you are," T'mar shouted to her as the great bronze's wings beat down and lifted them up. "I thought you might like to have a taste of what it will be like riding your own dragon."

My own dragon! Fiona thought, her eyes seeking out Talenth's weyr. Talenth will be bigger than this puny bronze, she thought with a pride so fierce that it surprised, then gratified her.

"Thank you," she called back as Zirenth rose up out of the Bowl. She saw T'mar's hand as he waved to the watch dragon perched near the Star Stones and then they were gliding down, into the valley below the Weyr spires.

"Are you ready?" T'mar called to her.

Fiona raised her arm and pumped it in the ancient dragonriders' signal of readiness.

A freezing blackness suddenly gripped her, but Fiona was ready for it. *Between* only takes as long as it does to cough three times, she reminded herself.

One.

Two.

Three.

They burst out high over Fort Hold and Fiona couldn't help shouting for joy at the sight.

"You'll do this on your own before you know it, Weyrwoman," T'mar promised her.

Fiona's shout turned into a noise of pure exhilaration as Zirenth banked sharply and spiraled on down to the landing between the Harper Hall and the Hold. Then Zirenth was on the ground, and T'mar jumped down and raised his hands to catch Fiona. She smiled as he deftly lowered her to the ground.

"You've got the longer journey," T'mar said as he stepped away from her.

"I'm the younger," Fiona reminded him with an impish grin.

T'mar had no reply and merely shook his head before waving her on her way.

"If I'm done before you, I'll come up to the Hold," T'mar said as he strode away.

Fiona turned away from him and toward the path up to the

Hold. It was a pleasant walk, although she was surprised to realize how tiring it was for her.

Too much time lazing around, she decided.

As Fiona climbed the path that led up to Fort Hold proper, she
eagerly examined the streets branching off on either side toward
the crafthalls and small cotholds, looking for any of the many Fort
Holder children she knew and had played with, but there was no
sign of them. It's lunchtime, she reminded herself, working to
keep her good mood.

Still, the memories of the rare times she'd managed to get away
from her father's watchful gaze—and where *had* he been?—were
among her happiest: hunting tunnel snakes in the bowels of the
Hold; getting wet and muddy at the nearest lake; chasing sheep
with the herders and herd dogs—all the things that a rambunc-
tious child, though perhaps not the Holder's daughter, would do
when not in fear of a scolding.

The first guard she saw at the Hold's main gate was someone
she did not recognize. Fiona forced a frown off her face—if she
hadn't Impressed, she would know who this new man was. She
was just about to introduce herself when another guard rushed
down from the watchtower, calling, "Lady Fiona!"

It was Jelir, one of the men who had survived the Plague with
her father and Kindan. He and Stennel had carried the dead off to
the massed graves, Fiona recalled.

"Your father's not here, my lady," Jelir told her as she approached him. He gestured back down the path. "He's down at
the Harper Hall." The guard next to him smirked, only to have
Jelir round sharply on him. "Nellin, this is Lady Fiona, the Lord
Holder's daughter."

Nellin sobered up immediately, murmuring, "Didn't mean no
harm, my lady."

What was so funny about her father being at the Harper Hall?
Fiona wondered. She shook herself, remembering her task. "I've
come for some herbals," she told the guards. "The dragons are
sick."

"We'd heard," Jelir replied. "All the fire-lizards are gone."

"Well, don't let us hold you up, my lady," Nellin said, waving
her inside. "From the sounds of it, you've got urgent business."

Fiona nodded and, with a final wave, made her way through

the Hold gates, through the courtyard, and up to the Great Hall gates, which were open to let in the afternoon air.

She was pleased to find Neesa ensconced in the kitchen, and for a brief moment, Fiona felt as though she were a young Lady Holder again, and not a Weyrwoman on an urgent mission.

"Lady Fiona, what a surprise!" Neesa exclaimed when she spotted her. "Can you stay long?"

"I'm afraid I can't," Fiona said. "I've come from the Weyr to beg for some herbals for the dragons."

"So it's real, then?" Neesa asked. "We know about the fire-lizards, of course."

"It's real," Fiona confirmed. "We've five up at Fort Weyr who are coughing. And already at least three have gone *between* from all the Weyrs, including Breth, Benden's queen."

"And the herbals will help?" Neesa asked, her eyes full of concern. "Thread'll be coming soon enough."

"We don't know if the herbals will help," Fiona said. "But they include echinacea and ginger—"

"Marla!" Neesa called. "Drat, where is she? She's as bad as your—"

"Pardon?" Fiona asked. She hadn't been looking at Neesa, but rather in the direction she was calling.

"Oh, nothing!" Neesa replied quickly. "It's just that your father is never around when needed either."

Fiona felt sure that there was more to it than that, but she really didn't have time to wheedle the rest of the news out of the head cook, particularly as a youngster, little younger than Fiona herself, came rushing into the kitchen at that moment.

"Marla, take Fiona down to the stores," Neesa ordered. "She's to have anything she needs. It's Weyr business."

Marla looked confused, frightened, and amazed all at once. "Weyr business?" she repeated.

"Surely you remember Fiona, the Lord Holder's daughter," Neesa said acerbically. "And wouldn't a curtsy be in order?"

Marla hastily curtsied, her face going bright red with embarrassment. "My lady," she said as she dipped down, then flushed even more. "I mean, Weyrwoman."

"Not to worry," Fiona said with a smile and a gesture to ease the other's discomfort. "I *am* in a bit of a hurry, so . . ."

Marla stared at her for a moment, still bemused. Fiona took matters in her own hands. "Follow me, I know the way."

She led the way down to the medicinal storeroom. "We need echinacea the most, then ginger, cinnamon, comfrey, and hyssop," she told Marla as she started pulling containers from cupboards built into the walls. The light in the room was dim. "Bring in one of the glows from outside."

"I don't know," Marla began hesitantly, but Fiona gave her a look that sent the young holder rushing out of the room.

She returned a moment later with a glow basket, which she hung on a hook high up.

"Much better," Fiona said, rummaging through another likely storage bin. "I won't take more than half of your supplies—"

"Half?" Marla squeaked, her eyes round.

"Dragons are big, Marla," Fiona reminded her with just a touch of exasperation in her voice. "They need much more per dose than humans."

"Did you think to ask the herders?" Marla said.

Fiona shook her head. "We'll do that if we need more."

"More?" Marla was astonished at the thought.

Fiona found a carisak and started to stuff it with herbs, each stored in their own jar or box.

"There!" she said briskly, shouldering the carisak. "That should be enough for a couple of days."

Marla was reduced to making small squeaking noises.

"I'll leave you to put the glow back," Fiona said as she made for the door. "No need to follow, I'll see myself out."

"Did you get everything?" Neesa asked as Fiona stopped back at the kitchen for a quick good-bye.

"I only took half of what were in the stores," Fiona told her, "just in case."

"Well," Neesa said consideringly, "you can always come back for the rest if you need."

"We don't even know if it works," Fiona told her. "What we heard from Benden was that they were trying it."

"What are the ingredients again?" Neesa asked. Fiona rattled off the list. "That sounds right to me," Neesa allowed, "not that I know all that much about dragons."

"I'm only just learning myself," Fiona said.

"You learn fast; you'll know it all soon enough," Neesa assured her.

"I don't know," Fiona said, pursing her lips. "I seem to be so tired all the time."

"I suppose that's natural, what with a new dragon and all," Neesa allowed.

"No," Fiona said, shaking her head firmly, "it's not." She explained what Fort's Weyrleader and Weyrwoman had told her, finishing, "So it seems that it's worse than normal."

"But not just for you," Neesa pointed out. "They said others were affected, too, weren't they?"

"Yes," Fiona admitted bleakly. "But what if—"

"If it's to do with this illness, then they'd have the same problem at the other Weyrs, wouldn't they?" Neesa suggested. Fiona frowned at that, thoughtfully. "So all you'd have to do is ask the other Weyrs, wouldn't you?"

"I suppose," Fiona conceded. She shook her head to clear off her morbid thoughts. She had a sackload of herbs to get back to the Weyr now. But before she could take her leave, a loud shout erupted from the Great Hall.

"Father?" Fiona called, recognizing the voice of Lord Holder Bemin in full rage.

"Fiona . . ." Neesa began, but Fiona had already raced out of the kitchen. Neesa followed the fleeing figure of the youngster and shook her head. She paused a moment, listening, then turned back to her pots. No matter what, she told herself, there'd be a meal wanted.

"Fiona?" Lord Bemin called out when he spotted his daughter rushing toward him from the kitchen. "What are you doing here?"

"I've come for some herbals," Fiona replied, dropping her shoulder to show the carisak slung on it. "What are you doing bellowing like that? I haven't heard you so angry since that time I got lost searching for tunnel snakes."

"Tunnel snakes would be better," Bemin responded, his expression sour, brows furrowed thunderously.

"Weren't you at the Harper Hall?"

"I was," Bemin snapped.

"Are you and Kelsa arguing again?" Fiona asked, her eyes dancing.

Bemin sighed and seemed to deflate where he stood. Fiona was surprised to see the worry lines around his eyes.

"She's not upset about her gold?" Fiona wondered. Kelsa had Impressed a gold fire-lizard a number of Turns back and was quite attached to her. Fiona was certain Kelsa's loss of Valyart had hit her hard. She also recalled that Kelsa and her father had made jokes about which bronze would fly when Valyart mated.

Even though she was the Lord Holder's daughter, or perhaps even more because she was the Lord Holder's daughter, Fiona had spent a lot of her youth with the herdbeasts and animals of the Hold; more than once she had helped a ewe birthing a lamb, or a herdbeast with a breech birth, so reproduction held no secrets for her.

And so it wasn't difficult for her to take in her father's stance and his bellowing, and come up with a shrewd guess: "Kelsa's pregnant, isn't she?"

"We were talking names," Bemin said by way of confirmation. "Kemma if a girl, Belsan if a boy."

Fiona did some quick thinking, her expression growing more radiant by the second. "You were going to tell me at the Hatching, weren't you?"

Bemin nodded.

Fiona let out a cry of joy and ran up to hug her father.

"That's great news!" she exclaimed. She stepped back. "When Talenth is old enough, I'll visit every day—" She frowned, then corrected herself. "—every sevenday at least!"

She saw that her father still looked upset. "What?"

"We fought," Bemin told her. "I wanted the child raised at the Hold, to be the next Holder, particularly if it's a boy."

Fiona could hear his unsaid words: particularly seeing as you're now at the Weyr. She could guess how the discussion, then argument went, her father getting more and more irritated at Kelsa's intransigence.

She snorted. "Father, you're talking about a kilometer's difference! Don't be such a ninny!"

Bemin looked surprised at her response and opened his mouth to reply, but Fiona remembered her mission.

"We can talk about this later," she told him briskly. "These medicines can't wait, and Talenth may wake up any moment now." She patted his arm and rushed by, headed toward the great doors. "Don't worry, it'll work out just fine!"

It was only when she was up on Zirenth's back with T'mar and the dragon was thrusting up into the sky above Fort Hold that Fiona wondered bemusedly at her temerity in giving her own father advice on romance.

Then Zirenth went *between* and she thought no more of it.

After delivering the herbs, Fiona raced across the Weyr Bowl toward the Queens' Quarters and up the ramp to her weyr to find that Talenth was just stirring from her long nap.

I itch, Talenth complained as soon as she spied Fiona. Fiona grabbed the bucket of oil and a brush and sought out the offending spot.

There! Talenth told her with a sigh of contentment. The patch was easily seen and soon dealt with. *Much better.*

Fiona smiled. "Only you could wallow in a simple oiling!"

Nonsense, I'm sure all dragons do it! Talenth corrected her, craning her head around to look at Fiona, her faceted eyes whirling with a touch of worry. *I'm not being mean to you, am I?*

Fiona rushed to Talenth's head and grabbed it, snaking an arm up to scratch the dragon's eye ridges. "No, of course not!" she told her dragon emphatically. "You're the most wonderful, marvelous, amazing friend a person could ever have!"

And you would tell me if I was being difficult, wouldn't you?

Fiona laughed. "As long as you'll tell me if *I'm* being difficult."

You? Never! Talenth replied, twisting her head down a little. *Just there. That feels great.*

Fiona chuckled at Talenth's so readily apparent pleasure and redoubled her efforts.

It had been less than two months, she mused to herself, and she couldn't imagine life without Talenth.

A loud cough from nearby startled her.

As one, dragon and rider turned toward the sound.

"Kalsenth," Fiona murmured, her heart suddenly heavy in her chest.

She's not getting better, Talenth observed. *What will happen if she doesn't get better?*

Fiona shook her head, not daring to answer.

SIX

Brave dragons, fly high, fly true
Gold, bronze, brown, green, and blue.

Fort Weyr, Seven Days Later, AL 507.13.22

"There's no need to worry about more herbals," Tannaz said to Fiona as she entered Kalsenth's weyr early that morning, bearing a steaming bucket full of the pleasant-smelling brew. "It's not working."

Fiona began a protest, but the older woman silenced her with a raised hand. "It hasn't worked at all these last three days."

Tannaz was a shrunken remnant of herself, eyes red-rimmed, hair oily and lank, her skin nearly hanging on her frame. She'd been up every night, twitching with every snort or cough her dragon made—and sometimes she'd started in terror to the sound of other dragons whose coughs echoed in the Weyr Bowl with an eery irrevocability, a harbinger of death.

Kalsenth's breath came and went in wheezes, punctuated erratically by louder coughs that wracked her great gold body from end to end; Fiona cringed to see the beautiful queen in such straits.

"Tell Cisca that I want to move to a higher Weyr," Tannaz said, turning away from Fiona and back to her dragon.

"Tannaz . . . ?" Fiona began but the older, smaller Weyrwoman waved her away with a hand thrown up dismissively.

In a mood that bordered on terror, Fiona left swiftly, calling to her dragon, *Talenth, tell Cisca that Kalsenth has gotten worse.*

After a moment's pause, Fiona's queen, who had clearly been dozing, responded, *I have. She says to meet her in the kitchen.*

Thanks, Fiona replied, altering her trajectory toward the Kitchen Cavern. As she made out the glow of the kitchen fires through the early morning fog, she spotted the darker form of a person near by.

"How's Tannaz this morning?" Melanwy asked. "How's her dragon?"

"Worse," Fiona told her brusquely. Melanwy had taken to skulking around Tannaz's quarters, always ready to help, but Fiona got the distinct impression that the old woman was personifying the old saying: *Misery loves company.* Fiona was growing to hate the older woman's presence but said nothing as Tannaz had made no protest.

"She's addled," Tannaz had told Fiona the only time the younger Weyrwoman had commented on it, her tone making it clear that she had expected more compassion from Fiona. "She thinks that I'm Nara, the old Weyrwoman, half the time." Seeing Fiona's still-troubled expression, Tannaz added, "I don't mind the company. You can't be here all the time; you've got your own dragon to tend."

Fiona couldn't help but hear the resentment in Tannaz's tone at that, the unspoken "Your dragon is healthy, at least."

"I'll see to her," Melanwy said now. As the old woman hobbled off, Fiona heard her add, "Haven't I always seen to her?"

"**F**iona, what is it?" Ellor asked as Fiona entered the Kitchen Cavern.

Fiona was still so unnerved by Melanwy's bizarre behavior that she could only shake her head.

"The Weyrwoman's over there," Ellor said, pointing. She pushed a tray into Fiona's arms. "There's *klah* here and something warm for this cold morning."

Still bemused, Fiona trudged over to the Weyrwoman and set the tray down, sitting only when Cisca gestured for her to do so. The Weyrwoman was so caught up in her own thoughts that it wasn't until she'd offered Fiona a cup of *klah* for the second time that she realized the younger queen rider hadn't responded.

"Fiona!"

Fiona looked up at her, dazed.

"What is it?"

"She's not going to make it, is she?" Fiona said quietly to Cisca. "Neither Kelsanth nor Tannaz, are they?" When Cisca said nothing, Fiona continued, her voice rising along with her anger. "And Melanwy's there every day, just waiting and hoping for the time when—"

"Drink some *klah*," Cisca said, her voice commanding. She pushed a mug into Fiona's numb hands.

Fiona obeyed, but it was as if someone else were moving her hands, someone else drinking. It wasn't supposed to be like this. Dragons were always healthy, they never got sick, they never . . . died.

"She's going to go with her, isn't she?" ahe asked, absently dropping her mug on the table.

"If she does, it'll be her choice," Cisca replied quietly.

"So what's Melanwy doing?" Fiona demanded.

"I think," Cisca replied after a moment, "in her own way, she's trying to help."

"Help?" Fiona couldn't believe it.

"In her own way," Cisca repeated. She looked up as K'lior pulled out a chair opposite Fiona. He looked haggard.

"I just left J'marin," K'lior told them.

"The herbal didn't help, did it?" Fiona demanded. She didn't notice the look that K'lior and Cisca exchanged and only barely heard K'lior's words: "No, it didn't."

"That's what Tannaz said," Fiona told them bleakly. She looked up at Cisca. "She said to tell you not to worry about the herbals and that she wants to move to a higher weyr."

"No," Cisca said determinedly. "She'll stay in her weyr." She caught Fiona's look and added, "I'll tell her."

T'mar approached them and, at K'lior's gesture, took a seat. "L'rian's Danorth is not getting better."

"None of them are," declared Kentai, approaching from the cavern's entrance. He grimaced as he added, "I just spoke with our Masterherder."

"Herder?" T'mar murmured in surprise.

"The herbal is very similar to one she uses for sick herdbeasts," Kentai continued, seating himself beside Fiona, across from T'mar. He shook his head. "She says that usually if the herbal doesn't work the first time, the beast will die."

"Dragons aren't the same as herdbeasts!" T'mar declared.

"No," agreed Kentai, "but the herbal is."

"I've spoke with Toma before," K'lior mused, "and she's always seemed very knowledgeable in her craft."

"We can't do *nothing*!" T'mar persisted, looking from Kentai, to Cisca, to K'lior, and finally at Fiona. "Thread is coming and we'll need all our dragons."

"I think we all know that, T'mar," K'lior said soothingly. T'mar simmered under the Weyrleader's gaze.

"Is there anything you suggest we do differently?" Kentai inquired.

T'mar glared at the harper, muttering, "If we had a healer . . ."

"If we had a healer he'd tell us no more than we know," Kentai retorted. He gestured to the Bowl outside and up toward the drumheights by the Star Stones. "I've been in constant communication and no one has a better solution than Kindan's."

"*He's* no healer," T'mar persisted rebelliously.

"No," Kentai responded agreeably, "he's not. But it was Kindan who thought of the ways that helped the Holders during the Plague, and Kindan is the only one who has bonded with a watchwher and Impressed a fire-lizard."

"I trust Kindan," Fiona declared hotly. "He saved my life."

T'mar gave her a surprised look, then lowered his eyes and muttered, "He's no dragonrider."

"But Lorana is," Kentai responded. "And it is her herbal we have been using."

T'mar gave the harper a mulish look but said nothing, instead reaching for a mug and the pitcher of *klah*. He knocked the mug over and broke it.

"Here," Fiona said, pushing her mug toward him. "Have mine."

"No, I'll get my own," T'mar declared.

"T'mar!" Cisca called to him in surprise. The bronze rider looked her way, his brows raised. "Are you sure you want to do that? It's never wise to turn down the favors of a Weyrwoman."

T'mar was about to respond angrily but caught himself. He shook his head and said to Cisca, "My apologies, Weyrwoman, I'm not myself."

Cisca nodded in acknowledgment, then looked pointedly toward Fiona.

T'mar turned toward the younger queen rider. "Weyrwoman, I apologize for my poor manners," he said. "If you'd accept my apology, I'd be most grateful."

The tension at the table was palpable and Fiona felt it as she never had before. It was hers to own; she could deny T'mar's apology and fan the flames or she could cool things off. She shook her head; she was too exhausted for anger to burn long in her.

T'mar caught her movement and mistook it. Affronted, he started to rise, only to stop when Fiona reached across the table and grabbed his hand.

"I was shaking my head at my own foolishness," she said, catching his eyes. "Please sit back down and *do* take my mug. We've all been through too much; we're all worried, and all tired."

She tugged on his hand and T'mar, with a lopsided grin, eased back into his chair.

"I'll pour, if you'll let me, dragonrider," Kentai offered. At T'mar's grateful nod, the harper filled the mug with the warm *klah*.

"I'm sorry to have snapped at you, too," T'mar said as he curled his fingers around the now-warm mug.

"If we're going to survive this," Fiona was surprised to hear herself say, "we are going to have to forgive our outbursts and accept our pain."

" 'Accept our pain,' " Cisca repeated, giving Fiona a curious look.

It was something that Kindan had said, Fiona realized, on one of the rare occasions when she'd managed to get him to talk about the Plague.

"Yes," she said, not caring to elaborate; she felt it would not be a good idea at this moment to mention Kindan again.

"We don't know how long this will last," Kentai said into the silence that fell. He smiled at Fiona. "I think our newest Weyr-woman is right: We are going to have to forgive our outbursts and accept our pain."

"So what are we going to do for the sick dragons?" T'mar wondered.

"Keep them as comfortable as possible; have someone be with them and their riders as often as needed," Fiona replied, remembering other words—this time from her father—about the Plague. In response to T'mar's scrutiny, she explained, "That's what Father said they did during the Plague."

"And I don't think there's much more we can do," Cisca agreed.

"Wait," T'mar surmised dully.

"And hope," Fiona added.

T'mar ran a weary hand through his hair and back down his neck, massaging his tense tendons. "It doesn't seem all that much."

"It's all we can do," K'lior replied.

"It's more than watching and waiting," Fiona added. "It's being someone who listens, someone who helps, a kind word, an understanding touch."

"You've done this before?" T'mar asked, his expression making it clear that he was dramatically reevaluating the young queen rider opposite him.

"Once," Fiona confessed. "With an old uncle."

She could see that the others wanted to know more. "He died holding my hand," she explained. Her face crumpled in memory as she added, "I cried for a sevenday."

The others looked at her expectantly. Fiona wiped her eyes and summoned a smile. "That was nearly two Turns back, just before I turned twelve."

"Your father made you do that?" T'mar asked, sounding offended.

"I am—was—a Lord Holder's daughter," she said. "It was my duty." T'mar's expression remained clouded, so Fiona went on, "I *asked* to be there." She forced back a sob. "If—if it were to happen to me, I'd want to know that someone would be with me, too."

Cisca rose and stood behind her, rubbing her shoulders soothingly. "Queen dragons never make mistakes when it comes to their mates."

"Obviously!" T'mar and Kentai agreed emphatically. K'lior merely nodded, with a special smile for Cisca.

"Very well, then," the Weyrleader said after a moment. "I believe that Weyrwoman Fiona has made an excellent suggestion: We shall arrange for someone to be in attendance of our sick dragons and their riders at all times."

"I'd best return to Tannaz, then," Fiona said, starting to rise. But Cisca pushed her back into her seat.

"She'll survive with Melanwy long enough for you to break your fast."

Before Fiona could draw breath to protest, K'lior added, "You're no use to anyone half-starved."

"There'll be fresh bread in a few minutes," Ellor called from her place by the ovens. "And some buns, too."

"There," Cisca said as though Ellor's words had closed the subject. "You can't leave until you've tried the buns and some bread."

"I'll stay if you'll stay," Fiona declared to T'mar. The older rider gave Fiona an odd look, then nodded.

"I'll get us some more *klah*," Kentai said, rising from his chair.

"Sit! Sit!" Ellor shouted. "There'll be someone along in a moment to do that." She turned back to her ovens, muttering to herself, "Never let harpers near the food."

By the time Fiona had finished her breakfast, the cavern had filled with weyrfolk. As dragonriders entered, they usually called out a greeting to the Weyrleader or Weyrwoman, or were greeted by K'lior or Cisca in turn.

"I didn't know there were so many children," Fiona said as she spotted a group of nearly thirty children arrive at once from one of the entrances at the far side of the cavern.

"Most of a Weyr is children," Kentai told her. He gave the dragonriders an apologetic look and rose. "Which reminds me: I'll need to get started with classes soon, if you'll excuse me."

"Of course," K'lior said. Cisca nodded and waved to him.

"You're wondering, why so many children?" T'mar guessed from Fiona's expression. Fiona nodded.

"The answer's simple," Cisca replied with a mischievous grin. K'lior must have kicked her under the table, for the Weyrwoman started and stuck her tongue out at him. She turned to Fiona.

"Given that there can be up to five hundred dragonriders in a Weyr, and that each of them is expected to do his—"

"—or her," K'lior interjected.

"—duty to the Weyr," Cisca continued with a scowl for her Weyrleader, "you'd expect there to be upward of a thousand youngsters of various ages."

"A thousand?" Fiona repeated, mulling the number over. She knew that Fort Hold proper had at least six thousand, and her father had told her that before the Plague there had been ten thousand, but she'd never really thought about how many of those would be children.

"We've fewer here now. I doubt we've got more than seven hundred," K'lior said thoughtfully.

"What happens to them all?" Fiona asked. "Where are they now?"

"Some are taking lessons," Cisca said, gesturing in the direction Kentai had taken. "Some are helping with the weyr."

"And some are doubtless getting into trouble," K'lior added with a grin.

"Doubtless," Cisca agreed. "And several are probably at this very moment on the Hatching Grounds, looking around and dreaming."

"I doubt it," K'lior declared. "I suspect it's a bit too early for that."

"What do they do when they grow up?" Fiona wondered.

"Some become dragonriders," K'lior said. "Some stay on and work at the Weyr; some become weyrmates."

"*Most* weyrmates work at the Weyr," Cisca corrected him.

"Some learn a craft and become apprenticed," K'lior went on.

"We've three in the Harper Hall at this moment," Cisca pointed out proudly.

"And two at the Smithcrafthall," K'lior reminded her.

"For which we are most grateful," Cisca agreed emphatically.

"Why?"

K'lior snorted. "Let us say, simply, that it is not as easy as one should like to get a tithe from the Smithcrafthall."

"D'gan," Cisca snarled. "The man's a cretin."

"Weyrleader D'gan?" Fiona asked. The Smithcrafthall was located near Telgar, and so came under Telgar Weyr's protection.

"He makes the rest of you look good," Cisca said to K'lior impishly.

K'lior shook his head and turned back to Fiona. "Some of them Impress or go to other Weyrs," he said, continuing the original thread of their conversation.

"And some go to holds," Cisca added.

"I can't think of any who came to Fort," Fiona said.

"You probably wouldn't," Cisca agreed. "They usually come as pairs or groups and prefer to stake out new lands. You wouldn't see many of them at the Hold proper."

"We're an independent lot, weyrfolk," K'lior agreed.

"But you'll never find weyrfolk unwilling to help," Cisca added, "if you ask for it."

"I think I should check on Tannaz now," Fiona said, feeling a bit out of sorts—the Weyrleaders were going on about how great weyrfolk were, and while *she* knew that holderfolk were every bit as kind and good, she didn't think it would be wise to point that out. Besides, no one had offered to help *her* since she'd been in the Weyr; she'd done all the helping.

As she rose from her chair, the bronze dragonrider she recognized as H'nez approached their table, saying, "More dragons coughing this morning, aren't there?"

Fiona was glad to leave; she liked him even less for that comment than she had before. As if K'lior wasn't doing everything he could!

Her anger stayed with her as she crossed the Weyr Bowl. The morning fog was all but gone, leaving only thin wisps of mist at the edges of the Bowl. Wishing for some way to vent her pique, Fiona kicked a stone out of her way. A moment later she found another, then another. What began as a way to relieve anger became a game and she proceeded to kick from one stone to the other until she realized that she was wasting her time and avoiding the task at hand. With an angry huff at herself, Fiona took her bearings and started toward her weyr.

She was halfway up the ramp to her ledge, wondering what she was going to say to Tannaz, wondering whether Melanwy would still be with her, when she heard a noise from her weyr and looked up.

There was a figure standing in the archway, looking startled.

For a moment, Fiona felt a rush of thoughts race over each other: Was it Kentai? Had someone heard Talenth coughing? Or . . .

The figure dropped its head in shame and started down the ramp toward her. It was a dark-haired girl who looked vaguely familiar, though Fiona couldn't recall having met her.

"I—I was just tending the glows," the girl mumbled as she reached Fiona.

Fiona's anger came back then, redoubled. She lashed out her hand and grabbed the girl's wrist. "No, you weren't!"

The girl's eyes flashed briefly, then she lowered them again and just stood there, trying to free her trapped hand with the other.

"What's your name?" Fiona demanded.

The girl stopped her struggling. At Fiona's commanding look, she swallowed and said, "Xhinna."

Still holding the girl's wrist, Fiona turned back to her weyr. "Come on."

"I've got chores to do," Xhinna protested. "I'll get in trouble."

"You're in trouble now," Fiona told her. "More won't matter." She paused to look back at the girl she was pulling along. "You wanted to get a look, didn't you?"

Xhinna tried out a look of incomprehension, but then gave it up; her face settled into a scowl as she murmured, "She should have been mine."

Talenth? Fiona called. *Are you okay?* She felt only the young dragon's sleeping mind. Aloud she said, "The dragon chooses the rider—you know that."

As they entered Talenth's weyr, Fiona cast a quick around the large chamber. The glows were still dim, left over from the night before, but she had expected that. Nothing had been disturbed.

"Have a good look at her," she instructed the dark-haired girl. "But don't wake her. She's still asleep and she'll want oiling the moment she's up."

"She's big," Xhinna said in awe as she sidled around the weyr toward the entrance to Fiona's sleeping quarters. Fiona saw Xhinna's darting glance into the other room, saw the look of longing in her eyes.

Recognition suddenly dawned. "You were the candidate who chased after her," Fiona exclaimed.

Xhinna's face darkened in shame. "I was afraid she was going to get away," she confessed miserably. "And it would have been my fault."

"Your fault?" Fiona thought that was going too far.

"I shouldn't have been there," Xhinna said, grimacing. "I wasn't Searched."

"Nor was I," Fiona remarked, not seeing any harm in that.

Xhinna swallowed hard and raised her eyes to meet Fiona's as she admitted, "I stole the robe from the laundry and snuck in with the others." Her eyes were bright with unshed tears. "Melanwy said I shouldn't have been there, that I might have ruined everything."

"Shh!" Fiona hissed, bringing a finger to her lips. "Melanwy's next door with Tannaz and Kalsenth."

Xhinna's eyes widened in fright and she mouthed a wordless, "Oh!"

"I thought," Fiona began softly after a long moment in which they both stood still, listening guiltily for any sounds that they might have been heard by Melanwy or Tannaz, "that all weyrfolk were allowed to be candidates at a Hatching."

"I'm not weyrfolk," Xhinna murmured in reply. Fiona gave her a surprised look, so Xhinna explained quickly, still in a furtive voice, "They found me all alone in the wild when I was just a baby."

"But you're younger than me," Fiona said in confusion. "It couldn't have been the Plague."

Xhinna shrugged. "No one knows. Perhaps my parents or my mother only just survived; perhaps something else happened, not the Plague."

"But you were raised here," Fiona protested.

"Not to hear the others tell," Xhinna said. "The boys tease me, the girls shun me, and Melanwy . . ."

Fiona urged her to continue.

"Melanwy wants to send me away," Xhinna said so quietly that Fiona had to lean forward to catch her words.

"But she's not the Weyrwoman!" Fiona protested.

"Nor was Cisca until a few Turns back," Xhinna replied. "And while Nara was around, Melanwy was headwoman. Everyone listened to her. She said I wasn't like most other girls." She paused for a long time before she raised her troubled eyes to Fiona's. "And she's right."

Fiona was disturbed by the other girl's intensity, by a nagging suspicion that Xhinna was trying to tell her some deep secret, something important. She examined the younger girl: dark hair fell just beyond her shoulders and framed a swarthy face and dark, intelligent eyes. Her nose was pretty and lightly freckled.

"I don't like Melanwy," Fiona told her honestly. "I know that she's old and addled and deserves respect but . . . she seems so *mean* all the time!"

Xhinna let out a gasp of surprise, her expression brightening.

Fiona turned back to Talenth, who had started twitching. Gesturing to her dragon, she asked the other girl, "Have you seen enough?"

Xhinna's expression made it clear to Fiona that the younger girl could never see enough of the queen dragon but Xhinna only said, "Yes, thank you." She turned away. "I'd best be going."

"Come back any time you want," Fiona called after her. Xhinna stiffened, as though stung by the words, so Fiona added, "I mean it."

The younger girl stopped and turned back, her expression full of surprise. "Really?"

"Really," Fiona replied. She grinned. "Although if you come when Talenth's awake, I'll make you help oil her."

Xhinna's face lit in a smile, her eyes dancing. Fiona was amazed at how much happiness transformed the girl's face.

"I could bring fresh glows," Xhinna offered shyly.

"As long as you don't get in trouble," Fiona replied. Then she remembered Xhinna's Hatching Ground admission and corrected herself. "I mean *more* trouble!"

Xhinna looked pained until she recognized Fiona's teasing tone, and then she grinned again. "I'm always in trouble," she replied. "At least with the glows, I can use you as an excuse."

"Absolutely!" Fiona agreed. She cocked her head as a new thought struck her. "In fact, perhaps we can arrange for you to help me."

For a moment, Xhinna looked absolutely stunned, then her face clouded once more. "Like a drudge?"

"No," Fiona corrected her, her tone turning a bit sharp, "like a friend." She paused and raised her eyebrows at the girl. "They do have those at the Weyr, don't they?"

"Some do," Xhinna allowed.

Fiona guessed that Xhinna added in her thoughts, "just not me."

"Who would I talk to?" Fiona asked.

Xhinna's face darkened once more before she answered, "Melanwy." Fiona's surprise must have shown, for Xhinna added, "Since the Hatching, she's had me report to her directly." Her tone changed to a remarkable approximation of Melanwy's croaking: " 'The honor of the Weyr *must* be maintained.' "

Fiona bit back a chuckle."That sounds just like her," she said. Then she asked, "Why aren't you with her now?"

"She sent me away," Xhinna responded bitterly. "She's in there with Tannaz, just waiting for—"

"What?"

Xhinna took a deep breath and a quick step back toward Fiona, to whisper, "She's just waiting for Kelsanth to die."

Then, as if the enormity of the admission overwhelmed her, Xhinna raced away back toward the Kitchen Cavern.

When Fiona was done tending Talenth, she walked back through her rooms and into the rear corridor. She paused for a moment outside Tannaz's quarters, then moved noisily into the room, calling, "Hello! Tannaz!"

She heard an answering voice coming from Kelsanth's lair and followed it.

Melanwy glanced up sourly from a chair set against the near wall while Tannaz stood wearily at Kelsanth's head, stroking the ailing queen's eye ridges.

"What do you want?" Melanwy demanded.

Fiona ignored her and walked over to Tannaz. "Is there anything I can get you?"

Tannaz looked over to her blearily, shook her head and turned her attention back to scratching Kelsanth's eye ridges.

"You need to eat, Tannaz," Fiona said to the older Weyrwoman. "Why don't we send for some food?"

"It's awfully dark in here," Melanwy declared loudly. She stirred in her chair. "Where's that dratted girl with the new glows?"

Fiona continued to ignore the old headwoman, keeping her attention on Tannaz. "Would you like to take a bath?" she asked, gesturing toward the bathing room. "I could watch her while you do."

Listlessly, Tannaz shook her head.

"I'm going to get you some food," Fiona declared, and turned to leave, only to find Melanwy blocking her way.

"Didn't you hear her?" the old headwoman blared angrily. "She said she didn't want any."

"She didn't say that, Melanwy," Fiona replied calmly, noting with surprise that she was nearly as tall as the old woman. "She didn't say anything."

"Then don't *get* her anything!" Melanwy ordered.

"I'll bring some food," Fiona replied firmly. Her temper flared and she stretched to her full height, her eyes flashing. "And you'll have respect for a Weyrwoman, no matter what your years!"

Either Fiona's words or her tone got through to the old woman. Melanwy stepped aside, wearily sitting back down in her chair, shaking her head. "It won't help, you know. She won't eat." Fiona looked at her. "I already tried."

Fiona was surprised to hear that admission from Melanwy but her anger still flared, so she snapped back, "But you're not a Weyrwoman." Melanwy's eyes widened. Fiona turned back to Tannaz. "If need be, I'll have her dragon *tell* her to eat!"

And, with that, she turned about, strode past Melanwy and Tannaz, and headed down the ledge to the Weyr Bowl, realizing that she could get to the Kitchen Cavern faster that way than going back through her own weyr.

When she arrived, she found Zirana and explained her need. "And do you know where I can find Xhinna?"

"Xhinna?" Zirana repeated in surprise, shaking her head. She gave Fiona a probing look. "What do you want with her?"

"I'll need help carrying this, and Melanwy's snarking about the glows," Fiona explained.

"Melanwy? Is she bothering you?"

"She's with Tannaz," Fiona replied in a tone that made it clear she thought that was worse.

Zirana frowned for a moment, then made up her mind. With a firm nod, she grabbed Fiona by the shoulders and pushed her toward the back entrance to the cavern. "You go back there, listen for children, you'll find Xhinna," Zirana told her. "I'll get the food ready."

"Thanks!" Fiona called back as she trotted away.

"She's no relative of mine, that girl!" Zirana called after her.

Fiona could almost hear Zirana thinking of saying more and then deciding against it. Why was the cook so alarmed about Xhinna?

She passed through the back archway and was surprised to find that she was in a large corridor with branches left and right as well as straight ahead. She knew that there were more living quarters carved into the hard stone of Fort Weyr than she'd seen so far, but even with her foray to the medicine stores, she hadn't quite realized their full extent. A breath of air and some light from the straight corridor informed Fiona that it connected somewhere with the outside of the Weyr and the road that led down to Fort Hold itself.

She cocked her head and listened. Faintly, from the right, she heard the sound of children laughing. She followed it. It was a number of minutes before she found herself outside a large room. Peering in, she saw more children than she'd ever seen at once in the Weyr.

Some were running around, others were grouped together, some were constructing with blocks, and some were playing games Fiona didn't recognize. Toward the back wall, she noticed a very large cluster of children sitting and listening raptly to someone who was pacing and gesturing before them. It was Xhinna.

Fiona moved closer and waited quietly for Xhinna to finish her storytelling. At last the younger girl stopped speaking, and as the children began murmuring to one another, Fiona approached. Some of the children saw her.

"It's the Weyrwoman!" "Weyrwoman Fiona!" Fiona was surprised by their whispers and the looks they gave her.

Then she felt a tug at the base of her tunic and looked down to see a small hand connected to a tiny, solemn-eyed child who couldn't have had more than four Turns.

"Are you really a Weyrwoman?" the little girl asked.

"Yes, I am," Fiona said, kneeling down to meet the girl eye to eye. The little girl backed up a step, startled.

A boy toddled up beside her, clearly a sibling. He was older but not by much. "Is your dragon going to die?"

"Dennon!" Xhinna's voice boomed above her as Fiona struggled to regain her composure. The question had shocked her, chilled her to the bone in a way that going *between* had never done. Xhinna squatted down beside Fiona, placed a hand on her shoulder, and gave her a brief squeeze, all the while saying to Dennon, "It's not polite to talk like that!"

"But you said Tannaz's dragon was going to die!" Dennon protested angrily. "And they say that Asoth and the others are going to die, too!"

"Your father's dragon will be all right, Dennon," Xhinna assured the boy, her tone suddenly quiet and soothing.

"B-but if a *queen* could die, then why not a blue, too?" Dennon blubbered. Beside him, his sister started to quietly cry.

"What's going on here?" a woman's voice called from the entrance. Fiona looked up and recognized Ellor.

"Xhinna, what are you doing?" Ellor demanded. "I thought you were going to watch them!" Under her breath she muttered, "The mothers only wanted a moment's peace!"

"It wasn't my fault," Xhinna replied, getting back to her feet. "Dennon started bawling."

"There, Dennon," Fiona said to the youngster, "it's going to be all right."

"Do you promise?" Dennon asked, his trusting eyes gazing into hers.

"Dennon," Xhinna rasped, "she can't—"

"I promise," Fiona said, raising her voice over Xhinna's. "Things will work out, even though there may be tears."

Remember that.

Fiona stepped back, looking around the room. That voice! She'd heard it before. She reached out to Talenth: *Did you say something?*

No, the queen replied. She *did*.

Who? Cisca?

No, Talenth replied. *I cannot say, I do not know her name. We haven't met yet.*

"Are you all right?" Ellor's voice was full of concern and Fiona realized that the cook had anxiously raced across the room to her.

"I'm fine," Fiona said, rising to her feet.

"Xhinna—" Ellor began, her voice edged with fury.

"She's to come with me," Fiona said. "I need her."

Ellor opened her mouth to protest, but Fiona cut across her. "Zirana sent me to get her."

Ellor looked like she wanted to argue, but the noise of the children distracted her. She blew out her breath in a loud sigh. "Very well," she said, glaring at Xhinna. "Go with the Weyrwoman and mind your manners!"

Fiona needed no more urging and, grabbing Xhinna by the arm, dragged the girl along with her.

"Thanks!" Xhinna said as they entered the corridor. "Now you see what I mean about how everyone always blames me, even when I don't do anything."

Fiona was quiet for a moment. When she spoke, it was with an honest, deliberate voice. "Those children didn't hear about dragons dying from anyone but you," she said. "You didn't set them off just then, but you certainly set them up for it."

Xhinna stopped dead in her tracks. Fiona turned back to her. Xhinna's expression was dead, haunted.

"I thought you were different," Xhinna whispered in shock. "I thought you might really like me."

"Oh, you're worse than a pricklebug, you!" Fiona roared back at her. She reached out and grabbed Xhinna's hand, tugging her along. "You take offense at the slightest bit of honesty." She sighed loudly. "It's like you *expect* everyone to be mean to you."

"That wasn't mean?" Xhinna asked with a sniff.

"It was true!" Fiona snapped. "You told those kids a story and you scared them. You're responsible for that. You made a mistake—it doesn't make you a bad person."

"It doesn't?" Xhinna repeated, as though the concept was new to her.

"No, everyone makes mistakes," Fiona said, increasing her stride as Xhinna started walking beside her faster. "It's what you do about them afterward that matters."

"You mean you don't hate me?"

"Because you wanted to be a dragonrider?" Fiona demanded. "Or because you like telling stories?"

"Because—" Xhinna took a deep breath before confessing in a rush, "Because I hoped that your dragon would die."

Fiona gaped at her, dumbstruck.

"I—I thought if—if I couldn't have her," Xhinna stammered, "then why should you?" She looked down and began to cry. "I'm sorry. It was mean of me, and I didn't mean . . . not really, b-but I thought if I had a dragon then maybe I'd . . ."

"Maybe you'd fit in," Fiona finished for her. Xhinna's head bobbed up and down, but she covered her face with her hands and her sobs continued unabated. Fiona groped for a response. The thought of losing a dragon, any dragon . . .

"You know I had a fire-lizard," she began. She thought she saw Xhinna nod, so she continued. "She was a gold. Her name was Fire." She paused, fighting to retain her composure. "I miss her . . . *so* much!"

"But you've got a queen!" Xhinna sobbed. "And I've got nothing."

"I'm not going to be sorry for you," Fiona told her brusquely. Xhinna stiffened in surprise. "You can still Impress—you're not too old."

"They won't let me on the Hatching Grounds," Xhinna protested miserably.

"They didn't let *me* on the Hatching Grounds," Fiona pointed out to her. "And I still Impressed."

Fiona felt herself losing her temper again. "Look," she said abruptly, reaching out to pry Xhinna's hands away from her face, "I don't have time for all this. Zirana sent me to find you. We've got to get food for Tannaz, and I'm going to get her to eat it, even if I have to force her dragon to make her; so you'd better come along now or you'll be in worse trouble."

She turned and started off back to the Kitchen Cavern. A moment later she felt a hand brush her arm. "I only thought that before I met you," Xhinna said softly. "About your dragon, I mean."

Fiona turned back to her with a small smile. "That's what I thought."

When Fiona and Xhinna arrived at Tannaz's weyr a half an hour later, Xhinna kept her eyes downcast and followed every one of Fiona's orders silently, just as they'd agreed.

"Pretend it's a game," Fiona had suggested with a grin. "You get a point for every order I give you that you can do without making any noise. This time I'll make it easy, but the next time—be warned!—I'll do my very best to make you laugh."

Treating it as a game made it easier for Xhinna to survive Melanwy's sour humor and bitter jibes.

"Seems you've found a leash for her, Weyrwoman," Melanwy admitted grudgingly as Xhinna dipped her head politely to the old headwoman. "She hasn't said a word once." Melanwy paused for a second, then added maliciously, "Usually no one can shut her up."

Xhinna's eyes flashed, but she caught Fiona's look and let the insult pass.

Tannaz ate, although slowly and mechanically, her sick dragon looking on as best she could.

"The food will do *her* good, too," Melanwy said, jabbing a gnarled hand toward the dragon. She glanced at Fiona. "Good on you to find a way to get her to eat."

"She's my friend," Fiona said simply. Tannaz glanced more alertly in her direction and almost managed a smile. Fiona smiled back at her and told her, "You should get some rest."

"I'll watch your dragon," Melanwy declared.

"Actually," Fiona said, trying to sound as diplomatic as she could, "perhaps *both* of you should rest and *we'll* watch Kalsenth."

"What about *your* dragon?" Melanwy protested.

"She's right next door," Fiona said with a dismissive shrug. "I can pop right round to her if she needs. Besides, she's sleeping. You know how they sleep," she added fondly.

"Weelll . . ." Melanwy drawled reluctantly, "I suppose a nap wouldn't do either of us any harm."

"Quite right!" Fiona agreed emphatically, gesturing for Xhinna to guide Tannaz to bed and raising an arm invitingly to the old headwoman. "I'll escort you to your quarters, if you'd like."

Melanwy glanced sourly after Xhinna, then shook her head and rose to her feet. "I can manage on my own," she muttered as she tottered off.

Xhinna helped Tannaz into her bed and covered her with a comforter, then returned to Kalsenth's weyr. The sick queen lay curled up with her head wrapped in front of her body, resting on her tail.

"You did well," Fiona told her, patting Xhinna on the arm. "And you know the reward for a job well done?"

Apparently Xhinna thought she did, for she groaned.

But Fiona surprised her. "You can stay and watch Kalsenth," she said, gesturing to the chair that Melanwy had vacated. "I'll be next door with Talenth—call or come get me if you need me."

"But—"

"You'll do fine," Fiona assured her.

"What if she dies while I'm watching?"

"She won't," Fiona said firmly. She tried not to betray any doubt. "At least, I don't think she will. Tannaz would wake up if that were to happen, I'm sure of it."

"But Melanwy wants to be here if she dies," Xhinna protested.

"She does?" Fiona asked, surprised.

"She wanted to go with Nara and Hinirth," Xhinna said. "She never forgave her for going *between* without her, so she's hoping to go with Kalsenth."

"Why not one of the other dragons?" Fiona asked.

"Only a queen will do for her," Xhinna replied sourly.

"Oh, I see!" It almost made sense. It wasn't as though Melanwy were very comfortable in her old age and she *must* know that her wits were out of kilter, which must be hard on someone used to being regarded as an honored member of the community. Going *between* with a dragon and rider would be an honorable, dignified end for her.

"Well, I'm hoping that she's chosen the wrong dragon," Fiona declared.

Xhinna turned her head in the direction of Tannaz's quarters, murmuring, "I hope so, too."

Against Xhinna's dire pleadings, Fiona brought the weyrgirl to dinner in the Kitchen Cavern with her. She made Xhinna sit next to her, closest to Cisca, in the place that Tannaz would usually have taken.

Cisca and K'lior nodded to the younger girl, and Cisca gave Fiona an inquiring look, but nothing was said until the desserts were served.

"Weren't you the girl who swiped a candidate's robes and snuck onto the Hatching Grounds during the last Hatching?" K'lior asked as he heaped a large helping of apple crumble onto his plate.

Xhinna tried to disappear by scrunching low into her seat, but her bright red face was evident to all.

"I wish *I'd* thought of that," Fiona declared.

"She wasn't the first, I assure you," Kentai added with a wry grin. "It's a long-established tradition in all the Weyrs."

"It didn't work, though, did it?" Cisca asked, not looking at Xhinna but at Fiona. Her look was odd: Fiona couldn't understand what she meant by it.

"The dragons always know," H'nez said from his place beside Kentai. "They know blue riders from bronze riders, too."

What was *that* supposed to mean? Fiona wondered.

"I thought all the weyrfolk were allowed to stand on the Hatching Grounds when they're of age," she said, glancing at Kentai for confirmation.

"We usually limit the number at each Hatching to not more than twice the eggs," Cisca said as she took a forkful of her cake. Noticing Fiona's curious look, she explained, "So as not to crowd the hatchlings or have too many pointless injuries."

"I won't do it again," Xhinna murmured, looking miserable.

"Yes, you will," Fiona declared, glancing fiercely in Cisca's direction. "As long as you've the right."

The senior Weyrwoman met Fiona's look steadily, then flicked a hand in acceptance.

"I don't want to make trouble," Xhinna persisted.

She looked ready to flee, so Fiona placed a hand over her wrist. "She helped me with Tannaz today," she said quickly. "I'd like her to stay with me, to help."

Cisca's furrowed her brow and gave K'lior a questioning look.

"Stay with you?" H'nez repeated.

"That way she could get things in the middle of the night if I have to stay with Tannaz or Kelsanth."

Cisca's expression cleared and, beside her, K'lior nodded. "I don't see any harm in it," he said to the Weyrwoman.

"You wouldn't!" H'nez said with a derisive snort.

"Actually," Cisca declared, glancing directly at H'nez, "I think

it's an excellent idea, particularly with Kelsanth in such straits."
She turned back to Fiona. "I almost wish I had thought of it myself. After all, the weyrlings in the weyrling barracks get plenty of
help, not just from each other but from their friends and family."

"A rider rides his own dragon," H'nez retorted.

"And makes his own straps, hauls his own firestone," K'lior
agreed equably. "But a rider doesn't make his own food, or raise
his offspring without help." He reached across to clasp Cisca's
hand. "Fiona is alone here in the Weyr. It makes sense that someone raised here should help, particularly as Tannaz is indisposed
at the moment."

"I think," Cisca declared, "that even if Kelsanth were not sick, it
would make sense to have someone available to help a queen
rider."

"Like a drudge?" H'nez said with a sneer as he regarded
Xhinna. "Certainly *she* fits the role."

"H'nez!" T'mar growled warningly.

Fiona glared angrily at H'nez, then turned away from him to
Cisca in a move that was an obvious dismissal and slight. The man
might be a bronze rider and many Turns older than she, but he
had a lot to learn about manners.

"Fioonna," Xhinna murmured fearfully beside her.

"Weyrwoman, Weyrleader, thank you," Fiona said with a polite
nod for each. She pushed back her chair and rose, nudging Xhinna
to do the same. "I think we'd best get back to my weyr so that we
can assist Tannaz as she needs.

"Harper," she said, nodding to Kentai. Her gaze skipped over
H'nez and rested on T'mar, as she said, "Wingleader." With that,
she turned sharply and, still clutching Xhinna's arm, marched out
of the cavern.

"Discipline is much lacking in this Weyr," she heard H'nez declare loudly after her.

"As are manners," Kentai agreed just as loudly. And, while she
wasn't sure if H'nez had recognized the harper's tone, Fiona was
certain as she walked away that the Weyr's harper was not referring to *her*.

They stopped to pick up dinner for Tannaz and Melanwy, then hurried off to the Weyrwoman's quarters. When they arrived, they found Melanwy urging Tannaz to "Get in the bath, now! You'll catch your death of cold."

Tannaz's eyes were flat, dark, unresponsive, but something in the intensity of Melanwy's words caused her to move listlessly toward the bathing room.

Melanwy spotted Fiona and Xhinna as she looked around for a place to put the towels. "Don't just stand there gaping!" she snapped. "Take these towels to the laundry and get more!" She waggled a finger warningly at Xhinna. "And mind you that they're not new towels; they'll just be dirtied by all this muck."

"Actually, I think they should be burned," Fiona said, surprising herself with her words.

"Burned?" Melanwy responded, eyebrows rising to the top of her forehead in outrage. "We don't burn towels at Fort Weyr, young lady, no matter what strange things you might have been taught at your Hold!"

"They're infected," Fiona replied. "They should be burned to prevent the spread of this illness to other dragons."

Melanwy's expression abruptly changed to contempt. "Well, of course," she sneered, "and we'll just send to the holders for more."

"Yes, we will," Fiona responded through gritted teeth, anger coursing through her. "And *you'll* address *me* as Weyrwoman!"

"You!" Melanwy repeated. "A mere strip of a girl, barely two months Impressed?"

"Yes, her," a new voice declared loudly from behind Fiona.

Fiona was so angry that she couldn't look back at Cisca—she kept her gaze locked with Melanwy's, making it clear that young or not, she was not going to stand for such poor manners.

"You're no better," Melanwy muttered under her breath. "Should've been Nara."

"But it's not Nara!" Cisca responded sharply. "Nara is dead, her dragon's gone *between,* and *I* am the senior Weyrwoman of Fort Weyr!"

There was the sound of dragons roaring in acknowledgment. Fiona was dimly aware that Talenth had been one of them.

It's all right, Fiona assured her dragon. *I'm all right.*

Of course, Talenth replied unperturbedly. Fiona got the distinct feeling that had Fiona not been all right, Talenth would have been in Kalsenth's weyr immediately. Her dragon's fierce loyalty filled Fiona with joy.

"I'm sure Melanwy had just forgotten, Weyrwoman," she declared, still staring at the old headwoman. She gestured to the archway to Tannaz's quarters. "You'd best help Tannaz with her bath—we'll take care of things here."

As if in a daze, Melanwy nodded and turned to obey. Fiona was surprised that the older woman hadn't continued to argue: it was as if Melanwy had suddenly lost her spirit. In the night outside the weyr, dragons bugled again.

"You need to be careful when you do that, Fiona," Cisca said quietly.

Fiona turned on her heel and found the Weyrwoman standing right in front of her. "Do what?" she asked, bewildered.

"Dragonriders can sometimes force people to their will," Cisca explained. "Not many, and most not as well as you just displayed. It's a dangerous gift and you can find yourself using it on others unwittingly. Later, Melanwy may feel that you forced her, stripped her of her will."

"You mean," Fiona asked with some fear, "I can make people do things they don't want to do?"

"Yes," Cisca said. "Dragonriders learn to recognize it and defend against it, but others . . ."

Xhinna had pressed herself tightly to the wall, her eyes going warily from Fiona to Cisca and back again.

"But," Fiona began slowly after a long silence, "doesn't everyone work to get people to do things they don't want to do?"

"There's a difference between cajoling and forcing," Cisca replied. She waved to Xhinna. "You cajoled Xhinna into helping you; you forced Melanwy. Do you feel the difference?"

Fiona hesitated, then nodded slowly. "I was angry at Melanwy," she said, "I *needed* her to do what I wanted so that I could calm down."

Cisca lowered her eyes and sighed, then looked up again with a grin. "Not that I can blame you this time," she admitted, "but you're going to have to learn *when* you are using that power, at the very least."

Fiona gave her a quizzical look.

"It can become second nature to you, like breathing," Cisca explained. "And then you'll always use it. If you do, you'll never know when people are responding because you made them or because they want to."

Fiona shivered at the idea, both thrilled and horrified . . . and wondering how often she'd done it before.

Cisca must have guessed her thoughts. "You may have used the power before, but you wouldn't have been nearly as strong as you are now that you've Impressed."

Footsteps echoed and then K'lior walked in.

"Queen riders are the strongest," he said, catching one of Cisca's hands in his. "Bronze riders are next." He grinned over at his Weyrwoman. "We learn to resist the power early on."

"You'll get more control over it when your dragon rises to mate," Cisca added.

"Mate?"

"Yes," K'lior replied. "When a queen bloods her kills and rises to mate, she's a mindless creature with only one intent." He nodded to Fiona. "You'll be the one to control her, to force her to your will—"

"And," Cisca continued, interrupting smoothly with a clenching of her hand around K'lior's, "when you learn to control your dragon, you learn to control your power at the same time."

"I don't understand," Xhinna murmured from her place at the wall.

"Fiona will," K'lior replied, nodding toward the young Weyrwoman. "When the time comes."

"But that's Turns away," Cisca said with a wave of her hand. She looked over at Xhinna. "Why don't you take those dirty towels to . . ." She trailed off, considering whom to suggest.

"I know it's not my place to say it, Weyrwoman," Xhinna said, pushing herself from the wall to stand upright. "But it seems that Ellor's always around when there's need and she knows much more than desserts." She swallowed nervously, then finished in a rush, "She'd make a great headwoman—you can ask anyone!"

K'lior made a strange noise in his throat, Fiona looked at Xhinna as though she'd never seen her before, and Cisca looked thoughtful.

Pressing her advantage, Xhinna continued, "As long as Melanwy still thinks she's in charge, she's going to cause trouble, Weyrwoman." She flicked her eyes up to meet Cisca's then, feeling that she'd overstepped herself, dropped her gaze to the floor again and muttered, "At least, that's what I've heard some saying."

Cisca gave Xhinna a considering look, then said, "Why don't you take these to Ellor and ask what's to be done with them?"

"Of course, Weyrwoman," Xhinna said, darting out of the archway and into the Bowl with all possible speed.

"She may have a point," K'lior murmured.

"She *does* have a point," Cisca agreed.

The sound of a dragon coughing reverberated through the night air. Cisca shook her head, then looked back at Fiona, but it was clear that her thoughts were elsewhere as she muttered to herself reflectively, "Ellor *would* make a good headwoman."

"I'll see to the glows," Fiona suggested demurely. After all Cisca's talk about power, she wanted to prove to herself that she could still do some things the usual way.

Cisca nodded. "We'll be in our weyr, if you need us," she said, turning to leave, but K'lior blocked her.

"Actually, I think we'll be in the Council Room," he said. In response to Cisca's questioning look, he explained, "I think it's time to set out watchriders."

"At this hour?" Cisca inquired.

"Immediately," K'lior replied with a firm nod, gesturing for Cisca to precede him. As they left, Fiona heard him continue quietly, "I think it would be a good idea to post several healthy dragons at the holds."

His voice was cut off as he and the Weyrwoman turned toward their quarters.

Fiona entered Tannaz's quarters with a bucket of fresh glows. While she replaced the old glows with new, she also found herself tidying up, making the bed, picking up clothes, and generally behaving in a manner that, she knew, would have surprised everyone back at Fort Hold.

You're a dragonrider now, she told herself sternly. It's time to behave like one.

But, deep down, Fiona knew that her behavior was more to convince herself that she wasn't some sort of monster.

"I'm rather glad that happened," Cisca said as she and K'lior entered the Council Room.

"With Fiona, or Melanwy?"

"Both, I think," Cisca replied, a thoughtful look on her face. She sighed. " 'Out of the mouths of babes!' Xhinna is right that we—I—should replace Melanwy as headwoman but . . ."

"You were afraid?" K'lior teased gently.

Cisca gave him a measuring look, her lips pursed tightly, before finally admitting, "Yes."

K'lior nodded and said nothing.

"Well, maybe not so much afraid as . . . considerate," Cisca corrected herself.

"That's what I thought," K'lior told her.

"And," Cisca said, persisting with her self-examination, "because I was hoping that the problem would solve itself without my pushing."

"And so it did," K'lior observed.

Cisca shook her head. "Only because Fiona lost her temper and pushed instead." She furrowed her brow, deliberating internally.

"She'll be careful now," K'lior said. "You scared her."

"I hope I didn't scare her too much," Cisca admitted ruefully. She smiled at K'lior. "Such power!"

"She said she was angry," K'lior remarked.

"Yes, but she compelled Melanwy," Cisca persisted. "Can you imagine the power that took?"

"Melanwy's—"

"—getting old, yes," Cisca said, cutting across his objection, "but she also has had tens of Turns more time to learn resistance to such compulsions."

"Are you suggesting that Fiona might be a problem?" K'lior asked, his eyes hooded.

"No," Cisca replied with a firm shake of her head. "I'm saying that she's going to be an awesome Weyrwoman when the time comes."

K'lior mulled that over silently until the sound of the wingleaders' footsteps disturbed him.

As usual, H'nez was first, followed closely by T'mar.

Really, K'lior reflected, it should be the other way around. Carefully he schooled his face to hide his thoughts as he examined his eight wingleaders.

H'nez was hotheaded, bold, decisive, and unwilling to admit error. Not quite foolish, but given to moods.

T'mar . . . T'mar was not himself, K'lior thought in agreement with Cisca's earlier disturbing observation. T'mar was more than ten—closer to twelve—Turns older than K'lior. In fact, except for an excessive level of restraint, he was the rider that K'lior himself had most hoped to emulate. But something had happened to T'mar, something that left him slightly off his peak, distracted . . . and it had cost him the leadership of the Weyr when Cisca's Melirth had unexpectedly risen after the death of Nara's Hinirth.

M'kury was a weyrmate of K'lior's; they had Impressed at the same time. M'kury was enthusiastic, outgoing, but perhaps overexuberant. He was also blunt in the extreme, which often rubbed people the wrong way. K'lior had no problem with it, as he had learned that M'kury expected no less in return. In fact, K'lior found it refreshing, even if occasionally overwhelming, to know that M'kury would never refrain from speaking his mind.

V'ney was almost the exact opposite; a person for whom manners were of paramount importance. His polish was well rewarded as he was liked—no, adored—by all his riders and had no lack of weyrmates, either. However, he was not as quick as H'nez or T'mar—when he was on form—when it came to handling a wing in flight. He could be counted to perform magnificently in ordinary maneuvers, but he—and his wing—tended to come apart when things got out of hand.

M'valer and K'rall were old, both having been wingleaders ever since K'lior could remember. And while they were steady, K'lior was concerned that they'd spent so much of their lives preparing—they were both nearing their fiftieth Turn as dragonriders—

that they would have neither the stamina nor the flexibility when it came time to fight live Thread.

The last two wingleaders came last to the Council Room and looked anxious and out-of-place as they entered. K'lior waved them in and gave them encouraging looks, but he could see the way they stiffened when confronted by H'nez's glower and K'rall's half-heard snort.

S'kan and N'jian were brown riders, and all of K'lior's work had not yet reconciled H'nez or K'rall to the fact that there were not enough mature bronzes to lead all the wings. And, in all honesty, K'lior wasn't sure that even if he'd had enough bronzes, he'd consider displacing these two as wingleaders. For, in constrast to the steady V'ney or the aging K'rall and M'valer, S'kan and N'jian were natural leaders—and natural wingleaders.

In fact, K'lior admitted to himself, it was a pity that queens were almost always caught by bronzes, for these two brown riders would both have made excellent Weyrleaders.

"It's not right, browns leading wings!" H'nez had complained when K'lior had first implemented his plan, and the grumbling had never ceased since. And no matter how hard K'lior or Cisca praised the brown riders or encouraged them, the resentment of H'nez, K'rall, and M'valer always kept S'kan and N'jian feeling unworthy.

K'lior gestured for the wingleaders to sit as he pulled out a chair for Cisca, but all except for M'kury waited until the Weyrwoman was properly seated. M'kury gave Cisca an unapologetic grin, which she returned; she was used to the prickly bronze rider and preferred his lack of airs to those of some others.

"So why did you call us at this late hour, K'lior?" M'kury began without preamble. "I was already well into a nice beer and looking forward to some—" He broke off with a meaningful glance toward Cisca.

"I'm not sorry to interrupt your revelry," K'lior replied just as briskly, "particularly as you have made it plain to everyone how tender your backside was after the last time you—"

"All right!" M'kury broke in with a hand upraised, conceding defeat. "Forget I spoke."

"Forgotten," Cisca said, her eyes dancing. She wondered which poor weyrfolk was dealing with M'kury's latest attentions—the young bronze rider seemed to have a different bedwarmer for every one of a sevenday.

"If your reasons for calling us were only to . . ." H'nez began suggestively.

"They were nothing of the sort," Cisca interjected hotly. "However some of us believe in exchanging pleasantries."

K'lior cleared his throat loudly. Cisca gave him a look that was not quite sorry but was, at least, attentive.

"I want to start posting riders to the holds," the Weyrleader announced without preamble.

The outburst was immediate and predictable. "The holds!" "Why now?" "You'd be dispersing our strength!"

"Not that any explanation is required, Weyrleader," M'kury cut in loudly and clearly, quelling the others into silence, "but I'd like it if you could explain your plan and the duration of the dispersement."

"We know that Thread is due very soon," K'lior began, ignoring the expected disgruntled body language displayed by H'nez, K'rall, and M'valer. He hid his surprise at T'mar's similar expression as he continued, "The weather is cold this time of year and may be cold enough that the Thread will freeze when it falls—"

"Blackdust!" M'kury exclaimed, slapping a hand to his forehead. "By the First Egg, why didn't I think of that?"

"Perhaps that's why you're not the Weyrleader," V'ney ventured in a tone that suggested that the exuberant rider might consider containing himself and letting K'lior continue.

M'kury smiled and gestured for K'lior to go on, but before he could, H'nez objected, "And what good would it do to send riders to the holds?"

"Not just the holds," K'lior said, "but all the obvious watchpoints where we might spot Thread or blackdust."

"That'd take two, maybe three wings to manage!" M'valer objected.

K'lior nodded. "I think that we can rotate through the wings, but, yes, I would imagine that to do it properly, with appropriate relief, we would need at least a wing for each major Hold: Ruatha, Fort, and Southern Boll."

"Surely you'd only need a single dragon for each?" M'kury suggested.

"At the Hold proper, yes," K'lior replied. "But I want us to cover every hold minor and every major outcropping or vantage point."

"Oh," M'kury responded. "Yes, I could see how that would eat up—"

"But not a whole wing, surely!" K'rall protested.

"Of course not," K'lior agreed. "We would want to rotate dragon and rider, give them a chance to rest, eat, and change vantage points."

"Why change?" M'valer wondered. "Wouldn't it make more sense to keep them in the same place?"

"Only if your eyes don't get tired of looking at the same place all the time," V'ney drawled in response.

M'valer glanced at the younger rider for a moment, then snorted. "Well said!"

"So," K'lior persisted, "we'll need to send out practically a full Flight of dragons." As expected, the riders perked up at K'lior's use of the word, "Flight."

K'lior nodded to H'nez. "I'd like you to oversee the first effort."

H'nez nodded, his expression veiled. K'lior could only guess at the many possible thoughts in the other's head, but he didn't doubt that surprise and a sense of entitlement were among them.

"Will you be ready by first light?" K'lior asked.

"Of course," H'nez responded automatically.

"Good," K'lior replied, nodding decisively. "I don't think we'll ask you to stay out for more than three days, then we'll rotate."

"I'd like to have K'rall's and M'valer's wings with me," H'nez declared.

"That was my thinking, too," K'lior responded. "But I want you to leave the ill dragons behind—I don't want to stress them any more than necessary."

"But they're only coughing!" H'nez declared, his irritation obvious. "I wouldn't let sick riders stay in their beds; I see no reason—"

K'lior cut across him, turning to K'rall and M'valer to ask, "Do either of you recall dragons coughing, in all your Turns at the Weyr?"

Mutely, K'rall and M'valer shook their heads. K'lior turned his gaze to H'nez. "Because this is something that rare, wingleader, I have decided that we *will* keep the sick dragons in the Weyr." He glanced at M'kury and added sardonically, "If it were only because they'd been out all night drinking beer or cavorting, I'd say differently."

M'kury grinned.

"But," K'lior continued, turning his gaze back to H'nez, "as dragons don't get colds or hangovers, I think it's best if we treat this carefully."

"Especially given the losses at the other Weyrs," Cisca added.

"And the fire-lizards," M'kury added, his usually chipper expression replaced by a much more somber look.

"Yes," K'lior agreed, "particularly because of the fire-lizards. It has been hard enough for our own weyrfolk to handle their loss. Seeing the dragons may help the holders and crafters cope with the loss of their own fire-lizards."

"Or it could irritate them," M'kury said bluntly. K'lior gave him a questioning look. "It could remind them that they lost their fire-lizards while *we*"—he gestured to indicate the whole Weyr—"have kept our dragons."

"They know that without the dragons all Pern would be Threaded!" H'nez declared with a contemptuous glare.

"I doubt they'll be thinking that until Thread actually does fall," Cisca put in. She saw some of the wingleaders—V'ney, T'mar, S'kan, and N'jian—nod in agreement. "Until then," she continued, "the loss of their fire-lizards might increase their resentment toward dragonriders."

"Are you saying that we shouldn't go on patrol?" H'nez wondered.

"No," Cisca replied, shaking her head, "I'm saying that we should remember it and behave accordingly." She gave K'lior a private look that he had come to recognize as a warning that he was shortly going to have a message relayed by his Rineth from her Melirth.

Cisca wonders if maybe you should send different wingleaders out first, Rineth told him an instant later. K'lior caught her eye and shook his head just enough for her to notice.

"The Weyrwoman's right," K'lior said out loud. "H'nez, I want you to take that consideration into account as you set up your patrols. Be sure to make a courtesy call at each hold, major and minor, and each crafthall."

"But—" H'nez protested only to have K'lior cut him off.

"It's good manners," K'lior said. "In fact, it makes good sense as we'll want to be recognizable to their ground crews." He paused. "In fact, H'nez, can you see to it that you identify the various ground crews, too?"

He pursed his lips for a moment as he considered that question himself. "Perhaps that's too much," he decided finally. "We can save that for the next Flight."

"No, Weyrleader, we can do that," H'nez declared, clearly upset that K'lior might think him incapable of the extra effort.

"Excellent," K'lior replied. He looked around the table for any objections, then started on the next topic. "Now, there is one other thing the Weyrwoman wants to discuss with us."

He gestured to Cisca, passing the discussion over to her.

"I'd like to ask Melanwy to care for Tannaz and Kelsanth full time," Cisca said straight out. At the dismayed looks of the riders, she added, "At least until Kelsanth recovers."

"Will she recover?" V'ney asked softly.

"We don't know," K'lior admitted after a moment's silence.

"What about that herbal they used at Benden Weyr?" T'mar asked.

"It didn't work; they lost their senior queen," M'kury declared, obviously surprised that T'mar didn't remember.

"We've more coughing," M'valer added reluctantly.

"Has any dragon recovered from this?" S'kan wondered out loud.

"Not that we've heard," Cisca replied. "Melanwy's old enough that looking after Tannaz and her dragon will be enough for her by itself, so I'm going to ask Ellor to stand in as headwoman."

"Ellor, the dessert cook?" H'nez asked. Cisca nodded and was surprised when the irritable dragonrider responded with, "Good choice. She's capable."

A murmur of agreement went around the table.

"Not that it's our business, anyway," K'rall pointed out. "Running the Weyr is the Weyrwoman's job."

"But it is a good choice," V'ney observed, daring the older rider to disagree.

"Oh, it is, it is," K'rall said quickly.

"Good," K'lior said. He rose from his seat, extending a hand to Cisca, who took it and squeezed it in relief. "Now, it is late and H'nez's flight will be leaving at first light, so I think *we*"—he indicated himself and the Weyrwoman—"will bid you a good night."

"Others," Cisca chimed in with a grin to M'kury, "might want to carefully consider whether it would be wise to resume their activities."

"No problem," M'kury declared. "They're both waiting for me in my quarters!"

SEVEN

Holder looks up to the skies
For signs of promise and demise.
Thread will fall across the ground
Unless brave dragons do abound.

Fort Hold, Morning, AL 507.13.23

The alarm klaxon from the guard tower startled Lord Bemin and he broke into a run, anxious to leave the Great Hall and discover the cause of the disturbance.

The moment he was outside, several huge shadows fell over him and he instantly knew the cause—dragons! A full wing by all rights, he noted quickly as he peered upward, half-hoping to see a small gold above him. But that was not to be, for he knew that Fiona's Talenth was still too young to go *between*. And then a dreadful thought crossed his mind and his face drained of color. He knew that some dragons had died from this new, unknown illness—could this wing of dragons be an honor guard bearing bad news?

He increased his pace, rushing toward where the largest dragon—a bronze—descended. The rider leapt off quickly but the dragon did not depart; clearly a brief visit was intended.

"My Lord—" Lord Bemin began as soon as he was in earshot, halting as he tried to remember the name of this bronze rider.

"I am H'nez," the rider drawled in response, glancing at Bemin as though he were a mere drudge, "rider of Ginirth." He paused for a moment as he examined Bemin and feigned ignorance. "And you are?"

"It has been a long time, Lord H'nez," Bemin replied stiffly, adding with an equally stiff but not very deep bow, "since you have graced this Hold with your presence. If my memory serves, the last time we met you were not yet a wingleader."

"I wouldn't know," H'nez said, "as I have no idea to whom I'm speaking."

Bemin's eyes narrowed in anger; he was wearing his hold colors and his rank was obvious. The dragonrider was being rude—but two could play that game.

"I had heard that dragonriders in the main have excellent eyesight," Bemin commented with another part-bow. "I did not realize that your eyes have gone so aged as mine that you cannot distinguish the colors of Fort Hold." He paused just for a moment and added with an obsequious expression, "That is where you wished to be, is it not?"

H'nez snapped to his full height, his eyes flashing. Beside him, his dragon rumbled ominously.

From within her lair, Fort Hold's watch-wher, usually asleep during the day, bugled a response.

"It is all right, Forsk," Bemin called to her. "We are honored by dragonriders from the Weyr."

Forsk made a sound that was not quite satisfied, feeling enough of Bemin's emotions to know that her bondmate was unhappy.

"So, you are the wherhandler here?" H'nez glanced from the Lord Holder to Forsk's lair and back again.

"Lord Holder Bemin, at your service," Bemin answered, extending a hand in greeting. His irritation with the dragonrider's haughty ways had evaporated as he had realized that no bearer of ill-tidings would have behaved so poorly. That H'nez paused for a long moment before extending his hand in response was not lost upon Bemin but did not detract from his joy at knowing that his daughter's dragon was still safe.

"To what do we owe the honor, dragonrider?" he asked, then added, "And may I offer the hospitality of my Hold to you and your riders?"

"You may," H'nez replied, adding with a sniff, "such as it is."

Bemin chose to ignore the remark, and gestured toward the Great Hall. "If you'd like, we could talk at the table in the Great Hall while we take refreshments."

"As much as that would please me," H'nez replied in a tone that indicated no such thing, "my duties require me to mount a watch on this Hold and all its outlying holds minor."

Bemin did not fail to notice H'nez's emphasis on the word *duties,* with the unspoken implication that Bemin himself had no such pressing worries.

"Perhaps when you've finished setting the watch, you'd accompany me to the Harper Hall," Bemin offered, managing with effort to keep the irritation out of his voice. "I'm sure that Masterharper Zist would be obliged for any news of Fort Weyr."

"I doubt I'll have time," H'nez replied curtly.

Bemin's eyes narrowed at the other's discourtesy, but, with a steadying breath, he tried again to be civil. "Will you need lodging for your riders?"

"Of course," H'nez said, as though it were obvious. "I shall stay here at your Hold. My riders will find lodgings where they are posted."

"Very well," Bemin replied. "If there is any other way in which I may be of assistance—"

"I'll be sure to let you know," H'nez answered dismissively.

"**W**hat are you doing here?" Kelsa asked Bemin in surprise as she made her way to the master's table at the Harper Hall the next morning.

"I spent the night here," Bemin replied. He gestured vaguely toward the journeyman's quarters. "In one of the empty rooms."

Kelsa looked from him to Masterharper Zist and back again, a challenging look in her eyes. "Why?"

"I wanted to show some flexibility," Bemin replied. "Masterharper Zist and I had a long talk—"

"You didn't tell him?" Kelsa broke in angrily, looking betrayed.

"I've been a harper long enough to know the signs," Zist growled at her, waving her anger away and gesturing at the large bowls of breakfast cereals piled in front of her. "As it is, anyone in this Hall who *doesn't* know you're expecting had better have a very good reason," he added, raising his voice enough to carry to every corner of the dining hall.

"I told you," Verilan murmured from his end of the table before immersing himself once again in an old Record.

"It wasn't the sort of thing you can hide, you know," Nonala added with a grin for Bemin. "I must thank you, Lord Holder."

Bemin raised his eyebrows questioningly.

"I won the bet," Nonala said, stretching out her hand toward Verilan.

"What bet?" Kelsa demanded airily. "How come you didn't bet me?"

"Because the bet was about how Bemin would react," Nonala explained. She gave Master Archivist Verilan a reproving look. "A noble man, as I said."

"I never doubted that," Verilan said quickly, looking up from his Record again while dipping into his pocket for a two-mark piece, which he passed over to Nonala's outstretched hand. He gave Bemin an apologetic look as he explained, "The bet was how long it would take before you . . . accepted Kelsa's requirements."

"Verilan thought you might hold out longer," Nonala explained. She gave the archivist the same sort of sisterly look she'd bestowed on him since they'd first met, him having all of ten Turns at the time. She grinned as she continued, "But *I* figured you'd waste no time."

"What are you talking about?" Kelsa demanded. She looked first to the Masterharper, then to Bemin for an explanation.

"I believe that your fellow master is telling you that Lord Holder Bemin will do whatever is necessary for the well-being of you and your child," Zist said finally.

"Oh," Kelsa said, looking toward Bemin. Her expression softened as she asked, "You will?"

"Yes," Bemin swore. "I love you."

Verilan rapped the table and stretched out his hand to Nonala, who ruefully returned the two-mark piece.

Kelsa's eyes slid to the pair of them and they halted the transaction with guilty looks on their faces until Nonala sheepishly confessed, "He bet me that Bemin would say he loved you the first morning he was at the Harper Hall."

"That's usually what happens," Verilan explained. "You'd know that if you read the Records more often."

Kelsa and Nonala shared a look of exasperated affection, shaking their heads nearly in unison.

"So you don't mind if she's raised here?" Kelsa asked Bemin when the moment passed.

"No," he replied promptly. "I'll make arrangements to be a part of her—or his—life, whether here or in the Hold."

"And if she wants to be a harper?"

"All the better," Bemin replied with a grin. "I have, as you know, changed my opinion about harpers in the past twelve Turns or more."

"But if the child would prefer the honor of being a Lord Holder," Zist added, looking challengingly at Kelsa, "I expect there to be no impediments."

"*Our* child," Kelsa declared firmly with an adoring glance at Bemin, "will have nothing stand in her way!"

"I would expect not," Zist agreed, "with such parents as she has."

"I'm impressed," H'nez allowed as he watched the conclusion of the ground-crew drill at Fort Hold two days later.

They were standing on a rise just beyond sight of Fort Hold proper in the first valley beyond. H'nez could see brightly colored flags waving in the distance and small gouts of flame as the ground crews practiced flaming the mock Thread burrows that he had helped to "plant" earlier that morning—" 'Cuz they're used to me and my ways," as Stennel, the head of ground crews noted.

"We'd be much quicker off the mark if we still had the fire-lizards," Stennel explained apologetically. "We trained them to spot the burrows and coordinate our plans." He shook his head regretfully. "As it is, we've got to rely on spotters in the heights, and I'm afraid we'll miss many burrows until they get too big for us."

"And how big is that?" H'nez asked, ignoring what to him was yet another whine about the fire-lizards. Didn't these holders realize that it was the *dragons* of Pern that protected them against Thread? The fire-lizards were nothing more than a minor amusement, even if, as Stennel maintained, they were occasionally useful.

"According to the Records, if we don't find the burrow in the first hour, then it'll be too big to fight with the flamethrowers," Stennel replied. "And then we'd have to get dragons to flame it."

"Hmph," H'nez grunted noncommittally.

"If we don't spot it within eight hours, the Records say that our best hope is to fire the whole valley around it," Stennel continued with a frown.

"Fire a whole valley?" H'nez repeated doubtfully. "I'm sure whoever wrote that Record must have been in error."

"It happened about ten times in the last Turn of the Second Pass," Stennel persisted.

"Who told you that?"

"It was in the Hold Records," Stennel replied. "I read them myself." He stood a bit taller as he continued with a touch of pride, "I wanted to know, as best I could, what we were to expect, my lord."

"Hmm," H'nez murmured, turning his attention to the distant lines of the ground crews as they moved back to their rallying point.

"Anyways, it makes sense," Stennel continued. "It matches up with what we've seen fighting fires."

"Fighting fires?"

Stennel flushed and shrugged. "You could consider a burrow rather like a fire in a high wind—either one will destroy every living thing around it in short order, my lord." He gestured to the ground crews in the distance. "These lads also fight our fires when we have 'em." He shrugged once more, grimacing. "We had the fire-lizards for that, too. They were great spotters.

"But they would never eat the firestone we use for the flamethrowers," he continued reflectively. He cocked an eye at the dragonrider, adding, "I'm sure glad they found the right stuff—although getting our stone is much harder now."

"Harder?"

"Aye," Stennel replied. "No one wanted to dig it before, when it was necessary for the dragons. Now it's only necessary for ground crews and no one *really* wants to go looking for it. Which is why the Mastersmith is working to see if he can adapt our flamethrowers to use proper firestone," he went on, shaking his head. "Last I heard, he hadn't much luck, but I don't get the freshest information all the time." He cast an inviting glance toward the dragonrider. But if he was hoping for illumination, he would be disappointed.

"I see," H'nez replied in a tone that showed that whether he saw or not, he certainly didn't *care.*

Stennel frowned. "I suppose fire's not so much an issue up in your Weyr, surrounded by all that rock."

"No," H'nez answered, "it isn't."

Why was it, he wondered, that holders were so easily irritated? They certainly weren't properly deferential, not even the women. With a frown, H'nez turned away, back toward his dragon. "Well, I've seen enough," he said, climbing up to Ginirth's neck. "I'll see you back at the Hold."

Stennel sketched a salute as the wind of Ginirth's wings buffeted him, and then H'nez was gone, *between.*

It's always good to show the holders their place, H'nez reflected as he and Ginirth emerged once more from *between,* this time over the courtyard of Fort Hold. A group of holder women and children scattered as he guided Ginirth down to a landing. He spotted Lord Holder Bemin striding out into the courtyard from the Great Hall in response to the commotion and allowed himself a grin as he noticed Bemin quickly school his irritated expression into a bland look.

"Does the ground-crew drill meet your approval, my lord?" Bemin asked as H'nez dismounted.

H'nez paused a moment, straightening his clothes, before answering indolently, "As well as could be expected, I suppose." He gave Bemin a measuring look. "I was surprised that you were not there yourself." He raised his eyebrows questioningly. "Was there business at the Harper Hall?"

Bemin flushed, which was not lost on H'nez. "I was busy with inventory," he replied tightly, waving a hand toward the Great Hall. "We have to be certain not only of our tithe to the Weyr but also to ensure that the holders themselves will prosper."

"Of course," H'nez agreed in a tone that was just short of insulting.

Lord Holder Bemin pressed his lips together, firmly stomping on his anger.

H'nez noticed and was amused. He started to add another jibe when the air above them suddenly darkened and was filled with the sound of dragons.

Bemin scanned the riders and their dragons' harnesses for signs of their Weyr, hoping that perhaps M'tal or some other Weyrleader had come to visit the Masterharper. Perhaps, he thought hopefully, I could have a word with him and he could rein in this irritating wingleader.

"V'ney!" H'nez exclaimed as he recognized the bronze rider descending. "You're a day early!"

The bronze rider, still descending, didn't hear him, of course, but H'nez's expression was so clear that when V'ney dismounted, he called out, "H'nez, you need to return to the Weyr."

"Why didn't you have your dragon send for me?" H'nez demanded, exasperated. Bemin was far enough behind that he saw both dragonriders' faces, and it was clear to him that V'ney had brought bad news.

"The sick dragons are—" V'ney stopped abruptly, placing an arm gently on H'nez's shoulder. "They're not expected to make it through the night," he finished quietly. "K'lior thought it would be best if the riders had the companionship of their wing."

H'nez's face was suddenly devoid of all expression. "Of course," he said immediately. "Thank you . . . I'll fill you in on the—"

"You haven't time," V'ney said. "You need to get your wing back *now*." He gestured to Bemin, who had quickened his pace to join them. "I'm sure the Lord Holder can set me right." He gestured skyward. "You get going."

H'nez opened his mouth to argue but stopped himself, settling instead for an abrupt nod of his head.

V'ney's bronze leapt up to the watchtower to make room for H'nez's Ginirth in the landing area.

"Wingleader!" Bemin called out as H'nez climbed astride his dragon. The bronze rider gave him a startled look. "I am sorry we part so sadly."

H'nez locked eyes with him, and for a moment the dragonrider appeared to be his usually arrogant self, but then he visibly deflated in sorrow and said, "I, too."

And then the dragon leapt aloft and was gone, *between*.

"My lord," V'ney said in the stillness that followed, "I'd like to apologize for any ill will wingleader H'nez might have engendered between your Hold and my Weyr." He shook his head and continued, "He's good with his riders and flies well—but he enjoys making trouble with everyone when he's on the ground."

"So I had noticed," Bemin said wryly.

V'ney snorted. "You mean that you couldn't understand why a dragon would choose to be ridden by an ass?"

Bemin's lips quirked upward. "I hadn't put quite *those* words to it, actually."

"Then you're a very tolerant person," V'ney allowed.

EIGHT

Weyrfolk, keep your duty dear
Provide for dragon and for Weyr.
When the Red Star comes on nigh
By your efforts will dragons fly!

Fort Weyr, Afternoon, AL 507.13.25

Xhinna cleared her throat so loudly that Fiona looked up from her position next to J'marin. The blue rider was resting fitfully, having exhausted himself in his ministrations to his ailing blue dragon.

Xhinna's eyes darted to the entranceway and Fiona followed her gaze. There was a rider standing in the doorway. H'nez. Fiona couldn't think of a single thing to say to him and merely glanced back down to J'marin.

H'nez crossed the room, his energy intense and compacted like a tunnel snake ready to strike, but he paused as he spotted the bucket full of green mucus and saw the half-cleaned trail near Asoth's nostrils. The blue dragon gave a rattly breath that startled everyone.

"Asoth!" J'marin exclaimed, raising his head up to look at the dozing blue. Assuring himself that his dragon was no better or worse than before, J'marin glanced around the room. He startled when he caught sight of H'nez and drew himself shakily to his feet.

"Wingleader."

H'nez waved him back down and crossed the last distance to stand beside his blue rider. J'marin looked at his sleeping dragon.

"I don't think I could take losing him," he told H'nez softly.

"What can I do?" H'nez replied. J'marin made ready to reply, then noticed Fiona and Xhinna. H'nez noted his reluctance. "Weyrwoman," he said respectfully, including Xhinna with a glance, "you must be very tired yourself. Why don't you excuse us and I'll stay with J'marin?"

Xhinna rose instantly to comply, but Fiona was reluctant to leave. Xhinna tugged on her sleeve.

"We're not wanted," she told her quietly.

"Speak to Talenth if you need anything," Fiona said to J'marin.

The blue rider nodded. "I will, Weyrwoman, you may count on it."

"You've got your entire wing at hand if you need it," H'nez assured J'marin as Fiona and Xhinna left.

"I know that," J'marin replied, "but the Weyrwoman's been a great comfort."

The rest of their words were lost to Fiona as she entered the corridor and made her way toward the stairs leading down to the Weyr Bowl.

J'marin's Asoth was no worse than the other three ailing dragons: M'rorin's blue Panunth, L'rian's green Danorth, and, of course, Tannaz's gold Kelsanth. T'jen's brown, Salith, was only slightly better off. It seemed to Fiona that Salith's symptoms were similar to those of the others a sevenday earlier. She didn't know if other dragons had the illness, but she'd heard enough coughing to believe that there were more infected dragons.

"Melanwy's up to something," Fiona muttered to herself as they made their way down the stairs. Behind her, Xhinna pointedly made no comment: Fiona had been over this ground with Xhinna so often that the weyrgirl had no more to say on the subject. "She's got H'nez involved, now, too."

"Wingleader H'nez makes his own decisions," Xhinna reminded her. Fiona snorted in disagreement, in response to which Xhinna continued, "I can see how he might listen to Melanwy, but I do not see how any plans of hers might be to his benefit. And H'nez always works to his own benefit."

Fiona made no reply. She was certain that Melanwy had, in the guise of consoling the riders of the sickest dragons, concocted some sort of plot. She knew that whenever she entered a room where Melanwy was, the ex-headwoman stopped talking. Even Tannaz now seemed to positively disdain Fiona's attempts at consoling her.

"Nonsense!" Cisca had declared when Fiona had raised her suspicions with the Weyrwoman. "Tannaz is under a lot of stress and can't be expected to act normally, under the circumstances." But she didn't dismiss Fiona's concerns completely. "All the same," she'd added, "if you can keep an eye on Tannaz, Melanwy, and the others, that would help." She had frowned thoughtfully, then continued, "At least you can provide them comfort."

Fiona had been making the rounds of the ill dragons and their riders every two days. Talenth was extremely supportive of the effort, often walking out into the Weyr Bowl to croon comfortingly to her ill weyrmates, much to the joy and amazement of all the riders.

Xhinna had remained firmly attached to her side, leaving only long enough to complete any errand Fiona requested of her. If their continued company caused any comment, Fiona did not hear of it. Certainly none of the blue or green riders had any words but kindly ones for Xhinna.

"Just because she's not right for a queen doesn't mean she wouldn't suit a green," L'rian had assured Fiona the only time the subject had arisen.

"A green?" Fiona had asked. "But greens only have male riders."

"That's because no one's ever thought to put a girl on the Hatching Grounds," L'rian replied, " 'cept in front of the queen eggs." His lips curved up briefly at the notion. "She might even Impress a blue."

"A blue?" Fiona repeated, surprised.

"The dragons choose," L'rian had assured her with a knowing look, "not the riders."

"She'd have to get on the Grounds to have a chance," Fiona had remarked.

"Seems to me," L'rian replied with a proper grin this time, "that she's the sort to *make* a chance, if given any encouragement."

Fiona gave him a questioning look.

"Well," L'rian replied in a slow drawl, "if she had a queen rider to encourage her, she might take the chance." He wagged a finger at her. "You bear that in mind, if the time comes."

"I will, green rider," Fiona promised.

Fiona could only vaguely imagine the surprised looks of Cisca and K'lior in the unlikely event of Xhinna Impressing a green, but the thought of *H'nez's* expression brought a smile to her lips.

"Come on," she called over her shoulder as they bounded down the stairs. "We can still get something to eat before we have to walk Talenth."

Talenth was now big enough to eat from the pens by the lakeside, and it had become something of a treat for the gold dragon to walk the two-kilometer distance there and back for her snacks. The first time Fiona had seen her dragon make her kill had been less horrifying and more comical as Talenth had to be practically ordered to dispatch the poor fowl she'd chosen as her first live morsel.

"You're supposed to chomp it down!" Fiona had shouted in exasperation. "Go on, kill it!" she'd added, startling herself with her own viciousness.

"Remind me never to make you angry," Cisca had remarked from behind her that day. When Fiona had twirled around, looking entirely too guilty, Cisca had merely chuckled. "They *do* tend to bring out the bloodlust in their riders, don't they?"

"Well," Fiona said after a moment to recover her poise, "I've seen the men work in the slaughter pens and this is far more dignified." She turned back to view Talenth, who was still mauling half-dead fowl, and turned back again to confess to the Weyrwoman, "Except, perhaps, this time."

"Go on," Cisca called encouragingly to Talenth. "You're hungry! Eat it!"

Startled, Talenth paused mid-strike, and the mauled bird scampered away.

"Oh, by the first Egg!" Cisca exclaimed in exasperation. She pointed at Fiona. "*You* go show her how!"

Fiona was just about to when Talenth, whether by design or blunder, neatly swallowed her intended lunch whole.

"Chew!" Fiona yelled.

"If she chokes, you'll have to go down her neck after it," Cisca teased.

But Talenth didn't choke and did chew, her back teeth making short work of both muscle and bone.

That was fun!

"It's supposed to be eating, silly," Fiona chided her, shaking her head.

"Well, now *I'm* hungry!" Cisca had declared, turning back to the Kitchen Cavern.

Now Talenth was so eager to join them that she was already waiting for them by the stairs.

"We would have come for you," Fiona told her.

But I'm hungry now, Talenth replied, turning toward the pens and charging off resolutely.

"You'd hardly think she was ..." Fiona paused, struck once again with an attack of muzzy-headedness. Why was it that she seemed normal most times, but not when she was confronted with sums or other deep thinking? Clearly it wasn't the illness, but it was *something*. It seemed like these days, since Impressing Talenth, if she didn't have someone like Xhinna to remind her, she'd never know where she was supposed to be. She needed more *klah*.

"She has sixty-four days since her hatching," Xhinna supplied smoothly. "Two months and eight days. She's just right for her age."

"Of course she is," Fiona said agreeably, picking up her stride to catch up with her dragon. Secretly, she was irked not only at her own forgetfulness, but at Xhinna's quickness in picking up on it.

It was obvious from the speed with which Talenth selected and dispatched her prey—a rather substantial young sheep—that the queen was really quite hungry.

"They say that when the queen is ready to rise, she's supposed to blood her kill," Xhinna said unexpectedly from Fiona's right side; Fiona had been so engrossed in Talenth's hunger that she hadn't heard the other girl catch up.

"They say it's the queen rider's responsibility to keep her from gorging," Xhinna added conversationally.

Fiona gave her a sharp look, snapping, "She's not gorging now, is she?"

Xhinna went red and shook her head quickly. "No," she said, "I didn't mean it like that."

"Queens get proddy, too," a deeper voice added from behind them. Fiona spun on her heel and found herself facing T'mar. The bronze rider grinned and gestured toward Talenth. "She's growing well."

He turned to Xhinna. "Ellor has requested you in the kitchen."

Xhinna's eyes widened as she tried to imagine what trouble she might have caused this time, and then, with a nod to both dragonriders, she took off in a sprint.

T'mar moved forward to stand beside Fiona. He glanced down at her and said conversationally, "I've discovered that when times are hard, I need my friends most."

Fiona glanced up at him, her expression blank even though she had a gnawing suspicion of his intentions.

"So it is a shame to see you treating the one person who is most attached to you so poorly," T'mar finished, catching her eyes with his own.

Spluttering, Fiona searched for words with which to deny the accusation but she couldn't find them: T'mar was right. She let out her breath with a deep sigh.

"It's just that everyone is always looking at me, judging me," she complained.

"And is this any different from growing up at Fort Hold?" T'mar asked politely.

Fiona shook her head.

"Of course, you haven't exactly gone out of your way to avoid notice," T'mar pointed out. Fiona glanced up sharply at him. "You generated quite a bit of gossip by having Xhinna stay with you."

"She helps me," Fiona declared simply.

"She's with you all the time," T'mar observed. "Night and day, it seems."

Fiona flashed him an angry look. "We're friends!"

"I know that," T'mar replied. "But have you considered what will happen to Xhinna when your Talenth rises and chooses a mate?"

From the look on Fiona's face, it was obvious that she hadn't.

"That's Turns away!" she declared.

"And in all those Turns, where will Xhinna's affections lie?" T'mar wondered, shaking his head firmly. "No matter what your intentions, it will be a brutal adjustment for her to make."

"But she's my friend!" Fiona blurted, her face twisted into a sad expression. "Why can't she still be my friend then?"

"She can," T'mar agreed. "But only if you keep her as a friend." He gestured back toward the kitchen cavern. "If you treat her like a drudge, just because you're out of sorts—and we all are—then what sort of friend will she be?

"And," he continued as he saw Fiona gulp as she absorbed his observation, "if you aren't careful to respect her emotions—all of them—what sort of pain will you cause when your dragon rises to mate?"

"And what about me?" Fiona demanded. At T'mar's puzzled look, she went on, "What about *my* emotions when my dragon rises to mate?"

"You've about three Turns to figure that out, Weyrwoman," he replied shortly. He shook his head. "Not as much time as you'd imagine."

I'm done, Talenth declared and Fiona looked over to her, seeing that the gold had cleaned herself as best she could in the lake.

"We'd best get you back to the weyr, then," she said aloud.

"She'll sleep," T'mar said by way of agreement. A small smile played across his lips and he nodded toward Talenth. "She's growing well, which speaks well for her rider."

"I thought you didn't like me," Fiona exclaimed in surprise.

T'mar snorted. "Just because I am willing to tell you how I see things doesn't mean that I don't like you."

Fiona gave him a look of incredulity.

"If you think about it," he continued, "I arranged to have this quiet talk and also to give you and your dragon some time alone together." He gestured toward her weyr and nodded to her. "I'll bid you a good afternoon."

And, with that, he strode off in the opposite direction.

" . . . So I just wanted to say that I'm sorry for snapping at you," Fiona apologized after she had recounted her conversation with T'mar to Xhinna as they lay in bed late that evening.

"It's all right," Xhinna said dismissively. "You're a queen rider; I'm just a weyrfolk—and not a proper one at that."

"No," Fiona corrected, "it's not all right. You deserve to be treated with respect and kindness." She reached over and hugged Xhinna. "You're my friend and I shouldn't forget that."

Xhinna returned the hug impassively and Fiona cocked an eyebrow at her. When the other girl said nothing in response, Fiona took it upon herself to say with a groan, "Look! We've been over all this before. You're my friend—I'm glad to have your company and your help."

"But T'mar's right," Xhinna said with a glum look.

"Yes, he is," Fiona agreed. "And some day, Turns from now, Talenth"—a fond smile played across her lips—"will rise and mate and things will be different for me in many ways." She was silent for a moment as all the ramifications of that time crashed upon her and she shivered fearfully. Quietly, she continued, "And then I'll *really* need my friends." She glanced imploringly at Xhinna. "Will you be there then?"

"Of course I will," Xhinna declared. She hugged Fiona tightly.

"Good," Fiona said, "because I'm sure I'll be a right proper wherry when that day comes!"

Xhinna snorted a laugh. "I don't doubt it for an instant."

"But now," Fiona added with a wide yawn, "it's late and we should sleep." She draped an arm over Xhinna and, in moments, was sound asleep.

"**W**ake up!" Fiona urged Xhinna. "Something's happening!"

A draft of cold air hit her as she leapt out of the bed, and she yelped as her bare feet touched the cold floor. The sense of urgency that had awakened her overwhelmed her fatigue.

Pulling on slippers and a robe, she ran to the ledge and looked out into the Weyr Bowl. "I'm right!" she declared. "Get up, Xhinna—now! Something's up!"

Startled into full wakefulness, Xhinna darted out of bed without any of Fiona's cold-feet histrionics and was at her side seconds later.

"See?" Fiona said pointing. "There are dragons down there and—listen!"

A male voice was issuing instructions softly in the night fog. "All here, then?" It was H'nez.

"Come on!" Fiona urged, darting into Talenth's weyr and out through the entrance into the Weyr Bowl proper.

"Help me with her," an old woman's voice demanded querulously.

"I'm all right," Tannaz replied, her voice sounding dead in the night air. "It's Kelsanth—she can barely move." Softly, she added, "Come on, dear, just a short walk and then we can go together."

"No!" Fiona's shout rent the night air. "No, you can't!" She turned back to her weyr. "Talenth! Talenth, wake up! Talk to Kelsanth, tell her she can't! She can't go *between*!"

"Fiona," Tannaz called. To the others, she said, "I told you, you were too loud."

"It doesn't matter," Melanwy said soothingly. "Just get Kelsanth down the ledge, now, and we can go."

"No!" Fiona cried again, willing Talenth to wake up. The young queen snorted in her sleep and lifted her head blearily.

Fiona?

Tell her to stop! Fiona shouted to her dragon.

"Fiona," someone else called softly through the night air. It was Cisca.

"They're going *between* forever!" Fiona cried.

"I know," Cisca replied calmly. "It's their choice."

"I didn't want to wake you," Tannaz called from her place in the Weyr Bowl.

Fiona turned and rushed out of her weyr, jumping off the ledge and landing hard on the packed ground below, her anger and despair carrying her quickly to Tannaz.

"You weren't even going to say good-bye?" Fiona demanded hotly. She turned to the other shining dragon eyes arrayed in the Weyr Bowl. She recognized them through some instinct beyond normal—Asoth, Panunth, Danorth—all the sickest dragons, including Kelsanth, who wheezingly trundled down the ramp from her lair.

"They won't last another day," Tannaz said imploringly. She gestured miserably to Kelsanth. "And I can't live without her."

"There must be another way!" Fiona cried. "There has to be!"

"There is none," H'nez declared.

"I have to agree," K'lior chimed in. His voice came from the ledge near his weyr. He was carrying a glow basket and Fiona saw it approach her, a shimmering ball of light in the night mist. "Once joined, a dragon and rider are together until death."

"I spoke with Mikal once," M'rorin called out from the dark. "He said that if he'd had the chance, he would have gone *between* with his dragon."

"But not everyone does," Fiona complained. "Salina stayed behind when her Breth went *between*!"

"Fiona," Cisca said, "it is their choice."

"I hope you never have to make it," Tannaz added quietly.

It was too much. Fiona broke down, great sobs engulfing her and her eyes blurring with tears. An arm wrapped around her shoulder and someone was embracing her, and then, suddenly, she was looking up into Tannaz's eyes.

"Let us say good-bye," the older Weyrwoman said quietly.

"I'll never see you again," Fiona wailed, crushing herself against Tannaz's tall frame, clinging to her. But her strength was spent, and after a moment, Tannaz pulled herself free of her grasp. Someone else replaced her.

"Be strong, Weyrwoman," M'rorin told her huskily. Fiona hugged him tightly, her senses informing her that all around her, the scene was being repeated with K'lior, Cisca, H'nez, T'mar, and the others.

"We must hurry," Melanwy called from above them, clearly having managed to climb onto Kelsanth. "There is not much time."

"Weyrwoman," J'marin said to Fiona, hugging her tightly and then pushing her away. "You will survive, you will thrive."

Fiona could say nothing in response, her stomach heaving with sorrow and despair.

"Don't forget what I said, Weyrwoman," L'rian whispered quietly to her as he gave her a hug. "Given a chance, let her on the Hatching Grounds."

"For this?" Fiona demanded, gesturely wildly around at the dying dragons.

"There must come better days," L'rian replied.

"Then *stay* for them," Fiona demanded.

"Not without my Danorth," L'rian said, shaking his head sadly. "There'd be no life without her." He gestured behind her to her weyr and Talenth, whom Fiona heard crooning anxiously in the background. "Could you live without your queen?" Before Fiona could reply, L'rian continued, "I can't live without my dragon. I'm a dragonrider." He reached down and, with one hand, gently raised her chin so her eyes met his. "Let me be remembered as a dragonrider, Weyrwoman."

"All right," Fiona agreed softly, her tears dimming her vision. L'rian hugged her quickly, stepped away, and patted her on the back. "Good girl!"

"We must get going!" Melanwy declared once more. "We'll wake the whole Weyr!"

"The loss of just one dragon will wake the whole Weyr," Cisca retorted sourly.

"Cisca," Tannaz called out from the darkness, now closer to her dragon, probably climbing onto her shoulders, "I'm sorry."

"You do what your heart tells you," Cisca replied, "and I can't argue with you."

At last all were on their dragons.

"Weyrwoman, we're ready," J'marin called to Tannaz through the night fog.

"Very well," Tannaz replied. At an unspoken command, four sets of dragon wings cupped air, four sets of feet leapt up, four dragons climbed briefly in the still night and then—were gone, *between*.

Fiona only vaguely remembered the massed bugles and keening of the Weyr; she only vaguely remembered collapsing as the grief, magnified a hundredfold by all the dragons of Fort Weyr, rebounded through her, but she dimly recalled Xhinna hovering anxiously nearby, and then being scooped up by strong, warm hands and gingerly carried back to her weyr and laid into her bed, and then sleep swept over her and she remembered no more until the dawn.

NINE

Blackdust, crack dust
Floating in the sky,
Dragonriders do trust
Thread will soon be nigh.

Fort Weyr, Morning, AL 507.13.26

The pall of disaster the next morning was shattered by the watch dragon's bugled cry.

Blackdust! The dragon's cry was echoed throughout the Weyr. *Fort Hold reports blackdust.*

The news galvanized the Weyr.

The Weyrleader wants you in the Records Room, Talenth relayed in a tone of surprise and pride.

"Mmph!" Xhinna complained as Fiona nudged her to get up. "What is it?"

"Dust fall at Fort Hold," Fiona told her shortly, jumping out of bed and pulling on her clothes. "The Weyrleader wants to meet with me."

"Where?" Xhinna called out as Fiona tore out of the room, still adjusting her tunic.

"Records Room!" Fiona called back over her shoulder, and then she was gone, leaving friend and dragon exchanging bemused looks.

"Where's Xhinna?" Cisca grumbled as Fiona stumbled into the Records Room. The Weyrwoman and Weyrleader were hunched over an old chart, peering closely at it in the dim light of their night glow. "I was hoping she'd bring *klah*."

"Still getting up," Fiona replied. She stood next to Cisca, leaning her arms on a chair back to look at the chart laid out on the table. She vaguely recognized the shape of Pern's Northern Continent and she could pick out the symbols for the major Holds and Weyrs, but she didn't understand the meaning of the wiggly lines that were drawn like snakes over everything. Unless the snakes were Thread or—"Do those lines show the Threadfalls?"

"Yes," K'lior agreed, glancing at her approvingly. "Master Archivist Verilan and your friend, Kindan, worked them out."

"If they're accurate," Cisca added, "then the next fall should be . . . here—High Reaches Tip." The tip of her tongue stuck out between pursed lips. "High Reaches again for the next Fall, at Southern Tillek."

"And then Benden Weyr and Bitra," K'lior said, pointing to another squiggle. Fiona saw that each line had a number next to it.

"But why is this one marked seven and not one?" she asked, tapping the line for the Fort Hold Fall.

"I don't know," K'lior confessed with a shrug. "I suppose that's a question for Kindan—"

"Verilan," Cisca corrected absently, still intent on the chart. "Kindan has enough to deal with at Benden."

"All Verilan was willing to say was that the charts were the best guess, based on old Records they'd found at the Harper Hall and the Weyrs," K'lior remarked. He paused, still scanning the chart, and then pointed. "This one here, the twelfth Fall by this chart, that's when we'll next see Thread."

"We must warn Benden," Cisca said. "If we're getting black-dust, I suspect it'll be even colder up High Reaches way, but Benden gets those warm winds from the sea." She frowned in thought, then asked K'lior, "How warm does it have to be for Thread to survive?"

"Or how cold to freeze?" K'lior replied, turning the question on its head. He shrugged. "I imagine that Thread probably freezes like any other living thing—" He nodded appreciatively as both Fiona and Cisca shuddered at his use of the word *living*. "—and goodness knows it's cold enough in the sky these days, but beyond that . . ."

"Well, now we know," Cisca said firmly, indicating the chart. "If these charts are to be believed—"

"Let's see if these other falls come as predicted," K'lior suggested.

"—then we've got a little more than fifteen days to prepare," Cisca concluded, riding over K'lior's interjection.

K'lior nodded and took on the distant look of a rider communing with his dragon. "I've called a wingleader's meeting for breakfast."

Xhinna rushed in at that moment, asking breathlessly, "Weyrleader, Weyrwoman, is there anything I can get you?"

K'lior and Cisca exchanged amused looks. Cisca shook her head. "You're just in time to escort us to the Kitchen Cavern where we'll all have breakfast."

The breakfast with the wingleaders was a somber affair. H'nez professed no faith in the Threadfall charts when K'lior mentioned them.

"Which is why we'll keep our patrols out," K'lior assured the grumpy wingleader.

H'nez accepted that decision with a contented look. "We must alert the Weyrs, of course," he observed.

"Of course," K'lior agreed drily. "Although I rather suspect that D'gan at Telgar will not take kindly to anything we have to say."

"D'gan has a problem," Cisca murmured angrily.

"What about High Reaches?" P'der asked. "D'vin wouldn't come to your council earlier."

"I've already alerted Lyrinth, the queen dragon there," Cisca replied.

"I'll go to Benden," T'mar offered.

"I'll go to Ista," P'der said.

"I can imagine how Weyrleader C'rion will feel to be briefed by a wingsecond," H'nez drawled.

"Are you offering to go instead?" K'lior asked, cocking his head.

"I've my wing to attend to," H'nez responded. "They suffered grievous losses."

"We all did," Cisca replied, her eyes flashing. H'nez did not reply.

"P'der, T'mar, when can you leave?" K'lior asked. The Kitchen Cavern had slowly been filling up as they conferred, and he could feel the concern and grief flowing in equal measures amongst the weyrfolk and dragonriders.

"I can leave now," T'mar announced, rising from his chair.

"I think—" H'nez's words halted T'mar's motion. "—that we need to consider the larger issue before we break up."

"And that is?" K'lior asked politely.

"The question is," H'nez replied as though speaking to a particularly slow weyrling, "how are we going to survive Threadfall with sick dragons?"

"*That* has been the question since the fire-lizards first took ill," Cisca retorted in exasperation. "*We*"—and she gestured to K'lior and herself—"have been trying to answer that ever since."

"I'll want all the wings at the Weyr ready for drill after lunch," K'lior declared. He glanced at P'der and T'mar, adding, "If you're not back by then, we'll work without you. We know that we'll have casualties when we fight Thread, so it makes sense to practice for that now."

"By the First Egg, that's more like it," H'nez declared. To T'mar he said, "You go and spend time with M'tal, while we do real work back here."

"His job is no less important, H'nez," K'lior said warningly. He waved T'mar and P'der away. "And now," he said, reaching for a fresh roll, "I think we should finish our breakfast and get ready for the work of the day."

"T'mar!" Cisca called as the bronze rider prepared to mount Zirenth. They were in the Weyr Bowl, less than half an hour after the end of their breakfast.

"Weyrwoman?" T'mar responded, turning around to face her.

Cisca crossed the distance between them so that she could speak in a normal voice. "You understand that there's a risk, going to Benden."

T'mar nodded.

"We can't say how the illness spreads," she continued, relieved at his easy response, "so don't stay any longer than necessary."

"I will," he assured her. With a grin he added, "I want to get back in time to see how my wing flies without me!"

"Fly well!"

"Always, Weyrwoman." With a last respectful nod, T'mar turned back to climb onto his dragon.

Let's go, he told his dragon. Zirenth flexed his hind legs and leapt into the air. He beat his wings once, twice, and was gone *between.*

Cisca turned at a sound behind her and spotted Fiona rushing from the Kitchen Cavern, looking distraught. "I wanted to say good flying!"

"Did you, now?" Cisca murmured to herself, giving the young rider a probing look. Louder, she responded, "He'll be back soon enough."

F iona spent the next several days with Xhinna and Cisca, with the Weyrwoman constantly presenting her with new and often arduous tasks that left her too tired to think—even with plenty of *klah.* After the first day, she realized that that was part of Cisca's purpose—to exhaust her.

That obvious ploy didn't bother her as much as it might have under other circumstances. Fiona realized how numb and useless she felt. The loss of Tannaz and Kelsanth was magnified by the losses of all the other riders and ill dragons that had gone with her—particularly those whom Fiona had visited for hours on end. No one knew of a cure for the illness. As far as Fiona knew, it was only a matter of time before all the dragons succumbed, including her own lovely, marvelous—and so young!—Talenth.

If the loss of her own dragon wasn't enough to terrify her, Fiona also realized that without the dragons of Pern, soon all the planet would be covered in burrows, with Thread sucking all life from the soil—and those Pernese that didn't succumb quickly to the falling Thread would slowly starve.

So she was secretly glad that Cisca kept her too busy to think and that Xhinna never left her alone for more than the barest few minutes.

Fiona knew, from the dreaded sounds of coughing, that more dragons had fallen ill, but she purposely did not try to discover who they were, preferring to concentrate on T'jen's Salith, the last of the original sick dragons.

T'jen was as tough as they came, as befit a Weyrlingmaster, even if he had relinquished his responsibilities when Salith took ill.

"You'll see," he had declared the day after Tannaz and the others went *between*. "We'll find a cure."

He was constantly consulting with Kentai about possible remedies and was dosing Salith with so many different herbals that it was a wonder the dragon was willing to put up with it.

"He knows we're trying," T'jen explained when Fiona was helping the dragonrider give his dragon a particularly noxious infusion. With a wry grin, he added, "Perhaps the smell alone will drive out the illness."

T'jen kept a steady eye on his weyrlings, even if he was no longer involved in their daily activities.

"See down there?" He pointed out from his place beside Salith, who was dozing on his ledge in the warm afternoon sun. "See the lads all lined up like that?"

"Yes," Fiona said, peering down at the strange assortment of youngsters. From her high vantage point, they looked more like dots than people.

"They're practicing drill," T'jen told her. "They learn to line up and move as a group, then they learn how to spread out like they will with their dragons when they start flying."

Curiosity caused Fiona to screw up her face as she asked, "How come I don't do that?"

"I suppose there's no reason you shouldn't," T'jen replied with a shrug. "Those in the queen's wing should also know how to work together." But, of course, Fiona reflected sadly, there was only Melirth and Talenth. And not only was Talenth too young, but Fiona and Cisca were too busy to devote any time to drill.

One evening her task came from Kentai—though Fiona didn't doubt that even this was a piece of Cisca's efforts to keep her busy. "Weyrwoman," the harper said to her at dinner. "Tomorrow I'd like to spend some time with you going over the medical procedures. We've scheduled training for the morning, and a drill in the afternoon."

"A drill?" Fiona asked.

"T'mar's wing and the weyrlings will play the sick and injured," Cisca informed her, her eyes twinkling as she mentioned the bronze rider.

"The drills are a lot of fun," Xhinna told Fiona. When Fiona looked at her, surprised, she added, "We've been doing them at least once a month for the past Turn."

"All because your Weyrwoman believes in being prepared," K'lior remarked, casting a fond look at Cisca.

After dinner, Fiona went to check on T'jen and Salith, and Xhinna, as usual, accompanied her.

T'jen's weyr was on the fifth level, on the east side of the Weyr, toward the southern end, almost above the lake. To get to it, they took the east stairwell and walked halfway around the corridor south to his lair.

"It's a good workout," T'jen had noted when Xhinna had arrived breathless on their first visit. "But worth the view."

He didn't exaggerate: T'jen's quarters had a magnificent view of the entire Weyr, with the Tooth Crag nearly straight ahead of him, and the Star Stones and Landing just at the limit of vision on his right.

It had become a habit, in the short time since they'd started their visits, that before entering, Fiona and Xhinna would stop for a brief rest so that T'jen wouldn't twit them about being out of shape—the ex-Weyrlingmaster was a stickler for exercise.

"You're going to be riding a dragon, young lady, you shouldn't be out of breath just climbing five flights of stairs and walking a quarter of the way around the Weyr," he had observed sharply when Fiona had commented on the distance.

Until now, however, they hadn't realized that their heavy breathing was audible to T'jen from their halting point near his weyr.

"Don't come in," he called wearily as they stood catching their breath.

"T'jen," Fiona repeated in surprise, "are you all right?"

"No, I'm not," he replied mournfully. "Send for the Weyr-leader."

Fiona was surprised by the request, knowing that T'jen's Salith could more easily alert K'lior, and then—

Talenth, Fiona thought even as her eyes filled with tears, *please tell Melirth that we need Cisca and K'lior at Salith's weyr.*

Melirth asks—Talenth halted and continued, *They come.*

Thank you, Fiona responded. Aloud, she said, "They're coming."

Xhinna gave her a quizzical look that slowly drained away as she figured it out. "How come the dragons didn't keen?" she asked Fiona.

"He passed away in his sleep," T'jen—who would from now on be known by his birth name, Tajen—said in answer. "I don't think the dragons know yet."

Fiona beckoned to Xhinna, and together they entered the brown dragon's lair.

"Oh!" Xhinna murmured in anguish as she saw Salith lying life-less, a final trickle of green mucus still snaking down his snout to puddle on the floor.

"I don't know what we'll do with the body," Tajen said sadly. Fiona could tell by his stance that the brown rider had followed their journey across the floor of the Weyr Bowl from his vantage point at Salith's ledge and, she guessed, had turned to Salith only to find the brown dead. Tears were flowing freely, ignored, down his cheeks. "I thought he'd go *between.*"

"Weren't you going to go with him?" Fiona asked quietly, mov-ing forward to stand beside him and pat Salith's huge head, idly moving her hand to his eye ridge as though in some half-formed hope that the dragon might revive with her ministrations.

"No," Tajen replied firmly, "we'd talked it over, Salith and I." He paused, his lips screwing up into a grimace. "I didn't want to set such an example for the weyrlings, even though I never wanted to lose Salith. Sometimes, all you have are bad choices."

The sound of feet rushing around the corridor alerted them to the approach of Cisca, K'lior, H'nez, T'mar, and M'kury. Cisca en-tered first, something in her stance and the way she moved mak-ing it clear that the others were to wait for her.

"Tajen," Cisca said quietly, "I grieve for your loss."

K'lior entered, bowed to the ex-dragonrider, and repeated her words. "Tajen, I grieve for your loss."

"Tajen," H'nez said, his eyes downcast and tear-streaked, "I grieve for your loss."

"He was a great dragon, you were a great pair," T'mar said when he approached. "I grieve for your loss."

M'kury came forward then, but even though his mouth worked, he could make no words, instead reaching out beseechingly with one hand to Tajen, who took it. M'kury grabbed the stricken brown rider and embraced him in a tight hug. When finally they broke apart, M'kury found the words: "I grieve for your loss."

"And I recognize your courage for remaining behind," H'nez added into the silence.

"It wasn't courage—" Tajen protested. "I needed to set the right example for the weyrlings. No matter what may come: 'Dragonmen must fly when Thread is in the sky!' "

He looked up at K'lior. "I don't know what we're going to do with the body, however."

"I do," Cisca replied. All eyes turned to her. She nodded to K'lior as she explained, "K'lior and I have talked about this already."

"We'll use slings and hoists to lift the body out of the weyr, and then dragons will bring it *between*," K'lior explained.

"It's too dark to do it tonight," M'kury observed, idly patting the brown dragon's body.

"No, we'll do it first thing in the morning," Cisca replied. She looked at Tajen. "Would you like us to keep watch with you?"

Tajen thought it over and shook his head.

"I'll stay," Xhinna said quietly. Fiona thought she looked surprised by her own words.

Tajen glanced at her, then said, "Thank you."

As the others shuffled out, Fiona managed to get Xhinna aside.

"That was awfully kind of you," Fiona said to her.

"You don't mind, do you?" Xhinna asked.

"No, Talenth and I will be fine," Fiona replied firmly.

"It's just that," Xhinna explained, "of everyone here, I might be the only one who knows how he feels right now."

Fiona looked at her blankly.

"Outcast, alone," Xhinna murmured as if to herself.

"You're not alone," Fiona declared stoutly.

Xhinna flushed, saying, "Before I met you, I mean."

"Should I send up some blankets?" Fiona asked, glancing toward Tajen's quarters. Xhinna smiled at her and shook her head. "I doubt I'll sleep tonight."

Fiona shucked off the sweater she'd put on earlier and handed it to Xhinna. "Then you'll need this."

Xhinna took it gratefully.

"We'll be up at first light," K'lior promised.

"I'll have the kitchens send up something warming," Cisca added.

As they made their way down the stairs to the Weyr Bowl, she said to Fiona, "You were right about her."

"Pardon?"

"Your Xhinna is a good person," K'lior said, glancing back at Cisca. The Weyrwoman nodded.

When she rose and dressed in the morning, Fiona found Talenth awake and waiting for her on her ledge. The dragon was peering curiously upward. Fiona looked up but could see nothing in the foggy morning mist; only the sounds she heard told her that the men were working to winch Salith out of his weyr.

They're taking Salith away, Fiona informed her dragon.

When I die, will you go with me? Talenth asked.

"It won't be for a long, long while," Fiona replied firmly, needing to say the words out loud. After a long moment of reflection, she added, "And yes, I'll go with you."

Good, Talenth responded feelingly. *I'd be lonely without you.*

"Right now, though, we've got other things to do," Fiona declared. "I'm going to be practicing this morning."

Practicing what?

"We're going to practice first aid," Fiona said.

Me, too? Talenth asked, her eyes whirling anxiously.

I think we can include you, too, Fiona told her. Talenth nudged her affectionately. "I need to get some breakfast."

With a wave, Fiona leapt from the ledge to the ground below, flexing her knees to absorb the impact, and then walked briskly off. She found the Kitchen Cavern more crowded than usual for this time of the morning and was glad to hear Cisca call her to the Weyrleader's table.

"Xhinna was up all night with Tajen," Cisca told her as Fiona sat and a weyrfolk laid a plate and mug in front of her. She cocked an eyebrow toward K'lior, who threw up his hands and glanced pointedly at H'nez. With a snort, Cisca turned back to Fiona and said, "K'lior and I were talking last night: we think Xhinna should be a candidate at the next Hatching."

Fiona gave her a surprised look, and then her face broke out into a wide grin.

"I wouldn't say anything to her about it yet," K'lior warned. "We have more important things to deal with today."

"Yes, today we have our drill," Cisca said.

"And I have mine," K'lior said, wiping his mouth and rising from his chair. With a nod to Fiona and smile for Cisca, he departed, trailed by P'der, his wingsecond, as well as T'mar and M'kury.

"Ellor is with Tajen," Cisca said to Fiona. "Salith was taken *between* this morning."

"I heard them working," Fiona replied, eyeing a breadroll without much enthusiasm. Cisca followed her gaze, grabbed the breadroll, and dropped it on Fiona's plate.

"Eat," the Weyrwoman ordered, grabbing a roll for herself. She leaned closer to Fiona and said quietly, "We must set the example."

The words rang a chord in Fiona; they were similar to words her father had used with her some Turns back when she had protested against visiting the elderly and sick of Fort Hold. "We are the model all others look to," Lord Bemin had said to her. "Some of these old ones looked after you when you were little; it's only fair to return the favor."

Fiona nibbled her lips nervously, then reached for the butter and spread it on her roll.

"Fresh today," Cisca said as she saw Fiona's look of delight at the taste of the butter and bread in her mouth. "Ellor had some of the kitchen up early to churn the butter specially."

"It's good," Fiona agreed, craning her neck around to see if she could spot Ellor and tell her directly. Then she remembered Cisca's words, that Ellor was with Tajen. "Did she make the butter for him?"

"She had an idea that he'd appreciate a good meal," Cisca said, wiping a stray crumb from her lip. "I know that he hasn't eaten well since Salith took ill." She shook her head sadly, then turned her gaze back to Fiona. "So, today we are going to drill on injuries—what do you know about first aid for dragons?"

"Nothing," Fiona replied in surprise. "Don't fellis and numbweed work on them as well as us?"

"They do," Cisca replied. "And when dealing with Threadscoring, the Records say that numbweed is 'most efficacious in relieving a dragon's pain' but caution that fellis juice is 'best administered to the rider.'"

"Why is that?" Fiona wondered aloud.

Cisca shrugged. "I imagine that more than anything, it's because it'd take such a large amount of fellis to have any effect on a dragon." She frowned thoughtfully before adding, "And I suppose it's not too good for an injured dragon to be drugged into sleep—except in the worst of cases."

"But why give fellis to the rider?"

"Because," Cisca replied, giving Fiona a mischievous grin, "you may have noticed that riders and dragons are linked."

Fiona nodded.

"And so," Cisca continued, "I imagine that calming the rider has a calming effect on the dragon, too."

"What is Threadscore like?"

"We only have the Records to go by," Cisca said. "According to them, however, the damage from Thread depends upon how long a rider or dragon is exposed to it before they go *between* and freeze it off."

"And if you don't go *between*?"

"Thread eats through flesh and bone very quickly," Cisca replied, grimacing. "There are Records about some terrible scorings—usually riders getting hit by clumps of Thread."

"Clumps?"

"Sometimes Thread falls in bunches, sometimes as separate strands," Cisca told her. She shrugged. "It seems to depend more upon the winds than anything."

"And when it hits in clumps?"

Cisca gave a long sigh. "A quick dragon or rider can get *between* quickly enough to avoid the worst of it," she said. "A single strand burns a thin line, like a hot poker across the skin."

"So you'd just treat that like a burn?" Fiona asked. "Numbweed, healing salve, and bandage?"

"Yes," Cisca agreed, impressed. "But if the score is deeper it must be cleaned carefully and stitched quickly."

"In a typical Fall, how many dragons are injured?" Fiona asked.

"There is no typical Fall," Cisca replied. "The number varies from a few to several dozen or more."

Fiona's eyes grew wide at the thought of so many wounded dragons and riders, but before she could say anything, a deep voice spoke from behind her.

"And that's why we drill." It was T'mar, and when Fiona turned to look at him, he smiled reassuringly at her. "So that we can keep those numbers as low as possible." He nodded to Cisca. "In fact, that's what brought me here—we're ready when you are."

Cisca rose and Fiona followed suit. "We're ready now."

Ellor, the new headwoman, saw Cisca rise and motioned for the rest of the assigned weyrfolk to join them. Together they filed outside into the Weyr Bowl, where the sun had risen high enough to burn off the worst of the morning mist and take the chill out of the air.

Kentai, who was already out in the Bowl, made his way toward them. "I think first we should practice with a dozen injured weyrlings," he suggested.

T'mar gestured to a group of weyrlings near the entrance to the Hatching Grounds. "I've already got some positioned."

Kentai, with Ellor's help, briskly organized the weyrfolk, while Cisca strode off to a table where he had left slates and writing tools. Following her, Fiona glanced up to her weyr for any sign of Talenth. She was surprised to see her dragon stick her head out, probably wondering what all the noise was about.

We're drilling on first aid, Fiona told her.

Great, Talenth replied cheerfully. *Can I help?* Then a moment later, she added, *What's "first aid"?*

When dragons or people get injured, Fiona replied, reminded once again that her dragon was still only a baby. *Usually during Thread-fall.* She went into a fuller explanation as she watched Cisca busily writing on several tablets.

Oh, Talenth replied, seeming uneasy at the thought. She strode further out onto her ledge and peered over at all the weyrlings. *What are they doing?*

They're going to pretend to be injured, Fiona replied.

Oh, me too! I want to pretend, too! Talenth responded immediately and so emphatically that Fiona turned to look back up at her. Eyes whirling anxiously, Talenth rushed toward the edge of the ledge and must have misjudged her speed, for she went straight off. Her face took on the most startled expression and Fiona screamed "Talenth!"—just before the weyrling spread her wings and glided easily down to the ground.

Did you see that? Talenth exclaimed excitedly. *I flew!*

"Well, you'd better stop flying unless you want to get injured for real!" Fiona yelled at her, her voice carrying clearly above the sudden silence that engulfed the Weyr Bowl as all the weyrfolk and weyrlings watched Talenth's excited first glide.

"You scared me right out of my skin," Fiona declared, surprised to hear those words coming out of her mouth: It was what Neesa had always said whenever Fiona had tried something new and dangerous.

I'm sorry. Talenth eyed her critically, tilting her head from one side to the other. *Your skin looks fine from here.*

Fiona laughed, striding over to Talenth and grabbing the dragon's head in her hands. "I meant that you scared me; I was worried that you might get hurt."

Talenth nudged her, nearly forcing Fiona off her feet.

That was fun, the young queen said. *Can I do it again?*

"Only if you're careful," Fiona said. "You looked so frightened, it seemed like you'd never remember you had wings!"

I was surprised, Talenth agreed. She raised her wings and turned her head to look at them. *I haven't used them much.*

Everything about you is new, Fiona replied with a huge grin on her face.

"Why don't you have her join the other hatchlings?" Cisca suggested, having arrived unnoticed behind Fiona.

"Or she'll probably distract everyone with her antics?" Fiona asked, silently relaying the request to Talenth, who looked up eagerly, head swiveling to find a likely spot.

"Yes," Cisca agreed with a laugh. "I remember when Melirth first did that trick—I'd thought that it was some peculiar trait of hers alone."

"To scare you out of your skin?" Fiona wondered.

"All dragons can do that," T'mar added from behind them, his gaze settled affectionately on Talenth. "She looks sound."

"When she isn't trying to break her neck," Fiona responded.

"Dragons are sturdier than you'd think," he corrected her. "They look fragile, but really, they're rather tough."

"Well, I'd prefer this one to keep herself in one piece as long as possible," Fiona replied and then, as her flip words registered, her spirits sank. She remembered Tajen—and Tannaz, J'marin, L'rian, and M'rorin.

"Talenth, over there by Ladirth, if you would," T'mar said aloud to the queen. Talenth looked over at the hatchlings, gave a chirp of recognition as a bronze arched his head up and back to look at her, and happily stalked off to join the others.

The youngsters—riders and dragons both—followed Talenth's progress with eager eyes, as they hadn't seen much of her at all until then. Once she'd arrived on station—and was prompted to remain there by a silent warning from Fiona—the collection of dragons and people returned to their drill.

"First, we're going to go from station to station and brief all the weyrfolk on first aid, bandages, numbweed, sutures, needles, and the other equipment," Cisca said to Fiona and Kentai. "Once we're done with that, we'll do a quick practice of some injuries, and then we'll take lunch and be ready for the proper drill."

They got everyone sorted out, and then Cisca showed each dragonrider one of the half-dozen slates she'd written on. When they got to the young bronze dragon and his rider, Fiona was surprised: F'jian needed Cisca to repeat her instructions no less than three times, finally being told, "If you still can't remember, ask Fiona."

F'jian had an open and friendly face, and Fiona could see that his poor memory troubled him, too.

"Another one of you muddleheads," Cisca remarked to Fiona as they moved off. The Weyrwoman regarded Fiona curiously for a moment, then added, "Although if this is you when you're not at your best . . ."

"I don't know," Fiona replied. "I think I have good days and bad days."

"We *all* do," Cisca said. "But compared to some of the weyrlings, you don't seem nearly as dazed as you did."

Fiona pondered that for a moment. "Maybe that's because I haven't been asked to do much more than I did back at Fort Hold."

Cisca looked thoughtful. "That *could* be it; I hadn't realized how much was expected of you there."

"If I wanted to be around my father, I was expected to behave," Fiona said with a shrug. "And because I wanted to be around my father very often, I learned quickly to behave very well."

"Hmm," Cisca murmured. "Well, I can't say I'm not glad of it, considering the times we're in, but I wish that you might have had longer to be a child."

"No one who survived the Plague could remain a child," Fiona told her, shaking her head.

Cisca turned back to survey the group of young dragonriders arrayed before them. "I hope the same is not true for this lot," she sighed. Then, with a characteristic headshake, she put the moment aside and turned back to the business at hand, waving to Ellor and calling out, "They're ready!"

What followed was more amusing than instructive: Many of the riders could only poorly explain their or their dragon's symptoms, most of the young weyrfolk were confused and disorganized, and the older ones weren't much better.

"This was to be expected," Cisca murmured for Fiona's ears alone. "Don't act alarmed, or they'll feel bad."

Fiona nodded; her father had said something similar to her when they'd held a fire drill not a Turn before.

Then Cisca said something that shocked Fiona: "Remember that *you* may be conducting this drill next time."

"I don't think I could manage if anything happened to you," Fiona protested. The loss of Tannaz was still too fresh in her mind.

"I don't plan on it," Cisca told her firmly, adding with a grimace, "but it's my duty as a Weyrwoman to be prepared for the worst." After a pause, she said, "And your duty, too."

A cold shiver went down Fiona's spine as she imagined seeing Cisca mounting a sick and dying Melirth for a final ride *between.*

Suddenly Cisca grabbed Fiona's arm and yanked her around so that she could meet her eyes squarely. *"That* is exactly what I need you to avoid," the Weyrwoman said sharply. In the distance, Fiona heard Talenth's plaintive cry, and she could almost feel the alarm spreading through the weyrfolk and weyrlings. "They look to us, Fiona. *We* set the tone. Our dragons reflect it."

A shadow fell beside her and Fiona felt her free hand grasped by someone else. Xhinna.

"It's all right." Fiona's words of reassurance echoed exactly Xhinna's words of reassurance. The two girls looked at each other in surprise for a moment and then burst out laughing. Fiona could feel their mood travel to the others, could feel Talenth's worry disappear.

"I'm sorry I'm late," Xhinna apologized.

"I'm glad you're here," Cisca told her. "You can stand with Talenth and keep her company."

"Get her to tell you about her first flight," Fiona suggested, still grinning.

"You know she talks to me sometimes?" Xhinna asked, clearly worried, turning from Fiona to Talenth and back again.

"Really?" Cisca responded in surprise. "How often?"

Xhinna shrugged. "Not that often."

"I ask her to," Fiona said, waving it away. But Xhinna's eyes still looked worried.

"Sometimes when you don't ask her to," Xhinna added quietly, casting her eyes down to the ground.

"Xhinna," Fiona replied slowly, firmly, "if Talenth wants to talk with you, then I'm glad."

Xhinna looked up, her eyes lighting in hope and surprise. "You are?"

"You are my friend," Fiona declared stoutly. "I'm glad that she likes you, too." Deep in her thoughts, she wondered again why Talenth only sometimes referred to Xhinna by name, but she knew it wasn't because her dragon loved Xhinna more than Fiona. It was something else . . . but Fiona couldn't imagine what it might be.

"Well, this is great," Cisca declared. "But, Xhinna, we're working on medical drills this morning."

"I heard," Xhinna said quickly, ducking her head again. "I'm sorry, Weyrwoman but—"

"No, don't apologize." Cisca held a hand up to halt her. "I was just going to ask if you'd be Talenth's partner while Fiona and I follow the drill."

"You don't mind?" Xhinna asked Fiona.

"Of course not."

"**V**ery well," Cisca called at the end of the second drill. "That went better than the first time." Rueful looks greeted that declaration. It *had* gone better than the first time, but only just.

"We'll take our lunch break now," Cisca told the gathered weyrfolk and weyrlings. "Then, before we work with the fighting wings, we'll do one last drill—only this time, the weyrlings will be our aidsmen and the weyrgirls will be the victims."

A snort of surprise erupted from the collected group while the older women chuckled appreciatively.

The drill after lunch was the best of the three.

"Right," Cisca called across the field as they finished the drill. "Weyrlings, send your dragons back to their lairs because I think—" and the air grew dark with the wings of the much larger fighting dragons "—that we might have more injured to deal with."

T'mar's wing arrived in good formation, except for his own dragon, who dropped precipitously in front of Fiona, causing her and many of the other girls to gasp in fright until Zirenth caught the air at the last moment and managed to land, with one wing precariously folded, as though grievously injured.

"Go! Help them!" Cisca's bellow echoed throughout the Weyr. Fiona and Xhinna rushed to T'mar and his bronze. Just as they neared, T'mar rolled dramatically off his perch and fell to the ground.

"Catch him!" Xhinna shrieked. Fiona caught him just in time and crumpled painfully under his weight. When she managed to get out from underneath him, she saw that his face was covered in a hideous red.

"He's been Threadscored." Cisca's voice reached her ears. "Quick, what are you going to do?"

Fiona wrenched her distraction over his face aside as she reached into her training; more into what she'd learned at Fort Hold over several Turns than what she'd learned today at the Weyr.

"Is he breathing?" she asked herself aloud, leaning forward to cup her ear over his mouth while simultaneously pressing his neck with two fingers to feel for a pulse. "Yes, he's breathing," she called aloud as she'd been trained.

"What's your assessment?" Cisca demanded.

"Threadscore of the face, possible involvement of the eyes," Fiona said, suddenly realizing that she'd pressed her ear against his "wounds" and berating herself silently for the error.

"What about the dragon?" Cisca asked sharply. Fiona looked up, aghast that she had forgotten to examine Zirenth. She was furious with herself for her mistakes—it wasn't like her to be so unclearheaded.

"The right mainsail is shredded," Xhinna called from the far side. "He'll need stitching."

"Assess!" Cisca bellowed at Fiona. All around her the shouting and quick movements were repeated as older weyrfolk demanded diagnoses and assessments from the young weyrlings and weyrfolk.

"T'mar's wounds are superficial—numbweed and fellis for the moment, first aid later," Fiona said, rising to her feet while being careful not to jar T'mar's head as she lowered it to the ground. "Numbweed and sutures for Zirenth's wing."

"Do it!" Cisca shouted right next to Fiona. Fiona was momentarily startled by her intensity until she realized that it was part of the process of the drill: The Weyrwoman was shouting in order to create the stress that would be present in a real emergency. Fiona scampered around to the far side of Zirenth and found Xhinna.

"Have we got the sutures?" she asked, examining the "wound," which was really an old torn sheet.

"Here," Xhinna said, lifting up a large needle and a spool of suture material.

"You do it!" Cisca shouted to Fiona. "Now!"

Fiona took two tries to get the suture material through the eye of the needle, all the while being berated by Cisca, and then carefully she began the process of joining the two torn halves of the "wound" together. She became totally absorbed in the task, imagining how much harder it would be to work up to the wing, worrying about any sudden flinches by the injured dragon that might further tear the injury. Finally, she was done.

She sat back on her heels for a moment, pleased with her work.

"What did you forget?" Cisca asked in a more normal voice.

Fiona furrowed her brow in thought, then groaned. "The numbweed!"

"Not to mention the rider," Cisca added tartly. Behind her stood T'mar, his face still dripping with his artificial injury. "The moment you are done tending the dragon you should . . ."

"Consult with the rider, tell him what you've done, and check him for shock," Fiona said, ruefully reciting the drill she'd been taught that morning. She looked at T'mar. "I'm sorry."

"I'll live," T'mar replied with a grin, wiping the "injury" off his face with a hand and licking it. "It's just sauce."

Fiona woke, suddenly. She reached out a tendril of thought to Talenth. The young gold seemed fitful in her sleep, as though she might wake at any moment. Fiona spent a moment in comfortable contact with her dragon, then focused her thoughts outward, listening.

A dragon and rider were moving quietly in the Weyr Bowl outside. The dragon coughed.

Fiona threw off her covers, eliciting a sleepy cry from Xhinna. She carefully pushed the covers up against Xhinna's exposed side and gingerly crawled out of bed, her mouth set tight to muffle any involuntary exclamations as her feet hit the cold weyr floor.

Quickly she found her slippers and gladly slipped into them, then paused long enough to pull on a nightrobe before moving into Talenth's lair.

"Maybe I *should* let you sleep on the outside." The voice made her jump with fright. Xhinna. Fiona raised two fingers, cautioning her to silence even as she gave the younger girl a thankful look. It was good to have company.

As they made their way out onto the queens' ledge, Fiona looked toward the entrance to the Hatching Grounds to judge the time. She could dimly make out four glows on either side of the entrance: it was just passing midnight.

Then something obscured one of the glows: Someone was entering the Hatching Grounds. Fiona frowned, wondering who would want to enter the Hatching Grounds this late at night.

A noise from the other end of the Bowl distracted her: the sound of a rider and dragon rising into the thick midnight air. The sounds ended abruptly as rider and dragon went *between.*

Fiona bowed her head. Another dragon and rider lost to the illness. A cough echoed around the Weyr in the night—still more dragons were ill, but they were not yet so desperate as to go *between* forever.

Beside her, Xhinna gasped as she realized what had happened.

Fiona saw the shadow pass a dimmer glow—the person was going further in. She took a step forward and leapt off the ledge to the ground below her, heading toward the Hatching Grounds.

A moment later, she heard Xhinna jump down and trot up beside her. Together they made their way into the Hatching Grounds. Once inside the entrance and past the glows, it was pitch black.

Fiona paused to let her eyes adjust. Ahead, she heard the sound of feet moving slowly ahead and saw a faint light—someone was carrying a small glow ahead of them. The glow grew brighter as the person turned to face them.

It was Tajen. He waited and Fiona took it as an invitation, so she caught up with him, Xhinna at her side. He nodded wordlessly to each, then turned once more, heading deeper into the Hatching Grounds. She had never realized before quite how large the Hatching Grounds were.

Feeling that she was being invited to participate in something deeply personal, Fiona followed reverently, silently.

It wasn't until they reached the sands on the far side of the Hatching Grounds, where a queen would lay her eggs, that Fiona began to understand. Beside her, Xhinna's breath caught, and

Fiona was certain that the young weyrgirl had reached the same realization at the same time.

It was not something that could be put into words. It was a feeling, a thought, a shiver.

In this great chamber was the fate of Pern decided. Here and in the Hatching Grounds of the other five Weyrs—four, now that Igen was abandoned—were boys made into dragonriders and girls made into Weyrwomen.

Fiona could practically feel all the Turns of fear and excitement from countless Hatchings radiate around her. There was something special about this place, and her skin tingled with the power she felt in it.

She remembered once more the excited feelings of *her* first visit to the Hatching Grounds Turns earlier, and even more felt the awe of the Impression that had just so recently changed her life forever. Her lips curved upward in a smile as she reached tenderly for her dragon, still sleeping in her lair. She remembered once more her surprise, fright, and pure pleasure as Talenth had first spoken in her mind.

"This cannot end." She was surprised at hearing the words: She thought she had not spoken aloud. And then she realized that she hadn't, that it had been Tajen's voice that had broken the respectful silence. "Not after hundreds of Turns, not after all the pain, the blood, the effort—" The glow's light dimmed and brightened again as it was obscured by Tajen's shaking head. "No. It cannot happen."

The glow's light became visible again as Tajen stood taller, shoulders back, spine braced defiantly.

"The creators of the dragons would never have allowed this," he said to himself. "They would have realized that the dragons could get ill; they would have provided a solution."

"Maybe they didn't know," Xhinna protested quietly, as though afraid to voice such a painful thought.

Tajen was silent for a long while, his shoulders slumping back down until he raised them again and protested, "But—the dragons!"

Fiona nodded in understanding and agreement. If the settlers of Pern, hundreds of Turns past, had been surprised by Thread, they had recovered quickly and developed the dragons as their defense. Having been surprised once, would they not have worked their hardest to avoid any future surprises? They had depended upon the dragons to save all of Pern; would they not have done everything in their power to ensure that that protection was never lost?

Still . . . perhaps their ancestors had felt certain that the dragons could never *get* ill.

The silence of the Hatching Grounds answered her. She felt once again all the hundreds of Turns of Impressions, of excitement, love, hope—

"No," she said loudly, firmly. "Even if our ancestors didn't think of this, we'll find a way to survive." She met Xhinna's eyes. "We must."

"And what," Xhinna began quietly, her voice shaking in sorrow, "if you lose Talenth?"

"I came here," Tajen said a moment later, into the unsettled silence that had fallen, "to consider what I would say to others when asked the same question." He gestured to Fiona for her answer.

"I told Talenth that I would go *between* with her when the time comes," Fiona said. Xhinna made a sound: half-sob, half-exclamation. "But I told her it wouldn't be for a long, long time."

"But you can't say that," Tajen told her quietly. "You can't be sure. You can never be sure that something won't happen to separate the two of you."

"You could have an accident," Xhinna suggested.

"But then Talenth would follow me *between*, wouldn't she?"

"No one really knows what *between* is," Tajen replied. "If a rider dies with her dragon, does the dragon go *between* to the same place?"

"*Is* there a place?" Xhinna wondered.

"The only ones who could tell us never come back," Tajen replied. He gestured toward the entrance and started them walking back out of the Hatching Grounds. "What does your heart tell you?"

Neither girl had an answer she could put into words.

TEN

Thread falls
Dragons rise.
Dragons flame,
Thread dies.

Fort Weyr, Morning, AL 508.1.13

"Wake up, Xhinna, wake up!" Fiona's excited voice startled Xhinna from her groggy slumber. "Thread falls today!"

Xhinna was up and out of the bed in a trice, her exhaustion forgotten.

"The bath's all yours," Fiona told her. "I've already been."

Xhinna paused on her way to the baths, wondering if Fiona could restrain her excitement long enough to wait for her before heading to breakfast. Clearly today was one of those good days when Fiona's energy was at its fullest.

"I'm going to check on the Weryleaders," Fiona said, turning decisively toward Talenth's weyr. "Be ready when I come back?"

"Sure," Xhinna murmured, her voice still morning-hoarse.

Thread! Xhinna thought as she stripped and lowered herself into the warm waters of the bathing pool. She had never thought that she would be eager for Thread to come, but she, like Fiona and everyone else in the Weyr, saw the arrival of Thread—of something dragons and riders could *see*, could flame, could destroy—as a relief from all the horror of the sickness that had claimed eighteen more dragons in the last nine days. At least thirty more were now sick.

More galling to the spirits of the riders and weyrfolk of Fort Weyr was the fact that Benden, Telgar, and Ista Weyrs had all already experienced their first Threadfalls. Xhinna and the other weyrfolk were all convinced that, as the oldest Weyr, the honor of the first Threadfall of the Third Pass should rightly have gone to Fort. It's really a silly notion, she told herself as she rubbed off the night's dirt in the warm waters.

After her bath, she dried herself as best she could, then brushed her teeth and returned to the living quarters to dress quickly.

Fiona burst into the room just then. "We're to meet in the Dining Cavern for breakfast," she blurted and, just as quickly, sprinted out again.

Quickening her pace, Xhinna finished tying on her shoes and sprinted out of their rooms, through Talenth's weyr, and, with a flying leap that secretly thrilled her, off the ledge and into the Weyr Bowl behind.

"Careful! You don't want to be the first casualty of the day!" Cisca called from behind her.

Xhinna waved in agreement but kept up her pace, hoping—and failing—to close the distance to Fiona with her shorter legs.

At least, Xhinna told herself as she arrived, gasping, at the entrance to the Dining Cavern and spotted Fiona beckoning to her eagerly, she's saved me a place.

As Xhinna slid in gratefully beside Fiona, another person sat opposite her: H'nez. The bronze rider cast a dismissive glance her way, murmured, "Weyrwoman" to Fiona, and reached for the *klah*.

Fiona intercepted his reach, pulling the pitcher out of his way. "Let me pour for you, wingleader," she offered politely.

"It's flightleader," H'nez responded, raising his mug. "I lead a Flight this day."

"I'm sure you'll do well," Fiona said.

"And who would doubt it?" H'nez demanded.

Flustered, Fiona could think of nothing to say in response and turned to Xhinna instead. "Would you like some, too?"

Xhinna noticed the angry look H'nez cast in her direction, as though it had been *she* who had cast doubts upon his prowess, and ducked her head, causing Fiona to miss her mug. The spill was minor and quickly mopped up, but Xhinna could feel her cheeks burning with shame.

"Good morning, Flightleader!" a cheerful voice called from the entrance. Xhinna recognized Tajen and was grateful when the ex-rider joined them at their table and occupied H'nez in conversation while she hastily ate.

"Slow down," Fiona chided her. "You'll need a good meal today."

"And a strong stomach," H'nez growled from across the table. "After what happened to Benden, I'm sure there'll be a lot of injured for you to sew up."

"H'nez!" Tajen protested. "That is no way to talk before a Fall."

The bronze rider's mouth twitched into a frown and he lowered his eyes. "None of them will be in my wing, of course."

"Pity about the rest of your Flight," Xhinna snapped tartly and then flushed in embarrassment at her words. Instantly, contrite, she said, "I'm sorry, my lord, my nerves got the better of me."

"As did mine," H'nez replied, his voice suddenly under control. Xhinna was surprised to see him regarding her reflectively. "Please forgive me, I think I am more excited than I'd realized."

"Nothing to forgive," Tajen said to both of them. "Let us all forget this moment."

"We've a Fall coming," Fiona added by way of agreement. She rose and gestured for Xhinna to follow, saying to H'nez, "Good flying, dragonrider!"

As they made their way out of the Dining Cavern, Fiona spotted Cisca beckoning to her. Certain that the Weyrwoman had heard the entire exchange and fearful of Cisca's ire, Fiona made her way reluctantly over to the Weyrleader's table.

She was right. "I look to you to keep tempers even, not frayed," Cisca chided her. Then she glanced over at H'nez and frowned, adding, "But I think in this instance, he needed someone to snap at." She gave Xhinna a saturnine look. "And *you* held your own."

"I was wrong," Xhinna replied glumly.

"Yes, you were," Cisca agreed. "And honest enough to admit it, which forced a bronze rider to examine his own actions." Xhinna's brows furrowed as she considered this. With a chuckle, Cisca added, "Now you are beginning to understand politics."

"**F**ly well!" Cisca called out later in the Weyr Bowl as K'lior mounted his bronze dragon. K'lior waved in acknowledgment and then Rineth leapt into the sky, followed immediately by P'der's brown Leranth and the other dragons of the Weyrleader's wing.

Farther in the distance, T'mar's wing and H'nez's wing lofted into the sky. Fiona's heart leapt in her throat as she waved to the dragonriders, wondering which of them would come back. She hoped T'mar would. Nervously she glanced toward Cisca, wondering if the Weyrwoman had noticed her look, and was surprised to discover an expression of fear and sorrow on Cisca's face.

"Weyrwoman?" Xhinna said from beside Fiona, obviously seeing the same thing.

Cisca forced herself into a smile and dabbed her eyes quickly before straightening once more. "Don't tell anyone!"

"What, that you're human?" Xhinna asked impetuously.

"I'm the Weyrwoman," Cisca declared. "Everyone looks to me for leadership."

"You're still human, my lady," Xhinna told her stubbornly.

"It's good to set the example," Fiona added in agreement, "but that doesn't mean you can't show your true feelings to me."

"Or me," Xhinna added. "I'll keep your secrets."

Cisca cocked her head at the younger girl consideringly, then nodded, saying, "Yes, you will, won't you?"

Xhinna nodded, then turned to the now-empty Bowl. "And there is no one in this Weyr who isn't worried about every dragonrider."

"Yes," Cisca agreed, her eyes scanning the empty skies above the Weyr. In the distance, near the Star Stones, she could see the watchdragon on his solitary patrol. She sketched a salute toward the rider and smiled when the dragon dipped its head in response. She turned back to the others. "Now, *we* need to get ready."

An hour later, Fiona and Xhinna struggled with the last of the heavy trestle tables as the first casualty arrived. Fiona was straightening up over the table when she caught a glimpse of something out of the corner of her eye. She jerked her head around in time to see a dark shadow against the nooning sun and, with a cry of horror, raced to the falling dragonrider.

Catch the head! she remembered from the drill they'd done days past. Arms outstretched, she raced to catch the rider's head and shoulders, only to misjudge and have the rider land full on her, crushing her to the ground. It was the last thing she remembered for a long while.

When she awoke, she was in her bed and it was dark. Her forehead was cold and wet; someone had put a cloth over it.

"Don't move," a voice told her warningly. She thought maybe it was Kentai.

"Don't speak," Xhinna put in sharply. "You took a nasty blow to the head."

"You'll probably have a concussion, so we're going to keep an eye on you," the Weyr harper added, reaching over to touch the cloth. "In a moment, I'm going to uncover a glow and I want you to open your eyes and close them the moment you see the glow. Don't nod or move your head."

"You were lucky Zirenth managed to ease T'mar's fall," Xhinna said, although it sounded to Fiona as though the younger girl were saying it more to reassure herself.

"Okay, open your eyes and close them when you see the glow," Kentai said calmly.

Fiona opened her eyes and immediately spotted the glow held in his hands about a handspan in front of her. She closed her eyes, feeling suddenly quite drained.

"Good," Kentai noted. "Now, without opening your eyes, can you lift your right hand?"

Fiona could and did.

"Lower it and raise your left," Kentai told her. Fiona did. "Excellent!" She heard the sounds of him rising and a rustle as Xhinna rose beside him.

"There doesn't seem to be any lasting damage," Kentai said softly—probably he meant his words for Xhinna's ears only, but Fiona's were strangely acute at the moment. "She should rest. Don't give her any fellis juice without checking with me."

"Okay," Xhinna replied, her tone a bit hesitant.

"How bad was it?" Fiona demanded, willing herself to stay still.

She heard a startled intake of breath, probably Kentai, and persisted, "How bad was it? I need to know."

"You're fine," Kentai said.

"Not me, the others," Fiona replied.

There was a silence.

"Tell me!"

"Seventeen were lost, twelve have serious injuries, twenty-three others have injuries that will keep them from flying for up to three months," Kentai reported grimly.

"And?" Fiona prompted.

"We've identified twenty-five more sick dragons," Kentai concluded. After a moment's pause, he added, "You must get better, Fiona. Your courage inspired everyone today."

"I was stupid!" Fiona groaned.

"You saved T'mar's life," Kentai corrected. "You risked your own to do it."

"How is he?"

"Alive, thanks to you," Kentai told her. "Now get some rest, I'm sure you'll have plenty of visitors tomorrow, T'mar included." He cleared his throat with a chuckle. "After all, it's not every day that a wingleader is saved by a Weyrwoman. It's usually the other way around."

"Go on, harper, I'll look after her," Xhinna said. Fiona heard the harper's footsteps fade away as he made his way through Talenth's weyr and out to the Weyr Bowl.

Talenth? Fiona called.

I wasn't worried about you, Talenth said, sounding to Fiona very much like she'd been worried sick. *I knew you were going to be all right.* She *told me so.*

She? Fiona wondered.

Shh, get some rest, a different voice echoed in Fiona's mind. *We're keeping an eye on you, you'll do fine.*

The voice sounded so calm, so assured, so sensible. Cisca? Xhinna? No, the voice sounded like neither.

Sleep, the voice said gently, firmly.

Fiona drifted off to sleep.

Fiona woke to the feeling that she was being watched. She stirred, then stopped as a voice spoke. "Don't move."

She heard the sound of someone rising from a chair—someone too big to be Xhinna; besides, the voice was male—and heard the person move awkwardly out of the room.

"I'll be back with the harper," the voice assured her. "You're to stay still until he examines you."

T'mar. Fiona opened her mouth to protest, but apparently the wingleader hadn't gone so far that he didn't notice, for he chided her with, "No, don't talk, either!"

And then he was gone, leaving Fiona alone with her thoughts. No, not quite alone. *Talenth?*

Fiona! her dragon responded instantly. There was a tone of contrition and embarrassment.

You're eating? Fiona thought to her, getting a fuzzy notion that her gold was over by the Feeding Grounds.

I was hungry, Talenth said. *She said I should eat.*

She?

Melirth, Talenth replied, her tone brightening, tinged with awe and pleasure. *She's very kind.*

Yes, she is, Fiona responded, wondering if perhaps it had been Melirth she'd heard the night before. But dragons rarely spoke so cogently, being more concerned with the here and the now.

Noise at the entrance to her quarters alerted her to the arrival of others.

Eat hearty, love, Fiona called to her dragon.

I am, Talenth replied, sounding as though her mental mouth were full. Fiona got the impression of warm, hot meat, and suddenly felt her stomach growl.

"Well, that's auspicious!" a voice called from the approaching footsteps. T'mar. "I've sent for food."

"She should start with liquids—a good light broth, first," Kentai corrected. "No *klah.*"

"No *klah*?" Fiona and T'mar objected in unison. There was a moment's silence as they reacted to their impromptu chorus, then T'mar continued solo, "From what Xhinna says, this girl practically lives on *klah*!"

This girl! Fiona muttered mentally. T'mar wasn't all that much older than Kindan, and Kindan was . . . much older than she.

"A concussion," Kentai lectured, rounding on T'mar, "which you avoided, courtesy of this child—"

"Child!" Fiona blurted out in protest.

"I beg your pardon, Weyrwoman," Kentai responded after a moment of dumbfounded silence.

"No *klah*?" Fiona prompted, quietly accepting his apology.

"It might make it more difficult to recover," Kentai explained. "*Klah* has been associated with headaches, and you'll want to avoid that."

"For how long?" T'mar and Fiona again asked in unison.

Kentai chuckled while Fiona fought to keep herself from blushing.

"We'll check at the end of the day," Kentai said. Fiona felt someone remove the cloth on her head, feel her forehead, and replace the cloth. "There's no sign of fever." She heard Kentai turn and grab something, then mutter to T'mar, "Close the curtains."

A moment later, Fiona heard the curtains that separated her quarters from Talenth's being closed, followed by the curtains to the outside corridor. By now, her room should be quite dark.

"Open your eyes, Fiona," Kentai said.

She found herself staring up at the harper, who was holding a glow. T'mar moved into view in the background, one side of his face covered in a bandage and his arm in a sling.

Kentai leaned forward, examining her intently. "What am I looking for?" he asked her.

"Pupils equally reactive to light," Fiona replied quickly, just as if it were a test. Then she realized that it was. "Are they?" she asked.

"Yes," Kentai said, nodding in relief. "Still, I want you to rest until tomorrow. Concussions can be tricky things."

"I had one once as a weyrling," T'mar said by way of agreement. He went pale as he continued, "I spent a whole day feeling like my feet were always two toes off the ground."

"Did you?" Kentai asked conversationally. "I don't recall the incident."

"Yes, well, you wouldn't," T'mar replied, sounding like he was regretting the admission. "It was the result of an unpleasant alter-cation."

"Did every weyrling fight with H'nez?" Kentai asked in exasperation.

"I suspect so," T'mar allowed. "At least, all the bronze riders did."

"How is he?" Fiona asked.

"His wing did better than some," T'mar replied, his tone full of self-recrimination.

"T'mar, aside from your injuries, only two of your wing were hurt," Kentai said. "That is no worse than most."

"Well, I've got ten days to get well again," T'mar said.

"Your arm might not be up to catching firestone," Kentai warned mildly.

"Oh, be certain of it, it will be," T'mar promised.

"So, tomorrow, I can get up?" Fiona asked, moving the conversation away from an obviously painful topic.

"Yes," Kentai agreed. "And we should leave you to your rest."

Fiona rested fitfully throughout the remainder of the day. The next morning, she felt well enough to get up and bathe without Xhinna's help; she was pleased to let her friend sleep in, after she'd been working so hard to help Fiona and also take care of as many of Fiona's duties as she could. But when Xhinna woke up and saw her toweling off, she was unusually quiet, and Fiona could see that something was bothering her.

"What?" she demanded.

Xhinna sighed and made a face; it was obvious that she felt she had some kind of confession to make. "There was a woman here while you were sick," she began. With a raised eyebrow, Fiona commanded her to continue. "Lorana," Xhinna said. "She Impressed a gold at Benden Weyr and she's been looking for a cure to the illness. She came here yesterday with the Weyrleader, B'nik, to look through our Records."

"And?" Fiona urged.

"They found something in the Records," Xhinna went on. "They were excited and surprised."

"What else?" Fiona prompted, seeing that Xhinna was getting closer to what was really worrying her.

"Her dragon got sick, she just found out, and she rushed back to

Benden," Xhinna finished in a rush, her eyes darting uncontrollably in the direction of Talenth's weyr.

"Talenth is fine," Fiona declared stoutly.

"Yes," Xhinna agreed hastily. "Of course."

Fiona threw on a robe and reached for her slippers. "Let's check on her," she said. "That way we'll *both* know."

But Xhinna didn't make a move to follow. Surprised, Fiona turned back and gave her a questioning look.

"You said that you'd go *between* with her," Xhinna began hesitantly.

"She asked me," Fiona replied softly, having a disturbing notion that she knew where Xhinna was heading.

"I don't know how I'd survive if you went *between*," Xhinna confessed.

"We're not going *between* for a long time," Fiona assured her.

"You don't know that," Xhinna replied, her face grim.

"You can come with us, if that's what you want," Fiona said.

"Thank you," Xhinna said, getting up at last. "I hope it won't happen and I don't know if I'll want to, but I just wanted to know . . ."

Fiona smiled and grabbed her hand. "We won't leave you behind," she promised.

From the moment that Kentai pronounced himself satisfied with Fiona's recovery, she had only one thing on her mind: to see T'mar. She hoped that she hadn't been too obvious about it when she'd offered to check on the injured riders, but judging from Kentai's raised eyebrow and Xhinna's amused snort, she wasn't sure.

To save herself from any snide comments, she made sure that she visited all the other riders first. But it didn't help.

"So now are we going to visit your boyfriend?" Xhinna asked after their last stop. "He's the only injured rider left, you know."

"He's not my boyfriend," Fiona protested heatedly. Xhinna wisely said nothing, but Talenth, who had apparently been attracted to Fiona's thoughts, asked, *What's a boyfriend?*

I'll tell you later, Fiona promised in a tone that sounded surprisingly like the same one her father had used Turns past when she'd been asking awkward questions. Unlike her own self all those Turns past, Fiona discovered pleasantly that Talenth was contented with the answer.

Zirenth's weyr was on the third level, above the weyrling barracks. Fiona could imagine that that location was part of the reason that T'mar had volunteered to add weyrlingmaster duties to his work as wingleader: the noise from the weyrlings below was audible even here.

"Good day, Zirenth," Fiona called loudly as they halted at the entrance to T'mar's quarters. "Is your rider about?"

"I am," T'mar intoned from just inside. "Is that Weyrwoman Fiona I hear?"

"And Xhinna," Xhinna added with a laugh.

"I'm checking on the injured," Fiona said, ignoring the laughing look in Xhinna's eyes. "You're the last for the day."

"Well, I'm glad to hear that," T'mar replied. "Please come in."

Xhinna sidled behind Fiona and pushed the young Weyrwoman irreverently in before her. Fiona realized that she was blushing and turned to chide Xhinna, only to hear T'mar laugh, "Leaving so soon?"

Flustered, Fiona turned back again. "No, it's just that I—"

"Come in, come in," T'mar invited her ebulliently. "Zirenth, we have company." He spread his hands in front of him demurely, adding, "If I had known, I would have sent for refreshments."

"They're on the way," Xhinna put in promptly.

"Are they?" T'mar asked in surprise, turning just in time to see a fresh tray being carried into view by the current. "Oh, yes they are!"

He picked up the tray with his good arm but Xhinna scooped it away from him with a courteous look and laid it on the nearby table.

Fiona took the moment to carefully appraise the bronze rider's injuries: the arm in the sling would heal with time; the bandage over the right side of his face was somewhat more concerning. T'mar must have noticed, for he chose that moment to say, "I appreciate your attentions, but I've been assured by both Kentai and Cisca that I will recover fully, even if I will add a scar to my forehead."

"It missed the eye then," Xhinna murmured clinically. "I'm glad."

"Burnt out just on the eye ridge," T'mar said, gesturing to the bandage. "If Zirenth had gotten us *between* an instant later, it would have scored through the bone. As it was, I was blinded on that side and so confused that when we came back into the Weyr Bowl . . ." He shook his head ruefully and gave Fiona a respectful nod. "Well, you know, as you took my fall."

"I was trying for your head and shoulders," Fiona responded lamely.

"I hate to say it," T'mar said, biting his lip, "but I'm rather glad you saved me as you did." Fiona gave him a surprised look. "I would have certainly broken both legs otherwise and been that many more months healing."

"Then I'm glad, too," Fiona replied. "Pern needs all its dragons and riders."

"Including queens," T'mar reminded her, raising a finger scoldingly. "Next time, let me fall if you must. The thought of you losing your neck to my stupidity . . ."

"Fresh *klah,* who wants it?" Xhinna interjected into the charged silence that fell as T'mar's words trailed off.

Fiona nodded curtly, her eyes fixed on T'mar. Was he just—

"Are you just worried about my queen?" The words were out of her mouth before she realized it. Beside her, she could feel Xhinna tense up in surprise. Fiona hid her shock by giving T'mar a demanding look.

T'mar took his time answering, first sipping from his *klah* and setting his mug carefully back down on the table before meeting her eyes. "As a dragonrider and a wingleader, it is my duty to worry about both rider and dragon."

"So this is just about my dragon," Fiona snapped.

"Fiona!" Xhinna cried.

"I nearly get killed for you and all you care about is my dragon!" Fiona continued, jumping to her feet and stepping back from the table. "Well, you can save yourself the next time!"

And with that she stalked off, leaving an astonished Xhinna and an open-mouthed T'mar behind her.

Are you all right? Talenth asked worriedly.

Yes, Fiona told her brusquely. *No*, she amended a moment later. *I don't know.*

What can I do to help? Talenth asked.

Why hadn't the others asked that? Fiona moaned to herself. She was trying so hard and never got any acknowledgment, she was so . . . She stopped in her tracks, feeling small and numb.

"I was stupid," she murmured, needing to admit it out loud. With a deep sigh, she turned around and walked back to T'mar's quarters. To Talenth, she said, *Thank you, you help just by being with me.*

I love you, too, Talenth replied. Fiona got the sense that her queen was tired, had been aroused by Fiona's emotions, and was now thinking of sleep once more.

I'll be down to oil you soon, Fiona promised.

I don't think I need it, Talenth responded drowsily.

Get some rest, then, sleepyhead!

She heard quiet conversation coming from T'mar's weyr as she approached. It stopped when she was close enough that her footsteps had probably become audible inside.

Fiona forced herself to enter. "T'mar, I'm sorry, I behaved badly."

"We're all under a lot of stress, Weyrwoman," T'mar replied calmly. He lifted a hand and opened it in a throwing-away gesture. "It's forgotten. Come sit back down with us."

Still feeling ashamed and somewhat shocked by her actions, Fiona sat back down. There was a long moment of silence, which she found pleasant, while they drank their *klah* and chewed on the rolls that had been sent up from the kitchen.

"Xhinna was telling me about our Benden visitors," T'mar mentioned at last.

"Lorana and B'nik," Xhinna said. "They came here with Kindan—"

"Kindan was here?" Fiona asked, surprised and disappointed. If he'd been there, why hadn't he come to see her?

Xhinna shook her head. "They dropped him off at the Harper Hall first."

"Did they find anything in the Records?" T'mar asked.

"Yes, they found a reference to a special place built at Benden Weyr."

"Why Benden?" Fiona asked.

"It was Weyrleader M'hall of Benden who convinced them to build the rooms," Xhinna said with a shrug.

"You're guessing," Fiona said.

"It happened over four hundred Turns ago," Xhinna replied. "Of course I'm guessing."

"It seems a good guess," T'mar observed. "M'hall was the eldest son of Sean and Sorka, and the first to establish a new Weyr."

"So?"

"So he was the senior Weyrleader, after the death of Sean, and people would have looked to him for leadership," T'mar replied. He shrugged. "I'm sure we'll learn more when they find the special place."

"They'd better be quick about it," Xhinna said, "if Lorana's queen, Arith, has got the illness."

There was an awkward, thoughtful silence.

"How much time does she have?" Fiona wondered out loud.

"We don't know," T'mar replied. He made a face. "You've talked with Kentai and Tajen and the others, you know as much as I do." He shrugged. "Maybe three sevendays, maybe less."

"Fiona said that if Talenth went *between* she'd go with her," Xhinna remarked.

"Yes," T'mar responded slowly, "I can understand that."

"I'm going with her if she does," Xhinna added stoutly.

"I wouldn't be so quick to make such a promise," T'mar warned her. Xhinna gave him a stubborn look and he went on. "No one ever says words with the thought that they might one day have to eat them."

"I won't!"

"You wouldn't be the first," T'mar observed mildly. "I've had to eat my own words countless times; that's why I give you such advice."

"How did they taste?" Fiona asked, surprised to find her humor returning.

"Awful," T'mar replied with a grimace. "But I was always glad after I'd eaten them."

" 'Be careful what you wish for, you might get it,' " Fiona repeated the old saying.

"Exactly."

"I'm not wishing for it," Xhinna protested irritably. "I just want to have plans."

"Why not plan for good things?" T'mar suggested.

"Like what?" Fiona challenged.

"Like when your Talenth can fly and take you *between*," T'mar suggested.

"What's that got to do with me?" Xhinna asked. After a moment, she turned excitedly to Fiona, "Would you take me with you?"

"Of course," Fiona promised. "We can go everywhere together."

"Not flying Thread," T'mar said.

"But we haven't enough queens for a queen's wing," Xhinna said.

"Yet," Fiona told her with a grin.

"Are you planning on repopulating the Weyr with queens so soon?" Xhinna asked mockingly. She dropped her eyes into her lap as she realized the full import of what she'd said.

Fiona remembered the times she had gone with her father to the stud sheds to watching the bulls breed. Somewhere in her future there were mating flights, many mating flights. A thrill, a sense of dread and excitement both, churned her stomach.

"That's for Turns not yet come," T'mar chided Xhinna gently. " 'Don't count your eggs before they've hatched.' "

"Dragon eggs," Xhinna said with a snigger and a mischievous glance toward Fiona.

Fiona turned her attention to T'mar, asking, "What's it like, a mating flight?"

T'mar smiled and shook his head. "That's not for Turns to come yet," he said again. "But it's marvelous and you'll be brilliant, I'm sure of it."

"Just don't let her gorge," Xhinna said warningly.

Fiona looked at her inquiringly.

"Your queen, don't let her gorge when she rises or the clutch will be too small." Xhinna felt the intensity of the looks the other two were giving her and explained, "I heard it from the other weyrfolk."

T'mar smiled. "They're right, of course. They've seen enough mating flights to know."

"What about you?" Xhinna pressed.

T'mar shook his head. "I'd rather not talk about it, if you don't mind," he said. "It's personal."

"Well, *I* remember the last mating flight and I felt this amazing feeling," Xhinna replied. "I'd never felt anything like it before. I just wanted to hug everyone."

"Yes," T'mar agreed quietly, "mating flights are like that: The emotions of the queen and her bronze flow into everyone."

"When is Melirth due to rise again?" Xhinna asked.

"Not for a while yet," T'mar replied. "Within the Turn, probably." He slapped his good hand on his thigh and rose from his chair. "Which reminds me, it's getting near enough toward dinner that we should head down to the Living Cavern and at least pay our respects to K'lior and Cisca, even if we're too stuffed to eat."

"Not me," Xhinna responded feelingly, rising and grabbing their tray deftly. "I heard what Zirana's making for dinner and I kept room enough!"

"The word from Ista is bad," Cisca said the moment she had a chance to catch Fiona's ear. "We don't know everything yet, but it sounds like they lost over two-thirds of their fighting dragons."

"How many do they have left?"

Cisca shook her head. "Less than a Flight, certainly. Maybe less than two wings." With a sad look she added, "I think they lost more to the illness than anything else. Too many riders don't want to miss the fight; too few are adept at knowing the signs of this illness."

"Do we know?"

"Not really," Cisca answered truthfully. "The cough is obvious, but the earlier signs . . . even Lorana wasn't certain. Not that we had much time to talk about it . . ."

Fiona gave her a puzzled look.

"We spent most of our time poring over old Records and little time talking," Cisca told her. She ran a hand nervously across her forehead, wiping hair away from her eyes. "Of course she left the moment she learned about her dragon." She paused in thought, then shook her head. "The cough's the most noticeable symptom."

Fiona saw that the others around the table were watching them and pulled back from Cisca. The Weyrwoman noticed and turned to K'lior.

"I was just telling Fiona about Ista," she told him.

"What's the news? Did they have a Fall?" T'mar asked. He was sitting across from Fiona.

"Yes," Fiona replied. She looked at the Weyrwoman, expecting her to fill in the details, but Cisca merely waved for her to continue the tale and reached for a platter of steaming meat. Fiona took a breath. "The Weyrwoman was just telling me that they may have lost as much as two-thirds of their fighting strength."

"Two-thirds!" M'kury exclaimed from farther down the table. "They were already light, and with the loss of C'rion . . ."

"J'lantir's leading them now," K'lior said.

"J'lantir," H'nez snorted derisively. "The man lost his whole wing!"

"But we found out *why*, didn't we?" M'kury retorted quickly. "And without them, we would have had even more holders die in the Plague."

"Holders!" H'nez snorted once more. "Who needs—"

"I was a holder, H'nez, in case you've forgotten," Fiona snapped angrily, her hands balled into fists under the table. "And without J'lantir, I wouldn't be here. Think on that."

"Actually," Cisca added drolly, "perhaps it'd be best if you just *think*, H'nez."

H'nez's eyes flashed and he tensed in his chair, his anger obvious to everyone. Outside a dragon bugled loudly, answered by another higher-pitched dragon: Melirth and Talenth. The sounds seemed to recall him to his senses, and with some effort, he relaxed in his chair.

"Everyone is tense," K'lior said soothingly into the silence that fell. "These are trying times and we—" He waved his hand indicating all the wingleaders and the two Weyrwomen. "—set the tone for the entire Weyr."

"I spoke without thinking," H'nez said, raising his eyes to K'lior, then Cisca, then Fiona.

"It was probably just the wine," M'kury said in a conciliatory tone. Then he noticed that there wasn't any wine at the table and raised a hand, calling, "We need some wine here. Make it Benden white, if you can."

"You and your Benden white," S'kan said, shaking his head. "You'd think you were in Benden, not Fort."

"Fort for the riders, Benden for the wine," M'kury said, holding out a hand to take one of the glasses being offered to the table. "Everyone has a specialty."

The rest of the wingleaders guffawed.

"And we know yours," M'valer said, gesturing to M'kury's glass as a kitchen drudge carefully filled it.

"And why not? We don't have another Fall for a sevenday," M'kury replied nonchalantly.

"Good point," M'valer acknowledged, raising his own glass for filling.

"Don't drink too much, though," K'lior cautioned.

"What about T'mar's wing?" M'kury asked with a sideways glance toward T'mar.

"Every wing is flying light," T'mar observed. "We need all the fit dragons we can get."

"We need fit riders, too," H'nez remarked sourly.

"My arm will be well enough when Thread falls."

"Not if you tear it up during drills," Cisca said pointedly.

"Why don't I ride with T'mar tomorrow?" Tajen suggested. He hadn't been sitting at the table but had come by partway through the conversation and had listened in, unnoticed. "I could catch the firestone for him."

T'mar started to say something, but K'lior spoke first. "That's a very interesting idea." The Weyrleader turned to Cisca. "Could we pair other uninjured riders with uninjured dragons?"

"You mean two riders together, or one rider on another's dragon?"

"That's unthinkable!" M'valer exclaimed, looking extremely outraged. "Don't ever think that I'll let my dragon be ridden by another!"

"Not even to save Pern?" Fiona asked him. M'valer hesitated and she pressed on. "Even if your dragon would allow it and wanted to do it?"

"You know how they get when Thread falls," M'kury added.

"Well . . . maybe," M'valer said finally. "But it would have to be in direst need."

"Why direst need?" Cisca asked reasonably. M'valer bristled, so she persisted. "How can we tell if without your dragon flying one Fall, we will have enough strength for the next?"

M'valer looked confused by this question, so Cisca continued, "No one can really say which dragon will be the most important in a Fall—"

"You've not ridden a Fall," H'nez objected.

"No, I've tended the injured," Cisca returned sharply. "And I'm saying that we need every fighting dragon that can fly, regardless of who is riding them."

"Well, it's a thought at least," K'lior observed, placing a soothing hand on Cisca's arm. She glanced over at him in surprise. Whatever response he gave was a secret between the two of them, perhaps relayed by dragon, but it seemed enough for Cisca. K'lior turned his attention back to T'mar. "If you've no objection, then I would be interested to see how you work with Tajen tomorrow."

T'mar gave the ex-dragonrider a quick, measuring look, then nodded. "I'd be delighted."

"Then it's settled," K'lior said, returning his attention back to his dinner.

"What about the weyrlings?" H'nez asked. "Who's going to handle them?"

"Well," Tajen replied with a shrug, "the ones who can fly will be handling firestone, and the younger ones will be working with the Weyrwomen here, so I don't think there's an issue."

"Who'll control the flying werylings and the firestone?" H'nez pressed.

"That would be my job as Weyrwoman," Cisca replied. She cast a glance at Fiona and smiled impishly. "Fiona will be responsible for the firestone, as we don't need to have any more riders falling on her."

That drew a chuckle all around and a shamed look from T'mar.

"With me holding on to you, T'mar, you needn't worry about falling," Tajen said, adding to the bronze rider's shame.

"If you want me to handle the firestone," Fiona said to Cisca, "then I should probably drill with the weyrlings."

"Well said!" Tajen exclaimed. "Why don't you plan on that tomorrow when the riders are practicing?"

Fiona nodded even as she felt her stomach go suddenly heavy

with worry. Tomorrow! Under the table, Xhinna patted her knee reassuringly.

"**Y**ou won't have much trouble with the older weyrlings," Tajen consoled Fiona early the next morning over breakfast. "There are only twelve of them with hatchlings from Hinirth's last clutch, and they're almost old enough to join the fighting wings."

"The two leaders are J'gerd and J'keran," T'mar added. "J'gerd's a wiry-haired lad, smiles a lot but he's thoughtful."

"J'keran is blond-haired and low-built," Tajen continued, glancing at T'mar for agreement.

"He's strong, just not tall," T'mar said. "They're both—" He glanced at Tajen. "—steady, wouldn't you say?"

"Steady's a good word," Tajen agreed. "Given time they'll make passable riders."

"They'll know what to do; you just keep on top of 'em," T'mar told her as he tipped back his mug for the last bit of *klah* and rose from the table. "You'll do fine."

And with that, they left.

Fortunately, Cisca took pity on her. It must have been the look in her eyes, Fiona thought ruefully as the Weyrwoman guided her toward the weyrling tables.

With well-honed good manners, all the young riders rose as soon as they spotted the Weyrwomen. Fiona knew some of them already, but she still felt that she was being confronted with a sea of faces.

Cisca gestured to one of the older weyrlings at the end of table. "This is J'gerd."

The lad smiled, and immediately Fiona recognized it as the telltale sign, along with his curly black hair, that had been given her by T'mar.

"You must be J'keran, then," Fiona said to a smaller, blond-haired boy standing beside J'gerd.

J'gerd's smile grew wider and he poked the other lad, saying jokingly, "Examine your conscience and tell the Weyrwomen whatever sins you've committed." While J'keran was still looking at him bemusedly, J'gerd added, "Quickly now, before it's too late!"

"You'd best be mindful of your own errors," J'keran replied steadily. Then he jerked his head toward one of the younger riders. "Either you or F'jian there would be my guess for any pranks."

"Sit, sit all of you," Cisca commanded. Obediently the riders sat back down, still looking at the Weyrwoman half-expectantly, half-fearfully.

"Fiona will be responsible for firestone drill this morning," Cisca said.

"Weyrwoman," J'gerd said with a polite nod toward Fiona.

"We worked together on the first-aid drill," F'jian piped up from his place at the tables. "If you'd like," he offered Fiona, "I could guide you around."

"So you can eat with the Weyrleader?" J'gerd replied with a shake of his head. "No, the Weyrwoman will need an experienced hand to help her, not some young . . ." But he trailed off as he realized that Fiona's queen was from the same clutch and any insult to F'jian's bronze might also be applicable to her queen.

"You have to forgive J'gerd," J'keran spoke up in the silence. "His lips often move a full minute before his brain."

That brought sniggers from the rest of the group and red-faced shame to J'gerd's face.

A subtle move from Cisca made it clear to Fiona that she was on her own to handle the situation. On her own and being tested.

"We need to make allowances all around," Fiona said after a moment, choosing her words carefully. "Some who speak too quickly should learn caution—" She saw J'keran glance victoriously at J'gerd. "—while others who do not speak at all risk never being heard." She was pleased to see J'keran and J'gerd exchange expressions as her meaning sank in.

"As such," she continued, "I think it best if the two of you came with me to the Weyrleader's table, while F'jian stays here and keeps order."

The young bronze rider sat suddenly bolt upright as he absorbed the meaning of her words.

"Come on, quickly," Fiona called, as she turned toward the Weyrleader's table, seeing K'lior rising. Cisca merely smiled and waved her on. If K'lior moved too quickly, she'd never be able to talk with him, Fiona realized with a rush of fear. She couldn't shout, it would be unseemly and almost certainly unheard in the noise of the Cavern so—

Talenth, ask Rineth to have K'lior wait for me, Fiona called to her dragon.

In front, she saw K'lior halt and turn slowly around, scanning for her. She picked up her pace and was soon beside him, J'keran and J'gerd a step behind her.

"K'lior, thanks for waiting!" Fiona said a little breathlessly. "I wanted to introduce the firestone crew to you."

"J'gerd, J'keran," K'lior said, nodding to each. He looked back to Fiona, saying, "Good choices."

He frowned for a moment before continuing. "Thread will fall over Ruatha and then on to the Weyr." He glanced at the three of them to make sure they understood. To the two lads, he said, "We'll use the usual recognition points and full load."

"Full load?" Fiona repeated, bewildered.

"Sometimes when we practice we don't fill the firestone sacks full," K'lior explained kindly. "But as we've a Fall coming and we're flying wing-light, we need all the experience we can get."

"Full load, it is," J'keran replied, sounding somewhat gleeful.

K'lior looked back at Fiona. "Is there anything else, Weyrwoman?"

"No, thank you, Weyrleader," Fiona replied formally, remembering at the last moment to bow rather than curtsy. Weyrwomen, as Xhinna was constantly reminding her, need not curtsy to anyone.

"Good Fall, Weyrleader!" J'gerd and J'keran called in unison as K'lior departed.

"We need to get ready, too, don't we?" Fiona asked, turning back to the older riders. "Won't they need firestone to take with them?"

"Of course, Weyrwoman," J'gerd replied, trying not to sound as if that weren't obvious. "J'keran, go and send the others to the barracks." He turned back to Fiona. "Do you have the key?"

"Key?" Fiona repeated blankly. It turned out that the firestone was kept in a locked room, a leftover precaution from the days not so many Turns before when firestone had been dangerously explosive—mere contact with water would set the "old" firestone burning.

The newer firestone, as Fiona knew from her time with Kindan, Kelsa, and the other harpers, had been discovered by C'tov of High Reaches Weyr and was, as far as any could tell, the real firestone that had been first discovered in ancient times when it was used by fire-lizards.

Fiona spun around looking for Ellor. She quickly spotted her.

"Here's yours," Ellor said, handing a simple key and length of chain over to Fiona. "Mind you don't lose it."

"Mine?" Fiona repeated in surprise.

"Certainly," Ellor said with a raised eyebrow. "You're a Weyr-woman: this is your Weyr."

With a nod, Fiona placed the chain over her neck and the key against her chest, pretending that she completely understood Ellor's meaning. She was certain that she was missing some deep importance in the headwoman's words, but she didn't have the time to think on it more. J'gerd and J'keran were right behind her.

"Let's go," J'keran urged, all pretense now dropped. "We don't want to be late."

"Especially not for H'nez," J'gerd agreed with a grimace.

Fiona said nothing but quickened her pace, breaking into a trot as she exited into the Weyr Bowl. She was about to slow down, uncertain of her direction, when J'keran sped past her. "This way!"

A knot of weyrlings were gathered outside the first-level door that housed the Weyr's supply of firestone.

"You'll need someone to count," a voice beside her chimed up unexpectedly. Fiona turned to see Xhinna, who gave her a reassuring smile and said, "You've got to keep a tally of all the firestone leaving the room."

"Could you do it?" Fiona asked. Xhinna's expression dimmed slightly, letting Fiona guess that her friend wanted a more challenging role. She leaned in closer. "What do you want to do?"

"I'd like to fill the sacks," Xhinna told her.

"That's hard work," a deeper voice spoke up. Xhinna and Fiona turned to see J'keran standing close by. "Usually we have the younger ones switch off."

"We've what—twelve weyrlings to fly firestone?" Fiona asked out loud.

"Eleven," someone else called out. "V'lex was injured in the last Fall."

"Thirty-three weyrlings to bag—"

"Thirty-four," Xhinna put in stoutly.

"You're not a weyrling!" one of the younger boys complained. "You're a girl!"

"*I'm* a girl," Fiona said warningly.

"Were you addled in your Shell, D'lanor? She's offering to help!" another weyrling put in, eyeing Xhinna with a combination of surprise and awe.

"And what will happen when you're all in fighting wings?" Fiona asked.

"Well, there'll be more weyrlings," J'keran suggested cautiously.

"Not unless Melirth rises soon!" J'gerd replied derisively.

"Why should we worry about that?" D'lanor wondered.

"You shouldn't," Fiona said. *I* should, she added to herself. "So, who should we set to counting?"

"Why not get V'lex?" someone suggested.

"Are you witless? V'lex can barely stand," J'keran rounded on the hapless weyrling.

"I can do it," Fiona suggested.

"Not a good idea, Weyrwoman," J'gerd said at once. "You'll need to be everywhere, keeping an eye on everything."

"And your dragon," J'keran added, glancing around in search of Talenth.

"You'll need her to coordinate with us," J'gerd explained. "When we're at the rendezvous."

"I could do it," a new voice piped up. "I'm good at counting."

Fiona discovered that the voice belonged to a young girl, younger than Xhinna. She had close-cropped strawberry-blond hair and vivid green eyes.

"Terin!" Xhinna exclaimed in surprise. "What are you doing here? Does Ellor know?"

"I asked," Terin replied stubbornly. "She said, 'Just as long as you don't get underfoot.'"

"Another girl," a weyrling in the distance murmured disapprovingly.

Fiona's doubts vanished with those words and the look on Terin's face.

"Very well, you can be our counter," she said. J'gerd gave her a doubtful look, then handed a slate to the young girl.

"Make a mark for every bag filled," he told her.

"I know," Terin replied testily. "My father is a bronze rider."

"No, he's not," a voice whispered loud enough to be heard by all.

"Enough!" Fiona bellowed, causing Terin to shrink visibly and the weyrlings to back away in surprise. "We've work to do, and we need to do it now." She turned to the younger werylings. "You know what to do. Get moving."

"They're going to need a full sack for every flying dragon," J'gerd told her. "And then we'll need twice that for the weyrlings."

"That's one hundred and sixty-four sacks to start," Fiona translated, "and . . ."

"Three hundred and twenty-eight for the weyrlings," Terin supplied from beside her. Catching the looks of surprise around her, she added, "I *said* I was good with numbers." She paused and looked at the weyrlings. "With Xhinna, that's just under five sacks each to start and another . . . not quite ten for the weyrlings."

"With that number, the werylings will be carrying close to thirty bags each, won't they?" Fiona asked, looking to J'gerd for agreement. He pursed his lips thoughtfully, then nodded. "That's too much weight, isn't it?"

"Each sack weighs—" Terin dodged past the first of the young weyrlings carrying two full sacks of firestone. "We should get out of the way."

"One sack at a time!" J'keran shouted at the weyrling.

Terin quickly made two marks on her slate and continued, "Each sack weighs two stone. So thirty sacks would be—" She paused to mark off another filled sack leaving the storeroom. "—sixty stone."

"Too much," Fiona said. *Talenth, tell Rineth that the weyrlings can only provide half the firestone at a time.*

Rineth has told K'lior, Talenth responded immediately.

"You'll carry half the load," Fiona told J'gerd and J'keran, "and come back for the rest."

The two riders nodded, and quickly exchanged looks of relief.

H'nez wants to know when his wing will have its firestone, Talenth relayed to her.

Ask Rineth in what order K'lior wants the wings provisioned, Fiona responded.

H'nez first, Talenth replied, her voice sounding slightly amused.

"Be sure to get the firestone to H'nez's wing first," Fiona called to the weyrlings as they rushed past.

"It'd be quicker if the younger ones just did the bagging and the older ones distributed," Terin said, her tone reminding Fiona somewhat of Xhinna.

"Excellent suggestion, Terin," Fiona replied, gesturing to J'gerd to implement it.

"Are you hoping to be Weyrwoman yourself, then?" J'gerd asked the young girl teasingly before hoisting a firestone sack and trotting off toward H'nez's waiting wing.

"Don't listen to him," Fiona said to Terin. "He's just annoyed that he didn't think of it himself." The younger girl's expression brightened.

Fiona could feel the tension from the dragons out in the Weyr Bowl and didn't need to see H'nez's irritated gestures to realize that the dragonriders expected their supplies to be delivered more quickly. She sighed and resolved to start earlier before the Fall when it really came. But "drills are how people learn," as her father often said. She smiled to herself at the thought of how surprised her father would be to see her in her current position. Lord Bemin had always been appalled when Fiona had taken it upon herself to order the Hold guard and other holders about—yet now she was ordering *dragonriders!*

Fiona stood at the entrance of the firestone room until Terin's count reached thirty sacks and then decided to follow the last sack to see how things were with the dragonriders.

Her eyes first went to H'nez's depleted wing. The older weyrling carrying the last load was struggling to bring it to the waiting blue rider at a trot, but the distance from the firestone room was such that it took several minutes to get there.

"Who's next?" Fiona murmured aloud to herself, determined to order the next wing to move closer to the firestone. Irritably, she realized that she didn't know. Probably M'valer and K'rall, H'nez's favorite wingleaders, Fiona decided with a grimace. Fiona guessed that K'lior was giving the prickly flightleader the opportunity to be first into the drill.

Talenth, have M'valer bring his wing here, she told her dragon. *They'll get their firestone that much quicker.*

A mild bugle in the distance alerted Fiona that her queen had relayed the message and that M'valer was surprised at it.

They come, Talenth replied a moment later. *Linth was surprised that I told him.*

"Upsetting the bronze riders, I see," a woman's voice said. Fiona whirled and was surprised to find Cisca looking down at her, an expression of approval on her face.

"This is quicker," Fiona said, gesturing to the wing of dragons that had arrived in front of the firestone room.

"I know," Cisca agreed in an easy, amused tone. "But having your new queen—'not months out of her shell'—order grizzled veterans around is something new to them."

"I suppose it must be," Fiona agreed reluctantly. "But they seemed so upset at not getting their firestone quicker—"

"Don't apologize," Cisca interrupted, holding up a hand. "You're doing your duty as a Weyrwoman."

"Was this another test?" Fiona asked, her feelings mixed between relief that she'd passed and annoyance that she'd been tested again.

"Every day is a test," Cisca replied soberly. "But we'll never learn new ways of doing things if we insist on telling everyone what they should be doing."

"Well, I think we should keep a full load of firestone bagged and ready at all times," Fiona remarked.

"A good idea," Cisca agreed, "and usually we do. I suspect that with T'mar's injuries, the issue was conveniently forgotten by the weyrlings."

"I can't say as I'd blame them," Fiona said. "They must have been exhausted bagging and flying the firestone and then, on top of it, helping with the injured."

"Sixty-two," Terin called loudly from the doorway. M'valer's wing had flown off and was replaced with K'rall's.

Cisca turned to the sound of the younger girl's voice and then looked back at Fiona, her eyes dancing. "Acquiring more outcasts?"

"She can count," Fiona replied with a shrug. "She says her father was a rider."

Cisca made a face. "She came to us from a small hold that was doing poorly," she said. "And yes, they made the claim but couldn't identify the parent."

"And they let her go?" Fiona asked, surprised.

"It was six Turns ago, during that harsh winter, and that hold couldn't feed itself," Cisca explained. Before Fiona could ask the question, the Weyrwoman continued, "Yes, it was one of your father's minor holds."

"It must have been Retallek," Fiona decided. "Father was going to replace the holder there as soon as the weather turned good enough to ride."

Cisca raised an eyebrow, urging Fiona to go on.

"There were none left alive when he got there," Fiona told her grimly.

"So she was lucky," Cisca murmured quietly.

"Yes," Fiona agreed with a deep sigh. She shook herself and said to the Weyrwoman, "I think I'll go inside and see if I can help."

Cisca acknowledged this with a wave and strode off.

Inside the firestone room, the air was getting dusty as the weyrlings heaped firestone into open sacks. She spotted Xhinna and waved to her, but the weyrgirl was too busy, wiping sweat out of her eyes and stooping to shovel another load of firestone into her bag.

"Water," Fiona murmured to herself. We must get them water. And why wasn't there more air coming in?

She started back to the entrance and pushed the double doors fully open, then looked around for someone to get water.

Talenth, she called, *could you ask Ellor to send someone with water for the weyrlings? They'll be parched.*

Ellor has sent the water, Talenth told a moment later.

Thank you, Fiona replied, sending a mental caress toward her dragon.

"One hundred," Terin said beside her as another weyrling passed by.

"Thank you." Fiona looked up and saw Tajen lifting a sack of firestone up to his perch behind T'mar on Zirenth.

"I've brought some water," a young boy piped up suddenly from behind Fiona. She turned and had to lower her gaze to meet the eyes of the towheaded youngster in front of her.

"Can you go inside and make sure that everyone gets a drink?"

The boy's eyes grew big and round as he realized he was talking to a Weyrwoman, but he shook his head slowly.

"Why not?" Fiona asked in surprise.

"Firestone explodes when water touches it," the boy replied in a half-whisper.

"Old firestone," Terin chimed in abruptly. "This is new firestone." She shook her head at him, looking superior, although Fiona doubted she was more than two Turns his elder.

"Go on," Fiona said, gently shoving the child to the door. "You'll be fine. Just make sure that everyone gets a drink; tell them it's my orders."

"Yes, Weyrwoman," the boy replied, his shoulders suddenly straighter as he realized that *he* would be giving the Weyrwoman's orders.

Fiona, who had been raised as a Lord Holder's daughter, had only a fleeting moment of surprise at how easily everyone followed her orders before she returned her attention the task at hand.

"One hundred and ten," Terin called out a short time later.

Fiona insisted on carrying the last sack herself and cheerfully handed it up to a blue rider, who gawked at her in surprise before tying the sack to his riding harness.

"Good flying!" she called up to him.

"Thank you, Weyrwoman," the rider returned, and then he was rising into the air, following the last wing as it took station above the Star Stones, then blinked *between* to the skies above Ruatha Hold.

"Everyone, take a break," Fiona called. "But stay on your feet. Ten minutes."

She had sent the weyrboy back to the kitchens for some snacks and set him the task of ensuring that everyone had a chance to eat while they were resting. She went into the firestone room and rousted out Xhinna and the weyrlings, urging, "Get some fresh air!"

To Terin, she said, "Good job." The youngster glowed.

"What do you think of firestone, now?" Fiona asked Xhinna when she had a chance to catch her alone.

"It's not so bad," Xhinna replied with a look of stout determination.

When the break was over, the younger weyrlings and Xhinna started back to bagging firestone while the older weyrlings put their harnesses on their dragons in preparation for hauling the firestone.

At last the last sack was loaded onto the dragons, and J'gerd waved to Fiona from his perch on brown Winurth, then called to the other weyrlings, "Test straps!"

The weryling dragons flexed their hindquarters and leapt into the air, their wings beating frantically as they lifted their loads. Just off the ground, they hovered.

Winurth asks if you can see any loose straps, Talenth told her. Fiona got a feeling of motion from her queen, and turned to see Talenth hurrying out on to her ledge to see all the commotion firsthand. As the young gold caught sight of the straining dragons, she added wistfully, *When can I do that?*

When the other weyrlings of your clutch can, Fiona replied sending a wave of commiseration along with the thought. She turned back to the weyrlings and assessed their situation. *Tell Winurth that I see nothing wrong from here.*

J'gerd waved down at her and made a pumping motion to the flying weyrlings. They rose higher. J'gerd dropped his arm suddenly and the weyrlings swooped, stopping abruptly, straining their lines.

Winurth says that everyone reports ready, Talenth relayed in a tone of curiosity. *What are they ready for?*

What, indeed? Fiona wondered. Suddenly she understood.

Talenth, tell Rineth that the weyrlings are ready, Fiona said, realizing that J'gerd could have just as easily had his own dragon relay the information to the Weyrleader.

K'lior says that they should meet high at the north Ruathan border, Talenth responded a moment later, relaying the message very carefully.

Good, Fiona responded. *Please tell Winurth.*

A moment later, J'gerd made another arm motion. In response, the weyrlings rose higher, gathered at the Star Stones, and then disappeared *between.*

Did they get there? Fiona asked a moment later.

Rineth says they are in a good formation, Talenth replied.

Fiona straightened her shoulders with pride and turned to Terin.

"They got there," she said. The youngster looked at her as if she'd just pronounced water wet.

It seemed only moments later that the older weyrlings were back, tying on their second load of firestone. Again they tested it. This time one sack fell off and a shamefaced green rider returned to the ground, retrieved the fallen sack, tied it securely, and tested once more. When all was in order, J'gerd gave the signal again and they went *between,* J'gerd first sketching a salute to Fiona. Fiona smiled and, gesturing for Terin to follow her, entered the firestone room.

Inside, she quickly collected all the younger weyrlings.

"Great work, everyone," she said to them, eyeing them all carefully. They were hot and sweaty, looking very much worse for their efforts. And yet, in a real Fall, they'd need to prepare at least eight bags of firestone for each dragon, and they'd only prepared three. "We've got at least an hour before we'll need to do more," she told them. Their faces brightened until Fiona held up a hand in caution. "But I think we should ready another load of firestone, just in case."

"But we won't need it!" a voice grumbled in the crowd.

"Today maybe," Fiona said. "But sure as Thread falls from the sky, the dragons will be needing firestone soon. What harm is there in being ready?"

"She sounds just like T'mar," the same voice grumbled.

"She should, she's a Weyrwoman," another voice answered. Fiona recognized that voice as F'jian.

"F'jian, take charge," she said. "I want to talk with the Weyr-woman." With that, she turned and moved out briskly, her thoughts racing even more quickly.

It seemed foolish to her, with the illness and so few weyrlings, for the Weyr to rely on them alone for firestone. And what would happen if the older weyrlings got the illness or were injured? Who would fly the firestone then? Perhaps some of the less injured dragons could do it. Or perhaps K'lior's thought of having healthy riders ride sick riders' dragons would fill the gap. She needed to talk to Cisca.

"They won't be up for it," Fiona blurted as soon as she found the Weyrwoman where she was supervising the laying out of the first-aid area along with Kentai and Ellor.

Instead of asking who or what, Cisca merely nodded. "What should we do about it?"

"Can we organize some of the weyrfolk?" Fiona asked. She lowered her voice to be certain that no one else heard her next words. "We don't know if the illness will affect the younger dragons. We must be prepared."

"Actually," Cisca corrected her, "we do know that it will affect them." Fiona looked puzzled, until Cisca continued, "We know that Lorana's Arith is infected."

"Oh, yes," Fiona replied sadly. She glanced toward her weyr, where Talenth was eyeing the bustle in the Weyr Bowl with great interest.

"We can do it," Ellor said. "We'll have to use more of the young-sters, though."

"Good idea," Cisca said. She turned to Fiona. "And with the work set more squarely on the weyrfolk, you'll be able to help me with more of my chores."

Oddly, the thought cheered Fiona. Cisca caught her look and winked at her.

"In fact . . ." she began, glancing around at the activity of the Weyr Bowl, "I think that perhaps you and I should make a quick inspection while we still have the time."

"Inspection?" Fiona repeated, wondering what the Weyr-woman was talking about. A rustle of wings surprised her further, even more so when gold Melirth settled on the ground next to them.

"Run and get your riding things!" Cisca ordered, turning to the chair on which she'd draped her wher-hide jacket, leather helmet, and gloves.

Fiona raced back to her quarters, waved cheerfully at Talenth, rushed into her rooms, and opened the closet where she'd placed the riding leathers that she'd been given, in all due ceremony, at Turn's End. She was surprised to realize that that had been less than three weeks ago. She grabbed what she needed and raced back out.

"She's big and you're small," Cisca said, eyeing her queen with obvious delight, "so I'll give you a hand up."

It was less elegant than that, but finally, with a certain amount of undignified pushing on the part of Fort's senior Weyrwoman, Fiona managed to catch the riding straps and crawl up on Melirth's neck. A moment later she was joined by Cisca.

"Are you ready?" Cisca asked, leaning over Fiona's shoulder.

"Where are we going?" Fiona asked, looking around the Weyr Bowl quickly, seeing the startled look on Xhinna's face and the eager looks of the younger weyrlings.

"I can't have you not doing your duty as Weyrwoman just because your dragon's too young to fly," Cisca told her sternly, adding with a chuckle, "And I haven't been in the air for *days*."

With that, Melirth leapt, her great wings easily propelling them up high and out of the Bowl. They paused only long enough to dip a wing at the watch dragon by the Star Stones, and then Fiona was engulfed in the cold of *between*.

Are you all right? Talenth asked anxiously.

I'm fine, Fiona replied and was surprised to realize that she was. It was the first time that *between* seemed merely normal, almost comforting. She had only an instant to adjust to the new feeling before they burst out again into the sunlight.

Above her, Fiona could see twelve dragons spread in a loose V formation. Each dragon had a pair of firestone sacks dangling below them.

"We're here!" Fiona cried, suddenly understanding Cisca. "We're watching the weyrlings deliver the firestone!"

"Part of your job, Weyrwoman," Cisca said into her ear. "Pay attention and see if they're doing it right."

Of course they were: they'd already done it once that morning. The purpose of the trip, Fiona realized, was not so much for *her* to check up on the weyrlings as for Cisca to show her how the weyrlings should be passing firestone.

The maneuver was quite tricky, Fiona decided as she watched one of the fighting dragons catch up with a weyrling, come alongside, get the weyrling's attention and then, with a heart-stopping flip of the wings, dive in a spiral to a position directly underneath the weyrling, near the firestone sack.

The load was transferred neatly from weyrling to dragonrider, and then the two veered away from each other, the weyrling's dragon lurching slightly from the sudden weight reduction.

"Well done," Cisca murmured in Fiona's ear. Fiona nodded in agreement. "Watch carefully: the trick's the same for the flamethrowers we'll be using."

"We don't have enough queens," Fiona protested, trying to imagine herself and Talenth accomplishing the maneuver.

"Yet," Cisca said with a laugh.

They watched until all the weyrlings had relinquished their loads and then Cisca called, "Hold on tight!"

Suddenly Melirth's great wings were pumping with more power than Fiona could imagine and the great queen lurched forward in the sky, arcing up to a nearly upside-down position before sweeping back in the other direction and taking up a position directly in front of the weyrlings.

Fiona felt more than heard the surprise and pleasure of the weyrling dragons behind her.

"We're taking them home," Cisca called. Fiona felt Cisca change her balance as she raised an arm and gave the universal signal to go *between*.

We're coming back now, Fiona told Talenth as the cold nothingness that was *between* engulfed her once more.

You had fun! Talenth said, sounding both pleased and accusing.

They burst out into the air above Fort Weyr, right at the Star Stones. The watch dragon bugled a greeting as Melirth zoomed past and then began a spiraling, leisurely descent back into the Weyr.

Yes, I did! Fiona agreed happily.

That evening Xhinna was so obviously sore from all her efforts that Fiona insisted the younger girl take her bath first.

"Don't put on your nightgown when you get out," Fiona ordered, "I'm going to put some salve on your back."

Xhinna didn't even protest as Fiona slathered her back with the sticky salve. Finally, Fiona sent her to bed and took her own bath. When she was done, she found Xhinna already asleep, lightly snoring.

Sometimes, Fiona thought happily to herself in a drowsy languor just before sleep overtook her, it's like we're sisters. It was a pleasant thought and Fiona squirmed up closer to Xhinna as she settled into sleep; it was still midwinter and the warmth of another body was perfect.

When Fiona awoke the next morning, Xhinna was still sound asleep. She decided to leave her; she knew that, despite Xhinna's protests, the girl had worked herself ragged the day before.

Stepping into Talenth's weyr, she checked on her sleeping mate, quietly oiled a new flaky patch that she'd been eyeing, and made her way out onto the ledge and into the Weyr Bowl.

The sun had crested over the easterly ridge of Fort Weyr, but there were still heavy banks of fog rising from the Bowl itself. Still, Fiona had no trouble negotiating her way to the Dining Cavern.

"Fiona!" Cisca hailed her as she entered. Fiona looked around and saw the Weyrleader and Weyrwoman seated by themselves at one of the regular tables. Cisca was beckoning to her. Fiona waved back and trotted over to sit beside them.

"We don't have enough weyrlings," K'lior began without preamble, not even looking up from the roll he was buttering. He was dressed in a worn tunic and looked haggard.

"No," Fiona agreed.

"K'lior! Let her eat!" Cisca said, pushing the rolls toward Fiona and offering, with a quirk of her eyebrow, to pour the *klah*.

"It's okay," Fiona said after her first gulp of *klah*. Cisca glanced pointedly to K'lior before glancing back to see if Fiona understood. Fiona didn't, but she gathered that the Weyrwoman wanted her to eat before she spoke again, so she took a roll herself and began to butter it quietly.

"Cisca," K'lior murmured warningly to his mate.

"Shh," Cisca said firmly in response. "Eat! Talk after."

"We need an answer before the others get here," K'lior grumbled before returning dutifully to his eating.

Fiona bit into her roll, still hot and melting the butter, chewed reflexively, swallowed, and asked, in defiance of Cisca's warning looks, "How many weyrlings would we need?"

"A Flight of flying weyrlings would be best," Cisca said, raising a hand to keep K'lior from answering.

"They need to have at least a Turn from the Egg, right?"

"More would be better," Cisca said in agreement. "In easier times, we wouldn't have them lifting firestone until they have at least two Turns."

"Don't want to overstrain them," K'lior put in.

"The younger ones will need another ten months before they can help," Fiona observed, realizing that she and Talenth would start their training at about the same time.

"Queens wait longer," Cisca told her warningly.

"In good times," Fiona pointed out.

"And these are not good times?" Cisca asked with a grin.

"You're to start training with the weyrlings, too," K'lior told Fiona abstractedly.

"I'm responsible for her training, Weyrleader," Cisca reminded him, adding a playful poke to remove any sting in her words.

"So tell her!" K'lior said, flinching from her fingers.

"You're to train with the weyrlings," Cisca said, turning back to administer another fast playful poke to her mate.

"Can I?" Fiona's eyes shone with excitement. "That'd be great."

K'lior snorted humorously.

"How did it work with T'mar and Tajen?" Fiona asked, returning to the original problem.

"Well enough," K'lior said. "But that solves only part of the problem."

"And we still don't know if one dragon will let another ride it."

"Can't you test that?" Fiona wondered. The other two looked at her. "Can Cisca ride Rineth?"

The two gave her startled looks. Fiona wondered what was wrong with her suggestion.

"Better a brown rider on a bronze," K'lior said after a moment. Seeing Fiona's perplexed look, he explained, "I'd be surprised if a bronze would let a woman ride him."

"Any more than I could see a man on a queen," Cisca said by way of agreement.

"Of course," K'lior added reflectively, "no one has ever tried, so I can't be certain it wouldn't work."

Cisca's eyes narrowed as she said thoughtfully, "I wonder if Rineth *would* let me ride him?"

K'lior shrugged. "I'd prefer it if you never have to find out."

"Me, too," Cisca agreed fervently.

"What did you do last Threadfall?" Fiona asked, her mind still working on the question before them.

"We used the older weyrlings and rotated a wing from each of the flights," K'lior told her.

"We left you to handle the problem yourself yesterday because we wanted to give you the chance to come up with a better solution," Cisca explained to Fiona.

"And we have so few dragons now that a wing would be a big loss to our fighting strength," K'lior added.

"Especially with the illness," Cisca added bitterly. She glanced at K'lior consideringly, then added, "I think we're going to lose Yerinth and Casunth today."

K'lior nodded, his expression set.

"H'nez will stay with F'vin, and M'valer says he has someone with S'pevan," Cisca added.

"Thank you for that," K'lior said, acknowledging Cisca's foresight.

"We've got another forty or more who are feverish," Cisca continued unhappily.

"How many will be ready for this Fall?"

"If it comes to the worst, a little more than a full Flight," Cisca told him. "But that would be spread out amongst the wings."

"A Flight," K'lior repeated with anguish in his voice.

"We'll find a cure," Fiona said, surprising herself. "We have to. What about Benden Weyr? Have we any news from them?"

"They found a room," Cisca said after a moment of silent communion with her dragon. "Melirth tells me that Gaminth says they are searching it."

"See? Then they'll find a cure," Fiona predicted confidently.

"In the meantime," Cisca said, looking pointedly at K'lior to get his full attention, "it is up to *us*, Weyrleader and Weyrwomen, to keep up our spirits."

"I agree," K'lior said. "If we lose hope, then all the Weyr will lose hope."

Fiona's mind was back on the issue of firestone. "How much firestone can one of the larger dragons carry?" Weyrleader and Weyrwoman looked at her expectantly, so she continued, "Could one of the browns or bronzes carry enough for a full wing?"

"Just detach a dragon from the wing to get the firestone?" K'lior repeated to see if he was following Fiona's line of thought. When she nodded, Cisca brightened, saying, "That could work!"

"It'd be difficult for the wing, though," K'lior said consideringly. "They'd lose cohesion, which would make fighting Thread harder."

"They'd have to train for it," Cisca agreed. K'lior frowned.

"But wouldn't they have the same problem if a dragon or rider got injured?" Fiona asked.

"Yes, they would," K'lior agreed. His expression brightened. "Your suggestion certainly could work."

"I think you should try it out tomorrow," Cisca said.

"Why not today?" K'lior asked in surprise.

A bugle and the sound of dragons keening erupted in the Weyr Bowl outside.

"Yerinth has gone *between*," Cisca responded.

A moment later the keening increased to a higher pitch.

"Casunth?" K'lior asked.

Cisca nodded sadly.

The loss of two more dragons to the illness cast a pall on the entire Weyr. Fiona found some solace in oiling Talenth's hide, and for a change it was frustrating that the queen's skin had very few of the dangerous dry patches.

She was happy to be interrupted by a voice from outside her ledge calling, "Weyrwoman? Wingleader T'mar sends his compliments and asks if you and Talenth would join the weyrlings in the morning drill."

"We'd be delighted!" She called to Xhinna, "Xhinna, we're going to drill with the weyrlings! Join us if you want!"

"I don't have a dragon!" Xhinna called back grumpily.

"You can pretend!" Fiona answered with a grin.

Talenth insisted once more on launching herself from her ledge and gliding down to the Bowl proper before trotting over to the weyrlings arrayed outside their barracks.

"Weyrwoman," T'mar greeted her as she joined the group. "If you'd please drill with the younger group."

"Can't we have her with us?" J'gerd asked. The rest of the older weyrlings added their agreement.

"No," T'mar told them firmly. "Talenth is of the same clutch as the youngsters; the drill is appropriate to her age."

"But she's bigger than any of them!" an older weyrling protested.

"That's because she's a queen, dimglow!" F'jian snapped in response.

"Where would you like us?" Fiona asked.

"A queen's position is either in front of a wing or in the middle of the wing," T'mar told her. "Today, I'd like you in the middle so that you and your dragon can observe the others.

"But," he continued, spreading his attention amongst all the younger weyrlings, "until you riders know your drill, your dragons will stand aside." A chorus of groans rose from the younger weyrlings, but was silenced by T'mar's order: "Form up!"

Fiona watched in surprise as the weyrlings started to line up in a large V formation until she heard a voice whisper loudly, "You're supposed to be in the center!"

Fiona flushed and then rushed to find her position. At the front, F'jian craned his neck around at the formation, then called to T'mar, "Ready for drill!"

"Weyrwoman, you need to be farther back, in line with the second-to-last row," T'mar called critically. Fiona scooted back quickly to the correct position.

"Very well," T'mar said, seeming satisfied. "Now we will drill." He took a deeper breath and ordered, "Wing, right wheel!"

Fiona was totally lost as the riders started moving forward and turning to the right. In moments she was completely outside the formation, scampering to get back.

"Halt!" T'mar bellowed. The group halted. "Weyrwoman?"

"I got lost," Fiona said. "Sorry."

"Perhaps you should watch some drill first," T'mar replied, beckoning to her to join him. To the weyrlings, he called, "Reform!"

As he put the weyrlings through their drills, T'mar explained everything to Fiona, from the formations to the arm motions, to the timing. When they were done, he called out, "Halt! Reform in a V ahead." To Fiona he said, "Now, Weyrwoman, are you ready to resume your education?"

Fiona took a deep breath and nodded. "I just hope my arms don't get too sore."

"If they don't," T'mar told her with a determined look, "let me know." He smiled at her distraught look. "It's your first day, your arms are certain to get sore." She made a grim face, to which T'mar added, "Just remember: All eyes will be on you."

Fiona nodded, shook her head to clear her mood, and smiled at the wingleader. "They always are!"

The drill was every bit as exhausting as T'mar had promised, but Fiona refused to admit it or ask for a break. It was only when the weyrlings themselves were grumbling loudly that T'mar finally relented.

"Okay, now get your dragons," he told them, "and reform here."

As Fiona sought out Talenth, T'mar told her in an undertone, "You're to stand in front of your dragon."

Fiona nodded and beckoned Talenth to follow her. As the weyrlings reformed, Fiona found her assigned spot and spent a few moments positioning Talenth.

This is fun! Talenth exclaimed, eyes whirling green in pleasure.

And, as the werylings recommenced their drill, with their dragons following dutifully behind them, Fiona realized that it *was* fun. For a while, anyway. They practiced the various maneuvers over and over again until even Talenth's enthusiasm waned.

"Well done!" T'mar called finally. "You can all take a break. Be sure to get water for your dragons." As he spotted some weyrlings heading to the barracks, he called out, "*Walk* to the lake, do not get water from the barracks. You need to cool off muscles—yours and your dragons'."

Fiona could see the sense in that as she trudged along with the others to the far end of the Bowl and the lake. The penned herd-beasts, afraid that they were on the menu, wailed and slunk away from the approaching dragons.

I'm not hungry, Talenth said, snorting irritatedly at the herd-beasts.

They don't know any better, Fiona replied. When her stomach grumbled she added humorously, *Maybe they realize that I am.*

I could get you one, Talenth offered.

I'll eat in the kitchen, Fiona assured her, patting her neck affectionately.

Without thinking about it, Fiona had Talenth wait to drink until all the other dragons had drunk their fill.

Manners, she chided her dragon when Talenth complained to her. *We set the example, we make sure that everyone else is fed—or watered—before us. That's the mark of a leader.*

Talenth absorbed Fiona's words trustingly and ceased her grumbling. *I'm a leader?*

You're a queen, Fiona told her. *Of course you are!*

A leader! Talenth glanced at the weyrlings ahead of her as they made their way back to the weyrling barracks. *Shouldn't I be in front, then?*

No, Fiona assured her, *you're fine where you are.*

"Fiona!" a voice called from just outside the weyrling barracks. Fiona spotted Tajen striding toward her.

"Good day to you, Talenth," he called as he approached. To Fiona he said, "I saw the drill today; you did well." He glanced at Talenth. "I just wanted to check her over; I haven't seen her in a while."

Talenth was delighted to show off her wings and have Tajen run knowing hands over her legs, examining her all over.

"She's growing well," he declared when he was done. He nodded to Fiona, adding, "And you've done well in oiling her. I see no signs of flaky skin."

"Xhinna helps," Fiona felt obliged to explain.

"I've heard that she has taken to gliding from her ledge," Tajen said. When Fiona nodded confirmation, he turned to the queen and said, "Are you ready to fly?"

Can I fly? Talenth asked Fiona excitedly.

"She certainly wants to," Fiona said.

"Well, I think if she gets on her perch and tries flapping her wings for a bit, she might extend her glide," Tajen replied. But he shook his finger at Talenth and added warningly, "But no more than a few beats, then glide back down. I don't want you straining yourself; you could damage your muscles."

Can I do it now? Talenth begged.

"Can we try now?" Fiona asked.

Tajen pursed his lips consideringly, then shrugged. "Only once, because both of you have had enough exercise this morning."

I can fly! Talenth exclaimed, prancing back to her weyr. Fiona and Tajen followed quickly behind her and stood below the ledge to watch as she climbed up, crawled into her weyr, turned, and raced to the edge, wings flared and ready for flight.

As she leapt off, she gave her wings one beat and bugled excitedly as she rose into the air. Another beat and then—"Hey, that's too high!" Fiona cried in alarm.

Sorry! Talenth responded, sounding not the least bit contrite.

Glide on back down! Fiona ordered, nervously eyeing the height to which Talenth had climbed. With her excitement unabated, Talenth leveled her wings and glided slowly back down to the ground, landing easily several hundred meters across the Bowl.

Did you see? Talenth called. *I flew! I really flew!*

Yes, you did, Fiona agreed, her mental voice full of pride. *You flew very well.*

Tajen walked quickly toward Talenth, with Fiona following a few steps behind.

"Ask her to spread her wings if she can, and hold them," Tajen requested of Fiona.

Talenth was willing but curious. *I think he wants to check your muscles,* Fiona guessed. She was right. Tajen ran his hands over Talenth's pectoral muscles and across her chest, gesturing for Fiona to follow behind him with her hands.

"I'm feeling for any heat and any signs of knotted muscle," he explained. He paused for a moment in his exploration, widening his movements around one particular spot, then pointing it out to Fiona. "Feel here."

Fiona did. The muscle seemed tighter than elsewhere.

"Nothing major," Tajen assured her, "just some normal tightness." He continued his inspection. "But if you were to feel the same tightness the next time she flies, you might want to tell me."

"Would that be bad?"

"I doubt it," Tajen said with a shrug. "Usually it's just the muscles getting their strength. Often one muscle has to do more work to compensate for weaker muscles until they get stronger. But if it persists, we may need to let her rest for a few days so that she doesn't strain herself." He smiled and beckoned for Fiona to come closer, murmuring, "Young dragons rarely do themselves an injury—the worst they do is get sore for a day or so—but it's always wise to keep an eye on them in case it's more serious."

Can I do it again? Talenth asked eagerly.

"Not today," Fiona replied, adding to Tajen, "She wants to do it again."

"Of course she does," Tajen replied with a grin. He caught Talenth's whirling eyes and said to her, "Tomorrow, if you feel up to it."

I will! Talenth declared fervently, climbing back up the ledge to her weyr. Tajen followed her progress with a thoughtful look in his eyes.

"Are you thinking she's doing too much?" Fiona guessed.

"No," Tajen said, shaking his head and smiling. "I was thinking how much her gliding exercise will help her muscle tone."

"Will that mean she'll be ready to fly sooner?" Fiona asked hopefully, working to keep her emotions from Talenth. She didn't want to raise the gold's hopes falsely.

"I don't think so," Tajen said. "But it might mean that she'll be more fit when she *does* first fly." He paused for a moment before adding, "But that wasn't what I was thinking."

Fiona's look challenged him to explain.

"I was thinking," Tajen answered, "that if it were to help her, it might also help the hatchlings." Before Fiona could respond, he added, "Those of her clutch, I mean."

"I don't know how the Weyrleader and Weyrwoman would feel about that."

"We can find out by asking them," Tajen said. "But first, I wanted to know if you or Talenth had any objections."

"No," Fiona said without really thinking over her answer. Tajen cocked an eyebrow at her, challenging her response. "No, honestly, I think it'd be fun."

"Then we should ask the Weyrleader and Weyrwoman, shouldn't we?"

"They'll be at lunch," Fiona said. "Just let me make sure that Talenth is settled in."

They found Cisca and K'lior at the head table on the dais.

"We figured that today we should be easy to find," Cisca murmured to Fiona as she joined them at the table. "I heard that your dragon flew today."

Fiona nodded, looking somewhat surprised that this was remarkable.

"You know that Melirth keeps an eye on her hatchlings," Cisca explained. "And Talenth was quite proud of herself."

"Yes, she was," Fiona agreed with a broad grin.

"In fact," Tajen inserted smoothly into the conversation, "we were wondering if perhaps it wouldn't be a good idea for all of Melirth's latest hatchlings to practice gliding."

Cisca beckoned to K'lior and quickly brought him in on the conversation. He frowned thoughtfully for a moment, then nodded, glancing at Tajen. "Would it help them fly faster?"

"I doubt it," Tajen responded. "But it certainly would make the transition easier. Their muscles would be more toned."

"I suppose," Cisca said carefully, glancing at K'lior for confirmation, "that if they drilled no more than once a day, it wouldn't be too great an inconvenience."

"And you could watch all the pretty youngsters," K'lior teased her.

"K'lior!" Cisca growled back warningly. "They're far too young for me, you know that!" She cast a sidelong glance at Fiona, "Though maybe for our junior Weyrwoman . . ."

Fiona blushed furiously, shaking her head in denial. Cisca's eyes danced as she enjoyed Fiona's discomfort, but then she took pity on the youngster and turned back to Tajen, asking, "Have you discussed this with T'mar?"

Tajen shook his head.

T'mar, who was seated farther down the table, looked up at the mention of his name. "Weyrwoman?"

With a nod, Cisca invited him to move closer. Once he was seated again, she explained Tajen's suggestion.

"I'm not sure that it *wouldn't* actually reduce their training time," T'mar said finally. "We don't know how much time is spent getting their muscles honed."

"Well, it wouldn't be Turns," Tajen said.

"No, but maybe months."

"Even a month might be all the difference we need," K'lior said with a tone of urgency.

"Tomorrow, Thread falls at High Reaches and Igen," T'mar observed.

"Ista is down to forty-six fighting dragons," Cisca said. At the startled looks of the others, she added, "B'nik of Benden has promised to support them."

"Which is why we must have all the fighting strength we can get," K'lior said. He glanced at T'mar and Tajen. "If the older weyrlings had to—"

"They would die," Tajen declared flatly. "They haven't even started flaming yet!"

"I think we will have to teach them soon," K'lior said heavily, leaning back in his chair and closing his eyes against the anguish he felt.

"Even with that," T'mar declared, glancing at Tajen for confirmation, "they'd need at least three months before they'd survive more than an hour against Thread."

"If that," Tajen agreed sadly. "If we had the queen's wing . . ." Tajen put in bitterly.

"We've got a queen," Cisca said.

"We can't risk Melirth," K'lior said immediately.

"If we do it properly, we won't *risk* anyone," Cisca replied. She glanced at Fiona, cocking her head questioningly.

"How much firestone could Melirth carry?" Fiona asked the Weyrwoman.

"More than a bronze," Tajen replied, glancing at T'mar, who considered the statement and then nodded reluctantly.

"She would still have to supply the firestone," K'lior objected, "and she couldn't do it any faster than another dragon."

"She could if she trailed the firestone at different levels," Fiona said. The others looked at her. "What if she trailed firestone at say, two, four, and six dragonlengths beneath her?"

"On both sides," Tajen added. "That'd be six dragons at once."

"And she can carry at least twice as much firestone as the weyrlings," Fiona guessed, glancing to the Weyrwoman for confirmation.

"Perhaps even three times as much," Cisca allowed, glancing toward K'lior with a concerned, measuring look.

"If anything happened to her—" K'lior began, then broke off, seeing another objection. "You're forgetting, all of you, that dragons have riders."

"And?" Cisca demanded, brows furrowed.

"There's a reason the weyrlings only have two sacks of firestone on tether at a time," K'lior told her. "It's because they couldn't manage the workload of more."

"So?" Cisca demanded. "I'll get someone to help me." She glanced pointedly at Fiona, who was delighted at the notion.

"No," K'lior replied, shaking his head firmly. "I might risk one of our queens at the trailing edge of Thread but not both Weyrwomen."

Cisca's elation deflated immediately. "You're right." Then she brightened again. "Perhaps Tajen?"

"Actually," Tajen began slowly as all eyes turned to him, "perhaps it would make more sense for T'mar and me to perform the experiment first."

"A bronze could carry nearly as much as a queen," K'lior reminded Cisca.

"And it would be safer for the Weyr," Cisca conceded against her will.

"Someone has to keep things running here," K'lior agreed with her.

"But if it works—" Cisca began.

"We'll talk about it," K'lior agreed. He raised a finger toward Fiona, adding, "But she won't ride with you."

"I could take Xhinna," Cisca said thoughtfully.

"*She'd* be thrilled," Fiona agreed.

Tajen turned to T'mar. "We should spend some time on this idea of the Weyrwoman's."

"It wasn't my idea," Cisca corrected him, nodding to Fiona. "It was hers."

Fiona flushed with pride.

X hinna's surprise at the long line of weyrlings clambering up the ledge to Talenth's weyr was quickly overwhelmed by her joy at watching the bronze, browns, blues, and greens happily launching themselves skyward, first in a glide and then, the second time, beating their wings several times to climb and climb before once more returning to the ground.

Fiona and Talenth watched with her from their vantage point on the ground, Talenth exclaiming happily at each launch and telling Fiona, *I flew higher than* that!—which, being true, required Fiona's firm agreement each time.

Can they come again tomorrow? Talenth asked excitedly after the weyrlings had finished their last flight and had gone back to their quarters.

You won't mind? Fiona asked. Apparently not, Fiona decided, as Talenth responded, *Can I go first?*

F iona woke suddenly, in the middle of the night. Xhinna was snoring beside her. Fiona directed her thoughts to Talenth and the dragon's response was so alarmed that Fiona instantly leapt out of bed. She paused only long enough to slip her feet in slippers and grab her robe before racing to Talenth's weyr.

Talenth was trembling in her sleep, limbs restless and eyelids fluttering.

It's all right, Fiona told her dragon as quietly as she could, concentrating on soothing her without waking her. Talenth uncurled, turned, and curled up again, still trembling.

It burns! Fiona heard. She snapped her head around, looking outside the weyr, trying to locate the source of that thought. But before she found it, she heard another voice call, *Arith!* And suddenly Fiona felt her legs give out and she collapsed against Talenth, all strength drained, her eyes streaming tears, her mouth open in a silent scream.

She seemed to lie there forever, all strength sapped, all hope gone, feeling only the trembling of her queen beside her. And then—

It will be all right. But it wasn't Talenth's voice. Fiona opened her eyes, looking around to find the source of the voice.

After a long moment, Fiona thought back, *How can you be sure?* But there was no answer.

ELEVEN

I reached out
And you were gone.
I cried out
But you had flown.

Fort Hold, Morning, AL 508.1.19

Cisca found her there, sleeping beside Talenth, early the next morning.

"Arith—"

"—has gone *between*," Fiona said grimly.

Cisca looked startled.

"Didn't you hear it happen?" Fiona asked her, surprised. Cisca shook her head. "I heard Arith cry, 'It burns!' and then Lorana cried, 'Arith!' and then Arith went *between* and . . . I collapsed."

"I've never heard of this happening before," Cisca said, looking troubled.

"And then I heard another voice," Fiona said.

"What did it say?"

"It said, 'It will be all right.' "

"I certainly hope so," Cisca agreed fervently, but she looked dubious. She looked off into the distance for a long, thoughtful moment and then seemed to come to a decision. "Whether it will or not, that's how we should act."

"Like it will be all right?"

"Yes," Cisca said. She leaned over and extended a hand to Fiona. "And so you'd best make yourself presentable. Meet me in the Kitchen Cavern. I'm sure others will want that reassurance— to see that it will be all right."

Fiona took Cisca's hand gratefully and stood up, feeling sore from her awkward sleeping position.

"So if Arith has gone *between*, what will Lorana do?" Fiona asked.

"She'll grieve," Cisca said, her eyes bright with tears.

"What about the cure, was she working on that?" Fiona wondered.

Cisca's eyes widened in horror. "Arith said, 'It burns!' What if the cure was what killed her dragon . . ." Cisca's voice trailed off. From her expression, Fiona could see that Cisca was speaking to Melirth, but then the Weyrwoman stopped abruptly.

"Benden flies today with Ista; I won't add to their worries," she declared. "We can find out later." She nodded to herself firmly, then told Fiona, "Get! Go have a bath, and meet me when you're ready."

"Yes, Weyrwoman."

F iona discovered just how fast news traveled in the Weyrs when she arrived at the Weyrleader's table for breakfast.

"If Arith went *between*, what does that mean for our weyrlings? They're nearly the same age," M'kury was saying as Fiona sat. Getting no response from the Weyrleaders, he turned to her. "What do you think, Weyrwoman?"

"I think it will be all right," Fiona replied, trying to sound as if she believed it.

"They were working on a cure, weren't they?" K'rall asked from his side of the table. His eyes rested on Fiona so she felt obliged— if utterly unqualified—to answer.

"I know no more than you," Fiona told him honestly.

"Well, I hope they hurry," M'kury said. "I've got three sick dragons in my wing."

"I doubt two of mine will last the day," K'rall said by way of agreement.

"How many will be left to fight the next Threadfall?" H'nez demanded.

"More than Ista," M'valer said morosely.

"Fighting Thread is hard enough without this illness eating away at our strength," V'ney observed, disheartedly spooning up some cereal.

"Too right!" M'kury agreed sourly. "And the illness itself—it's hard enough when you can tell with the sneezing, but Jakoth, he was fine one moment and then just gone—how can we tell if we're taking sick dragons against Thread?"

"It will be all right," Fiona ventured again, wishing she could find the same conviction as whoever had spoken to her earlier.

V'ney looked across at her, disbelief written on his face. "No offense, Weyrwoman, but you're young, and the young are always convinced they'll live forever."

"Lorana's Arith was not much older than your Talenth," H'nez observed. He turned to K'lior. "Are we certain that none of the weyrlings are sick?"

His implication was not lost on Fiona, who suddenly found it harder to be optimistic and lost her appetite for her roll. Cisca shot her a quick look, her eyes dropping to Fiona's food, and getting the hint, Fiona forced herself to take a bite.

"None that we've noticed," T'mar said. The other wingleaders looked less than reassured at this, so he continued, "Tajen has been keeping a special eye on them."

The implication that Tajen, who had lost his dragon to the illness, would be a diligent observer was not lost on the wingleaders.

"That's good," V'ney said.

K'rall wasn't so pleased. "Ah, but his dragon was coughing up that green infection before—"

"Wingleaders," K'lior said, raising his voice to cut across K'rall's words, "in six days we ride Fall over Ruatha Hold and our own Weyr. For now, I think that should be all that concerns us."

The wingleaders nodded in reluctant assent, returning their attention to the food on their plates.

After breakfast, K'lior had the wingleaders assemble their wings for more practice drills.

"You'll have the weyrlings today, Weyrwoman," T'mar informed Fiona as she strode out into the Weyr Bowl with him after breakfast. Fiona couldn't hide her surprise, and T'mar chuckled.

"Just tell them to go about their chores, then drill them like we did the other day and—if they're good—let them have another romp on the Weyrwomen's ledge," he told her.

"What about you? Tajen?" Fiona asked worriedly.

"We're going to try your trick with the firestone," T'mar told her with a grin. He laughed when he saw her stricken expression. Turning away to wave to Tajen, he called over his shoulder, "The rewards of a job well done!"

Another job, Fiona thought, remembering that her father had often said the same thing to her. The thought of him braced her and she squared her shoulders and turned toward the weyrling barracks.

J'gerd and J'keran were joking with F'jian, the young bronze rider, off to one side.

"Weyrwoman," J'keran said, nodding respectfully when she approached.

"You're to finish your chores, then drill the older wings," she said, glancing at J'gerd to see that he understood. The curly-headed youth pursed his lips in readiness of some objection, then thought the better of it and nodded in acceptance. Satisfied, Fiona turned to F'jian. "When the younger weyrlings are done with their chores, let me know. We'll be drilling on the ground."

F'jian nodded, somewhat surprised at hearing her give orders— he was a good head taller than she and at least a full Turn older. "Yes, Weyrwoman."

Xhinna joined her before the chores were done, so Fiona took her aside for a hasty conference.

"T'mar says I'm to drill the younger weyrlings today," Fiona told her, allowing her panic to show.

"You'll do fine," Xhinna assured her. As Fiona began to shake her head, Xhinna added, "Just pretend like you mean everything as a test—especially any orders you get wrong."

With Xhinna by her side, murmuring encouragement, the drill went well enough, especially when Fiona had the brilliant idea to have Talenth join in again and also tried alternating who gave the drills—she even surprised everyone by giving Xhinna a chance.

" 'Just pretend like you mean everything as a test,' " Fiona quoted back at her as she rushed off to lead Talenth. The other girl's eyes flashed angrily, but then she grinned.

Despite the weyrlings' initial mutinous murmurs, Xhinna proved as adept at drill as Fiona had expected, giving her orders in a well-timed cadence that actually made the drills work better.

"That was amazing!" Xhinna told Fiona when they finally called halt, her eyes shining with joy. "I could almost feel how they'd be in the air and—" She cut herself off abruptly and dropped her eyes to the ground.

Fiona could guess what the other girl was thinking: that it was something she'd never experience. She wanted to say something to reassure her, to give her hope, but she couldn't think of anything that wouldn't sound false or silly.

"Help me walk Talenth to the lake," she said instead, leading them to the tail of the long line of weary but exhilarated weyrlings.

Why is she sad? Talenth asked, turning her faceted eyes toward Xhinna.

She wants to Impress, Fiona told her.

Xhinna, you could Impress one of my hatchlings, Talenth told the younger girl but "loudly" enough that Fiona could hear, adding hurriedly, *when I have them.*

Xhinna stopped in her tracks, jaw agape as she looked at the young queen. She raced up and wrapped her arms around Talenth's neck, reaching up toward her head to scratch her eye ridges. "Thank you, Talenth!"

Of course, it will be a while before I'm old enough, Talenth added privately to Fiona. Fiona smiled at her dragon and raced around to her other side, to scratch her other eye ridge. Talenth stopped, momentarily lost in draconic rapture, then realized that the weyrlings were leaving them behind and started forward once more, alternating hopeful looks from side to side in an effort to keep both girls scratching.

The high point of the day for Fiona was back at the Weyrwomen's ledge watching Talenth and the other weyrlings practice flying again. Finally, though, the practice was over, and she dispersed the tired but happy weyrlings back to their barracks. She had just finished oiling and settling Talenth comfortably in her weyr when T'mar and Tajen returned on bronze Zirenth. She raced over the ledge, jumping high with all the enthusiasm of a weyrling, landed on bent knees, and tore off toward them.

"How did it go?" she cried as she approached.

Tajen was first down and he met her grin with one of his own. "It went well."

"Help me down, will you?" T'mar called irritably from his perch, flapping his injured arm in its sling like a wounded dragon. "I can't manage yet with this on me!"

Tajen shortly had the bronze rider on the ground.

"I can't wait to get better," T'mar said, sourly massaging his shoulder with his free hand.

"I wouldn't have guessed," Tajen observed drolly.

The bronze rider's eyes flashed, then the anger faded as he realized he was being teased. "It's just—"

"It was too much for your arm," Tajen finished, meeting T'mar's stubborn look squarely. "You shouldn't have tried so much this first time."

T'mar started to argue but caught himself and sighed, shaking his head. "You're right," he agreed glumly. "But we need every dragon—"

"And rider," Tajen interjected.

"—and rider," T'mar agreed, "to fight the Fall."

"We need every *healthy* rider and dragon," Fiona corrected him. "It's no use having sick dragons or injured riders trying to fight Thread."

T'mar glanced from Tajen to Fiona and back again, deciding not to argue the point.

"Anyway," Tajen said, returning to Fiona's original question, "it went well."

"It would have been better if both of us were uninjured," T'mar added.

"That slowed things down," Tajen agreed with a wave of his hand. "Even so, trailing six sacks of firestone was much quicker than trailing two at a time."

"Why did we never do it this way before?" Fiona wondered.

"Because it only makes sense in certain circumstances," T'mar replied. "It works when there are grown dragons fit enough to haul firestone but not fit enough to fly a Fall."

"And when the Weyr is short of able weyrlings," Tajen added.

"Yes," T'mar agreed, glancing toward the Hatching Grounds and quickly back at the others as if questioning why there weren't more weyrlings old enough to haul firestone. "And it's hard work: hard on the dragon, hard on the riders."

"More weyrlings is definitely the better choice," Tajen agreed.

There was a sound above them and all three craned their necks upward: The rest of the Weyr was returning.

Fiona watched in wonder as the dragons of the six fighting wings dispersed, first dropping their riders off and then heading either to the Feeding Grounds or their weyrs for a much-needed rest. Her expression changed as she noticed how ragged each of the wings appeared—small, disordered . . .

"It's the illness," Tajen said.

Fiona looked over at him and saw that he'd been watching her.

"The wings are disarrayed because of sick or lost dragons." His voice choked on the word "lost," and Fiona realized that rarely did anyone refer to the dragons as "dead"—it was just too hard to say.

"But they'll fight well enough," T'mar declared, glancing over toward K'lior as he and his riders dismounted.

"I wonder how it went with the others today?" Tajen asked. No one doubted that he meant the other Weyrs.

"We'll find out soon enough," T'mar said, slapping the other man on his shoulder. "Let's get cleaned up and meet with K'lior."

Cisca wants you. The "voice" was that of a grown female dragon: Melirth.

Where? Fiona asked, craning her neck around the Bowl and not spotting the Weyrwoman.

The Records Room.

Fiona turned to explain her summons to the two men but they were already on their way to their quarters. She walked briskly back to the Weyrwomen's ledge and on to the Records Room, where she found K'lior, Cisca, and Kentai. The harper had chalk in hand and was writing on a slate. Fiona saw that he had divided the slate into two columns: on the left he listed the names of the Weyrs, and on the right he listed numbers.

"This is the fighting strength of the Weyrs as best we know," Kentai said out loud.

"Does that include dragons with the illness?" K'lior asked.

"We can't say for certain," Cisca replied. "I got the numbers by asking the Weyrwomen of each Weyr."

"So Benden has one hundred and seventy-five," K'lior began. "How many did they lose against Thread today?"

"They started with one hundred and eighty-five," Cisca replied. "But we don't know how many were injured, or how seriously."

"Ista has only thirty-four?" Fiona exclaimed as she examined the numbers. Cisca nodded bleakly.

"And this one hundred and fifty for Telgar . . ." K'lior asked skeptically.

"That's the number Lina's Garoth gave me," Cisca replied with a shrug. "It wasn't too clear if that included dragons with the sickness or not."

"I wonder if D'gan wouldn't just think they were all slacking," K'lior agreed with a sour look on his face.

"Why isn't there a number for High Reaches?" Fiona asked.

"Because Sonia would only say that they had enough dragons, wouldn't be able to lend any, and wouldn't need any more," Cisca replied, her annoyance undisguised.

"That doesn't seem very nice," Fiona remarked.

"D'vin and Sonia have been very aloof for a number of Turns," K'lior said.

Kentai meanwhile had totaled the numbers and he frowned at the tally.

"Four hundred and ninety-five?" Cisca said, standing up to read over his shoulder. "Between four Weyrs we have less than Telgar *started* this Pass with?"

"'That number stays in this room," K'lior said, his voice full of authority. Kentai raised an eyebrow questioningly, and K'lior answered, "Oh, I've no doubt that others can do the sums, but I would prefer to leave them to do it on their own."

"Leave it for gossip rather than fact?" Kentai guessed.

"That and it would be best if this news didn't come from us," K'lior said.

"Everyone knows about Ista, though," Fiona said. "Even the weyrlings are talking about it."

"I wish we knew how many injured there were at the Weyrs, and how soon they'd be fighting again," Cisca said, frowning at the numbers.

"We can guess from our own, though," K'lior said. "We've got thirty-five dragons who won't be flying the next Fall."

"We can't know for certain, though," Kentai reminded him. "There are too many variables."

"So, are you saying we shouldn't guess?" K'lior pressed. "That we shouldn't make plans?"

"No," Kentai replied with a quick shake of his head. "I'm saying that we shouldn't put too much faith in our guesses."

"There are some things we know, though, don't we?" Fiona asked, looking hopefully at the adults. Cisca quirked her mouth into a half-smile and motioned for her to continue. Fiona hadn't planned on saying more, so it was a moment before she continued, "We can say that Ista Weyr can't fly a Fall unaided, right? I mean, it takes at least three wings usually to fly a full Fall, doesn't it?"

"Yes," K'lior agreed. "Fortunately, Benden has agreed to help out."

"And we know that High Reaches Weyr won't help anyone," Cisca added, her expression grim.

"And I'm not sure if Telgar can be counted on for much," Kentai remarked.

"So what we know is that we're pretty much on our own," K'lior surmised. He glanced at each of the others in turn for agreement, then continued. "And we know that our fighting strength today is just a bit more than four wings." He paused for a moment and murmured to himself, "We could send out a Flight and have a wing in reserve."

"They could haul firestone," Cisca suggested.

"Or carry extra firestone and join the fight after they've replenished the rest of the Flight," Fiona suggested hopefully.

K'lior turned to jab a finger toward her. "*That* is an excellent idea!"

"It is at that," Cisca agreed warmly.

"What about the dragons that are ill?" K'lior wondered, glancing toward Cisca. "Could they haul firestone?"

Cisca shook her head. "M'tal said that they lost too many of their feverish dragons *between* in their first Fall."

"If they weren't ill, we'd have fifty more dragons at this moment," K'lior said with a grimace. "*Then* we'd have two full Flights!"

"But we don't," Cisca said.

"I just wonder how many of the other Weyrs are in the same situation," K'lior replied.

Cisca shrugged, conceding the point. "If Tannaz hadn't gone *between*, Kalsenth would be rising soon . . . she might even have risen by now."

Fiona reflected on that. "What if she rose during Threadfall?"

"According to the Records, no queen has risen during Threadfall," Kentai told her.

"Does that mean that the queens know when Thread is coming?" Cisca wondered.

"I suspect it's simpler than that," K'lior replied. To Cisca's raised eyebrows, he explained, "Thread falls every three days, so there are more Threadfree days than not."

"Hmmm," Cisca murmured appreciatively.

K'lior pursed his lips and turned to the door. "I think we've spent all the time out of the glowlight that we can without it being noticed," he said to the others. He nodded at Cisca. "Your idea of using the reserve wing to carry extra firestone is a good one— we'll need to practice it in the morning."

"What if the riders ask about Arith and Benden?" Cisca asked, turning to follow him.

"It will be all right," Fiona said. The others looked at her, surprised. "That's what we're supposed to say, isn't it?"

Cisca glanced at K'lior, a smile on her lips. The Weyrleader reflected the smile as he turned back to Fiona. "Yes, that is exactly what we'll say!"

"Firestone?" H'nez repeated, his expression outraged. "A fighting wing to haul firestone? What are weyrlings for?"

"If they trail multiple sacks, they could replenish the fighting wings in a third the time of the weyrlings," K'lior said, trying to remain reasonable.

"Coddling weyrlings, by the First Egg!" M'valer muttered disapprovingly.

"We've only got eleven fit to fly," Fiona told them.

"Eleven's not enough," S'kan said decisively.

"So who's in reserve?" H'nez demanded, his irritation un-dimmed.

"My wing, I should think," T'mar declared. "I've already got experience with this new rig, so I can train them."

"But your wing's light!" M'kury complained. In fact, every wing was light.

"We'd have enough dragons if we made the sick ones fly," K'rall grumbled, glancing toward H'nez for approval. The other bronze rider made no response, his eyes cutting quickly toward K'lior and then back again.

"Sick dragons don't survive," T'mar replied.

"And when there are none but sick dragons left, what then?" K'rall demanded.

"Then," K'lior replied in a controlled, even tone, "we'll reconsider our options."

"By then, Pern will be lost," V'ney said, shifting morosely in his chair. His wing had been hurt the worst by both the illness and bad luck in the Fall, and he had only twelve dragons left.

"We have survived for over five hundred Turns," Cisca said. "I don't see why we won't survive this Pass."

"We'll have the wings work together," K'lior declared. "T'mar and N'jian will be reserve, H'nez and M'valer, M'kury and S'kan, V'ney and K'rall."

"And you?" H'nez pressed.

"I'll take point," K'lior replied as though it should have been obvious. "We'll start practice at first light."

Fiona found herself and the weyrlings working hard over the next three days as they helped the Weyr prepare for the next Fall, but no matter how tired they were after a drill, the young hatchlings always found the energy to leap off the Weyrwomen's ledge and beat their wings into the sky in tentative imitation of the larger, older fighting dragons, always encouraged by their weyrling riders and the invariable group of envious weyrchildren who formed a cluster over by Fiona and Talenth.

On the morning of the Fall, Xhinna and Terin approached Fiona with a new concern.

"How are the dragons going to fight when it gets dark?"

Fiona stared at them. "I don't know," she admitted. Then she brightened. "I'm sure K'lior will have an answer."

She found K'lior with Cisca and Kentai, and broached the subject. His response surprised her.

"I didn't even *think* of it!" K'lior exclaimed. "I was so busy concentrating on the wings and—"

"I should have thought of it," Kentai said, looking glumly at the parchment written in Verilan's careful script. "There must be something in the Records. . . ."

"We all should have thought of it," Cisca said, not wanting the harper to hoard the blame. "But what does it matter?"

"Can the dragons see well enough in the dark?" Fiona asked, allowing relief to creep into her voice. The relief vanished when she saw the look that Cisca and K'lior exchanged.

"If it's cold enough, won't the Thread freeze in the night air?" Kentai suggested. He started over to a stack of Records, fumbling through them while murmuring, "I recall reading about it not long ago . . ."

"But if it doesn't freeze," K'lior began slowly, his eyes locked on Cisca's, "and we can't see it—"

"The Thread will fall and burrow," Cisca finished for him. "Of course, all the Thread that falls up as high as the Weyr will freeze in the snow—"

"But that doesn't mean some won't burrow somewhere," K'lior interjected.

"And in the morning . . ."

"The Thread will spread," Kentai finished with a heavy sigh.

"We can fight burrows," Cisca declared.

"If we have the strength," K'lior agreed.

"The ground crews—" Kentai began.

"—will not cover the high hills and mountains," K'lior finished with an angry shake of his head. He paused, clearly communing with his dragon. "I've asked T'mar and M'kury to join us. Together perhaps we can come up with some plans."

"You'll have to tell the others," Cisca cautioned him.

"I'd prefer not talk about this with H'nez until we have a plan," K'lior admitted. Cisca shrugged; she had no problem with that approach. K'lior took the time while they were waiting for the two wingleaders to say to Fiona, "You have a habit of finding difficult friends, don't you?"

Fiona looked up and saw that he was smiling at her.

"Don't stop," Cisca told her heatedly. "We need these sort of friends; they keep us from making terrible mistakes."

"Indeed," K'lior said, his expression thoughtful. He raised an eyebrow toward Cisca in some secret communication that seemed to Fiona as though they were dragons communicating telepathically.

"Yes," K'lior said after a moment. "I think we should encourage this Terin to stand on the Hatching Grounds."

"Nothing short of a full revolution for you, is there?" Cisca wondered, her eyes dancing at Fiona.

" 'Need drives when Thread arrives,' " K'lior quoted in reply.

"What about the watch-whers?" Fiona asked. "I know my father's Forsk will be eager."

"Watch-whers?" K'lior repeated, running a hand through his hair in exasperation. "What could they do?"

"They can see at night," Fiona replied, undaunted. "And I know that father has been training with Forsk, getting guidance from Kindan, M'tal, and Nuella."

K'lior groaned. Cisca looked at him worriedly. "The watch-whers," he explained. "When M'tal was here at the Hatching, he wanted us to train with the watch-whers."

"And you said no," Cisca guessed.

"And I said no," K'lior agreed disconsolately. "Could you imagine H'nez . . . ?"

"He would have been apoplectic," Cisca agreed.

"Well, there's nothing we can do about it now," K'lior said with a heavy sigh. "We'll fight the Thread tonight and see if perhaps we can train with the watch-whers before the next Fall."

The last rays of the sun illuminated the Weyr Bowl as dragons and riders launched into the sky, wing by wing, to form up at the Star Stones and wink out, *between.* Fiona watched them with mixed emotions, not certain how they would fight Thread they couldn't see.

"Don't worry," T'mar had assured her just before his heavily-laden wing departed. "We'll be fine."

But it was hard not to worry when Fiona caught sight of Cisca's set expression; hard not to worry as she and the remaining weyr-folk scrambled to set up the aid tables; hard not to worry as the younger weyrlings raced each other to bag more firestone; hard not to worry as the sun's rays faded out completely and the Weyr Bowl was illuminated only by the massed glows, eery splotches of blue, green, and yellow dotted in the dark.

"F'jian," Fiona called as she approached the firestone room. The young bronze weyrling looked up from his work. "As soon as they're finished bagging, get the weyrlings over to the Dining Cavern for *klah* and a chance to warm themselves at the ovens. We won't be needing anyone for at least an hour; then we'll want them to help with the injured."

"Of course, Weyrwoman," F'jian said, sketching her a quick salute.

Fiona made her own way to the Dining Cavern to get a pitcher of warm *klah* for those waiting in the Bowl. Inside, she saw Cisca pacing nervously near one of the ovens.

"It will be all right," Fiona murmured to her. Cisca nodded, her eyes still anxious, then visibly steeled herself, lifted her head high, and nodded.

"Of course it will," she replied with feigned certainty. She smiled. "It had better," she continued. "I told K'lior as much."

"And as Weyrleader, he knows not to gainsay you," Fiona agreed with a grin.

"Exactly!" Cisca agreed lightly. Fiona smiled at her and moved on to the *klah* hearth. Her ears were good and tuned to the noises of the night, so she was able to hear Cisca's low murmur, "Fly well, my love."

Fiona felt the pang, the mixture of emotions—joy, sorrow, worry—which the Weyrwoman had for K'lior and wondered if she herself would ever feel that way about another.

The moment K'lior's Rineth touched ground on Fort Weyr's Bowl, Cisca was beside the bronze dragon, numbweed at the ready, directing a group of weyrlings to attack the Thread-scored burns. Other groups of weyrfolk scattered around Fort Weyr's Bowl as more injured dragons landed by the light of glows.

"What is it?" Cisca asked suspiciously, taking in the joyous look on K'lior's face as he dismounted beside her. "Tell me."

K'lior closed his eyes to refresh his memory. "It was amazing," he said.

"And?" Cisca prompted impatiently. K'lior paused dramatically. "Tell me right now, bronze rider, or you'll—"

K'lior held up his hands in surrender, smiling and shaking his head. He touched a finger to her lips but Cisca snapped at it with her teeth.

"Now," she growled.

"We were getting torn up," K'lior said after a moment. "Casualties were high—"

"There can't be more than two dozen," Cisca objected, surveying the Bowl critically. "That's bad, but not high."

"It would have been higher if we'd fought alone," K'lior said.

Cisca's eyes widened in shock. "You *didn't*?" She glanced toward the top of the Bowl, as if expecting burrowed Thread to come over the crest at any moment.

"We had help," K'lior told her.

"High Reaches?" Cisca asked. "I'm surprised, considering the way—" She stopped, catching the look in K'lior's eyes. "Not High Reaches?"

"Not High Reaches," K'lior agreed.

"Who then?"

"No dragons at all," K'lior replied, his eyes shining in wonder.

"But ground crews couldn't protect the mountains," Cisca objected.

"No ground crews," K'lior agreed. He paused as long as he could, judging Cisca's growing agitation, until he said, "Watchwhers."

"Watch-whers? They came?" Cisca said, and K'lior nodded solemnly. "They helped?"

"They more than helped," P'der, K'lior's wingsecond, said as he approached them. "They *ate* the Thread!"

"And they see better in the dark than dragons," K'lior added, his face bursting into another great grin.

"They know which of the Thread is frozen and which is still alive," P'der added, shaking his head in admiration. "Those big eyes of theirs . . ."

"You should have seen them," K'lior told her. "We were being torn apart by Thread, couldn't see, couldn't help our dragons, and then all the sudden we saw these points of light rise up from below us—"

"Their eyes," P'der interjected, nodding enthusiastically. "They reflected the night sky so much they were like jewels coming up from the ground."

"And then she told us that they could handle the rest of the Fall, that we should go back," K'lior finished.

"She?" Cisca asked with a raised eyebrow.

"Nuella, of course," P'der said. "The queen watch-wher's rider."

"The WherMaster," K'lior added in agreement.

"Of course, there were hardly enough watch-whers," P'der added. "If they had had to fight a full daytime Fall, when all the Thread is warm enough to be alive, they would have been overwhelmed."

"*We* would have fought the Fall, then," K'lior said.

"I don't know," P'der said, shaking his head. "There are some times, particularly down Boll way, when those warm winds keep the evening hot."

"Let's hope that doesn't happen, then," K'lior said. He looked at Cisca. "Remind me to talk with Nuella in the morning. It was amazing."

"So you got to see watch-whers flying at night?" Cisca asked. K'lior nodded. "Eating Thread?" K'lior nodded again. Cisca huffed angrily at him. "And you didn't tell me?"

"You know that we agreed that the queens wouldn't fly until the sickness is gone."

Cisca glared at him.

"The next Fall's at night, down at Boll," P'der observed helpfully.

"I'll be there," Cisca said, daring K'lior to contradict her.

"It'll be late in the evening," K'lior said, thinking aloud. "The Thread will probably all be dead, so there's probably no harm in it."

Above them, sounding all around the Bowl, there was a chorus of dragon coughs. K'lior exchanged looks with his Weyrwoman and wingsecond.

"There are over fifty coughing from the sickness," Cisca said somberly.

"We lost three *between* in the Fall," P'der added.

"So we have just over a hundred dragons fit to fly the next Fall in three days' time," K'lior surmised. Cisca and P'der nodded gloomily. K'lior straightened up, threw back his shoulders, and gave them both a cheering look. "With the watch-whers' help, that will be more than enough."

"And we'll have six days' rest after that Fall," Cisca added with a similar attempt at cheer.

"P'der, have the wingleaders meet me in the Council Room in the morning. We can go over our organization then."

P'der nodded curtly and strode off toward his quarters.

K'lior gestured to Cisca, who took his hand, and the two strolled around the Bowl, checking on injuries and doing their best to cheer up riders and dragons both.

"You should have seen it," K'lior said. "There I was, wondering how we were going to manage, when this voice comes out of the night sky—"

"Which voice?"

"Nuella's," K'lior said, "only I didn't know it at the time. Nearly scared me off my perch."

"How could she call to you?" Cisca asked.

"She was right above me," K'lior told her.

"So she called down over her watch-wher? She was riding the watch-wher?"

"She was riding the watch-wher," K'lior affirmed. "But she didn't call over it."

Cisca gave him an irritated look.

"She was flying upside down," K'lior told her, his face once again wide in a grin. "So she just leaned her head back and talked to me. She was about as far from me as you are, actually."

"Upside down?" Cisca repeated in amazement.

"Well, she's blind," K'lior answered, as if that explained everything. "Probably didn't notice."

"Even blind, she'd have to notice that she was upside down," Cisca replied acerbically.

"Yeah, she probably did," K'lior agreed wistfully. "But she was having the time of her life."

"I'll bet her mate'll have her ears for that stunt," Cisca predicted.

"Only if he finds out about it," K'lior said softly.

Cisca stopped mid-stride, gripping K'lior's hand and turning toward him. "Don't *you* go getting any ideas!"

"I wouldn't dream of it," K'lior replied innocently.

"**Y**ou did a good job," H'nez told Fiona as she checked on his Ginirth late the next morning. "His wing looks like it's already healing."

Fiona smiled and shook her head; she'd already heard the same line from S'kan about his Lamorth.

"You, as a wingleader—"

"Flightleader," H'nez corrected immediately.

"—flightleader, then," Fiona accepted the change without rancor. "You know that Ginirth's wingtip will need time to recover. You won't be flying the next Fall."

Actually, Fiona wondered, why should any of the dragons fly the next Fall? From what she'd heard, the watch-whers were well up to the task.

"You're right," H'nez agreed absently. He raised a hand to Ginirth's eye ridge and scratched where the dragon liked it the most. "I was hoping to convince myself otherwise."

"You figured that if you could convince me, you'd convince yourself?" Fiona recalled some of the old ones she'd known as a child back at Fort Hold—they'd tried much the same trick with her father and had had no more luck with him than H'nez was having with her. "It's an old trick, flightleader, and one not only practiced by dragonriders."

H'nez smiled and shook his head. Then he sobered again, gesturing with his free hand toward Ginirth. "So how long do you think before he'll be ready to fly again?"

"How long do you think the wound will take to heal?" Fiona asked in return.

"Maybe a sevenday, maybe less," H'nez told her.

"I'd say he'll be ready then," Fiona replied.

H'nez brightened. "Did you hear that, Ginirth? Less than a sevenday!"

"I said *maybe* less," Fiona reminded him.

"Less than a sevenday," H'nez repeated stubbornly.

Fiona rolled her eyes in exasperation, then returned to her examination. Satisfied, she straightened up and made her way back from Ginirth's withers, where his wingtip rested, to the bronze dragon's head, searching in her carisak for a jar of salve.

"Numbweed," she said, handing it to H'nez, "if he needs it."

H'nez nodded and pocketed the small jar, still scratching Ginirth's eye ridge.

With a backward wave, Fiona left him and headed down to the Dining Cavern for lunch, her rounds completed.

T'mar shouted to her as she reached the entrance, so she changed direction toward him.

"The watch dragon reports that the Harper Hall is asking for a dragon," he told her, "so Zirenth and I are going—did you want to come?"

"Yes, please!" Fiona was anxious to check on Forsk and her father. She searched the cavern, looking to ask Cisca. T'mar noticed and said, "I've already asked the Weyrwoman for you."

"Oh, thank you."

"We can go after lunch," T'mar said, gesturing her toward a seat.

Fiona sat and regarded T'mar thoughtfully. "You must still be exhausted from last night."

Outside, a number of dragon coughs echoed in the Weyr Bowl. T'mar glanced at her expectantly.

"Fifty," she told him, grimacing. "That's our best guess."

"Guess?"

Fiona shrugged. "The ones who are sickest are easy to tell," she replied. "It's the ones who are just coming down with the illness that are hard to know about."

"Maybe they'll have good news at the Harper Hall," T'mar said hopefully.

Fiona nodded. They finished the rest of their meal in silence. Afterward, she raced to her quarters to get her flying gear.

"I'm going to the Harper Hall," she told Xhinna, quickly throwing open her closet.

"You'll need to put your leggings on," Xhinna told her. "And boots, scarf, and jacket."

Fiona was dressed and racing back toward T'mar in less than ten minutes. The wingleader was also dressed in flying gear: wherhide jacket, gloves, and cap.

With a quick word of thanks to Zirenth, Fiona clambered up the bronze's foreleg to perch on his neck, searching among the flying straps for hooks to secure herself. When T'mar climbed up behind her and saw what she was doing, he laughed. "You don't need to do that—we're not fighting Thread!"

"I just want to practice," Fiona explained. "Besides, didn't I hear you telling the weyrlings the other day about the dangers of turbulent air?"

T'mar groaned in acknowledgment. "But as long as I'm holding on to you"—and his strong arms braced her from either side—"you've nothing to worry about."

Fiona laughed, then elbowed his arms away, finishing her work of clipping on to the fighting straps. "I do, if you aren't going to clip in!"

"Very well, Weyrwoman," T'mar agreed with a sigh. When he was done, he wrapped his arms around her once more, recalling for Fiona memories from when she was a child on a cold day and her father similarly wrapped his arms around her. She leaned back against his chest and closed her eyes, warm with the memory.

The sudden leap into the air and the sound of Zirenth's great wings propelling them swiftly up and out of the Weyr Bowl did nothing to disturb Fiona's happiness, and even when they went into the cold nothingness of *between*, she felt safe.

The weather over Fort Hold and the adjoining Harper Hall was much as at Fort Weyr—wispy drifts of snow could be seen at the edges of buildings and the base of the cliffs, and the air was crisp, cold, and dry with the harsh winds of winter. The sun was bright and the sky cloudless as they descended to the landing midway between the Harper Hall and Fort Hold. Fiona took a quick breath of the frigid air through the scarf wrapped over her face and let it out just as quickly—it felt as though it still had the cold of *between* in it and it hurt her lungs. She took a second, smaller, shorter breath and felt better.

The air on the ground was warmer, and as soon as they dismounted, Fiona and T'mar unbuttoned their wherhide jackets. T'mar waved affectionately as Zirenth leapt up again, seeking out a perch on the cliffs above Fort Hold.

"I don't know why he bothers," he said with a chuckle and a shake of his head. "I told him we wouldn't be long."

"Perhaps he doesn't believe you," Fiona suggested with a grin. "After all, they serve Benden wine."

"That would be enticement enough for M'kury," T'mar said, "but I'm made of sterner stuff."

"Wouldn't you want some nicely mulled red wine on a crisp day like to day?"

"*Klah*," T'mar corrected tersely. "As you mentioned earlier, I am still exhausted from last night."

"So why didn't you send someone else?" Fiona asked. T'mar didn't answer, merely shaking his head.

They were scarcely under the Harper Hall's arches when someone shouted and Fiona felt herself lifted off her feet. She had to control her impulse to kick out with her foot when her assailant cried joyfully in her ear, "Fiona! What a delight!"

"Verilan?" Fiona cried, astonished that the Master Archivist would engage in such a display of emotion and exercise.

"Fiona!" Verilan cried again, hugging her tight. Presently he put her back down and pushed her away from him, saying, "Let me look at you!"

Fiona felt herself blushing, both surprised and touched by Verilan's exuberance, particularly as her strongest memories of him were of numerous scoldings for "playing in the inks—again!"

"You're taller," he said, finishing his examination. "You've grown—what?—two centimeters?"

"Nearly three," T'mar put in from behind her. Fiona craned her neck around in surprise—since when did he keep tabs on her? The explanation came quickly enough, as he continued, "I heard Ellor groaning about it just the other day."

"That's not quite a record," Verilan responded. "I believe greatest growth in a three-month period for a girl your age was recorded at Telgar Hold some eighty Turns ago when Lord Holder Predder's eldest daughter grew three and a half centimeters—"

"Verilan," Fiona broke in, fearing that she had somehow unleashed another outpouring of the Archivist's prodigious memory, "we're here because of the signal."

"Yes," Verilan said, visibly pulling himself out of his recitation. "Master Zist had it set." He gestured vaguely toward the Masterharper's quarters. "You should go there."

"Verilan?" Fiona said, her tone pleading for more information.

"I think you'll find your father there," he added.

"Is he all right?" Fiona asked immediately, despite reason telling her that if he were injured he'd be in the Infirmary, not the Masterharper's quarters.

"All right?" Verilan repeated, pursing his lips thoughtfully. "I think that depends upon one's criteria for such things."

Fiona shook her head in exasperation, grabbed T'mar's wrist, and tugged the bronze rider into a trot behind her. "We'd better hurry!"

T'mar made no comment at the incongruity of being led by a young, blond Weyrwoman who was not only half his age but also more than a full head shorter than himself; he had seen enough of Weyrwomen in his time to realize that he was probably lucky not to have to endure worse. He even kept his silence when Fiona banged on Zist's door and announced herself.

"Isn't T'mar with you?" Zist asked as he pulled open the door. "Ah, yes, he is!"

"Where's my father?" Fiona demanded, scanning the room and quickly identifying its occupants. Her worries faded as she spotted Bemin seated with Kelsa at Zist's round table.

"What's going on?" Fiona demanded, her eyes switching from Zist, to Bemin, to Kelsa and back before finally settling demandingly on Kelsa.

"Your father and I—" Kelsa began diplomatically, then broke

off, pushing herself to her feet and patting her stomach in a manner that seemed both odd and subtly familiar to Fiona. "Well, we're going to have a baby."

"About time," Fiona said. She saw Bemin start to speak and cut through: "Since I already knew—" She paused at the surprised expressions on Kelsa's and Master Zist's faces and realized that her father hadn't relayed their earlier conversation to either; her guess was confirmed by Kelsa's glare at her father. "—I presume this meeting is to let me know formally and also, by its venue—" She waved a hand around the room. "—to tell me that there are still some issues to work out."

Zist wore an expression of approval that warmed Fiona; his approval was hard earned, more often than not.

She turned her attention to Kelsa. "Let me guess: You're not certain you want to be a lifemate with him, and you want to raise the child here?"

"Actually, we've been through that," Bemin said.

"We really just wanted to ask your blessing," Kelsa added in an uncertain tone—a rarity in the outspoken Songmaster.

"I think it's great," Fiona told her enthusiastically. She looked at her father. "I'd been hoping you'd do something like this."

"You were?" Bemin replied, surprised.

"I think Mother would have wished it," Fiona said. In a quieter voice she added, "And I think so would Koriana."

She was surprised at her feelings when she spoke of her long-dead, mostly forgotten older and only sister. Ever since she could remember, Fiona had been told how much she looked like her sister, how kind Koriana had been, and how in love Kindan had been with her. It had seemed like Fiona would forever be in Koriana's shadow . . . until she was freed by her Impression of Talenth. And yet . . . Fiona thought of Kindan, remembered her half-hope that he would be here, remembered how her heart pounded whenever she heard of him, how happy she was whenever he smiled at her—was all that just her following the shadow of her dead sister?

"But you couldn't have known I'd come," Fiona realized, glancing over at the Masterharper. "So that wasn't the only reason."

Zist smiled at her and nodded. "No, it wasn't," he agreed.

"It was my idea," Bemin added, smiling at his daughter. "I'd heard about your casualties and . . ."

"Healer Tintoval accepted," Kelsa finished for him, gesturing to the healer, whom Fiona only now noticed in the room.

"As we've got the Healer Hall here, Fort Hold really only needs one journeyman healer to make the rounds," Bemin declared.

"That's only temporary," Zist reminded him, "until we get more trained journeymen and masters."

Fiona looked at the young healer. "You don't mind that I took your stores for the dragons, do you?"

"Not at all," Tintoval told her, waving the issue aside. "I'm only sorry to hear that it didn't work."

"Have we heard any more from Benden?" T'mar said, turning hopefully to the Masterharper.

Zist shook his head. "Kindan will be doing his best."

"I'm sure of it," Fiona agreed ardently.

"As am I," Tintoval said. "And so will K'tan," she added, referring to the healer at Benden Weyr.

"Are you sure about this?" Fiona asked. "You wouldn't want to go to Benden instead?"

Tintoval shook her head. "Benden has a healer."

"Tintoval is weyrbred and familiar with dragons," Zist added.

"But not with healing them," Tintoval interjected.

"All healers say that, at first," T'mar assured her. He bowed to her. "Healer, on behalf of my Weyrleader and Weyrwoman, I wish to extend our hopes that you will come to regard Fort Weyr as your home."

"Thank you," Tintoval replied, obviously touched by his sincerity.

"I also have news that you might want to hear," T'mar said, turning back to Master Zist.

"Well, why don't you have a seat, and you, too, Weyrwoman, and we'll hear it over some fresh *klah* and dainties," Zist invited, gesturing them toward the empty seats at the table.

"We shouldn't stay too long," Fiona cautioned as she sat down. "T'mar fought Thread last night and like all the dragonriders, he's still exhausted."

"We saw," Bemin replied. "In fact, Forsk saw it rather close up."

"Oh," T'mar said, deflated. "So my news is known to you."

"That the watch-whers flew against Thread?" Zist said. "Yes, we know that. What we don't know is how it worked out for the Weyr."

"What sort of casualties do you have?" Tintoval asked.

"Eleven severe, thirteen light," Fiona recited quickly.

"You've helped?" Tintoval inquired and, on receiving Fiona's nod, continued, "How many sick dragons do you have?"

"We've fifty," T'mar told her glumly. "But we may lose some of them any day."

Selora, the Harper Hall's head cook, arrived with a tray holding a pitcher, mugs for all, and a plate piled high with delicious-looking, bite-sized dainties. They continued the conversation over hot *klah* and snacks, talking about dragon injuries, human injuries, and the night flight until Fiona, with a brush of her foot against T'mar's leg, alerted the bronze rider that it was time to go.

"Masterharper, Lord Holder, Master Kelsa," T'mar said, standing and nodding to each in turn, "we really should get back to the Weyr. I'm sure Tintoval will want to get settled in, and that Cisca and K'lior will want to greet her personally on her arrival."

"Yes, yes, we've been keeping you too long," Bemin agreed, rising to his feet and bending over to help Kelsa solicitously to hers.

"I'm not that far gone, old man," Kelsa growled at him, but Fiona noted that her tone was more grateful than grudging.

"In my experience, Master Kelsa," Tintoval advised, "it's best to get them used to helping as early as possible; that way, when you really need help, it'll already be there."

"Hmm," Kelsa murmured, glancing consideringly at Bemin.

Tintoval left to retrieve her things, and as T'mar called for Zirenth to meet them at the Landing, Fiona said good-bye to her father and Kelsa, making sure to hug each of them an equal number of times and assuring Kelsa once again, "I am *so* glad you're doing this!"

T'mar insisted upon putting Tintoval up front, with Fiona squashed between them.

"We don't have enough straps," Fiona remarked as she buckled herself on.

"You didn't really need them on the way here," T'mar replied, airily waving a hand, "and you don't need them now."

Fiona ignored him. Secretly she latched a hand onto the bottom of Tintoval's jacket and wrapped her other arm under and around the straps in front of her, assuring a secure grip.

Even so, she lurched slightly as Zirenth leapt into the air, and then they went once more *between* and back to Fort Weyr.

Back over the Star Stones at Fort Weyr, Zirenth gave a grunt of surprise and dropped precipitously as they flew into a pocket of lighter air. Tintoval flew up out of her perch, and it was only Fiona's tight grip that kept her from falling off. But the effort strained the arm clutching the healer and sharply wrenched the one wrapped in the fighting straps. Fiona groaned in pain. T'mar grabbed her the moment he felt the lurch, but without being anchored to the fighting straps, he could only use one arm himself.

On the ground, T'mar had no sympathy for Fiona's groans. "You shouldn't have done that! Tintoval was safe enough."

"Only because I held on to her!"

"You could have fallen, too!" T'mar retorted.

"So you admit she was in danger!"

"We can't afford to lose you," T'mar replied, his tone pained.

"And we can afford to lose a healer?" Fiona demanded, her fury in full flight.

"Better than a queen rider," Tintoval interjected. "We hardly had enough queens, and with the losses at Benden and here—"

"So this is all about my queen?" Fiona demanded. "All that matters is her?"

"Yes," T'mar told her, his voice going steely cold. "We've only the two, in case you haven't noticed."

"And we've only the *one* healer," Fiona retorted, jerking her thumb at Tintoval.

T'mar gathered breath for a response, but a bellow from Melirth put a halt to all conversation. They turned to see Cisca storming toward them, her eyes flashing dangerously.

Fiona felt herself cringing, overwhelmed by the barely controlled power emanating from the Weyrwoman.

"Come with me," Cisca ordered Fiona and turned away once more, certain of obedience.

For a moment Fiona thought to stand her ground, but then—

What's wrong? Talenth demanded anxiously.

Nothing, Fiona lied. *I was just scared.*

Talenth emerged from her lair, eyes whirling red, finding Fiona and crooning at her anxiously.

It's all right, Fiona assured her, projecting warmth and love toward the young queen. *I'm getting over it.*

Cisca, walking quickly, led her into the Council Room. K'lior was already there, seated, and looking grave.

The instant the two looked at her, Fiona, feeling that her safety lay in taking the offensive, declared, "T'mar wasn't worried about the new healer!"

"That won't work," K'lior told her, his tone steady but firm.

Fiona glared at him for a moment more, then dropped her eyes guiltily.

"What did you hope to accomplish back there?" the Weyrleader demanded, waving a hand back toward the Weyr Bowl.

"Well—I—" Fiona spluttered.

"You didn't think," Cisca told her. "It's not uncommon at your age—"

"At my age!"

"Yes, at your age," Cisca repeated. "News of your behavior will be heard by everyone soon enough."

"But T'mar was—"

"—wrong," K'lior finished for her. "He should have used the straps."

"He said he didn't have any," Fiona protested.

"He could have borrowed some from the Harper Hall," K'lior replied. "Master Zist is used to dealing with dragonriders and is smart enough to keep some on hand."

"As, no doubt, does your father," Cisca added.

"Then you agree—"

"I do not agree with your public humiliation of a wingleader," K'lior interjected harshly. "T'mar's a good man; he would have learned his lesson without your childish outburst."

"Childish!"

"Childish," Cisca agreed, but her tone was softer than K'lior's and she shot the Weyrleader a look that Fiona couldn't fathom. K'lior shrugged in response, leaving Cisca to continue, "An adult would have realized that T'mar would punish himself harshly for his error and—"

"—an adult would accept the realities of being a queen rider," K'lior finished.

"And let someone else die?" Fiona demanded in anguish and fury, her eyes filling with tears.

"If need be," Cisca answered softly. She gestured to herself and Fiona. "Without us, there would be no queens. And without the queens, there will be no Pern."

"So our queens are nothing but brood mothers?" Fiona demanded sourly. "And you and I are—" She found she couldn't finish the sentence and so said instead, "But what about Tannaz? Why did you let her go *between*?"

"It wasn't my choice," Cisca told her. She shook her head sadly. "You know that it wasn't really Tannaz's choice, either. Kelsanth was dying; there was no cure."

"There's no cure now," Fiona reminded them grimly. But she remembered the words she'd heard: *It will be all right.* The words had been spoken with such faith that she couldn't set them aside.

"We can't give up," K'lior told her firmly.

"Why not?" Fiona demanded petulantly. "Tannaz did. There's *still no cure.*"

"We can't give up because we are dragonriders," K'lior told her.

"Did your father give up during the Plague?" Cisca demanded.

"Yes, he did," Fiona replied, her voice a near whisper. "After my mother and my brothers all died, he kept hope, but when Koriana . . . ," She trailed off, remembering her father telling her about the Plague, about how Kindan had refused to give up even when Lord Holder Bemin himself had surrendered to despair.

It will be all right. Was it Kindan who had spoken to her? No, the voice had sounded different. But the words had Kindan's faith, his surety, his steadfast refusal to admit despair . . .

"Kindan didn't, though," Fiona said out loud, raising her head and glancing first to Cisca and then to K'lior. "He never gave up."

"Nor will I," K'lior vowed.

"Nor I," Cisca said. She lifted her chin up challengingly to Fiona. "So, Weyrwoman, daughter of a Lord Holder, Plague survivor, who will you follow: your father in his despair, or Kindan?"

Stung by the question, Fiona loyally declared, "My father

vowed never again to give in to despair." She met Cisca's brown eyes. "He has never failed his Hold."

"And you, Weyrwoman? What of your Weyr?" K'lior asked softly.

Before Fiona could answer, Cisca raised a hand and cautioned her, "Since Impression, you've been a Weyrwoman—that is unquestionable. The question is: What sort of Weyrwoman will you be? Will you be a leader and an inspiration, or will you be a whiner and an embarrassment? Will you bear your responsibilities, or bow under them?"

"But—to let her fall!" Fiona wailed. A torrent of emotions broke over her and she began to cry.

Realization dawned on K'lior's face. "You aren't angry at T'mar—you're angry because you would have let her go!"

"I held on!" Fiona declared, holding up her aching arm as proof.

"Of course you did," Cisca replied proudly. "You're a Weyrwoman." She glanced to K'lior. "We've never questioned that."

"But," K'lior persisted, "if it had come to letting her go or falling with her—"

"I would have let her go!" Fiona cried, dropping her head into her hands and shaking it in shame and sorrow. "I would have let her go."

Strong arms wrapped around her and she was pulled tight against Cisca's tall body. "Of course you would," Cisca agreed with her, "because that's what you would have had to do to protect Pern. You would have hated yourself for it, probably never have forgiven yourself, but you would have done it." Cisca pushed her away and put a finger under Fiona's chin, gently raising it so she could see the girl's eyes. "And that's what makes a great Weyrwoman: doing what has to be done even when she hates it."

"That's why you let Tannaz go," Fiona said with sudden understanding.

"Yes," Cisca replied, the words torn out of her, and again she crushed Fiona in a tight embrace, the sort of embrace a mother gives her daughter; the sort of embrace Fiona had always longed for. A short moment later, however, Fiona pushed herself away and glanced toward K'lior. "And that's why you called me in here."

The Weyrleader nodded, a corner of his lips turned up in a bitter smile. "Better to know your mettle now than when we are in worse straits."

Fiona nodded. She stood as tall as she could and said to K'lior, "Weyrleader, I apologize for my outburst at Wingleader T'mar. I was distressed and took my temper out on him. I regret it."

"Perhaps not all *that* much," Cisca said, eyes dancing. "I know that it's sometimes tempting to see bronze riders cringe at the lash of a harsh tongue."

"Cisca!" K'lior said reprovingly. "Not everyone has your evil sense of humor."

Cisca shook her head, catching Fiona's eyes. "Remember Melanwy?" Fiona nodded glumly, remembering how she'd influenced Melanwy's actions. "As Weyrwomen, we have incredible power. The best way to guard against abusing it is to be honest and listen to our fellow Weyrwomen."

"So if I think you are being unfair, I should tell you?" Fiona replied.

"Of course," Cisca agreed forcefully. Then she smiled. "I reserve the right to ignore you, of course."

"In which case," K'lior said with an evil grin at his Weyrwoman, "come to me and I'll handle her!"

Cisca snorted derisively. "And Melirth will deal with *you*!"

"But of course," K'lior agreed.

"Seriously," Cisca said, turning again to Fiona, "it is often hard for a young Weyrwoman to accept the realities of her position."

"To let healers die that I might live," Fiona said by way of example.

"If that is what is needed to protect your queen and the future of Pern," Cisca responded emphatically.

"It just doesn't seem fair," Fiona said softly.

"It isn't fair," Cisca agreed. "It's up to us—Weyrwomen and Weyrleaders—to make it as fair as we can."

"And when we can't," K'lior added, "it's our responsibility to make certain that no sacrifice is in vain."

Fiona nodded; K'lior's words sounded like something her father would say in similar circumstances.

"So," Cisca said, "are we ready to greet our new healer?"

"I think we are," K'lior said, heading toward the doorway.

"I expect you to deal with T'mar on your own," Cisca murmured in Fiona's ear as they made their way back in to the Weyr Bowl.

The reason Fiona gave Cisca and K'lior for insisting on showing Tintoval around the Weyr was to make up for her previous behavior, and she was glad that they didn't question her, particularly as they exchanged dubious looks that made it clear to her that they guessed her other reason—to avoid T'mar as long as possible.

"There are at least fifty dragons with the illness," Fiona said as Tintoval startled at the coughs echoing around the Weyr Bowl.

"My training is with people," Tintoval remarked worriedly.

"With Thread injuries such training works for both dragons and riders," Fiona assured her.

"And the sickness?"

Fiona made a face. "Maybe you can help."

Tintoval shook her head. "I think our best hope is still at Benden."

"Maybe," Fiona agreed, "but that doesn't mean we should stop trying."

"No," the healer agreed wholeheartedly. She paused as Fiona turned toward a stairway. "Are we going to visit the sick dragons now?"

"Not all of them," Fiona told her. "I doubt we'll get to see more than ten before dinner."

"Dinner doesn't matter to me if that'll help," Tintoval offered.

"If only it were that easy," Fiona replied, shaking her head. "But my father always says that 'hungry stomachs make dull minds.'"

"Does he?" Tintoval replied. "I thought that came from Master Zist."

Fiona stepped out of the stairwell and turned right, heading toward the third weyr.

"S'ban's blue Serth started coughing about a fortnight back," she murmured to the healer as they slowed at the entrance. She shook her head sadly, raised a warning hand to Tintoval, then called out, "S'ban, it's Fiona with the new healer!"

"A new healer," the voice inside began hopefully. "Does he—"

He broke off as they entered. S'ban was dressed elegantly in wherhide breeches and a thick blue sweater accented with a gold chain around his neck. For a moment his face showed his surprise at Tintoval, and then it darkened.

"I'm not sure that Serth will tolerate a woman's touch," he warned them. When Fiona opened her mouth to argue, the blue rider amended quickly, "I mean, a woman who is not a queen rider."

"S'ban, this is Tintoval," Fiona said by way of introduction. "She's just been posted master and assigned here." The blue rider looked, if anything, even more disturbed at the news.

"I grew up at Benden," Tintoval added, moving deftly around S'ban toward his dragon's lair. When she spotted Serth curled up miserably with his head just barely free of a thick puddle of mucus, she called, "Why, aren't you the biggest blue I've ever seen!" Over her shoulder to S'ban she remarked, "My father's dragon was a blue—Talerinth."

"I met him!" S'ban exclaimed brightly. "T'val was his rider. We competed at the Games before—"

"Yes," Tintoval said shortly. "Talerinth was burned by a fire-stone explosion and they went *between*." She grimaced at the memory, adding, "I had six Turns at the time. I was named Tinto-val because father convinced my mother that I was going to be a boy—you know how mad blue riders are for sons!"

"We like daughters, too," S'ban replied consolingly, moving up to her and looking at her sideways as he continued, "Is that why you chose to be a healer?"

Tintoval nodded faintly, confessing, "I didn't know at the time that healers can't mend broken hearts."

S'ban reached for her hand and patted it awkwardly. "I'm sure if anyone could, it would be you."

Tintoval smiled at him and, shaking her head to dismiss the issue, turned back to the ailing blue. "Serth, do you mind if I look at you? I can't promise to help, but I'll do my best not to hurt."

She strode forward to the listless blue's head and forced herself to ignore the poorly stifled sob of his rider.

Seeing that the healer was able to handle herself, Fiona quietly made her way past S'ban, found the bucket and mop she'd brought on an earlier visit, and quietly went to work cleaning up the green ooze near Serth's head.

"You don't have to do that," S'ban protested when he saw her. "I'll do it later."

"I want to help," Fiona told him, continuing undeterred. She gave him a lopsided smile. "Weyrwoman's right."

Tintoval glanced up at her with a surprised look, then returned to her examination of the blue dragon.

"His breathing is labored," she noted. She glanced at his flanks. "And irregular."

"We tried some mint salve to ease the breathing," Fiona told her.

"And?"

"It only helped for a short while," Fiona replied. "I was afraid it could make things worse, open up the lungs to more infection."

"I use it at night, to help him sleep," S'ban said worriedly. "Should I stop?"

"Does he sleep easier when you do?" Tintoval asked.

"He seems to," S'ban replied cautiously.

Tintoval glanced to Fiona, who shrugged. Then she turned to the blue rider. "I think that if it helps him to sleep, you should keep on doing it. Sleep is one of the body's best defenses against illness."

S'ban nodded in acceptance, but cast a questioning glance toward Fiona.

"It makes sense to me," Fiona told him. "Besides, I learned Turns back never to argue with a healer."

"Or a harper, I'll guess," Tintoval added drolly.

"I owe my life to a harper turned healer," Fiona declared.

"That's right," Tintoval said, nodding. "You were at Fort Hold when Kindan—"

"And you can be certain, S'ban, that Kindan will do no less now to fight this illness than he did to fight the Plague," Fiona cut in, building smoothly on the healer's start.

"He'll need to be quick, if Serth is going to survive," S'ban added, his expression bleakly honest.

"Tintoval," Fiona murmured to the healer five hours later as they checked in on their tenth sick dragon, "it's time for dinner."

The healer nodded silently, her attention still on the sick brown dragon she was examining.

"Go on, healer, you need to keep up your strength," G'trek told her.

"Will you come with us?" Tintoval asked respectfully.

G'trek shook his head. "No, I think I'll stay with Korth, in case he needs anything."

"Send word by Talenth if you have need," Fiona said.

The brown rider nodded. "You can be certain of it, Weyr-woman."

Outside, as they walked briskly toward the stairwell, Tintoval asked, "Wouldn't he need his dragon to ask to talk to you?"

Fiona shook her head. "I'll ask Talenth to listen for him."

"And she's old enough to remember that?"

"Well, yes," Fiona replied, surprised at the healer's question and startled that she'd never considered Talenth's memory remarkable.

"Queens grow quicker than other dragons," Tintoval commented half to herself. "I just never realized quite how capable they are."

"I never thought that she couldn't do that," Fiona confessed.

"Perhaps that's why she can," Tintoval replied. At Fiona's surprised look the healer shrugged. "In trying times most people rise to the occasion."

Fiona shook her head ruefully, thinking again of Kindan and how he had risen above his despair to save everyone during the Plague. "Like Kindan."

"He was the first one to encourage me to consider becoming a healer," Tintoval told her. "I had barely eight Turns, but he recommended me to K'tan as an understudy." She shook her head in bemusement at the memory, continuing, "Two Turns later I was at the Harper Hall."

"I'm surprised we never met," Fiona said.

"We did," Tintoval told her with a grin. "But you had all of five Turns and you spent all your time in Kindan's lap." She winked at Fiona. "I seem to recall it was your birthing day."

"It was! I fell asleep," Fiona remembered. She had never felt more comfortable than curled up on Kindan's lap.

"Kindan had a smile on his face the whole time," Tintoval recalled, adding, "I was quite jealous, of course. Even your father couldn't prise you away."

"I never got to see much of him," Fiona said, reminiscing. "And I knew on my birthday no one would make me go away."

"Wise of you," Tintoval agreed. "I was never quite that bold."

Fiona suddenly found herself uncomfortable talking about Kindan like this. She felt as though her memories got tarnished by being shared so openly.

"And now, neither of us have him," Tintoval continued with a distant look in her eyes. "He has eyes only for Lorana, the new queen rider."

"So I heard," Fiona said shortly.

"But she was here!" Tintoval recalled. "Didn't you meet her?"

"No," Fiona replied, heat rising to her cheeks as she remembered the reason.

"You weren't too jealous, were you?" Tintoval asked with a sly grin.

Her taunt trapped Fiona into either replying or, by her silence, tacitly accepting the jibe. "Actually, I was suffering from a concussion," she said finally. She told the healer the whole story of how she caught T'mar's full weight, adding, "Perhaps you would have done differently?"

"For T'mar?" Tintoval asked with a broad smile. She shook her head. "No, for *him* I would have done the same thing." She wagged a finger down at Fiona. "You've got quite an eye for the men, if you don't mind my saying!"

"I do mind!" Fiona retorted hotly. "I was only trying to save him!"

Tintoval took a step back from the irate queen rider and spread her arms wide in apology. "Your pardon, Weyrwoman," she said, "I didn't mean to upset you."

Fiona shook her head and gestured for the healer to keep moving as they exited the stairwell and started across the Weyr Bowl. The way was dimly lit with glows and Fiona could make out small groups of riders and weyrfolk heading toward the Dining Cavern.

"And, actually," Tintoval continued a moment later, "you raised an interesting problem that I hadn't considered."

"I did?"

"Yes," the healer agreed. "The issue of handling riders who are too injured to maintain their mount."

"I think it's pretty rare," Fiona said with a shrug. "Usually the fighting straps keep them secure, but T'mar was unlucky."

"Perhaps we could discover a better way to catch them," Tintoval murmured thoughtfully. "Maybe something like Kindan's parachutes?"

"Wouldn't they have to be awfully big?" Fiona wondered. They were entering the well-lit Dining Cavern and she paused, glancing around for sight of T'mar.

"Oh, this feels just like home!" Tintoval exclaimed, her face brightening as she scanned the large room filled with dragonriders and weyrfolk.

T'mar wasn't at the Weyrleader's table.

"I'm sure that Cisca and K'lior will want to talk with you," Fiona said, gesturing for the healer to follow her. As they made their way to the back of the cavern, she was pleased to see so many people she recognized and a bit surprised by their reaction to seeing Tintoval for the first time.

"A woman healer!" "Who would have thought?" "I hear that she was weyrfolk at Benden." "Benden, eh? So why is she here, then?" "Well, they've got a healer, haven't they?"

K'lior and Cisca greeted the healer warmly and gestured for her to sit beside them. Fiona glanced to see if there was a place for her, but a sharp look from Cisca dissuaded her and she made her apologies, climbing back down from the raised platform and scanning the large cavern again for T'mar.

She found him seated with his wing at a table near the northern entrance.

Well, there was nothing for it, Fiona told herself grimly. She straightened her back and raised her head, recalling her father's instructions. "When apologizing, do it quickly and be forthright," Lord Bemin had told her Turns back over an incident involving one of the cook's favorite serving bowls. "And be certain that you mean it. There's nothing worse than a half-hearted apology."

But she could have died! Fiona protested to herself, wondering how her father would have responded.

"She didn't," he would probably have said, "and you weren't angry with the bronze rider because of that." She could imagine him sighing and drawing her close. "Lying does not become a Lady Holder, particularly if she lies to herself."

Yes, Father, Fiona thought in an end to the imaginary conversation, you're right as always.

She was at T'mar's table. The riders there all stopped talking when they saw her.

"Weyrwoman," T'mar said, inclining his head respectfully.

"Wingleader T'mar," Fiona began, "I wish to apologize to you for my outburst this morning. I should not have been angry with you." She bit her lip and forced herself to continue. "The truth you spoke was not one I was prepared to hear. I regret my harsh words."

T'mar regarded her for a moment, then gestured for her to take a seat. His wingman hastily rose and moved to the end of the table, brushing aside Fiona's protests with a shake of his head and a smile.

T'mar waited until she was seated, then leaned in close to her. "You are not weyrbred; you learned something today that our children know as soon as they can talk."

"I am holdbred," Fiona agreed, "but my father is a Lord Holder and many of the same truths apply to Lady Holders as it does to Weyrwomen." She frowned. "It's just hard to accept."

"Harder as a Weyrwoman, I believe," T'mar told her. "As a Lady Holder you could renounce your claim, but as a Weyrwoman . . ." He shook his head.

"Is it always this hard?" Fiona asked him frankly. "Am I the only one . . . ?"

"No," T'mar assured her. "I think every Weyrwoman battles with this issue." He waved a hand toward Cisca. "I know that she did, before Melirth rose."

Fiona pursed her lips, her chest tight as she worried about how she would deal with Talenth's first mating.

"You've Turns yet, Fiona," T'mar said, guessing her thoughts from her expression. He grabbed her hands with one of his and clasped them tightly, reassuringly. "You'll do fine, I'm certain."

"Cisca . . . ?" Fiona asked tentatively.

T'mar grimaced and shook his head. "If she chooses to tell you, she will," he replied. "Let's just say that there was a great deal of relief that Rineth flew her."

Fiona noticed that T'mar glanced down at the table immediately thereafter, as though reliving some painful experience.

She was wondering how she could learn more—perhaps Ellor would tell her?—when the night was pierced by a strange noise, not the sound of a dragon but of something else, a noise Fiona instantly recognized: a watch-wher!

"I didn't know watch-whers came here!" she exclaimed, craning her neck toward the entrance.

"They don't," T'mar said, pushing himself up and away from the table.

Fiona saw that Cisca and K'lior were also rising and looking toward the entrance.

Talenth, Fiona thought quickly, *ask the watch-wher's name.*

Her name is Nuellask, Talenth responded immediately. *Can I meet her?*

Wait, Fiona replied, *she might be frightened.*

Of me? Talenth asked in amazement. Fiona assured her that that was probably not the case while still managing to keep her young queen from prancing out into the Bowl.

"It's Nuellask," Fiona said, following T'mar. "She's Nuella's gold watch-wher."

"Thread's not due for two days," T'mar said. "I wonder why she's here?"

"Maybe she wants to coordinate with us," Fiona suggested.

Cisca caught sight of her as they reached the exit and, shaking her head at the exodus, told Fiona, "Keep them back."

Fiona nodded and found herself herding curious riders and weyrfolk back to their meals, all the while wishing she had a better chance to see Nuella and her gold watch-wher.

After a few minutes, T'mar returned, beckoning to Fiona. "Cisca wants Nuella to meet you."

With a relieved smile, Fiona ceded her job to T'mar and headed out into the darkened Weyr Bowl.

Even in the dim light, Fiona had no trouble locating the knot of riders clustered around the small gold watch-wher. The watch-wher arched her neck high over the humans as Fiona approached and then snaked it down to bring her head with its huge eyes to bear directly on Fiona, issuing a soft, high-pitched greeting.

"I'm Fiona," she told the watch-wher, reaching a hand forward, fingers outstretched tentatively to scratch the watch-wher's nearest eye ridge. As Nuellask crooned in delight, Fiona smiled. "Forsk likes to have her eye ridges scratched, too."

"Did you spend much time with her, then?" a strange woman's voice asked from close beside her.

Fiona shook her head, then expanded, "Not really. She was up at nights, and Father always insisted that I be asleep." She grinned in memory. "But sometimes, when I was lonely, I'd go into her lair and curl up with her when I was tired."

"From catching tunnel snakes, no doubt," the woman, whom Fiona realized must be Nuella, guessed with amusement in her tone. "Kindan complained of it to me on several occasions."

"Complained?" Fiona repeated, feeling irked with Kindan. "I got a quarter mark for each head!"

"And never got bitten, except the once," Nuella added approvingly.

Fiona looked at her in surprise. "How did you—how did Kindan know about that?"

Nuella laughed. "No one keeps secrets from harpers for long."

"But I treated myself and kept the cut hidden!"

"You still needed stores and you had to ask someone, even if hypothetically, about treating snakebites," Nuella replied, her voice full of humor. She held out a hand, which Fiona took and shook eagerly. "I'm Nuella, as you've no doubt guessed." She continued, "And rest assured, no one would have known except that Kindan was keeping such a careful watch over you."

Fiona was too embarrassed to reply.

"*I* thought it was a particularly good idea to ask Kelsa if there'd ever been songs written about treating snakebites," Nuella confided approvingly.

"She wrote one just afterward," Fiona remembered, then groaned, glancing over to the older woman in horror, "and she consulted Father on it! You don't suppose she told *him* . . . ?"

Nuella laughed and shook her head. "I have no idea," she replied. "All I know is that after the song was written, Kindan showed up at my camp very agitated and tried to slyly teach the song to me."

"He was afraid *you* were going to go after tunnel snakes?"

Nuella shook her head, her grin slipping. "I'd already done that," she confessed. "I think he was just trying to be certain that I knew how to handle the bites if I ever did again."

With a shock of horror, Fiona realized that Nuella was referring to her first watch-wher, the green Nuelsk, who had died of snakebite. She risked a glance at the older woman—who had nearly twice as many Turns as she—and was surprised by their similarities: both were blond and freckled. Nuella's eyes were more of a pure blue than Fiona's, but they could have been sisters or, at least, half-sibs.

"It seems that Kindan's friends are always doing brave things," Cisca remarked as she strode over to them, K'lior and H'nez trailing just behind her.

"Kindan sets the example," Fiona said in unison with Nuella. The two glanced at each other in surprise, then laughed.

"Can I see your dragon?" Nuella asked when she recovered. "Nuellask said she'd like to meet her."

"Of course," Fiona said, calling to Talenth. The little queen eagerly scampered out of her lair, launching herself for a quick glide in the night. Shaking her head, Fiona called, "Show off!"

Talenth said nothing in response, just striding quickly over to the gold watch-wher. The two exchanged cautious sniffs, then inspected each other eagerly.

Can I play with her? Talenth asked hopefully. Fiona could see the attraction: Nuellask was just a bit bigger than the little queen.

She's much older than you, Fiona warned her. *I don't think she'll want to play.*

"And you're supposed to be sleeping, aren't you?" Nuella added with a laugh. Sensing Fiona's surprise, the wherhandler told her, "Nuellask gave me an idea of your queen's eagerness."

"She wants to play," Fiona admitted.

"I could see the attraction," Nuella agreed. She turned toward Talenth, shaking her head. "I'm afraid that Nuellask and I have to get back to our lair. We'll be flying Thread in two days' time."

Talenth hung her head until Nuellask chirped at her soothingly.

"I'm sure you'll meet again," Nuella promised the queen dragon, "when you're older." She turned to Fiona, adding, "When you're both older."

Before Fiona could respond, Nuella turned toward the knot of riders, saying to K'lior, "Then it's agreed, Weyrleader, that the watch-whers will ride the Fall?"

"After your last performance, I wouldn't have it any other way," K'lior replied feelingly. "But if there's any danger—"

"Your H'nez will be on duty at Southern Boll," Nuella interjected. "If there's any need, we'll contact him."

"I still think it's a bad idea," H'nez grumbled. "The Records say nothing of watch-whers fighting Thread—"

"Actually," Cisca interrupted smoothly, "they do."

"When?" H'nez asked abruptly.

"As of last night, when I wrote the report," the Weyrwoman told him.

H'nez was not amused. "If they're so useful, why was there no mention before?"

"I doubt anyone ever thought to mention it because it was obvious," K'lior told him. "Watch-whers watch at night and guard holds—we all know that. Probably no one thought it worth mentioning that at night they also guard the holds from *Thread.*"

"We haven't trained for this," H'nez protested.

"I accept responsibility for that," K'lior said.

"If all goes well, we won't need you," Nuella assured H'nez.

"Not need . . . ?" H'nez repeated, his tone full of disbelief.

"If the weather holds, the Thread will all be dead," Nuella said, "and then neither dragon nor watch-wher will have to fight."

"That would be good," K'lior said. "And it would give us time, afterward, to train together."

"I thought dragons didn't like flying at night," Fiona said.

"They don't," Cisca agreed. "But they hate missing Thread more."

"I must return," Nuella said, turning back toward her watchwher and feeling for the saddle. Nuellask gave her an encouraging chirp, turning her head to guide Nuella. After Nuella mounted, the others stood back as the queen watch-wher beat her tiny wings, rose slightly in the night air, and was gone *between.*

"Let's hope the Thread freezes," K'lior said.

The new day dawned cold with snow flurries falling, clothing the Weyr in a damp blanket of slush and mist—snow rarely stayed long in the warm Bowl of the Weyr. Farther up, in the weyrs, it was a different matter.

"I don't know how this cold will affect the sick dragons," Tintoval said when she met Cisca for breakfast that morning. "I know that dragons are usually not bothered by cold but—"

"—dragons don't usually get sick," Cisca finished for her, nodding in agreement.

"We could ask them," Fiona suggested. The other two looked at her in surprise.

"I suppose we could, at that," Cisca said.

"But would they know?" Tintoval wondered. The two Weyrwoman glanced at her. "People who have a fever feel cold when they're really hot, and those who've suffered from being frozen sometimes think they're too warm."

"Would it hurt to keep them warmer?" Xhinna wondered. "Even if they felt all right, would it hurt?"

"I think we should worry about the riders," Fiona said. "If they're cold, then it's likely that their dragons are, too."

"And they don't have the illness, so they'll know," Tintoval added approvingly.

"I wouldn't be too sure of that," Cisca cautioned.

"Why?"

"Dragons and riders share a bond," Cisca replied, "and a dragon's confusion can fuddle a rider."

Tintoval bit her lip and nodded.

"It's better than nothing," Fiona said.

"Yes, it is," Cisca agreed.

"I'm going to be busy getting ready for the Fall," Fiona said to Tintoval. "Do you think you can manage on your own?"

"If not, see me," Cisca said.

"Can I have Xhinna?" Tintoval asked.

Fiona turned to her friend. "Do you think you can survive a day without trying to beat the weyrlings at sacking firestone?"

Xhinna spent a moment torn between her desire and her sense of duty. Duty won. "Of course, Healer."

"I'm glad we've got the right firestone," T'mar remarked as he and Fiona watched the younger weyrlings preparing spare sacks of firestone. "In this weather, the older stuff would have to be salted and then rolled in grease before we could bag it."

"And even then it was still dangerous," Tajen added as he eyed the weyrlings' efforts critically. "This is *much* better."

"We've got enough for a full Flight," Terin reported after a final glance at her tally slate. "Do we need more?"

T'mar glanced up at the darkening sky, still flecked with falling snow, and shook his head. "I don't think we'll need it."

"The weather will be different down at Southern Boll," Tajen cautioned.

"But it's still winter there," T'mar said.

Tajen flipped open his hand in a gesture of agreement.

H'nez, M'valer, and K'rall departed on Thread watch shortly before dark.

"Send word at any sign of black dust," K'lior reminded them before they departed.

"I expect all the Thread will drown," M'valer said with a sour look.

"That would be good," K'lior said. "We could use the rest."

"Rest!" H'nez exclaimed. "We'll be up all night."

"I've never found that a problem," M'kury called from beside K'lior. He turned to the Weyrleader. "Perhaps you should send me instead?"

H'nez's disgusted snort echoed around the Weyr Bowl, undampened by the muffling snow.

"Good flying, wingleaders!" K'lior called in the ceremonial salute.

A moment later, the three wingleaders were gone, *between*.

When K'lior returned to the Living Caverns, Cisca greeted him with, "Why the troubled look?"

"I don't know," K'lior replied, shaking his head. "I suppose I'm concerned with the way H'nez and the others are so convinced they've nothing to worry about. They don't seem ready. Alert."

"I can understand them," Cisca replied. "With this beastly weather, as long as the watch-whers are on duty, there'll be no call for dragons."

K'lior pursed his lips, then nodded absently.

"But it's warmer down south," Fiona remarked.

"We shouldn't worry," Cisca decided. "Not with Nuella minding the watch-whers."

Her words did little to assure either Fiona or K'lior, who exchanged worried looks.

"Nuella's been training for this for a long while," Tintoval said in reassurance. "She'll have no trouble managing the watchwhers, I'm sure."

"I said no," Zenor repeated forcefully, turning Nuella toward him. Behind her, Nuellask gave them a questioning *chirp.* "You can't do this."

"But I must," Nuella replied calmly. "You know that."

"The first time, yes," Zenor agreed. "You needed it for peace of mind, if nothing else. But Nuellask"—and he shot the gold watchwher an acknowledging nod—"knows what to do now, so she doesn't need you."

Nuella drew breath to argue, but Zenor placed a restraining finger on her lips. "You've got children, Nuella. What would they do if anything happened to you?"

"They would survive," Nuella answered softly, pushing herself against Zenor and nuzzling in tightly. "They have the best father on all Pern—"

"So it's my duty to ensure that they keep their mother, too," Zenor finished.

"If anything happened to Nuellask and I wasn't there—"

"It would hurt terribly, I know," Zenor said. And Nuella had to admit that he *did* know. Not only had he helped her through the torment of losing her first watch-wher, Nuelsk, but he had also survived the wrenching loss of his own two fire-lizards.

"But you would survive," Zenor concluded. And this, Nuella

knew bitterly, was also true. The bond between watch-wher and whermate was strong, but it was nowhere near as deep as that between a rider and her dragon.

"I *have* to go, Zenor," Nuella said at last, pushing herself away from him more reluctantly than her brusqueness showed. "It's my duty."

"She's right," a small voice piped up from behind Zenor. " 'Dragonriders must fly when Thread is in the sky.' "

Zenor glanced over his shoulder to smile at Nalla, their eldest.

"Mummy hasn't got a dragon," little Zelar corrected.

"It's the same thing," Nalla protested.

"You two were supposed to be in bed," Zenor said with a sigh. He turned, still holding Nuella's hand. "But as you're not, you can give your mother a kiss good-bye. She'll return it when she comes back."

Nuella's hand tightened thankfully on Zenor's. The two youngsters needed no further urging and rushed to their mother. Nuella bent over to receive their hugs and kisses.

"Now off to bed with you," Zenor said, making shooing motions. "I'm surprised Silstra let you stay up this late."

"She doesn't know," Nalla returned as she was leaving. "She was watching the baby."

"Well, Sula, then."

"*She* was making bread," Zelar said, rolling his eyes.

After they had left, Zenor helped Nuella into the saddle he and Terregar had constructed specially for her. He strapped her in tight.

"No flying upside down this time," he chided her.

"It musses up my hair," Nuella responded, not—Zenor noted—necessarily ceding to his request.

"Bring her back," Zenor said to Nuellask. "She and I have more babies to make."

"Gladly!" Nuella responded with a laugh. "I want six, at least."

"Excellent," Zenor agreed, his eyes dancing.

"And Nuellask wants a few more clutches herself, I'm sure."

"Which is a good thing," Zenor said, "as it seems that your babies start with hers."

Nuella smiled and said nothing. Zenor gave her hand one last tight clasp and then released her, stepping well back from the watch-wher.

"Fly safe," he called fervently.

The gold watch-wher gave a loud cry, alerting all the other watch-whers in the compound, then sprang up into the air on her hind legs and disappeared *between*.

The night was silent, the air was still. Zenor shivered at the sudden cold.

The night air of Fort Weyr was torn by a cry Cisca had never heard before, but she reacted before she could think.

"Melirth!" she shouted as her eyes caught sight of the plummeting object. The great queen was airborne before any other dragon in the Weyr could respond, and swiftly brought herself up under the stricken flier.

Cisca grabbed a pot of numbweed automatically and raced across the Bowl. "K'lior!"

Alerted by her previous call, K'lior had already started toward her along with the rest of his wing's riders.

At the last possible moment, Melirth moved to let the injured flier tumble gently to the ground. Two cries of pain, one female, one draconic, filled the night air.

"It's Boll! You've got to come!" Nuella cried out as she heard the voices approaching. "The Thread is still alive! The air's too hot; the watch-whers are getting slaughtered."

Rineth! K'lior's call was all that was needed.

Cisca clenched her jaw tightly as she caught sight of Nuella's back, Thread-scored to the bone from right shoulder to left pelvis. The score continued on the left side of the gold watch-wher.

Get the healer here, Cisca told her dragon, oblivious to the sounds of the dragonriders forming up. She took a dab of numbweed and gently smeared it down the length of Nuella's burn.

Nuella hissed first in pain, then relief. "Please, how bad is Nuellask? She says she isn't hurt much but . . ."

"You took most of the score yourself," K'lior announced as he joined his mate. Tintoval and Fiona rushed up, with Xhinna following slightly behind them.

"Always the rider, never the dragon," Cisca added in a mixture of exasperation and admiration.

"We have to go back," Nuella said, trying to find the buckles that strapped her to her watch-wher.

"You're not going anywhere," Cisca pronounced. "Except maybe to bed."

"We'll take it from here, Nuella," K'lior reassured her.

"No!" Nuella said. "You can't see the Thread, your dragons can't see the Thread, it's too dark. Only the watch-whers can see the Thread, and they scattered when we got hurt.

"We've got to go back, to rally them and get them to point out the Thread for your dragons," she finished, struggling feebly.

Cisca and K'lior exchanged looks.

"Your watch-wher is not hurt too badly," K'lior said consideringly. "She could guide us."

"No, you'll need me, too," Nuella said. "Nuellask needs me to help her get the watch-whers under control."

Cisca made up her mind and reached for the buckles of Nuella's saddle. "If that's the case, there's no time to lose," she said. "You'll fly with me."

She turned to K'lior. "Go on, we'll be along presently."

"But the queens shouldn't fly!" K'lior protested as Melirth moved closer to her rider.

"*This* one is," Cisca declared, unbuckling the last of Nuella's straps and helping the WherMaster out of her saddle. She turned to Fiona, her eyes flashing in the night air and the younger Weyrwoman nodded in reluctant acceptance of the unspoken request—that if anything should happen to Cisca or Melirth, Fiona would continue on regardless.

"You'll be all right," Fiona declared staunchly, adding, "Talenth and I will guard the Weyr while you're away."

Cisca grabbed Fiona in a quick, grateful hug before releasing her and turning back to Nuella.

"You'll ride behind me," she said, as she guided Nuella toward Melirth.

"That's fine," Nuella told her, trying not to wince as the torn leather of her flying gear rubbed against her wound. "With your eyes, I won't have to worry about Thread."

K'lior and the dragonriders of Fort Weyr arrived over Southern Boll Hold in darkness. K'lior ordered the Weyr to hold in place, waiting for his eyes to adjust. He had just started to make out the watch-whers in their desperate fight against Thread when Melirth burst from *between.*

Cisca wants to know what are you waiting for? Rineth relayed, getting Cisca's impatient tone down pat.

We can't see, K'lior responded.

Cisca says that the watch-whers will see for us, Rineth said, sounding confused. *Nuella suggests assigning a half-wing to each watch-wher.*

Precious moments were lost as the plan was implemented. The first watch-wher bolted *between* when it found itself guidon for over half a dozen flaming dragons, but it soon returned, giving the dragons a partly apologetic, partly challenging *blerp* and directing them toward another clump of Thread.

Even with the watch-whers guiding them to the clumps, the night fight was awful. Dragon after dragon bellowed in pain as unseen Thread scored and they ducked *between.* Some did not return.

The watch-whers fared worse. K'lior soon learned not to wince at the painful high-pitched scream of a fatally Threaded watch-wher.

Nuellask was everywhere, rallying the watch-whers, chiding the dragons, chewing Thread. She paid the price for her leadership and several times bellowed in pain before going *between* to rid herself of Thread.

When Nuella at last relayed that the Thread had moved on to fall over the sea, where it would drown, K'lior gratefully gave the orders to return to the Weyr.

Tell Nuellask that all injured watch-whers should follow us, K'lior added. *And remind me to send a sweep wing to look for burrows in the morning.*

For all their work, K'lior was certain that Thread had fallen through to the ground in the darkness. He shuddered at the thought of what the ground might look like in the morning.

Take us to the Hold, Rineth, K'lior said. *I must speak with the Lord Holder.*

Contrary to K'lior's fears, Lord Egremer was effusive with his praise of the dragons and their riders.

"We'll have ground crews out at first light, I promise," he said. He looked nervously northward, toward where Thread had fallen. "How bad is it, do you suppose?"

K'lior shook his head. "We did our best," he said. "But the warm weather meant that every Thread was alive. The watch-whers were overwhelmed and we'd never trained with them, so our coordination was lousy."

Lady Yvala's eyes grew wide with alarm.

"We'll have sweepriders out at first light," K'lior promised. "As soon as we see anything, we'll let you know."

"I'd hate to lose the stands of timber to the north," Lord Egremer said. "They're old enough to be harvested, but I was hoping to hold off until mid-Pass, when we'll really be needing the wood."

K'lior nodded. "We'll do our best."

"And we're grateful for all that you've done," Egremer replied.

Wearily, K'lior mounted Rineth and directed him home.

The morning dawned gray, cold, and cloudy. Even Cisca was subdued.

"The reports are in from T'mar on sweep," she said as she nudged K'lior awake, handing him a mug of steaming *klah*. K'lior raised an eyebrow inquiringly. Cisca made a face. "Five burrows."

K'lior groaned. Cisca made a worse face and K'lior gave her a go-on gesture.

"Two are well-established. They'll have to fire the timber stands."

K'lior sat up, taking a long sip of his *klah*. He gave Cisca a measuring look, then asked, "Casualties?"

Cisca frowned. "Between the illness and Thread, twenty-three have gone *between*. F'dan and P'der will be laid up with injuries for at least six months. Troth, Piyeth, Kaderth, Varth, and Bidanth are all seriously injured and will also take at least six months to heal. There are eleven other riders or dragons with injuries that will keep them from flying for the next three months."

"So, we've what—seventy dragons and riders fit to fly?"

"Seventy-five," Cisca corrected. "And we've got over three seven-

days before our next Fall. I'm sure that we'll have more dragons fit
to fly by then."

"Three sevendays is not enough time," K'lior grumbled, rising
from their bed and searching out some clothes.

"No, you don't," Cisca said sharply, getting up and pushing
him toward the baths. "You smell. You're getting bathed before
you do anything else."

K'lior opened his mouth to protest, but Cisca silenced him with
a kiss.

"If you're nice," she teased, "I may join you."

K'lior tried very hard to be nice.

Lord Holder Egremer scowled at the line of smoke in the distance. Forty Turns' worth of growth, gone. Three whole valleys
had been put to flames before the dragonriders and ground crews
could declare Southern Boll Hold free from Thread.

The rains would come soon and the burnt land would lose all its
topsoil. He could expect floods to ravage the remnants of those
valleys. In the end, there might be a desert where once there had
been wide forests.

It would be worse for his holders. They had expected years of
work and income culling the older trees, planting new, and working the wood into fine pieces of furniture. Now Southern Boll
would be dependent upon its pottery, spices, and the scant foodstuffs it could raise for its trade with the other Holds.

The Hold would take Turns to recover.

"I'm sorry, Egremer," a disconsolate K'lior repeated. "If there's
anything the Weyr can do to help—"

Egremer sighed and turned back to the Weyrleader. K'lior was a
good ten Turns younger than himself, and while Egremer wanted
desperately to blame someone, he knew that it would be unfair to
blame the dragonrider.

He forced a smile. "I appreciate that, K'lior," he replied. "And
there might be more that you can do than you know."

K'lior gave him an inquiring look.

"If I could have the loan of a weyrling or two, to help scout out
the damage and maybe haul some supplies . . ."

"Weyrlings we have a-plenty," K'lior said. He shook his head. "It's full-grown dragons that are scarce."

"I'd heard that your losses are high from the illness," Egremer replied. "Is there anything we can do for you, Weyrleader?"

For a moment, K'lior made no reply, staring off into space, thinking.

"Nothing," he said at last, angrily. "You can't give us more mature dragons, or heal our wounded more quickly."

Egremer's face drained. "How long do we have, then?"

K'lior's face grew ashen. "Fort is lucky. We don't have another Threadfall in the next three sevendays. We'll probably be able to fight that," he answered, adding with a shake of his head, "but I can't say about the next Fall."

The despair that gripped the Weyrleader was palpable. Egremer looked for some words of encouragement to give him but could find none. It was K'lior who spoke next, pulling himself erect and willing a smile back on to his face.

"We'll find a way, Lord Egremer," he declared with forced cheer. "We're dragonriders, we always find a way." He nodded firmly and then said to Egremer, "Now, if you'll excuse me . . ."

"Certainly!" Egremer replied. "I'll see you out. And don't worry about those weyrlings, if it's too much bother. Having them would only save us time."

K'lior stopped so suddenly that Egremer had to swerve to avoid bumping into him.

"Time!" K'lior shouted exultantly. He turned to Egremer and grabbed him on both shoulders. "That's it! Time! We need time."

Egremer smiled feebly, wondering if the dragon's sickness could affect riders as well. K'lior just as suddenly let go of the Lord Holder and raced out of the Hold.

"Thank you, Lord Egremer, you've been most helpful," he called as he climbed up to his perch on Rineth.

"Any time, Weyrleader," Egremer called back, not at all certain what he had done, but willing to use the Weyrleader's good cheer to elevate that of his holders rather than depress them more by looking at the Weyrleader as if he were mad.

"Cisca, it's time!" K'lior yelled up from the Bowl to their quarters as soon as he returned *between* from Southern Boll. "That's what we need, time!"

Cisca stepped up to the ledge in Melirth's quarters and peered down to K'lior. "Of course we need time," she agreed, mostly to humor him.

"No, no, no," K'lior shouted back. "The weyrlings and the injured riders—they all need *time* to grow and recover."

"Make sense, K'lior," Cisca returned irritably.

K'lior took a deep breath and gave her a huge smile. "We'll time it. Send them back in time somewhere so—"

"So they can recover!" Cisca finished with a joyful cry and a leap. "K'lior, that's brilliant!"

"There's only one place we can go," K'lior told the assembled wingleaders. "Igen. It's the only Weyr that's empty. And we can't go back too far—we don't want to have to worry about the Plague."

"I'd recommend going back ten Turns," Tintoval, who was there at Cisca's invitation, said.

"Why not just three?" M'valer asked querulously.

"Three gives no margin for error," Tintoval replied.

The bronze riders exchanged looks, and K'lior said, "Ten Turns, then."

"If this works, won't you want to offer the same chance to the other Weyrs?" Tintoval asked.

"It makes sense," Cisca said. "But there's no reason we can't have an overlap."

"Not with D'gan," T'mar murmured. M'valer glared at him, but before he could say anything, M'kury said with a smirk, "No, indeed!"

"No one knows if this is going to work, anyway," H'nez said. K'lior glanced sourly in his direction—H'nez had been late in joining the fight the night before.

"That's why we're going to try it ourselves before we suggest it to the other Weyrs," K'lior said. He grimaced. "It's a pity we've only got twelve weyrlings able to go *between*."

"But we've got seventy-seven injured riders and dragons who can manage," Cisca pointed out. "Together, that will give us nearly three full Flights of dragons."

"*If* they survive," H'nez reminded her. "If something happens to them—"

"Then we'll be just as shorthanded as we are now," Cisca cut him off.

K'lior turned to T'mar. "When can you be ready?"

"In two hours," T'mar replied. "When do you need us back?"

"Excuse me," H'nez said, "but I think I should be the one to go."

K'lior turned to him with a raised brow.

"I've had the most experience leading Flights of dragons; I'll be the best at training them and handling their injuries," H'nez explained.

"T'mar is handling the weyrlings now," K'lior said. "And the decision as to who goes is mine."

H'nez flushed angrily. "Then pick me."

K'lior eyed him with distaste for a moment, then turned his attention back to T'mar. "The healer will need to stay here."

T'mar nodded in agreement.

"Weyrleader!" H'nez snapped through gritted teeth. All eyes turned to him. "If you will not let me lead the Flight back to Igen, then I demand that you send me to another Weyr."

"H'nez!" M'valer gasped.

K'lior merely nodded. "I can not send you until this illness has been cured," he told H'nez. "At that time, however, you may go to any Weyr that will have you. In the meantime, as we have more wingleaders than wings, you are to fly in M'kury's wing."

H'nez nodded stiffly, rose from his chair, and rushed out of the room, ignoring K'rall's and M'valer's outraged expressions.

"I could go," Fiona spoke up in the silence that followed H'nez's dramatic exit. Everyone looked at her. "I know some healing and I'm a Weyrwoman."

T'mar smiled kindly at her, shaking his head. "Talenth is too young to go *between*."

"Three Turns is a long time for the Weyr to wait for its next queen," M'kury said, glancing at the other riders.

Cisca pursed her lips and shook her head. "We can't risk losing the only other queen we have."

"If Talenth were older, able to go *between,* I'd be happy to send you," K'lior said. He shook his head. "As it is, I can't allow it."

"They're going back in time?" Xhinna repeated in surprise when Fiona filled her in later as they were oiling Talenth. "And that will work?"

"No one knows," Fiona said. "But they hope so."

"How will they know how to get there?"

Fiona smiled. "They're going to use the Red Star as a guide."

"The Red Star?"

"Yes, they'll fly to Igen in our time, sight the Red Star in the Star Stones, and work out what the image should be for ten Turns back," Fiona told her.

"And when they come back, they'll be three Turns older?" Xhinna said, grappling with the thought.

"In three days, they'll be three Turns older," Fiona agreed, her tone wistful. "T'mar's leading them."

There! Talenth cried as Fiona found a particularly itchy part. Fiona smiled indulgently and scrubbed harder with her oily rag. *Oh, that's much better!*

"When we're done oiling Talenth, Cisca wants us to meet with Tintoval and make a chest of medicinal supplies," Fiona said.

"What if something goes wrong?" Xhinna asked. "What if they don't come back?"

Fiona shook her head. "In that case, we'll think of something."

"There are two more sick dragons today," Xhinna noted darkly.

"That brings the total up to eighteen," Fiona said, pursing her lips tightly. "And two more dragons went *between.*" She'd lost track of how many dragons had succumbed to the illness; she knew it was over fifty, but she couldn't say by how much. More became ill every day.

"Even if everything goes well, there will be less than two full Flights of dragons."

"I know, Xhinna," Fiona replied, grimacing. "We just have to do what we can."

"I heard that the Benden Weyr healer's dragon went *between* today."

Fiona nodded. Cisca had sent her after breakfast to check on Tintoval; the healer had known K'tan—no, Ketan—it had been his recommendation that had sent her to the Harper Hall.

"How do you bear it?" Xhinna asked, glancing over from her place near Talenth's neck, her oiling temporarily forgotten. She gestured to Talenth. "How can you stand the thought of losing her?"

"I *won't* lose her," Fiona declared. She patted Talenth forcefully. "No matter what happens, I won't lose you."

Talenth chirped happily. *I love you.*

"I wish I were going to Igen," Xhinna said wistfully. "I'd like to be away from all this for three Turns."

"You could ask T'mar," Fiona said, though her heart wasn't in it. Xhinna shook her head. "I'll stay with you."

"I think Talenth's all done for now," Fiona said, leaning back from her place over Talenth's itchy patch. "Let's go find Tintoval."

The sun was well past its zenith when all the arrangements were complete and the riders and dragons were arrayed in the chilly Bowl, ready to go to Igen and back ten Turns in time. In the end, after much discussion, it was decided that T'mar should take only the forty-seven most lightly injured dragons and riders, as well as the older weyrlings. It would be too dangerous for the thirty more seriously injured dragonpairs to make the leap *between* times, a point that Fiona emphasized in her discussions with F'jian and the other disgruntled young weyrlings.

"Fly well," K'lior called to the assembled riders. From perches on high, the rest of the dragons of Fort Weyr looked on.

"I'll see you in three days," Tajen said as he helped T'mar settle the last of his gear on Zirenth's neck. "Try not to get too tanned."

T'mar laughed and waved his farewell. Tajen stepped back, joining K'lior, Cisca, Fiona, and the others. T'mar turned on his perch, making one final assessment of his charges, then raised his arm and pumped his fist in the ancient signal to ascend.

Sixty dragons leapt into the air and beat their wings, climbing up out of the Bowl to array themselves near the Star Stones, with T'mar's Zirenth in the van. They remained there for one more instant and then were gone, *between.*

Dinner that evening was subdued. Fiona kept Xhinna near her for company. Kentai arranged for the children to sing during the meal, which should have lifted everyone's spirits but even the spritely "Morning Dragon Song" seemed only to punctuate the fact that T'mar and nearly ninety other riders—including those whose dragons were too ill—weren't sharing the meal with the rest of the weyr.

Three Turns, Fiona mused as she ate without speaking. What would T'mar be like then? All her vague, half-formed images of the bronze rider blurred and dimmed; she'd already known he was too old for her, and these added three Turns just emphasized that difference. If she'd entertained any hopes of a deeper relationship someday, those hopes were now dashed.

As she and Xhinna walked back to their quarters after dinner, F'jian and J'nos caught up with them.

"It's not fair," F'jian complained. "They should have let us go, too!"

"Look on the bright side," Fiona said to him. "At least now you're the senior weyrling."

F'jian paused in his surprise. But then, after a long moment, he declared, "I'd still prefer to go to Igen with the others." .

"We can't even ride our dragons yet," J'nos reminded him. "How could we survive going *between* times?"

F'jian didn't reply, his face set in a stubborn look. "If you could go, you would, wouldn't you, Weyrwoman?" he asked.

Fiona pursed her lips and hesitated before answering. "I wouldn't risk Talenth for it."

"But if it wasn't a risk, what then?" F'jian persisted.

"And is staying here, with the illness, any less of a risk?" J'nos added.

"It doesn't matter," Fiona said with a shrug. She drew herself up haughtily, remembering her responsibility to set the example and grateful that she had the height on the two weyrlings. "We can't go, so our job is to make the best of what we can do, not moan about what we can't."

F'jian sighed. "I suppose you're right." His expression brightened. "Can the weyrlings practice gliding again tomorrow?"

"We'll have to ask Tajen," Fiona said, "but I see no problem."

"And we'll have to practice bagging firestone by ourselves," Xhinna said eagerly.

"We've pretty much been doing that already," J'nos replied.

"The others will be back long before the next Fall," F'jian reminded Xhinna.

Xhinna grimaced.

They reached the weyrling barracks, and the two weyrlings waved their good-byes. Fiona and Xhinna trudged along in silence, lost in their own thoughts until they reached the weyr.

I wish I could go, too, Talenth said, peering out of her weyr as they climbed the slope up to the queens' ledge.

"I know," Fiona said aloud, pausing long enough to scratch Talenth's eye ridges. "Our time will come."

Behind her, Fiona could sense Xhinna's wistful gaze. She turned to her and beckoned for Xhinna to come to Talenth's other side. For several minutes both girls were engrossed in indulging the young queen. The moment was broken when Xhinna failed to stifle a yawn and Fiona found herself unconsciously echoing her an instant later.

Grinning, Fiona said, "I guess we need to get some sleep."

Go! Talenth urged them, butting first Fiona and then Xhinna toward their quarters. The gold dragon curled up but did not put her head under her wing in her usual sleeping posture. Fiona noticed and Talenth told her, *I will go to sleep soon. I want to think.*

Since when did dragons spend time thinking, Fiona mused as she changed into her nightclothes and crawled into bed. And what did they think about? she wondered just before sleep overwhelmed her.

Fiona woke, suddenly alert. Xhinna lay beside her, a comforting bundle of warmth, her breathing deep and steady. Without turning her head, she glanced toward Talenth's weyr.

The queen was awake, alert, her gaze intent on something outside in the Bowl.

Fiona. The voice wasn't Talenth's, but Fiona felt she recognized it. Slowly, cautiously, she eased her way out of bed, still not certain that she wasn't imagining things. Sliding her feet into her slippers, she picked up her robe from its place beside the bed and tiptoed away.

Talenth turned her head toward her, then back out to the Bowl, eyes whirling rapidly.

What is it? Fiona asked.

She wants us to come with her, Talenth told her.

The night air was cold, frozen, quiet, expectant. Fiona found herself warming her nose with the fingers of her left hand as she crept into Talenth's weyr and peered out into the snow-covered Bowl. Flecks of snow drifted down steadily, adding to the carpet already covering the ground.

Fiona scanned the snow-muffled stillness for a long moment before she spotted a darker shape—a dragon. By her size, she was a queen.

Fiona glanced at the shape for another moment before turning decisively to walk down the queens' ledge—she never considered jumping down as she usually did, feeling somehow that it was inappropriate.

As she got closer, she made out another shape, a human, standing close beside the dragon.

"Get dressed," the rider said as Fiona approached. "We must be quick. We can't wake the others."

Something about the rider seemed familiar. "Why? Where are we going?"

"Igen." The word was like a challenge and Fiona shivered, feeling her heart lurch.

"I can't leave Talenth."

"She comes, too," the rider said. "And the weyrlings." The rider glanced toward the barracks. "They're coming now."

Fiona glanced toward the barracks but saw nothing. Who was this woman?

"We have to hurry: They need to see you and Talenth go or they won't follow."

"Follow?"

"They need to come with you to Igen."

"How do you know?" Fiona asked, a sudden thrill of suspicion running down her spine.

"It's happened already," the rider told her.

Fiona gasped as realization struck her. "You're from the future!"

The rider nodded. "You must hurry."

Fiona darted back inside and pulled on her clothes as quickly as she could. When she returned, she suddenly realized that Xhinna had slept through the commotion.

"Xhinna," she cried. "I need to—"

"She stays," the rider declared in a tone that brooked no argument.

A figure raced into sight from the direction of the Living Caverns.

"You may come," the rider said as the figure resolved itself into the form of Terin.

Talenth crept out of her weyr and, with a furtive glance toward Melirth's quarters, hopped down from her ledge.

"We can't go *between*," Fiona protested. "And Talenth is too young to carry my weight."

"You'll ride with me," the rider told her. "As for *between* . . . you'll have to trust me."

Two shapes appeared from the direction of the weyrling barracks. F'jian and J'nos.

"Hurry!" the rider told Fiona, racing back and mounting her dragon. She leaned a hand down to Fiona. "I know *when* we're going!"

"Talenth will be safe, won't she?" Fiona asked, her voice catching.

"My word on it," the rider told her, grasping Fiona's hand and pulling her up. "Quickly, they must see us go *between*."

Talenth!

I have the image, I can see where to go, the little queen told her calmly.

"Doesn't she have to be flying?" Fiona asked the rider in front of her worriedly.

"Talenth, jump!" the rider said in response. At the same time, the queen they were riding leapt into the air. Fiona only had a moment's glimpse of Talenth jumping after them, and then she was engulfed in the greater darkness of *between*.

Talenth! Fiona called frantically.

I am here, Talenth assured her calmly. *We are fine.*

It will be longer than normal, we are going back in time, Fiona heard the rider say.

Don't you need to go to Igen now first?

I've already been there, the rider replied, her voice certain.

Who was this person? Fiona wondered. Who rode a gold and could bring them back in time?

A growing sense of wonder overcame her as she considered the most obvious answer: Could this be Fiona herself, come back from the future?

TWELVE

A sea of sand,
Harsh clime for man.
Mountains rise high,
Igen Weyr is nigh.

Igen Weyr, Morning, AL 498.7.2

The cold, black nothing of *between* was suddenly replaced by heat
and a bright sun.

Whee! Talenth cried delightedly. *Look how high I am!*

Fiona glanced over and saw that Talenth was indeed nearly
twice as high as she'd ever been before. *Careful! Just glide down.*

Okay, Talenth said, sounding disappointed. Nevertheless, the
young queen glided carefully down into the strange Bowl beneath
them.

"This is Igen Weyr," the strange rider called.

"It's awfully warm," Fiona said. "I thought it would be cold and
windy, even here."

"We are slightly more than ten Turns back in time," the rider
replied with a hint of humor in her voice. "I thought you'd prefer
to start with warmer weather. This is the second day of the seventh month of the four hundred and ninety-eighth Turn since
Landing."

The gold touched down and the rider turned to Fiona, the

bright morning sun rising behind her casting her face in shadow. "Get down."

Fiona obeyed reflexively and was surprised to see the rider and dragon leap skyward as soon as she'd found her feet. In an instant they were gone, *between*.

There's no one here, Talenth declared, peering around the sandswept Weyr.

Fiona wheeled slowly around on her heel, scanning the Bowl and the weyrs carved into its walls.

Where were T'mar, the injured riders, and the older weyrlings?

Fiona felt a moment of panic as she wondered if she'd somehow been betrayed, misled by an unknown rider and purposely abandoned here with a dragon too young to fly. She spotted a canvas-covered mound not too far away and walked over to it.

As she approached, she realized it had been recently erected. She lifted up a flap and saw crates and barrels—supplies of some sort.

So at least she doesn't mean me to starve, Fiona thought hopefully.

She turned around, scanning the abandoned Weyr. The air was hot and getting hotter, smelling of sand and roasted dust. Overhead the sun was intense even though only still rising, already beating down unyieldingly.

The floor and sides of the Bowl were of a different stone than she had expected, accustomed to the stark whiteness of Fort Weyr. This Weyr was carved into orange rock. Fiona knelt and picked up some loose earth in her hand; it was sandy, fine, and dusty, unlike the packed ground of Fort's Bowl.

Aside from the canvas mound of supplies, the Weyr had a forlorn, abandoned feel to it.

Fiona turned around again slowly, scanning for the queen's quarters, searching for the entrance to the Hatching Grounds, the location of the Kitchen Cavern, the weyrling barracks—and suddenly the Weyr was alive to her, she felt the stone in her blood, felt the warm welcome of the hot sun and the fine sand.

This could be home.

A sudden rustle above her caused Fiona to crane her neck upward. A clutch of dragons burst forth from *between*, with the gold in the lead. Fiona saw F'jian mounted on his bronze Ladirth, looking both terrified and thrilled at the same time as his dragon glided down quickly to the ground.

Talenth, watch out! Fiona called, fearful lest one of the inexperienced riders or dragons come crashing down on her. Talenth scurried to the side of the Bowl and Fiona scampered after her a moment later.

"Did you see us?" F'jian shouted as soon as his Ladirth came to a halt. "We flew!"

"We only glided," J'nos corrected him as he slid down Pilenth's foreleg onto the ground. He stood beside his brown, patting him loudly, a broad grin splitting his face from ear to ear. "But we went *between*!"

"If we hadn't seen you do it, we wouldn't have dared to try," F'jian said to Fiona in awe.

"Where is everyone else?" J'nos asked, peering expectantly around the Weyr.

"I wonder," Fiona mused, "if she could bring you back, could she bring back the more severely injured riders and dragons too?"

The other weyrlings gathered around them, all wondering the same thing.

"We should ask the queen rider," Fiona said, gesturing to the far side of the Bowl where the huge gold dragon had alighted.

"Who is she, anyway?" F'jian asked.

"And we won't get in trouble, will we?" J'nos wondered anxiously. "After all, she's a queen rider."

"Let's ask her," F'jian said. Fiona nodded in agreement and found herself leading the others toward the Weyrwoman and her queen dragon.

"Hello!" she shouted, feeling alarmed as she sensed that dragon and rider were preparing to go *between* once more. "Can you bring back the other injured dragons and riders?"

"For that I'll need help," the woman returned.

"I don't think that we could give you any help," Fiona began reluctantly, gesturing to the dragonets. "They're too small; it's a wonder they managed to get here at all."

"Oh, it's no wonder," the gold rider replied in amused tones. "And I'm sure you'll be able to help with what needs doing."

Before Fiona could respond, the queen dragon leapt into the air, beat its wings once, and disappeared *between*.

It seemed only a moment later that she reappeared and the air was full of dragons—gold, bronze, brown, blue, green—all guiding or aiding injured dragons and riders to settle upon the warm sands of Igen Bowl.

Fiona felt dizzy and swayed where she stood, even as one of the queen riders laughed and waved merrily in her direction.

"Are you all right?" J'nos asked, grabbing her and propping her upright.

"I think it's just the heat," Fiona replied, looking around for the gold rider who had first brought her here. "We should go thank her."

But before they'd gone half a dragonlength, a gold dragon leapt into the air and was gone, *between*. Fiona heard the loud rush of many wings, and suddenly the weyr was empty of all save the weyrlings and the injured dragonpairs from Fort Weyr.

"Where'd they go?" J'nos cried.

"Who was she?" F'jian demanded.

Fiona shook her head. "I don't know."

The others took this news in slowly, muttering amongst themselves.

"You don't think it's a trick or something, do you?" F'jian asked after a while.

"We're here—she did what she said she would," Fiona said. "Besides, she rode a queen."

The woman had never claimed to be a Weyrwoman—but she must have been one. Who else but a Weyrwoman could ride a queen?

"What are we going to do?" J'nos asked, looking around with growing alarm.

"*You* are going to go over to the weyrling barracks and start cleaning them," Fiona told him sternly. "The Weyrwoman said that this is Turn four ninety-eight, so this Weyr has been abandoned for nearly seven Turns—you'd best watch for tunnel snakes."

"Tunnel snakes!" J'nos blanched. "I don't know how to handle tunnel snakes!"

"If you find any, let me know," Fiona told him. When the brown rider's eyes bugged out, she explained, "I used to hunt them back at my father's Hold."

Fiona was surprised and pleased by the hushed exclamations of the other weyrlings as this news spread.

She turned to F'jian. "Get some others to help stow what's under that canvas in the Kitchen Cavern. Send in a detail first to be sure there are no tunnel snakes there, either."

F'jian nodded and started calling out names, while moving toward the canvas-covered mound.

"And send another group to see to the older riders and dragons; we'll need to get them out of the heat."

Fiona wondered if hot, dusty Igen Weyr might have other dangers than tunnel snakes. She dismissed the worry, telling herself that the weyrlings would report anything out of the ordinary.

They had been working for about a quarter of an hour when the air above them was once again filled with dragons. Fiona glanced up and waved, her face splitting into a huge grin—part from relief and part in reaction to the evident astonishment of the riders flying above.

T'mar had arrived.

Talenth, tell Ladirth and Polenth that we need everyone out here to help with the injured riders.

I told them; they're coming, Talenth replied promptly.

Fiona made a face as she berated herself for not already detailing a crew to clean out weyrs for the injured riders.

F'jian joined her, glancing up as the injured dragons and riders made hasty landings. "Most of the supplies are medicines and bandages," he told her.

"No food?" Fiona asked, frowning.

F'jian pursed his lips and shook his head. "Some *klah* bark, some herbals, but nothing to eat."

Fiona frowned in turn, then dismissed the worry. "Get the weyrlings to help these injured riders. Put them in the weyrling barracks for the moment—just to get them out of the sun."

A shadow passed low overhead and Zirenth landed nearby. "What are you doing here?" T'mar shouted.

"When did you leave?" T'mar demanded, leaping down beside Terin, who had just returned, breathless, with a flask of water.

"Late at night after you left," Fiona said. She had been too eager when the mysterious queen rider had made her amazing offer to consider how T'mar would react, and once she'd arrived at Igen, she'd been too busy organizing the weyrlings to think about it anymore.

"F'jian and the other weyrlings are here, too," she told him, partly to give T'mar all the news at once and partly in hopes that he might be distracted by the information.

"How did you get here?" he repeated, reaching out to grab Fiona's shoulders with both arms, as if to assure himself that she was real.

"The Weyrwoman brought us," Fiona said.

"*What* Weyrwoman?" T'mar demanded. "Not Cisca?"

Fiona shook her head.

"Then who?"

"I don't know," Fiona told him honestly. "She never gave me her name."

T'mar frowned, looking deep into Fiona's eyes. "It wasn't you, was it?"

"From the future?" Fiona asked.

"No, you on your own!" T'mar exclaimed. "How could anyone know to come from the future?"

Fiona's temper rose. "*Anyone* from the future would know! If it's been done, then they'd know, wouldn't they?"

"And they brought you here, conveniently, before we arrived," T'mar said, his tone simmering near the boil.

"And they got us some supplies," Fiona said, gesturing to the remains of the mound that the weyrlings had mostly stored.

"Supplies?" T'mar repeated, brows creased in a frown.

"Mostly medicine and bandages," Fiona said. "The weyrlings will be storing it in the Living Cavern once J'nos has finished checking for tunnel snakes."

"Tunnel snakes?"

Fiona's lips turned up in a quick grin as she confided, "I don't think he'll find any, but I told him to keep an eye out for them. "

"This Weyr's been abandoned so long, there probably *are* tunnel snakes," T'mar said in a tone that indicated he hadn't considered the possibility himself.

"Well, there probably aren't any in the Living Cavern; we would have heard J'nos's shriek by now," Fiona said. Seeing

T'mar's thoughtful look, she pressed on. "And I've got another party clearing the weyrling barracks. We're putting the injured dragons and riders in there until we can clear out some weyrs."

"Weyrwoman Fiona, what are you doing here?" someone called in surprise from the gathering throng of dismounting riders. Fiona recognized J'keran, one of the older weyrlings.

"Same as you," she told him with a grin. "Are you ready to start cleaning?"

"Cleaning?"

"Unless you were planning on sleeping out here in the Bowl," T'mar said.

"Get over to the weyrling barracks," Fiona said. "F'jian's got some of the younger weyrlings working there already, but I'm sure they'll benefit from the oversight of more mature riders."

"I'm on it!" J'keran said, looking relieved at the notion of ordering around the younger weyrlings.

"I'll be by to check that everyone's working," Fiona warned him. She turned to Terin, saying, "Terin, I want you to take stock of the supplies, then see how they're coming with the weyrling barracks." Terin nodded. "As soon as you're done with that, find F'jian and get a crew to clear out the Hatching Grounds—there really might be tunnel snakes there, so have everyone be careful and send in some of the smaller greens."

"Send in the greens," Terin repeated to herself, then nodded and trotted off to the Living Cavern to start her chores.

"Hatching Grounds?"

"I was thinking that for the time being it would be quicker to clear than individual weyrs," Fiona said.

"Good thought."

"And I don't know about you, but I didn't bring any bedding," Fiona continued. From the look on T'mar's face, it was obvious that the wingleader hadn't thought of it either. Fiona hid her surprise, asking, "Did you bring any food?"

T'mar shrugged, shaking his head.

"Well, then we're going to get hungry."

"T'mar," a rider called from the distance, "should we post a watch dragon?"

"Of course! But not you, P'der, you need to rest," T'mar replied.

"I can rest as easily up there," P'der said.

"No, you cannot!" Fiona shouted at him. "You are going to get well and that means you are going to rest or Cisca and K'lior will have my head!"

"Fiona?" P'der called, squinting to better see her. "What are you doing here?"

"Keeping you from doing something stupid," Fiona returned tartly. She searched around for one of the weyrlings and beckoned him over. "P'der here is recovering from serious injuries to his neck and back," she told him. "He's to rest, lying on his stomach." She frowned, thinking about how to treat the stubborn scores that had nearly flayed the man. "If he has to sit up, he's to sit with his chair reversed." The weyrling looked from her to P'der, Klior's wingsecond, to T'mar, then back to Fiona, and she gave him an irritated growl. "Once he's settled, see Terin and find some numbweed. If there's only reeds, then set a pot to boil—we'll need a lot of it."

The weyrling blanched at the thought of making numbweed, a smelly, difficult job that all weyrfolk avoided if at all possible.

"We're just here to get older, D'lanor," she told him with a reassuring smile. "These injured riders are here to get well. So it's our duty to look after them, eh?"

D'lanor replied with a hesitant smile of his own.

"P'der," Fiona said, cocking her head in the direction of the Living Cavern.

"Yes, Weyrwoman," P'der replied, and turned to follow the weyrling.

"So, Weyrwoman," T'mar said, stressing the title and smiling as he said it, "who should we set on watch?"

"That, wingleader, would be up to you, wouldn't it?" Fiona retorted. And, before he could respond, she turned briskly on her heel and headed over to the weyrling barracks.

An hour later, Fiona sat exhausted by a smoky hearth, taking her turn stirring a smelly pot full of numbweed grass. The air not only was full of the noxious fumes that made her eyes water and her nose run but was also stiflingly hot. Fiona resolved to herself that in future she would boil numbweed only in the cold of the night.

A noise behind her caused her to turn her head and she saw Terin approaching.

"The weyrling barracks are all clean," the younger girl reported. "The crew cleaning the Hatching Grounds will be done in another hour or so. I set a group to clearing out your quarters."

"My quarters?" Fiona repeated in surprise. Then her brow furrowed. "How did you manage to get them to obey you?"

"You're the senior Weyrwoman," Terin replied with no hint of duplicity. "I just made it clear to them that it's what you needed." She smiled as she added, "You know how it is with weyrlings; the boys practically fell over themselves to help."

"And, after all those firestone drills, they're used to following your orders," Fiona guessed.

"It's not like there are any other weyrfolk around," Terin agreed. "Shards, you and I are the only two women here!"

Fiona coughed and gestured to the exit into the Bowl. "We need to get out of here."

"I'll have J'keran get someone to take over," T'mar called from the entrance. He gave Fiona a sheepish look as she neared the entrance. "I'm sure that there has to be some weyrling who's earned it."

"Don't you dare!" Fiona cried, eyes widening angrily.

T'mar took a half-step back, his confusion evident.

"This numbweed is for everyone," Fiona told him. "*Everyone* works on it. I will not have people taking it as a punishment. What sort of numbweed do you think you'll get with an attitude like that?"

"I hadn't thought of that," T'mar confessed with a frown. "Very well—"

"Shall I set up a roster?" Terin offered.

"Yes," Fiona said with a firm nod. "Every person who's able will be on it—except for you."

"Why not me?" Terin asked, looking ashamed.

"Because you're going to be doing all the tallying around here," Fiona told her firmly.

"You'll be our Records keeper," T'mar told her with a suitably grave expression.

"Headwoman," Fiona corrected.

"Headwoman?" Terin and T'mar echoed in disbelief and surprise.

"Can you think of anyone else more qualified here?"

"I suppose not," T'mar admitted after a moment. He turned to Terin. "Headwoman it is."

"Me?" Terin squeaked.

"Yes, and you'd better get to that list; we don't want the numbweed to burn," Fiona said. With wide, serious eyes, Terin nodded and scuttled off. Fiona shouted after her, "And don't let anyone give you trouble!"

"I won't!" Terin called back over her shoulder, her pace increasing as she raced over to the weyrling barracks.

Talenth, Fiona called to her dragon, *where are you?*

I'm in the Hatching Grounds, Talenth said. *I'm helping scare the tunnel snakes away.*

Be careful! Fiona warned.

Of course, Talenth replied quickly, but Fiona could hear her dragon's disappointment.

She amended her warning: *If you get bit, let me know.*

Okay, Talenth replied more cheerfully. *Is that all?*

No, Fiona said, remembering the real reason she'd contacted her dragon. *I want you to tell all the dragons that Terin is headwoman.*

Okay, Talenth replied instantly. *They know.* A moment later, she added, *Zirenth thinks it's a good idea.*

"Your dragon thinks it's a good idea for Terin to be headwoman," Fiona reported to T'mar.

"I know," T'mar replied with a grin. "I told him."

A weyrling rushed up, ducked his head in acknowledgment of T'mar and even more in acknowledgment of Fiona. "I'm to stir the numbweed."

T'mar clapped the weyrling on the back and guided him into the Kitchen Cavern. "Let me show you how it's done." He turned back to Fiona as he pushed the weyrling forward, saying, "Would you wait here for me, Weyrwoman?"

"Okay," Fiona replied, surprised at T'mar's deferential tone. When he returned, he gestured for her to precede him out into the Bowl. Zirenth landed in front of them, turning his head toward them, his multifaceted eyes whirling with eagerness.

"I think it would be a good idea to familiarize ourselves with the surroundings before it gets dark," T'mar told her, gesturing for her to mount his bronze dragon. Moments later, Zirenth leapt into the sky, his huge wings beating steadily, slowly gaining altitude and clearing the Weyr Bowl.

"Shards!" T'mar exclaimed as he noticed the size of the gap between Zirenth's claws and the top of the Weyr. "I hadn't realized how much the heat would affect him."

"Why would it?"

"Hot air is thinner, so it requires more work to get the same height," T'mar told her. He reached past her and patted Zirenth's neck affectionately.

"We should probably warn the injured dragons not to strain themselves," Fiona said.

"Yes," T'mar agreed distractedly. His tone was more focused when he told her a moment later, "Done."

Zirenth found a good updraft into which he swerved to circle up high above the Weyr.

"I can see the sea," Fiona said, pointing off to the east.

"This land is so dry and hot," T'mar remarked worriedly.

"Does anything grow here?" Fiona wondered. "Wasn't that why Igen was abandoned?"

Fiona could feel T'mar behind her shaking his head. "The last Lord Holder made some poor choices in dealing with the drought and planted more thirsty crops rather than switching to those adjusted to more arid climes."

"My goodness! That answer was something I'd expect more from a harper than a dragonrider!"

Behind her, she felt him shrug. "Just as Lord Holders, we find it useful to keep abreast of things."

"I suppose we could fish," Fiona said, gazing westward over the uninviting terrain, "but I'm not sure that we'd catch enough to feed the Weyr."

"And it would get very dull," T'mar agreed. Zirenth dipped out of the thermal, gently curving his flight westward. "I think we can do better."

"But we can't get near the holders," Fiona protested. "We don't want the dragons near the fire-lizards."

"Why not?" T'mar asked. "The fire-lizards are not sick back in this time."

"And we don't want to risk them getting sick," Fiona pointed out. "But even if we could be absolutely sure that none of our dragons carries the illness, fire-lizards have the strangest memories, and we *don't* want them remembering us being here at Igen, in this time."

"Of course," T'mar agreed. "But I think that will be the least of our problems."

Fiona scanned the harsh landscape below and nodded. Zirenth turned eastward, back toward the Weyr.

"There has to be some place where the Weyr kept its herds," she said.

"Herds?" T'mar snorted. "How do you know they kept herds? It's just as likely that they fed directly out of the holders' stock, saving everyone the trouble of delivering livestock across *that*." He gestured to the badlands below him and then, just as suddenly, gave a startled grunt. Zirenth dove instantly, his motion surprising Fiona, who found herself grateful for T'mar's sudden tight hold on her waist.

"What's that?" the bronze rider asked, pointing to a dusty spot below.

"It looks like some workbeasts," Fiona said, raising one hand to shade her eyes as she peered against the harsh sunlight.

"Traders?" T'mar mused.

"Don't get too low, or Zirenth will have hard work getting us back to the Weyr," Fiona cautioned.

T'mar chuckled. "Just as long as he can get us high enough to go *between* we'll be fine."

Fiona said nothing in response, abashed that she hadn't thought of it herself.

"They look like they're heading for the Weyr," T'mar said as they got lower. "Six, maybe seven cargo drays and one house dray."

Fiona remembered trader caravans coming to Fort Hold when she was younger and her face lit up: They always brought strange and wonderful things, even for those used to the marvels that often came to the Harper and Healer Halls.

The house dray—which Fiona would have called the domicile

dray—was covered with bright decorations, and the front of all the drays were shaded with colorful canvas hoods. They looked much more gawdy than the ones she had seen before.

Her spirits fell as she had a new thought. "Traders trade. What will they want to trade with us?"

"We'll find something," T'mar declared.

"They must have started here some days back," Fiona said as they descended close enough for her to see how slowly the ponderous workbeasts were moving. "How did they know to come?"

"Perhaps the same person who guided you guided them," T'mar suggested. "We'll know soon enough."

A large man in the lead dray climbed up to the top of the wagon, waving in recognition of the dragon descending toward them. Fiona and T'mar were not surprised to see him signal the other drays to halt. As they circled lower, Fiona saw that what she thought was a seventh dray was actually four workbeasts harnessed together two by two.

"Let's not leave them in this heat long," she said as Zirenth nimbly touched down on the hot dusty ground. She immediately shucked off her jacket and wished she had worn cooler clothes. How were they going to survive this heat for the next three Turns?

T'mar leapt down first, turning back to hold his arms out to Fiona who, suppressing a grimace at his gallantry, fell into them and then pushed herself away as soon as her feet felt the earth beneath her. T'mar smiled and gestured toward the traders.

"Should we tell them about *timing* it?" Fiona whispered to T'mar as they trudged through the thick sand toward the first dray.

"Let's see if we can avoid it," he said in reply. A sudden thought made him add, "I wish we'd thought to have you wear your rank knot."

"You're wearing yours," Fiona said, thinking that should be enough. T'mar did not reply.

"T'mar, Zirenth's rider, and Fiona, Talenth's rider," he declared as the lead Trader approached.

"Well met," the man replied. Fiona was surprised to see how big the man was, taller than T'mar by a head and so broad-shouldered she thought he could easily lift one of the workbeasts single-handed.

"Azeez at your service," he said, bowing low to them. He ges-

tured toward his dray. "The sun is high; we would be more comfortable talking in the shade."

Fiona saw that the other traders had left their drays and were
trudging to the first one, climbing into the cabin from the back.

"We don't want to disturb you," T'mar said. "Especially in this
heat."

"This heat?" Azeez cocked his head up and peered at the sun
above. "This is not heat."

"We're from the north," Fiona said. "We're not used to such
heat."

"I can see that," Azeez agreed. "You are not dressed for it."

Fiona nodded politely, surreptitiously studying his clothing: he
wore long, flowing robes, and his head was topped with a piece of
cloth that draped down over his ears and neck and was tied into
place with a brightly colored piece of knotted rope.

"Traders learn to adapt to the climate," Azeez said, motioning
politely for them to precede him.

"Is there much here to trade?" T'mar asked.

"There is always trade," Azeez replied, his tone making Fiona
wonder if he was quoting some wise saying. They reached the
dray and Azeez beckoned for them to climb up. "It will be quicker
to go in through the front."

By courtesy Fiona went first, spending a moment locating the
doorway and its latch before she entered the dim cabin.

Voices stopped mid-word as she entered.

"Sit! Sit!" one of the traders urged her, pointing to a cushion just
beyond the door. Fiona sat quickly and was surprised to recognize
how relieved she felt when T'mar settled next to her—she felt
young and awkward, a feeling that increased as she glanced
around at the faces peering at her and realized that no one else
there was as young as she.

"I'm T'mar and this is Weyrwoman Fiona," T'mar said, nodding to the others.

"Fiona!" one of the traders exclaimed in surprise. "That's not a
common name."

"Lord Bemin's daughter is named Fiona, isn't she?" wondered
another trader, an old woman by the sound of her voice.

T'mar glanced at Fiona, and she could tell that he was thinking
that they would not be able to keep their origins hidden after all.

"I'm that Fiona," she said. "We are here from the future. But I think we should keep that a secret."

The traders began to talk excitedly amongst themselves until Azeez called them to order. Several of the traders—Fiona noticed the old woman in particular—appeared to find her claim unbelievable.

"Some of our dragons were injured fighting Thread and we've come back in time to speed their healing," Fiona said. "Do we have you to thank for the medicines we found at the Weyr?"

"We brought them," Azeez said cautiously, glancing sternly at the other traders.

"How can going back in time speed their healing?" the old woman demanded.

"It has to do with timing," Fiona began.

"—you must understand that this is highly confidential," T'mar interjected.

"It will take the same amount of time for their wounds to heal," Fiona continued, glaring at T'mar, "but while we hope to stay here for three Turns, we will return to our time only three days after we left."

" 'Healed and ready to fight,' " the old woman said, her tone indicating that she was repeating words she'd heard previously. She looked at the other traders, who shared glances and nodded to one another in some strange understanding that Fiona couldn't fathom.

"Three Turns, you say?" Azeez said, looking thoughtful.

"If this works, we'll tell the other Weyrs back in the future so that they can heal their injured, too," T'mar said.

"So they will come when you leave?" the old woman guessed.

"So we hope," Fiona told her. She swallowed hard, adding, "Things are not going well for us."

"The Weyrwoman who spoke to us earlier warned us that you would not accept the presence of fire-lizards," Azeez said, his eyes darting from Fiona to T'mar, gauging their reactions.

"I had to give up my fire-lizard," Fiona admitted bleakly.

"Can we trade on the future?" the old woman asked Azeez. "Isn't that worth more than treasure?"

"Excuse me," Fiona said irritably, "but it seems awfully awkward to be talking with people and not know their names."

The old woman glanced to Azeez, a smile crossing her lips fleetingly.

"Our pardon," Azeez said, inclining his head respectfully. He pointed to the old woman. "This is Mother Karina—I mean, Trader Karina—"

"I think you were right the first time," Fiona said, interrupting him. She glanced at the old woman, who sucked in a gasp of surprise and quickly dropped her eyes.

"'Dragonriders can always see lies,'" Karina said, glancing sourly at Azeez.

"Why are you called Mother?" Fiona asked, her tone polite but demanding. "It means more than just the word, and more than trader."

She sensed surprise and nervousness in the other traders.

"We traders of the desert are different from others," Karina explained. "We love our hot dry weather, we eat spicy hot food to cool us, we know how to travel from one oasis to another, how to survive when there is no water, what to do in a sandstorm—"

"Sandstorm?" T'mar repeated the unfamiliar word.

"Winds do not come over the mountains," Karina said, gesturing to the east, "but pick up from the south and west, sometimes blowing for thousands of kilometers, blowing all before them, including the sand."

"The wind can strip the hide off a person in minutes," Azeez said with a shudder.

"Even dragons are not safe," Karina warned them. "But you can go *between* when we cannot."

"What you describe sounds dangerous even to dragons," T'mar said. "I shall be certain to warn my riders. Thank you."

"I have met traders before who ride in brightly colored drays," Fiona said. "Would I have met any of you desert traders?"

"No, we prefer the plains of Igen and Keroon," Azeez replied.

"So you trade with other traders?"

Karina chortled. "Traders trade with everyone."

Azeez glanced at the other traders, who shifted in their seats, their faces expressionless; yet Fiona felt that they had reached some unspoken agreement.

"Our caravan brings you food," Azeez said to his guests.

T'mar began to reply but Fiona, reacting to a feeling in her gut, interrupted before he had half a word out. "What do you wish in trade?"

T'mar glanced at her in surprise, but her glare silenced him and he sat back slightly on his cushion, silently relinquishing the conversation to her—although not without some hidden reservations, she felt.

Karina gave Fiona an approving look, but it was Azeez who spoke. "You must understand, our tithe we give to the Lord Holders in trade; they pass on our goods to the Weyrs."

"And Igen Weyr has been empty for Turns," Fiona mused.

"Lord D'gan feels that the tithes rightly belong to Telgar now," Azeez said. Fiona got the feeling that he was quoting a conversation with one of the local Lord Holders—and from his tone, the Lord Holder had not been pleased.

"The holders would be hard-pressed to provide us with tithe," Fiona remarked, glancing toward T'mar. The wingleader nodded, reluctantly agreeing with her appraisal.

"One hundred and twenty-four dragons, even if forty-six of them are still weyrlings, will require a lot of feeding," Karina commented. "And if you are successful, we are to expect similar amounts in the Turns after you leave."

"The Weyrwoman told you this?" Fiona asked. Karina nodded. "Then she must have had an idea how we could accomplish this."

Karina smiled mischievously. "She said that you would know what to do."

"She assumes a lot," T'mar replied sourly. Fiona glared at him again.

"There are things a dragon and a rider can do that no others can do. Might that be worthy of trade?" she suggested.

"Some things are worth more than gold," Karina responded guardedly.

Fiona smiled; she had heard her father say that many Turns earlier—or, rather, some Turns in the future. "Knowledge," she said.

"That is one," Karina agreed. Azeez shifted slightly in his seat. Karina caught his eye—again Fiona felt some secret communication pass between them—and nodded.

"Our riders will need to patrol around the Weyr—" T'mar began.

"Lord D'gan claims that Telgar provides all the protection we need," Karina said.

"Igen was abandoned," T'mar persisted, and Fiona could tell that his remark touched a nerve with the traders. "While we are here, we will patrol and provide aid as needed."

"That is something," Karina agreed. "But for cattle and livestock, we will need to trade with holders and farmers."

Fiona smiled at the old woman. "You have something in mind."

"Your patrols will help in emergencies, but the farmers lose stock to the wild canines that roam the land." Fiona could sense what Karina didn't add: "Since the Weyr was abandoned."

"What could help against that?" Fiona asked. "Don't most of the wolves attack at night?"

Karina nodded. "If we could trade the farmers something that would watch at night—"

Fiona burst out laughing. "Watch-whers! You want watch-whers!"

"They are good against tunnel snakes, too," Azeez admitted. He grinned. "We may not need them in our drays, but we know their value to holders."

"But—" Fiona was about to say that Nuella's presence at the Wherhold near Plains Hold should be enough protection when she realized that, in this time, Nuella had not yet come to Plains Hold. In fact, she realized with a thrill of excitement, there had always been a mystery surrounding Nuella's move. Perhaps now she knew the reason.

"I see," she said finally. She thought, *Zirenth, tell T'mar to say nothing. It's important—I'll explain later.*

I have told him, the bronze dragon replied.

Beside her, T'mar gave a startled motion, which he covered by crossing his knees and glancing toward her.

"What would it mean in trade if we could convince watch-whers to relocate here?" She saw their startled looks and smiled. "Ah, you were just hoping that we could get an egg or two, weren't you?"

"If the watch-whers could stop the night attacks, there would be far more livestock than you and your dragons would need," Karina said.

"Since the Plague," Azeez began and then stopped as he noticed the dragonriders' startled reaction. "Ah, but that was Turns ago for you, wasn't it?"

"Yes," Fiona answered hastily, realizing that the traders were not aware of the dragon illness of the future.

"Ten Turns or more," Karina told Azeez. She noticed Fiona and T'mar exchange uneasy looks and smiled, saying, "You have dragons that you say were injured from Threadfall, and we know that won't happen for another ten Turns or more, so you must come from at least that far in the future."

"I think I see how you can trade on that information," Fiona guessed.

"You can?" Karina raised an eyebrow.

"Of course," Fiona told her. "You know now that ten Turns in the future the dragons will be so injured that they need to send us back in time, so you know that their need for numbweed will be great and you can trade that knowledge profitably to those who grow and harvest numbweed, helping them make greater profit and helping yourself to your rightful profit in carrying the goods in tithe."

"You could be a trader," Karina said. Fiona accepted it for the compliment it was.

"My father raised me well."

"You mean, your father *will* raise you well," Azeez corrected her, smiling.

"I think I might prefer *is* raising me well," Fiona countered, smiling back.

"You were talking about the Plague?" T'mar said politely to Karina.

"Since the Plague, there are fewer farmers, and many farms lie fallow, untended," Karina said.

"Might there be any cattle left from abandoned holds?" Fiona asked.

"There could be," Azeez admitted, "but if there are, they would be mostly in hidden valleys in the low mountains."

"The sort of terrain that only dragons could traverse," T'mar said, grinning at Fiona. "I think we could entertain our weyrlings with such a prospect."

"Do you know of any abandoned fields nearby where we could graze our herds?" Fiona asked.

"There are more fields in Keroon than here in Igen," Karina told her. "For your dragons it is a short journey."

Fiona pursed her lips thoughtfully, then turned to T'mar. "Do you know if any of the older weyrlings have experience tending livestock?"

"It would be better to find holders for that," T'mar replied, holding up a hand to forestall Fiona's quick retort. "Remember, we will be here only for three Turns, and others will follow after us."

T'mar's words reminded Fiona of one of Neesa's admonishments: Always leave a place better than you found it.

"So," she summarized, "while it is possible that we might find some cattle in hard-to-reach valleys, we'll need to trade watchwhers for enough food to feed the dragons in the Turns to come." She glanced at Mother Karina. "That doesn't seem enough. Is there anything else we could trade?"

"Gold and precious metals are always in demand," Karina told her.

T'mar looked thoughtful. After a moment, he looked at Azeez. "In our Weyr, we often knit sweaters to pass the time. They are highly regarded by the holders looking to us."

"Such gifts would not be best to trade from this location," Karina responded, "particularly if you wish to remain hidden."

T'mar pursed his lips in sour acceptance of her point.

"What could we make for trade that might not arouse suspicion?" Fiona asked.

"Nothing too bulky, obviously," T'mar said.

"Why not?" Fiona countered. "Dragons can carry heavy loads. We could deliver our goods anywhere on Pern."

"As long as you weren't seen," Azeez reminded her.

"Would it not serve you well to have us carry goods for you?" Fiona asked, directing her question to Mother Karina.

The old woman leaned back and roared with laughter. It was several minutes before she recovered enough to speak. "You *should* be a trader!"

Fiona glanced at Azeez and the others and perceived a mixture of shock, irritation, astonishment, and admiration.

"We could save you days on your most perilous journeys, and we all know that time is precious to a trader, not to mention saving you wear and provisions," Fiona persisted, feeling that she had to win their approval in addition to that of Mother Karina. She could see them reflecting thoughtfully on her words. "You could create havens to store goods, and we would move them for you between one store and another in only the time it takes to go *between*."

"You said your dragons were injured," Azeez said.

"Our older weyrlings are too young to carry all that an adult dragon could carry," T'mar said slowly, "and many of our older dragons will need half a Turn or more to recover, but there are enough able now to carry everything in this caravan safely anywhere on Pern."

"Anywhere on Pern," Azeez repeated, his eyes wide.

"In only the time it takes to cough three times," Fiona added.

"How would we arrange this with you?" Karina asked, and Fiona realized that she had made the deal.

"Our weyrlings must drill to learn recognition points all over Pern," T'mar said. "There is no reason we could not arrange for one to be placed at your disposal while the others are drilling."

"The only thing is that you would need to keep your fire-lizards away from the dragons," Fiona warned.

"But fire-lizards like dragons!" one of the younger Traders exclaimed in surprise.

"There is a reason," T'mar told him.

"And you can't tell us," Karina guessed. She turned toward the agitated young man. "Tenniz, we shall do as they ask."

The lad nodded, clearly troubled, and leaned back; his eyes went unfocused, and he looked as if he were lost in thought.

"I think," Mother Karina pronounced slowly, "that we have a trade."

"For our services you will provide . . . ?" Fiona prompted.

"We will provide you with a twentieth of the profits we make on all goods carried by your dragons," Karina said with a smile.

"I think, given the time we will save and the extra goods you'll be able transport *anywhere* because of us, that we should at least get the full tithe—a tenth—of all profits," Fiona responded. She ignored T'mar's grunt of surprise, keeping her eyes focused on Karina.

"Who bargains for you, wingleader?" Karina asked T'mar.

"The Weyrwoman bargains for the Weyr," Fiona replied. "The Weyrleader leads against the Fall; the Weyrwoman leads in all else." Beside her, she could sense T'mar's reluctant nod.

Karina smiled at Fiona's boldness, then exchanged a glance with the other traders. Tenniz was still lost in thought, so Karina prompted, "Tenniz?"

"I see a sickness," Tenniz spoke, his eyes still unfocused, his words brilliant in a way that Fiona could not quite understand—shiny with purpose, almost as though he were in another place. "Thread is falling, yet fire-lizards and dragons are not flying against it, coughing out their life force, dying."

"You have a sister," Fiona responded, shivering with insight and urgency. "Her name is Tannaz. She must go to Fort Weyr."

Tenniz glanced up at her, his reverie broken in astonishment. He searched her face and suddenly, tears fell from his eyes.

" 'The gifts of the future can be bitter,' " Karina quoted.

"She was my friend," Fiona admitted, her eyes locked with Tenniz's.

"We are only given so much time to treasure the gifts in our lives," T'mar added solemnly.

"If Tannaz was your friend, then I am your friend," Tenniz declared, reaching out a hand to Fiona. Fiona leaned forward to take it, but Azeez barked, "Stop!"

She turned to him in surprise, her hand outstretched in midair.

"Among traders, the hand of friendship has a special meaning," Azeez told her. "Once given, it can never be returned."

"So be it," Fiona said, clasping Tenniz's hand tightly. The lad surprised her by rising from his chair, levering her up by her arm, and clasping her tightly to him. Then he pushed himself away, leaned down, and tenderly kissed her on the forehead. Sensing that this was part of some ritual, Fiona stretched up to kiss him the same way.

"The traders of the desert are not like others," Karina said to T'mar. "While all traders owe allegiance to the Lilkamp, we trace our line back to those who roamed the ancient Earth, trading, searching, reading the ways of the world."

"You have the blood of dragonriders in your veins," Fiona guessed.

"Many traders do," Azeez said with some pride. "Many riders

who have lost their dragons take to wandering and find themselves becoming traders by choice."

"We desert traders have a bit more," Karina said, and Fiona could feel the other traders swell with pride. "We brought with us a talent different from that required to ride dragons."

"You can see the future." Fiona saw Karina's look of surprise fade into an approving grin.

"You who travel back in time as though it were merely a road less traveled would see that, as with all roads, it can be mapped," the old woman said.

That gave Fiona an idea. "Such an ability would be invaluable in predicting sandstorms," she offered.

"It is good for trade all around," Azeez admitted with a wicked grin.

"It was Tenniz who knew about the Weyrwoman," Fiona said with certainty. She glanced at her new friend. The dark-haired, dark-eyed, dusky-skinned man—who looked so much like Tannaz that Fiona's heart lurched in sorrow—met her eyes and nodded. "Do you know who she is?"

Tenniz shook his head. "Sometimes," he began slowly, "when I feel the future, I get a sense of big events—like boulders or holes in the horizon." He looked to see if Fiona followed the meaning of his words, then continued. "She stands out like a beacon, a light that goes on for Turns."

"Is it hard to learn how to use your gift?" Fiona asked, already suspecting the answer.

"It is not enough to see the winds of time," Tenniz said softly. "It is also important to know when to speak and when to stay silent."

Fiona absorbed this slowly. "Sometimes it must be very painful for you."

A sound, near to but not quite a sob, burst from Tenniz.

"I think I can understand," T'mar commented. "Impressing a dragon is a great gift, but it has a price, and sometimes that price is a terrible sadness."

Tenniz glanced at the older dragonrider in surprise.

"I think that we all have gifts," Fiona declared. "Sometimes not knowing the future is a greater gift than knowing the future."

"It can be so," Karina agreed. "Our lives are what we are willing to make of them. Our gifts are our own to cherish or despise."

A sudden indrawn breath from Tenniz startled them all. Fiona glanced at him worriedly and found herself locked again by his gaze, knowing that he had seen the future once more and that it concerned her—and worried him.

"You are with the beacon," Tenniz told her, his voice full of awe. "She is *so* powerful, she can change everything. And you will change her."

Tears dripped again from his eyes and his jaw trembled with fear. "You will face difficult choices. You will control all Pern. You are in the beginning and at the end." His expression grew bleak. "I can see the beacon going out in your presence."

"What does *that* mean?" T'mar asked in alarm.

Tenniz could only shake his head, looking pityingly at Fiona.

"Thank you," she said to him, gulping down her fears. "I would rather know than not."

Tenniz dropped his eyes. For a moment Fiona felt a wild, uncontrolled panic—how could she destroy all Pern? And why would she destroy the one person who had helped her the most? Then she took a steadying breath and squared her shoulders, recalling her father's proud gaze, the admonition of brave Tannaz, and Kindan's joy when she Impressed Talenth—and Talenth herself.

"I shall do what is right," she declared. "I am the daughter of Fort Hold's Lord, a queen rider, and I *will* serve and save Pern!"

Fiona was drained, listless, when they returned to the Weyr less than a quarter of an hour later. She tried—and failed—to stifle a yawn.

"You should rest," T'mar told her, glancing worriedly as she lurched to stay upright.

"I'll rest when we've got everything prepared," she said, forcing herself upright. "I am the Weyrwoman; it's my duty."

T'mar smiled affectionately at her. "Go rest for an hour," he told her. "I can take care of the Weyr for that long." He made a shooing gesture at her. "Go, get some rest."

Fiona's protests died on her lips as Terin trotted over to her and grabbed her by the hand. "You're no good to us exhausted," the younger weyrgirl declared.

"But—"

"All you'll do is drive the weyrlings to exhaust themselves in turn," Terin told her. "And then we'll *all* be cranky."

Sensing the futility of further protests and recognizing that she was too tired to argue anymore, Fiona let herself be led away by her small headwoman.

"I found some blankets but no sheets," Terin said apologetically as she led Fiona up an incline and into a darkened weyr. "There are no charged glows—in fact, I think all the glows are dead—so we'll have to see if we can find some wild glow to replace them."

"Look for dank places, near slow waters," Fiona told her.

"We'll get to that later," Terin said, although Fiona could tell from her tone that the youngster had filed the information away and would act on it accordingly. She led Fiona to a pile of blankets and sat her down. "No mattresses, either. We found enough cots for the injured riders, but we'll have to get mattresses soon."

"We make them from willow reeds," Fiona said. "You'll find them near the glow goo."

"Shh!" Terin said, gently pushing Fiona down on the makeshift bed and covering Fiona with the topmost blanket. "You're not as bad as some of the others, you know," she commented absently as she tucked the blanket against Fiona. "Some of the riders practically fell asleep on their feet."

"Is no one working?" Fiona asked, but fatigue overwhelmed concern and she couldn't muster the energy to sit up again.

"Oh, no! I wouldn't let that happen," Terin told her primly. "But the ones who were always slow and dizzy seem to be the ones who are doing best here." She cocked her head as if just realizing what she'd said. "That's odd, isn't it?"

Fiona could only nod, working her head against the rough blankets to find a more comfortable spot, her eyes already closed. Sleep came to her quickly.

"Fiona." The voice that woke her much later was deep, male. T'mar. Fiona rolled over, ready to leap out of bed. T'mar held up a restraining hand. "The traders have been spotted; they'll be here in about a quarter of an hour."

Fiona sat up and wiped the sleep from her eyes.

"F'jian and some of the other weyrlings are getting up to help," T'mar reported as he stood back to give her room. He quirked his eyebrows as he said, "They were all overcome with a similar exhaustion."

Fiona found her shoes and slid her feet into them, then rustled her hair into a bunch and shoved it behind her as best she could without a mirror. She didn't think the traders would take affront at her appearance, but she *did* have her duty as Weyrwoman. She turned back in time to catch T'mar stifling a grin.

"I'm not surprised they're exhausted," Fiona said as she gestured for the wingleader to precede her. "We did a lot of work today, and none of them have ever gone *between* before."

"Ah, but not all were so fatigued," T'mar told her. "In fact, the ones that took it the best were the same as the ones Tajen had remarked upon when he was Weyrlingmaster."

"What about you?" Fiona asked, recalling Cisca's concerns about the bronze rider. "Have you slept at all?"

Before T'mar could respond, his knees suddenly buckled, and she reached out to prop him up. Fiona helped him back to the makeshift bed and sat him down.

"Put your head between your knees," she ordered, pushing down on his head to overcome his resistance. "Don't sit up until I tell you."

"But the traders—"

"Terin will see to things," Fiona declared with false assurance. "Anyway, you'll be up in a moment, so just hush and rest."

Fiona spent the next few minutes exploring her memories of the amazing day she'd just lived.

"Some of the weyrlings are probably tired because they were awoken in the middle of the night back at Fort Weyr," she said after a few moments' thought. She slowly released the pressure on T'mar's head and let him sit up, her eyes examining him as best she could in the dim light. "Do you feel like standing?"

"Whether I do or not, I have a duty," T'mar replied, forcing himself to his feet again.

Fiona eyed him critically. "We'll get you to the Kitchen Cavern and have you sit," she decided. "You can order just as easily from there as anywhere."

T'mar didn't argue and silently allowed her to keep a steadying hand on his arm as they made their way down the queens' ledge and over to the Kitchen Cavern.

"Ah, you're up!" Terin exclaimed brightly as she saw Fiona arrive. "We've done what we could, but we've got no proper food to greet guests."

"They'll be bringing the food," Fiona assured her. "I suspect, however, that it won't be food we've had before."

Terin shrugged. "As long as it's not numbweed, I'll eat it."

Fiona sniffed the air and was vexed to be able to still catch a faint whiff of the noxious but marvelous weed.

Terin noticed and frowned. "I think next time we'll brew it in the Bowl."

"Maybe down by the river," T'mar said. Terin gave him a quizzical look, so the bronze rider expanded: "The Igen River is over those mountains—no time at all a-dragonback."

Terin shrugged, dismissing the issue from her list of worries.

"You know," she said to Fiona in the tone of one relaying a confidence, "I'm the only girl here." She caught Fiona's widening eyes and amended hastily, "The only one who isn't a dragonrider."

"You're going to have to draft the dragonriders to help you," Fiona told her.

"But—"

"You're headwoman," T'mar reminded her. "You won't have any problems."

"I've only ten Turns!" Terin protested.

"It's not the Turns that matter—it's how you behave," Fiona assured her.

Terin pursed her lips, not looking relieved.

T'mar nodded. "You've a maturity about you that makes people willing to discount your years." He caught her worried look and added, "Besides, they're used to obeying the headwoman—and certainly none of *them* would be willing to take on your duties." He grinned.

"But some of the boys—"

"If anyone gives you a problem, *I* want to know of it," T'mar told her firmly.

"And I," Fiona added fiercely. She glanced at T'mar and turned, grinning, to Terin. "I told Talenth to tell the other dragons that you're headwoman. I doubt you'll have any problems."

"Oh!" Terin exclaimed. Her expression brightened with mischievous glee.

"I expect you to behave responsibly," Fiona warned the younger girl. "Or you'll have to answer to me."

Terin's glee cooled noticeably and her next words were very demure: "Yes, Weyrwoman."

They are here, Talenth said. *They are at the gates.*

"Have the watch dragon let them in," Fiona said aloud, to let Terin know. She glanced at the young headwoman. "Do we have the storerooms clean?"

Terin's eyes widened in horror. "No, we were too busy clearing quarters for the most injured riders," she confessed.

"No matter," T'mar assured her. "I'm sure I can find enough warm bodies to prepare at least part of the storerooms before we eat."

At this Fiona's stomach rumbled, and she suddenly realized that she was ravenously hungry. T'mar smiled.

"You go greet our benefactors, while I take care of the storerooms," the wingleader said, rising from his chair. Fiona glanced at him nervously, but the bronze rider made it clear by his stance that he was no longer in need of aid.

Fiona met Azeez just as he called the caravan to a halt.

"Welcome to Igen Weyr," she said with a slight bow. The words seemed to grow larger in the cooler air, and she felt as though they meant even more than she'd intended.

Azeez jumped down from his dray and bent his head toward Fiona in response.

"It is good to see this Weyr in use again," said Mother Karina, striding forward. She nodded to Fiona. "It is right that you are its first Weyrwoman."

Fiona didn't know how to take the old woman's statement—was it a compliment or a pronouncement?

"Get the beasts settled and the stores unloaded," Karina ordered Azeez. Before Azeez could respond, she continued, "Everyone is hungry; send up the lunch supplies first." She glanced at Fiona. "Has your headwoman got her weyrfolk ready?"

Fiona's eyes widened in a mixture of fright, astonishment, and humor: How would Karina take to meeting Igen's headwoman?

"Let's find out," she replied, trying not to worry as she gestured for Karina to lead the way.

In the Kitchen Cavern, Terin was busily supervising a mixed array of convalescent riders and reluctant weyrlings.

"I've got water boiling," the girl said as soon as she caught sight of Fiona. She saw Karina behind her, hid a gulp, and made a curtsy. "Terin, headwoman at Igen."

"This is Mother Karina," Fiona said, waving a hand to introduce the older woman.

"How many Turns have you?" Karina demanded of Terin.

Terin's expression clouded fearfully, then she drew in a breath and drew herself up taller, saying proudly, "I've ten Turns."

"A good age," Karina told her in approving tones. "I was that age when the traders called me Mother."

Terin gave a noncommittal nod in response, not quite sure how to handle this information. Then she said, "All the *klah* bark is old and moldy." She gestured to a sack.

"The lads have brought more," Karina said dismissively.

A noise from behind Karina caught their attention and they saw two traders coming forward with sacks over their shoulders.

"J'keran!" Terin called immediately. "Send five strong weyrlings back with these traders—they have our lunch."

"Immediately!" J'keran replied, gesturing for another weyrling to take over his duty at his boiling pot.

Karina gestured to the boiling water. "And what were you hoping to put in your pots?"

"Food for injured dragonriders and growing weyrlings," Terin replied promptly. A small grin slid over her as she added, "And anyone else that feels need."

Karina cocked her head at those words. "Is that so? Is it a habit of the Weyr to feed those who wander nearby?"

"Always," Terin replied solemnly. "We'll share the last crumb."

"Big words from such a small girl," Karina replied.

"Only the truth," Terin replied, her eyes flashing. "I am an orphan myself. I was taken in as a baby, my parents dead from the hunger." She raised her head in challenge to the older woman. "So you see, I have reason to be my word."

"Be your word? And what does that mean to you, youngling?"

"It means you can count on me to stand by the words I speak," Terin replied. "And as I've been appointed headwoman here by Weyrwoman Fiona, and that appointment's been approved by senior wingleader T'mar, you can take my word to stand for that of all the riders here at Igen."

"There must be a *lot* of trader stock in the weyrfolk!" Karina declared with a laugh. She held out a hand to Terin. "It is a pleasure to make your acquaintance, headwoman."

"Thank you," Terin replied, her expression lightening once more as she took Karina's old, withered hand in her much younger, smaller grasp and shook it firmly.

"So, do you know how to prepare lentils, headwoman?" Karina asked. "Or how to make desert bread?"

"Could you show me?" Terin asked politely.

Karina nodded and gestured for Terin to precede her to the kettles.

In short order J'keran and the traders arrived with barrels and more sacks of goods. The first barrel contained *klah* bark, which was quickly put to the boil. The first sack contained some small hard disks that none of the riders had ever before seen.

"These are lentils," Karina explained. "They are full of protein and good eating, hardy enough for our desert climes. They make an excellent soup—which can be our first course."

She started to lead Terin away, talking about garlic, ginger, and carrots. Fiona was torn between following and checking on the work unloading supplies.

Glancing back at her, Karina said, "Go on, Weyrwoman! Terin and I can handle this."

The relaxed smile on Terin's face was the final assurance Fiona needed, so, with a half-wave, she took off into the corridors toward the storerooms.

"We'll be done shortly, Weyrwoman," T'mar told her when she arrived. Quietly, just for her ears, he added, "I hope that we'll eat soon—we're building quite an appetite."

"Terin and Karina are working on it," Fiona replied. "But it'll be close to another hour." Seeing T'mar's face fall, she added hurriedly, "But we've got fresh *klah* for those who need it."

"We can wait until lunch," he decided.

Fiona nodded and left, wondering what to do next. She decided to check on the injured riders and their supplies, and ended up in the small herbal room, sorting through medicines. It took Talenth to break through her concentration.

T'mar says that lunch is ready, the gold dragon told her.

Good! Fiona replied, suddenly aware of the amazing aromas that were filling the Weyr. *How about you?*

I'm not hungry, Talenth assured her. *A little itchy, maybe.*

Her words reminded Fiona that she needed to be sure there was enough oil on hand for all the young and old flaky dragonhide. She almost turned back to check the stores, but her stomach grumbled again and she headed for the Kitchen Cavern.

In addition to the promised lentil soup, there was something she'd never encountered before: a spicy mixture of onions, sweet potatoes, and black beans, all wrapped up in a very thin, soft flatbread. It was both sweet and piquant.

"It tastes good," Fiona said as soon as she swallowed. "Good, but different."

"Hot food for hot climes," Tenniz told her with a grin. "You'll get used to it soon enough." His eyes held some hint of mystery, but Fiona was too busy enjoying the new tastes and smells to linger upon it.

"Early afternoon in this climate tends to be too hot for work," Azeez said to T'mar, "so usually we take a nap."

"That make sense," Fiona said before T'mar could object. "It will be particularly good for the injured riders and those with injured dragons."

"Why the dragons?" T'mar wondered, frowning.

"If their riders are resting, they'll rest, too," Fiona reminded him.

"But we don't have—" T'mar began, gesturing toward Azeez.

"We have gear we could set up in your unused living quarters," Azeez assured him.

Karina shot him a glare and Fiona noticed.

"You've stayed here before," she stated. Tenniz looked down, avoiding her eyes, but Karina nodded.

"No one was using it," Azeez said.

"We kept the water flowing," Karina said.

"I'm glad you did," Fiona said. "I'm sure the Weyr would have been much harder to clean if you hadn't used it." She turned to T'mar, then added, "I see no reason why you can't continue to use it while we're here."

T'mar thought about it, then nodded. "We will be using less than a third of the weyrs, and would be glad of your company."

"Let me be clear," Azeez said. "We're traders; we need to move to trade. We'd only be here occasionally, for no more than a night."

"Not if I can help it," T'mar replied, then laughed as he caught Azeez's bemused look.

"We talked about this when we met," T'mar continued. "We could carry supplies for you." Azeez nodded, still no closer to comprehension. "And you would need to store them, occasionally?"

"We could store them here?" Karina asked, eyes alight with the prospect.

"Whatever we can do to help," T'mar offered.

"For a reasonable fee, of course," Terin added from her place at the table. She caught Karina's eyes challengingly and locked with them until the older woman threw up her hands in surrender.

"Another with the soul of a trader!"

THIRTEEN

The stars shine so cold at night,
The sun burns so hot by day,
The wind whips in wild delight:
The weather at Igen is fey.

Igen Weyr, Early Morning, AL 498.7.3

Talenth woke Fiona early the next morning. *The watchdragon says*
that they are getting ready to leave. Fiona propped herself up on an
elbow and looked at Terin sleeping next to her on their makeshift
bed of blankets, considering whether to wake her. She decided
against it; the younger girl had had a busy enough first day as
headwoman.

She made a mental note to send a party of weyrlings to get mattress fillings and started to crawl over Terin to the edge of the bed,
but stopped when she saw her open her eyes.

"What is it?"

"The traders are leaving," Fiona told her quietly.

Terin rubbed her eyes and sat up. "I'll come with you."

"It's still dark outside," Fiona cautioned as she rose and hastily
pulled on the clothes she'd been wearing the day before. Terin followed suit and in short order the two followed the gleam of Talenth's eyes into the queen's new lair.

Did you want to come, too? Fiona asked her dragon.

Will it be fun? Talenth asked. Fiona shrugged. Talenth glanced around her lair and decided that she'd got herself too well settled to want to move. *I'll stay here, then.*

One of the moons was high enough to provide some dim light in the Weyr Bowl outside—enough for eyes to see, if not in color. Fiona picked out the shape of the watch dragon on the heights near the Star Stones to the east. The night air was chill, fresh, expectant. She made out a shape: T'mar.

He must have seen them, for he stopped and waited for them to catch up. Together, the three of them made their way to the Kitchen Cavern.

"*Klah* or tea?" Terin asked, grabbing a glove to snag a pot of water from the hearth.

"You will find that it's best to change your hours when you live in the desert," they heard Mother Karina say from somewhere behind them. They turned to face her. "Night is your friend."

"Thread falls when it will," T'mar told her.

"Thread does not yet fall," Karina reminded him. "Even when it does, Igen Weyr prepares in the early morning and late evening. Avoid the sun whenever you can."

Azeez entered behind her. Karina turned to him.

"Everything is ready," Azeez told her respectfully.

"The night awaits," Karina said, turning to follow Azeez.

"Let us see you on your way," Fiona offered, trotting after them.

They made their way through darkened corridors dimly lit by half-charged glows until they reached a deeper darkness where the heights of the Weyr Bowl shaded them from the moon's light. Stars glittered beckoningly in the night sky.

Azeez climbed up to his perch on the first dray. "We shall see you soon."

"Expect us before the next sevenday," Karina amended.

Whips cracked, encouraging the large herdbeasts to start moving. With Azeez in the lead, the drays began to move slowly out into the dark night. When they could no longer be seen, T'mar turned to lead the way back.

"So, *klah* or tea?" Terin repeated when they returned to the Kitchen Cavern.

"*Klah*," Fiona replied. "And I'll help you get started with breakfast."

T'mar raised his eyebrows in a wordless question.

"I don't think that I'll be able to get back to sleep," Fiona explained. "And while we haven't enough charged glows to do much, I think I'd prefer to start adopting Karina's suggestion."

"Karina's suggestion works well for those who bring wares from one place to another," T'mar said, "but not so well for those who need eyes to see what wares to gather."

Fiona nodded in agreement."We must see if there are any light mirrors in storage," she said. "We could do with more light in the lower quarters, and I'd like to examine the Records."

"You could bring them here, into the Kitchen," T'mar suggested.

"They're heavy; I don't think I could carry many."

"Get the weyrlings to help."

"They'll be busy enough tending the injured," Fiona said. "We should plan how we're going to do it." She gestured for T'mar to take a seat. "Terin, do you have a spare slate and some chalk?"

Terin's cheeks dimpled—if there was one thing on which Fiona could rely, it was that Terin would never be far from her tools.

"Our worst injured are N'jian, P'der," T'mar began, ticking off the list on his fingers as Terin delivered the slate to Fiona, "F'dan's Ridorth, K'ranor's Troth—"

"Hold it!" Fiona interjected. "You're going faster than I can write, for one, and for two, we should be talking injuries and treatments."

T'mar replaced the frown on his face with an apologetic look. His brows rose in surprise as Fiona snagged the cuff of her sleeve and used it to erase the half-filled slate.

"Very ladylike," he teased her.

Fiona glared at him, but without any real feeling. "I think we should have separate slates: one for injured riders, the other for injured dragons."

"It's a pity that we couldn't bring the healer," Terin remarked.

"But—" Fiona began to protest, then paused. "Actually, you're right."

"It would have made sense if we'd decided to bring the most injured back in time," T'mar corrected. "As it was, we deemed it too risky." He glanced up at Fiona, the merest hint of accusation in his eyes, as he added, "Until we got our unexpected help."

Fiona shook her head in irritation. "You *know* that I have no idea who it was—"

"I do," T'mar cut across her. "But it is not something I would put past your older self."

"I can't say for certain that it wasn't me from some time in the future," Fiona admitted, not bothering to hide her frustration, "but it doesn't matter—they're here now and we'll have to care for them as best we can."

She glanced down at the two slates she now had, one of which had been silently placed in front of her during her latest exchange with T'mar.

"So," she said, turning back to the problem at hand, "we've got P'der and . . ."

"N'jian," T'mar supplied, his face devoid of feeling. "His right side was severely Thread-scored."

"Fortunately they went *between* before the Thread ate far into his chest," Terin said. Fiona glanced over to the younger girl— Terin looked queasy but persisted. "His injuries are to the skin and muscle of the chest and abdomen."

"His right side looks like a slab of meat badly butchered," T'mar said, grimacing. He continued bleakly, "Whether he survives or not is up to us."

"What do we need to do?" Fiona asked.

"We need to keep his wounds clean, keep him flat on his back, give his skin a chance to grow again, and then—slowly—help him to recover his strength," T'mar replied. He gestured for the slate, but then pointed at the other one instead, writing down a list of dragon names. After a moment he glanced up at Terin. "We'll need more slates—at least two."

Terin nodded and rushed off, grabbing a glowbasket as she passed out into the darkened storeroom corridors.

"Troth, Piyeth, Kadorth, Varth, and Bidanth are all the worst in-jured dragons," T'mar said as he wrote down their names.

"When it gets light enough, I'll start a search of the Records," Fiona told him. "I'll look for descriptions of treatments, as well."

"As well as what?"

"Just about everything," Fiona replied with a shrug. "Watering holes, cattle and herdbeast plains, crops grown, glow supplies, herb gardens, local medicines, weather reports—"

"Whoa!" T'mar interjected, raising a hand to fend her off. "You'll need a Turn before you find all that."

"I hope not," Fiona replied with a shake of her head; she regretted the movement instantly, as her longer bangs whipped across her face, causing her to irritably blow them aside and run her hands through her rebellious locks to pull them back once more behind her ears.

When she was finished, she was surprised by the look on T'mar's face. "What?"

"Nothing," the bronze rider replied, glancing hastily down to the slates.

"What?" Fiona persisted.

T'mar reluctantly looked back up at her. "It's just that you looked cute when you did that."

Fiona felt her cheeks flush and a thrill run through her at his words. Cute!

T'mar looked away again and ended the awkward silence by clearing his throat. "Of the dragons, I'm most worried about the damage to Troth's and Varth's wing joints—if they don't grow back fully, they'll never be able to fly again."

Fiona nodded, suppressing a shiver.

Terin returned at that moment with a stack of slates, her glowbasket perched precariously on top. She returned the glowbasket to its place, trotted over to the table, picked up two, and blew the dust off them, coughing. She placed those two slates in front of Fiona, scooping up the rest and saying, "Whew! These were left behind when they abandoned the Weyr. They're all musty and dirty, so I'm going to wash and dry them."

"You know," T'mar said as he took one of the proffered slates, "we really need a slate for every injury, so that we can keep track."

"Seventy-seven slates?" Terin called from her place by the hearth. "I don't think that's practical."

"Why?" Fiona returned, glad to be distracted from T'mar.

"How would you cart them all around?" Terin asked. "And how would you keep them from being erased?"

"We should set up a Flight board," T'mar declared. Fiona didn't hide her confusion, so he explained, "We have them back at the Weyr."

"This *is* a Weyr," Fiona reminded him.

T'mar gave her an irritated look.

"I think it's a pity it was abandoned," Fiona said.

"You haven't been here a full day," T'mar reminded her. "Perhaps you should wait to make up your mind."

"Our ancestors founded it for a purpose," she disagreed. "I'm sure they considered its location carefully."

"Times change," T'mar said with a shrug. "They might not have foreseen such a drought."

"You were saying something about a Flight board?" she said, returning the conversation to the subject at hand.

T'mar nodded. "Every wing has them and there's a master board—or two—one in the Records Room and the other here, in the Living Cavern."

"I remember," Terin piped up from her corner, pulling out another freshly washed slate and laying it on a drying board. "It was at the Weyrleaders' table, on the wall behind."

"That's it," T'mar agreed. "Although that was only a summary board. It shows each wing with totals fit to fly or injured. With one look, the Weyrleader knows the fighting state of the Weyr."

"K'lior had it cleaned off before we left," Terin put in, pulling another clean slate out of the washbowl.

"I imagine he—or Cisca—decided it was too depressing," T'mar said. He glanced over at Fiona, shaking his head. "Do you realize that we have no fewer than *three* of our nine wingleaders here with us?"

Fiona was surprised.

"Myself, N'jian, and K'rall," T'mar told her. "Not to mention K'lior's wingsecond, P'der."

"K'rall?" Fiona repeated in surprise. She couldn't recall the sour old bronze rider's face among those she'd seen.

"His face was scored," T'mar said. "He should recover in two months or so."

"We had to dose him with fellis juice, to keep him from moving his mouth." Terin sounded amused.

"Until the youngsters get old enough to fly, we'll have to keep the older weyrlings for flights and other work," T'mar declared, glancing at Fiona, who nodded in agreement. He took another breath. "In that case, we can split the thirty-three youngsters into three groups—"

"Four," Fiona corrected instantly. "We'll need a work party for housekeeping chores here at the Weyr."

"And that would give them some rest, as well," Terin added.

"F'jian and J'nos would be the first two leaders—"

"Are you sure you want J'nos?" Terin interjected. The other two turned to her and she shrugged as she explained, "Did you see how dozy he looked yesterday? He could barely walk." She paused, her lips pressed together firmly and her eyes thoughtful. "He wasn't the only one, either. It's like—"

"Like all those who weren't dozy before suddenly became dozy!" Fiona exclaimed in surprise.

T'mar looked at her with eyes narrowed, then slowly nodded. "You think that *timing* it has caused this?"

"We're in two places in one time—our younger selves are now at Fort, where we belong, and our older selves are here, where we never were—why wouldn't that cause strain and distraction?" Fiona responded.

"I don't feel dozy!" Terin declared.

"That's because you aren't a dragonrider," Fiona told her. She regretted the words the moment she saw how Terin's face fell sorrowfully.

"At least, not yet," T'mar told her.

"Not everyone Impresses," Terin said with a pout.

"There are no guarantees," T'mar agreed. "But I'm sure you'll get your chance"—he glanced slyly at Fiona—"when her queen rises."

Terin's eyes widened and she glanced apprehensively toward Fiona.

"Of course!" Fiona said. "You and Xhinna—"

"I wish she was here," Terin interjected.

"We could use her help," Fiona agreed. She turned back to T'mar, saying, "So this distraction could be caused by *timing*?"

T'mar pursed his lips. "It could."

"You don't sound certain."

"I'm not," the bronze rider agreed. "It doesn't explain why you were . . ."

"Dozy?" Fiona supplied when his words trailed off. "And you? Weren't you also dozy?"

"Do you think it was an effect from *timing* it now?" T'mar wondered. A short moment later, he shook his head and answered himself, "But that doesn't explain why some were affected and not others."

"Maybe everyone reacts differently," Fiona suggested with some uncertainty.

"I can understand being distracted when in the same time twice," T'mar said, his lips pursed again, "but I don't understand why we would feel it when we *weren't* in the same time."

"Perhaps—" Fiona began but cut herself off. T'mar gave her a questioning look, but she only shook her head in response. She didn't want to suggest that perhaps they were twice in the same time not now, but back in the "present" Third Pass. T'mar continued to look at her thoughtfully.

"It doesn't matter," she said. "We know that if we're distracted we can still function: if not at our best, then well enough."

"The others will be waking soon," Terin said as she walked back to them, leaving a drying tray full of clean slates. "We should decide on those shifts."

"I think we can use J'nos," Fiona said. "He'll need watching until he gets over being—" She cut an amused look toward Terin who grinned back at her. "—dozy."

"T'del and Y'gos would be the obvious candidates for the other two positions," T'mar said.

"Why?" Fiona asked, realizing that she couldn't remember T'del among the many weyrlings.

They ride browns, Talenth answered.

"Browns are usually wingseconds," T'mar replied.

"Or wingleaders," Terin added. T'mar accepted the addition with a nod.

"Why not go by ability?" Fiona wondered.

"Brown and bronze riders are often the ones with the most leadership ability," T'mar said.

Fiona cocked her head challengingly.

"Oh, you get the occasional blue or green rider who makes a good leader," he explained, "but more often their skills lie in different areas."

"Like cavorting!" Terin snickered. "It's a wonder we don't have more of them."

"Greens are sterile," T'mar reminded her.

Fiona tapped the slates. "We need to concentrate."

T'mar heaved a sigh and gave Terin an apologetic look. "Maybe we could send you to the traders when there's a mating flight."

"I remember the last mating flight," Terin said. "I'll be fine."

Oh, but you're getting older! Fiona thought. Suddenly she realized that so was she. In fact—"Terin, when's your birthing day?"

"The twentieth of the seventh month," Terin replied promptly, surprised by the distraction.

Fiona laughed. "You're going to have another Turn soon!"

"What?" Terin cried in dismay. "My birth date is months away!"

"Not here!" Fiona told her. "Here, we're in the seventh month already."

"And when's *your* birthday, then?"

"The eighth day of the seventh month," Fiona told her, her face changing expression as she realized that that date was only five days away.

"And how old will you be?" T'mar asked.

"Now or then?" Fiona asked.

"Which is now and which is then?" Terin asked with a laugh.

"You'd have fourteen Turns at your next Turning," T'mar remarked. "So here you'd have only four Turns, wouldn't you?"

"This is very confusing," Fiona said glumly. "Do I Turn on my birthday here, or wait until the right amount of time would have passed in the future?"

"Why not do both?" Terin asked, giggling. "You could have a Turning for now and a Turning for later."

"What matters is how old your body is," T'mar declared. Fiona shot him a glance. Undeterred, he continued, "It's how we'll judge the dragons and their readiness to fly or go *between*."

"And that speaks to when *your* dragon will rise to mate!" Terin exclaimed, dissolving into a full-on giggling fit.

What, Fiona wondered anxiously, if Talenth rose to mate back in this time? There were only two bronzes: T'mar's Zirenth and K'rall's Seyorth. Well, three, if she counted F'jian's Ladirth, she corrected herself reluctantly.

"She's too young," Fiona heard herself say.

"Not in three Turns' time!" Terin retorted, her giggles dying away. She took a breath and, when she caught sight of Fiona's expression, forced herself to stop altogether, murmuring, "Sorry."

Fiona's eyes flashed as she dredged up a heated retort, but it died on her lips as Talenth said, *When will you be done? I itch.*

"I've got to oil Talenth," she said, rising.

"I'll warm some oil," Terin said, glad of an excuse to change the topic.

"I'll finish here," T'mar said, waving to the charts.

Later, when Terin arrived with more oil, the younger girl tried to apologize to Fiona. "I'm sorry about back there," she said. "I didn't mean—"

Fiona waved her apology aside. "You were having fun," she told her. "There's no harm in that."

Terin dipped her head and diligently applied herself to searching out and oiling any flaky patches of Talenth's skin.

Afterward, they returned to the Kitchen Cavern. Terin snagged the first weyrlings and set them to cooking and sculling duties. "And be sure there's *klah!*"

"Make sure we send out a party to find more glow," Fiona said as she rose after her breakfast. "I think the light's good enough to see in the Records Room."

"I've detailed the work party to concentrate on getting more of the lower weyrs cleared for the injured," T'mar said. "I'm going to take the older weyrlings on a patrol—we'll look for your glows while we're out."

Fiona nodded, saying as she departed, "Be sure to check with Terin for anything else we might need."

The Records Room was a room off of the Weyrwoman's quarters, as in Fort Weyr. Fiona searched in the dimly lit room for the large mirrors that she knew should be there and found a pair. She snagged the first one and went back into the corridor, mounting it in the holder built into the wall and angling it so that it picked up the morning light and bounced it into the room. Satisfied, she returned to the Records Room and placed the other mirror so that it reflected the light up to the glittering white ceiling, providing the room with nearly the same illumination as light through a window.

In the center of the room was a long, low table surrounded by chairs. Fiona was surprised at first that the chairs, at least, hadn't been taken along when the Weyr had been abandoned but, on reflection, realized that Telgar Weyr would already have had sufficient furniture for its Records Room. Some of the Records had obviously been taken, though—a few of the storage cabinets were empty—and she could only hope that enough remained for her purposes.

She found a couple of likely stacks, settled herself at the table, and began to read.

It didn't take all that long for Fiona to recall her father's choicer oaths in regards to reading Records. "A boring necessity best delegated," was the most innocuous of his pronouncements. For a brief moment she toyed with the notion of delegating the work, but curiosity overwhelmed boredom and she soldiered on, stifling a yawn.

She had gone through twenty slates—finding only two of value—before she found a truly tantalizing reference: "Of course, we used the surveyor map to locate the most recent vein of minerals."

Surveyor map? What was a "surveyor?" She shook her head. It was the idea that mattered, not the word. If there was a map that showed minerals, what else might have been marked on a map? She looked around the room, eyes narrowed. Where would such a map be kept?

In a locked cabinet, Fiona decided. She rose and walked around the room, exploring. At last she ended up back at the cabinet where she'd first started. Had she looked carefully enough? She squatted down in front of it, studying the open cubbies. Yes! The bottommost cubby had a door, and there was a keyhole in that door! So, where was the key?

She spent many fruitless minutes hunting through the other cabinets before she wondered if perhaps some blockheaded Telgar-bound rider had pocketed the key. If that were the case, how could the door be opened?

Returning to the closed cubby, she knelt and carefully inserted a fingernail into the keyhole. She gently tugged. She was so surprised when the door swiveled open that she fell back on the stone floor.

The cubby was filled with tightly rolled . . . maps?

Fiona pulled out the top roll. It was as long as the cubby was deep. With a triumphant cry, she brought it to the table, pushed aside the boring Records, and unrolled it.

It was a map made of strange material, smooth, almost silky— definitely something made by the Ancients. She placed a slate on one corner to hold the edge down and then spread it out fully, trapping the far edge under another slate.

Talenth! she called excitedly. *Tell T'mar to come to the Records Room—quick!*

"**A**nd see, there, that's the symbol for gold, isn't it?" Fiona said an hour later as she and T'mar pored excitedly over the map, each with a mug of *klah* nearby.

"Where?" T'mar asked, diverting his attention from a place where he'd spotted good pastureland—a possible gathering for wild herdbeasts.

"There," she said, pointing again to a series of turns in a river. "Over by Plains Hold."

"I wonder that the Mastersmith hasn't seen this," T'mar said thoughtfully.

"I wonder why we don't have one of these at Fort Weyr," Fiona countered.

"Fort was the first Weyr," T'mar mused. "I suspect they had this already at the Harper Hall and didn't see the need at the Weyr."

"Mmph!" Fiona snorted. "I don't recall anything like this in the Hold Records."

"But didn't Kindan find similar Records when he was searching for the new firestone?"

Fiona shrugged—she didn't know and didn't care—and tapped her chosen spot on the map to gain T'mar's attention. The wingleader, with a quick grin, bent to inspect the markings.

"I think you're right," he said as he straightened up again. And then, in surprise, he bent down once more, eyes wide. "That's exactly where the Wherhold is!"

"No," Fiona corrected triumphantly. "It's exactly where the Wherhold *will* be."

"And when Zenor is mining the gold—"

"—and Igen is getting a dutiful tithe—" Fiona added, her face splitting into a huge grin.

"—we'll have enough to trade for our needs!"

Despite the excitement of their discovery, neither T'mar nor Fiona were able to devote much attention to it for the next several days, spending the bulk of their time engaged in the effort required to settle up a Weyr—and one full of convalescents, at that.

Fiona found herself crawling into bed in the heat of the afternoon only to wake at the first cooling of the evening. Her whole sleep schedule was rearranged—she spent more time sleeping in the day than at night—and it did her temper no good at all.

But she had cause to be pleased, not annoyed: After only five days in their new Weyr, enough weyrs had been cleared to house all the injured dragons and riders; the work teams had been trained in the basics of first aid and dressings; T'mar and his scouting parties had located several good grazing areas and had filled them with herdbeasts; they had started a well-composted herb garden and had located and identified several varieties of wild crops and fruits that they could harvest to add to their stores. All in all, as Fiona woke early on the morning of her fifth day, leaving Terin to sleep in for once, it seemed that things were well in hand.

She turned the glow enough to manage her toilet, then turned it over again to its dim side, slid quietly past the sleeping Talenth, and made her way to the Kitchen Cavern, where she discovered the last of the evening crew getting ready for rest and the beginnings of the day crew coming on watch.

T'mar, because of his need to scout the surrounding lands, was on the day crew, and she was not surprised to see him enter the Kitchen Cavern not long after she had set herself down at the Weyrleader's table with a basket of warm rolls, some preserves, and a pot of *klah*.

"I wish we had butter," T'mar grumbled as he joined her, leaning over to examine the various preserves.

"To have butter we'd need milch cows, cowherds to herd them, milkers to milk them, a churner to churn the butter, and a cool place to store it," Fiona said as she chewed her roll. But, she admitted to herself, a little butter would be nice.

"We could trade," T'mar said.

"We have nothing to trade with yet," Fiona pointed out. "Anyway, in this heat, how long would butter last?"

"There must be a way to keep it cool," T'mar said.

"Some of the storage rooms might work . . ."

"Not for long, you'd need some ice—"

"Ice!" Fiona's shout caused everyone in the room to turn toward her. "T'mar, that's it! We can get ice!"

"What?"

"It isn't enough to have a tithe of gold," Fiona continued on excitedly. "We need something we can trade with anyone at any time."

"Most people will do without ice if they've other needs," T'mar warned her.

"But those that want it will pay dearly," Fiona said, her enthusiasm unabated. "Think of it, particularly here in this heat! Not only can you keep food fresh, but if you set up a fan—and we've no lack of wind here to drive one—you could cool a room!"

T'mar stroked his chin thoughtfully, staring absently in the distance in front of him.

"Some of our riders would do better if their quarters were cooler," he murmured. Then he shook himself out of his musings and turned his attention back once again to the young queen rider in front of him. "It's the middle of summer and we're in one of the hottest places on Pern, where were you planning on finding ice?" he demanded. A moment later he added, "And without getting us caught. Don't forget that none of the riders in this time know of our presence here."

Fiona waved aside his objections with an airy flick of one hand. "Where, bronze rider, is it cold all Turn?"

"You can't make ice *between*!" T'mar objected.

"No, not *between*," Fiona said, her tone exasperated. She pointed toward with her finger. "North! In the Snowy Wastes!"

T'mar looked at her as if she were sun-touched.

"Think of it, it's just a jump *between* for us and then we're back again with as much ice as we can carve out of the ground."

"Where would you go?" T'mar asked. "This idea is so good, I'd be very surprised if D'gan or one of the other Igen riders hasn't already thought of it—in which case we stand a very good chance of running right into them."

"Then we go where they don't," Fiona said. "We go north of Benden or Nabol."

"We could use the coastline to guide us," T'mar mused appreciatively. "That would give us an easy mark to follow." Then he frowned again. "Except that the coast is often fog-shrouded, which could spell disaster."

Fiona gave him a questioning look.

"A dragon needs a good visual image to go *between*," he told her, remembering that she had yet to take Talenth *between* on her own.

Fiona knew what happened without a good image—at best, the dragon would not go *between*. At worst . . . it would be lost forever, trapped *between*.

"Wait a moment," T'mar exclaimed. "Why didn't I think of it before?"

"What?"

"The Far Watchers!" T'mar told her, his expression triumphant. "Every weyrling is drilled on them; they're not part of the standard recognition points so we don't drill them often, but even so . . ."

"Far Watchers?" Fiona repeated, confused.

T'mar gestured to her apologetically, explaining, "They're two very tall peaks at the northern edge of the Benden Mountains—weyrlings are taught about them to get an idea of the sort of weather that's too cold for Thread to survive." He grinned. "To the north of the peaks the ground is always frozen, covered in layers of ice." He nodded to her as he continued, "Layers of marvelous, easily cut and hauled, tradeable ice."

"So when can we go?"

"*We*," T'mar said, "aren't going anywhere. Now that you've given me the idea, I'll take a group of the older weyrlings there later today when we have a chance." He gestured toward her. *"You* will want to arrange a special storage room for the ice, maybe two, as we'll need to experiment to find the best way to store it as long as we can."

Fiona began spluttering in protest until T'mar said the one word that was certain to silence her. Rising from his chair, he nodded to her, his eyes twinkling. "Weyrwoman."

Fiona forced her temper back under control, giving him a seething look as she nodded his dismissal.

"Until later, wingleader," she replied, stressing the last word with a tone that hinted threat and revenge while emphasizing her superior position—a mannerism she'd learned from her father when he dealt with recalcitrant holders minor and lofty craftsfolk.

When Terin arrived later in the day, Fiona had her detail a work party to clear out the innermost supply room.

"And make sure that we can get in and out of it easily," she added. "I'm off to check on the injured riders."

"Say hello to K'rall for me," Terin said in a waspish tone—the older bronze rider was a very bad patient who was completely unwilling to have young Terin tend to him and refused to accept that she was headwoman, even when Fiona had asked Talenth to relay the information to Seyorth, his dragon.

Fiona he treated with a mixture of awe and condescension, not forgetting for a moment that she was a queen rider but constantly harping on about her youth. As she got to know him more, Fiona started treating him like one of the old guards at Fort Hold: she was polite, deferential, but very definitely in charge.

And she was grateful that of all the older wingleaders, she had to deal with him rather than H'nez, whose manners brought out the worst of her famous Fort Hold temper.

She stopped in the kitchen long enough to prepare a light tray and grab a first-aid bag, then headed around the Bowl to K'rall's weyr. She mused at this other difference in Igen Weyr living—at Fort Weyr, no one thought twice about walking directly from one side of the Bowl to the other, but here, in hot Igen, everyone was careful to use the interior corridors and the back entrances to the weyrs.

Fiona made a mental note to herself—again—to get canvas and

fittings for awnings that could be placed above the weyrs to provide shade. She and Terin had seen the small indentations above
either side of every weyr in Igen and had quickly divined their
purpose, but a search for the corresponding poles and canvas had
proven fruitless. She couldn't imagine why the cooler Telgar Weyr
clime would require such things, but perhaps the Igen weyrfolk
had decided to bring this bit of familiarity with them.

Fiona imagined how the Weyr would look festooned with
brightly colored canvases—from above it might look like a mini-
Gather, quite colorful. She wondered if riders would insist on having the awning colors match their dragons' colors or if they would
go for more elaborate designs. In fact—and Fiona made another
mental note—such work could easily be extended to tents that
might be profitably traded with desert folk everywhere. Perhaps
there was a new trade for the Fort riders, used as they were to
knitting garments in their spare time. But first they'd have to trade
for the fabric . . .

She stopped outside K'rall's door, listening and gathering her
breath and thoughts.

"K'rall?" she called when she was ready, and marched through
the door.

"Are you decent?" she asked as she placed the tray on his dining table, keeping to the newly established ritual of asking a question that would both alarm and please the older man.

"K'rall?" she called again, looking around the room, her eyes narrowed. She went to the hanging glows and turned them up, glancing around the room. She heard a noise from the lavatory. "I'll just
wait outside," she called. "Knock on the table when you're ready."

She went back outside and waited.

Talenth? Fiona asked her half-awake queen. *Could you ask Seyorth how K'rall is this morning?*

Seyorth says that K'rall wants to get the bandages off, Talenth told
her. *He says that K'rall is grumpy this morning.*

Tell Seyorth that K'rall needs to keep the bandages on, Fiona replied.
There was no point in telling a dragon that the bandages would
have to be maintained for at least a month—dragons didn't remember such lengths well. A month and forever were closely related in a dragon's mind.

I've told him, Talenth replied a moment later. *Why is it that all the bronzes are so polite to me?*

It's because you're their queen, Fiona told her, smiling to herself; they had this discussion at least every other day. Talenth was both overjoyed by and slightly nervous about the apparent adulation showered upon her by her fellow dragons.

It's good to be queen, Talenth decided. Fiona smiled and shook her head affectionately.

K'rall's voice interrupted. "When she rises, make sure she doesn't blood her kills."

"You haven't taken off your bandages have you?" Fiona demanded, bustling into the room. His strange reference to Talenth's future rising made her wonder if he wasn't also feverish. Although it was also possible that the older rider had said it merely to distract her.

"It itched," K'rall said, turning to look at her. Fiona had to work hard to school the revulsion out of her expression—the right side of K'rall's face was a mess.

"Shards!" she exclaimed. "Now we'll have to redo the sutures."

Talenth, have one of the weyrlings bring some fellis juice, Fiona ordered. *Whoever's on duty in the pharmacy.*

Turning her attention back to K'rall, Fiona clenched her jaw and took the seat opposite him.

"You've got a nasty wound, K'rall," Fiona told him, examining the mauled side of his face with all the detachment she could muster. "You didn't suffer just a single burn, you know."

K'rall lowered his eyes—he was lucky to still have the right one—unwilling to face either the truth or the Weyrwoman.

"*If* you behave, you'll get back the full use of your jaw," Fiona said. "If not, we'll be feeding you porridge for the rest of your life."

"I had to see," K'rall said slowly, his words slurred. "I had to know."

"*You* had to listen to your Weyrwoman!" Fiona shouted at him, losing her temper. Before K'rall could voice an angry retort, Fiona softened, and reached out to take his hand. "I'm sorry, but I don't want to see you disfigured."

K'rall raised his other hand toward his face—Fiona grabbed it with her free hand and gently put it back on the table. She shushed him, saying, "You are a dragonrider, you bear your wounds with pride." She nodded fiercely, feeling both the strength and truth of her words. Whatever her feelings about his personality, Fiona would never deny K'rall's courage. "If you let me," she continued, "I will see to it that the damage is slight."

She saw his eyes light in disagreement and shook her head at him. "Your wounds are not so different from the others'," she told him. "And I learned enough at the Hold and the Hall to know how to treat them.

"You need rest, you need to keep your muscles still, so that they can grow and recover, and you need to keep the bandages on until the skin has healed." Fiona found herself marveling at her words and her tone of voice—where had she learned to speak like this? Then she realized: She was speaking like her father had, like Cisca did.

"We must play our part, Fiona," Bemin had said to her once, on the sad day when they'd buried one of the old Fort guards. "Even when we don't want to, we must act as though we know all the answers and can do whatever is asked of us." He had smiled at her as he added, "And, after a while, it is no longer playing."

Fiona now understood the meaning of those words. She was no longer playing.

She saw K'rall's unspoken question lingering in his eyes. It was difficult for her to answer.

You must play your part.

"You are a handsome man, K'rall," Fiona said, not surprised to hear his breath catch or see his eyes rise to meet hers. She met them squarely. "I'm of the age where I notice such things more and more"—she felt heat rising in her cheeks, but she persisted— "and I've seen the way some of the women back the Weyr watched you." She smiled. "I think that won't change when you get back."

"You can't know," K'rall murmured.

"Nor can you," Fiona told him firmly. She heard the scuttling of feet moving quickly toward them and heaved an internal sigh of relief that the weyrling from the pharmacy had arrived. "Now finish your breakfast and then lie back down—we're going to have to redo those stitches and then dose you with fellis juice—you need to rest." When K'rall opened his mouth again to protest, she threw up a hand. "One more word, bronze rider, and I'll stitch your mouth shut. By the First Egg, you *will* recover fully and you *will* obey me!"

K'rall looked ready to protest once more—probably to say that he would never disobey a Weyrwoman—but he must have realized that speaking was just what Fiona had ordered him against doing, because he merely sighed and slowly ate his porridge.

At last Fiona left him, replacing herself with one of the nursing weyrlings under strict orders to let her or Terin know if there was any change in his condition and to keep a good eye on his breathing—she was a bit afraid that she'd been too liberal with the fellis juice.

Fiona felt it was her duty as Weyrwoman to check personally on the wingleaders every day—and she made certain that she checked up on every injured rider or dragon every two days—so her next visit was with N'jian.

The brown rider's Threaded chest had been a particular worry for T'mar, who fretted that the cold of the long trip *between* times might have exposed N'jian to infection, so Fiona kept a careful eye on him during the first days at the Weyr. Fortunately, he seemed to have taken no ill from the journey, but his recovery would be slow and difficult. With the muscles of his chest and abdomen shredded by a strand of Thread that had been frozen just seconds before it would have devoured his innards, N'jian could only rest on his back or left side, and all movement was painful for him.

Fiona wondered if the rider wouldn't be well-served by floating in a warm bath, perhaps with some healing salts, but she was still sufficiently worried by the state of his wound to want to hold off until he'd recovered more. As it was, he was starting to develop sores on the parts of his body that supported his weight.

Fiona had decided that he could stand long enough to eat breakfast—he didn't need her to warn him against sitting as standing was a sufficiently painful procedure in itself.

He wore nothing more than a long, loose tunic over his bandages, partly because it was difficult for him to dress and also because that made it easier to tend his wounds.

Fiona schooled her expression into a smile as she decided to inspect his sores today.

"I'm going to want to look at the sores and see what we can do

about them," she said as she entered the room, glancing meaningfully at the weyrling who was already there. Without a word and
no visible sign of relief—something that Fiona had had to drill the
weyrlings on—the lad left them alone. Fiona had realized from
her own thoughts that having wounds examined in private would
be less embarrassing than in public, so unless she needed to consult with a weyrling or provide instruction, she conducted her ex-
aminations alone.

She went about the inspection with a sense of distraction that
she worked to instill into all the weyrlings—they were to show no
sign of embarrassment at tending naked flesh. It was hard enough
to recover from wounds without being made to feel ashamed of it.

Fiona realized that she had learned some of this detachment
from Cisca, some from her father, and also some from her brief
time with Tintoval, who managed to profess such a passion for her
duties that no one was bothered by her necessarily intimate exam-
inations.

Still, Fiona would occasionally in the privacy of her thoughts
marvel that she had been examining a *grown* man until she firmly
told herself to get over it—these were people, with feelings and
pride, people who had risked their lives and their beloved dragons protecting others; she would see them only as such.

"Let me get those cleaned up and bandaged and you'll be good
for the day," she told N'jian cheerfully.

"I'm sorry to be such a burden—"

"You flew Thread, you're *not* a burden," Fiona said brusquely,
cutting him off. "You get well; you'll be fighting soon enough."

N'jian accepted her assurances silently, wincing only when
Fiona touched a particularly sore wound.

"If you feel the need, later, you might want to relax in the pool,"
she told him when she was done and ready to leave. "Just let
someone know and they'll get the bandages back off."

Since she had tackled her two most challenging patients first,
the rest of the morning got easier once she'd finished with N'jian.
Still, she was glad to finally find herself back in the Kitchen Cavern relaxing with a mug of *klah* in front of her.

With a contented sigh of her own, Terin sat beside her, helping
herself to the pitcher of warm *klah* that she'd placed on the table
along with a basket full of warm rolls.

"Mmm," Fiona said as she bit into one of the rolls, "this is excellent."

The sound of dragonwings caught her attention and she turned toward the entrance, expecting to see a glimpse of the returning dragonriders. But an overwhelming sense of alarm caused her to jump to her feet.

Come quick! T'mar needs you! Talenth cried.

Warn the weyrlings! Fiona called back. *Have them meet me!*

"Terin, come on, something's wrong with T'mar!" she shouted over her shoulder as she dashed out into the Weyr Bowl.

She arrived just in time to catch T'mar as he slid off Zirenth's neck.

"T'mar! What happened?" Fiona cried as she knelt over him, shading him from the sun. She felt his forehead to see if he was feverish, but it felt cool. She glanced up in time to see the older weyrlings being helped down from their mounts. Only a few could stand unaided.

"Weak," T'mar murmured. "Dizzy." Feebly he moved a hand, attracing Fiona's attention to the carisak it held. "Go' the ice."

Fiona quickly organized parties to carry the riders into the Kitchen Cavern, lying them down on the ground all the while assuring their dragons that they would be okay.

"What happened?" F'jian asked as he directed another pair of boys carrying the last of the older weyrlings into the cavern.

"I don't know," Fiona said, still clutching the cold carisak that T'mar had given her. "They went to get ice."

She looked around and saw that all the weyrlings had carisaks that bulged. "Get a party to put those carisaks in the storeroom," she instructed F'jian. "Terin knows which one I mean."

Talenth, who's on watch? she asked, hoping that whoever it was was one of the responsible ones she could trust in this emergency.

J'per.

Shards! J'per was worse than any of the youngest weyrlings. No wonder T'mar had left him on watch.

Is he awake? Fiona asked acerbically, recalling how often J'per had been chided for sleeping on watch.

He is now. Talenth replied slyly. Fiona didn't need to ask her queen to elucidate for Talenth expounded, *I had Ginoth rustle his wings—that woke him!*

Good! Fiona turned her attention back to T'mar. Was there something about the Snowy Wastes? Could it have frozen them all more than the cold of *between*? Or—Fiona shuddered—could it be that some illness lived in the Wastes, something that affected riders this quickly? If T'mar and the older weyrlings died, what would she do?

"T'mar," Fiona said urgently to the listless rider. *Zirenth, what happened?*

Tired, the bronze dragon responded. *They all got very tired.*

Zirenth seemed unconcerned, which gave Fiona an immense sense of relief. She had Talenth check with the other dragons of the party and found the same thing—the riders had suddenly become overwhelmed with exhaustion, and none of the dragons were overly worried.

"Let's get them to their weyrs," Fiona said, rising from her knees. "They need rest; they've been pushing themselves too hard."

F'jian and the other young weyrlings worked hard to move the older riders to their weyrs, relieved to have something to do.

J'per reports dust in the distance, Talenth relayed when Fiona had finished settling T'mar in his weyr.

Traders?

I've sent J'per to find out, Talenth responded, seeming pleased with her action.

I need to know when they'll arrive, Fiona told her.

I've told them, Talenth responded. In a few moments, she added, *J'per thinks that they will be here at nightfall. He says that they look like they are camping in the shade.*

Very good, Fiona said. *Thank him and have him return to his post.*

Distantly she heard the rustle of wings that heralded Ginoth's return to his watch at the Star Stones. Fiona turned back to the sleeping T'mar for one final check. He was resting easily, so Fiona decided that she could leave him under Zirenth's care.

Let me know if he wakes, she told the bronze dragon. Zirenth raised his sleepy head long enough to meet her eyes and nod, then he curled back up into a comfortable sleeping position.

Stifling a yawn of her own and feeling that she'd had too much excitement for one day, Fiona returned to the Kitchen Cavern.

"We have a fair bit of ice now," Terin reported. "What do you want me to do with it?"

"Use it to cool any of the injured that most need it," Fiona said. She cocked her head questioningly. "How long will it keep frozen?"

Terin shrugged. "There wasn't enough to fill the room, so I think it'll melt faster."

"Can you put it in pitchers or something so that we can collect the meltwater?"

"There's a lot of ice for that," Terin replied.

"I was just thinking that it'd be nice to serve Azeez and Karina some *cold* drinks," Fiona said.

Terin's eyes widened in appreciation. "I'm sure that the traders would enjoy that." She grinned. "In fact, I think it's our duty to see what such cold drinks might be like."

Fiona shook her head. "Not for me," she said, "I'm ready for my nap. Maybe later."

"I suppose a nap's not a bad idea," Terin agreed. She made a shooing motion toward Fiona. "You go; I'll keep an eye on things here."

As Fiona settled a clean sheet over herself, grateful that the weyrlings had found mattress stuffing before their excursion to the Snowy Wastes, Fiona replayed T'mar's return in her mind one more time before drifting off to a fitful sleep.

When she woke, hours later, the sun was on the horizon and the day fading away.

Talenth, she called, as she slipped into her shoes, *how is T'mar?*

Awake and waiting for you in the cavern, Talenth replied. *I told him you are coming.*

Does he have any idea—no, wait, I'll ask him myself.

Fiona hurried along to the Kitchen Cavern. T'mar, seated at the raised Weyrleader's table in the back of the room, nodded to her as she entered. J'keran and J'gerd were seated with him.

"We were just discussing our trip," T'mar informed her as she sat at the table.

"And?"

T'mar shook his head. "We've no idea why it was so exhausting for us."

The dragons are fine, Talenth volunteered.

"Well, you'd been out riding before, hadn't you?" Fiona said. "Perhaps going from the intense heat to the extreme cold and then back again—"

T'mar interrupted her with a shake of his head. "I've made journeys like that before without this ill effect."

Fiona sighed, at a loss for ideas. It was almost as if whatever had affected her and T'mar and some of the other weyrlings a while back had affected those who went to the Wastes even more. Sudden inspiration caused her to gasp, but she shook her head when T'mar narrowed his eyes at her expectantly. Instead, she cut her eyes to the two older weyrlings.

"J'gerd, J'keran, for now if there are no more problems, I'd like you to get the older weyrlings ready to receive the traders," T'mar told them. After they had left, he turned to Fiona. "Well?"

"It's just that you and I have been talking for a while now about the dangers of being in the same time twice," Fiona began slowly. "What if that happened this time?"

T'mar frowned.

"When was the last time you went to the Snowy Wastes?" she persisted.

T'mar shrugged. "I think the last time was in the winter when we practiced recognition points."

"And *when* do you think you went to the Snowy Wastes today?"

T'mar frowned. "It was—"

"Was it now, in *this* Turn, or *then,* ten Turns in the future?"

T'mar's jaw dropped and his eyes widened as his certainty gave way to confused possibility.

"And wouldn't that mean that you and the weyrlings had gone *between* times twice today?" Fiona continued, triumphantly. "And that you were double or triple-timing yourself ten Turns in the future?" She paused to let her point sink home. "And wouldn't *that* cause you to be extremely tired and dizzy?"

"Yes," T'mar agreed slowly, "that seems reasonable." He frowned. "But I *only* know recognition points in the future!"

"Is that a problem?"

"It is when it comes to drilling the weyrlings—your weyr-lings—as they get older," T'mar said bitterly. "If it caused this much trouble with the older weyrlings, imagine what it would do with those going *between* for the first time."

"The second time," Fiona corrected absently. "They've gone *between* once already."

T'mar glowered at her.

"So how hard is it to learn the recognition points for this time?" she asked.

"It's not so much that as *unlearning* the old points," T'mar replied. "And we've no way to know *when* we are."

"How will we get back to Fort Weyr at the right time?"

"I hadn't really thought of it," T'mar admitted. "I had only thought to come back when we left; I don't know how we'd come back three days later."

"I'm sure we'll think of something," Fiona said. "For the time being, though, I think we should concentrate on our current problems." She grinned at him. "Like how best to make use of your ice!"

"You sound like you have some suggestions," T'mar returned with a grin of his own.

"I do," Fiona agreed, raising her hand high and beckoning to Terin. "And I'm sure Terin will have more."

A zeez and Mother Karina greeted the wingleader and Weyr-woman effusively as T'mar and Fiona ushered them into the Kitchen Cavern.

"We have news!" Azeez cried as soon as he saw them.

"And we brought supplies," Mother Karina added.

"We have some news of our own," T'mar told them. "But first, come sit with us."

"You must be tired after your journey," Fiona added solicitously as she gestured to the high table. She smiled at T'mar as she continued, "We've had a chance to explore our surroundings and prepare some refreshments."

"And something to trade, I imagine," Azeez said as he carefully seated Mother Karina and then himself.

"*Klah*?" Fiona asked, offering the pitcher.

"It's too hot for *klah*," Mother Karina replied.

"Tea, then?" Fiona offered, picking up another pitcher. "We've made a nice infusion of herbs and some of the orange rinds you left us. It's quite refreshing."

"What's in the third pitcher?" Mother Karina asked, eyeing it suspiciously.

Fiona poured herself some of the *klah* before responding. "In this heat, I have to agree that warm *klah* is not too pleasant," she began, reaching for the third pitcher. "But iced *klah*—" and she poured two lumps of ice into her mug "—is entirely different."

She raised the mug and passed it to Mother Karina. "Perhaps you'd agree?"

"Ice?" Karina repeated, eyeing the bobbing lumps in the mug. "It's the middle of summer—where did you get ice?"

"Perhaps you'd care for a new treat, made with sweet cane and orange peel," Terin suggested, bringing forth a covered dish and ceremoniously displaying a bowl full of crushed ice sprinkled with the orange flavoring. "It's quite tangy."

"You have this much ice, that you can make sweets with it?" Azeez asked in surprise.

"You should try the ice," Fiona said, spooning out a portion into a bowl and putting it in front of him.

"Most of our ice we use to keep our injured riders cool," T'mar added. "A large block properly placed can cool a whole room."

"A block of ice?" Karina repeated. "For cooling?"

"I imagine you could use it in your caravans," Fiona said. "We could probably arrange a trade—"

"Weyrwoman, you most certainly could," Azeez agreed, dubiously lifting a spoon of the shaved ice to his mouth. He chewed it slowly, carefully, his expression growing ever more enraptured. "This is marvelous."

"So you think we could trade with it?" T'mar prompted.

"Of course," Karina agreed. She took a sip of the iced *klah*. "This is good!"

"How many kilos can you get for us?" Azeez asked.

"Can you deliver it where we ask?" Karina added, glancing sharply at the other trader.

"Obviously quantity and delivery will have to be discussed,"

Fiona said with an airy wave of her hand. "But for now, perhaps you would like to tell us of your journey?"

Dinner that evening was an ebullient affair with weyrlings and those older riders able to walk mixing together with the traders, each group finding the other alien and fascinating.

"It is good to see dragonriders in this Weyr again," Azeez said as he leaned back from the table, replete with Terin's best cooking.

"Not that traders were ever invited to dine at this Weyr," Karina added darkly.

"Times change," T'mar said, not doubting that D'gan would never have considered issuing such an invitation when he'd been Weyrleader at Igen.

"Yes, they do," Azeez agreed.

"We have news," Karina said, glancing to Azeez.

"It is not all good," Azeez warned. "We have spoken with our traders and they agree to try your plan of transporting special goods by dragon." He paused, eyeing T'mar before continuing. "We have also spoken with some holders. The news there is not so good. They are shorthanded from the Plague and many of their fields lie fallow. What food they get they either consume themselves or give in tithe to Telgar Weyr. They have nothing to spare."

T'mar shifted uneasily in his chair, his expression dark.

"What about the wild beasts, those that were left to roam after the Plague?" Fiona asked.

"Those that you can find, you can have," Azeez said with a shrug. "None could stop you."

"But how will you find them?" Karina asked. "If holders see you herding them on your dragons, they are quite likely to count them as tithe to the Weyr."

"And I suspect D'gan will not be happy," T'mar observed.

"He'll probably accuse them of lying, which will cause them further hardship," Mother Karina said.

"So we are on our own for cattle," T'mar surmised.

"No," Azeez said shaking his head. "But you cannot expect to get cattle from the local holders."

"We could buy them somewhere else?" Fiona asked.

"You could trade for them," Karina agreed. "If you had something to trade."

Azeez held up a restraining hand before T'mar or Fiona could speak. "Ice will only go so far," he told them. "It is a luxury, and if there is too much of it, questions will also be asked."

"What about the watch-whers?" Fiona wondered. "If we get them, what then?"

"You could trade a watch-wher egg for a quarter-herd or maybe even a half-herd of livestock," Azeez said with a shrug of his shoulders. "But can you get one?"

"What if we could get gold?" Fiona asked.

The two traders abruptly sat upright and leaned forward. "Gold would buy many things," Azeez agreed. "It might not buy cattle directly, but it could buy things that could buy cattle."

"Where would you get gold?" Karina asked, her eyes narrowed suspiciously.

Fiona smiled at her and tapped her nose knowingly. "Craft secret."

"How soon could you get it?" Azeez asked.

"Not any time soon," Fiona admitted. "For the time being, we'll have to trade in ice."

"That will work for a month, maybe two, but for Turns . . ." Azeez shook his head.

"We will need to do most of our trading at night," Mother Karina said. "Not only to keep your ice cold but to keep our trades from prying eyes."

Fiona saw T'mar sit bolt upright and was convinced that he had the same startling thought that crossed her mind, but she glanced at him warningly as she said, "Well, if you want us to trade at night, you'll have to teach us how to navigate by the stars."

Azeez and Mother Karina exchanged a quick look, then Azeez shrugged in acquiescence. "It will be our pleasure."

"That knowledge has already been traded for," Karina said as she caught Fiona's look of surprise. She and Azeez exchanged glances, and then the old woman sighed sadly.

"It made sense for us to trade on the knowledge we gained from you," Karina admitted, her eyes downcast. "But it gives us mixed feelings." She paused, consideringly. Finally she raised her eyes to meet Fiona's. "We traded some fire-lizard eggs, knowing what we know of the future. One was a queen egg."

"It wasn't mine," Fiona said, her eyes all the same blurry with tears. Quietly she continued, "I got my fire-lizard eight Turns later. I named her Fire and loved her very much." She wiped her eyes and shook her head to clear her mood. "I wouldn't be surprised if she was from your queen's clutch. Do not regret it. I don't."

"Well," Mother Karina said, wiping her eyes as well. "It was a wrench to let the egg go."

"And," Azeez said, "as we traded on the knowledge you've given us, we consider that we owe you trade."

"I see," Fiona said, glancing toward T'mar.

"We come from a time ten Turns in the future," T'mar reminded the Traders. "Don't make the mistake of trading on that too much."

"I'm not sure you made a good trade," Fiona said by way of agreement. "Not only did you lose a chance at many clutches, but you also lost the joys of a fire-lizard."

"Your dragons will not accept fire-lizards near them," Azeez said. "We decided to resist the temptation."

"Beside," Karina added, "without fire-lizards, we will need to develop different means of communications."

"Not to mention that they hate the sandstorms," Azeez reminded her drily.

"We should talk more of trade," Fiona said, gesturing for Terin to bring her slates. "We have a list of things we can offer."

"And a list of things you need, no doubt," Mother Karina added with a gleam in her eyes.

T'mar waited until the next morning, when the traders were gone, to ask the question he had for Fiona. "What is it that you didn't want to say in front of the traders?"

"Well," Fiona said, her lips curved upward with satisfaction, "it's just that I realized that these traders have spent Turns navigating the desert by the stars."

"And?"

"Well, we know that the Red Star is one of those stars," Fiona continued, "and that the moons and planets and other stars all move in the sky in determined patterns."

"Yes," T'mar agreed impatiently.

"So," Fiona continued, smiling sweetly, "why can't we use the stars to tell us *when* as well as where we are?"

T'mar stared at her for a long moment and then, slowly, his lips curved up in a grin to match hers.

"And with the stars to guide us, we can come back to Fort Weyr three days after we left!" he exclaimed. He grabbed Fiona in a great hug. "I couldn't use the Red Star for such accuracy, but I'll bet the traders can teach us how to use the planets! Well done, Weyrwoman, well done!"

Fiona basked in his praise.

Weyrwoman.

FOURTEEN

First flight,
Wings delight.
Weyrlings soar,
Dragons roar.

Igen Weyr, Morning, AL 498.7.8

"The weyrlings want to start gliding off the queen's ledge again,"
Fiona said as she met T'mar for breakfast two days later.

T'mar frowned thoughtfully then shrugged. "They're *your*
weyrlings, do with them what you will."

Fiona mouthed "my weyrlings" in surprise and T'mar laughed
at her.

"Good training," he told her teasingly. "You never know when
you'll need it."

Fiona tried to come up with some response but was so overwhelmed that all she could do was splutter while T'mar watched
her with dancing eyes.

"You know," she finally managed, "you're absolutely right,
wingleader. They *are* my weyrlings."

"They won't be ready to really fly for another ten months," he
reminded her. "That much I will not countenance."

"Won't you, wingleader?" Fiona asked, drawing out the last
word meaningfully.

T'mar smiled at her, shaking his head. "You know that flying too early would strain their wings, make them unable to fly for any time at all." He paused, adding slyly, "It would make for a bad mating flight for your queen if she couldn't outfly her bronzes."

"Talenth will outfly any bronze here!" Fiona retorted hotly. From her weyr, Talenth bugled challengingly in an echo of her rider's declaration.

"I'm sure she will," T'mar agreed in soothing tones. "Provided you take care not to overstrain her before her time."

He stood up. "Now, if you'll excuse me, J'gerd and I are going to meet the traders for our first instruction in the stars."

"Now?" she asked, frowning. "The sun will be up in a couple of hours."

"Indeed," he agreed. "But this is the time Azeez requested, so we go now."

"Fly well," Fiona said, reaching for the *klah.*

"You'll be flying your own dragon soon enough," T'mar assured her. Then he grinned, "After all, you Turn four today!"

Fiona glanced at him in utter bafflement. T'mar gestured to Terin by the hearth. "Have you lost track of time?"

"Terin, what's he talking about?" Fiona demanded in exasperation. T'mar smiled once more, turned about and, with a wave, departed into the Weyr Bowl.

"Well, he's right," Terin replied.

"Four?"

"Today is the eighth day of the seventh month in this Turn," Terin said, sounding as though the date should be obvious to her Weyrwoman.

"My birth date!" Fiona exclaimed. "But I haven't Turned, I've only been here for—"

Terin interrupted her with a giggle, clearly thrilled with herself, exclaiming, "Ah, but *here,* in this time, you've Turned four!"

Fiona contented herself with a glower for her headwoman, as she tried to make sense of events. They had left Fort Weyr in the spring of the 508th Turn after Landing and gone back in time to the summer of the 498th Turn. When they had left, Fiona had . . . she paused to think through the numbers . . . five months and nine days to her birth date so she wouldn't reach her fourteenth Turn until then, even though the date would be the third day of the twelfth month of this Turn—she'd celebrate her birthing date in the middle of winter!

Fiona groaned.

"Head hurts, doesn't it?" Terin said with no sympathy. She moved the cauldron she was tending away from the hearth, dusted her hands on each other, and sauntered over toward Fiona, grabbing a stack of slates on the way.

"I've done all the figures," Terin said as she sat beside Fiona, sliding a slate over. "I'll Turn eleven on the fifteenth day of the twelfth month—twelve days after you—"

"But you'll Turn one in twelve days' time," Fiona interjected, finally seeing the humor in the situation.

"Exactly," Terin agreed. "I've got the dates for the weyrlings— young and old—but I'm still working on getting the dates for the older riders."

Fiona raised an eyebrow inquiringly.

"Well," Terin continued, "I was thinking that we should celebrate both Turnings, just to keep things in perspective."

"But you know, when we come back, we'll still have this problem," Fiona warned. "I'll have nearly seventeen Turns by then."

"And I'll be as old as you are now," Terin said in agreement. She smiled as she added, "I'll be nearly a full Turn older than Xhinna!"

Xhinna! Fiona's face fell. How would Xhinna react when they returned? What must she be feeling now?

"She knew I was going," Terin said, guessing at the thoughts causing Fiona's expression. "I'm not sure she thought it through, though. And . . ." Her words trailed off miserably.

"She expected to be with me," Fiona completed grimly. "But the Weyrwoman said—" She cut herself off with a brisk shake of her head. "Well, there's nothing for it now. We've Turns to go before we return."

"Only three days for them," Terin objected.

"Turns for us," Fiona persisted. "And that's what matters at the moment." She shook her head again to clear herself of future worries and glanced at the chart. "So, what sort of birthing day are you planning?"

"I wouldn't want to spoil the surprise," Terin replied.

"Not for me," Fiona said with a grin. "For you!"

Fiona took her "Turning day" celebration that evening in good part, dealing with all the taunts and gibes of the younger and older weyrlings with graceful aplomb, consoling herself all the while that Terin and the others would have their comeuppance later.

And, truth be told, the dinner and dessert were quite magnificent.

"I tried some of the hotter peppers that Mother Karina boasted about," Terin said when Fiona asked about the particularly spicy bean and tomato dish that Terin served with the cornmeal rolls that the desert traders favored. "And cumin and a dash of nutmeg." She frowned, gesturing toward the stores. "We'll need more nutmeg."

"Whatever you need, headwoman, we'll get it for you," T'mar declared, pouring out his third helping of the spicy bean dish. "This dish is worth every effort."

Terin glowed with pride.

She glowed quite differently—red with embarrassment—twelve days later when Fiona, having banished her from the kitchen, presented Terin with *her* "Turning day" feast.

The days between the two "Turning days" had been hectic and full of activity for Fiona, Terin, and the dragonriders. Still, Fiona had managed to find the time not only to reinstitute the early morning weyrling glides from the queen's ledge but also to inveigle T'mar and F'jian into turning their hands to cooking meals.

T'mar started with Terin's bean recipe and added roast herdbeast marinated in a hot spicy sauce of his own invention. F'jian preferred to highlight garlic in his cooking, spicing up chicken breasts with a sweet and sour sauce that filled the entire Kitchen Cavern with its tantalizing scent.

For herself, Fiona concentrated on sweet juices, trying some of the newer fruits that the traders had brought in from Keroon and Ista—pungent fruits with an amazing tang. She mixed these with rice from Ista and produced a pudding that tantalized everyone. Of course, Fiona presented the dessert to Terin as baby food—and delighted as Igen's headwoman turned nearly as red as the food in front of her.

After the meal, as the younger weyrlings happily cleaned up—mostly by gorging on the leftovers, Terin sidled up to Fiona and asked with a mischievous look, "And when is T'mar's Turning Day?"

Fiona didn't know and it took her several days and some gentle questioning to discover it, as T'mar firmly deflected every effort.

K'rall was her source. He had made great progress in his recovery in the three weeks since they'd arrived, and Fiona was now allowing him to talk for an hour each day—and K'rall, deprived of speech for so long, proved to be quite garrulous.

"So who's next with their 'Turning Day'?" he asked after Fiona had checked his injuries.

"I don't know," Fiona admitted. She cocked her head at him and smiled winningly. "Maybe you can help me . . ." and she explained her dilemma.

K'rall started to laugh, but gritted his teeth as a spasm of pain in his jaw and Fiona's flashing eyes warned him that he was still recovering from his wound.

"Give me a slate and I'll write down what I know," K'rall said. Fiona didn't have a spare slate with her but promised to return in the evening. After a few more polite remarks and an awkward silence, she rose to leave and continue her rounds of the convalescents.

"Is there anything else we can do for you?" she asked as she made to leave.

"Maybe you could," K'rall told her thoughtfully. "I realize that I'm not supposed to use my jaw too much, but it's been three sevendays now and my poor Seyorth is beyond restless. Is there something a rider and dragon could do for this Weyr?" he finished in a wistful tone.

Fiona started to suggest that he consult T'mar but thought better of it. She *was* the Weyrwoman, after all.

"I'm sure we can think of something!" she told him with a grin. Then she recalled her earlier discussion with the dragonrider and the fear he had of the reaction to his scarred face. "Why don't you come down and join us this evening for the meal?"

K'rall opened his mouth in protest, caught the admonishing look in Fiona's eyes, and closed his mouth, slowly nodding in acceptance.

"I'll have Terin get you a slate and you can write down those dates while you're there," Fiona told him. She turned and started to leave, then called back over her shoulder, "We eat at the Weyrwoman's table, in the back."

K'rall's amused snort followed her down the hall.

T'mar was not amused when Fiona informed him that evening as they made their way to the Dining Cavern. Fiona could feel his discomfort even as he tried to form a reply.

"He had to recover sometime," she told him. "And you've been complaining for more than a sevenday at how overworked your wingleaders are."

T'mar nodded glumly and Fiona cocked a sideways glance at him. "Are you worried that he'll challenge your authority?"

T'mar said nothing.

"That's silly," Fiona said. "*I'm* the authority here."

"I don't know if K'rall, recovered, will feel that way," T'mar told her. "You've yet to have fourteen Turns."

Fiona had spent much time thinking about this, so she had a ready answer. "It's not age, it's authority that matters here."

T'mar looked at her questioningly.

"As long as Talenth is the oldest queen, the dragons will defer to her," Fiona said. "And in deferring to her, they defer to me."

T'mar pursed his lips sourly. "You sound like a hardened, tough old rider."

"I'm not," Fiona replied. "But I'm a Lord Holder's daughter, I've been trained from birth to lead others." She grimaced. "I don't think I know anything else."

"You're young; you're going to make mistakes."

"What, and older people don't make mistakes, too?" Fiona snapped, eyes flashing. She shook her head, dismissing her anger. "Being young, I *know* that I make mistakes, I know that I have much to learn, and I'm willing to ask for help when I need it." She paused. "So, wingleader, will you help me with K'rall?"

T'mar let out a long sigh and broke his stride, turning toward her. For a moment as their eyes locked, Fiona felt that T'mar was seeing her in a different light, and it both thrilled and scared her.

And then . . . the moment was gone and the tall bronze rider nodded.

"Of course, Weyrwoman."

And Fiona realized that the look he had given her was not for the Weyrowman but for her, Fiona, herself.

K'rall did not arrive until dinner had already been served, and then he made his way quickly, head down, to the table at the rear of the dining cavern. He could not avoid the cheerful calls of the small numbers of ambulatory convalescents, but he acknowledged them only with a curt nod.

T'mar rose when he noticed the older rider, as did Fiona. Seeing their Weyrwoman rise, the rest of the table followed suit. K'rall sat hastily, but Fiona remained standing, sweeping her gaze over the other tables and commanding them with her presence to rise as well.

A hush fell throughout the huge room.

"It's good to have you join us again, bronze rider," Fiona said, looking at K'rall. He raised his eyes to hers and then recognized that everyone was standing in his honor. Fiona raised her glass to her lips. "I drink to your continued recovery."

There was a moment's silence, then the hall filled with a chorus of: "K'rall!"

Fiona sat down slowly, her cheeks burning as she darted a glance at T'mar, who shook his head imperceptibly, confirming her own feeling that she'd overdone it. Well, she'd made a mistake—she'd learn from it.

"I'm sorry, K'rall," she said softly to the bronze rider. "I meant to welcome you, not embarrass you."

K'rall glanced over to her and smiled. "I'm not embarrassed," he told her. "I was just a bit taken aback, is all."

"I was telling the Weyrwoman how glad I'll be to have more wingleaders recovered," T'mar said. "I don't know if she's told you much of our circumstances here, but there's much to do and few hands to do it with."

"I haven't told you much," Fiona admitted to K'rall, "because I didn't want worrying to slow your recovery."

"I'm a wingleader, my lady, worrying is part of my job," K'rall told her, his face set grimly but his eyes resting upon her warmly. "Tell me what needs doing, and I'll see how I can help."

Quickly, with useful interjections from T'mar and J'keran, and occasional nods from the younger F'jian, Fiona sketched the state of the Weyr's affairs, deftly handling K'rall's indignant outburst when she dealt with the problems of demanding a tithe and describing their successes to date.

"I see," K'rall said when she had finished. He took a moment to slowly chew a bite of his meal, then turned back to her. "And what is it you'd like me to do?"

"One thing that I absolutely require is for you to start rounds with the other injured riders," she replied promptly. K'rall raised his eyes at that but Fiona persisted. "It's vital that injured riders see other riders recovered from their wounds—"

"Gives them hope," K'rall murmured approvingly. His eyes twinkled and his craggy features creased as he said, "You've your father's way with words, my lady."

"Shh!" Fiona chided him. "You don't want to strain those muscles too much."

K'rall winced in agreement.

"Speaking of *between*," T'mar interposed himself deftly into the conversation, "we've discovered a problem with our training."

K'rall contented himself with a raised eyebrow in response.

"Our training on recognition points—" T'mar began then caught himself. "—*my* training on recognition points was—or will be—nearly eight Turns in the future." He paused, but K'rall gestured for him to proceed. T'mar plunged on, explaining about the ice—which prompted a surprised yet approving look from the other bronze rider—and the problem with timing it.

"I hadn't thought of that," K'rall admitted. He stabbed his fork toward Fiona and T'mar. "But you've a solution . . ."

T'mar nodded and explained about the traders and learning to navigate by the stars.

"I would like to learn this," K'rall said when T'mar had finished. He glanced at Fiona. "You think we can use the stars to guide us *between* times?"

"I think *someone* has done it—or will do it—already," Fiona replied firmly, recalling their arrival at Igen Weyr.

K'rall nodded in agreement. "Any idea who the mystery Weyr-woman is?" He paused, then added, "Or will be?"

T'mar glanced significantly at Fiona, who bristled at the impli-cation and replied heatedly, "No one knows!"

"Time will tell," T'mar responded teasingly.

After dessert, Terin placed a clean slate and chalk by K'rall's arm and Fiona eyed him meaningfully. K'rall glanced at T'mar and smiled, took the slate, and filled it in quickly before passing it back to Fiona.

Fiona looked at it for a moment, then passed it over to Terin, tapping at one point significantly.

"Oh, *that* will do!" Terin crowed ecstatically.

Terin and Fiona kept their plans secret until the first day of the next month. That morning they cornered K'rall and J'keran and brought them into the secret.

"He's going to hate it!" K'rall declared, his face drawn in as wide a grin as he could manage. Fiona smiled in agreement, then narrowed her eyes as she scrutinized the muscles in his face.

"We'll need to get some moisturizer or salve for you," she de-clared, motioning to Terin in the private shorthand they had de-veloped to indicate when Fiona wanted the headwoman to make a mental note.

"This is where it'd be nice to have a healer," Terin said, frown-ing thoughtfully.

"Bah!" K'rall snorted. "I'm well-healed and have you to thank for it. A bit of a pinch is all I feel, and I'm sure that'll fade as I work the muscles more."

Fiona had reluctantly approved K'rall's pleas to be allowed full expression of his face again. In the week since his first dinner in the Dining Cavern, her respect and affection for the gruff old rider had grown immensely. K'rall was less conservative in his thinking than Fiona had initially guessed. In fact, she realized that a lot of what she'd branded as hidebound in his behavior was more a re-sult of caution and a certain amount of fear of failure. And a lot of that fear, Fiona had decided, had vanished with his first Thread injury and its slow recovery.

Father always said that many sticks-in-the-mud were saplings trying to grow new leaves after winter, Fiona reminded herself. She smiled softly at the memory, and was shocked to realize that if she were to go to Fort Hold *now*, she'd find a father only forty Turns and still in mourning—scarcely a Turn had passed here since the Plague had taken his wife and other children from him. A part of her desperately wanted to go to him, to assure him that she would grow up healthy, wise, and strong under his parenting. She realized how much such knowledge could mean to him at the moment and the notion surprised her.

"What is it?" K'rall asked, seeing Fiona's expression. "A burden shared . . ."

"I was thinking of my father," Fiona admitted, knowing that the older rider would understand.

"Your Talenth is still far too young to fly, let alone *between*," K'rall admonished her. "And she's far too sensible to try."

"True," Fiona agreed sardonically. While Talenth was well into her fourth month, it surprised Fiona sometimes how maturely her marvelous queen comported herself. Talenth was insistent that she be last to use her ledge for the now traditional morning weyrling glide and she was the first to greet a newly healed dragon when it tested its wings for the first time in his or her recovery. Fiona cocked her head at the older rider but stifled the question on her lips.

"Something else, now," K'rall rumbled, feigning a hint of exasperation. "What is it?"

"Why are there so many more injured greens?"

"I don't know," K'rall admitted with a shrug. "Perhaps it's because there are so many more greens than bronzes or browns"—he held up a hand to restrain her from interjecting—"and the blues are smaller, so they're harder for Thread to hit."

Fiona nodded, and K'rall smiled affectionately at her.

"Now, if you'll excuse me, Weyrwoman, I've duties—*more* duties—to attend!"

She waved him away, certain that she'd gained another convert to her secret plan.

Fiona waited until after dinner that evening as the younger weyrlings were clearing the dishes and preparing to bring around the desserts and then, with a nod to K'rall, she rose from her position.

"If I may have your attention," she said in a loud, carrying voice. A bugle from a dragon in the Weyr Bowl outside ensured that the Dining Cavern was stone silent.

T'mar eyed her suspiciously and she grinned at him.

"As you know," Fiona began, unable to keep her face straight, "we have taken to celebrating events in here, in *this* time as well as those that would occur back in our own time at Fort Weyr." She paused to allow the riders to digest her words. "You may recall that this started with my birthing day and continued with Terin's."

She glanced toward T'mar. "And while it will be some time before we celebrate another birthing day, tonight we celebrate something that I think, for a dragonrider, is far more significant." She nodded to Terin, who pulled out a nicely decorated cake and started walking ceremoniously toward the high table.

"Tonight we celebrate the fact that this is the same day, in the same time, that a young Candidate stood on the Hatching Grounds—" Fiona paused dramatically, long enough for the instructed weyrlings to trot toward various other riders with smaller confections. "—and one, in particular, Impressed a bronze."

T'mar's gasp of surprise was matched by Zirenth's delighted bugle. Several other riders were equally surprised to have small cakes placed in front of them by grinning weyrlings.

Fiona reached for her glass and raised it high. "To all those who Impressed this day!"

She was instantly joined by a thunderous roar of approval that rang around the room.

"I never even thought . . ." T'mar began when he could find his voice again, but it broke and he just sat there, silently shaking his head in shock, surprise, and pure elation. Words came to him again at last as he reached out a hand to Fiona, saying, "Thank you."

Fiona grinned and nodded in response, thrilled that she had put one over on the all too aware T'mar.

"I'm surprised we never thought of this back at the Weyr," K'rall murmured to Fiona as she sat back down.

"Yes, I was surprised, too," Fiona agreed. "I suspect it will soon become a Weyr tradition."

"It is already at Igen," K'rall responded, and, eyes twinkling, he raised a glass in toast to Fiona.

B y the next sevenday, supplies were once again beginning to run low at Igen Weyr, and so it was with a sense of relief that Fiona heard the watchdragon's report that the trader caravan had been spotted.

"They'll be here in the morning," T'mar said that evening. He glanced over to K'rall. "Do you think we are ready?"

"To collect ice in this time?" K'rall asked. He had been drilling the older weyrlings in recognition points by flying himself and his Seyorth on long reconnaissance flights up the Igen mountain range, selecting prominent locations for references. Fiona fondly recalled the look of pure boyish pleasure two days earlier when K'rall had returned with a clump of ice—again she found more to admire under the older rider's gruff exterior.

"It would be nice to have something cooling for the traders," she said.

"How many hundredweight would you like?" K'rall asked. "I'm certain of six of the older weyrlings, but I'd not want them to haul more than a hundredweight each." He glanced toward his weyr as he added, "Seyorth will easily handle two hundredweight."

"I think I should come along, then," T'mar responded. "That way, between the eight of us, we'd have ten hundredweight—a half ton."

"Even Karina will be amazed!" Fiona said with glee. She caught T'mar's reticence and prompted, "What?"

"Ice will do for some things but it won't answer for our main need," he told her.

"I think you're right, T'mar," K'rall agreed. "Having a watch-wher egg would be our greatest asset with the local holders."

"I thought we had to wait on the traders for that," Fiona objected.

"We do, which is why I'm glad to hear they're coming," T'mar said. He rose from his chair, gesturing for K'rall to precede him. "But until they arrive—we've got some chilly work to do."

While T'mar and K'rall organized their riders, Fiona and F'jian organized the canvas and ropes the riders would need to haul back the ice.

"Fly well!" Fiona called as the eight dragonriders mounted their dragons.

T'mar and K'rall sketched salutes at her and then, at K'rall's command, the small wing lifted and went *between*.

"I hope they're not too tired when they return," F'jian remarked as they returned to their duties. Fiona gave him an inquiring look. "Well," he said with a shrug, "they're going to have to *time* it to get back before the traders arrive."

Fiona nodded glumly, then lifted her head up. "Which means we need to get the storeroom ready *now*."

F'jian groaned in response and Fiona slapped his shoulder affectionately. "Just wait until your dragon is old enough to fly . . . then you'll be able to collect the ice *and* store it yourself."

"That might not be so bad," F'jian responded wistfully.

"The ice is indeed marvelous but we can't trade it," Azeez said first thing the next morning after T'mar had proudly displayed it.

K'rall and T'mar both opened their mouths in what would certainly have been an indignant outburst but Fiona cut across them, directing her comments to Mother Karina, "Where does this ice need to be for a good trade?"

Karina smiled and nodded toward Azeez.

The byplay wasn't lost on Fiona who smiled in response. "You thought I wouldn't foresee this?"

Azeez stiffened as Karina laughed and shook her finger at him. "I told you she was trader!"

"That's as may be," Azeez replied tetchily, "but it doesn't alter the situation."

"Of course it does!" Karina replied, biting off more laughter. She pointed a finger toward Fiona, saying, "Go on girl, tell us what you've devised."

"Some of this ice we'll trade, to be delivered when and where you say," Fiona said, putting extra emphasis on the *when*. Karina nodded, expecting no less. "But we'll hold back a hundredweight for trade with the wherhold."

"Ah!" Karina exclaimed.

Fiona eyed Azeez. "You know where it is."

"Yes," Azeez agreed. His eyes shifted away from her.

"What is it you don't want to say?"

Azeez sighed. "They have little reason to like dragonriders."

"And what do you recommend?" T'mar asked, bristling with ill-suppressed anger.

Azeez said nothing, glancing first to Karina, then to Fiona.

"Send a girl," Karina said finally.

"No," Fiona corrected her firmly, "you want to send me—a Weyrwoman."

K'rall and T'mar gasped.

"Kindan mentioned some of the problems that Aleesa had when he knew her—not too long ago in this time," Fiona explained quickly.

Karina frowned at her thoughtfully.

"He said that the Telgar Weyrleader felt that the watch-whers were unnecessary and a burden detracting from his rightful tithe," Fiona recalled. "And so Aleesa hates dragonriders, fearing that they want to destroy the watch-whers forever."

"She's touched in the head," Azeez declared. He started in surprise when Fiona nodded in agreement.

Again, Karina laughed. "Come, Azeez! And how many times do I have to remind you that little pitchers have big ears?" she teased, jerking her head at Fiona. "This one grew up dandled on a Lord Holder's knee, listening to every conversation of importance for a whole Hold while being groomed to take over." She laughed as she caught Fiona's look.

"Oh, lady, do you think I didn't guess?" Her eyes twinkled as she continued. "Anyone who heard Lord Bemin's staunch support for Lady Nerra over her older—and completely useless—brother would have to be witless not to divine his reasoning."

Fiona thought of mentioning Kelsa and her future half-sib but decided that Karina knew far too many secrets already. Let Tenniz tell her, if it came to him.

"You are holding something back," Karina said with a cackle. "You look just like Tenniz when he doesn't want to tell one of his Sightings."

"I am," Fiona admitted. "See if he can see it himself." She glanced curiously at Mother Karina. "And where is he, by the way?"

"He is busy with trader matters in another location," Karina replied with a negligent wave of her hand. She smiled challengingly at Fiona. "Perhaps you can see where yourself?"

Fiona snorted in response to Mother Karina's jest.

Beside her, T'mar cleared his throat. "If you are saying that we should send Fiona—"

"I think it's an excellent idea," Fiona said, cutting him off. "When do we go?"

"The sooner the better," Azeez replied. "Our information is that Aleesa is dying."

Fiona nodded; from what little she'd heard of the events that had unfolded—would unfold—the news was not unexpected to her. She caught Karina eyeing her carefully and shook her head slyly.

"Her gold has clutched and there's a queen egg," she said.

Azeez gasped while Karina merely smiled, saying, "We were only told that Aleesk had clutched. Nothing was mentioned about what or how many eggs."

"I don't know how many eggs, only the queen," Fiona confessed.

"You know how this all happens, don't you?" Azeez asked accusingly.

With a shake of her head, Fiona replied, "No, I only know how it ends, not what events transpired along the way."

"Just like Tenniz," Karina murmured quietly.

"Except that, unlike Tenniz," T'mar interjected, "we know because this is our past."

"But we only know those things that were important to us or brought to our attention," Fiona added. She glanced at T'mar, then K'rall, reading their glum expressions.

"We must find another way," K'rall urged, glancing down at her. "We cannot risk—"

Fiona silenced him with an upraised hand. "Karina already

knows enough to trade for Turns to come," she told him. "No sense in giving her more for free."

She turned her attention to the traders.

"Do you know where the wherhold is now?" she asked. "Well enough that we can fly to it?"

"We know a place where you can land," Azeez admitted. "But we have no traders that we'd trust with this secret nearby, else we'd have them introduce you and bring you into the camp."

"From what we've heard, you must hurry," Karina added.

"But we've got all the time we need," K'rall said airily.

"No," Fiona said. "We've seen the effects of too much *timing*."

"Even now, I can feel the effects of just being in this time twice," T'mar said, rubbing the back of his neck wearily. His eyes narrowed as he added, "I didn't feel this drained until recently."

"When?" Fiona asked urgently. She made a conciliatory gesture to the traders who looked unnerved.

"Since Hatching Day," T'mar said with growing certainty.

"That makes sense," K'rall said. "Until you'd Impressed you wouldn't feel time the way a dragonrider does."

"Terin isn't affected at all," Fiona observed in confirmation. Then she shook her head. "We should have this conversation later."

"Agreed," T'mar said. K'rall nodded emphatically.

"For now, the question is how long will I need to be gone and who will handle my duties while I'm away?" Fiona stated.

"I hadn't realized we had decided that you would leave," K'rall protested.

Fiona sensed T'mar stiffening beside her, ready to add his weight to K'rall's argument. She spoke before he could. "As Weyrwoman, I am responsible for the well-being of this Weyr." She paused and let out a deep breath. "If we do not do this, I do not see how we can feed the Weyr, heal the dragons, and return to help."

"We could find something," K'rall suggested.

"We know what happened," Fiona said. "The only thing we don't know is *how*."

"But that 'how' could mean your life!" T'mar exclaimed, shaking his head. "I don't see that it's worth the risk."

"It's my choice to make, though, isn't it?" Fiona stepped away from the two wingleaders, standing beside Karina and looking back at them.

"As I recall, Kindan said that one of those wherholders actually shot an arrow at M'tal's Gaminth," K'rall replied grimly.

"Which is why it's well that Talenth is too young to fly, isn't it?" Fiona interposed sweetly. "It will just be me: one unarmed, harmless young girl."

"There's still time to back out," T'mar told her the next day as he lowered her down Zirenth's side at their landing point. Azeez had assured them that they were out of sight of the wherhold but less than a kilometer away.

"I wouldn't linger, all the same," Mother Karina had observed when they had discussed the plan.

Fiona glanced back up at T'mar, shaking her head. She'd made her pledge; she wouldn't back out. "I'd know."

"I'll bet your father wishes you were a boy," T'mar replied, shaking his head in admiration.

"I'm quite happy being a woman," Fiona said, smiling.

T'mar looked ready to respond but thought better of it. "Zirenth and I can be here whenever you need."

"I'll be fine," Fiona assured him, reaching up for the carisak that she'd handed him as she'd clambered down. T'mar handed it over to her and she hoisted it, scampering away from Zirenth.

"Circle around north," T'mar instructed her, "so that if they see me leaving, they won't suspect you were brought here by dragon."

Fiona waved in acknowledgment and started off. As the wind from Zirenth's wings buffeted her, she turned back to sketch a quick salute to T'mar, but she wasn't sure if he saw it before he went *between*.

She turned back again to resume her trek and paused with a deep sigh.

Talenth? she called.

I'm here. Her queen's instant response calmed her in a way that no words of her own or any other's could.

How are you doing?

Well, Talenth replied, her tone surprised that Fiona need ask. *But if you're going to be gone much longer would you ask Terin to oil me?*

Of course, Fiona responded, grinning to herself. She was becoming accustomed to Talenth's draconic ways, particularly the young queen's fading memory. She didn't bother to explain to Talenth that it would be easier for the queen to ask Terin directly, preferring to send the request to Seyorth, who'd agreed to listen for her. The older bronze sounded both quite pleased that she'd asked him and quite amused with the young queen's self-absorption.

It is done, Seyorth told her. He added humorously, *The headwoman was surprised to hear from me.*

Thank you, Fiona told him, a smile crossing her lips as she imagined Terin's frightened squeak when the bronze dragon spoke in her mind.

Anything, Weyrwoman, Seyorth responded. Fiona was stirred by the depth of commitment the bronze's reply involved and thrilled to hear him so easily label her Weyrwoman.

With one parting mental nod, Fiona turned her attention back to the ground in front of her. It was wild, uneven, and took her longer to traverse than she had expected. By the time she was near the wherhold, she was hot, sweaty, and thirsty.

She debated digging into her carisak for her flask and wondered why she hadn't hung it from her side the moment Zirenth had gone *between,* but finally decided that she should wait and ask for water when she met someone.

She had just started forward again when an arrow flew across her path.

"Now that is just enough!" Fiona shouted loudly, her anger and irritation echoing around her. Dimly, in the distance, she heard the strange bugle of a watch-wher, answered by several others. Shaking her head, she said to herself, "Shards, I didn't mean to wake them!"

She glanced around for a sign of the bowman who had shot at her but saw nothing.

"I need to talk with Aleesa!" Fiona shouted toward where the arrow had originated. "It's important."

"You need to leave," a man's voice responded, not from where the bowman had fired, "while you still can."

"What makes you think Aleesa is here?" a woman's voice demanded from where the arrow had been fired.

"Oh, this is too much," Fiona muttered angrily to herself. She was scared, but she was angrier than she was scared and she knew that *that* meant someone was going to come off the worse for it—and *not* her. Loudly, she said, "Look, I'm sorry about the fire-lizards but—"

Another arrow whizzed past her, this time coming from the man's position.

"No, by the First Egg, you will *not* scare me!" Fiona shouted, her voice echoed by the bugles of watch-whers. Her anger flowed from her like a storm as she raged on, "I am Fiona, Talenth's rider, Weyrwoman of—"

"Of what?" the woman's voice demanded.

"We have no use for a Weyrwoman," the man added.

"You have use for *me*!" Fiona roared back.

"I know all the Weyrwomen's names, there is no Fiona," the woman declared.

"I am Lord Holder Bemin's daughter," Fiona snapped back.

"Your first story was better: Bemin's daughter can't be more than two Turns," the woman said bitterly.

"I come from the future," Fiona said, backtracking. "I *am* Bemin's daughter and I Impressed a queen dragon." She couldn't help adding, out of a sense of honor, "And, anyway, in this time I've just turned four."

"You?" the woman snorted. "A queen?"

"Is she here?"

"Of course not!" Fiona snapped. "She's not old enough to fly."

"So, Fiona from the future, rider of a gold and daughter of a Lord Holder," the woman began, her voice dripping with sarcasm, "if your dragon is so young, how did you get here?"

"What's your name?" Fiona asked. She guessed that this person was Arella; she'd heard Kindan speak of her. The man was probably Jaythen.

An arrow whizzed by her in response. "You need to stop asking questions and leave."

Didn't Kindan say something about Arella having a watch-wher?

Talenth, would you bespeak Arelsk and say who I am, Fiona thought to her dragon.

Arelsk is a green, did you know that? Talenth asked conversationally, indicating that she'd passed the message. *She is quite nice, really.*

"If you are Arella, as I think, then check with Arelsk," Fiona said out loud, sending a mental appreciation back to Talenth. "My Talenth has spoken with her."

A moment later, bushes parted in the distance and a woman rose with a bow in her hand. She strode toward Fiona, her bow still cocked, but the arrow pointed to the earth.

"Why are you here?"

"Your mother is dying," Fiona said, not knowing how much time they had, "and Aleesk has clutched a gold."

Arella stopped midstride, raised her bow toward Fiona, then lowered it again, her face the picture of surprise. "How did you know?"

"For me, it's already happened," Fiona told her. "I did not lie: I am from the future, I Impressed a queen, and I am Lord Bemin's only surviving child." She was surprised at how important this last statement was to her. She gestured to the other bowman's position. "Is that Jaythen over there? Or Mikal?"

Some of Arella's wariness returned. "Mikal is dead."

"The Plague?"

Arella shook her head. "It weakened him, but he survived. Old age took him."

"He was babbling about something from the future," Jaythen said as he rose from his hiding place. He glanced askance at Fiona as he added, " 'A queen too young to fly.' "

"Those were his last words," Arella said, eyeing Fiona carefully.

"No, his last words were: 'You must listen to her,' " Jaythen corrected her, striding toward the other two, glancing up and down at Fiona. "I couldn't see how a queen could talk," he admitted. "Now I wonder what you have to say?"

A smile crossed Fiona's lips as she sent a silent thank-you to the late ex-dragonrider, wondering to herself if his Sight came from trader blood. "First, could I get something to drink? I'm parched."

Half an hour later, Fiona was seated cross-legged on the dirt-packed floor of a dimly lit cavern, drinking from a mug of cool water, aware of many eyes inspecting her, most of them young.

"There's more of them every time a green or gold rises," Arella murmured as she affectionately tusseled the hair of one of the younger boys, who bore a marked resemblance to her. She eyed

Fiona speculatively. "You've not experienced a mating flight yet, have you?"

Fiona shook her head. Jaythen snorted at some secret joke, and Fiona eyed him disdainfully.

"Bet you'll have less of a swagger when you do!" Jaythen declared knowingly. Fiona glowered in response.

"Jaythen!" Arella growled at him, shaking her head and apologizing to Fiona: "Men don't know anything."

"I've noticed," Fiona replied, keeping her eyes firmly on Jaythen.

The wherhandler held her eyes for a moment longer, then laughed. "You've nerve enough, that I'll grant!"

"'Needs drive when Thread arrives,'" Fiona responded, quoting the old saying.

"There's no Thread here," Jaythen declared.

"Yet." Fiona's tone was implacable. Jaythen bristled, but Arella calmed him by placing a hand on his knee, her eyes challenging Fiona to continue.

"Where I come from we've been fighting Thread for nearly three sevendays now," Fiona told them. She paused at the brink of telling them of the dragon sickness—so far no one in this time had been told of it. And yet, how could she explain why she'd had to banish the fire-lizards?

"We've been losing dragons not only to Thread but also to a sickness," she said finally, plunging into the heart of the matter. She continued quickly, "The fire-lizards caught it first, which is why I had Talenth send yours away—we don't know how, where, or when they got the illness." She shrugged. "We don't even know if they gave it to the dragons."

"How many dragons have this illness?" Arella asked, ignoring the suspicion roiling from Jaythen in nearly visible waves.

"I don't know," Fiona told her honestly. "At—" She paused again, then plunged on. "—at Fort Weyr we had eighteen that were feverish when I left and—"

"Eighteen?" Jaythen cut her off, snorting derisively. "That's nothing!"

"How long are they ill?" Arella asked.

"We don't know for certain," Fiona told her. "None have recovered."

"It's only eighteen," Jaythen said dismissively.

"There's more," Arella decided, gesturing for Fiona to proceed.

Fiona took a deep breath before continuing, "The Weyr is understrength. We've only seventy-two fighting dragons—"

"What?" Arella cried in surprise. "There are more than that at Fort Weyr today!"

"Did you lose that many dragons to Thread?" Jaythen asked.

Fiona shook her head. "We lost most of them to the sickness."

Arella turned to Jaythen with an expression of horror. His sneer slid off his face and his whole demeanor changed as he asked quietly, "How many?"

"Since we first identified the illness, we've lost one hundred and eleven dragons," Fiona told them grimly. "Some died from Threadscore, but most from the sickness."

"What about the other Weyrs?" he asked respectfully.

"I don't know about all of them," Fiona replied. "Some have cut themselves off from the rest of Pern." The two wherhandlers nodded in sympathy. "We're not the worst hurt. That would be Ista—I hear that they have barely one wing's worth of fighting dragons."

"How can they protect the holders?" Arella asked.

"Benden and Fort Weyrs have agreed to fly in their aid," Fiona said. "But we don't know how much longer we can hold on. We've less than a Flight ourselves and even with—" She cut herself off abruptly. Should she tell them about the watch-whers and their night flight?

"Even with what?" Arella prompted.

"Our last two Falls were at night," Fiona said in preparation.

"Dragons don't see well at night," Jaythen remarked thoughtfully.

"Watch-whers do!" Arella exclaimed. She jerked her head toward Fiona and grinned. "Mikal and M'tal, Benden's Weyrleader, have been prodding Mother to train the watch-whers to fight Thread at night." Her grin faded and she shook her head. "But she refuses."

"Maybe she'll change her mind," Fiona said hopefully. She *knew* that watch-whers had flown Thread at night but she didn't know if those watch-whers had any relation with the ones here, now, at the wherhold.

"I don't think she will," Jaythen said.

"My mother is old and set in her ways," Arella explained. "The Plague and Mikal's death have been hard on her."

Jaythen, who had been silently grappling with his own thoughts, spoke up again. "What I want to know, future girl, is what we have that you want."

"If you're really from the future then you know what happens," Arella said, eyeing Fiona speculatively.

"Not entirely," Fiona admitted. "I know what happens to *me* and to those around me that I care about."

Arella gave her a dubious look, so Fiona continued. "As you say, I've four Turns in this time—do you expect that I would be learning every single thing that goes on in Pern at such an age?"

"A Lord Holder's daughter?" Jaythen snorted. "I'd expect you to know more than your Turns would suggest."

"I do," Fiona agreed. "But I learned most of that when I was older." She paused reflectively. "At this age I was just discovering Forsk's lair." She smiled at the memory. "She was the biggest thing I'd ever seen and her eyes were—"

"You met Fort's watch-wher?" Jaythen interrupted.

"I used to sleep with her," Fiona told him, smiling fondly. "Father got so annoyed, but not nearly as angry as when I took her off after tunnel snakes."

"You caught tunnel snakes with a watch-wher?" Jaythen repeated, astonished.

"Not until I was older," Fiona confessed. "I think I had just turned six when I caught my first one." She grinned. "Don't tell Father or he'll forbid me altogether. But I earned a quarter-mark each!"

"Are you saying he *didn't* forbid you?" Arella asked with all the protectiveness of a parent.

"Well, he was always surprised at how I always seemed to have spare pocket money," Fiona confessed, "but I was careful never to spend too much."

"And he never forbade you?"

"No," Fiona said, smiling at the memories. "I was very careful to arrange it that he never got around to it." Arella gave her a perplexed look and she explained, "I mean, whenever the subject came up, I made it clear that I understood the dangers involved and my responsibilities to be an example for the Hold."

"And never quite got around to saying that you wouldn't go after tunnel snakes!" Jaythen snorted appreciatively. He turned, grinning, to Arella. "Almost as devious as some others I could mention!"

"Doubtless all women," Arella agreed with an evil grin. "Something you should bear firmly in mind."

Jaythen's grin slipped. Arella savored his reaction before turning back to Fiona.

"But, as you did with your father, you have avoided answering the question of what are you doing here."

Fiona thought for a moment, weighing her options and choices. Finally, she chose the direct approach. "We want to trade for your queen egg."

"Why? If, as you say, you have a queen of your own, what makes you think you can have two?" Arella replied.

"What are you offering in exchange?" Jaythen demanded.

"The queen is not for me," Fiona said to Arella. To Jaythen she said, "I'm offering you a permanent hold of your own, a place where you will be welcomed and honored by all."

Arella leaned back hard against the wall behind her, her eyes closed, an expression of hope lighting her face.

"Who are you to make such offers?" Jaythen demanded angrily, jabbing a thumb toward Arella. "Who are you to raise her hopes so high?"

"I am Fiona, Talenth's rider," Fiona declared, raising her head and voice in pride, "Weyrwoman."

"Weyrwoman?" Arella repeated, opening her eyes and leaning forward even as she wiped the tears from her cheeks. "We know all the Weyrs. Which Weyr claims one so young as you as its Weyrwoman?"

"Anyway, that's a Weyr in the future," Jaythen added dismissively. "Your promises can't be kept until then."

"I am Weyrwoman of Igen Weyr, here and now," Fiona told them.

"Igen has been abandoned!" Jaythen exclaimed. "How can you—"

"We came back in time," Fiona cut across him angrily. "Our injured riders and dragons and our weyrlings, even our youngest. We're here now to recover and mature. We'll stay here until the youngest weyrlings are ready to fight Thread."

"That'll take Turns!"

"Yes," Fiona agreed. "And through all those Turns, *I* will be and am Weyrwoman of Igen Weyr."

"So if the egg wouldn't be for you," Jaythen said, returning to her offer, "then who?"

"I think it's dangerous to know too much of the future," Fiona said. "But I'm pretty sure that you'd approve of her. Anyway," she continued, and then stopped.

"What?" Arella prompted.

Fiona sat still for a moment, debating whether she should tell them. Finally, she nodded to herself. "You must keep this a secret, all right?"

Jaythen and Arella eyed her suspiciously, neither agreeing nor objecting.

"I only saw the queen when they flew Thread at night," Fiona said.

Arella turned to Jaythen, eyes glowing. "I told you! I told you they would fly against Thread!"

"You swear this, on your honor?" Jaythen asked Fiona.

"Of course!"

Something seemed to ease inside him, as though his heart had started beating more strongly, and his expression grew less guarded and more hopeful.

"Who flew the queen?" Arella asked.

"Nu—the woman to whom I want to give this egg," Fiona replied.

"That's the second time you started with 'Nu,'" Arella observed slyly. "You can't mean that miner girl."

"She's already got a green; do you expect her to bond with another?" Jaythen demanded.

"The person I know has been bonded with a gold for all my memory," Fiona answered honestly.

"This queen egg will hatch soon," Arella said. "And if we don't find her someone with whom to bond, she'll—"

"Be lost *between*," Fiona finished.

"We think that some watch-whers go wild and live by themselves," Jaythen told her, shaking his head. "But not golds. Aleesa says that a gold must have a person."

"So, future girl," Jaythen surmise grimly, "you've come to bargain with something Aleesa won't want, in hopes of delivering a queen egg to someone who already has a watch-wher of her own—are you sure you don't want to amend some of your tale?"

Fiona glanced at Arella and saw the same look on her face as on Jaythen's—and neither looked promising.

"This will happen, I know it," she swore firmly even as she wondered if, somehow, the future came about in an entirely different way—one that didn't involve her or Igen Weyr. And if that was so, how would the weyrlings be fed or supplies for the wounded be found? Desperately, she asked, "Can I talk to Aleesa? Please?"

Arella glanced to see Jaythen's reaction and, when he shook his head, sighed and repeated the motion.

"My mother is old and tired," Arella said. "What you offer is nothing she'd want to hear and I won't have you upsetting her."

Jaythen rose, gesturing toward the cave's exit. "It's best if you leave now."

Tears of rage and disappointment threatened to overwhelm Fiona. She sat there, shaking her head. "No," she murmured to herself. "No, it *has* to be this way!"

With the speed of a tunnel snake, Jaythen whipped around, wrapped his hand tightly around her arm, and yanked her off the floor. "No, it *doesn't,* holder girl!" he shouted, propelling her toward the exit.

Fiona turned back, determined not to leave only to find herself twirled tightly against his chest, a gleam of metal suddenly visible down by her neck, just below her line of sight.

"Don't think I won't!" Jaythen whispered in her ear, his words filled with a desperation and a longing that seemed like madness to Fiona.

"Jaythen!" Arella screamed. The room was suddenly full of children, all peering wide-eyed at the scenario.

"She comes here and makes promises she can't keep and then thinks to defy us!" Jaythen yelled, his words deafening in Fiona's ear. He twitched and Fiona felt a sharp pain at her throat, as Jaythen pressed his blade tightly against her skin. Fiona gasped.

Talenth! she cried.

"Jaythen, you can't, she's a dragonrider!" Arella cried imploringly.

"Dragonrider!" Jaythen spat out the word. "And what have they done for us? Sent us packing, disdained and denied us at every chance, or used us like pawns for their own ends." He eased his knife back for a moment, then pressed in again tightly, as he added, "Killing this one—even if she is a rider—would only be a partial payment for all the wrongs they've done us these Turns past."

A sudden raucous bugling and crying erupted all around them, echoing deafeningly.

"Jaythen, if you kill me, more than one will die," Fiona found herself saying. "More than all who live here, more than all who are now in Igen—maybe all Pern."

She paused, her blood pounding in her veins even as she forced herself to speak calmly, quietly, using all of the power that Cisca had cautioned her against, saying, "Put the knife down."

"You'd best do it now," an elderly voice said harshly from behind them. "Or by the First Egg, I'll send your Jaysk *between* forever." Aleesa.

The clatter of the knife as it fell on the stone floor was so strange to Fiona's hearing that it took her a moment to understand what it meant. Gently, slowly, she raised her hand and pushed Jaythen's away from her throat, moving to the opposite side of him as she did.

"You'd best run now, girl," Aleesa said. "And forget that you ever learned the way here."

Fiona shook her head stubbornly. "I can't do that." She found herself looking at a frail old lady who reminded her eerily of Melanwy—it was the eyes, she thought. There was only the slightest hold on life left in them, as though she'd already taken her last ride *between*.

"Please, we need your help," Fiona begged, adding when it looked like the old woman was going to deny her, "We can help you, too."

Aleesa laughed, a dry, heaving, cackle that was totally without mirth. "How can *you* help *me*?"

"Not you," Fiona replied. She gestured to the others in the room. "Them. The watch-whers and wherhandlers."

Aleesa eyed her consideringly for several moments, then nodded slowly.

"Aleesk woke me," she said. "She said she'd heard the dragon, the voice that Mikal mentioned when his mind was wandering on its last path."

She smiled knowingly at Fiona, slowly raising a finger and wagging it at her. "He told me something else, in secret."

She turned to Arella, her attention focused on her so tightly that it was as though neither Jaythen, nor Fiona, nor any of the others existed. "Do what she says," she ordered her daughter. "Do whatever she asks, take whatever she offers."

Arella gave her a long, troubled look, which Aleesa met unwaveringly. Finally, Arella nodded in acquiescence.

"So we just give in?" Jaythen asked warily, glaring over Fiona to Aleesa. "Again we let the dragonriders do as they please?"

"No," Aleesa told him forcefully, pointing her finger straight at Fiona, "you'll do what *she* says." When Jaythen drew breath to argue, she cut him off with a chopping motion. "You know better than to raise a hand to a woman, or did you forget why we helped Kindan?"

"You helped *me* that day," Fiona said, forcing her voice to be calm and controlled, turning around and raising her eyes up to the older man. "If Kindan hadn't defeated Vaxoram, none would have survived at Fort Hold."

"Or here," Arella said. "If it weren't for Kindan standing up for a woman's right to follow her dreams, there would have been no one to remember us, no *dragonriders* to come to our aid."

Jaythen let out a low, wordless growl.

"Nothing can change, Jaythen," Fiona said to him imploringly, "if you will not allow for change in your mind."

"Things change," Jaythen said, shaking his head. "They get worse every new dawn."

Fiona stared at him in utter bafflement for a moment, then looked at Arella. "Does he speak for all of you?"

"No," Arella said. "But his words ring true."

"Then let it be different," Fiona declared. She reached a hand to Jaythen. "Make a difference. Choose to change things and make things better instead of worse."

"Shards, you're worse than Kindan!" Arella exclaimed.

Fiona shook her head in resignation. "This I know," she said, catching Arella's eyes. "I know that there will be a wherhold, in my time, somewhere near Plains Hold. And I know that Nuella will be the leader."

"Nuella rides a green," Arella said, shaking her head but sounding wistful.

"I don't think she does anymore, or for not much longer," Fiona replied sadly. "I don't know what happened, a cave-in or snakebite or both, only that she lost Nuelsk."

"So what is her watch-wher called?" Aleesa asked, eyeing Fiona carefully.

"Nuellask," Fiona replied.

Aleesa mulled her response over silently for several moments as if debating with herself. Finally, she said to Fiona, "You speak of the future. I will tell you of the past. When Mikal passed away, he said several things, some of which sounded feverish." She shook her head in reverence for the man and the memories. "I didn't understand his last word because I thought it was two words, like a question, but he spoke it like a statement."

"Nuellask," Fiona guessed. "They say there are some who can travel to the future without a dragon or watch-wher."

Aleesa heaved with dry, wheezing laughter. "They say!" she repeated, smiling and pointing at Fiona. "You know more than you let on, little weyrling. You know someone, but you don't want to say who."

"Craft secret," Fiona admitted. She tossed her head up in apology. "If it were my craft, I would feel differently, but as it is not, I will respect their wishes."

"Ha!" Aleesa snorted. "You have just declared them traders!" She smiled triumphantly as she observed the look on Fiona's face. "I've a good idea who, even, but keep your secret, youngling." She turned to Arella. "I like this one—she's got nerve and she's not afraid to use it." Her gaze returned to Fiona. "Just be careful, weyrling, that you don't stick your neck under any more knives."

Fiona found herself rubbing her neck unconsciously, her eyes darting toward Jaythen and then to the knife still on the ground. Would she have talked him out of it if Aleesa hadn't appeared? She wasn't certain, but she thought so. Fiona swallowed as the import of her thoughts struck home. She could see how she'd be willing to risk all again, risk without thinking, simply because she was *certain* that she wouldn't fail.

"Ah!" Aleesa chuckled, her eyes taking in Fiona's reaction. "You *do* learn!"

"I'm stubborn and will fight for what I believe," Fiona admitted. "But I am willing to listen, willing to reconsider."

"Except in this," Aleesa guessed.

"No, even in this," Fiona replied. "Only in this, I have knowledge of what will be that compels me."

"You know what will be but not *how* it will become," Arella guessed, her lips pursed thoughtfully.

"I think I have the right idea of how it will become," Fiona persisted.

"And *that*, my little weyrling, is your danger," Aleesa told her, nodding firmly.

Fiona felt her face growing hot with embarrassment but she said nothing; there was nothing to say.

Aleesa seemed to sag where she stood; then with a small noise, she turned and started back into the cavern from which she'd appeared, saying faintly, "I am tired. I go to rest."

Respectfully the others waited until the noise of her slow movements faded into silence. Then, Arella turned back to Fiona.

"What do you need?"

"If she won't take the egg, weyrling, then our deal is done and we're through with you," Jaythen declared when Fiona had gone over her plan with them.

"Agreed."

"And if you can't get the wherhold, what then?" Arella asked.

"What would you like instead?" Fiona asked unconcernedly. She *knew* they would get the wherhold. She didn't know quite when or how, but she knew that the wherhandlers would get the wherhold. What worried her was that, try as she might, she could remember no mention of Jaythen or Arella in all the conversations she'd heard about the place.

Arella shrugged, undecided. "Something just as good?"

"The best we can find," Fiona countered. "I only saw one place on the charts where there was gold."

Arella snorted in reply. "I doubt we'd need the gold ourselves."

"It wouldn't hurt," Jaythen corrected her.

Trying to stifle a yawn, Fiona wracked her brains for anything else that needed resolving.

"You've nerves, I'll grant you that," Jaythen said, eyeing her approvingly. "But they've caught up with you now and you'll be useless until you've slept."

Fiona wondered if that was all the apology she would ever get from the wherhandler and decided, with another yawn, that at this particular moment she didn't care.

"Come on," Arella said, rising from her cross-legged position on the floor, "we'll find you a place to sleep." With a look of warning, she added, "I'm afraid it'll probably be in a room full of squirming children and they'll think nothing of using you as their pillow."

Fiona smiled. "I think I'd like that, actually."

Moments later, Fiona was the center of attention for a group of sleepy-eyed children.

Wake me if Aleesk stirs, Fiona reminded Talenth drowsily.

I will, Talenth promised, sounding tired but intrigued.

Not long after that, with a smile on her lips, Fiona drifted off to sleep in the warmth of massed bodies.

It seemed to Fiona that she had slept for hours but it was still pitch black when she opened her eyes to Talenth's urgent call: *Fiona!*

Aleesk? Fiona responded, moving carefully around the children, snagging her shoes as she left and slipping into them just outside the room.

She is outside, Talenth told her. *Her rider is with her.*

It's their time, Fiona replied with a dread certainty. Aleesa had reminded her too much of Melanwy, particularly in the way she seemed so tired, so pained by living.

Wake Arella and Jaythen, Fiona told Talenth. *Tell them to come outside.*

Fiona increased her pace, her hands outstretched to protect her from any walls she might not remember as she retraced her steps to the wherhold's main entrance, taking a spare moment to marvel at how much she'd learned from her times hunting tunnel snakes.

The smaller moon provided a sliver of illumination that lit the small bowl outside the wherhold. Fiona had no trouble spotting the gold watch-wher as she ambled into the clearing.

"You need to say good-bye," Fiona called out softly in the night. She heard a groan from the dark shadow beside Aleesk.

"I had hoped to go in peace," Aleesa replied, turning around, her face now visible in the moonlight.

"First you must say good-bye to your daughter," Fiona told her. She sensed Aleesa's annoyance and added, "That's one thing I still miss with my mother, that I never got to say good-bye."

"You had only two Turns when the Plague took her!"

"Less, and yet I still wish it," Fiona said.

A noise from behind her announced the arrival of Arella and Jaythen.

"Mother," Arella said as soon as she identified Aleesk in the distance.

"It's time for me to rest," Aleesa said. "I wanted to try Nuella's trick and go *between* with my Aleesk." She patted the gold watch-wher affectionately. Aleesk gave a quiet noise in agreement.

"But—" Arella's pleading voice broke off.

"It's my time," Aleesa said. "Mikal told me—that was my secret." Fiona felt the old woman smiling toward her. "He said I'd be seen off by a Weyrwoman, with all honor."

Fiona felt tears welling in her eyes as she clasped her hands together and bowed low to the old woman and her watch-wher.

"WherMaster, on behalf of all Pern, I honor you," she said, her voice catching on the word "honor."

"Arella," Aleesa said, looking toward her daughter, "I'm sorry I was such a hard mother. You deserved better."

Arella could make no reply, her eyes streaming with tears. She shook her head helplessly.

"Jaythen," Aleesa went on, then shook her head in exasperation. "You are the most difficult, stubborn, angry excuse for a man I've ever known." She paused long enough for him to react, before adding, "But I love you like you were part of my heart." She continued sadly, "You should not be the leader of the wherhold but its hunter and protector."

"I think I'd like that," Jaythen admitted. "I'm not good with people."

Arella snorted in agreement before turning back to Fiona. "Now, I've said my good-byes. It's time for me to leave."

Fiona rushed forward beyond Aleesa and knelt at Aleesk's side, her hands cupped together. "Let me help you mount."

"I'm sorry we didn't have more time together," Aleesa said as she accepted Fiona's aid and climbed up on the back of her gold. "I'm sure our fights would have been legendary."

Fiona stepped back as Arella and Jaythen strode up to stand beside Aleesk, Arella still crying wordlessly. Jaythen raised his hand in a stern salute.

"Fly well!" he called.

And in that moment, Aleesk leapt in the air, her wings beating once, twice, and then she was gone, *between,* leaving only a bitterly cold wind behind in her place.

Arella wailed, burying her head in Jaythen's chest.

"I'll be back as soon as I can." Fiona's promise rang in her ears as she watched Zirenth spiral upward and blink once more *between.*

"We'll give you a fortnight," Jaythen had told her. "After that, we'll be gone. You'll never find us."

"You'll go faster with dragon help," Fiona had told him.

"Yes, we would," Jaythen had admitted dubiously.

Now, as Fiona trudged up the gravel road toward Mine Natalon, the bulk of a well-insulated egg thumping hard against her shoulders in the backpack she wore, she found herself wrapped in doubt. How could she be so sure that the queen in *this* gold egg was the one with which Nuella had bonded?

And why would Nuella want to leave this place, the mine of her father? And hadn't Kindan said that she had a mate, Kindan's childhood friend, Zenor? What would entice him to leave his home and family?

And why *now?* Only she—Fiona—and the dragonriders at Igen had any need for urgency. Nuella had Turns.

Fiona swore angrily to herself as she continued to trudge up to the coal mine. Stubborn! Why must you be so stubborn?

She was so certain that she was on the right course, had found the path from the *now* of this past to the *then* of her future. But the only way she'd know for certain was if she *knew* that the dragonriders at Igen had found their food, found their supplies, and had founded the wherhold—and that knowledge was in *her* future, and so unknown.

What, Fiona wondered irritatedly to herself, was the use of being able to go *between* times if you couldn't be certain how the future came to be?

A smile crossed her lips as she realized how silly the notion was—and then the smile faded as she again tried to grapple with the complexities of traveling *between* times.

One day at a time, she told herself, repeating one of Kindan's favorite sayings.

The sound of barking alerted her to her nearness to the mine hold. A thrill of excitement, mingled with the tang of dread, coursed through her veins as she realized that she was committed now, that there was no going back.

She recalled what she'd seen of Nuella, Threadscored, insisting that she *had* to lead the watch-whers in their night flight, and picked up her pace, anxious to meet the young girl who would become that brave, inspiring woman.

She was surprised to see many houses in the open, most of them in varying states of disrepair. Then she remembered: the Plague. Still, in two Turns, surely there would have been more recovery than this?

She looked upward, toward the mountains, and saw the flat face of a proper hold, carved into the mountainside. A faint wisp of smoke rose in the mid-morning air, her first sign that the place wasn't totally abandoned.

A dog ran around her, its tail raised, barking happily.

"Hello," Fiona said to it, trying to identify the breed. Her father had kept several varieties of dogs spread throughout Fort Hold: sheepdogs for the sheep, cattledogs for cattle, guard dogs, vermin hunters, fowl hunters, and pets.

This dog looked like it might be either a hunting dog or a guard dog. But something about it—

She was startled when the dog, circling around behind her,

jumped on her back, knocking her over. Her start turned to fear as she heard its growl.

The sound of an arrow whizzing through the air ended in a sharp shriek from the dog.

"Run, girl!" someone shouted. "He's injured—he'll maul you for certain!"

Fiona needed no more urging. Scrabbling to her hands and knees, she staggered to her feet, the weight of the backpack with the queen egg packed in warm sand making her movements awkward.

Another arrow whizzed.

"Faster! Dump your pack!"

"I can't!" Fiona cried in despair, her feet feeling leaden as she tried to pick up speed and set her course toward the stone stairs leading to the proper hold. She felt teeth bite into her calf and stumbled, nearly fell, then picked herself up again.

"I can't shoot—I'll hit you!" the archer shouted. "Drop the pack!"

"No!" Fiona shouted, unwilling to give up her mission even as she felt blood flowing down her leg and into her shoe. She had to get away! She had to get—

Talenth! Fiona cried. *Send the dog away!*

There was a moment of shock as Talenth recognized that something was horribly wrong with her rider, and then Fiona heard a loud wail and the dog let go. There was the thunk of an arrow hitting flesh, but Fiona barely heard it.

You're hurt! Talenth cried in despair.

I'm fine now, thanks to you, Fiona assured her. *I've got a scratch but I'll be fine.* Even as she said the words, she wasn't certain. A wave of nausea overwhelmed her, and she just had time to realize that she didn't know if *she* would survive to return to the future before she stumbled. Instead of rolling, she took her full weight on her hands and felt the shock spread up through her arms and into her shoulders even as her strength gave and she collapsed, burying her face in the cold hard dirt, and then she remembered no more.

FIFTEEN

Rider to your dragon hew
Lest any harm should come to you.

Igen Weyr, Morning, AL 498.8.12

Talenth! Fiona's first thoughts were for her dragon.

I am here. Talenth sounded calm, but her voice carried an undertone of relief. *You are all right! She said you would be.*

Fiona wondered briefly if her dragon meant Nuella or the voice that they had heard before, the voice of the mysterious Weyrwoman.

The egg?

It will hatch soon, Talenth told her. *It is good you are better.*

"Lie still," a voice—male—ordered her firmly.

Fiona groaned and struggled to get up.

"Lie still or I'll dose you with more fellis juice," the voice ordered with a hint of exasperation.

"I don't like sleeping face down," Fiona said, her words muffled by the pillow under her.

"Then you should have thought of that before you got mangled," she was told. She heard someone move in a chair beside her, heard the rasp of a glow stone being turned, and from the corner of her eye she could tell that the room filled with a soft blue glow. "Don't move your leg," the man cautioned her, "but tell me how you feel."

"Fine," Fiona responded irritably. "I've got to get up, I've got to—"

"Rest," the man interjected. "You've got to rest."

"But the egg!"

The man's breath stilled chillingly.

"The egg is all right, isn't it?" Fiona asked, worried by the silence. "Talenth told me—"

"She did, did she?" the man asked, sounding amused. "You spoke of her a lot in your sleep but no one here has ever heard of a Talenth."

"What else did I say?" Fiona asked, wondering how much she might have to tell and how much she might have revealed already. "How long—"

"You've been here two days," the man told her. "Most of it dosed with fellis juice to keep you from jumping up and tearing your leg irreparably."

"The dog bit me," Fiona said, her tone calculating. "His teeth dug in but I don't think he got a tendon. I think he only mangled the calf." She paused, considering the wound critically. "It should heal in a sevenday, maybe two."

"It should, if it's not infected," the man agreed, sounding impressed with her diagnosis. "Are you a healer, too?"

"I've had to tend the sick and injured," Fiona replied, carefully guarding her words as she realized that the man still hadn't answered her question.

"Ah, yes," the man said in a tone that sounded agreeable but was tinged with lingering doubt, "part of your duties as Weyrwoman, no doubt."

Fiona stifled a groan. "You don't believe me."

"I don't put much credence in words murmured in delirium," the man corrected her. She got the impression that he hadn't altered his opinion now that she was awake.

"Do you think I'm still delirious?" Fiona asked, then added, "*Was* I delirious?"

"You certainly sounded like it," the man told her. "But now that you seem to be awake and—" His hand touched her brow quickly, professionally. "—not fevered, I may have to alter my opinion."

"What did I say?" Fiona repeated her original question. "And," she added tetchily, "who did I say it to?"

"You said it mostly to me, Zenor," the man replied.

"Mostly?"

"There were others earlier," Zenor told her calmly.

"Well, Zenor—wait a moment!—you're Kindan's friend!"

"Yes," the man said. "You mentioned him in your sleep, too." There was something odd in his tone, humorous but somewhat more than that—Fiona couldn't place it. "And the mystery Weyr-woman. Is that you?"

"I don't know," Fiona confessed.

"You were most urgent," Zenor said. "You said that you were from the future, that you had to see Nuella, that you hoped you weren't too late and—"

Fiona groaned loudly, furious with her indiscretion.

"You *did* seem worried about the future—you kept saying you had to get back."

"Shards!"

"And something about gold, which aroused quite a lot of interest, particularly mine," Zenor told her.

"Did I tell you about the wherhold?" Fiona asked, abandoning any hope of keeping all her secrets.

"You said that Aleesa had gone *between* on Aleesk," Zenor told her. "Like Nuella."

"Nuella's gone *between*?" Fiona gasped, pushing herself up in a panic.

"No, lie back down!" Zenor ordered, pushing her shoulders back down to the bed. "You're as bad as she was."

"Was?" Fiona repeated, her eyes wide with worry.

"You should sleep," Zenor told her firmly, shifting in his seat. "You're not the only one I have to tend."

"Who else?" Fiona asked, surprised and feeling guilty that she was taking him away from those who needed it.

"Nuella," Zenor replied tersely. "She's asleep in the next room, dosed with fellis juice like you."

Fiona's question flew between them, unspoken.

"There was a cave-in. Nuelsk saved her—" Zenor bit back a sob. "—we think. But a tunnel-snake bit Nuelsk as she tried to get out. She managed to save Nuella before she died."

"Just like Dask saved you Turns back," Fiona said in amazement.

"Turns back?" Zenor repeated, surprised. "It wasn't that long ago."

"No, I guess it wouldn't have been, for you," Fiona agreed.

"I suppose Turns aren't the same for you, then?" Zenor demanded. Fiona hid her surprise: he acted much younger than she'd thought he was and then, realizing her error, she asked, "How many Turns have you?"

"I'll be turning seventeen soon enough," Zenor told her proudly.

"And I'll be turning fourteen soon enough," Fiona replied, both stung by his tone and amused by the realization that "soon enough" meant anything just under a full Turn. Zenor had only sixteen Turns in this time! She had always thought of him as older, like Kindan. Come to think of it, in this time Kindan had little more than sixteen Turns himself. A thrill of recognition, nearly a challenge, ran through her—she was almost old enough for Kindan!

Idly she wondered what it would be like if she arranged to meet him, now, as old as she was with him as young as he was. Her pleasure at the thought faded as she wondered if she looked enough like her late sister, Koriana, to cause Kindan pain. Probably, she admitted to herself, he would recognize her as Koriana's kin and then what would she say to him? And what if he fell in love with her and she had to leave him—how would he survive having his love dashed a second time?

But no, Fiona assured herself, Kindan hadn't seen her or hadn't recognized her if he had met her in this time, or he wouldn't be at Benden Weyr, he'd be with her instead—*if* they'd fallen in love back in this time. The questions were so confusing, they made her brain hurt.

"You should get some rest," Zenor said, rising from his chair. "I need to check on Nuella."

Too tired to protest, Fiona drifted off into a hazy, fitful sleep.

"How's the egg?" Fiona asked when she next woke.

"We've got it near a hearth and it's still warm," Zenor assured her. Fiona was surprised to see a red-haired girl about her age standing beside him, bearing a large tray. The resemblance to Zenor was obvious.

"This is Renna," Zenor said by way of introduction. As Fiona started to turn over, he stopped her with a firm hand on her back. "You still shouldn't move."

"I *hate* sleeping on my stomach," Fiona complained, adding, "I don't think I can eat like this."

"Let me look at your leg," he said, going to the end of her bed and gently unwrapping her bandage. He leaned forward and sniffed deeply, smelling for any sign of infection. From his pleased reaction, there was none.

"With puncture wounds, the greatest danger is of infection," Zenor explained, half to Fiona and half to Renna. He deftly rewrapped the bandages and moved to the front of her bed. "Let's see how you feel sitting up."

Fiona was horrified to discover that she felt worse sitting up. The wounds on her left leg felt as though they were bleeding or, worse, her muscle was oozing out through the openings. It must have shown on her face, for Zenor moved to push her back down, but she raised her arm to forestall him.

"I'll get better," she promised. She smiled wanly at Renna, who gave her a dubious, slightly green look in response. "Perhaps I'm just hungry."

"Sit there; we'll bring the table over," Zenor said, gesturing for Renna to give him a hand. Together the two lifted either end of the table and carried it closer to the bedside.

"That egg will hatch soon," Fiona said as she gingerly raised a mug to her lips.

"I agree," Zenor said. Renna glanced between Fiona and her brother, her face set in a thoughtful frown.

"It's a gold," Fiona continued, having discovered with some surprise that the mug contained not *klah* but cool fresh water. "The last queen watch-wher on Pern."

"How can you be certain?" Zenor demanded, frowning.

"I can't and I'm not, but Aleesa thought so," Fiona said.

Renna's expression suddenly changed and she turned to Zenor, saying, "She's not suggesting that Nuella—"

Zenor waved her to silence. "I've explained about Nuella."

Renna turned to Fiona. "She's not ready—she's still recovering—it's only been a few days!"

Fiona was too weak to argue with the fiery redhead. A twinge from her wound prompted her to ask, "Why did that dog attack me, anyway?"

"Most of the dogs went wild after the Plague," Zenor said with a wave of his hand. "Too many were abandoned when their owners succumbed."

"Those of us who could settled inside the hold," Renna said, her face reflecting painful memories.

"I'm sorry."

"If the dragonriders had helped—" Renna began hotly, her blue-green eyes flaring angrily at Fiona.

"I was only a baby," Fiona began in protest before realizing that her explanation would only further confuse things.

"You don't look that young," Renna snapped back heatedly.

"Kindan said that the dragonriders had to wait until the Plague had passed to protect the weyrfolk," Fiona said.

Renna snorted. "They waited, all right! They're still waiting."

"What?" Fiona asked in shock, shaking her head. "No, that's not true! They dropped masks and fruit at all the holds—"

"Except those looking to Telgar," Renna told her harshly. "D'gan left us to live or die on our own."

"And that fool Fenric locked himself in his hold until Nerra recovered enough to throw him out," Fiona said, recalling her father's words on the subject as he explained why he had supported Nerra's claim to Crom Hold.

"Yes," Zenor agreed, giving Fiona a keen look.

Fiona didn't hear him, her mind absorbing Renna's words. She asked her quietly, "How bad was it here?"

"Dalor survived," Zenor answered. "So did Nuella, myself, Renna, Nuella's baby sister Larissa—mostly the young."

"It affected those in their prime more than the young or the old," Fiona said, remembering countless discussions with Kindan, her father, and the older hold survivors.

"Except in our case, the very youngest succumbed shortly afterward," Renna added bleakly. At Fiona's surprised look, she explained, "There was no food."

"We've only half the people that were here before the Plague,"

Zenor said. "Natalon had already had us starting to relocate to the new hold; afterward, we abandoned all the old houses."

Renna rose. "I'd better go check on Nuella."

Fiona waved at Zenor. "You go, too! I know you're sweet on her—"

A muffled gasp from Zenor and a startled guffaw from Renna made her realize that she'd broached a touchy subject and she did her best to hide her surprise.

"Kindan told me," Fiona said quickly, hoping to cover her gaffe.

Renna opened her mouth to speak, then thought better of it, shaking her head. She gestured to Zenor. "You should go. I just realized that our patient here probably needs some help getting to the necessary."

Zenor gave her a mulish look, but it dawned on Fiona that she *did* need help, and her expression settled Zenor's suspicions enough that he gave his sister a curt nod before he left.

"Just so you know," Renna said in a tight voice, "the last thing Nuella said to Zenor was, 'Why did you let me live?' "

"But I thought that Nuelsk saved her," Fiona said in surprise.

"She pushed but Zenor pulled," Renna said tersely, wrapping an arm around Fiona and guiding her to her feet. "So, your coming here with a queen's egg and sounding like Zenor and Nuella are mated is just as addled as expecting a dragonrider to say a kind word."

"*I'm* a dragonrider," Fiona said in protest.

Renna raised an eyebrow. "Really?" she asked skeptically, waving a hand toward the hills outside. "Where's your dragon?"

Not waiting for Fiona's response, she guided her toward the door and down the hall to the necessary.

By the time they returned, Fiona was so tired that she uttered no protest when ordered by Renna to lie down on her stomach once more.

"You need your rest," the redhead said, closing the room's shutters.

"Thank you," Fiona told her.

"See?" Renna replied with quirk of her lips. "You can't be a dragonrider—you're too polite!"

Fiona didn't have the strength to argue.

When she woke again, Talenth was calling her.

Fiona!

Talenth?

When are you coming back? Talenth asked. *I itch!*

Oh, I'm sorry! Fiona replied. *Can you ask Terin to oil you? I'll be back soon.*

She heard a noise in the room and craned her neck around. In the dim light that slipped past the shutters, she made out someone sitting beside her. It was a woman with gold hair.

"You must be Nuella," Fiona said, starting to roll on her side and then thinking better of it as a stabbing pain reminded her of her wound.

"Why are you here?" The question came out of a voice husky with disuse and despair.

"I heard about Nuelsk," Fiona said. "I'm sorry."

"But you want me to take the queen egg," Nuella said accusingly. She heard Fiona's surprised gasp and added, "I hear very well—better than Zenor thinks."

Fiona spent a moment absorbing the young woman's words. How old was Nuella, anyway? Fiona wondered. She'd seemed very old when she met her at Fort Weyr, but that was ten Turns in the future . . . Nuella was about the same age as Kindan . . . she'd have about sixteen Turns now.

"You said you had a queen of your own," Nuella said proddingly.

"Talenth," Fiona replied unable to keep the warmth out of her voice.

"Could you imagine losing her?"

"I lost my fire-lizard," Fiona replied. Fondly she recalled Fire, and her breath caught.

"How?"

Fiona hesitated before responding. "I think it's dangerous for people to know too much about their future."

"We're talking about your past."

"My past is your future," Fiona said. "Did you hear me when I was talking in my sleep?"

"No."

Fiona decided that she really hated thinking face down. "Will you help me sit up?"

"No," Nuella replied. "If Zenor has you lying down, then I think you'd best stay that way."

"But it's so hard to *think*!" Fiona complained. It was hard enough to think at all, and had been ever since she'd Impressed Talenth. From that moment on she'd been fighting the dizziness and fatigue that she'd come to associate with being twice in the same time. Was it because she'd timed it back here, to this now? Or was it something else?

Fiona forced herself to focus. Now wasn't the moment to consider this issue. Nuella. She had to talk to Nuella. She was here, now. She wished she had some *klah*.

"How did you survive the Plague, then?" Nuella demanded.

"I was a baby; I don't remember much of it," Fiona replied instantly without thinking. She groaned as she realized what she'd said and then let out a deep sigh.

"I wish I hadn't said that," she said then. "I come from ten Turns in the future. In my time, there's been no hint that we came back in time to here. I hate having to ask so many people to keep this secret."

"Well, if nobody knows in your time, you must have chosen wisely," Nuella observed.

Fiona mulled on that for a moment, started to nod, felt the pillow against her face and thought better of it. Besides, Nuella couldn't see her movement anyway. "I hadn't thought of it that way," she said. "Kindan trusted you, so—"

Nuella snorted derisively. "Kindan!"

"What?" Fiona asked, surprised at Nuella's tone. "Are you angry with him? I thought you wanted Nuelsk."

"Do I have her now?" Nuella cried, her voice breaking. "Is she here with me now?"

A door opened and light spilled into the room as Zenor strode in angrily.

"Nuella!" he exclaimed. Then, to Fiona, he said, "What have you said to her?"

"Stop, stop, it's not her fault!" Nuella cried.

"What did you say?" Zenor persisted, shutting the door and pounding up to Fiona's bedside. "Don't you know she's been through enough?"

"Stop protecting me!" Nuella insisted.

This is too much! Fiona thought miserably. Her wounded calf throbbed horribly and she felt nauseated by the emotions whipping around her.

Talenth! Send T'mar, Fiona called to her queen. Just the act of reaching out calmed her. *Send him now!*

He comes! Talenth replied. *You sound sad.*

A loud bugle, muffled by thick walls, announced the arrival of the bronze.

"That's T'mar," Fiona said. "He'll take me back." She started to rise, wondering how she would find her things and where they had put the queen egg. "I can't handle this anymore."

A hand gently pushed her back down as Nuella said, "Stay."

"You need to rest," Zenor declared.

"I can't rest here," Fiona said, resisting Nuella's hand. She bit back a sob. "I'm sorry, I've done you nothing but harm since I came here."

"Tell me about the future," Nuella said, her hand still resting gently on Fiona's back.

"Why should I?"

"Nuella, she's probably lying!" Zenor declared.

"No, she's not," Nuella told him. "How many people do you know who can order dragons around?" She said to Fiona, "You can tell T'mar that—"

A loud noise outside announced T'mar's presence.

"This place is nothing but children!" T'mar shouted, his anger obvious. "Out of my way! Out of my way, all of you! Where is Fiona!"

"In here," Fiona called. Zenor rose and opened the door.

"Fiona!" T'mar cried, shoving Zenor out of his way and rushing to her side. Taking in her bandaged leg, he asked, "What happened?"

"A dog bit me," Fiona told him. And then, suddenly, it was funny to her. She started laughing.

"A dog *bit* me, can you imagine?" It was the funniest thing she'd ever said, she decided. Her chest hurt from laughing while lying on it and her leg twinged every time her chest heaved. "Oh, Shards! It hurts to laugh!"

T'mar turned wide eyes to Zenor. "She's not feverish?"

"No," Zenor said, eyeing Fiona with concern. "She wasn't the last time I checked."

"It's the strain," Nuella said. "She's laughing to relieve her emotions."

"That's it!" Fiona agreed, then proceeded into another round of laughter. "If I don't laugh, I'll cry!"

Suddenly that seemed like a very excellent idea and tears started streaming down her face.

Nuella's hand on her back became firmer, moving more slowly. "It's okay. It's okay, Weyrwoman, we believe you. We believe you now."

"What, all I had to do was cry?" Fiona demanded through her tears. "Or was it laugh?"

"Both," Nuella said. "Zenor, I think she should sit up, maybe drink something."

"I want to feel her temperature," Zenor said by way of agreement. "Fiona, if you can sit up for a moment, you might feel better."

"I don't know," Fiona said, even as Nuella's hand moved to her far shoulder and applied a gentle upward pressure.

"I think they're right," T'mar said, his voice approaching her. His strong hands grabbed her shoulders and gently guided her upright.

"Most of them died in the Plague, T'mar," Fiona said as soon as she saw his face, lined with a harsh look that seemed ready to turn into an unbridled anger. "Telgar sent no aid, nothing."

T'mar sucked in air in a hiss. "I'd heard," he said shortly. He turned to Zenor and Nuella. "I cannot tell you how sorry—"

"But we stole their Weyr!" Fiona exclaimed, her eyes suddenly dancing once more with humor. "We came back in time and took Igen Weyr."

Zenor gave T'mar a questioning look that turned into one of surprise when the bronze rider nodded in acknowledgment.

"We ought to take Telgar, too," Fiona declared in a murmur to herself. "It'd serve them right." The idea appealed to her so much, she caught T'mar's gaze and continued, "When we get back, why don't you go there for their next mating flight? You'd make a great Weyrleader." She had a moment to marvel at the words pouring out of her mouth before she added, "Better than D'gan, better than H'nez."

"This is not like her," T'mar said to Zenor, his mouth set in a frown.

"It's stress," Nuella said. "She has been through a lot and the bite has—"

"—added physical stress to her mental exhaustion," Zenor finished.

"I can't be exhausted," Fiona declared, trying to rise on her feet and stopping as a sudden pain tore up her left leg. "Ouch, that hurts!"

"Fiona, you must rest," Nuella said. "Lie back down and rest."

Zenor ran a quick hand over Fiona's forehead and nodded gravely. "You're flushed, and peaked."

He rose quickly and crossed the room to a side table, quickly emptying several containers into a mug and returning with it. "Drink this."

Fiona took a sip and made a face. "It's wine and fellis juice."

"You need your rest," T'mar said. "You heard the healer."

"He's not a healer," Fiona said even as a frantic part of her fought to get control of her mouth. "He's a goldsmith."

"Goldsmith!" Nuella repeated. She heard T'mar's gasp of surprise and her expression grew thoughtful.

"You must rest," Zenor said to Fiona, gently easing her back down to the bed. "I'm sorry that we distressed you; your recovery will be delayed because of it."

"T'mar, tell them, make them understand," Fiona begged, fresh tears somehow forming at the edges of her vision. "Tell them whatever they want to know."

"As you wish, Weyrwoman," T'mar agreed, leaning down toward her to plant a soft kiss on her cheek.

"You kissed me!" Fiona declared in muzzy surprise. "I like that."

Exhaustion overcame her before she could say more, and she slipped into a deep sleep with a contented sigh.

T'mar's voice greeted the moment her eyelids fluttered open. "The egg has hatched."

"Oh, Shards! I'd hoped to be there," Fiona exclaimed.

"Don't sit up," T'mar said warningly. "Your wound is still healing."

"Nuella . . . ?"

"She says that the queen is the most beautiful creature she's ever known," T'mar told her, his tone conveying both wistfulness and sardonic surprise.

"And?"

"She and Dalor—did you know they are twins?—have agreed that she and Zenor can leave as soon as the queen is able."

"What about the rest of it?"

"What rest of it?" T'mar asked, surprised. "Isn't that all we need?"

"No," Fiona said. "They have to form the wherhold, they have to take Arella, Jaythen, and all the other watch-whers."

"I know nothing of this," T'mar said, sounding somewhat aggrieved. "Is there anything else you need to tell me?"

"Oh, I'm too tired to think straight!" Fiona complained grumpily. "I—"

"Rest," T'mar ordered, rising from his chair. "We can talk more later."

"No," Fiona said, "I need to get back. I miss my dragon; I miss the warmth of the Weyr."

"It's warmer here than at Fort Weyr," T'mar said. Before Fiona's irritated groan escaped her lips, he continued, "But I know what you mean: Igen is a better place for you."

"Can you take me?" Fiona asked hopefully. "I can come back later."

"Let me check with Zenor," T'mar replied, heading for the door.

It seemed like forever to Fiona before the door opened again. T'mar entered, followed by Zenor, Nuella, Renna, and another man.

"Tevris and Tesk will manage," the new man answered Nuella. "And, to be honest, we're better off with fewer mouths to feed."

"Do you want us to take Larissa?" Nuella asked.

"I don't know if it'd be safe for her—" Zenor replied doubtfully.

"I'm sure it will," Fiona interjected. "The wherfolk have loads of kids."

"And we could use the practice," Nuella added. From his lack of response, Fiona guessed that Zenor was growing red.

"*We* need the practice, too!" Renna declared. "Don't we, Dalor?"

So the other man was Dalor, Fiona thought. She could hear the blush in his voice as he asked, "We do?"

There was a moment's awkward silence after which Dalor, probably reeling from Renna's glare, corrected himself. "I mean, we do!"

"Fewer mouths," Nuella reminded him quietly.

"Renna?" Dalor said, passing the decision off to her.

"Well," Renna said with a sigh, "she's probably closer to Nuella."

"She could come back later," Zenor suggested.

"Yes, she could," Dalor agreed, happy to find a workable compromise.

"We should go now," Fiona said, rising painfully from the bed. She was surprised when no one stopped her.

"We can loan you some crutches," Zenor said.

"We can't go until dark," Nuella said.

"Isn't your watch-wher sleeping?" Fiona said. When Nuella nodded, she turned to T'mar. "Zirenth can carry her, can't he?"

"Easily," T'mar agreed. "Shall I send for the weyrlings?"

"Yes," Fiona said, smiling at Nuella. "I don't doubt you'll have some things you'll want to bring with you."

"If you don't get them all now, you can come back for them," Renna said.

"I'm not sure we want to attract too much notice from D'gan," T'mar objected.

"One trip or two won't be a problem, will it?" Fiona said, daring T'mar to object. The wingleader frowned but reluctantly agreed.

"Good!" Fiona said, and turning once more to Nuella, added, "I think you'll like Igen Weyr."

"The Weyr?" Nuella repeated in surprise.

"We'll go there first," Fiona said. "Then, when it's dark enough, we'll go to Aleesa's." She smiled. "We've found, with the heat, that our hardest work is best done in darkness, like the watch-whers."

"What about the hold you promised?" Zenor demanded. "I can't see us staying at a Weyr forever."

"And you won't," Fiona promised. "But we've still some things to arrange."

"Such as . . . ?"

Fiona noticed that T'mar was also intent on her answer. "We'll need smithcrafters to help with the gold, so we'll have to visit the Smithcrafthall."

"Smithcrafters?" Nuella asked, puzzled. Inspiration struck. "Oh, I suppose Zenor is enough of a miner that we needn't worry on that account."

"You need the smiths to refine and work the gold," Fiona explained.

"And we still need to negotiate with the holders," T'mar added.

"I don't think that will be a problem," Fiona said.

"We'll take that jump when we come to it," T'mar allowed.

It took some time, more than Fiona wanted, for Nuella and Zenor, ably aided by Renna and less ably aided by the infant Larissa, to assemble their belongings.

It was nearing midday when T'mar finally gave the signal to Zirenth and the weyrlings he'd called to help in the transport.

Between couldn't come soon enough for Fiona, even though the cold seemed like a fresh bite into her injured calf, and then—

You're here! Talenth cried joyously, and Fiona smiled as she saw her beautiful gold prancing about in the Bowl below.

I'm here, Fiona agreed warmly.

As soon as T'mar had lowered her to the ground, she hobbled over to Talenth and grabbed her head in both arms, surprised that they barely reached around.

You've grown!

Of course! Talenth agreed. *Isn't that what I'm supposed to do?*

Fiona found no argument with her insistence that Nuella and her watch-wher be temporarily housed in one of the unused queen's weyrs. She was thrilled by the way her offer was received by Nuella and, even more so, by Zenor, whose attitude toward dragonriders in general and Fiona in particular seemed to have undergone a complete and permanent revision.

"This is marvelous!" he said as he examined the bath and Fiona demonstrated the hot and cold taps. "And the water is hot all the time?"

"It should be," Fiona allowed. "At least it is in Fort Weyr."

She was touched by the way Zenor carefully arranged the room and then led blind Nuella around it, proudly boasting, "Once she knows where things are, she gets around just fine."

The sun was just going down as Fiona led them to dinner, seating them at what she'd begun to think of proprietarily as the Weyrwoman's table.

She was pleased to be greeted by the weyrling riders and the walking wounded, and even more pleased by the respectful manner in which they treated her guests.

"Watch-whers, eh?" K'rall said when he heard about Nuella. Then he peered more closely at her as recognition dawned. "Why, you don't look—"

"K'rall!" Fiona cut across him warningly. "Remember we are ten Turns in the past and what's happened to us has yet to happen for Nuella and Zenor."

K'rall cast her an affronted look that faded only after he digested her meaning. He harrumphed, then gave her a look that might have been a smile, before nodding respectfully to Nuella and Zenor. "Let me just say that I am honored you chose to come here."

Zenor beckoned to Fiona, who leaned close enough for him to mutter, "Don't hold back so much that you scare us away from the future."

Fiona thought about that for a moment. "I'm sorry—nothing terrible, just frightening."

"Oh," Zenor said with a grin. "So nothing more than I've come to expect with Nuella."

"I suppose that's right," Fiona found herself agreeing. After all, she'd heard not only Kindan's ballads but also his stories firsthand. "Nothing quite so startling as being the first person to take a watch-wher *between*."

Dinner proceeded uneventfully after that, except that both Zenor and Nuella were surprised by the spicy dishes served them.

"It's the heat," Fiona explained. "Mother Karina, the oldest trader, explained that in hot climates it's good to eat spicy-hot foods that aid in sweating."

"The sweat cools the blood," Zenor guessed. "Does that mean we need to drink more here?"

"Definitely," T'mar agreed. "And here's one of the special dishes that Terin has prepared for Fiona's return."

He gestured to a bowl that Terin had placed proudly on the table. It looked a bit like a white pudding or a solid cream but Fiona was certain that she had never seen its like.

"I'm sorry that we don't have more than enough for a taste for each of us," T'mar apologized as he scooped up a spoonful and put it on Fiona's plate. "Terin has a nice cobbler to accompany it."

Fiona's nose crinkled, taking in the scent of warm cinnamon and apples wafting across the air as Terin proudly carried a warm pot to the table.

"We think the two will go together well," T'mar said with a wink at Fiona.

Dubiously, Fiona took a nibble-sized portion of the white solid onto her spoon and put it in her mouth.

"It's cold!" she exclaimed, nearly spitting it out. "It's like ice, only it's creamy."

"Iced cream," Terin said with a huge grin. "It took me a long time to convince J'gerd to help make it." She leaned close to Fiona as she whispered, "We had to use a full kilo of ice!"

"It's amazing!" Fiona said as she helped herself to a full mouthful. She turned an eye toward T'mar. "Something to trade?"

"Oh, indeed!" T'mar agreed wholeheartedly, contently mixing the iced cream and the warm cobbler into a cool mash.

"I've never heard that dragonriders trade," Zenor observed mildly as he dubiously tried the iced cream. His brows rose in delighted surprise as he savored it and swallowed.

"No one is supposed to know we're here," Fiona said, unable to conceal her worry that too many people already knew, "so we can't ask for tithe."

"Besides," T'mar added with an airy wave of his hand, "if we did and D'gan found out about it . . ."

"I couldn't imagine he'd be happy with the prospect," Nuella said. She took another bite of the iced cream, savoring it slowly before saying, "And if this need to trade has driven you to create *this*, then I think it's great!"

"At Fort Weyr the dragonriders knit sweaters and scarves, that they give to holders and crafters that are beholden to them," Fiona said, feeling an urge to defend dragonriders.

"Your father is a Lord Holder," Nuella replied. "You can't tell me that he never griped about the tithe."

"No," Fiona admitted. "But he never skimped on it, either."

"Speaking of tithe," Zenor said, glancing toward Nuella, "we have a list of questions about this hold you're proposing—"

"And a list of needs, no doubt!" K'rall interjected. Fiona glanced nervously in his direction, afraid that the old rider was affronted, but she was surprised to see a huge grin on his face. "No more than your due, I'm certain."

The byplay was not lost on Zenor, who gave Fiona an appraising look before continuing, "Our biggest need will be smithcrafters."

"Yes," T'mar agreed. "And we'll want you to have them because, unlike the other holds, we are hoping you will give us tithe."

"We haven't even settled!" Zenor protested hotly.

"We think that once you have, you'll find that there's more than enough for you and yours," T'mar told him. He shook his head emphatically. "We are not Telgar. We will not demand more than a fair tithe."

"Also," Fiona added, "don't forget that we'll be supplying you with stakehold, an investment of our own, as it were, and should expect—as traders—to see a return on it."

"You can't have it both ways, Weyrwoman," Zenor cautioned her. "Either we tithe or we trade."

"Trade and tithe," Fiona told him. "You'll find that we have many things worth trade." She gestured to the iced cream bowl, now empty. "And we won't stint our friends."

"Very well," Zenor said after checking Nuella's expression.

"Your biggest need is food, anyway," Nuella said. "Your Weyr and our wherhold will make a large dent in the available herds." She turned her face toward Fiona. "How many watch-whers are there at Aleesa's?"

Fiona was chagrined to admit that she didn't know. "Two, for certain," she said. "Both Arella and Jaythen have them. Arella is bonded with a green and Jaythen is bonded with a bronze."

Zenor frowned.

"What about the other eggs in this last clutch?" Nuella asked.

"They were all spoken for already," Fiona told her.

"That's both good and bad," Nuella said to Zenor.

"Why?"

"It means we've less to worry about when it comes to transport, but also less to bargain with," she said. "There are a lot of holders who've come to see the value of watch-whers."

"That's part of the reason why we want to see the wherhold established here," Fiona told them. "The holders around here were hard hit by the Plague and there are many wild herds that have attracted predators. The watch-whers can guard the herds—"

"I'm used to the mines," Nuella remarked. "I suppose it would be nice to be out in the night air."

"You'll have Jaythen and the others to help," Fiona assured her.

"You mentioned gold," Zenor prompted.

"We saw it marked on the Weyr maps," Fiona said.

"I'd like to see them."

"Why don't you go with Fiona, and I'll check on Nuellask," Nuella suggested.

"I'd like to see this map myself," K'rall said as the others rose.

T'mar and Terin accompanied them. While they walked— slowly, in deference to Fiona's crutches—Fiona held a quick consultation with them on the injured dragons and riders.

"We've three more riders that are now healed and ready for duty," T'mar reported, "and N'jian has recovered from the worst of the bedsores—we've got him resting in his pool most of the day, with a weyrling and his Graneth keeping a watchful eye on him."

"I'd like to see your injured," Zenor said from behind them. "Maybe I can learn some things."

"Or teach them," Nuella added with a touch of pride. "Zenor became quite the healer during the . . ." Her voice trailed off as she realized what she was saying.

"The Plague happened over nearly twelve Turns in our past," T'mar told her. "I was about the age you are now."

"It's done, we survived, and we press on," Zenor said in a tone that suggested a change of topic.

"Kindan said much the same thing," Fiona said in surprise.

"He might have learned it from Master Zist," Nuella said. She smiled. "After Kindan left, Master Zist picked Zenor to help him."

"Scared me witless," Zenor agreed. "I was afraid he was going to make me a healer or—worse—a harper."

"I would have missed you," Nuella said fervently.

"I was never so glad as when Kindan sent his fire-lizard calling Zist back to the Harper Hall," Zenor admitted.

"They've had a hard time finding enough healers, since," Fiona said as they began the slope upward to the queens' weyrs.

"Is that why you've none with you?" Nuella asked.

"There's only one at Fort Weyr, and that just recently," K'rall said.

"Perhaps we should send some people from the mine to the Healer Hall," Zenor said thoughtfully.

Fiona said nothing, deciding not to tell them that they hadn't.

When they came to the top of the ledge, T'mar said to Nuella, "I could escort you to your quarters while Fiona shows the others the Records."

"I'd like that," Nuella said, reaching out a hand toward T'mar. He grabbed it and led her on, telling her, "I've only seen a watch-wher once before and not up close."

"Oh," Nuella responded with interest. "Whose?"

"Yours, actually," T'mar replied with a chuckle. "I suppose I'd better not tell you too much or it'll spoil the surprise."

"Don't tell me too much because if Zenor hears, he might want to put a stop to it," Nuella retorted with a laugh of her own. "From your tone, I was probably doing something that would frighten him."

"Is that something you do often?"

"At least once a sevenday," Nuella replied with an impish grin. "It keeps him on his toes."

"Hmm," T'mar said thoughtfully.

"See here?" Fiona said, pointing to the map she'd unrolled on the table beneath them. "Those marks are for metals and minerals." She pointed to one in particular in the legend and then to where she knew the wherhold would be established. "See how large it is there, right at the river's bend?"

"Gold is heavy; it would tend to accumulate in bends," Zenor said judiciously. He looked up from the map, his eyes full of longing. "I'd like to see this site."

"According to this," K'rall said, gesturing to a dotted line on the map, "the land is bound to Keroon." He circled a spot not too far away on the map, saying, "That's Plains Hold there."

He glanced at Fiona. "What would your father say if Fort Weyr were to annex part of *his* Hold to some newcomers?"

"Actually, he'd want to know which part and who the newcomers were," Fiona replied. "A lot of holds lie empty and he'd be glad of the extra tithe."

Zenor nodded understandingly. "As a miner, I'm used to tithing to the Hold."

"There's plenty of good land there," K'rall said judiciously. "I've flown over it when . . ." He trailed off as he exchanged an understanding look with Fiona. He'd flown over it when the wherhold had been established. The thought of what his knowledge might mean for Zenor and the new holders both excited and alarmed her—was it right to tell them?

"I see more and more why timing it is dangerous," K'rall said with a heavy sigh. He glanced at Zenor. "What we know about the future could help you or hinder you—and we've no way of determining which!"

"I prefer going into a tunnel that's well-shored," Zenor replied. "If I know what to expect, then I can make plans."

"You can also come to grief expecting support where there is none," Nuella added from behind him. They all turned to see that she and T'mar had arrived. She searched out Zenor and grabbed his hand, saying, "After I checked on Nuellask, I decided that I wasn't too tired after all, and T'mar offered to bring me here."

"K'rall is concerned about telling us too much of our future," Zenor told her.

"I trust the dragonriders here," Nuella said, emphasizing the word "here." "They'll tell us what we need to know."

"So it's up to us to decide, is it?" Fiona asked sourly. She heard K'rall's and T'mar's gasps at her tone but ignored them, turning to Zenor. "Ask what you want; I'll tell you if I want."

"Will we survive?"

"At least until my time you'll not only survive, you'll thrive," Fiona told him. Oddly, she discovered that that revelation perked up her own spirits—probably it meant that their endeavor here at Igen Weyr would succeed.

"Will we have trouble with the holders?" Nuella asked.

"I don't know," Fiona said. "But if you do, you overcame—will overcome—them."

"How many of the wherpeople join us?" Zenor asked.

"I don't know," Fiona admitted. She thought of saying more and decided that this question-and-answer session was best.

"Will I mine gold?" Zenor asked.

"I don't know," Fiona admitted. She'd only ever heard of all the gold jewelry he'd made, never of his actually mining it.

"Will we find gold?"

"Oh, yes!" Fiona agreed avidly. "Your wherhold will be known throughout Pern for it."

"Can we ask more questions later?" Nuella said, tugging on Zenor's arm. "I think we've heard enough for the moment."

"Of course you can," T'mar assented with an approving look toward Fiona. "Anytime."

"Will the dragonriders support us?" Nuella asked as they started up the stairs, Zenor carefully bracing her.

"*We* will," K'rall declared stoutly. T'mar and Fiona looked at him with surprise, so he explained, "There isn't a rider here who doesn't owe his life or his mate's life to the efforts of the watchwhers. Why, when you fought that night—"

"I think that's more than they wanted, K'rall," Fiona interrupted him calmly.

The bronze rider started in embarrassment and nodded his head. "I might have said too much."

"No," Nuella told him staunchly, "I think you said just the right amount."

K'rall gave her a brisk nod of acknowledgment: the one reserved for equals among dragonriders. Zenor noticed and stiffened in response, afraid to ask further and glancing nervously toward Nuella.

Nuella laughed; she had caught enough of his emotions through the movements of his hands and the stiffness of his body.

To Zenor she said apologetically, "It sounds like I'll continue to give you worry, love."

"I won't complain," Zenor vowed.

"Much," Nuella corrected him with another laugh. Zenor joined in loudly.

"I think we should visit the Smithcrafthall tomorrow," Fiona said as they entered her quarters. "While it's light."

T'mar groaned and Zenor looked at him questioningly. "The heat in daytime can be excruciating," T'mar explained.

"I hear it gets better in winter," Fiona said, not wanting them to be too alarmed.

"I like the heat," Nuella said. "And you say you keep watch-wher hours? Work in the dark and sleep in the light? I can see how that would work."

Zenor absorbed her remark with a thoughtful look, which was quickly replaced by one of excitement as he asked, "Do we know if Terregar or Silstra survived the Plague?"

"I don't," Nuella said.

"I don't know who they are," Fiona said with a shrug.

"I thought you were an expert on all things Kindan," Nuella teased her. "She's Kindan's oldest sister."

"I still remember their wedding," Zenor said wistfully. "It was nighttime and Dask flew over holding a basket of glows, looking like a flying star."

"A flying star," Nuella repeated. "Something to think about for our wedding."

"Our wedding?" Zenor echoed faintly, his face going white.

"I think it would be a good to have one before we have children, don't you?" Nuella continued, enjoying the strangled noises that he made in response.

"Actually," K'rall interposed uncomfortably, "you might want to reconsider weddings. At least with dragonriders, because of the mating flight, riders tend to partner impermanently."

Zenor's objection was a loud and immediate, "No!"

"No?" Nuella repeated.

"I mean, no, I am not going to accept anything less than a permanent pairing," Zenor told her. "That is, if you want."

"Are you proposing?" Nuella asked, her face blossoming with a glowing look.

"No."

"What?" Nuella's exclamation was both outraged and unyielding.

"I will propose," Zenor said, temporizing, "but I want to do it at the right moment."

"And *when*," Nuella asked coldly, "would that be?"

Zenor stopped and turned to grab Nuella by the shoulders. "When I have something worthy to offer you."

"You are worthy," Nuella assured him, gently removing his hands from her shoulders and gesturing for him to continue walking. "But if you must wait, don't wait too long."

"Certainly!" Zenor agreed emphatically. A moment later, however, when he was certain that Nuella wouldn't notice, he shot an appealing glance to T'mar and K'rall, who responded with nods which affirmed that they would help him however they could. Zenor let out a sigh of relief, which he covered by feigning a yawn. "We should rest; we'll have a busy day tomorrow."

SIXTEEN

Good earth,
Fresh soil,
Hardy ground,
Less toil.

Igen Weyr, Morning, AL 498.8.14

"It'll be hot," T'mar cautioned as Zenor mulishly repeated his demand that they visit the wherhold site before setting off for the Smithcrafthall.

"I understand," Zenor said. "But I want to see what's there."

"You might not find anything in a short search," K'rall said.

"But if we had a sample to bring with us, we'd have a much stronger argument," Zenor said.

The two wingleaders nodded reluctantly. T'mar asked K'rall, "Will you take him, or do you want to lead the ice party?"

"I'll take him," K'rall decided. "I'll take S'gan and D'teril— they've recovered well enough to fly and their dragons need to stretch their wings."

"Take some of the older weyrlings, too," T'mar suggested.

K'rall gave the bronze rider a thoughtful look. "Who would you suggest?"

"Y'gos or T'del," T'mar replied instantly. "They're both steady riders and their browns should be up to the heat."

"Hmm," K'rall murmured. "Should I be concerned about Harith and the heat?"

D'teril's Harith had scored a wingtip in the Fall over Ruatha.

"Fiona says he's fully recovered," T'mar replied, adding, "I checked them out the other day and they seem more than anxious to get back in the air."

K'rall smiled sympathetically. "Well, I'll keep an eye on him," he decided. "Wouldn't be the first time a blue flew too early!"

"No, it wouldn't," T'mar agreed with a grin. Blue riders were eager fliers, and often their dragons became so overcome by their riders' enthusiasm that they overexerted themselves and strained their muscles.

"Fiona and Nuella have decided that they'll go to the old wher-hold this evening," Zenor said, glancing out from the shade of the Dining Cavern to the roiling heat in the Weyr Bowl, "so it would be good to have some news to send with them."

Four dragons—two blues and two browns—launched themselves from their weyrs into the hot air over the Weyr, reveling in the currents that swiftly lifted them up over the Star Stones. K'rall's Seyorth landed nimbly in front of K'rall, who gestured to Zenor. "We're ready."

Zenor smiled in delight as K'rall helped him climb up the bronze dragon's huge front leg to a riding position on Seyorth's neck. K'rall followed a moment later and, sketching a salute to T'mar, urged his great bronze skyward.

T'mar had a moment to enjoy the view of the small wing of five dragons before they veered away from the Star Stones and winked *between.*

He heard footsteps behind him and turned in time to see the envious look on Terin's face as she gazed at the space where the dragons had been.

"There's a group of weyrlings going to cut those reeds for you later," T'mar said. "Perhaps you'd like to go with them."

Terin nodded eagerly.

As the chill of *between* enveloped him, Zenor tensed, gasping for air that wasn't there. Before his panic could overwhelm him, daylight burst around him and air entered his lungs once more.

"I'm sorry," K'rall said, "I should have warned you."

Zenor couldn't speak, but shook his head in a feeble denial. Seyorth wheeled and dove suddenly, causing Zenor to tense in panic once more. And then—

—he let out his breath and looked at the ground rising below him. He was riding a dragon!

He hadn't had any time when they came to Igen Weyr from Mine Natalon to really appreciate the experience—and he'd been too concerned with Nuella's well-being to notice anything around him, even the cold of *between*. But now . . .

"There!" he called excitedly over his shoulder. "Land there!" He turned red with embarrassment as he realized he had just ordered a bronze rider, but it faded when he heard K'rall's enthusiastic, "Hold on!" from behind him. Seyorth flicked his wings, spilling air, and they plunged even more steeply downward, giving Zenor a near vertical view of the river's bend rapidly rising up to meet them.

Just when Zenor started to feel the first tinges of panic returning to him, Seyorth leveled up, circled once, and deftly landed less than a dragonlength from Zenor's chosen point.

"Wow!" Zenor exclaimed. "That was fantastic."

"I never grow tired of it," K'rall admitted, patting Seyorth affectionately before handing Zenor down.

The air churned as the other four dragons landed and their riders jumped off.

"What are we looking for?" S'gan called as he strode over to join K'rall. He nodded affably to Zenor.

"We're looking for two things," Zenor said. "A good site for a wherhold—they like caves and hate the sun—and traces of gold."

"Gold?" S'gan repeated, his brows rising in surprise. He spun around, eyeing the ground carefully. "Where would we find that?"

"The river's bend is probably the best spot to look," Zenor said, nodding in the indicated direction. He allowed himself a moment to take in the surrounding scrub, greener near the river but certainly not desert. He could imagine growing crops or grazing cattle here.

"Let's go!" S'gan replied enthusiastically, taking off in a lope.

As Zenor made to follow, K'rall laid a hand on his arm. "Let's not go too quickly; this is likely to be a long search, isn't it?"

"It is," Zenor agreed with a smile, matching his pace to that of the older dragonrider. He noticed that D'teril, the other blue rider, was racing after S'gan, but that the two younger brown riders were taking their cue from K'rall. "Are they always like that?"

"Blues are quick, agile," K'rall explained. "They tend to Impress those with similar traits."

T'del, one of the brown riders, cocked a questioning look toward K'rall.

"Not all blues are the same," K'rall said in response. "But if you were to place a bet in a race, bet that the fastest rider is a blue."

"Blues start quick, browns finish," T'del said, grinning.

"True."

Zenor slowed as they reached the river bank, and carefully began to pick a path to the river's edge.

"I don't see anything," S'gan called from his spot on the shore.

"It'll be in the water, under the dirt," Zenor replied absently as he took a cautious step into the water and squatted down to grab a handful of muck from the river bottom. He examined it carefully and grunted with pleasure when he noted that it was grainy, not fine. Gold was less likely to sink far down in grainy soil. He eyed the overhang on the far side of the river, then turned to K'rall. "Can we get over there?"

"Certainly," K'rall said, slogging down into the river and carefully picking his way to the far side. When he got there, he gestured to Zenor, who was watching at him in surprise. "You were thinking we'd *fly*?"

Zenor snorted and shook his head in acknowledgment of the twitting, then made his way across, following K'rall's course. Once there, he began to pull up clumps of sand, letting the water wash them away and examining the results. K'rall watched him dubiously.

"I'm hoping to get lucky," Zenor admitted. "Really, I'd expect to find little glimmers of gold—just dust but . . . ." He shrugged and grinned, and then, suddenly, his expression changed to one of complete shock.

"What is it?"

"Gold," Zenor said shakily, raising up his hand to show a large nugget. He pocketed the piece and redoubled his efforts. In an instant the others had clambered over to join him.

"Show us how to do it," S'gan begged. Once Zenor had shown them, the four younger riders churned up the river until the water downstream was yellow with sand.

K'rall eyed them all tolerantly, satisfying himself with a couple of attempts before giving up to watch the others.

"Have you seen enough?" he asked half an hour later as Zenor, thoroughly drenched, stood up and stretched his sore muscles.

"Yes," Zenor said, smiling at the dragonriders, who looked ready to drain the entire river in their attempts to find more gold. "I think we've got something to show."

"Then perhaps we should see if there is a potential holding site nearby," K'rall suggested, splashing back across the river.

"Come on," he shouted over his shoulders to the other riders. With a chorus of groans, they reluctantly followed.

Once out of the water, Zenor realized how much sandy grit his trousers had retained and regretted it, except for the heavy bulge in his pocket. He eyed the ground and headed off toward a low rise not far away.

"You could dig that out, probably," K'rall observed. "Or you could quarry some rock and build."

"Maybe both," Zenor mused. "Quarry for the hold, use the caves for the whers."

K'rall grunted agreement.

"How long would it take?" D'teril asked as he came, panting, up beside them.

"It depends on the soil," Zenor said, digging a toe into the earth. He turned to K'rall. "Can we take some samples?"

K'rall shrugged. "We didn't think to bring tools."

"A sturdy stick will do," Zenor said. He grabbed a branch from a nearby tree and broke it off, then strode around, poking the stick in the ground and occasionally stooping to dig a sample. Finally, he threw the stick away and turned to K'rall. "I've seen enough."

"Will it do, then?" the bronze dragonrider asked with a smile.

"There's good topsoil in places, particularly near the river," Zenor replied. "And the hills have good solid rock in them." He nodded. "I think we can make a holding of it."

Armed with good news and several nuggets of gold, Zenor and the riders returned to the Weyr.

"It'll be cooler at Telgar," T'mar said enticingly to Fiona as they stood outside the Dining Cavern under the burning hot Igen sun at noon.

"But I'm on crutches!" Fiona said. She'd been glad just to spend the morning with Talenth, idly oiling her and listening to the gold dragon commiserating with her over her injury. She felt dizzy and useless.

K'rall gave T'mar a warning look, then chimed in, "Well, if you're not up to it, Weyrwoman, I suppose—"

"I didn't say I wouldn't go!" Fiona snapped, her pride piqued. "I just said that I'm on crutches."

"We'll be sure that there's something nice and cool for you when you return," Terin offered. At K'rall's gesture, she pulled out two jackets. "And I found these. I think you and T'mar should wear them."

"What are they?" Fiona asked, peering at the jackets. "They look hot."

"Hot but fashionable," Terin said with a grin as she picked one up by the shoulders and proudly displayed the back. "What all Weyrwomen and Weyrleaders should wear."

"I'm not a Weyrleader," T'mar said, holding up his hands in a warding gesture.

"Close enough," K'rall allowed. "Especially with regards to the markings."

Fiona glanced more carefully at the large diamond woven onto the back of the wherhide jacket: It was sandy and showed three mounds—the Igen Weyr markings.

"Oh, wouldn't that rile D'gan!" T'mar exclaimed.

"We thought it might provide some amusement," K'rall said, including Terin with a gesture.

"And given all that I've heard about Telgar, it might be a good idea to be quickly seen as from another Weyr," Terin added.

"I'll roast in that!" Fiona declared in a feeble attempt to avoid wearing the jacket, but she knew, even as she spoke, that she not only would wear it, she *wanted* to.

"So put it on only when you're in the air," Terin replied sensibly, tossing the jacket to her. Fiona caught it awkwardly, groaning. Terin took pity on her and walked over. "Of course, if you want, I could help you with it now. Maybe that would be easier."

Fiona made no protest as Terin, aided by K'rall, helped her into the jacket.

"There!" Terin declared proudly. "All set."

"You look a proper Weyrwoman," K'rall said approvingly.

"I'm too young."

"It's not the age," K'rall said solemnly, "it's the decorum."

Fiona couldn't argue with that, particularly as the words made her beam with pride. She turned to T'mar, who bowed slightly to show his approval.

"So, how far will I have to walk?" Fiona grumbled quietly to T'mar as Zenor approached.

"Not far," T'mar said. "We'll be sure to land you as close as we can to the Smith Hall."

"Are you sure that I'm needed?" Fiona asked, directing her question to both T'mar and Zenor.

"I can't say for certain," Zenor told her, "but given that Nuella can't come, I'd be grateful for the support."

Nuella was sleeping with Nuellask. The watch-wher was too young to be left alone for any length of time.

"And I'd honestly prefer it if you were there as Weyrwoman," T'mar told her. He looked awkwardly at the wherhide jacket he'd looped over his forearm. "I'd prefer not to claim honors I haven't earned." He met her eyes. "You have the right to claim to be Igen's Weyrwoman."

Fiona's eyes danced in delight even as she shook her head demurely.

"You do," T'mar assured her. "And I don't doubt that your time at your father's Hold will help in our dealings."

"Please give me a hand up, then," Fiona said, directing her words to K'rall. T'mar hid a smile as he clambered up to his position on Zirenth's back and reached down to grab Fiona. Zenor came up next, and then Fiona's crutches were strapped on to Zirenth's harness. T'mar made certain that all the flying straps were secure, with Fiona in front, Zenor in the middle, and himself in the rear.

"Fly well!" K'rall called with a wave as Zirenth rose into the air.

As they flew toward the Star Stones, Zenor followed Fiona's gaze and saw a gold head sticking out of the queen's weyr. "We'll be back before dinner," he said to cheer her up.

"I know," Fiona said with a sigh.

"I'll make certain that no one shoots arrows at you or sets dogs on you," T'mar promised, his voice light.

Fiona sighed again, more deeply. She hadn't thought that the reason for her discomfort was *that* obvious. She certainly wanted the best for the Weyr, but she was getting close to the point where she'd be willing to trade a sevenday's coddling for another injury.

"You are carrying the weight of the Weyr on you, I know," T'mar said, seeming to divine her thinking. He reached forward and patted her lightly on the shoulder.

"I'll survive," Fiona declared, wishing she'd drunk more *klah*.

"You will," T'mar agreed. "Things will settle down soon enough. Perhaps you'll even be bored."

Fiona snorted in disbelief.

With a thought from T'mar, Zirenth went *between*.

The cold, black nothingness of *between* surrounded them and Fiona was glad of her warm wherhide jacket. Then they were surrounded by light and sound again. The air was cooler, the scene greener, the smells less sharp, more earthly.

It took no time for Zirenth and T'mar to get their bearings and then they whirled into a steep spiral toward the ground below, buffeted by the tricky winds that flowed in the narrow river-fed valley.

"We came in low enough that we shouldn't have been spotted at either the Hold or the Weyr," T'mar shouted as they descended.

"If we did, no one at the Weyr would comment on it. Dragon-riders from all over come regularly, I'm sure," Fiona shouted back. "I'm sure they visit here as often as they visit the Harper Hall."

She turned her head to look forward again, eyeing the ground rising up below her.

The first thing she noticed was the Smithcrafthall itself. It was a huge building set tight against the raging Three Forks river, close enough that two large waterwheels dipped into it. There was a lot of activity farther downstream, and Fiona peered at it for a moment, trying to determine what the people were doing.

They landed in the clearing nearest the Smithcrafthall. T'mar leapt down and helped Fiona dismount, handing her the crutches before turning back to help Zenor.

"That's odd," Fiona said as she surveyed the huge doors of the Smithcrafthall. "I would have thought there'd be a crowd gathered to see us."

The huge four-panel doors were built so that very large objects could traverse into and out of the Smithcrafthall. Fiona hobbled toward a smaller side door.

"They're not keeping guard," Zenor muttered.

"Why would they?" T'mar asked.

Zenor shrugged, his expression troubled. "I would."

At the door, T'mar moved in front of Fiona and pushed it open, then gestured for her to precede him.

She was met by a cacophony of sound, the bashing of metal with metal, the hiss of hot liquids into molds, the tinkling clatter of small tools on rough-finished goods. No one glanced up as she entered, and she was surprised to find no one near the door.

"Where is the Mastersmith?" Fiona asked but her voice was lost in all the noise. She turned to Zenor. "Who is the Mastersmith now?"

"Veclan," Zenor replied, surprised that she needed to ask. "Isn't he for you, too?"

Fiona shook her head, then turned back to the room before them. It was huge, and she began to be less surprised that their entrance had gone unnoted. When she could pick out people among the metal, braziers, furnaces, and jigs, they all seemed to be intent on one task or another, eyes down, gaze intent on their chores.

"Where would we find him?" T'mar asked.

Zenor shrugged. "I've never been here."

"Where would we find Dalor?" Fiona asked. "He's leading the mine now."

"In the thick of things," Zenor replied, grinning. "Dalor is always where there's a problem to be solved, and then he's on to the next one."

Fiona nodded; it made sense and was much the same with her father or, come to think of it, with herself at the Weyr.

She began a careful survey of the work floor, looking for a knot of men. She found one and raised her crutch to point it out before proceeding as quickly as she could with her sore foot trailing behind her. She probably would have walked on it and ignored the crutches, but she knew that both Zenor and T'mar would chide her for it, and to be honest, she knew that the calf still needed rest no matter how much the infirmity galled her.

The knot thinned as they approached, then reformed protectively around the oldest member. He reminded Fiona a bit of Master Zist when he was in one of his foul moods, and she had to force herself to keep moving forward. As he took in T'mar's shoulder knot and recognized him as a dragonrider, his bushy eyebrows narrowed in a sour frown. His gaze settled for a moment on Zenor and his expression altered a bit.

"Mastersmith Veclan?" Fiona began, shouting more loudly than necessary, hoping that her words would carry over the din to those beyond the small group. "I am Fiona of Igen Weyr, we've come to offer you an opportunity we think might benefit Hall and Weyr."

Veclan looked surprised, and his gaze went from Fiona to T'mar, to Zenor, and then back to Fiona. His thoughts were obvious: Why was a young girl doing the talking?

"Igen Weyr?" the man next to Veclan repeated scornfully. "Why don't you say Telgar?"

"I wasn't speaking to you," Fiona snapped at the rat-faced man. "I was talking to the Mastersmith."

"Then you should learn manners, weyrgirl," the rat-faced man growled back.

"Weyrwoman," Fiona corrected, her tone carefully set so as to make her correction sound reflexive, as though she'd spoken absently. She eyed the man a moment, noted the journeyman badge on his breast, then said to Veclan, "I do hope it's customary for the Mastersmith to do the talking in his own Hall." She turned to the other man, adding, "And out of courtesy I would speak to you by name."

"I am Journeyman Stirger," the man replied testily.

"Mastersmith," Fiona began again, then realized how tired she was of shouting and gestured around the hall, "I hate to distract you from your work, but is there a quieter place we could talk?"

"What happened to your leg—did you trip on the way down a dragon?" Stirger drawled.

"Lady Fiona was attacked by dogs that had gone wild at my mine," Zenor said, stepping forward to catch Stirger's eyes, his hands raised aggressively.

"Your mine?"

"Perhaps someplace quieter?" Fiona repeated.

Mastersmith Veclan eyed her a moment longer, then nodded. To Stirger he said, "Check on the castings."

"But Master—"

"Kindly ask Silstra to join us in my office," Veclan said to Stirger. The journeyman waved a hand in acknowledgment and turned rudely away from the others without further word.

Veclan pointed out the way and nodded to indicate that Fiona should go first. When she turned and he caught sight of the symbol on the back of her jacket, he gasped. "You dare to wear that here!"

"It's her right," T'mar spoke up from behind the old Smith. "Hers is the senior queen at Igen."

"The only queen," Fiona called over her shoulder, feeling compelled to add in honesty, "And she's not yet had her first Turn."

Veclan held his questions until they reached a small office and he ushered them inside. The office housed two tables, one standing off to the side, and the other at the head of the room, clearly his workdesk. Both were cluttered with drawings and half-finished castings or other metal works. When Zenor shut the door behind them, the noise from the work floor diminished appreciably.

"So, Lord D'gan has decided to reestablish the Weyr?" Veclan asked as he gestured to the nearer table. Zenor pulled a chair out from under a pile of rubble and held it for Fiona, then set to work carefully moving the drawings and other items to clear a space for the others. T'mar looked at him, shaking his head, and set to helping as best he could.

"That's not necessary," Veclan said, "and you'll only upset Silstra. She's convinced that I can't keep the place tidy by myself and she'd feel lost if I didn't allow the rubbish to pile up."

"Silstra?" Zenor perked up in surprise, his nagging feeling from the first time her name had been mentioned hardening into a firm suspicion. "Is she married to Terregar?"

"How do you—" Veclan began in surprise, then shook his head. "You are from her mine."

"Her brother Kindan was my best friend," Zenor told him. "I helped wash Danil's watch-wher the night before the wedding." He shook his head reminiscently. "That was Turns past." He looked up to Veclan. "Do they have any children?"

"They lost their first to the Plague," Veclan told him sadly. "But they've another."

"Silstra was the best cook and organizer and she knew all about healing and—" Zenor's enthusiasm was cut short as the door burst open and a young woman rushed in.

"Silstra?" Zenor asked, his eyes wide.

Silstra paused, taken aback. She glanced at Zenor, who stood up.

"Zenor!" she cried. "You survived!" She saw the other two then, and her eyes narrowed. "But what are you doing here with dragonriders?"

"We have a proposal for you," Fiona said, taking a deep breath as Silstra's fierce gaze latched on to her. "Zenor is part of it." She nudged him, hissing, "Show them!"

Zenor paused for a moment and reached into his pocket, extracting a heavy bag. He glanced at Fiona one final time, then loosened the bag, upended its contents into his palm.

"We'd like some help in setting up a hold and craft hall," he said as the Mastersmith lurched forward, eyes wide, to examine the nuggets resting in Zenor's hand.

Veclan motioned questioningly to Zenor, who obediently dumped the contents of his palm into Veclan's outstretched hand. The Mastersmith held the nuggets close to his face for a moment, then turned to Silstra. "Get Zellany."

As Silstra turned to go, Fiona added, "And could you bring Terregar, as well?"

Silstra paused and turned back, eyeing Fiona dubiously. "Why do you want my husband here?"

"This concerns him," Fiona told her.

"If it concerns him, it concerns me," Silstra replied tartly.

"Of course," Fiona agreed.

Silstra shot a glance toward Veclan, then demanded of Fiona, "And what business has the Weyr with our crafting?"

"We're here mostly to help," Fiona said, forcing herself to relax. "Our trade—"

"Trade?" Silstra snorted. "Weyrs don't trade!"

"*This* one does," Zenor told her stoutly.

"Would you please get Terregar and whoever else the Master needs," Fiona begged, "and then we'll answer all your questions."

Silstra glared at her for a moment, then glanced toward Veclan for confirmation before turning once more and leaving.

"Well, maybe not *all* their questions," Zenor murmured to Fiona, eyes twinkling.

An hour later, Fiona felt drained. Her wounded calf throbbed and she turned pleadingly to Zenor.

"Let's go, milady," he said, rising from his chair. He glared at Stirger, who had invited himself into the meeting halfway through and seemed only to delight in creating discord. "It's obvious that there is no trade here."

"Dragonriders don't trade," Stirger declared once more.

"We would," Fiona responded, rising from her chair and propping her crutches under her arms. She turned to Silstra.

"I am sorry we couldn't come to an agreement," T'mar said, also rising.

Zenor glared at Silstra. "Kindan would have listened."

"Doubtless," Stirger drawled. "After all, he is a harper, and likes a good tale."

Fiona bit back an angry retort, instead venting her anger and disappointment in a sigh. She turned to Veclan and Zellany, the other master at the Smith Hall, searching for some final words, but found none and shook her head in sorrow.

"We're not coming back," Zenor said to her as they made their way to the door. "We can find another way."

Fiona said nothing, too weary to argue. She started forward then stopped, turning to Zenor. "Didn't you want to ask them about the ring?"

"What ring?" Silstra demanded, glancing about the room as though looking for something missing.

"I can make it myself, I'm sure," Zenor said. "Gold's not that hard to work."

"You're going to use your gold to make this—this—" Stirger spluttered, gesturing toward Fiona. "A ring for her finger?"

"No," Fiona said, turning toward Silstra. "He's going to make a ring for Nuella, before he asks her to marry him." She smiled grimly. "And we were going to fit out our dragons to carry glows to honor them on their wedding night, the way Dask honored you on yours."

Silstra went pale and sat down hard in her chair. Terregar glanced at her in shock, then turned to Fiona. "And what do you care? Dask was only a watch-wher!"

"Watch-whers will fly Thread at night," T'mar declared hotly. "Dragons and dragonriders will owe their lives to them."

"I'd ask that you keep that to yourselves," Fiona said. "It won't happen until the Fall over Southern Boll." She smiled as T'mar reached around her to open the door. The noise of the hall outside was almost welcome after all the bitter talk.

"Wait a moment!" Veclan's voice boomed out.

Fiona paused, then stepped through the door. Behind her she heard quick, heavy steps and muffled gasps, and suddenly Mastersmith Veclan stood before her.

"My lady, would you please come back inside?"

"The air in that room is too foul with malice; I prefer the smoke and noise out here."

"I am an old man," Veclan replied, "and my time is more precious to me than it ever was."

"You are worried about a successor," Fiona replied. "You needn't be."

"And why is that?" Veclan asked, frowning.

"Because the choice is obvious, once you believe what I said," Fiona told him.

"And what is it that you'll gain for your Weyr?" Veclan asked.

"We're not doing this for the Weyr," Fiona replied. "We're doing this for Zenor."

"Zenor?"

Fiona nodded. "For him, his wife to be, and their children."

"I don't understand."

"And I don't want to tell you more than I must," Fiona replied. "But think: with his wife riding a gold watch-wher, what better trade could he have than mining gold for her? In her honor?"

"Why not ride a watch-wher beside her?" Veclan mused.

Fiona shrugged. "I don't know."

"I still do not understand what the Weyr gets from all this."

"Honor more than anything," Fiona replied without thinking. She gestured toward Telgar Weyr. "I have heard too many stories about the Weyrleader there. Honor has been lost by him; it is up to the rest of the Weyrs to rebuild it."

"No gold for you?" Veclan wondered, eyeing Fiona shrewdly.

"I *have* a gold!" Fiona exclaimed hotly. "And not all the metal of Pern is worth one instant with her." She started to move around him. "I've wasted enough time away from her."

"Very well," Veclan called to her back. "Go back to your Weyr, Weyrwoman. You'll need more than one dragon to bring all our gear anyway."

Fiona slowed and stopped, not believing her ears. Hopefully, she turned back to look into the Mastersmith's eyes. "You mean you will help us?"

Veclan nodded, smiling.

"Why?" Fiona asked in surprise. "What changed your mind?"

"The way you spoke of your dragon," Veclan told her. He shook his head admiringly as he added, "I wanted to believe you when you spoke of honor, but it was when you spoke of your gold that I realized you were telling the truth."

"Of course she is," Zenor exclaimed from behind him. "She's the Weyrwoman of Igen Weyr!"

"She's certainly a Weyrwoman," Veclan agreed with a firm nod toward Fiona. "And she's the first Weyrwoman I've ever met who's willing to *trade*."

When Fiona returned to the Weyr hours later, the first thing she did was hug her beautiful Talenth. Then, even though her every nerve was still humming from the emotions of the day, she carefully searched every speck of her dragon's hide for any slightest imperfection and oiled it thoroughly. She had never until that moment appreciated how much enjoyment she got from such a simple task.

You are the most beautiful, marvelous, amazing dragon on all Pern! she declared stoutly.

I know, Talenth replied, without any trace of arrogance.

"I have one more journey today, and then I'm not going anywhere," Fiona promised as the last rays of the sun were cut off by the high stone walls of the Weyr Bowl.

It would be good to have you watch my flying, Talenth admitted.

I've missed that, Fiona agreed. *I'm sure you're getting quite good at it.*

I was thinking that perhaps we could start flying just before dark, Talenth suggested hopefully.

"I'll want to check with T'mar," Fiona said aloud. "I wouldn't want you to strain yourself."

Talenth's eyes whirled a contented green. *If you make this journey, will we get better food?*

What, you don't like sheep? Fiona teased.

All the older dragons talk about cattle, Talenth told her wistfully. *They say that I'm big enough to eat one on my own.*

Oh, I don't know about that! Fiona cocked her head to one side as she examined Talenth's head critically. *You'd want to chew, that's for certain!*

I always chew, Talenth declared, sounding hurt.

Love, you only chew when I make you, Fiona reminded her, smiling broadly.

And you always remind me, so I always chew!

Fiona shook her head, willing to let her beautiful queen have the last word on the subject.

She turned her head as she heard a noise outside and recognized Nuella and her small watch-wher.

We've got company, Fiona told Talenth. *Nuella is here with her little Nuellask.*

Little? Talenth repeated in confusion. *Did we meet them before?*

Fiona tried to find a way to explain that they'd met the older Nuellask in the future. Dragons had poor enough memory without adding the confusion of time travel.

We met them when they were older, she explained at last.

Older, so bigger, Talenth mused. *Smaller now?*

Yes, because she's younger, Fiona agreed.

Am I older than her now?

Yes, you are, Fiona replied. *She's just hatched, so be gentle.*

Talenth arched her neck and blew a wisp of air from her nostrils to the small watch-wher.

She hears me! the gold dragon exclaimed joyfully. *Yes, I'm a dragon, a queen like you. No, you're not a dragon, you're a watch-wher.* A moment later she told Fiona, *She wants to know what is the difference between a dragon and a watch-wher.*

"Talenth is talking to Nuellask," Fiona said to Nuella, who had stood silently during the exchange. "Nuellask wants to know what is the difference between a dragon and a watch-wher."

Nuella smiled, her eyes glowing with an obvious love for her new mate. "What are you going to tell her?"

Talenth, Fiona said, *tell her that watch-whers like the night and dragons like the day.*

I don't mind the night, Talenth said with an air of protest.

I know, Fiona replied indulgently. *But you spend more time sleeping at night than you do during the day. Nuellask spends more time awake at night than during the day.*

Oh, Talenth responded, sounding mollified. A moment later, she said, *I told her.* She paused in thought for moment before continuing, *I don't know if she understood.*

That's all right, Fiona looked at the small ugly creature and felt a sense of wonder that such a beast was related to the dragons. She carefully tamped down her feelings to keep Talenth from picking up on them and alarming the baby watch-wher. *Do you like her?*

She's nice, Talenth told her. *Can she sleep with me?*

She's likely to twitch, Fiona cautioned, thinking that watch-whers were probably enough like newborn dragonets that sleeping would be her principle occupation.

"Talenth wants to know if Nuellask can sleep with her," she told Nuella.

Nuella laughed. "Youngsters are the same whether two legs or four, always wanting to play together or sleep together." She caressed the baby watch-wher's head affectionately before adding, "We'll see how she feels when we get back."

Fiona nodded. "Are you ready to go?"

"I think the sooner the better," Nuella replied, gesturing toward Nuellask. "You never know when she'll fall asleep."

Talenth, tell T'mar that we're ready to go, Fiona told her dragon.

He knows, Talenth replied a moment later. *They come.*

Fiona heard the rustle of dragon's wings and saw Zirenth land nimbly. The sound alerted Zenor who rushed over from the next weyr.

"All set?" he asked, glancing from Nuella to Fiona. He gestured at the watch-wher. "Are we bringing her?"

"Of course," Nuella told him. "She's still small enough that I can just about hold her in my arms."

"Another sevenday and she'll be too big," Fiona said with a laugh.

"I've got a bucket of scraps," Zenor said, wagging the bucket hanging from his hand, "just in case she gets hungry."

"Can Zirenth handle four and a watch-wher?" Fiona asked T'mar.

"Certainly," he said. He couldn't hide the pride in his voice.

In a few minutes they were all settled, Nuellask nestled comfortably between Zenor and Nuella, Fiona behind her, and T'mar in the rear, Fiona's crutches once again strapped below him. T'mar had quickly constructed a harness of spare rope with which to hold the watch-wher securely and had been scrupulous in ensuring that all the humans were properly strapped.

"Precious cargo," he murmured to Fiona before signaling Zirenth to rise.

Between was a refreshing break from the dying heat of the Igen day, quickly replaced by the cool night air of the wherhold.

"Nuellask liked it," T'mar reported to Nuella. "She asked if we could do it again soon."

"Soon," Nuella promised the small watch-wher. "Right now we're going to meet some new friends."

"Should I come or wait here?" T'mar asked Fiona as he set her on her crutches.

"Come," Fiona said. "I'm not sure I can get around all that well in the dark."

The baby queen watch-wher let out a sudden squawk that reverberated in the night air and startled them all.

"Zirenth says that she felt others," T'mar reported.

"Good girl, Nuellask!" Zenor said. "You let them all know who's the queen!"

Nuellask chirped in pleased acknowledgment.

"Well, we don't have to worry about making ourselves known," Fiona murmured to T'mar as they moved forward. Zenor guided Nuella, who herself was guiding Nuellask, while T'mar hovered close by Fiona's side.

"That's a pleasant sound," a voice called from the darkness in front of them. Fiona recognized Arella's voice.

"Why are you on crutches, girl?" Jaythen growled from a place so close to them that Fiona stumbled in surprise. "Did you trip?"

"A dog bit me," Fiona replied testily.

"I'll bet the dog died of shame right after," Jaythen replied with a raspy laugh.

"An arrow," Fiona told him. "But he wasn't dead until after Talenth spoke."

"Your dragon killed a dog?" Jaythen asked incredulously.

"No," Fiona said. "She startled him enough that the bowman could get a proper aim."

"And the girl bonded?" Arella asked. "Is that her?"

"I'm Nuella."

"I'd heard you were blind," Jaythen said, surprised.

"I am," Nuella said. "But in the dark everyone is blind, except the watch-whers."

"You're the one who rode a green *between*?" Jaythen demanded.

"Yes," Nuella replied, adding, "Are you always this demanding of your guests?"

"Don't get many guests," Jaythen replied.

"I can see why," Zenor murmured.

"We came to discuss the move," Fiona said.

"You did it? It's settled?" Arella asked.

"We've found a good site, and the Mastersmith has agreed to send some crafters," Zenor said.

"Mastersmith?" Jaythen repeated. "What does he have to do with the wherhold?"

"Not with the wherhold," Zenor corrected. "With the gold we'll be mining there."

"Gold?" Jaythen repeated, and there was no mistaking the surprise in his voice. "There's gold there?"

"There is," Zenor replied. "We came to talk about how soon you can move there."

"How many are there?" Nuella asked, turning her head in search of faint sounds. "I hear the children and one man. Are there others?"

"She's good," Arella declared approvingly. "There's only four adults: me, Jaythen here, Jifar, and Serella."

"Silstra and Terregar will join us from the Smith Hall," Zenor said. "They have one youngster, and we've Nuella's sister, Larissa."

"We've five children," Jaythen said. "We lost three to the Plague."

"Would have lost more if Kindan hadn't sent the dragonriders," Arella added.

"Kindan was my best friend growing up," Zenor said. "He gave his watch-wher to Nuella."

"So you're a miner, then," Jaythen commented. "No watch-wher of your own?"

"I've enough to do keeping her out of trouble," Zenor said, jerking a thumb toward Nuella, who elbowed him goodnaturedly in response.

Jaythen laughed. "I'll bet you do."

"Come in," Arella said, "and we'll talk plans."

Fiona smiled to herself, convinced that the wherfolk would follow Nuella's lead and accept Zenor's aid.

"I think things wouldn't have gone so well if we hadn't brought the watch-wher," T'mar said much later as he helped Fiona negotiate the ramp up to her weyr. Talenth raised her head wearily but still asked, *Can the watch-wher sleep with me?*

She's already asleep, Fiona told her apologetically. *And I think she wants to sleep with her mate.* She saw the glow of her queen's eyes and added, *How about I sleep with you tonight instead?*

Will you?

"You can leave me here, wingleader," Fiona told T'mar as she curled herself up against Talenth, "we girls are spending the night together."

"I'll get you a blanket," T'mar offered.

"If you see Terin, please tell her she's welcome to join us." Fiona pulled off her jacket and bundled it under her neck, idly wondering if she was treating the Weyrwoman's garb inappropriately. She shook her head at herself and nestled more tightly against the fur lining; she was too weary to let decorum concern her.

She was already asleep by the time T'mar returned, carrying a sleeping Terin in his arms, a pair of blankets draped over his shoulders. He smiled down at the young Weyrwoman and arranged the drowsy headwoman next to her before covering both with blankets, which he carefully tucked in around them.

He stood then, examining his work and nodding in satisfaction. As he looked at the two girls who had done so much in such a short time, his eyes softened, then lingered for a moment on Fiona. Truly a Weyrwoman, he thought.

He stepped back quietly and turned off the glows that Terin had left lit for their return.

SEVENTEEN

Thread burn,
Thread score,
Rider heal,
Dragon soar.

Igen Weyr, Late Evening, AL 498.9.8

"That's the last of it," K'rall reported as he and his wing of convalescents dispersed in the last of the evening light.

That wing, in the last three sevendays, had grown to thirty-one
as more than two dozen riders and dragons had recovered from
their injuries. There were only sixteen of the original forty-seven
lightly injured dragonpairs remaining, and Fiona hoped to see at
least half of them returning to duty in the next sevenday. That
would still leave the thirty severely injured, who would need at
least another four months to heal.

"Good," she said, gesturing toward the Kitchen Cavern and the
Weyrleader's table. Terin and T'mar were already seated. They had
finished eating before K'rall's return and were engaged in what had
become a routine meeting to handle the planning of the next day's
events. As she sat down and Terin pushed a pitcher of iced *klah*
toward her, she added, "We've enough ice to trade when Azeez arrives in the morning, and enough to provide the wherhold."

"We've two rooms full of ice, we should have enough," Terin

added, shaking her head. "Any more and the whole place will freeze."

"Don't say that," K'rall said holding up a cautioning hand, "or you'll have every rider in the Weyr demanding his own cooler."

"Not if they want to eat, they won't," Terin said with a frown, turning toward the large cookpot simmering on the hearth.

"Has Zenor had much luck mining?" K'rall asked T'mar. K'rall had led the group that had flown the Smithcrafters and their gear to the newly established wherhold.

"They've been too busy settling in," T'mar replied. "I doubt they'll be able to start serious exploration for another month or more."

"In the meantime, we've more mouths to feed than we've food," Terin said grimly.

"I thought that holder Kedarill had pledged a herd to the wherhold," K'rall said.

T'mar shook his head. "Kedarill was willing to let them herd as many head of cattle as they could find," he explained. "Finding is the problem."

At Fiona's urging, Zenor had taken the lead in negotiating the establishment of the new wherhold with the holder of Plains Hold. Kedarill had greeted the proposal enthusiastically, and his enthusiasm had redoubled with Zenor's revelation of gold and the Mastersmith's support. Kedarill was certain, and T'mar agreed, that Ospenar, Keroon's Lord Holder, would fully concur with his minor holder's decision, especially after M'tal, the Weyrleader of Benden Weyr, had made an enthusiastic tour of the new wherhold.

The new wherhold was on land that looked to Benden Weyr under the new boundaries established after Igen was abandoned, and so M'tal's approval made Ospenar's acceptance all but foreordained.

In involving Benden's Weyrleader, Fiona, Nuella, and T'mar had been careful not to mention the Igen dragons, while at the same time providing a plausible explanation for the future appearance of any dragon at the wherhold—that they were from Benden Weyr.

"We've loaned them some from our herd in the meantime," Fiona said, sighing deeply at the memory of the twenty head of cattle that had been hauled off by dragon to the fresh pens at the wherhold.

"I thought your plan would keep us from this," K'rall said, glaring at T'mar.

"We've enough for the next sevenday," Fiona said in T'mar's defense. "By then the wherhold should have found their own cattle, and maybe some gold with which to repay us."

"We could cut back," Terin suggested.

"It's not the riders, it's the dragons," T'mar reminded her with a reluctant shake of his head. "If it weren't for the dragons, we would have enough cattle to supply us easily."

"A Weyr's not much use without dragons," Fiona muttered, wondering if perhaps her earlier castigating thoughts of the old Igen Weyrfolk were perhaps premature. She savored a mouthful of *klah*, hoping it would keep her awake.

"It'd be different if we had a proper tithe," K'rall assured her.

"But then we'd be a proper Weyr with four times as many dragons," Fiona replied. She made a face and concluded, "So I'm not sure if we'd be any better off."

"Do you think that the holds could support the Weyr in a fair tithe?" T'mar asked K'rall speculatively.

The older dragonrider pursed his lips tightly. "No, I think that as they are they wouldn't support a full Weyr." He nodded toward Fiona as he added, "But if the Weyr were to *trade*, perhaps then."

"So what if we were to scour the area for any more wild herdbeasts?" Fiona asked, sipping some more *klah*.

"I don't know if that would work," T'mar said.

"Maybe not if we looked just here, but what about across Pern?" K'rall suggested.

"I'd not want to rob anyone of their proper herd," Fiona objected.

"Nor would we," K'rall said. "We would look in the wild places, the sort of places we've found unclaimed cattle before."

"We're going to need more livestock as the injured recover and the weyrlings get old enough to fly," T'mar said. "Even if we survive now, we'll have too many mouths to feed later."

"It seems a waste to leave good riders growing old when they'll be needed in their prime when we return," K'rall remarked dolefully.

T'mar motioned for him to continue and the old rider added, "Three Turns doing nothing more than practicing is at least two Turns, maybe even two and a half Turns, too many."

"So why not send them back?" Fiona asked, her face brightening. "They won't age, and they can eat in the future."

"If we send them all back now, we'll be too short-handed to look after the injured," T'mar told her. "Besides, we'll need some older, steadier riders to train the youngsters—drill them on recognition points, teach them to flame, and show them the tricks they've learned flying in formation."

"But that doesn't require a full wing for three Turns," K'rall said. "I think Fiona may have part of our solution—send some of the able-bodied forward in time to meet us when the weyrlings are old enough to learn to fly in formation." His eyes gleamed with excitement as he went on hurriedly, "That'd save on not just cattle but everything, and the riders would be better off, too. And you'd save on all the clothing and gear that you'd need in the meantime—you could use that extra for more trade."

"How would you know when to arrive?" T'mar asked.

"We use the stars, like the traders trained us," K'rall replied. "We'd come back a month before the end of the third Turn. If you weren't ready then, we could train with you."

"So you're offering to lead the wing?" Fiona asked.

K'rall nodded curtly. "If we use this next sevenday to set things in order, we could leave at the end of it."

"What if we find we need you?" T'mar asked.

K'rall shrugged. "Send someone forward to bring us back again."

"What about when the others recover?" Fiona asked.

"N'jian can train with them, as I've trained with this lot, and then bring them forward," K'rall said. He gave T'mar a broad smile as he caught the other's surprise at the recommendation and nodded toward Fiona. "I know that sounds strange coming from me, but this Weyrwoman's done a lot to broaden my horizons." He pursed his lips tightly before admitting to T'mar, "And so have you."

T'mar gave the older rider a grateful look. "I'm sure you would have done the same."

"I'm not so sure," K'rall said, shaking his head. Glancing

frankly at Fiona, he added, "I'm afraid I might have decided that this one here was too young for such duties."

"And perhaps I am," Fiona said. Before K'rall could argue with her she continued, "We won't really know until we return to our time, ready and able to fight Thread with four full wings."

"She's right," T'mar said. "The test comes when we're needed."

"I just hope all this—this—" He framed his head with his hands to indicate the muzzy-headedness that affected them all. "—noise will go away when we get back."

"I've been dealing with it since I Impressed," Fiona said. "I'm sure you'll handle it."

"It's got something to do with timing it, I'm certain," K'rall said. "And that's another good reason to take people forward as soon as they're able—this strain puts everyone on edge; we'll have fights if we're not careful."

"T'mar and I, and some of the other weyrlings, have managed without fighting," Fiona said.

"But you prove my point," K'rall told her. "You and T'mar and some of the weyrlings have been fighting this since before we came back in time and it's cost you—you could have done so much more without the distraction." He shook his head irritably, adding, "But that's not my point. If it affects you so differently from most, there's no telling if it won't affect others even worse."

"Well, we've had no fights yet," T'mar said not quite refuting the older rider.

"We've been here just more than two months," K'rall reminded him. "What will you be like three Turns from now?"

T'mar smiled and shook his head. "I suppose you'll have to find out."

"Of course," Fiona said, "if you leave now, you'll miss the wedding." There was no need to specify which wedding: all the Weyr was talking about Zenor and Nuella.

"But he hasn't even proposed yet!" K'rall exclaimed.

"He hasn't made the ring yet, so he can't propose," Fiona said.

"He's started practicing," Terin said with a smile. "I heard from Arella that he's been cursing nonstop since Stirger set up that solar forge." With a shrug, she added, "Of course that might have been for the price he charged."

The others smiled. Journeyman Stirger was a prickly, ill-tempered, opinionated, arrogant, and stubborn man, but he was honest enough to admit it. He was also quick to apologize and admit his mistakes. His apology to Fiona had almost had her forgive him, and had caused her to realize that she had some of her father's tendencies to hold on to a grudge longer than sensible.

"Ah, but once Stirger thought up the idea, it was Zenor who figured how to mass produce them and market them," Fiona said. "And with that he's recouped Stirger's price twice over."

"And found himself rated apprentice to the Smithcraft," T'mar remarked, remembering the dazed look of the young man when Mastersmith Veclan had sent down the package containing smith garb and badges.

"At least Terregar is there to keep order," K'rall remarked. He had a grudging respect for red-haired, hot-tempered Zenor, but Terregar's steadiness was more in keeping with K'rall's temperament and though he had more than ten Turns on the smith, they had forged a bond of friendship.

"Terregar!" Fiona exclaimed with a snort. "It's Silstra that runs the place." She shook her head as she mused, "I'm surprised Veclan was willing to let her go; she was doing much the same at the Smith Hall."

"Ah, but she's a wise woman and she'd been training her replacement," Terin said, with a touch of wistfulness. She'd spent some time helping Silstra. The older woman had been to the Weyr on Fiona's invitation, and her sharp eyes missed nothing as she examined the Kitchen Cavern, the supply rooms, and the rest of the Weyr, she was both free with her praise and profuse with her advice. Terin glanced around the large Kitchen Cavern now as she added almost mournfully, "And she managed to get Sula from Mine Natalon to handle the hearth so as to let her concentrate on other holding matters."

"And you watched her every move, memorized the best of them, and ever since have been hounding the weyrlings like a queen dragon about to mate," K'rall said, wagging a finger at her while his eyes danced with humor.

"It's only sensible," Terin muttered not quite sure whether his words were meant as ridicule or praise.

"Which brings us back to cattle," T'mar said.

"So it does," K'rall agreed, lowering his hand back to his lap. He was silent for a moment. When he spoke again, there was sorrow in his voice. "While I'd hate to miss the wedding, I don't think we can afford to wait."

T'mar made a face but could offer no dissent. He lowered his head, resting his chin on an upraised hand, his elbow propped on the table in his favorite thinking position.

"It'll mean more work for the older weyrlings," Terin said.

"The younger ones won't be ready to fly for at least another seven months," K'rall observed.

"Six months, ten days, to be exact," Fiona corrected with a wry grin. "We make the count every day just to be sure."

K'rall smiled indulgently at her. "It's been many, many, many Turns since Seyorth was a weyrling, and I still haven't forgotten how we were always counting down the days."

"How about this," T'mar said, looking up at the others. "We stop by the wherhold tomorrow morning early, and if we can't glean a definite date, we let K'rall and the others leave tomorrow evening."

"We can be ready in a day," K'rall agreed. "I certainly would hate to miss the wedding."

They found Zenor no more ready to forge his gold wedding ring in the next sevenday than he had been in the sevenday before and so the next evening, reluctantly, K'rall and the other convalescent riders readied themselves for the jump forward in time.

Fiona made a special effort throughout the day to say something in parting to each rider and every dragon that was going forward, while attending to her other duties. Even so, when the thirty-one dragons and riders gathered at dusk in the Weyr Bowl, she had a sinking feeling in the pit of her stomach as though she were saying good-bye forever.

"When we meet again, Weyrwoman, you'll be flying *between*, a true dragonrider," K'rall said, his eyes gleaming with pride.

Fiona nodded, not trusting her voice. K'rall eyed her for a moment and then grabbed her into a great big hug. Almost as quickly he released her again, seeming abashed at his actions. Fiona leaned forward and up to kiss him on the cheek. "Fly well, K'rall!"

T'mar stepped over to K'rall, repeating the instructions for a final time: "Come *between* on the night of the first day of the third month in the Turn—"

"Five hundred and one after Landing," K'rall finished for him. He gave T'mar a tight nod. "We'll meet you then." He turned to Terin, who huddled unobtrusively behind Fiona. "When we meet again, you'll be as old as the Weyrwoman is now!"

Terin nodded, her eyes gone wide at the thought. K'rall gave her a moment more to speak and, when she remained mute, shook his head. "Can I hope we'll get a welcome feast?"

"Of course!" Terin said, suddenly bubbling with words. "I'll cook your favorite meals, and we'll have ices and—"

"Glad to hear it, lass." K'rall cut her off with a wave of his hand. "I'll leave it for you to surprise us."

With a final nod to T'mar and Fiona, the older rider clambered up his dragon's foreleg and settled himself into his riding straps, tightening them with exaggerated motions to make certain that Fiona knew he was being careful.

"Wouldn't want to fall off in a jump of three Turns," he called down.

"Fly safe, dragonrider!" Fiona returned, stepping away from Seyorth, her hand grabbing Terin's and guiding her back.

In the dim light, Fiona barely made out K'rall's hand gesture signaling the wing aloft. And then the rustle of thirty-one pairs of wings blew loose sand through the still-hot evening air as the dragons rose into the night sky, climbing heavily and circling over toward the Star Stones.

For a moment, Fiona could almost make them out, a blur of wings and motion, and then they were gone *between*—and Turns ahead.

Fiona and the younger weyrlings found themselves busier in the days after K'rall and the other convalescents went forward in time, surprised at the return of all the work that they'd gladly shared.

For herself, Fiona was happy to be forced to spend more time at the Weyr and leave the issues of the wherhold to T'mar and the older weyrlings. Still, the Weyr felt emptier, particularly with the thinned numbers at mealtimes.

To make up for it, she began encouraging P'der, K'lior's wingsecond, and N'jian, the last remaining injured wingleader, to join her at the Weyrwoman's table.

"It's part of your therapy," she told each of them in turn as she slowly ground down their resistance. She made it easier by moving them into lower level weyrs vacated by the departed dragonriders—she moved everyone lower to fill in the empty weyrs. "A change will do you good. And besides, the air is colder lower down."

By the end of their third month in the past, the worst of the injured dragons were ready to start limited activities, and early mornings and late evenings were filled with the sorry sounds of dragons as they painfully learned to move regrown muscles.

"Start by having them just walk from one end of the Bowl to the other," T'mar said when Fiona asked for therapy suggestions. "Then, when they can do that without too much pain, have them glide off the queen's ledge."

"We'll have to schedule that carefully," Fiona said thoughtfully. "We don't want the sun up, but we want to give the weyrlings a chance for their glide and some breakfast."

"I'm sure you'll have no trouble with that."

Fiona's look made it plain that she thought it was easier said than done. However, when T'mar made to comment, she raised her hand up angrily, forestalling him. "I'll manage."

Her solution was very popular: With the consent of the riders, she arranged for the younger weyrlings to "assist" them in exercising their dragons, including some of the more tedious warming-up exercises and culminating in the glide off Talenth's ledge.

I like having everyone around me, Talenth said when Fiona wondered whether it was too much for the young dragon. *Anyway, I'm their queen.*

Fiona laughed at that, but not without a nagging thought crossing her mind: How would Talenth react on her return to Fort Weyr and her position as a lesser queen? Come to think of it, Fiona realized that she wasn't sure how well *she'd* manage adjusting to a secondary role. She shrugged off the thought as F'jian and one of the recovering greens made a particularly long glide; the problem was Turns ahead.

The hot summer that had so alternately impressed and dismayed the dragonriders turned colder, and finally, as the four hundred and ninety-eighth Turn since men first settled on Pern neared its end, the weather turned bitter and frigid.

"Is there any chance of getting more heat up here?" F'dan asked petulantly one morning as Fiona completed her inspection of his wounds.

"No," Fiona told him bluntly. "You're fully recovered. If you want to be warm, then get off your arse and hike on down to the Kitchen Cavern—the exercise will do you good."

F'dan snorted at her tone and her choice of words. His had been a hard recovery, and he had learned early on in his physical therapy that Fiona had heard enough swearing from her father's guards that he could only rarely cause her to blush. She had responded by teasing him about it, using his own words against him.

"I'd be happier back at the Weyr," he said wistfully.

"Talk to T'mar, then," Fiona said. "If he thinks you're ready to go, he'll probably send all the older riders off into the future."

"Not before the wedding, I hope!" F'dan said, looking shocked. "Not with all the practice we've had!"

The wedding was one of the constant topics of conversation at the Weyr ever since Fiona had first broached her wild idea to T'mar and P'der.

"I think we should do something special for Nuella and Zenor on their wedding," Fiona had said, unaware that her eyes were gleaming in a way that telegraphed to any who knew her that she had a plan already set in her mind. T'mar and P'der exchanged glances: They *knew*.

"And what would that plan be, my lady?" P'der asked, carefully keeping his expression neutral.

"Well, do you remember Silstra's wedding?" Fiona asked.

"I believe I've heard of it before," P'der had said, his eyes dancing. Fiona flashed him a quelling look that did little to dampen his humor. Well, perhaps she and Terin *had* rather gone on about stories they'd heard about the wedding, but even Silstra, normally quite reserved, had reminisced fondly about the late-night wedding, and the way it had been illuminated by a basket of glows carried by Dask, her late father's watch-wher.

"Good," Fiona said tartly in response to his teasing tone. "Then perhaps you'll see why I think having the whole Weyr illuminate the procession would be a fitting tribute—"

"Fiona, that's excellent!" T'mar had declared, his face beaming.

"She doesn't know what she'll be doing ten Turns from now, but we do—an excellent tribute!" P'der had concurred.

The plan, Fiona was pleased to recall, had been enthusiastically adopted by every dragon and rider in the Weyr. Glow swamps had been raided, and glow balls large enough for a dragon to hold in forelegs had been shaped from the nearby river clay; practice had become a new drill involving ever more complex maneuvers and routines until the nights were a-gleam with swirling patterns that kept all enraptured.

"I wish we'd thought of this in our time," T'mar had said as he and Fiona watched the entire flying Weyr perform an intricate maneuver involving formations of red, blue, and green glows. He had purposely excluded himself from the drill, guessing that he would have duties at the wedding which would keep him earthbound.

"Pretty, isn't it?" Fiona had asked by way of agreement.

"Not just that," T'mar replied, shaking his head, "but we can adapt it to fighting tactics, as well—and see where we've got gaps in our wings."

"We could aid the dragons in night flights, too," P'der added. "I'm sure the glows don't bother the watch-whers."

"That's something I hadn't considered," T'mar admitted appreciatively. He nodded toward the final formation as it flew overhead. "We'll have to remember this."

"It'd be hard to forget," P'der had replied.

"And do we have any idea when the wedding will take place?" F'dan now asked.

Fiona shook her head with a grimace. "I'm not sure that Zenor has asked."

"But I thought he'd finished his ring a fortnight back!" F'dan exclaimed.

"He did," Fiona said, smiling. "Of course, he'd melted down three perfectly good attempts before deciding on this one, so . . ."

"Weyrwoman," F'dan told her seriously. "I would take it as a personal favor if you would sit down with the young man and impel him forward in his quest."

"So that we can have the festivities before you leave?" Fiona asked, smiling.

"But of course," F'dan replied. "After all, we blues are known for our conviviality!"

"Are you offering me a ride?" Fiona asked teasingly. F'dan had complained of aches and pains nearly every time he'd ridden his Ridorth—except when practicing with the glows.

"Do you know, Weyrwoman, I believe I am," F'dan said, rising from his seat and bowing courteously to her. "It would be our honor—Ridorth's and mine—to escort you on this quest."

"I'll have to check with—" Fiona began, meaning to say that she would have to check with T'mar, but she cut herself off. After all, wasn't she the Weyrwoman here? True, it was only by dint of her being the only queen rider at Igen Weyr but, really, after all these more than six months at the Weyr, wasn't she entitled to the perks of the title as well as the duties?

She checked herself and her impulse. She was Weyrwoman, and she'd spent the last six months learning the role—both here and back at Fort. There was a reason to check with T'mar.

"I'll check with T'mar first," Fiona said. "I'd hate to foul any plan he might have made already."

"Of course," F'dan agreed, walking toward her and offering an arm. "Shall we go down together?"

"Certainly," she said, taking the proffered arm and smiling. She knew that his offer of an arm was more for his benefit than hers; by the time they'd reached the level of the Bowl, she didn't doubt that she'd been holding *him* up and not the other way around.

T'mar was not in the Kitchen Cavern when they arrived.

"I'll just sit over here," F'dan said, pulling a seat near the large hearth.

"Don't get too comfortable," Fiona warned him. *Talenth, where's T'mar?*

Inspecting the weyrling barracks.

"Come on, he's with the weyrlings," Fiona told F'dan, cocking her head toward the Bowl.

F'dan made a great effort out of getting up from his chair, but Fiona glared at him, arms crossed, not buying the act for a moment. He'd recovered enough that he could rise from a chair unaided—it was only walking long distances that taxed his strength.

"Better," she murmured archly as he caught up with her. The blue rider shrugged unrepentantly.

They found T'mar, J'keran, and J'gerd inspecting the weyrling quarters. T'mar made a great show of dismay at the merest speck of dust or the slightest error of placement.

"Attention to detail," he said, shaking his head at the collected riders. "If you are not constantly alert, you risk getting yourself Threaded—or, worse, getting your dragon Threaded."

"He's right, by the egg of Faranth," F'dan added urgently. "If I had been just a moment more attentive, I would have spotted the clump that got me."

"Every rider makes mistakes," T'mar said with a wave toward F'dan. "With a six-hour Fall, it can happen at any moment. The better practiced you are at keeping your eyes open, on insisting on following every ballad and instruction, the better chance you have of surviving even the worst encounter."

"We were lucky to get *between* so quickly," F'dan agreed.

"May we have a word, wingleader?" Fiona asked. T'mar glanced at her, then said to J'keran, "Will five minutes be enough?"

"Certainly, wingleader," J'keran said promptly.

T'mar turned to Fiona and F'dan, raising his hands invitingly.

"F'dan suggested that perhaps we should see if Zenor needs some help," Fiona said.

"With?"

"Proposing!" F'dan exclaimed. "Before we all expire from old age."

T'mar's eyes twinkled, and his lips curved upward as he asked Fiona, "And you are qualified in this matter, how?"

It was a good question, but Fiona was only willing to admit that to herself. "I'm the Weyrwoman around here and have a certain weight at the wherhold."

T'mar grinned, shaking his head. "So you are proposing to

frighten him into marriage?" He shook his head. "It seems to me that fear is his current problem. I can't see that increasing it will help any."

"But we'll have to go back soon, and if he doesn't propose we'll miss the wedding!" F'dan objected.

"So you two hatched this scheme just so the Weyr could show off night flying?" T'mar asked sardonically.

"Well . . . yes," Fiona agreed. "It would be a shame to have the older riders leave without seeing the fruits of their labors."

"I would think that recovering from their injuries and returning to fight Thread would constitute the fruits of their labors," T'mar said, his voice taking on an edge.

"T'mar!" Fiona said, her tone just short of a whine. "This is our chance to honor Nuella and set a proper example, to show that the Weyrs can work with watch-whers. It's not just fun."

T'mar looked at her thoughtfully for a moment, then ran a hand wearily through his hair. "I suppose if I said no, you'd just go anyway."

"No," Fiona told him, shaking her head emphatically. "I'd want to know why, and if I thought your reasons were totally unacceptable, *then* I might go." She blew out a breath before adding, "But I expect that any reasons you have would make sense and I wouldn't go just out of spite."

T'mar gave her a frank look of gratitude.

"Was F'dan here your last convalescent for the morning?" he asked finally.

"For the day," Fiona corrected. "And he's fit enough that I've accused him of shirking. That's partly why we thought to fly to the wherhold."

"The watch-whers will be sleeping soon, if not already," T'mar remarked.

"All the better to see Zenor without their knowing," Fiona replied, her lips curving upward impishly.

T'mar chuckled, shaking his head.

"Very well, if you're set on this," T'mar told her. "Go now, before the others find out and we have an impromptu performance."

Fiona smiled back gratefully, turning and dragging F'dan by the arm before the wingleader could change his mind.

"But you know," T'mar called over his shoulder, forcing them to halt and turn around, "as F'dan hasn't been there yet, he'll have to fly the whole way."

Fiona's smile broadened, as she said, "Of course! All part of my plan, wingleader."

Beside her, F'dan groaned.

"This will teach you to stint on your therapy," Fiona told him unsympathetically.

"It's not that much farther," Fiona said to F'dan as he groaned once more.

"I'd forgotten what it's like to ride for hours!" the blue rider moaned. "I'm sore in places that haven't been sore in Turns."

"Nothing a good brisk walk on the ground and a warm bath later won't cure," Fiona assured him gruffly, glad to have someone else's pain to distract her from her own: This was the longest she'd ever flown a-dragonback, and while F'dan might not have been sore in places in Turns, Fiona was certain that she'd grown new muscles just for the occasion that had the express purpose of becoming painfully sore.

She leaned back against him to peer up and out over the right side of Ridorth's neck.

"There!" she called, pointing with her right hand, her left tightening its grip on the arm F'dan had wrapped protectively about her waist. "See those foothills?"

In response, Ridorth began a turn and a steady descent toward the ground. Moments later they landed and Fiona quickly unsnapped her straps, threw her leg over Ridorth's neck, and slid quickly down to the ground below, landing with knees flexed.

"Don't try that fool stunt again, Weyrwoman!" F'dan shouted at her as he climbed down the approved way, using Ridorth's foreleg. "I'll not be tending you if you break your legs!"

"Sorry," Fiona mumbled, her cheeks hot.

"Can you imagine what they'd say at the Weyr if I returned you injured?"

His tone was bantering now, but Fiona had no illusions that his first angry reaction was the most honest.

"I was stupid."

"Not stupid, just foolish," F'dan corrected her, stepping around to her side. "And perhaps a bit young, still."

Fiona cocked her head up at him: The blue rider wasn't tall by most standards, but he still stood a head higher than her.

"You forget that, don't you?" F'dan said. Her look answered him and he continued sagely, "You know, you've the whole Weyr on your shoulders *only* if you won't ask for help." He stepped behind her, quickly resting his hands on her shoulders. "And while there's no one who doubts your courage, you've not cause to bear such a weight."

"Cisca does."

"Weyrwoman Cisca relies on the help of others and admits her mistakes," F'dan said as he returned to his place by her side. He leaned down to wag a finger in her face, saying kindly, "Which is not to say that you don't have the same qualities, Weyrwoman. Just to say that you shouldn't forget your friends."

Fiona gave him a questioning look but found herself afraid to speak.

"Bold as I am, I count myself among them," F'dan added. He looked ahead—giving Fiona time to wipe her suddenly teary eyes—and scanned their surroundings critically. Then he looked back down to her, raising his eyebrows. "Where to, my lady?"

Fiona glanced around. North of the river she made out the outlines of a large stone shed with a sloped roof and long overhang; her guess that it was a barn was reinforced when she noted the thin line of a stone fence adjoining it. Closer, by the river, there was a long, low building, again in proper stone and with the requisite roofing. The building looked odd and she squinted at it. The roof overhung the river and—

"There!" Fiona declared, setting off toward the knot of men working beside the building.

Shortly her hunch was rewarded when she caught sight of a red-haired man in the group.

"What are they doing?" F'dan murmured as they got close enough to make out the details.

"I think they're setting up a waterwheel," Fiona said, watching a group of men struggle with hoists and tackle.

Their presence wasn't noted by the workers. Fiona, with a smile, indicated to F'dan that they should remain quiet, watching the work. It took the toiling men and women a good quarter of an hour to get the wheel mounted and seated on the stone shaft, and then they all stood back appreciatively as the water rolled off the plume to start the wheel turning, at which point there was a quiet cheer. A handsome bearded man with just a hint of gray in his beard stood away from the group and called, "Well done, lads! Now we can get to the *real* work."

He was met by a chorus of good-natured groans.

"Finding the gold, that is," he explained.

"That's Terregar," Fiona told F'dan.

"*That's* Terregar?" F'dan asked, eyeing the other man with renewed interest. "His work in gold and jewels is—"

"Just starting now," Fiona reminded him abruptly.

"So this is a good time to set him a commission, isn't it?" F'dan asked with a grin.

"Probably," Fiona agreed. "Have you anything in mind?"

"A ring, I should think," F'dan said, glancing down at his barren fingers meditatively. He looked over to her, adding, "You might consider it, too."

"The way you lot fly, it'd only get dirty with blood or ichor," Fiona exclaimed.

"You never know when a pair might come in useful," F'dan replied judiciously.

Fiona jerked her head toward the group and started forward, calling back to F'dan, "Come on, while they're still on break." To the group she called, "Zenor!"

The red-haired lad cocked his eyes toward the sound and his face broke into a smile as he identified her.

"Weyrwoman!" he called back. "You're just in time!" He gestured to the waterwheel, now turning at a steady pace. "Did you see?"

"We got here just as you were mounting it," Fiona told him. Out of the corner of her eye, she saw Terregar point out a new task to the rest of the workers and then detach himself in their direction.

"We're a bit busy," Terregar called as he approached, his glance falling to Zenor.

Zenor glanced reprovingly at the older man's brusqueness, then turned to Fiona. "To what do we owe the honor?"

"We were wondering about rings," F'dan said, essaying a grin toward Terregar.

"Actually, we were wondering about one in particular and its current disposition," Fiona said, having noted the flash of Terregar's eyes at F'dan's words. She glanced toward the smith. "Although if you were looking for commissions, I'm sure we could arrange a fair trade."

Terregar's angry look faded. He glanced down to the ground, abashed. "I'm not used to fair dealings with dragonriders," he said, glancing up again. "I'm sorry."

"As are we," Fiona replied. "Although once we are fighting Thread, we won't have time for fair trade."

"I don't know," Zenor objected, "I think the sweat of your brow, the blood of your bone, the ichor of your dragons, the risk of your lives or worse, is hard to price."

Fiona smiled at him. "I suppose there is that."

Terregar eyed Zenor thoughtfully, clearly reassessing his own beliefs.

"You could be a harper," F'dan declared appreciatively.

A sound from above, more felt than heard, heralded the arrival of a dragon from *between*. Fiona glanced up in surprise; it was a bronze.

"That's not one of ours," F'dan declared, eyeing the landing dragon carefully.

"We're not supposed to be here," Fiona yelped, looking to Zenor and Terregar for aid. "They can't know we're from the future!"

"Here," Terregar said, shucking off his tunic and throwing it toward Fiona. "Put this on and go to the others."

"You can't hide me," F'dan said as the others turned to him. "My blue is yonder."

"Just be who you are, only from this time," Fiona called as she strode off quickly to join the work group.

"I was much younger then!" F'dan called back.

Fiona shrugged and then turned her attention to her new role as smith worker.

"There's a strange bronze landing," she explained before the other workers could finish their greeting. "I need to blend in; they can't know we're here from the future."

"Weyrleader D'gan would have a fit," one of them said in agreement. He glanced at Fiona assessingly. "Ever panned for gold?"

Fiona shook her head, grinning from ear to ear.

"We'll set you up, then," the man said, reaching for a pan and tossing it to her. "I'm Klinos, that's Jenur, Aveln, Torler, and that," he finished, gesturing to the youngest of the group, a lad of about ten, "is my son, Finlar."

"Mine, too," Jenur put in with a growl. She was the only woman in the group and clearly used to Klinos's ways. "Or did you forget that you had help?"

"You're always a help, love," Klinos said obtusely. "Finlar, this is the Weyrwoman, only we want to keep that a secret from the other dragonmen."

The youngster grinned up at Fiona. This was a challenge that he was sure to revel in.

"He'll show you the way of it," Klinos said, nodding affectionately toward Finlar.

"Come on Weyrwo—"

"Fiona will do."

Finlar's eyes got as wide as the mining pan in his hands. In a hushed voice he said, "Fiona."

Behind, the others laughed.

"Go on with you, teach her right!" Jenur called after them. "Be sure she finds some good nuggets."

"Most of 'em have already been found," Finlar complained.

"Let's do what we can," Fiona suggested.

Finlar led her down to the river bank and stood for a moment, eyeing it critically.

"Do you mind getting wet?" he asked and, when she shrugged, started out straight into the river. He glanced back when he noticed that she hadn't followed and called, "It's okay, it's pretty flat here. No big holes."

Reluctantly, Fiona followed, wondering if perhaps they weren't making more of a spectacle of themselves than prudence suggested. The water quickly rose to her knees and then to her waist.

"It's cold!"

"Nah, just chilly," Finlar corrected. "You get used to it quickly."

He peered around and started trudging farther upstream and more toward the far bank. Fiona followed him, wondering if she shouldn't be reining him back. As if reading her thoughts, he peered back over his shoulder and said, "It's okay, I know what

I'm doing." After a moment he added, "Besides, if I didn't, me ma would skin me alive."

Fiona grinned.

"Okay, now lean down, get a good mix of bottom and water," Finlar told her, matching his actions to his words, "and then stand back up, swirling the water around to spill the dirt out." He began a swirling motion with his arms and allowed the dirtier water to spill over the edges. "If you're lucky, when you're done, you'll find a nugget. If not, you'll find gold dust, little flecks of the stuff." With pride he added, "You always find gold flecks."

Fiona repeated Finlar's steps twice before she felt she had a good grasp of the mechanics. Her first pan revealed only small flecks of gold.

"Throw it back, you'll get better," Finlar said as he inspected her pan.

"But . . . it's gold!"

"The mill's for those small flecks," Finlar told her dismissively. "That's why we're building it."

Seeing her continued reluctance, he leaned over and used his pan to force hers back into the water, spilling the contents. "Trust me, you'll find better!"

Fiona sighed but dutifully scooped up another pan. It didn't *seem* right to her so she dumped it, moved another step closer to the shore, and tried again.

"That's it," Finlar said encouragingly. "Use your senses." His dropped his voice. "Sometimes I think we can feel the gold."

Maybe they could at that, Fiona thought as she lifted up the re-filled pan: This one felt right. Moments later she was jumping up and down squealing, "Look, gold! I found gold!"

"Shh, you're supposed to be blending in," Finlar hissed at her desperately, glancing back to the far shore. What he saw made him groan. "Oh, no! Now we're for it."

Fiona was so thrilled with the sight of the two nuggets in her hand, each just about the size of the fingertip of her smallest finger, that it was moments before Finlar's panic registered.

"They're waving us over!" Finlar cried in despair.

"I found gold!" Fiona exclaimed, still oblivious to the danger.

"You're supposed to act like you've been doing it for the past half Turn," Finlar growled at her.

"Look," Fiona said eagerly, extending her pan to him. "Aren't they beautiful?"

"They?" Finlar repeated, his brows furrowing as he bent closer. "You found two?"

"Right there," Fiona said, ducking her chin toward their location in her pan. She glanced up at him, grinning broadly. "Aren't they pretty?"

"Most of the times we don't find two," Finlar said with awe in his voice. He turned toward the far bank and waved. "Come on, we'll show them!"

Fiona walked carefully over, keeping her attention divided between her pan and the placement of her feet: There was a lot of gold dust in the pan, too, and she didn't want to lose any of it.

Finlar reached down and grabbed her arm to help her up the bank, where waiting hands reached down to hoist her up.

At the top, Fiona found herself looking into the amber eyes of a tall, middle-aged man with speckles of gray in his otherwise warm brown hair. He was a dragonrider not just by his garb but by his bearing. She raised her head to greet him, but a nudge from Finlar reminded her of her secret and she dropped her eyes again.

"You're always being so bold," Finlar chided her. "You'll shame the hold the way you go on." To the dragonrider, he said, "Please forgive her, my lord."

The muted sound of laughter in the distance told Fiona that F'dan could only just contain his mirth at her position.

"My lord," Fiona said, bowing in a low curtsy, keeping her pan steady in one hand. "Please forgive me: I was overexcited and too bold."

"Nonsense," the dragonrider assured her, his eyes dancing. "You had every right." He gestured to the pan. "May I see?"

She relinquished it to him, feeling for a moment once more like a holder and wondering if she'd lose her treasure to this man. She tamped hard on her pride and could feel, in the distance, F'dan's mixed emotions of approval and humorous appreciation.

"As you can see, Lord M'tal," Terregar spoke from his side, as the dragonrider poked his finger to nudge the two visible nuggets, "we've had a lucky find."

M'tal! Fiona cringed inwardly. Benden's Weyrleader himself.

She'd seen the man before, of course, but he was younger now than the last time she'd laid eyes on him.

"And set up a new crafthall?" M'tal asked, looking toward Terregar.

"And the wherhold," Zenor added stoutly.

"It was about the wherhold—and Nuella—that I came," M'tal replied. He pushed the pan back toward Fiona, telling her, "Well, I'm sure your master will be pleased with your work this day."

Fiona glanced toward Terregar, who gave her a look suffused with dread and wonder, and then she piped up, "If you please, my lord, I'd take it as a great favor if you'd accept these pieces for Journeyman Kindan."

"Kindan?"

Fiona dropped another curtsy and pressed the pan back into M'tal's hands. "We've all heard his songs and the ballads about how he helped in the Plague," she said. "It seems only right—to me, at least."

M'tal cocked his head, glancing toward Terregar and Zenor approvingly. "You teach your crafters well."

"We haven't a harper of our own yet, but we do what we can," Zenor responded, carefully avoiding any glances in Fiona's direction. Fiona noted that Terregar was eyeing her with renewed interest, clearly reevaluating her.

"Journeyman Kindan is famous throughout Pern," Fiona said. "It seems only right, if it's not too much to ask."

"It's not," M'tal said, picking the two nuggets out of the pan and returning it to her. "And I thank you for the notion."

Zenor eyed the two pieces carefully, saying, "If my lord would, I believe I could fashion those into a ring or small pins."

"A harp, perhaps?" M'tal asked.

Zenor paused for a long moment, consideringly. It was Terregar who spoke up, "A harp it shall be, my lord." To Zenor he said, "Any lack we'll make up from other pannings."

"A gift from the Wherhold for Kindan's gift of his watch-wher to our lady Nuella," Fiona declared grandly. Finlar's gasp at her side alerted her to her mistake: Her wording was too grand for a mere crafter girl.

"Well spoken," M'tal said as he passed the nuggets over to Zenor. "Very well spoken for one without a harper."

"We're a mixed lot," Terregar told him quickly. "Some from the Smith hall, some from outlying holds and crafts nearby."

"Mmm," M'tal murmured. He glanced at Fiona. "And who should I name to Journeyman Kindan as his benefactor?"

"Fi—" Fiona began but broke off even before she felt Finlar cringing beside her. "Please just call it a gift from the crafters and holders of the wherhold, my lord."

Terregar glanced at her in surprise mixed with admiration. Zenor gave her a knowing nod; he'd formed his opinion of her back at Mine Natalon.

M'tal turned back to Zenor. "As I was saying," he began, "my visit here was more to coordinate with Nuella and the wherfolk than to admire your gold."

There was a subtle shift in the atmosphere as the crafters absorbed his words.

Zenor gave him an expectant look.

"Do you recall how Nuella visited all the holds, Turns back before she bonded with Nuelsk?"

Zenor nodded. "Indeed I do, my lord," he replied. "However, if you are here to ask that of her again, I should inform you that she's just recently bonded with a gold—"

"Has she, by the First Egg!" M'tal exclaimed, his face breaking into a huge grin. "I'd heard about the accident at the mine, of course, but I hadn't hoped—" He cut himself off, motioning courteously to Zenor. "Please continue."

Zenor cast a nervous glance toward Fiona: What should he say?

Fiona thought quickly, passing her pan to Finlar, who grasped it in surprise. "I could go see if she's awake, sir," she suggested quickly to Zenor.

"Yes, do that," Zenor said gratefully, glancing back to the Weyrleader. "Perhaps we should wait for Nuella."

"Perhaps," M'tal said, glancing toward Finlar and the two pans, "I could try my luck in the river?"

As Fiona sped away she suppressed a giggle at the sight of Benden's Weyrleader drenched up to his hips as he happily panned for gold. It was only when she was halfway to nowhere that she realized she wasn't exactly sure where to find Nuella.

She scanned around nervously, then settled on the hills. She was certain that Zenor and Terregar would have quarried their stone from the hills, excavating quarters for the watch-whers at the same time as providing housing for the crafters.

Quickly she discovered that she'd made the right choice. She paused as the dark archway cut into the side of the hill came into view: the craftwork was perfect, the stones laid dry to form a tall archway that was properly recessed the regulation dragonlength into the hill, with room clearly set for two large steel doors, one set behind the other to provide double protection against Thread. She thought she could feel both Zenor's mining craft and Terregar's smith craft at work in its formation—a proper blend for Nuella's queen.

Again Fiona found herself admonishing herself to remember that Nuella had not yet made her amazing night flight. The adoration of the Fort riders for the watch-whers was something that had already subtly disturbed the wherhandlers, unused as they were to anything but derision from dragonriders.

Glows lit the way inside, and Fiona turned to the sound of voices and the smells of cooking.

"Who are you and what are you doing here?" a woman's voice demanded brusquely from the nearest hearth. "You're soaking. Why aren't you out in the sun, drying off?"

Fiona's heart leapt as she took in the flour-smudged face, the stern look and the amazing smells arising all around her. This slim person was clearly of the same mold as her beloved Neesa, the head cook at Fort Hold since before Fiona was born.

"You must be Sula," Fiona said, recalling Zenor's glee at arranging to bring her with them from Mine Natalon.

"Of course I am. Now get out of here," Sula responded sharply. "Don't think to nab a dainty on your way out, either!" To herself she began muttering, "I work all day and all night and these kids just gobble it up without a word of thanks."

"If you've dainties, you might want to send them down to the river," Fiona said over Sula's mutterings. The cook glanced at her sharply, and Fiona explained, "Weyrleader M'tal is here, looking for Nuella."

Sula clasped flour-whitened hands to her cheeks, adding to the smudges already there, as she exclaimed, "Why didn't you say so immediately!" She began bustling about the kitchen, twice as busy as she'd been before. "Oh, my!" She raised her voice to a bellow. "Silstra! Silstra, get over here, we've got company!"

She glanced again at Fiona. "Well, what are you still doing here? You've delivered your message, you—"

Silstra bustled into the room, her face set to scold whoever had caused her to be disturbed. She stopped the moment she caught sight of Fiona and dropped a curtsy. "Weyrwoman, what are you doing here?"

"Actually, I was here to get Zenor to propose," Fiona admitted, "but Weyrleader M'tal has dropped in and wants a word with Nuella."

"Did he recognize you?" Silstra asked, her expression going anxious.

"No," Fiona replied. "They sent me into the river to pan and I found some nuggets and—" She cut herself short. "He thinks I'm a crafter or holder, and I've been sent to get Nuella before M'tal starts asking questions that Zenor and Terregar can't handle."

Silstra snorted. "Then you'd best be quick—neither of them are good at lying."

Sula, who had been staring bug-eyed at Fiona ever since Silstra had identified her, finally found breath enough to gasp, "My lady, I'm so sorry! I didn't—"

Fiona stopped her with a raised hand and a grin. "You reminded me of our cook back at the Hold. It felt like being home."

"Shards!" Sula exclaimed, shaking her head in dismay. "That a cook would talk so to a Lady Holder!"

"If she hadn't, I'd be the size of a barge," Fiona replied, still grinning. "I was always stealing from the kitchen."

"I had you marked for a rascal," Silstra murmured approvingly. Sula gasped in surprise. "You couldn't manage your Weyr at this age if you hadn't been a hellion as a child."

"I only hunted tunnel snakes," Fiona said in her defense.

"Exactly!" Silstra said. She turned to Sula. "But the Weyrwoman's right about your dainties. Do be a gem and set out a platter that I can bring down."

"And some iced *klah*," Sula said in agreement, nodding toward Fiona. "We're so glad that you weyrfolk brought us that."

"It's the only way to survive in the heat," Fiona said. "But I think you'd best send down warm *klah,* as it's really chilly out and, also, we don't want to have to explain the ice."

"Oh!" Sula exclaimed, smudging yet more flour onto her cheeks with her hands. "I hadn't thought of that."

"I'll lead you to Nuellask's weyr," Silstra said, turning so quickly that Fiona had to scurry to follow her. On the way, Silstra said over her shoulder, "I'm glad you're here; I've about run out of things to say to Zenor." She shook her head, adding fondly, "The lad's afraid he's not good enough for her."

Fiona thought briefly of Kindan, wondering if he felt the same, and then realized that her previous mention of him and her meeting now with his oldest sister brought a pang of longing and familiarity to her heart.

"It seems to me that he loves her," Fiona replied. "Isn't that enough?"

"Sometimes," Silstra said. "I think he's afraid that she'll say no, fearing that she'll end up having to choose between him or her queen."

"She won't," Fiona declared. "At least, she hadn't in my time."

"Don't tell her that," Silstra cautioned. "I can see how right you are to keep the future clouded. If she knew what she did, she'd feel trapped and without choice."

"Yes," Fiona agreed. "That's one reason."

Silstra paused outside a darkened archway. "Nuellask is in there."

Talenth? Fiona called. *I'm here at the wherhold. Could you ask Nuellask if I can come in?*

A moment later a curious chirp echoed in the corridor.

"She doesn't usually do that," Silstra muttered, surprised.

"I asked Talenth to speak with her," Fiona explained.

"Who's there?" Nuella called groggily from the entrance.

"It's Silstra," Silstra replied. "Weyrwoman Fiona is here with me."

"M'tal's down by the river," Fiona added. "He's asking questions."

"M'tal?" Nuella repeated, her voice perking up. "I dreamed about him."

"Should I have him come to you here?" Fiona asked. She added, "He doesn't know about me—he thinks I'm a crafter."

"Well, he's right on that," Nuella said, her voice approaching them. A moment later she stepped out, one hand outstretched. "Nuellask is sleepy; we can leave her here," she said as she reached her hand toward Fiona, who grabbed it in response. Nuella smiled. "It's good to have you here again, Weyrwoman."

"We've been busy at the Weyr," Fiona said, "or I would have come more often."

"You are always welcome," Nuella told her.

"So I did right, then?" Fiona asked, suddenly feeling her age and all the worry that she'd had about forcing the queen on Nuella and the wherfolk to move here.

"You did," another voice chimed in from down the corridor. It was Arella. She added teasingly, "Didn't you know that?"

"No, not really," Fiona admitted in a small voice. "I only knew that there was a wherhold, not who was in it—"

"But you knew you were doing right at the moment, when you forced us to change," Nuella corrected her. She waved her free hand dismissively. "You should understand how much being tied to the future hurts you."

Fiona made a surprised sound.

Nuella and Arella both burst out laughing and Fiona found herself bristling, her cheeks hot with shame.

"They mean well, Weyrwoman," Silstra assured her in a tone that told of long suffering with the wherwomen's humors.

"If you just trust yourself, Fiona, you'll do fine," Arella explained when at last she recovered from her laughing bout.

"This wherhold is thriving—will thrive," Nuella added approvingly. "And it is because of you, only because of you, that it is so."

"But I knew it would!" Fiona declared, feeling that that should detract from her honors.

"No," Nuella corrected with a shake of her head. "As you said, you only knew some things. You were responsible for making this, even if the future gave you hints."

"M'tal's here," Silstra said to Arella.

"He's down at the river," Nuella added, raising Fiona's hand invitingly. "So, Weyrwoman, what shall we tell him?"

"Hmmph!" Fiona snorted. "After all you've just said, it seems to me that you'll figure it out."

Nuella snorted, then nodded. "I'm sure I will."

"He doesn't know about Fiona or the Igen riders," Silstra added.

"F'dan brought me," Fiona said, "but he's going to say that he's from Fort Weyr."

"As that's the truth, there's no problem with that," Nuella agreed.

"I'll get back to Sula—she's doubtless in a tizzy by now," Silstra said, nodding to each of them in turn, then marching quickly away.

As they made their way down toward the river, Arella and Nuella quizzed Fiona on her meeting with M'tal. Both giggled and glanced at each other when Fiona, red-faced, explained about her gift for Kindan.

"He's quite a looker," Arella told Nuella knowingly.

"I know," Nuella agreed. "But I prefer redheads."

"We know," Arella said with a grin.

"He's a handsome lad," Fiona agreed. She saw Arella's encouraging nod and, not wasting time to wonder how the wherhandler had divined her intentions, plunged on, "He'd be quite a catch."

"Only if he's willing to be caught," Nuella said with a sigh. "I was hoping maybe when Nuelsk rose . . ."

Arella burst out laughing, pointing a finger accusingly at Nuella. "I never would have thought that of you!"

"Why not?" Nuella asked, her innocence vanishing. "I've heard enough about mating flights to hope—"

"You are a sly one!" Arella exclaimed.

Fiona felt uncomfortable with the tone of the conversation, not scandalized but troubled all the same, feeling somewhat as though she were on the edge of a deeper understanding that only experience could provide.

"As it is," Nuella persisted, "I don't know if I can wait until Nuellask rises."

"Ah, but it'd be so much better with a queen!" Arella said, grinning lecherously.

Something in Nuella's silence calmed the other wherhandler, who shook her head, glancing toward Fiona with a meaning Fiona couldn't fathom.

"M'tal doesn't know my name," Fiona told them as they drew near the millhouse.

"Probably for the best," Nuella agreed. "Fiona's not that common a name."

"He'll have met me by now," Fiona said in agreement. "I mean the 'me' of four Turns."

"If watch-whers can go *between* like dragons," Arella asked, her lips pursed thoughtfully, "can they go *between* times like dragons, too?"

Nuella and Fiona gasped at the notion.

"Weyrwoman?" Nuella said, throwing the question to her.

Fiona shook her head. "I can't see why not."

"What's it like, then, going *between* times?" Arella asked.

"It's hard," Fiona told her. "It's harder on riders than dragons or weyrfolk. Terin doesn't feel it at all. But the riders—we feel like there's a noise or tension, a tingling, a jangle on the senses. It comes and goes and we're never sure when. Some days are better than others, and the days aren't the same for all dragonriders. It leaves us both tired and edgy. *Klah* is good when we're tired, rest when we're edgy." She frowned as she admitted, "There've been fights. Fights that shouldn't have happened."

"Fights?" Arella asked, surprised.

Fiona nodded. "We—T'mar and the wingleaders—handle them. If a douse of cold water won't bring them to their senses, we put them in a ring with a stuffing suit and let them have at it."

"Stuffing suit?" Arella repeated.

"A set of clothes full of stuffing so that they can hit each other without breaking bones," Fiona explained. "They usually wind up exhausted, all the fight gone out of them." She gave Arella a grim look as she added, "And then they're put on the worst details for the next fortnight or more."

"I can imagine," Nuella said thoughtfully. To Arella she said, "Remember that."

"Aye," Arella responded. She explained to Fiona, "We're still sorting out how we're going to handle the wherhold."

"Arella's been used to more watch-whers in the same place than I have," Nuella said. "So I look to her for knowledge."

"You're the senior," Arella reminded her. "You've got the gold."

"You're following Weyr traditions?" Fiona asked.

"It seems right," Nuella explained. "At least until we learn differently."

"Besides, all the watch-whers obey the queen," Arella added.

"And dragons," Nuella reminded her. Fiona noted Arella's sour look as the woman acknowledged that remark. For a moment Fiona wondered what it would be like the other way around, if the dragons obeyed the watch-whers, and then she realized that they already had—in the night flight Nuella had led.

"I'm not so sure," Fiona said much to Arella's surprise. "I think the watch-whers are willing to listen to the dragons much the same way the dragons are willing to listen to their riders."

"So, no difference," Arella said with a dismissive shrug.

"No," Nuella responded. "The Weyrwoman has a point. A dragon doesn't *have* to obey her rider."

"Think of a hatching," Fiona said suggestively.

"Or a mating flight," Arella added appreciatively. "If your dragons are anything like our watch-whers, then a mating flight requires the greatest control a handler—rider—ever needs."

"It's in the Ballads," Fiona said in agreement, suppressing an internal shudder—could she control Talenth when she rose? She forced herself to be calm; the event was still Turns away. Besides, Fiona couldn't imagine Talenth ever fighting her.

"Shh," Arella hissed warningly to Fiona. "We're getting near."

They found the group indoors, with Terregar leading M'tal on an impromptu tour of the new building.

"We've only got the beams for the second floor but we're hoping to trade with Lemos for enough wood to lay in decent flooring," he was explaining as they entered.

"I hate to say it," M'tal replied, "but Telgar's got better wood at lower prices."

"I'd prefer not to trade with Telgar," Zenor replied. "Besides, we figure that here we're beholden to you, so that it's good manners to work with other holds beholden to Benden."

M'tal gave him a thoughtful look. "In old times this land would have looked to Igen Weyr for protection," he said.

He found himself looking at a sea of hopeful faces and added, "I see no reason why Benden Weyr shouldn't avail itself of such a great tithe. I'll have a word with C'rion."

The group gave a collective sigh of relief, untempered by M'tal's mention of tithe.

"Ah, Lady Nuella," M'tal cried as he caught sight of her. "How kind of you to join us!"

Nuella's face split into an honest grin as she rushed toward the sound of his voice, hands outstretched. "My lord!"

"M'tal," the dragonrider corrected her. "My friends call me M'tal."

Beside her, Fiona felt Arella's surprise. She guessed that even though the wherhandler had met Benden's Weyrleader several times before, this impulsive, uncontrolled display of affection for one attached to the watch-whers removed any lingering suspicion that all dragonriders fell into two groups: those who despised the watch-whers, and those who sought to use them for their own purposes.

"M'tal," Nuella corrected herself, folding herself into his arms and hugging him cheerfully.

"It's been too long, I'm afraid," M'tal said when they broke apart. "When I'd heard about your Nuelsk, I thought that I should wait until you were settled before asking you—"

"What?" Nuella wondered.

"Actually," M'tal said, gesturing around with a free hand, "I'd meant to inveigle you into something like *this*." He smiled and shook his head in awe. "Only I'd no notion of anything quite so grand as your current undertaking."

Nuella turned her head toward Fiona, then hastily, as if realizing her error, back to M'tal. "It all just sort of happened, my lord."

"I wish we had known about the gold here sooner," M'tal said wistfully. "It would have eased the pain everywhere, for people are willing to work that much harder in the hopes of getting beautiful jewelry."

He glanced toward Terregar. "How did you find it?"

"It was on some old maps at the Smith Hall," Fiona improvised quickly, taking in the look of impending terror on Terregar's face. "I was cleaning—"

"Hiding," Terregar corrected acerbically, grinning at Fiona with gratitude hidden in his attitude of long-suffering affection.

"Ah, so you're craftbred!" M'tal said to Fiona. He turned back to Terregar, adding, "Quite an honor to the Smithcraft. Master Veclan must have been sorry to let her go."

"Actually," Fiona said in all honesty, "I think he was grateful to see the back of me."

Terregar snorted.

"Lady Silstra is preparing a platter, my lord," Fiona said, aiming her glance halfway between Terregar and M'tal and throwing in a sloppy curtsy for good measure.

"I've kept you all too long," M'tal said, turning toward Nuella and politely reaching for her hand. "If I can just have a word with this kind lady—" He paused and glanced at Arella. "—and Arella, too, I'll let you go back to your work."

The look on Arella's face when she heard M'tal name her was one of surprise suffused with delight.

Nuella glanced toward Fiona, who caught the look and said, "I'm sorry for having disturbed you, my lady."

"Well, it was an important interruption," Nuella said dismissively. "Just see that all your interruptions are as important."

Fiona nodded, then remembered Nuella's eyes and amplified, "I will, my lady."

With one final scrutinizing look and a sardonic mutter of, "Very much an honor to your craft!" M'tal took his leave of Fiona and the others.

There was a moment of silence as the remaining workers waited for the Weyrleader to move out of earshot, and then they all gave a collective sigh of relief.

"That was awkward!" F'dan declared as he stepped out of the crowd.

"Did M'tal notice you?" Fiona asked.

"He did and I told him my rank and Weyr," F'dan assured her. He glanced toward Terregar. "I wonder if my presence here might have inclined him more toward offering protection."

"I'm sure it did," Terregar said, his lips curving upward. He turned his attention to Fiona. "And now that that latest excitement is out of the way—and, I hope you do not take this badly, I must confess that excitement seems to follow you, Weyrwoman—what was it that you came to see us about?"

"Rings," F'dan reminded him.

"We've already negotiated your price."

"A day's work here from both me and my blue," F'dan told Fiona. From the look on Terregar's face, Fiona guessed that the smith was still recovering from his shock while simultaneously calculating how to use F'dan and Ridorth to his best advantage. Fiona found herself liking this bearded man and could see why Silstra had found his quiet competence so attractive.

"With an option for another day for the same price," Terregar reminded F'dan.

"Such option to expire upon our departure from Igen," F'dan said, repeating the last part of their agreement.

Terregar nodded. "You drive a good trade, dragonrider."

"I learned it from the best," F'dan said, and surprised Fiona by glancing in her direction.

"And what is it you want to trade today, Weyrwoman?" Terregar asked, his attention once again returning to her.

"Actually, all we want is a moment of Zenor's time, if we could," Fiona said, glancing toward the red-haired man. With a smile she added, "And perhaps to see the ring."

Terregar's eyebrows rose. Did Fiona detect a gleam of humor in his eyes?

"It's better in the sunlight," Terregar said. "Zenor, why don't you take them outside?"

Zenor, seeming distracted, led them through the doorway and into the midday sunlight. A wind swept the worst of the heat from them, but all the same, Fiona felt they couldn't stay long before they'd be driven back inside.

"Come on, Zenor, give," she said peremptorily, holding out a hand, palm open.

Zenor reached into his tunic and pulled on the leather thong tied around his neck. He looped it over his head and dropped it into Fiona's outstretched hand.

"I don't think it's good enough," Zenor said morosely even as Fiona's mouth opened in a large "Oh!" of astonishment.

"Zenor, it's amazing!" she exclaimed, holding the gold band up close so that she could examine every intricate detail. "Three bands wound together, how did you do it?"

"I had help from Terregar," Zenor said. "Although he did say that I was as addled as a wherry to even think of such a piece."

"It's never been done before," F'dan explained. "There's never been enough gold of such quality, nor"—he nodded respectfully toward Zenor—"anyone so deft at such workings."

"I was always good at making things," Zenor said with a diffident shrug of his shoulders.

"You know," Fiona said judiciously, returning the ring to Zenor, "you're right. There's something wrong with that ring."

"I knew it," Zenor groaned. F'dan gave Fiona a startled look of disbelief. "I just knew it," Zenor continued. With a pleading look he asked Fiona, "What is it?"

"It's not on Nuella's finger!" Fiona exclaimed, her eyes flashing in irritation.

"Huh?"

"You can't see your work in its proper light until it's in its proper setting," she told him. "And that ring was made for her finger. That's its proper setting."

She reached for his hand, latched on, and tugged. "Come on."

"Where are we going?" Zenor asked, lurching after her like a herdbeast being led to pasture.

"I think I'd best see to Master Terregar," F'dan said hastily, taking off in the opposite direction. "I'm not sure I should be seen more by Weyrleader M'tal today."

Fiona ignored his words, concentrating on keeping Zenor in her grip.

Halfway toward the wherhold, Zenor grasped her intention and suddenly dug in his heels.

"No, I can't, it's not the right time," he told Fiona feebly. "I'm not ready."

Fiona released his wrist and turned around to face him.

"Do you love her?" she asked.

"Huh?"

"Do you love her?" Fiona repeated. "Kindan told me long ago when he was talking about you, her, and Nuelsk, that when he left he told her that if she kissed you then everyone would know that she loved you." She paused to let that sink in. "So, knowing that, do you love her?"

"Well, of course!" Zenor cried in response. "But she's got the new watch-wher and we're settling in and—"

"None of that matters," Fiona told him calmly. "You need to seize the moment, Zenor, or you might lose her forever." She paused as a sudden revelation burst upon her. "You're afraid of losing her, aren't you? You almost lost her in the Plague."

"And what if something happens to me?" Zenor asked. "What then? You've seen how hard it was for her after Nuelsk. It was just as hard after her parents and—"

"Zenor, you've answered your own question," Fiona broke in gently. Zenor gave her a puzzled look. "You can't deny her the joys of today to save her from the pain of tomorrow. All you are doing is denying her any chance at happiness, not any chance at pain."

Zenor's eyes grew wider as he absorbed the sense in her words.

"Today is an excellent day to see if that ring fits," Fiona urged him quietly.

"Yes," Zenor agreed, drawing himself up to his full height, his eyes roaming off into the distance . . . or the future. "You're right."

He started off, his gait purposeful and long, leaving Fiona to trot after him.

Zenor didn't break his stride as they entered the dimly lit hold, nor did he pause to find his bearings, setting a course directly for the kitchen. Presently Fiona heard the tenor voice of M'tal.

"Nuella," Zenor began the moment he burst into the room, halting all discussion.

Nuella looked toward him expectantly. Zenor closed the distance between them and he reached for the leather thong around his neck, pulling it off in one fluid movement even as he sank to his knees, his free hand grasping Nuella's.

There was a moment's silence as everyone took in the scene, then Zenor placed the gold ring in Nuella's palm. "Will you marry me?"

Nuella gasped in surprise, her eyes suddenly wet with tears. "Marry you? Of course, with all my heart!"

"That went very well, my lady," F'dan said as he hoisted Fiona up in front of him and busied himself with tightening her riding straps firmly. "You have quite the social knack, if I may observe."

"I just had to think of all the moaning you'd make if I failed," Fiona replied teasingly. Really, it was a joy to spend time with F'dan because he treated her like a full-grown person, able to take on any burden, sometimes demanding more of her than she thought she could give. And he did it all with a manner that was always respectful, always supportive. And, of course, he swore like some of her father's guards—when they thought no one from the Hold was listening.

"We lowly blues are always willing to take on the tasks we're called to," F'dan replied drolly as Ridorth leapt nimbly into the air. "Of course," he added, "I'll certainly need a long massage for all the kinks I've got in my poor recovering body this day."

"I'll send a weyrling," Fiona retorted icily. Massaging was one of the therapies that she'd initially feared the most but had ultimately found to be the most enjoyable and relaxing work. It had taken her two sessions to cure her of any lingering squeamishness when dealing with human flesh, particularly male human flesh, and to become absorbed in the art of gentling muscles back into health.

"Oh, be sure to send a pretty one," F'dan teased. "I like it when you send a pretty one."

Fiona snarled playfully but said nothing as the darkness of *between* took hold of them.

"I'll do your hair if you do my leg," F'dan offered as they burst back out into the daylight over Igen Weyr. Beneath them Ridorth bugled a response to the challenge from the watch dragon perched on the heights near the Star Stones.

"Wash, brush, and trim?"

"Deal."

It had given Fiona a sublime sense of relief when she discovered that riders of blues and greens, while deferential to her as a Weyr-woman, treated her womanness as something unimportant to their relationship with her. Fiona had always understood intellectually why that was so, but it was only when she recognized it on a subconscious level that she truly allowed herself to open up to them. These older men, who did not see her as a potential mate, were free to see her as the person she was.

Of all the riders, perhaps because of his lengthy recovery, Fiona had become fondest of F'dan and was most comfortable being herself with him.

"You are truly a beautiful girl, you know," F'dan said as he toweled off her hair while she sat before him. Fiona couldn't help blushing with pride. F'dan threaded a lock of her gold hair through his fingers. "Your hair is silky, your freckles mark your face and shoulders delicately, your nose is—" He sniffed. "—well, you'll survive with your nose."

"What's wrong with my nose?"

"Nothing." F'dan chuckled. "Just teasing." He finished toweling and picked up a comb, running it slowly through her hair. He held up the ends and peered at them. "Yes, you need a trim. You're getting all raggedy." He hissed through his teeth as he added, "And this sun's not good for the condition—you're all dried out. Aren't you using that oil we'd discovered?"

"We ran out," Fiona replied drowsily. She *loved* when he played with her hair.

"Mmm," F'dan murmured in a tone that informed her he would check on the veracity of that statement.

"We used the last of it on *your* leg, if you recall," she told him, not quite finding the energy to sound testy. She'd insisted upon their return on massaging his leg first and was glad she had: the exercise had done him much good, but his muscles had definitely been tight and had needed the massage to relax them.

"Really," F'dan responded, sounding not at all convinced. "How convenient for you, then."

Fiona growled back in keeping with the banter.

"I'm surprised you don't demand that I stay here with you the next three Turns," F'dan commented. "Otherwise who will take care of you?"

"I can take care of myself."

"It's a good thing that you've arranged to have the wedding before I leave, then," F'dan murmured as he began to tackle her long locks. "Perhaps you'd prefer me to cut it short so that you won't have to worry about it when I'm gone?"

"That's an excellent idea," Fiona said, knowing it would surprise the blue rider. "In this heat it's far too much bother."

"But your hair is so soft!" F'dan objected.

"I don't see *you* wearing your hair long in this heat," Fiona retorted.

"I'll grow it out again as soon as I return to the Weyr," F'dan told her. "In colder weather it's wise to have long hair."

"Ah, then you agree," Fiona said triumphantly. She held up a hand with index finger and thumb measuring a gap. "This long, if you please."

"You might as well be a boy at that length," F'dan remarked sourly. "You'll take away my only joy."

"Well, short, then," Fiona said willing to compromise. "But if I don't like it, you'll cut it my way."

"Very well," he agreed, not bothering to keep the reluctant tone out of his voice.

Fiona was glad to hear him pick up the scissors, for she knew that she'd be seated for a long time and, truth be told, the stress of the morning had left her quite tired.

Then, dimly, she heard something out of the ordinary and roused herself enough to question Talenth.

A bronze has arrived, Talenth told her, *and the watch dragon has challenged him.* A moment later, she added, *It is Gaminth of Benden Weyr.*

"Gaminth?" Fiona repeated, sitting up and startling F'dan, who just narrowly avoided clipping her bangs at the root. "M'tal?"

"I heard, too," F'dan told her irritably. "You're not done, and until I'm done with you, you're not fit to be seen." He paused, adding drolly, "Unless you'd really like Benden's Weyrleader to see you with your head half-shorn."

Where's T'mar? Fiona asked Talenth, sighing irritably but allowing herself to be pushed back into the chair.

He and the older weyrlings are getting ice, Talenth responded.

Who's the senior bronze? No, forget that. Fiona remembered that T'mar's Zirenth was the only healthy adult bronze still here. *Where's N'jian?*

N'jian went with them. Talenth replied, sounding much less worried than Fiona. *J'keran is greeting him.*

J'keran asks where you are, Perinth said suddenly to Fiona.

I'll be done in a moment. Have him offer the Weyrleader some refreshment but nothing with ice, Fiona replied.

Nothing with ice, Perinth repeated to himself.

Tell Terin that she's got company, Fiona said to Talenth.

She's getting ready, Talenth told her. *She says to remind you that the traders are due this evening.*

"Oh, dear!" Fiona groaned out loud. "F'dan, hurry!"

"You hurry a haircut, you get bad results," F'dan told her with mock seriousness. "You're just over half done."

"You've got five minutes, and then I'm leaving now matter how I look," Fiona warned him.

"No," F'dan told her sternly, "you're a Weyrwoman. Even Weyrleaders who arrive unannounced can wait for you."

"They might," Fiona agreed. "*I* can't."

"Probably true," F'dan muttered to himself, stepping back and eyeing her hair judiciously before his next cut. "So the practice will be good for you."

Fiona seethed with impatience as F'dan continued his careful clipping. Slowly she forced herself to relax and as she did, she realized that for all his words, the blue rider had sped up his work.

Finally, F'dan stood back for one last careful inspection of his handiwork and sighed.

"Well, it will do," he said. "You can't expect good results if you rush."

Gesturing to Fiona to rise, he placed his hands on her shoulders and turned her about to face the mirror.

"I'm gorgeous!" Fiona exclaimed, beaming with pride at her new look.

"You were always gorgeous, Weyrwoman. Now you're stunning," F'dan corrected.

Fiona leaned forward to the mirror to examine F'dan's scissor work. Her hair was short but framed her face and skull like a golden cap. The hair on her forehead parted into two separate bunches, with the angled break at the center of her forehead.

"I look like a baby," she complained. "I'm too young!"

"You only look your age," F'dan said. He brushed stray hairs from her clothes, then stood back again, inspecting his handiwork.

"There!" he proclaimed proudly. "Fit to greet a Weyrleader!"

He spun her on her heels and, with an affectionate pat on her butt, sent her on the way out of his quarters.

Over her shoulder, Fiona called back, "Thanks, F'dan!"

"Any time, Weyrwoman, any time," he told her feelingly.

She took the steps down to the Bowl two at a time. The midday heat forced her to slow down as she crossed the Bowl to the Kitchen Cavern; even so she arrived with her newly trimmed hair plastered to her face with sweat.

She was seen first by Terin, who was facing toward the entrance, talking to a tall man. M'tal? Fiona thought. If it was him, why wasn't he wearing his Weyrleader's jacket?

She was too far to hear Terin's words distinctly, but her gesture made it obvious that she had announced Fiona's arrival to the man.

The man who turned to face her was not the same M'tal she'd seen earlier that day. His face was more lined, his hair had more gray, his eyes looked—

"You're from the future, too!" Fiona exclaimed as she closed the distance between them.

"M'tal, Gaminth's rider of Benden, at your service," M'tal replied, bending low and reaching for Fiona's hand. Fiona raised it as her training compelled her and was pleased when the dragonrider gently kissed the back of it and released it to her, his eyes surveying her warmly.

"I can see your sister's face in you," he told her. "She was not much older than you the last time I saw her."

"And when was that, my lord?"

"M'tal," he corrected her gently, adding, "B'nik leads the Weyr now." He paused, then continued, "I last saw your sister more than ten Turns back when the black-and-yellow quarantine flag was first seen at Fort Hold." He smiled sadly. "I can still see her in my mind as she raced off to her Hold and father."

"I had less than two Turns at the time," Fiona said with a deep sigh.

"And yet, now, you seem to have grown rather quickly," M'tal said with a grin. "I'd heard you'd Impressed; I hadn't heard that K'lior thought to send you back in time here."

"Lord K'lior had not ordered it," Fiona replied. "But why are you here now?"

"I'm here through an oversight on my part," M'tal admitted frankly. "I must have got my coordinates mixed. I'd hoped to meet you when you were leaving Igen to return to our present."

"So we did return," Fiona murmured to herself. Before M'tal could comment further, she silenced him with a raised hand. "Please, say no more about it, I've learned that knowing too much of the future is a heavy burden."

M'tal nodded in agreement and frank approval. He started to say something else, then seemed to collapse on himself, reaching out hastily to prop himself upright.

Fiona and Terin reached out to guide him into a chair.

"You'd best not tarry too long, my lord," Fiona warned him. "Being back in time is hard on us riders."

"So I'm discovering," M'tal replied weakly. "Do the effects wear off?"

Fiona shook her head. "They haven't so far," she told him. "But some feel it more than others and some of us have felt it practically since Impression."

"Since Impression?" M'tal repeated, eyes narrowing suspiciously. "That doesn't seem right."

"It's like a constant noise in our heads, like chalk rubbed the wrong way on slate," Fiona said. She gestured toward Terin, only to discover that the young headwoman had gone over to the hearth, to prepare a quick pitcher of *klah*. "Those who have not Impressed, like Terin there, don't feel the effects."

"And how many weyrfolk came back in time with you?"

"Only Terin," Fiona admitted.

"So it might just be that she's immune to the effects," M'tal observed.

"Perhaps," Fiona agreed politely.

M'tal flashed a grin at her. "Clearly you don't think so." He waved a hand in a throwaway gesture, then continued, "I don't see many of your injured."

"We've been here long enough for most of them to recover," Fiona replied. "Only our most severely injured remain, and they'll return right—"

"After the wedding!" M'tal exclaimed, slapping his forehead with his hand. "Of course, I'd forgotten. You were the source of the glows!"

"Please, we haven't done that yet," Fiona told him urgently.

"But Zenor has asked Nuella, hasn't he?" M'tal asked. "I seem to recall that this was about the day he did—perhaps that's why I came back to this time."

"He asked her just this morning," Fiona admitted.

M'tal leaned forward, scrutinizing her face carefully, and then exclaimed, "You were the girl! You were the one who forced him to ask her! And gave me the gold for Kindan!" He blew out his breath in a long, surprised sigh, shaking his head. "I knew that I'd seen you before, when I'd seen you before. You reminded me so much of Koriana that I couldn't forget you." He paused and admitted impishly, "I'd even had some thought of introducing you to Kindan . . . but I wasn't sure if that wouldn't cause him more grief."

"You did?" Fiona asked excitedly. For a moment she allowed herself to be lost in the possibility: What would have happened? How would it have worked?

Terin dropped the tray of mugs and *klah* on the table, rattling Fiona back to reality.

"I'm glad you didn't," Fiona said as she placed a mug in front of the bronze rider, picked up the pitcher, and poured him a full helping of the warm *klah*. "I cannot stay in this time; I belong back at the Weyr."

"You say your injured have left already?" M'tal asked.

"Only those with the lighter injuries," Fiona told him. "They've gone ahead in time to meet us here in another two and a half Turns when the younger weyrlings"—she felt herself blush—"and my queen have matured."

"You brought the younger weyrlings back?" M'tal asked, his brows raised in surprise. "The ones from Melirth's last clutch?" When Fiona nodded, he asked, "How?"

"We're not sure," Fiona admitted. "There was a queen rider who guided us back, and then she and a group of riders brought back the most injured riders and dragons."

"Otherwise it would have been only the thirty lightly injured and the twelve older weyrlings," Terin interjected.

"And you don't know who this queen rider was?" M'tal asked.

Fiona shook her head, then bit her lip hesitantly. M'tal noticed and raised his brows again invitingly.

"T'mar and I wonder if it wasn't me from the future," Fiona admitted reluctantly. "From beyond *our* future."

"Well, you could have done it because you would have known that you could have done it," M'tal murmured thoughtfully, glancing over to Fiona for agreement.

"That was the thought," Fiona replied. "But . . . it didn't feel like me." She groped for words. "I didn't feel doubly strained, like I think I would if I were in the same time three times over."

"Hmm," M'tal murmured, then, once again, he made the throwaway gesture with his free hand. "I doubt we'll find an an-

swer in our time, either, but we're certain to find one *some*time."
He downed his *klah* and rose to his feet. "I think it would be best if
I left now. I know what I need to know."

"We can help you," Fiona said, nodding urgently to Terin who
was already on her feet on the other side of the bronze rider.

M'tal made to wave them off, but then, with a startled look, he
found himself reeling and gladly leaned on them for support.

"Maybe you *are* in this time thrice," Fiona told him.

"Perhaps," M'tal agreed feebly. "In which case, the sooner I
leave, the happier I'll be." He smiled. "Of course, I shall be sorry
to miss more of your company."

"Are you well enough to go *between*?" Terin asked as they
helped him up to his perch on Gaminth's neck.

"Yes, I think so," M'tal said, waving them back and adding
testily, "This blasted heat doesn't help."

He glanced thoughtfully at Fiona for a moment, as though
mulling over his words, then gestured to her sadly. "I should tell
you, Kindan is attached to Lorana."

"I'd heard," Fiona shouted back up to him. "Give him my regards."

"Certainly!"

Gaminth leapt into the air, slowly climbed up out of the Bowl,
passed the Star Stones, and winked *between*.

"So we know one thing, that we make it back safely," T'mar said
when Fiona recounted the events to him later that evening at dinner. A trading caravan with Azeez and Mother Karina had arrived
just in time to join them, so the Dining Cavern was more full and
lively than it had been for a while.

"Yes," Fiona agreed. "And we know that some people seem to
take timing it even worse than we do."

"Which begs the question—why?"

Fiona shrugged.

"It might be that some are just more susceptible," N'jian spoke
up from the far end of the table.

"Or it could be that some are traveling in time more than others," T'mar observed darkly.

"Does anyone have a good understanding of timing it?" Fiona wondered.

"No," N'jian replied before T'mar could answer. "All I know is that it's not encouraged, and I think with good reason."

"Shards, you'll have no arguments there!" Fiona exclaimed, glancing at J'keran, who was bravely stifling a yawn, and F'jian, who looked no better.

"Did Nuella set a date for the wedding?" Mother Karina asked as she approached the table with her latest dish. It had become the custom that whenever the traders arrived at the Weyr, they would share in the Weyr's chores. Terin was particularly grateful for the relief—Mother Karina usually forced the youngster to sit and watch when she was cooking.

"You can't learn everything on your feet," Mother Karina always said.

It was now Terin to whom she served the first portion, ostensibly in her role as headwoman but, Fiona guessed, more because the old trader had taken a motherly interest in the Weyr's youngest. Terin took the mothering with a mixture of annoyance and delight: delight at the attention; annoyance that someone would feel it required.

Her eyes widened as she sampled, chewed, and swallowed, she raised a hand to fan her mouth and reached for a mug of cool water with the other. "Whew!" she exclaimed. "Spicy!" After a moment, she amended with a look of surprise, "But not really hot."

Mother Karina beamed at her, passing the plate toward Fiona and T'mar, who reached for it simultaneously. Fiona reluctantly waved for him to take it first; in her unspoken tally of new dishes, it was the bronze rider's turn to have first taste. A Weywoman's duties included ensuring the fair treatment of everyone in the Weyr.

T'mar passed the plate to Fiona who took a small helping before passing it on.

"It smells marvelous," she declared.

"It is from a different cooking style than we normally use, but still one for a hot climate," Karina explained.

"Meat sliced thin, cooked quickly, onions, fresh vegetables . . . and something else," Fiona said as she carefully savored the tastes in her mouth.

"We trade it from Ista and sometimes from Nerat Tip," Karina said. "It is called coconut. There is a kind of milk inside, as well as a white flesh that can be flaked off."

"It gives the dish a slightly sweet flavor," Terin said, eyeing the distant plate hopefully.

"I'll get you more," Karina said, rising and heading back to the hearth.

" 'You need feeding,' " Terin quoted to Karina's fleeting back in a voice that carried only to Fiona's ears.

"Is that so bad?" Fiona asked. Terin narrowed her eyes, then grinned and shook her head.

"When *is* the wedding?" she asked, repeating Karina's unanswered question.

Fiona, mouth full, shook her head and shrugged.

"It would be good to find out," N'jian said seriously. "I would hate to miss it, but we are wasting valuable time and resources here now that we're all healed."

"When you leave, how many will be left?" Azeez asked rhetorically.

"T'mar, Terin, myself, the twelve older weyrlings and the thirty-two younger weyrlings," Fiona said, ticking off her fingers with each number.

"Forty-seven then," Azeez said, glancing up toward Mother Karina, who had returned and was determinedly refilling Terin's plate in spite of the other's murmured protests.

"And thirty weyrs free," Karina said, looking up from her serving.

"Winter's getting harsh," Azeez added.

"Would you two kindly stop dancing around and get to the point?" Fiona asked with an edge of amused exasperation in her voice. T'mar glanced at her and then nodded toward Azeez.

"We were wondering if we could trade our services for your empty weyrs," Azeez said in a rush, glancing from T'mar to Fiona.

"Trade?" Fiona repeated, turning her eyes toward Mother Karina. The older woman nodded, gesturing toward Terin and pulling up a seat to sit beside her. "This one, for sure, could use some help."

"I'm doing fine!" Terin protested loudly.

"You are," Fiona agreed diplomatically. "Except that you hardly sleep, and when you do you're tossing and turning and you're always to bed last and up first."

"I toss and turn?" Terin asked in surprise, a hand rising to her cheek in mortification.

"And talking," Fiona added. She grinned at her friend. "Do you think that *every* time I end up sleeping with Talenth it's because I want to?"

"I could move out—"

"No, you will not!" Fiona declared loudly. She turned to Karina. "I see no problem with this notion."

"Traders and weyrfolk," N'jian muttered, shaking his head. "It's not been done."

"I'll bet it has," T'mar said. "Remember that when our ancestors crossed here from the Southern Continent, everyone lived in the same place—" He nodded toward Fiona. "—Fort Hold. It wasn't until much later that Fort Weyr was established."

"So the traders and the dragonriders were certainly living together for part of the time after the Crossing," Azeez agreed.

"We have nothing to hide," Fiona said, glancing quellingly toward N'jian.

"Our ways are different, Weyrwoman," he responded unapologetically. By way of illustration, he jerked his head toward a group of blue and green riders who were laughing together over some shared joke.

"Trader ways are different, too," Fiona countered. She waved a placating hand toward the brown rider. "Oh, I don't say there won't be problems or the occasional difference, but I think it will be a great help to the Weyr."

Her emphasis on the last word was not lost on N'jian who considered her response for a moment before nodding reluctantly.

"We asked because we would like to help with the wedding," Mother Karina explained.

"Traders don't like settling in one place for too long," Azeez said.

"Not all traders mind a bit of a rest," Karina corrected him. She turned to Fiona. "It's customary for new mothers to rest in one place for three months—longer if possible."

"We'd be delighted to help," T'mar said with a nod toward Fiona.

"And the wedding?" Karina inquired.

"The older riders shouldn't tarry too long," N'jian reminded T'mar.

"We can't hurry their wedding," Fiona reminded him.

"With all respect, Weyrwoman," N'jian replied, his lips twitching upward even as he sketched a bow from his chair, "*you* can."

"And did," T'mar added.

Fiona threw up her hands in surrender. She turned to Mother Karina. "You've met Nuella, haven't you?"

Karina nodded. "We came from there."

"By dragonback," N'jian added. "They left their caravan and several traders behind."

"Setting up a new depot?" Fiona guessed.

"Did you get any ideas from Nuella or Silstra, then?" Terin asked, her fork hovering near her mouth.

"Eat, child!" Karina ordered. She waited until Terin had emptied her fork before continuing. "I spoke with Silstra—she is quite a trader—and she thinks that sometime before Turn's end would be best."

"Turn's end would be the latest we could keep the older riders here," T'mar said.

"That doesn't leave much time," Fiona said, startled.

"Indeed," Karina agreed. "Which is why I offered our services to Silstra." She allowed herself a small smile. "And as soon as we can get our mothers settled into the Weyr, we'll be able to set them to making suitable wedding clothes."

"That's right!" Fiona exclaimed in sudden memory. "Kindan said that traders were at Silstra's wedding!"

"Silstra thought it fitting," Karina allowed, looking pleased.

"So we've less than seventeen days," Terin declared before hastily swallowing her next mouthful.

"It would help to get an exact date," Fiona said thoughtfully.

Terin rose quickly and pressed her hand on Karina's shoulder before dashing to the hearth. Fiona didn't have time to wonder at the odd gesture, because Karina leaned in close at that moment to say conspiratorially, "And who would be best at getting that date?"

"I suppose it would be me," Fiona confessed with mixed emotions. She wasn't sure she could soon handle another day as exciting as this one had proved. T'mar glanced at her—or, rather, at a point over her shoulder—and grinned.

"What?" Fiona demanded, perplexed. Her confusion grew as everyone at the table started to rise and noises from behind indicated that all those in the Cavern were getting to their feet.

Terin approached with F'dan—they were bearing a large platter between them. On the platter was a large cake with icing, and too many candles to count quickly.

"Happy birthday, Fiona!" Terin cried as she put the cake in front of her.

"But—it's not my birthday!" Fiona exclaimed loudly, her voice not carrying over the roar of the riders cheering her on.

"Yes, it is," T'mar told her, grinning wildly. "You've been here one hundred and seventy-eight days now, and that, added to your time at Fort Weyr, is a whole Turn." He gestured toward the candles. "You've turned fourteen."

"Make a wish!" the crowd urged.

"Blow them out!"

Still confused and overwhelmed with surprise, Fiona gave a gracious sigh, drew a deep breath, and blew the candles out.

Afteward, as everyone finished congratulating her, she looked over to Terin and smirked widely.

"What?" the young headwoman asked nervously. "You aren't mad, are you?"

"Oh, no," Fiona exclaimed, her eyes dancing impishly. "I'm just recalling that you've twelve days until *your* Turning!"

*S*oon *enough,* Fiona reassured Talenth as she hovered over the Star Stones perched on Zirenth's back. You'll be flying soon enough.

I wish I could go with you, Talenth repeated morosely.

Well, how about the first place we fly to will be the wherhold?

I'd like that, Talenth agreed.

I have to be there, Fiona told her again. *Nuella has asked me to stand by her side.* She paused, adding worriedly, *You will be okay without me?*

I'm tired, Talenth replied sounding testy. *I'll sleep.*

Sleep and grow strong, Fiona told her encouragingly.

I wish I was bigger.

Soon enough, love, soon enough, Fiona assured her, sending a tender caress with her thoughts. *How are the children?*

The littlest ones are in your bed, I think they think I'm too big for them, Talenth told her, her spirits lifting. *But the older ones are warm and comfortable.*

Mother Karina had been speechless when Fiona had suggested that the trader children spend the night in her weyr, those wanting to sleeping with Talenth.

"I sleep with her all the time," Fiona assured her. "She's completely safe. And I'm sure she'd love the company."

"But trader children . . . sleeping with a queen!" Karina repeated, eyes wide in amazement.

"She likes the company and," Fiona added with a wry grin, "it makes her feel older to have youngsters to watch over."

Karina and the other traders had difficulty looking at the queen, who was much bigger now than any of their herdbeasts, and thinking of her as young. But as Fiona knew all too well, Talenth had only been out of the egg little more than ten months now.

"Anyway, she's going to have to learn," she said, hoping to clinch the argument; learning had a special place in Karina's thinking.

"Why, are you planning on having lots of children?" Karina asked, and her eyes twinkled at Fiona's sudden blush.

"That's for the future," Fiona told her, trying to will the heat out of her cheeks. "I was thinking that once we're back at the Weyr, she'll appreciate the company of the younger weyrfolk."

"And you'll have a steady supply of helping hands," Terin observed tartly.

"Are you complaining?" Fiona asked, brows raised. When Terin shook her head quickly, Fiona added, "Anyway, it's not so much for me as for her and the children." Her eyes glowed. "I remember sleeping with Forsk when I was a child . . . I never felt so loved or peaceful."

"You're an odd one," Karina said. "You seem happiest when in the center of a pile of warm bodies."

"It keeps the cold away," Fiona replied. More honestly, she added, "It feels like family would feel to me."

Karina eyed her speculatively. "And you didn't have that growing up the only child of the Lord Holder."

Fiona said nothing.

"Well, if it pleases you, Weyrwoman," Karina allowed at last, "I'll see if the children are up for it."

"Up for it!" Terin exclaimed in disbelief. "You'll be able to trade a whole sevenday's chores *and* their best behavior for the honor."

"And they'll think they got the better of the bargain," Karina had agreed with a grin.

So now, as Zirenth went *between* in the last of the twilight, saluted by the luckless rider perched on his watch dragon near the Star Stones, Fiona still felt anxious over leaving Talenth behind, but was comfortable in the knowledge that her queen was surrounded by awed, amazed, and—she was certain—soon to be loving companions.

The cold, silent nothingness of *between* was replaced in a sudden rush by the warm, noisy air over the wherhold as Zirenth spiraled quickly toward the landing place. Before them a specially erected trellis, lined with glows, stretched outward from the entrance of the wherhold to a raised platform at the end of the walk, where Zenor and Nuella would exchange their vows. Here and there, Fiona picked up the brighter glows of watch-wher eyes, brilliantly reflecting what little light there still was.

She deftly picked her way past the trellis and headed into the wherhold where, as she had half-expected, pandemonium reigned. The smells arising from the kitchen and the tenor of the overwhelming babble assured Fiona that whatever problems there were did not emanate from that location.

"I'm here!" Fiona called loudly, her voice echoing down the corridors. Hearing no response, she turned toward Nuellask's lair.

She had just about arrived when a pair of arms reached out and pulled her inside.

"Good!" Silstra cried as she slid Fiona out of sight.

"What is it?" Fiona asked as her eyes adjusted to the faintly lit gloom.

"Did you know that M'tal would be here?" Nuella demanded, her voice pitched much higher than normal.

"No," Fiona admitted. "But I should have guessed, come to think of it."

"*And* C'rion of Ista!" Silstra added, looking far more panicked than Fiona would ever have guessed possible.

"And Kindan," Nuella added, her tone somewhat mollified.

"Kindan?" Fiona squeaked. "What if he recognizes me?"

"We figured it out," Nuella said, gesturing for Silstra to explain.

"You'll be the crafter girl you pretended to be when M'tal met you," Silstra said tentatively.

"But M'tal said that he thought I looked so much like Koriana he thought about introducing me to Kindan!" Fiona wailed.

"What's the harm in that then?" Silstra asked, cocking her head assessingly. "You're nearly the same age—it might be good for him."

"I'm the same age *now*!" Fiona exclaimed. "When I go back to my time, he'll be ten Turns older. Besides—" She cut herself off hastily.

"You know something of the future involving him," Silstra guessed shrewdly.

"I want you beside me," Nuella said. "I don't think I can do this on my own."

"That's silly, and you know it," Fiona declared undiplomatically. She regretted the words as soon as they left her mouth and her expression showed it. "What I mean is that you're more than able, Nuella. I'm flattered that you want me by your side but—"

"If you can't be there..." Nuella began, her eyes wide with fear. "Then Silstra will have to manage everything; Sula's doing the cooking and there's no one else—"

"What about Terin?" Silstra asked, glancing toward Fiona in a way that made it clear she'd already tried this suggestion.

"Won't Kindan be with Zenor?" Fiona asked suddenly.

"Y-yes," Nuella allowed.

"Then there won't be a problem," Fiona told them. "He'll be so busy with his duties and I'll be so busy with mine that we won't have any time to exchange pleasantries."

"That's good for the ceremony, but what about after?" Silstra wondered.

"I'll get T'mar to take me dancing," Fiona said, almost glad to have a reason to spend time with the bronze rider.

"That's another thing—all those dragons!" Nuella sniffed. "How are we going to explain them?"

"We won't," Fiona said with a shrug. "Any colors the riders are wearing belong to Fort Weyr but I doubt they'll be seen in the dark."

"So how will you explain them?" Silstra asked.

"If pressed, we'll say that they're from Fort Weyr," Fiona said. "That's no lie."

"And if not pressed?"

"Well, it would seem to me that C'rion will think that M'tal arranged it and M'tal will think that C'rion arranged it," Fiona replied, her lips curving upward.

"That will only work if you keep the riders away from the Weyrleaders," Silstra said.

"Yes," Fiona agreed reluctantly. "I suppose you're right."

Talenth, Fiona called, *please tell T'mar that M'tal and C'rion are here.*

He says that he's already seen them, Talenth replied a moment later.

"T'mar knows," Fiona explained. She wiped her hands together briskly, as if wiping that problem off her hands. "Now, is there any other way I can help you?"

"Just hold my hand and don't let go," Nuella implored, reaching out a hand.

"Never," Fiona vowed, clasping it firmly.

"Well," Silstra said glancing around the room. "I think that everything is in order." She glanced toward Fiona. "I'll go tell Kindan to start the music." At the door, she turned back. "When you hear the music, start out."

"Oh, he's playing?" Fiona asked excitedly.

"He sang at Silstra's wedding," Nuella said. "And I met him, when I was hiding, pretending to be Dalor."

"Hmm, maybe that'll work for me, too," Fiona said.

"How do I look?" Nuella asked.

Fiona knew that for blind Nuella, the question was more than perfunctory. "How about we try an experiment?" she suggested as a bold thought came to her.

Talenth, could you relay an image to Nuellask? Fiona asked.

I can try, Talenth responded eagerly.

"Let me look at you," Fiona said, turning to eye Nuella carefully in the brighter light of the hallway.

Nuella was dressed in a fine white dress with delicate white slippers, her blond hair wrapped up around her head in a French braid bound with pretty blue ribbon.

Fiona concentrated on her and concentrated on sharing the image with Talenth.

Do you see it?

A woman in a dress, Talenth told her. *Is that Nuella?*

Yes, Fiona agreed. *And if you can give Nuellask the image and ask her to send it to Nuella—I know she's very young.*

She tries . . . now, Talenth replied. *This is fun, she likes it too!*

"Close your eyes, Nuella, reach out to your watch-wher," Fiona instructed. "What do you see?"

Nuella gasped in astonishment. "Is that me?"

"As best I can *see* you, as best Talenth can share the image, and as best Nuellask can send it to you," Fiona said.

Nuella grabbed Fiona's hand tightly in hers. "Oh, thank you!" Her free hand reached down to her dress. "Oh, it's as beautiful as I'd hoped!"

"Well, then," Fiona said, her lips curved up in a huge grin, "the music has started. Let's not keep your red-haired lad waiting."

Her face split in a huge beaming smile, Nuella walked with Fiona out into the crisp night air.

The music swelled and suddenly was the only sound as the gathered crowd grew hushed.

Ahead, at the raised platform, Fiona could make out the figures of Zenor and Kindan, standing side by side. Zenor had never looked more handsome. Kindan stood beside him, resplendent in harper's blue, his gaze resting proudly on Nuella.

"*Definitely* you should marry him," Fiona whispered as they reached the first of the stairs. She added, warningly, "Step."

Nuella took the step easily, and Fiona guided her beside Zenor, took the hand with which she'd been guiding her, and placed it into Zenor's outstretched hand.

As Fiona moved to the side, Kindan moved around in front of the pair. From the shadows, C'rion and M'tal appeared on either side. Terin appeared with a small plush pillow bearing two gold rings, each crafted of three bands twined together.

"We are here for a joyous occasion," Kindan told the gathered crowd. "It is all the more joyous for me because we celebrate the joining of two of my dearest friends in a new life at a new and prosperous hold, the craft of their hands, and the bonding of their hearts."

Kindan paused and looked out down the trellis pathway. "Terregar? Silstra?"

Fiona looked in surprise as Terregar and Silstra, arm in arm, walked quickly up the path to stand before Nuella and Zenor.

As the hush of the crowd dissolved into excited whispers, Kindan spoke up loudly.

"Tonight also," he said, "it is my pleasure to announce another union." At his gesture, Terregar handed a rolled parchment up to Zenor; a short moment later, Silstra handed a similar parchment to Nuella.

"Actually, two unions," Kindan corrected himself, his eyes dancing mischievously. He gestured to the rolls Zenor and Nuella clutched in bewilderment. "By order of Mastersmith Veclan, I am pleased to announce that the Plains Wherhold has been designated a smithcraft, the Goldhall of Plains Hold."

Zenor's eyes went wide with amazement while the crowd gapsed in surprise.

"And by order of Lord Holder Ospenar and holder Kedarill, I am also pleased to announce the establishment of the Wherhold of Plains Hold."

Kindan went down on one knee before them, intoning quickly, "My lord, my lady, it gives me joy to be the first to greet you!"

Zenor shook his head, shocked, while Nuella's eyes streamed with tears of joy.

Their shock and joy redoubled as Kindan rose and C'rion and M'tal bowed to them. "To the Wherhold!"

Their cry was echoed loudly by the collected holders, their elation echoing all around them.

Kindan had to wait a long time for the crowd to be quiet once more.

"And now, my lord," he said nodding toward Zenor, "my lady," he bowed toward Nuella, "I understand that you have come to express vows before this company." He turned to Nuella. "Is this so?"

"It is," Nuella declared loudly.

"And you, my lord?" Kindan asked of Zenor.

It took Zenor two tries before he could sound out, "It is."

Kindan smiled at him and Fiona was pleased to see M'tal rest a comforting hand on Zenor's shoulder as Kindan continued through the vows. At last the rings were exchanged, and the newlyweds kissed.

Kindan stepped back then, shouting to the crowd, "Zenor and Nuella!"

Now, Fiona called to Zirenth.

She was lucky to be facing away from the wherhold so that she saw the long trails of glows in the sky as they approached. As T'mar's Zirenth, bearing a basket full of green glows, and N'jian's Graneth bearing a basket full of yellow glows, flew into view of the rest of the crowd, Kindan called out, "What? Watch-whers?"

"They fly well," M'tal noted approvingly. "I'd always known that watch-whers were up to such things."

"Dansk flew with just one basket," Kindan said as he looked to the sky in awe. "I'd never thought of seeing so many watch-whers in flight . . ."

The massed wing of forty-two dragons, all the older werylings and recovered riders, flew overhead in a graceful display of color, then reformed and swung back around, performing intricate maneuvers, making tight circles and trails in the sky to the delight of all the observers, at a height such that only the glows themselves, and not the dragons carrying them, were visible.

"That's some flying," C'rion exclaimed, glancing toward M'tal.

"I didn't know watch-whers could do so well," M'tal remarked.

"They are very capable," Kindan declared. "Although . . ." He shaded his eyes, squinting into the dark sky above.

Quick! a voice implored Fiona.

She didn't need any urging and, feigning a loss of balance, tumbled into Kindan.

"I'm sorry," she exclaimed, "I got dizzy."

"Not a problem," Kindan said, setting her back on her foot and resuming his scan.

Talenth! Tell T'mar it's time to finish! Fiona thought, glancing toward M'tal, who had stopped staring at the sky long enough to look her way.

"Oh, it's you again," he said, smiling at her. He pointed up to the sky. "Some sight, isn't it?"

"Indeed, my lord," Fiona said. "I hear that Arella and Jaythen practiced forever on it."

She wasn't lying, as presently two lights separated from the others descending in a steep dive, resolving themselves into the shapes of a green and bronze watch-wher, each triumphantly carrying large glows in their foreclaws and—to Fiona's surprise—bearing riders on their backs.

With their descent, the final performance was over and the dragons of Igen disappeared *between*.

The party swelled as the Igen dragonriders, garbed as plain holders, arrived from their landing behind the wherhold. Under the pretext of helping the newlyweds settle in, Fiona escorted Zenor and Nuella, glad to get out of the sight of Kindan and the Weyrleaders.

"I'm so glad we primed Arella and Jaythen," Fiona sighed as she helped Nuella out of her gown and into more comfortable party clothes.

"They were thrilled to fly with dragonriders," Nuella replied. "I just wish that Nuellask were older."

"On your wedding night?" Fiona exclaimed in exasperation.

"Well," Nuella considered, "maybe not." She paused for a moment. "But I'm getting one of those saddles when she's older."

"I don't doubt it," Fiona said in agreement. "Come on," she said, hastily changing the subject before Nuella might question her tone, "let's get you out there for the dance!"

Nuella followed her lead gladly until Fiona could return her to Zenor and the two of them led off in the first dance in the square laid out beside the garlanded trellis.

"Who's good on the drums?" Kindan called out, searching the crowd. He spotted Finlar and gestured to him. "You look like a strong likely lad—are you up for it?"

"I can try," Finlar replied, breathless with excitement.

From among the other children, Kindan quickly gathered a makeshift orchestra and set to singing and calling tunes until relieved by Silstra and Terregar, who proved to have very good voices.

Fiona found T'mar and danced with him once before finding herself tapped by N'jian, then F'dan, J'keran, and what seemed the entire Weyr one after the other until she honestly declared herself exhausted.

In a lull between sets, she pored over the food laid on the groaning tables, piled her plate high, found herself some sweetjuice and sat in a quiet corner, glad to be unnoticed for the moment.

When someone suddenly spoke beside her, she jumped.

"M'tal tells me that you know Arella and Jaythen." It was Kindan.

"I do," Fiona admitted.

"And Nuella, you were her honor maid."

"Yes," Fiona said, feeling very uncomfortable. She glanced around anxiously for T'mar or any of the dragonriders but could not make out any of them in the dim light and motion of the dancing throng.

Kindan peered closer at her. "You remind me of someone," he said. "Are you related to Nuella?"

Panic enveloped her. In desperation, she lifted her cup to her lips and let it slip, splashing juice down her front. "Oh, no!"

Kindan looked around futilely for something to help dry her off.

"I must go or this will stain," she said, jumping up and scurrying away as fast as she could.

"Will I see you again?"

"Certainly," Fiona called over her shoulder. She found T'mar, who took one look at her frightened expression and stained dress and picked her up in his arms.

"It's Kindan," she breathed into his ear. "I need to get away, back to the Weyr."

"Very well, it's getting late anyway," T'mar said. With a grin, he added, "And I think we've done well by the Weyr this evening."

"Indeed!"

When T'mar dropped her off, Fiona slipped quietly into her weyr. Eyes accustomed by the starry night to the light of the dim glows, she found her nightgown, quickly changed, and, seeing her bed full and squirming with the youngest of the trader children, snuggled herself into the crowd of older children nestled up against Talenth's warm hide.

I'm back, Fiona said drowsily to her beautiful queen. Talenth heaved a slight sigh and drifted into a deeper sleep.

No one was quite prepared for the next morning. The trader children were desperate to stay with Talenth the whole day, while the adults—trader and rider alike—were all weary from the excitement and drink of the evening before.

Neither T'mar nor Fiona pushed the others hard that day but as the sun sank once more on the horizon and they gathered for the evening meal, T'mar told the diners in the Kitchen Cavern, "I think it is time for the older riders to depart."

"They're all recovered," Fiona agreed.

"We were only waiting for the wedding," N'jian remarked. He cocked a glance toward T'mar. "Same plan as with K'rall? Meet you here at the third Turn?"

"Yes," T'mar said. "Use the same coordinates."

"The stars will guide us," F'dan murmured in his seat next to Fiona.

The next day was marked by a flurry of activity as the older riders collected their gear, sorted out their quarters, and prepared for the jump *between* times to the Igen Weyr nearly two and a half Turns in the future.

"You'll have sixteen Turns when we meet again," F'dan said as Fiona hugged him goodbye. "You'll be full grown, a lady in your own right."

Fiona laughed at the description.

"I doubt I'll have changed all that much," she said.

"You'll be a dragonrider when next we meet," N'jian told her, glancing down from his mount on Graneth.

"And your queen won't be long from rising," F'dan reminded her. He pushed her away from him to look her in the eyes. "Be careful, Weyrwoman."

"I will," Fiona promised.

The dragonriders mounted, the dragons rose in the starry night, circled up to the Star Stones, and blinked *between*.

EIGHTEEN

Weyrling and rider,
First jump, no higher.
Glide to ground,
Then go round.

Igen Weyr, Early Morning, AL 499.13.11

Fiona started pestering T'mar on her fifteenth birthday. She tried to be subtle.

"I've fifteen Turns now," she told him. "Isn't that a great age for someone on their first flight?"

"It is," T'mar agreed, grinning. "Let me see how Talenth seems in the morning."

In the morning he said to her, "No, she's strong, but I think you should wait."

And so she waited. And waited. She let another fortnight go by before she broached the subject once more. "Isn't Ladirth well-formed?" she asked as the weyrlings gathered for their late-night gliding.

"Yes, he is," T'mar agreed with a long-suffering sigh. "And he'll be a fine flyer too, when the time is right."

The next month passed with Fiona valiantly refraining from a single comment, although she caught T'mar eyeing her speculatively several times. She spent more time with Terin, with the younger weyrlings, with the traders, while T'mar was busy training the older weyrlings in formation flying, flaming, and recognition points.

"Tomorrow have the weyrlings set the riding straps on their dragons," T'mar told Fiona the next day when the weyrlings had finished their early morning glide.

Fiona's eyes lit, but that was nothing compared to the shouts of joy when she told F'jian and the rest of the weyrlings.

"Too much exuberance," T'mar muttered disapprovingly when he heard the outburst. Fiona stuck her tongue out at him, which was very un-Weyrwoman-like but satisfying all the same.

The next morning, the weyrlings were lined up extra early, eyes gleaming, but T'mar disappointed them, merely inspecting their riding straps and murmuring quiet corrections to each individual rider. Fiona wasn't spared the ordeal.

"Have them try again tomorrow," T'mar said after ordering the harnesses removed before the weyrlings had their practice glides.

The next day things were much better, but T'mar ordered them once again to remove their harnesses before the dragns flew.

"If one harness is wrong, they are all wrong," T'mar said when the chorus of groans arose from the collected weyrlings.

"Whose harness was wrong?" Fiona asked.

"You don't know?" T'mar replied, shaking his head sadly.

Fiona's face burned with shame.

"Tomorrow, we get here before T'mar and we check everyone's harness," F'jian said.

The next day, to everyone's intense relief, T'mar allowed the dragons to fly with their harnesses on.

"We'll keep that up for the next sevenday," he said, sounding pleased.

"I'll bet they never did this to the other weyrlings," Fiona muttered rebelliously to F'jian.

"Maybe not," F'jian said with a shrug. "But if it makes us safer riders, what's the harm in it?"

Fiona couldn't say anything in response, suddenly recalling her angry exchange with T'mar Turns back and ahead at Fort Weyr.

At the end of that sevenday, T'mar made the weyrlings fill sandbags to their weight. He inspected them on a balance beam and, for the next several days, until all the weights balanced for all the weyrlings, made the weyrlings empty their sandbags individually before allowing their dragons to fly unharnessed.

The older weyrlings, meanwhile, found the whole exercise hilarious and were now lined up every morning, jeering the weyrlings and cheering on the wingleader.

"We'll get up *before* everyone," Fiona swore one morning. Her words were met with a growl of approval from the rest of the weyrlings.

The next morning, every weyrling was checked twice, once by his partner and once by Fiona, who was herself checked three times—first in secret with F'jian alone, and twice more in public by F'jian and J'nos.

"We need to set the example," she had explained.

The effort proved out—for the first time the dragons were allowed to walk around the Bowl with the sandbags attached to their harnesses before T'mar—to the groans of all the younger weyrlings and the guffaws of all the older weyrlings—ordered the sandbags removed again.

This practice lasted another sevenday and became so routine that all the younger weyrlings exclaimed in delight when T'mar refrained from ordering the sandbags to be removed.

F'jian smiled excitedly at Fiona as his Ladirth climbed the queen's ledge in preparation for his first full-weight glide, but Fiona was troubled.

"I don't think this is right," she said to F'jian's surprise. "Don't you think T'mar would insist on them flying first with a lighter load to strengthen their muscles?"

"But they've been gliding for Turns!" F'jian protested. Fiona glanced toward T'mar and noted how the bronze rider stood, impassively looking their way.

"T'mar," she called. "Shouldn't we start with less weight?"

T'mar's face slowly creased with a smile and he nodded.

"It was another test!" F'jian groaned beside her as he rushed to remove half the sandbags from Ladirth's load.

Two full sevendays passed before the dragons were permitted to glide with their riders' full weight in sand.

And then—

"No sandbags tomorrow," T'mar said as the last dragon glided back down to the ground, landing lightly, his eyes whirling in shades of green with pleasure.

"No sandbags," Fiona repeated, having learned always to repeat the wingleader's orders for confirmation.

The rest of the day crawled by, broken only by the excited chatter of the younger weyrlings.

"You first," T'mar said to Fiona as the weyrlings formed up the next morning. "Climb up on Talenth—mind your head!—she's got the largest wingspan, and even though you're nearly the lightest rider, if she can manage without strain, so can the others."

For all her anticipation, for all that dragonriders had been flying dragons for hundreds of Turns, for all the experience Fiona had had flying on the backs of others' dragons, she still couldn't help feeling nervous and excited as she climbed up on Talenth's back.

Ready? Talenth asked excitedly.

Wait a moment, Fiona said, turning to look down at T'mar—he looked smaller from this height—asking, "Can you check my straps, wingleader?"

T'mar smiled as she passed another one of his silent tests and walked around Talenth's neck, inspecting the straps from both sides and tugging on them.

"They look in order," he said. He leaned closer and said in a voice pitched for only her ears, "Are you ready?"

Fiona's heart leapt into her throat and for a moment she felt light-headed. This was it! Then she nodded. "Ready."

"Just a regular glide, nothing more," T'mar said to her. "Talenth can't get much speed with you on her back, so she'll just have to glide off the ledge."

"I know."

T'mar nodded and waved for her to proceed. Fiona found herself hesitating, not frightened really, but wanting to savor the moment. She would never have a first flight again.

"Go, Weyrwoman, fly!" the other weyrlings urged.

Okay, Talenth, just take a nice drop off the ledge, she said.

Talenth rumbled a sigh and then trotted as quickly as she could to the ledge and went over. She spread her wings and glided no more than ten meters before landing daintily.

"Next!" T'mar barked, not even waiting for Fiona to move off.

Go to the back of the line, Fiona told Talenth, hiding a grin.

We're going to go again? the gold dragon asked excitedly.

If we can.

They could and did.

"Three times," T'mar said when Fiona landed for the second time, unable to keep a huge smug grin off her face. "Always do things three times."

And so they did.

We flew! Talenth cried excitedly as they watched the last of the weyrlings complete their third glide.

We glided, Fiona corrected her, leaning forward to pat her neck affectionately. *Flying will come later.*

Indeed, it took another two months before T'mar declared that he had a special announcement to make after dinner.

"Tomorrow we'll begin weyrling training," he told the assembled riders as they finished their dessert.

Fiona, F'jian, J'nos and all the younger weyrlings cheered but their voices were drowned out by those of the older weyrlings and dragonriders.

"You worked hard for it," J'keran told Fiona. "You deserve it." He motioned for her to lean toward him and added quietly, "I think T'mar was harder on you lot because of your gold."

"I had guessed as much," Fiona replied, adding, "It might also be because he wants to be sure that these weyrlings are better prepared to fight when they return."

"If that's the case, then when they're ready to learn flaming and fighting, T'mar will be working both sets of weyrlings extra hard," J'keran said, a pained look on his face.

"Better learn than burn," Fiona replied, quoting the old training motto.

"You say that before your muscles are burning from the workout," J'keran warned her. "When you start catching sacks of firestone in midair and flying six-hour Falls, you'll find you have muscles that you never knew you had—and all of them sore." He frowned for a moment, then brightened. "Of course, T'mar probably won't force *you* to train like the weyrlings."

"Queens fly Thread," Fiona returned, feeling her cheeks heating.

"Only if there are enough for a queen's wing," J'keran responded as he leaned back and spooned up his last bite of dessert.

Fiona turned to T'mar. "I want to train with the weyrlings."

"Of course," T'mar replied as if the matter were already settled.

"Fighting and flaming," she said.

T'mar's eyes narrowed. "If we can find a flamethrower, certainly."

"It'll be Turns before it's an issue," J'keran remarked as he swallowed his last bite.

"Good, then I'll have Turns to track down a flamethrower," Fiona declared.

Fiona tackled the issue of finding a flamethrower the very next day, taking time with Terin to thoroughly examine the storerooms without result.

"They probably took them to Telgar," Terin said.

"Is there anywhere else they might be?" Fiona wondered aloud. She couldn't imagine why a Weyr without queens would be worried about taking flamethrowers with them.

"The Hatching Grounds?" Terin ventured. "That's the only place we haven't been that might have the room."

"What about the queen's weyrs?" Fiona asked. "We've only thoroughly looked through three: there are two more."

Terin shook her head. "Only one—I assigned the other to F'jian yesterday."

"But they'd still be cleaning it out, wouldn't they?"

Terin nodded. "I'll have them keep a lookout for anything that might be a flamethrower."

"I'll talk with Azeez when he comes in."

The deal with the traders had worked out brilliantly in the Turn and a half that the Fort riders had been back in time. While much of the trade occurred outside the Weyr at depots established much as T'mar had suggested in areas safe from sandstorms and easily serviced by caravans, there was still a lot of storage in use at the Weyr as dragonborne goods were moved from one outlying depot to another. Indeed it was rare to see an actual caravan at the Weyr these days. Instead, traders came in on dragonback and left the same way. By mutual agreement, only the original traders were allowed to stay at the Weyr, so as to keep the secret among a select group.

"A flamethrower?" Azeez repeated when Fiona brought it up over dinner. He frowned thoughtfully. "Are they the same as are used in the holds?"

Fiona glanced questioningly toward T'mar. "Probably," the wingleader said.

"You don't want a flamethrower," Azeez told Fiona, shuddering.

"Of course I do," Fiona replied hotly. "They're used in the queen's wing."

"All the flamethrowers I know use the old firestone," Azeez said with a grimace. "They're prone to explode."

"They won't work with proper firestone?" T'mar asked, curious.

"No, they rely on mixing stone and water to produce flame," Azeez said.

For countless Turns firestone—now called old firestone or sometimes flamestone—had been reluctantly chewed by dragons until the last old firestone mine had exploded. The search for a new vein of the ore had led C'tov, aided by Kindan, to discover— or rediscover—the original firestone that had long ago been chewed by fire-lizards.

"Flamestone's very dear," Azeez said. "It'll be hard to get and transport here, particularly without someone noticing."

"I don't want it here," T'mar said. "There have been too many accidents with that stuff, and the weyrlings could get careless, never having dealt with it before."

He caught Fiona's mulish look, so he added, "The burns from that stone are horrific."

Fiona grimaced. "There must be some way."

"It'd be better to find a different sort of flamethrower," Azeez remarked.

"Who could—" T'mar began.

"Stirger!" Fiona cut in excitedly. "It'd be the sort of challenge that would warm his ratty heart."

"You're not seriously suggesting that we ask the smith—" T'mar began only to be cut off once more by Fiona.

"If it were done right, it could be sold to the holders, too," she said, turning to glance at Azeez. The trader took on a calculating look and then grinned devilishly back at Fiona.

"Yes, it could be quite profitable," he replied. "I believe that D'gan is currently operating the only remaining old firestone mine."

T'mar snorted derisively. "He would be!"

"Probably forced some Shunned to do it for him," Fiona agreed acerbically. "Getting a better flamethrower would free them, wouldn't it?" She glanced to T'mar for confirmation.

The bronze rider made no response, his lips pursed thoughtfully.

"Well?" she prompted.

"I was thinking," T'mar said, rousing himself. The others looked at his grim expression. Fiona motioned impatiently for him to continue. "I don't recall any word of a new flamethrower being mentioned in our time."

Fiona's lips fell into a frown of her own. "Father would have mentioned it."

"So this invention will have to wait until your return," Azeez said hopefully. "It does not mean that Stirger could not develop it for you now."

"He'd have to agree to keep it a secret," Fiona said sourly.

"Is there anyone else who could invent such a thing, then?" Azeez asked. "Someone you could trust more to keep such a secret?"

T'mar cocked his head thoughtfully for a long moment. "I can't think of anyone."

"I can," Fiona said excitedly. "Terregar and Zenor both."

"If you could pry them away from their mining and smithing," T'mar retorted.

"We'll just have to be very persuasive," she said.

The two men glanced at each other ruefully and chuckled.

"What?" Fiona demanded, glaring at them.

"I rather suspect it'll be you that's persuasive," T'mar said, his lips curved upward in a smile.

"Weyrwoman," Azeez said by way of agreement.

Fiona found in the next two months that she didn't have the time to pursue anything other than her duties—and her training. The first drills were easy enough, with the weyrlings walking around the Bowl and repeating their twice daily gliding lessons, steadily building up the weights carried by the young dragons. They were helped happily by the young traders who wintered with them and were thrilled to be counted as "dragon baggage," as J'gerd had humorously labeled them, or "dragon riders" as they gladly labeled themselves.

After two sevendays T'mar changed the drill dramatically.

"Today we will see if you can fly," he told the collected weyrlings that morning at breakfast. The older weyrlings followed this announcement enthusiastically, remembering their first flight more than two Turns back.

Breakfast and chores were finished at breakneck speed, and Fiona, F'jian, and J'nos had the weyrlings assembled in proper formation well before T'mar strode out into the Weyr Bowl, trailed by the older weyrlings.

"Who wants to be first?" T'mar shouted to the collected group. Every hand shot up.

"It should be the Weyrwoman," F'jian said, lowering his hand reluctantly. Fiona was startled to see all the other weyrlings lower their hands, murmuring, "Yes, Fiona! Let her go first."

T'mar hid a grin, while behind him, the older weyrlings voiced their agreement.

Fiona looked down from her perch on Talenth and saw Terin standing, silhouetted by the light of the Kitchen Cavern, hunched over, her face unreadable in the distance.

"I'll do it if Terin rides with me," Fiona called back. T'mar's brows furrowed and all the weyrlings murmured in shock. "It's only fair, after all she's done!"

As T'mar opened his mouth, Fiona added, "She doesn't weigh much; I'm sure that Talenth can carry her, too!"

T'mar turned to Terin. "Terin, come here!"

Slowly at first, then faster, the youngest headwoman trotted over to the bronze rider. T'mar gave her a gentle look and then motioned for her to turn around. Grabbing her under the elbows, he lifted her experimentally then put her back down, his eyes going to Talenth.

"Weyrwoman, how much do you weigh?" he asked.

"Seven stone," Fiona called back. "And Terin's not more than five. Talenth has already handled twelve stone."

"Very well," T'mar said, swatting Terin lightly on the butt, sending her on her way.

Terin's delighted cry echoed around the Weyr.

"But only for the first flight," T'mar called as Fiona reached down and helped her friend clamber up. "You don't want to over-fly her."

"No, of course not," Terin agreed, her eyes gleaming as Fiona helped her around in front of her and tied the straps around her.

T'mar walked over and examined the fit of the straps from where he stood. Satisfied, he stood back and called up to Fiona, "Just up to the level of the Bowl, then glide back down."

"Very well," Fiona replied. Then her face split into a huge grin as she said, *Talenth, let's fly!*

Talenth took two steps and then launched herself skyward, her wings beating gently in the heavy morning air. All too quickly she was at the level of the Bowl.

"All right, back down," Fiona called, adding, when it seemed like Talenth was too enraptured to hear her words, *Talenth!*

The queen let out a roar of pure joy and dipped a wing, sending them into a tight spiral, to level up again and land, deftly, right where she'd started.

"A gentle glide was what I believe I requested," T'mar re-marked drily as Talenth folded her wings contentedly back against her sides.

Fiona gave him an apologetic shrug and set to getting Terin back down to the ground.

"Again?" she asked, her eyes gleaming as Terin raced over to the bronze rider.

"This time glide back down, gently," T'mar said. "Remember, you are the rider."

Fiona felt herself redden, but she nodded in meek acceptance.

This time no tricks! Fiona told Talenth before giving her the sig-nal to fly. In no time at all, they were at the level of the top of the

Bowl again and it was time to descend. Talenth raised her wings to cup more air and climb higher but Fiona told her, *If you don't behave, we won't get to fly more.*

All right, Talenth agreed reluctantly.

Fly too much too soon and you'll be sore for months, Fiona explained.

I feel fine, Talenth complained as she glided in to another perfect landing.

"One more time, then it will be someone else's turn," T'mar said.

"Could we go higher?" Fiona asked hopefully.

T'mar shook his head. "Slow and steady is the way that works best."

I tried, Fiona reminded Talenth as they found themselves once again in no time at all level with the top of the Weyr Bowl and descending in a gentle glide.

It was fun, Talenth said, landing in the exact same spot and folding her wings about herself complacently. *I could do that all day.*

It's harder when the sun's out and the air's hot, Fiona reminded her.

I'm sure I could manage, Talenth declared.

I'm sure you could, Fiona agreed indulgently, *but what about the blues and greens? They'd want to follow your lead and they'd get hurt.*

I hadn't thought about that, Talenth replied, looking toward the smaller dragons eagerly awaiting their turn to fly. *I suppose I should set the example and be careful.*

You are their queen, Fiona said in agreement. She remained perched on Talenth as all the remaining weyrlings made their first flights, glad of the higher vantage point and happy to be able to share the moments directly with Talenth, extolling the skills of each new dragon and rider, leaning forward to lay her cheek on Talenth's soft hide, and enjoying in every way she could her time with her mate.

From their weyrs, Zirenth and the older dragons watched and bugled their approval of each new flight. When everyone was done, T'mar had the older dragons assemble into a wing in preparation for the day's work.

Fiona was surprised to find herself looking down over Zirenth as the great bronze dragon approached.

You're bigger than Zirenth! she told Talenth excitedly.

Well, of course, Talenth responded calmly. *I'm the queen.*

Fiona laughed and slapped Talenth affectionately on the neck before climbing down and guiding Talenth back to her weyr, where she quickly removed the riding straps and checked Talenth's skin for any signs of flakiness. She didn't find any, but took the time regardless to oil Talenth's chest and belly to a fine sheen, reveling in the scent and sight of her beautiful queen's hide.

That evening Terin and Mother Karina outdid themselves in a special feast for the new dragonriders. Just before the end of the day, T'mar ordered all the new riders to gather at the edge of the shallow lake at the eastern end of the Weyr.

"There is one final tradition for new riders that must be observed," he intoned solemnly. He arranged the thirty-three riders in three tightly spaced ranks, with Fiona in the middle of the first rank.

"Close your eyes," he ordered. "Keep them closed until I say you may open them."

There was a rustle and breeze from dragon wings above them and then suddenly—

"Shards!" "Oh, that's cold!" "Eeek!"

Before Fiona could twitch a muscle, she was drenched, head to toe in something that was very cold, very wet, and very, very smelly.

"Eugh!"

"You may open your eyes, dragonriders," T'mar intoned solemnly. When Fiona opened her eyes, she found that the weyrlings were surrounded by the older riders, who were all laughing hysterically.

"Well, what are you waiting for?" T'mar barked to the drenched dragonriders. "Into the water with you!"

Fiona needed no urging and found herself rushing past the other still-befuddled weyrlings to dive into the shallow lake and wash off the worst of the stench that engulfed her.

"When you're quite done," T'mar drawled, enjoying himself as much as the older weyrlings, "you may disperse to your quarters." He paused. "You will have much work to do tomorrow."

Over the next few sevendays, the weyrlings were flying for over an hour at a stretch. They were drilled on imaging—producing accurate images to share with their dragons. They learned about air currents and how to ride them up or down; they learned about steep and shallow turns, about dives, about weather—and they were drilled intensely on everything, quizzed anytime day or night. The older weyrlings took particular delight in attempting to catch out Fiona, F'jian, or J'nos.

A fortnight after they had started flying in earnest, T'mar had them flying to the valleys where the Weyr kept its herdbeasts, to the riverside where they gathered rushes, and back to the Weyr, shepherded by the older riders until they were able to fly in trios by themselves, watched by the strategically placed older riders.

Once T'mar pronounced himself satisfied with their efforts in this new routine, he made it a part of their regular drill, stretching their flying time until they were able to fly six hours nonstop.

"Now tomorrow," T'mar told Fiona over dinner one night, "we'll do one straight, long flight—where should we go, Weyrwoman?"

"The wherhold," Fiona replied instantly. "I'd like to introduce Talenth to Nuellask."

"I'd guessed as much," T'mar gestured for J'keran to join them. "We'll be flying to the wherhold tomorrow," he told the other bronze rider.

"Are we bringing anything with us?" J'keran wondered.

"Check with Azeez and Terin," T'mar said. "No more than six dragonloads. If any of the younger dragons get too tired, we can have the older ones help."

"They can just land, can't they?" Fiona asked in surprise.

"Not on the water."

Fiona acknowledged this with a wry grin and a shake of her head.

"The Weyrwoman will ride in the middle of the formation," T'mar explained to the riders in the dark of morning as they gathered after a hasty breakfast. "F'jian, your wing will take the lead; J'keran, yours will follow the Weyrwoman."

F'jian gulped at the prospect of leading all of the Igen dragons himself. T'mar noticed and clapped him on the shoulder, saying, "Don't worry, if you get off course, I'll be right there to correct you!"

If anything, F'jian looked more worried.

"You'll be using the stars and the sun," Fiona reassured F'jian when she managed a quiet word alone with him as they prepared their riding straps for the long flight. F'jian nodded, his expression still bleak. In exasperation, she added, "And you know what to do if all else fails, right?"

"No."

"Ask," Fiona told him, shaking her head. "I don't doubt your weyrmates will be telling you long before you get worried."

"Mount up!" T'mar called.

In moments the massed wings were aloft. They circled the hapless D'lanor and Canoth, who were left behind on watch, before F'jian's bronze Ladirth bugled loudly and set off on the long flight toward the wherhold.

Talenth flew well and Fiona allowed herself to loosen up, twisting on her perch to peer at the dragons behind her, then turning back again to scan those in front. The younger weyrlings kept a good formation, she noted with pride.

They cleared the saddle between the Igen Mountains and flew toward the Igen river. At first, Fiona couldn't make it out and then, slowly, where she expected it, she discerned a ribbon of blue water tinged with the gold of the rising sun.

The sun erupted over the horizon and the view changed from a vision of grays and blues to a world of colors: gold, sand, blue, green, brown, and, in the far distance, a hint of snow on the northernmost mountains. Fiona reveled in the sight, turning her gaze from one vision to another.

Before them the vista stretched endlessly and seemed only to crawl toward them, like a trundlebug on a hot day.

It seemed to take forever to get anywhere.

Fiona realized worriedly that she needed to use the necessary and wondered how long she could hold out. She started scanning furiously for Plains Hold and bit back a curse when she found it—so far ahead of them.

Minutes crept by slowly while the pressure in her bladder continued to build and she swore at herself for not taking the time to make a final visit before mounting her dragon. If only she hadn't been so worried about F'jian!

Finally the flight started to descend, slowly, leisurely. And then—by the First Egg!—she spotted the wherhold. She almost cried out in relief and desperately willed the flight to drop faster, to reach the ground sooner so she could slink off to the necessary.

It was not to be: T'mar indicated that they were to overfly the wherhold in a large circle to announce their presence.

Why don't we just have one of the dragons talk to Nuellask? Or Arelsk? Fiona demanded tartly.

Manners, was the response relayed from T'mar through Talenth.

Fiona gritted her teeth, determined not to reveal her plight even as she felt the beat of Zirenth's wings above her and saw the bronze dragon descend into the formation—which widened to allow him—beside her. When he signaled for the rest of the flight to descend while signaling for her to remain aloft with him, she could no longer hide her urgency.

"Not fair!" she shouted.

T'mar indicated that they should land by the watermill and Fiona consented with glee: There was a restroom there, too, and it would not be crowded with desperate dragonriders all waiting their turn.

She had dismounted and was racing for the stone building before T'mar could say a word.

"So, how do you like flying with a full bladder?" he asked when she rejoined him at last.

"How did you know?"

"I didn't," T'mar confessed, grinning broadly, "until now."

"Oh!" Fiona growled, too rushed to say anything more. "So why did we land here?"

"Why *did* we land here, Weyrwoman?" T'mar repeated challengingly.

Fiona swore silently to herself, meeting his mocking look squarely while she thought. "It's a test, obviously," Fiona replied, trying not to sound like she was playing for time—which she was, of course.

T'mar nodded.

"F'jian, as the leader of the first wing, is acting wingleader," Fiona decided, beginning to relish the challenge. "So the test will be to see whether he makes his courtesy to the lord and lady, properly attends to the well-being of the dragons and riders, and then . . ." She paused as her thoughts raced ahead of her and she sent a silent message to Talenth. "They'll come here to water the dragons and check for new orders."

T'mar nodded but raised one hand, motioning for her to continue.

"And the test for me . . ." She trailed off, thinking hard, and then inspiration struck. "Is to see if I'm willing to let F'jian figure this out on his own!"

As if in response, they heard the rustle of dragon wings and the sky darkened as the small flight rushed into a landing near the river's edge.

"Very good," T'mar said with a congratulatory nod. "And why is it that you need this test, Weyrwoman?"

"Because a leader who doesn't let her juniors learn on their own is no leader at all," Fiona replied.

T'mar's lips curved upward approvingly. "And so, what are your orders, Weyrwoman?"

"Orders?" Fiona repeated, arching an eyebrow and matching his grin. "I expect I'll be asking F'jian what he plans to do next."

"Very good!"

F'jian, when asked, looked stumped for a moment before turning inquiringly to J'keran, who cocked his head back toward the Weyr.

"I think we should return to the Weyr," F'jian said, spreading his gaze between T'mar and Fiona.

"And, without asking J'keran, why do you think that?" T'mar asked.

"Because we've flown three hours already," F'jian replied slowly, "and the dragons are watered and we shouldn't have to fly more than six hours in a day as we haven't flown more than that so far."

"Very well," T'mar said. "Make it so." He turned to the gathered riders and raised his voice, "And on the way back, I want you to keep your eyes open for good recognition points. You'll be going *between* soon enough, so we shall start drilling on passing images."

The younger weyrlings' eyes lit up at his words and, while remounting their dragons, they babbled excitedly among themselves.

Fiona waited until F'jian's wing was aloft before ordering Talenth up and into her position, glancing behind her to be certain that J'keran and the older riders had taken their positions astern. Satisfied, she scanned the skies for the sight of the large bronze shape that was Zirenth, found it, and allowed herself a moment of congratulations before turning back to look down at the watermill as they passed over it.

It would make a good recognition point, she decided, fixing the bend of the river and the angle of the building in her mind. The wherhold itself was a smudge of buildings and low hills to the southeast.

The flight back to the Weyr seemed longer than the flight out, perhaps because she was tired, or perhaps because she was so eager to get back to the Weyr.

She glanced around in front and behind at the flight, found T'mar again, and scanned the ground below. The wind in her short hair kept her cool. In fact, the air at their height was cool enough that Fiona almost wished she'd brought the heavy wher-hide Weyrowman's jacket, while at the same time she worried whether the riders would get burned flying for so long under the hot Igen sun. She regretted not packing sunblock in her carisak.

She glanced around again and it suddenly hit her—she was flying! She was flying on Talenth!

Talenth, we're flying! Fiona called excitedly. *Remember how long we've wished for this?*

It feels good, Talenth agreed, pausing her stroke for a moment so that she could take one great big downstroke to catch up in a spurt with the receding wing in front.

Squawks from behind warned them that J'keran and the older riders were not pleased with the maneuver, so Fiona quietly urged Talenth back to her routine of slow, steady strokes.

But from that moment on, Fiona's view of their journey changed from one of duty to one of adventure, and time seemed to shrivel into nothing as they soared back to Igen Weyr.

True to his word, T'mar quizzed the riders on their return for the recognition points they'd chosen, demanding that they send the image to Zirenth. Red-faced, each rider was informed, usually by

Zirenth's amused snort, that his image was not sufficiently well-formed to use for a journey *between*.

Only Fiona's image of the watermill at the wherhold passed muster.

I see it, Zirenth told her directly. *I could go there*.

Fiona kept her expression neutral, not wanting to further depress the weyrlings.

After that, sending images was added to their daily routine. Then one night, over a month after they'd started this routine, T'mar arose after dinner and announced, "Tomorrow the younger dragons will turn two."

Fiona glanced excitedly at the younger weyrlings gathered at her table. She'd known it; she'd been counting down the days, hoping that perhaps they would start—

"Tomorrow, in the morning, we will start drilling on going *between*," T'mar said. After that, his mouth continued to move, but no one could hear him for the roar of approval that echoed throughout the Kitchen Cavern.

"**Y**ou stay here," Terin told Fiona acerbically after the fourth time she was awakened by the Weyrwoman's tossing and turning. "If you go to Talenth, you'll keep *her* awake, too!"

As the younger girl grabbed spare blankets and hauled herself off, grumbling under her breath, to the queen's lair, Fiona muttered an apology and tried to force herself to sleep . . . but it wasn't possible.

Sleep, Talenth murmured to her sometime later and, whether it was her tone or some special ability that she'd only just acquired, Fiona finally drifted off.

She awoke with the very first noises of the morning, dressed quickly, and ran to the Kitchen Cavern.

T'mar arrived at his usual time and refused to be rushed, even though Fiona could feel the tension of the other weyrlings nearly overwhelm her own sense of excitement.

"If you all cannot calm down, we will try again tomorrow," T'mar said after the werylings had groaned at seeing him pour a third cup of *klah*.

Fiona willed herself to be calm, sending her eagerness into the very rock of the Weyr, forcing her breathing to slow, concentrating her loving thoughts on Talenth. Around her, she felt the other riders do the same.

"Better," T'mar intoned, slowly raising his cup to his lips. Only Fiona saw how his brows twitched as he tried to keep from laughing.

"I'll bet you were worse on your first day," Fiona said accusingly.

"Another habit of a leader is to ensure that those who learn from her don't have to repeat her mistakes," T'mar observed drily. Fiona gave him a brittle look. The bronze rider was clearly enjoying himself, but she couldn't argue with his dedication.

T'mar sent the older weyrlings out first. They flew off singly, winking out *between* to the recognition points he had assigned them.

"Break into groups of three," T'mar ordered as the younger weyrlings gathered in front of him. Fiona aligned herself with F'jian, but T'mar shook his head at her, saying, "You're your own group, Weyrwoman."

The weyrlings smiled but, prudently, made no comment.

"We've twelve recognition points," T'mar told them. "Twelve groups. We work round-robin."

J'keran appeared suddenly over the Star Stones, and landed just as T'mar pointed toward him, saying, "J'keran at the Star Stones is your return point. You will jump to your recognition point and then back here to the Star Stones and land. Once you've landed, you'll rotate to the next group until you've jumped to all of the recognition points."

The weyrlings surged eagerly toward their dragons, but T'mar's voice rose up. "You will jump one at a time. We will wait until we know that the jump was successful before another person goes *between*." He paused, glaring around at the riders. "Is that understood?"

"Yes, wingleader!" Fiona and the thirty-two weyrling riders shouted back dutifully.

"Do you really understand?" T'mar asked again, lowering his voice dangerously.

"Yes, wingleader!" they shouted once more.

"Very well," T'mar said. He glanced around, pointing at D'lanor.

"You will jump first," he said.

D'lanor gulped, his eyes wide with sudden fright.

"J'gerd has your position." T'mar paused. "What is your destination?"

D'lanor closed his eyes and repeated the drill of asking his Canoth to ask J'gerd's Winurth for the image.

"It's dark!" he said, opening his eyes in surprise. "I can't see enough!"

"Yes, it is," T'mar agreed, smiling at the distraught rider to assure him that he'd done well. "Try again."

D'lanor closed his eyes once more. This time when he opened them, he was smiling. "The wherhold."

T'mar nodded and paused, no doubt, Fiona guessed, checking with J'gerd, Winurth, Zirenth, and Canoth to confirm that D'lanor had good coordinates.

"Very well, mount your dragon, fly up to the Star Stones, and, when you get the signal, you may jump *between*."

Time seemed to stand still as Fiona and the other weyrlings watched D'lanor climb to his mount on Canoth, carefully check his straps, solemnly salute T'mar and Fiona, launch into the sky, and climb up toward the Star Stones.

Fiona didn't know what the signal was and so was shocked when Canoth and D'lanor suddenly disappeared *between*. She wasn't the only one, for around her the other weyrlings gasped softly in surprise.

She could hear her heart beating loudly, feel the blood pumping through her veins as she waited, breathless.

"There comes a time," T'mar said softly in her ear, having sidled over to her unnoticed, "when you have to trust."

Fiona glanced up at him bleakly, then nodded in understanding, forcing her lips straight, taking a deep breath and letting it out slowly.

She was just about to ask T'mar or Talenth if D'lanor had made it when suddenly there was a change above the Star Stones and D'lanor and Canoth burst out of *between*, back from their first flight.

To the cheers of his weyrmates, an elated D'lanor glided back down to the Weyr Bowl.

T'mar pointed to the next group. "J'nos, you will go to V'lex."

J'nos repeated the drill, discovering that V'lex was hovering over Plains Hold. Again, dragon and rider rose to their position by the Star Stones, again they disappeared *between*, and again their weyrmates held their collective breath until, triumphant, the dragonpair returned to the Star Stones.

It seemed, as this was repeated over and over, that the fear and the thrill should lessen, that it should grow anticlimactic, but it didn't.

"Weyrwoman," T'mar said finally. She was the last to go. The others all looked at her expectantly. She looked to T'mar for instructions and he surprised her with, "Where do you want to go?"

Fiona's eyes went wide. In her panic, she reached out to Talenth.

We can do this, Talenth assured her, not at all concerned. *We already did it once when we came here.*

The calm in her mental touch was enough to reduce Fiona's fright to something manageable.

"The wherhold," Fiona replied. "I'd like to pay my respects to Lady Nuella while I'm there."

"Very well," T'mar agreed. "Who do you contact?"

"J'gerd," Fiona replied instantly, sending the thought to Talenth. J'gerd's image came back: the wherhold in the bright midday sun. "I have the image."

Through his bronze dragon, T'mar checked with J'gerd, Winurth, and Talenth. "Very well, mount up—and good flying."

As Fiona checked her straps in the growing morning light, she saw that Azeez, Mother Karina, and many of the young trader children had gathered to watch. Before she urged Talenth upward, she saluted T'mar and then, with a gracious wave of her arm, saluted the traders.

Let's fly, Talenth! Fiona called, and her beautiful, great, wonderful golden queen was airborne with one quick leap, surging upward to the Star Stones. Fiona had a moment to look down at J'keran and wave, and then T'mar's words echoed once more in her mind, "There comes a time when you have to trust."

Very well, she would trust. She shifted the image in her mind, moved the sun to the far end of the sky and farther, brought the stars and the two moons to shine and passed it to her dragon. *Talenth, let's go here!*

Her heart leapt in her mouth as the cold nothingness of *between* enveloped them and she began counting in her mind, remembering that *between* only lasts as long as it takes to cough three times. Three times! Was it more? Had she—

They burst out of the nothingness into the warm night, Talenth bugling joyously, answered by a chorus of watch-whers below.

Talenth, please convey our greetings to Nuellask, then let's land.

As they descended, Fiona caught sight of many large eyes glowing up at her and directed Talenth to land near the smaller pair in the middle.

"Weyrwoman!" Nuella called gladly as Talenth landed and Fiona jumped down. "I heard you would be coming."

"This is my first time *between*," Fiona cried as she rushed over to hug Nuella. "I wanted to come to you and Nuellask."

"Why is it, Weyrwoman, that you make your first flight *between* at night when all the others came by day?" Nuella wondered.

"Well," Fiona said with a shrug, "Nuellask would be asleep at midday, and it didn't seem fair to disturb you like that."

Nuella chuckled.

"Well, you've done it and now you'd best get back and take T'mar's rightful ire," Arella told her, shaking her head, muttering as she turned away, "If all Weyrwomen were like you . . ."

With a final hug, Fiona took her leave of Nuella and climbed back on Talenth.

So soon? Talenth asked in surprise as Fiona urged her upward again.

I don't want us to get caught, Fiona replied, giving Talenth the original image she'd received from J'gerd and instructing her to go *between* once more.

The time was shorter or Fiona had grown more used to it, for she emerged in the hot midday sun near J'gerd. She waved and he waved back, grinning, while she had Talenth wheel in a tight circle on her wingtip and gave her the coordinates for J'keran and the Star Stones.

They burst back out exactly where Fiona had imagined and she cried with glee, waving carelessly to J'keran before starting her descent into the Weyr Bowl.

It was only as she surveyed the ground below her that she noticed that something had changed. The hatchlings had been dispersed to their weyrs, their riders arranged in a tight knot, T'mar and the older weyrlings standing grimly in front of them.

Fiona's sense of triumph faded as she took in the scene. What had happened?

She dismounted and strode over to T'mar with a questioning look on her face.

T'mar turned away from her angrily, addressing the younger weyrlings.

"There is always some *idiot* who thinks they are special," he told them icily. "Some dimglow who thinks that drills are too much effort, that they know everything."

He turned back to Fiona, glaring at her.

"Fortunately," he went on, turning once more to the weyrlings, "we have a solution for this sort of behavior." He paused for a long while, long enough for the sense of dread and shame to lodge deep in Fiona's chest, sucking all the joy of her unauthorized adventure right out of her.

"Our Weyrwoman has volunteered to man the Star Stones for the next month," T'mar told the collected group gravely. "That will enable the rest of us to continue our training." He paused. "We are done for today. Go about your duties."

As the riders dissolved into smaller groups, none passed near Fiona, none looked at her, none spoke to her or acknowledged her existence in any way.

Talenth, I'm sorry! Fiona called to her dragon.

You are the Weyrwoman, Talenth responded in a tone of confusion. *You are my rider. You can do nothing wrong.*

This time I did, Fiona admitted miserably. *I am the Werywoman. I neglected my duty to the Weyr; my duty to set the example.*

When the others were out of earshot, T'mar approached her. "There's always one idiot," he repeated. "I knew it would be you."

"That's why you sent me last," Fiona guessed, her heart falling deeper into her chest.

T'mar nodded curtly, his eyes boring into hers as they welled with tears, and then he glanced away and strode off briskly without another word.

If T'mar's treatment was bad, Terin's outburst that evening was even worse.

"What if you *hadn't* come back?" the young headwoman demanded. "How would I survive? How would I live?"

Nothing Fiona could say would console the girl, who stormed out of her weyr and slept elsewhere that night.

As Fiona curled up tightly in her cold bed and tried to find some warmth, she reviewed the day, castigating herself for her foolishness, for her selfishness, for her stupidity in thinking that she could fool T'mar. Sleep overwhelmed her at last.

The next month passed slowly for Fiona. She apologized the very next day to every rider in the Weyr, twice to T'mar, and three times to Terin. Azeez and Mother Karina eyed her pityingly, but she said nothing to them, taking her punishment as it was meant.

However wrong she'd been, she was the Weyrwoman, and she refused to allow her shame to keep her from her duties. In fact, she redoubled her efforts in response.

She duly took the hot and bothersome duty of watch dragon at the Star Stones, convinced that she was probably the only Weyrwoman ever so condemned.

As the rest of the weyrlings drilled in recognition points, Fiona found herself continually worried about their return, continually standing as an example of what not to do. She wore her best garb as a tribute to their efforts and, wordlessly at first, then verbally, expressed her praise and growing confidence as the weyrlings came and returned again and again from their journeys *between* until she wondered how she could ever have thought the journey dangerous.

In the last sevenday of her punishment, Fiona found herself actually looking forward to the duty, finding it a time where she could spend hours in thought and moments in short communication with returning riders. Her thoughts were occupied by considering the stores for the Weyr, the trade with the outlying holds, and the functioning of the Weyr.

Terin had returned to sleeping in the queen's weyr on the third day of Fiona's punishment, her complaint of, "It's too cold with the others!" fooling neither of them. Now she took to climbing the long flights of stairs up to the Star Stones to bring Fiona food and snacks and, occasionally, to share in the watch, often perched in front of Fiona on Talenth's neck.

Fiona turned as she heard Terin's approach and wondered idly how she was going to handle the younger girl's imminent womanhood. Fiona had noticed how Terin had started eyeing the older weyrlings and had teased her gently about it, adding her own cogent observations to ease Terin's embarrassment but she was worried that, being the only eligible partner for most of the riders at the Weyr, Terin might find herself overwhelmed with offers or worse—frightened by the intensity of emotion if one of the older greens took to the skies in a mating flight.

It was something that concerned Fiona about herself, too. Neither Talenth nor the greens of her clutch were old enough yet to rise, but those of J'keran's older dragons might rise again at any moment. How would Terin react when the emotions of a mating flight combined with her growing emotions as a woman? How would Fiona?

And, Fiona admitted with a deep sigh, how would she react to Talenth rising? She wasn't ready for it, she admitted to herself, and it scared her.

Terin bounded into view and Fiona shook her worries out of her head, producing a grateful smile and leaning down from her perch to help the younger girl climb up.

"They're doing in and outs," Fiona told her, meaning that the weyrlings were now practicing jumping rapidly *between* the Weyr and all the other recognition points.

"They'll be exhausted tonight," Terin replied, pulling a roll out of her carisak and passing it back to Fiona.

"And hungry before that," Fiona agreed.

"I've got the young ones tending the meal," Terin said. "Stew, so there's little chance they'll burn it."

"That's good!" Fiona agreed.

"What are the traders going to do when we leave?" Terin asked.

"They'll manage," Fiona replied, unconcerned. To ease Terin's worried look, she added, "They've managed before, haven't they?"

Terin shrugged in agreement. "What about us?"

Fiona raised an eyebrow inquiringly.

"What are we going to do when we get back?" Terin expanded. "I mean, I know everyone calls me headwoman—"

"And with good reason," Fiona cut across her firmly, surprised to hear the younger girl bring up that old worry.

"But when I get back, I'll just be another weyrgirl," Terin said. She frowned as she added, "And what about Xhinna?"

"I don't know," Fiona replied slowly. She hated to admit to herself that she'd forgotten about Xhinna in the course of the crowded last two Turns. Musingly, she said, "You'll be as old as she is when we return."

"It'll only be three days for her."

"For everyone," Fiona agreed, bringing up the image that she'd already started rehearsing of Fort Weyr with the sun and the moons in exactly the right position. For all that she regretted her rash jump *between* times to visit Nuella, she was glad to know that she could trust her imaging and certain that she could, even now, without further practice, easily jump forward once more in time back to Fort Weyr.

Fiona thought back to Terin's remark. How would Cisca view Fiona when they returned? Talenth would be ready to mate; Fiona would have had all these Turns of experience running a Weyr—could she ever be happy again following someone else's orders? Or did she, now that she'd tasted it, see herself only as senior Weyrwoman?

"There'll be a place for you," Fiona said realizing that her brooding silence was only making Terin more anxious. "And I guarantee, when Talenth clutches, I'll have you on the Hatching Grounds."

"What about Xhinna?"

"Her, too," Fiona said. "You both deserve it."

"But she'll never Impress a queen!"

"No, probably not," Fiona said with a thoughtful shake of her head. "But even K'lior and Cisca feel that she could Impress a green or maybe even a blue."

"A blue?" Terin repeated in surprise.

"No one will know until we try," Fiona replied with a shrug.

A flurry of dragons came through, landing at the end of their exercise. Soon everyone had returned, dragons were dispersing back to the weyrling barracks, and only Zirenth remained with T'mar, who sat eyeing the events from his lofty position atop his dragon.

Fiona was surprised when Zirenth launched himself again and flew up toward the Star Stones. She waved cheerfully at the wingleader, but instead of waving back, he brought Zirenth in for a landing beside Talenth.

T'mar dismounted and climbed up Talenth's foreleg, one arm holding onto the riding straps to support him.

"Have you noticed anything odd about Sarinth?" T'mar asked her meaningfully.

Sarinth was V'lex's green.

"She seemed eager to please today," Fiona replied, eyes narrowing thoughtfully. "And . . . maybe a bit more distracted than usual."

"She's going to rise, isn't she?" Terin asked, her eyes wide.

"It's possible," T'mar said with a deep sigh.

"I've seen three mating flights," Terin boasted, her eyes shining. "They were fun!"

"You're getting older," Fiona reminded her.

"I'm more concerned about the traders," T'mar replied, "particularly the children."

"Didn't they have fire-lizards before?" Fiona asked rhetorically. T'mar's expression remained grim, so Fiona added diplomatically, "I don't see any reason why we can't talk with them tonight."

T'mar looked only partly relieved. "Have you . . . ?"

Fiona smiled at his awkward discomfort and shook her head sadly. "Fire was too young to rise, but there were plenty of fire-lizards at the Harper Hall." She glanced into his eyes and, in that moment, quashed her fears. "I think I'll manage."

"Good," T'mar replied, lips pursed tightly. "Good." He paused a moment before saying, "You've done well here with the weyrlings."

"It's been fun," Fiona agreed. "I've learned a lot."

"I thought you might," T'mar said with a sly grin. Fiona glanced at him sharply, then roared with laughter.

"There's . . . always . . . one!" she choked out between gales of laughter, pointing her finger at him accusingly.

T'mar went bright red, then hung his head for a moment before raising it to meet Fiona's eyes, nodding in honest admission.

Terin glanced back and forth between the two of them mystified over the exchange until Fiona explained, "T'mar was speaking from experience when he said there's always one idiot who thinks he is special."

"*You* were the idiot?" Terin asked T'mar in surprise.

T'mar nodded guiltily, recovering enough to say to Fiona, "Did you learn your lesson as well as I did?"

"I think so."

"Good," T'mar replied. "Then tomorrow—if we aren't interrupted—you may join us."

Early the next morning the air was punctuated by a raucous cry, startling Fiona, Terin, and Talenth awake.

Sarinth is blooding her kills, Talenth reported, her tone a mixture of confusion and excitement.

Fiona felt the same excitement as she glanced toward Terin, who returned her look with a grin. "This is going to be fun!"

"We should go help," Fiona replied. *Talenth, stay here.*

Talenth agreed reluctantly as Fiona and Terin dressed hastily, trotted out of the weyr, and jumped over the ledge into the Bowl below, where they made their way toward the cluster of riders loosely gathered around the feed pens at the lake's edge.

"Don't let her gorge!" a rider called encouragingly to V'lex, who looked confused and overwhelmed by his dragon's passion.

"I can't—she's—" V'lex replied miserably, his hands held out beseechingly, his chest heaving rapidly.

Fiona parted the crowd, dragging Terin behind her. "Grab his other hand," Fiona told her as she reached for V'lex's left hand, pivoting around to stand in his sight.

"V'lex," she said, "look at me."

V'lex forced his eyes to focus on her.

"You can do this," she told him encouragingly. "Breathe, V'lex." She took a deep breath herself in illustration. "That's it! Now focus on Sarinth. She must only blood her kills—she can't gorge."

"She's fighting me!" V'lex wailed. Fiona caught the fear in his voice, the sense of amazement that his normally so agreeable green had turned into an uncontrollable, red-eyed, voracious, vicious beast.

"Reach out, V'lex, reach out with me," Fiona said, feeding her power through him. Faintly she felt an echo from Terin.

V'lex stiffened as the jolt of power coursed into him and, in the distance, Sarinth bugled in surprise and irritation. Fiona was only vaguely aware of the encouraging noises around her, that Sarinth had given up her first kill to pounce on a second and, after a brief fight, reluctantly only drank the blood of this kill, too. She pounced on a third, dispatching it with one sudden blow to the neck, fastened her jaws on its throat and sucked eagerly, her skin glistening.

Around her blues and browns made encouraging noises, their riders splitting their attention between the green dragon and her rider.

With a taunting cry, Sarinth leapt skyward, instantly chased by a flock of eager blues and browns.

"She mustn't go *between*." The rough male voice barely made itself heard over the eager noises of the dragons. It was T'mar.

Some instinct had Fiona reach out toward Terin and drag the younger girl to her side, leaving V'lex exposed to the growing attentions of the other riders even as she herself continued to pour her power into the green rider.

And then—in an instant—Fiona felt a backlash flow into her, and suddenly she had an image from high in the sky, looking down on the Weyr and the puny blues and overmuscled browns as she soared over them, taunting them with cries as she climbed higher and higher in the cool morning air, the sun rising over the horizon in tribute to her prowess.

"Fiona!" a voice, harsh with emotion, burst over her. "Fiona, you must see to the traders!"

Fiona felt herself being brusquely shoved, pushed out of the warm huddle of bodies pressing around V'lex, felt Terin's grasp tighten in panic on her hand and then—she was out of the throng, looking back longingly.

T'mar's head appeared amongst the others as he called, "Go, see to the children!"

And then the instant of connection, of soaring emotions Fiona had only dimly felt before, seeped away from her and she was herself, back on the ground, a loud group of dragonriders behind her, Terin gasping wide-eyed for breath still clinging tightly, painfully to her hand, and—in the distance—a knot of young traders, looking more alarmed and frightened than excited over the behavior of the dragonriders.

"Did you see the green dragon jump into the sky?" Fiona asked the knot of youngsters as she closed upon them.

Some nodded, others shrank back behind their elders. Fiona took a deep, steadying breath and continued, "She's on her mating flight, and she jumped into the sky daring the boy dragons to see if they could catch her."

She smiled, adding, "She's only thinking about how high she can fly, how much better she is than them, and—"

Suddenly an overwhelming emotion, a sense of elation and climax flowed into Fiona and she was temporarily speechless. Beside her she heard Terin gasp and some of the older trader children also cried out while the youngsters all pointed skyward, crying, "Look, they're falling!"

Fiona, with her back to the scene, shook her head. "They're just playing. The brown caught the green and it's part of their mating game."

"Will they make more dragons?" a little boy piped up.

"Greens don't lay eggs," a girl corrected him, her eyes locked on the spectacle above them.

"Firestone makes them sterile," Fiona agreed absently, willing herself back under control, feeling her skin tingle as another wave of emotion rolled over her. She took another deep, calming breath, felt Terin's fingers cling desperately to hers and drew the younger girl to her in a tight hug.

"Sometimes it's nice to hug a friend, just because you feel like it," Fiona said over Terin's shoulder to the youngsters. Some nodded solemnly, seeking out friends and hugging them with all the innocence of children. Encouraged, Fiona directed them into a larger hug, more children joining in until she, Terin, and all the trader children were one giant hug.

There was one sudden, final, joyful shout from the distant dragonriders, one final thrill pouring through the knot of children, and then Talenth said, *Winurth flew her.*

Afterward, Fiona and Terin herded the trader children through a quick bath in the Weyrwoman's quarters, by which time the older traders were ready to look after them. Once Fiona had returned the last of their charges, she turned to Terin. "Let's take a moment in the bath ourselves."

"Do you want to go first?" Terin asked.

Fiona shook her head. "Just this once, we'll share the tub."

As Terin's eyes widened, Fiona added hastily, "We'll be needed soon—we won't have much time."

They were quickly in and out of the tub, spending more time drying and combing hair than bathing. Fiona insisted on Terin going first and, as the younger girl sat with her eyes closed as she luxuriated in having her hair parted, combed, and braided, Fiona remarked, "You did well."

"I was scared," Terin confessed, lowering her head so that Fiona could finish braiding. "I wasn't sure what I wanted at the moment—I felt so overwhelmed, not myself." She paused thoughtfully, then declared, "I want to be myself, not someone dragon-flamed."

Her words echoed in Fiona's mind long after.

Tell T'mar we're coming, Fiona told Talenth, signaling to Terin to stop drying her hair.

"We've got to get going," she said aloud as she rose from the chair and started for the entrance to Talenth's weyr. "With a mating flight there are two very happy riders and . . ." She gestured with an open hand.

"They'll all need breakfast," Terin agreed, striding quickly to catch up to her.

They found T'mar at the entrance to the Kitchen Cavern.

"I'll start the *klah*," Terin said, rushing past.

"No rush," T'mar called after her. "We'll take this as a rest day."

Fiona cocked an eyebrow upward and grinned impishly.

"And how did you enjoy your first mating flight as Weyr-woman?" T'mar asked.

Fiona started to recount Terin's trenchant observation to him but thought better of it, changing her expression to one of mild amusement.

"Has Sarinth chewed firestone?" Terin called from her place by the hearth.

"Firestone?" T'mar repeated, frowning. "No, we won't start to practice flaming until they've mastered the recognition points."

"You might want to reconsider that," Fiona observed. "I'm not sure if we would want to wait for Sarinth to clutch."

"Oh," T'mar said, dumbstruck. He turned toward Terin and sketched a bow in her direction. "Well caught, headwoman."

"I just thought . . ." Terin began only to break off, blushing. "It's just that . . ." She glanced helplessly toward Fiona.

"We women tend to concentrate on such things," Fiona said drily, recalling one of Kelsa's choice phrases.

"Well," T'mar said with an expression of one rapidly reprioritiz-ing, "I suspect we'll need to start firestone drill shortly."

"We'll need firestone," Fiona replied.

"Hmm," T'mar said, his face creased into a thoughtful frown. "That may be difficult."

"Rather," Fiona agreed, heading over to the spare hearth to start rolls. She turned back to him, flashing a taunting smile. "I'm sure you'll figure out something."

"That *is* unexpected," Azeez allowed as T'mar laid out the prob-lem to the trader over the evening meal. He twitched a smile toward Fiona and Terin as he added, "We'd already discussed how to handle it—an exchange of finished gold for firestone—but we hadn't planned to deal for another three months or so."

T'mar turned to the smirking Fiona in amazement. "You'd al-ready *planned* . . . ?"

"Weyrwoman," Fiona said, her eyes dancing as she pointed at herself.

"Indeed," T'mar responded with a snort, half-amused, half-respectful. "So, *Weyrwoman*, how was it that you forgot to allow for rising greens?"

It was Fiona's turn to blush. She couldn't speak and mutely shook her head.

"With dragons, we could retrieve the stone more quickly," Azeez said thoughtfully, "but we hadn't expected to begin trading . . ."

"Perhaps we can find something else besides gold," Terin suggested.

"Foodstuffs?" Fiona ventured. She shook her head, negating her own suggestion, then brightened as a new thought came to her. "Spices!"

"Recipes," Terin declared.

"Ice," T'mar offered.

The two women shook their heads at him and he gave Fiona a challenging look that she answered with, "They're in the north."

"Iced cream, then," T'mar said in a stubborn tone.

"Recipes," Terin repeated.

"We would like to establish direct trade with the Fire Hold," Azeez allowed.

"It won't last beyond our leaving," Fiona observed, shaking her head.

"Profit when possible," Azeez said, quoting a trader maxim.

"I don't want us to get involved in trader politics," T'mar declared, glancing frankly toward Azeez. "Especially to the detriment of traders beholden to Fort."

"You have conflicting loyalties," Azeez observed.

"We've already established loyalty with you," Fiona said, adding, "Do you think it won't last when we return to our own time?"

"In your time, Fiona, you are not the senior Weyrwoman," Azeez reminded her. "You may not control your loyalties."

Fiona flinched—the remark struck all too true.

"Then let us help you while we can," Terin said, glancing toward Fiona for approval.

"Recipes won't work," Azeez said, changing the subject back to the original issue, "but recipes with spices would."

"Because you could only sell a recipe once?" Terin guessed.

"Correct," Azeez agreed approvingly. "Have you any recipes that require unusual spices?"

"Curry with pistachio," Fiona suggested immediately, citing her favorite culinary find.

"Pistachios aren't limited to Igen," Mother Karina replied with a thoughtful frown, "but they are not common to the cold north, either."

"Ginger and some of the hotter chilis," T'mar suggested.

"I'm sure we can come up with a list for trade," Azeez agreed. "When and how will we start?"

T'mar pursed his lips in a sour look. "I don't know," he admitted, "I'd hate to think of depriving the Weyrs of their needed—"

"The Weyrs have need of us, too," Fiona cut across him, gesturing to the weyrlings around them. "If we don't get them trained and ready to fight, there will be no point in our coming back to this time."

"I wonder, though, is there any other source of proper firestone?" Azeez asked, glancing toward Fiona. "If the Igen charts marked gold, wouldn't they also mark firestone?"

T'mar and Fiona exchanged astonished looks and rose from the table, eager to put thought into action.

"The map has lasted this long," Mother Karina said in a tone that halted their motion, "I'm sure it will keep until after you've eaten."

"And the food's hot now," Terin added, grinning at the older trader.

T'mar gave Fiona a sheepish look and the two returned to their seats, but they were unable to keep themselves from eating more quickly than usual. Terin, Azeez, and Mother Karina noticed and laughed at them.

T'mar flushed, but Fiona ignored them, concentrating on finishing her meal.

"Another excellent and tasty meal, Terin," she said as she rose from her place, searching the cavern for a nearby glowbasket she might purloin. T'mar was at her side before she reached the entrance to the Weyr Bowl.

"Would you like us to wait for you?" Azeez called after them, his amusement unrestrained.

"Whatever," Fiona called back, waving a hand airily over her shoulder.

Talenth greeted them solemnly as they entered her weyr. Fiona paused long enough to call out a greeting and an apology as she and T'mar moved through the Weyrwoman's quarters and into the Records Room beyond.

"We should have brought more glows," T'mar observed as he laid the map out on the long table and tried to make out the markings in the light of the glow Fiona had brought. Fiona leaned close to the map, frustrated herself, and nodded in agreement, only to gasp in surprise as the level of light in the room doubled.

"I thought you might need more," Terin said brightly as she entered, cradling a large basket in her arms. She placed it heavily on the table and leaned over the map, joining the other two in their examination.

"What's this?" Fiona asked, tapping a mark on the mountains not far north of the spot that marked the location of Igen Weyr. T'mar leaned closer and then peered down at the legend at the bottom of the map.

"Silver, I think," he said, returning to the spot on the map to fix it in his mind.

Terin examined the legend carefully. She pointed at one mark. "This is the mark for firestone."

"So we just need to find that on the map . . ." Fiona murmured, scanning the map from the bottom to the top, right to left. She paused at a spot near Nerat Tip. "Here's one."

"I doubt M'tal would be happy with us poaching in Benden territory," T'mar remarked.

"Not if he never knew about it," Terin said suggestively. Fiona and T'mar gave her a remonstrating look and the young girl sighed. "I suppose that wouldn't be too friendly, would it?"

"Here's one," T'mar said, pointing to a spot south of the Weyr. He frowned as he measured the distance with his eye. "It's less than an hour's straight flight from here."

"That's odd," Fiona said, peering closer to the spot. "Why would dragonriders have forgotten the old firestone if Igen had a mine so near by?"

"I suspect we won't know until we look," T'mar replied.

"Tomorrow?" Fiona asked, cocking an eyebrow upward.

T'mar nodded.

"Do we tell Azeez?" Terin wondered.

"Let's see what we find, first," Fiona suggested.

Fiona invited Terin to ride with them, but the young girl demurred, asking quite rightly, "And who will keep an eye on everything if we're *all* gone?"

They left at first light, wearing the light clothes favored by the traders under their warm wherhide jackets and riding gear, and carrying extra water. T'mar had decided to bring half the young weyrlings; the rest were working and drilling under F'jian's and J'keran's watch.

T'mar had set J'nos directly in charge of the traveling group of weyrlings, who had been ecstatic at the thought of a playful excursion until T'mar had reminded J'nos that they needed to bring shovels, picks, and other digging tools.

Talenth was first into the air and took up a position high above the Star Stones as she waited, radiating impatience, for the others to catch up. T'mar joined on Zirenth shortly, the bronze rider smiling and waving at them.

He says that we were right to take the high position as we're the most powerful, Talenth told Fiona smugly. Fiona laughed and patted her beautiful young queen enthusiastically.

Taking their cue from the Star Stones, Fiona oriented Talenth in the direction she thought they should fly. A few moments later, Zirenth aligned to the same direction and T'mar gave Fiona the signal that she should lead.

With a laugh of pure delight, Fiona urged Talenth onward. The queen responded eagerly, her wings swiftly boosting them to a breathtaking speed. A sudden worry nudged Fiona and she craned her neck around to see that the smaller blues and greens were struggling to maintain their speed.

Slow down; we'll let the others catch up, Fiona said to Talenth, her pride in her gold's great strength seeping through her admonishment.

I suppose, as leader, we shouldn't lose them, Talenth agreed reluctantly.

We need to go higher, too, Fiona said as she eyed their distance to the ground. *Let's start a slow climb.*

The idea of a climb pleased Talenth, who broadened her downstroke to lift them slowly higher. Fiona compared her view of the ground below with her memory of heights and elevations—and the chill of the air—and had Talenth level off when she was satisfied.

We continue south with the river in view on our left, Fiona said to Talenth.

T'mar says that this is high enough, Talenth relayed with the smug tones of someone proven right.

Fiona nodded in response but said nothing, concentrating instead on the view ahead and trying to ignore the chill air rushing over her. She was glad that T'mar had insisted that they wear full riding gear; on the ground it had been hot and stifling, but in the air it was just enough to keep Fiona from a severe chill. She adjusted her scarf up higher over her nose—"I've seen them freeze clean off!" F'dan had told her once when they were discussing the dangers of dragonflight.

The sun to their left lit the Igen river gold, then silver as it rose higher into the sky. It was a beautiful day and Fiona's heart leapt to be here, now—a Weyrwoman on her gold dragon.

Talenth, she thought fondly, *I love you.*

I love you, too.

They're lagging, Fiona told Talenth as she scanned the weyrlings struggling along behind them two hours later. *Ask T'mar if we should land and let them rest.*

T'mar says that we should land when we find the site, Talenth replied.

Fiona pursed her lips tightly to hold in a sharp retort and bent further over Talenth's neck, peering at the ground below for any sign of the landmass they were seeking.

The map had shown a spot on the southern end of a saddle between two hills, the northern one higher than the southern, with the firestone on the eastern side of the saddle. But that map had been drawn hundreds of Turns back, and while the mountains wouldn't have changed in that time, the sands of Igen could have blown so much dust into the area as to fill in the saddle itself. That would make sense, else why would the Igen riders have abandoned the mine?

Her gaze caught on something—there! What was that? She peered down further, raising a gloved hand to shield her eyes from the sun. It looked like a large "X" in the ground below her. It was directly in the saddle between two mountains and the area looked recently worked.

Fiona had Talenth turn a tight circle over the spot.

Ask T'mar if we should land, Fiona said to Talenth even as she urged her gold lower.

Yes, was the response Talenth relayed.

Let the weyrlings land first, Fiona instructed Talenth. *We'll go look around a bit.*

They flew to the far side of the southern hill, then circled to the west and came back around to the big "X." Fiona could spot a road that led toward the river and followed it to a well-constructed pier that looked recently used—there were coils of rope neatly placed at the far end, ready to moor a cargo ship.

T'mar says we should join them, Talenth told her.

They circled back and landed near the others. The heat in the valley was oppressive, and Fiona shucked off her riding gear before she dismounted, grateful for the flowing robes of lightweight white material she wore beneath. She pulled the hood up over her head to shade her hair and neck from the sun and then jumped down lightly to the sandy ground below.

"It looks like someone's been here before us," T'mar remarked as she joined him. He gestured to the roadway. "This is recent work."

"No sand on the road," Fiona agreed. She gestured uphill, toward the dark tunnel entrance. "Is anyone in there?"

T'mar shook his head. "Why don't we find out?"

With J'nos and the weyrlings trailing behind them, they climbed the rise to the dark tunnel.

"It looks like there's a door at the far end," T'mar said as they got closer, his brows furrowed thoughtfully.

"And it's closed," Fiona agreed. They crossed into the darkness of the tunnel. Something light just inside caught her attention and she turned to it. It was a slate with white chalk written on it: "Please be sure to close the door when you're done."

"Do you recognize the writing?" Fiona asked, raising the slate toward T'mar. The wingleader took it and examined it cautiously before handing it back to Fiona, who replaced it in exactly the same spot.

"Could it be Pellar's?" Fiona asked. She'd never met the man, but as everyone knew that he was mute, used slates, and mined firestone, he was an obvious choice.

T'mar frowned before replying, "Actually, it looks something like *your* writing."

Fiona turned back and snatched at the slate, eyeing it minutely. It could be, she finally decided. "Or Terin's."

"Why don't we see why we should keep the door closed?" T'mar suggested, putting his hand on the handle and pulling the door open.

It was dark inside.

"Did we think to pack glows?" Fiona asked, turning back to J'nos.

"Here, Weyrwoman," one of the other weyrlings replied, passing up a small glowbasket. "It's not very big."

"It'll do," Fiona told him gratefully, stepping through the door as she unbundled the glow and let its feeble light play on the tunnel beyond.

"Someone," T'mar murmured as he looked around the scene in front of them, "has been very busy."

The tunnel ahead was blocked by a workcart, clearly ready to resume its role in mining as soon as the bags of firestone placed in and all around it were moved away. Bags and bags and bags of firestone—

"There's more than we need!" J'nos exclaimed delightedly as he eyed the bags of firestone stacked to the left and right of the tunnel entrance. "There's enough for all the dragons we have to fight a full Fall!"

"There's another slate," T'mar said, gesturing toward the center of the cart. Fiona rushed toward it, glow in hand. The writing on the slate read, "Take what you need."

"Someone has been very thoughtful," Fiona said as she passed the slate back to T'mar. The bronze rider crouched down to bring the slate closer to Fiona's glow and read the message with a low whistle of surprise.

"By the egg of Faranth!" T'mar said when he had breath again. He peered quizzically at Fiona. "You haven't been back in time again, Weyrwoman?"

"Not that I remember," Fiona replied, shaken by T'mar's observations on the slate's handwriting. Even more than the note outside, this slate looked like it was written in her hand.

"Perhaps sometime in the future?"

"That would explain the dizziness!" Fiona exclaimed. T'mar gave her a quizzical looked so she continued, "T'mar, what if we were in the same time more than twice? Remember how shaken M'tal was; what if our dizziness is because we're triple-timing or worse?"

"And only some of us," T'mar said thoughtfully. "Others don't feel it because they didn't—or won't—do it."

"Exactly!"

"That's a possibility, Weyrwoman," T'mar agreed. A moment later he added, "But it's a possibility for the future. For now, we've got other concerns."

"Like mating greens who haven't chewed firestone," Fiona said.

"Precisely." T'mar turned to J'nos, saying, "Organize a party to start loading the dragons. We'll take this load back *between*."

The work was hot and sweaty, but in less than two hours, each of the dragons was loaded with five sacks of firestone—Zirenth and Talenth each carried eight—and the tired riders mounted their dragons.

T'mar says that you are to give the coordinates, Talenth told her as they rose into the hot midday air. Fiona swelled with pride at the honor, then set the image of Igen Weyr at midday firmly in her mind and sent the image to Zirenth for confirmation. She caught T'mar's pumping arm gesture of acknowledgment, had Talenth send the image to the rest of the wing, then said, *Let's go.*

They burst out into the sky over Igen precisely where and when Fiona had chosen, were greeted cheerfully by the watch dragon, and descended swiftly to a landing in the Weyr Bowl near the unused firestone shed.

With the rest of the weyrlings to help, unloading proceeded

more quickly than loading and they all retired to the Dining Cavern for a well-deserved late lunch.

"We've got ninety-six sacks of firestone," T'mar said to Fiona as they started in to their meal of cold cuts and bread, "so we can afford to use two sacks each."

"So that's enough to flame for about an hour and a half?" Fiona asked, piling some cold chicken onto her bread and liberally spreading it with one of the marvelous curry pastes that Mother Karina had introduced to the Weyr.

T'mar nodded, watching Fiona's behavior with an amused look.

"What?" Fiona demanded, seeing his look. "Can't a girl be hungry?"

"Of course," T'mar responded smoothly, his eyes twinkling. "But it would be a shame if Talenth strained herself."

"I am not fat!" Fiona declared hotly, suddenly folding the bread in two and forcing it into her mouth.

"Merely a growing girl," T'mar agreed, his grin belying his demure tone.

"Hmph!" Fiona snorted around her mouthful. She chewed quickly and took a long swallow from her mug of iced water. "Flying that far is hard work."

"For a dragon," T'mar responded.

"You're just afraid that I'll get taller than you!"

"I like tall women."

Fiona fumed, her lips thin, but realized that any further response would only fuel the wingleader's jest.

"So we'll start with the firestone after lunch?" she asked, desperate to change the topic.

"Not you, unless you want to make Talenth sterile," T'mar replied.

"I thought I might watch."

"I'm sure you'd be welcome," T'mar said, adding with his former humor, "and you could use the exercise!"

Talenth was sleepy after lunch and lay inside her weyr peering out at the activity.

Lazybones! Fiona chided her.

You *didn't fly this morning*, Talenth reminded her haughtily.

I helped haul the firestone, Fiona countered. Talenth made no response, but Fiona caught a faint hint that her queen felt none was necessary.

"I'm not fat, am I?" Fiona asked Terin, who stood nearby, eager to watch.

Terin eyed her for a moment then said, "Well, you're taller than me."

"So I'm fat?" Fiona demanded, horrorstricken.

"I don't know," Terin replied thoughtfully. "You might just be growing. I think you'd have to ask Mother Karina." She shrugged. "But what if you are?"

Fiona had never thought of herself as fat; she'd always been skinny—everyone at the Hold had pestered her to eat more. "You're only skin and bones!" they'd always said.

But perhaps her time here in Igen had put more than meat on her—and she just hated the idea. Especially, she hated the way T'mar teased her about it.

"Look!" Terin cried as a gout of flame erupted from the throat of one of the greens. Fiona and Terin both watched, excited, as T'mar proceeded along down the line of dragons, signaling each in turn to flame.

Apparently satisfied, T'mar mounted his bronze Zirenth and signaled the rest of the dragons to rise with him.

T'mar asks if we'll take watch, Talenth relayed, lifting her head and snaking it between Terin and Fiona where they stood.

"Certainly!" Fiona replied. "T'mar wants us to take watch, want to come?" she said to Terin.

Terin readily agreed and, shortly, the two were mounted on Talenth as she beat swiftly up to the watch heights and daintily landed beside the blue watch dragon. The rider, his face barely visible under his wide sun hat, waved cheerfully, hefting one of the two firestone sacks at his side, and eagerly joined the rest of the weyrlings.

"I suppose from now on we won't be able to call them weyrlings," Fiona said.

"They've still got to learn how to fight as a wing and as part of a larger Flight," Terin pointed out.

"That won't take long," Fiona replied.

Fiona was right; in less than three months the dragons and riders were drilling as groups, wings, and even as a small flight.

They returned to the firestone mine several times for more firestone, finally sending a half wing down under J'nos for a sevenday to mine more.

"We were very careful," J'nos explained. "We only worked where it was easy and never dug too far in."

At the same time, T'mar arranged for Fiona to resume her lessons flying *between*, often inviting her to join him as referee in the wing and flight exercises.

Spurred by T'mar's comments earlier about her weight, Fiona took to flying every day, often helping the traders by carrying loads slung under Talenth to their various depots scattered around central Pern. She was careful to arrange that such favors were returned in full, particularly ensuring that Terin was never left to bear the burden of the Weyr's management unaided.

T'mar had taught and drilled Fiona and Talenth on all the recognition points throughout Pern from the massive Red Butte to the spires of High Reaches Weyr—from a safe distance—from Nerat Tip to Southern Boll, from Ista Hold to the icy Far Watchers until Fiona could instantly and accurately recall the images for any place at any time.

"We're drilling now," T'mar explained as they planned for a night jump to Fort Hold not long after Fiona's "sixth" Turn, "because you'll need to know this when we return to our time, and with Thread falling, there may not be any chance to practice." He did not add, but Fiona guessed, that the other reason he wanted her and Talenth fully trained was in case something happened to Cisca or her Melirth. "We must pay particular attention to time," he reminded her.

Fiona nodded and took a steadying breath to still her racing heart. She was going back to where she lived, when she lived there.

T'mar says for us to send Zirenth the image, Talenth told her.

"All right," Fiona replied, concentrating on the image in her mind.

T'mar says we will lead them, Talenth reported a moment later with unalloyed pride in her voice.

Fiona's eyes widened and she took another deep breath before nodding to herself.

Ready? she asked Talenth. When her gold dragon rumbled in acknowledgment, Fiona said, *Let's go!*

The cold, dark nothingness of *between* enveloped them. Fiona scarcely noticed it, she was concentrating so hard on her destination. In a moment they burst out into the sky above Fort Hold, the Harper Hall visible to their left, and Fiona ordered Talenth to start a slow rightward spiral down, checking over her shoulder to be certain that Zirenth had followed them. She smiled as she caught sight of the bronze trailing behind her, his multifaceted eyes barely returning the moonlight.

Below them, from the Hold, Fiona heard the high-pitched bugling challenge from Forsk, the Hold's green watch-wher.

Tell her it's okay, Fiona said to Talenth. Immediately, Forsk's challenge changed to a warble of greeting. She looked down behind her, to where the watch-wher's lair was slowly receding away, and waved at the bright eyes of the watch-wher.

Ask Zirenth if he's ready, Fiona replied.

T'mar says to go to Fort Weyr, high, Talenth said.

"More drill!" Fiona exclaimed laughing. She drew forth her image of Fort Weyr, checked the night sky around her, and had Talenth relay the image to Zirenth.

Good, Talenth said. Fiona smiled and gave Talenth the word to go *between.*

An instant later they were high above Fort Weyr in the same night at nearly the same time. A wave of dizziness engulfed Fiona and she nearly fainted, gripping the riding straps tightly and leaning forward against Talenth's neck.

T'mar! Fiona cried. *Too many times!*

She only sensed T'mar's feeble response, finding the shadowy form of the bronze behind her. Without waiting, Fiona formed the image of Igen in her mind and ordered Talenth and Zirenth to jump *between* back to safety.

The watch dragon bugled worriedly as they reappeared in the warm Igen air and swiftly descended to the Weyr Bowl below, dragons and riders scrambling toward them anxiously.

"Get T'mar!" Fiona shouted above the din as she struggled to shake off the severe lethargy that had turned her legs to stone and kept her shivering in fright.

"Come on down, Weyrwoman," F'jian called, raising his arms wide. "I'll catch you!"

Sluggishly, Fiona undid her straps and threw her leg over Talenth's neck to slide down off it and into F'jian's waiting arms.

He caught her easily with one arm under her knees and the other under her shoulders.

"Are you all right?" he asked worriedly, peering down into her eyes.

Fiona found herself looking up at him, seeing the intensity of his gaze, sensing his concern, and suddenly she felt more than all right, in fact—a bugle from Talenth startled her back to reality.

"Yes," she said shakily, gesturing for him to set her down. "Thanks for catching me."

"My pleasure," F'jian replied with more warmth than Fiona found comfortable. Had he been about to kiss her? Had she been about to kiss *him*?

They were the same age or nearly, but Fiona was startled by the flood of emotions that surged within her. I'm not ready, she told herself firmly. Her body disagreed.

NINETEEN

White wine for wonder,
Red wine for blunder.

Wherhold, Late Evening, AL 500.8.18

Fiona grinned to herself as she gripped Terin tighter to calm her as Talenth steepened her spiral downward to the landing area outside of the Wherhold.

"I thought dragons didn't see in the dark," Terin called back over her shoulder nervously.

"They see," Fiona assured her. "Just not as well as watchwhers."

Terin's response was a wordless noise, not quite a squeak.

Terin's noise was nothing compared to T'mar's when Fiona had told him her plans earlier that day.

"There's nothing to worry about," Fiona had assured him. "You and the rest are going to be drilling, Karina is here to keep the pots stirred, and Terin and I need some time with Nuella." She'd paused, waiting until he opened his mouth in protest before adding, "It's the polite thing to do."

T'mar's protest had turned into a strangled noise.

"As Weyrwoman, it's my duty to maintain relations with our

holds," Fiona had added, her tone as demure as she could make it without laughing.

T'mar seemed ready to burst with objections and Fiona's expression dared him to try but the wingleader had finally managed to say only, "As you will, Weyrwoman."

Fiona had savored his assent for the victory it was. Ever since her almost-kiss with F'jian, and T'mar's comments about her weight, Fiona had been very careful of her behavior around the male riders. It wasn't that she didn't trust them, it was that she didn't trust herself—or know how to handle her feelings.

Thus the trip to the Wherhold and Nuella, who was nearest her age.

She jumped down first and then helped Terin dismount. The other girl was a bit shaky but recovered quickly.

A figure approached them from the shadows and called out, "Weyrwoman?"

It was Zenor.

"Zenor!" Fiona cried gladly. "How's the baby?"

"Nalla's doing fine, Weyrwoman," Zenor replied with a broad grin. "She's even sleeping through the night, now." His grin slipped as he added, "Mostly."

Nalla was born within the expected time after Nuella's wedding, just—close enough that Zenor had to endure many good-natured taunts from envious wherholders.

"To what do we owe the honor?" he asked, as he gave her a strong hug and then moved to hug Terin, who squeaked in awkward surprise at the gesture.

"We're here to beg shelter," Fiona told him. She gestured for him to lead the way. "In particular, we want to talk with Nuella."

"Watch-wher business?" Zenor asked.

Fiona felt herself blush. "No, it's more . . . personal."

"Ah . . . girl business!" Zenor said knowingly.

"Sort of," she admitted.

Zenor wrapped an arm around her shoulders comfortingly and led them to the quarters that he and Nuella shared. The air held a touch of the strange odor that Fiona associated with newborns—a mix of many things, including powders, incense, the warm musk of watch-wher, and a faint whiff of used diapers. It was not quite unpleasant nor quite appealing.

From her other side, Terin leaned close and murmured, "It smells like babies."

"It should," Zenor replied, much to Terin's chagrin. "Although it should really smell like just one baby, sometimes it seems as though Nalla is determined to make the stink of three babies."

"Fiona!" Nuella's voice called welcomingly from inside the room. "And is that Terin?"

"It is," Terin said, moving forward into the room. "Fiona's come to talk about boys."

"Oh," Nuella said. Fiona and Zenor entered the room at that moment, and Nuella turned her face toward them, adjusting her grip on Nalla as she did. With a grin toward Zenor, she added, "They have their uses, most times."

Zenor helped Fiona to a seat and then asked her frankly, "Would you like me to leave you alone?"

"No, stay, Zenor," Nuella said before Fiona could reply. She nodded toward Fiona. "Anything you say here stays between these walls. Zenor is an excellent listener, a good counsel, *and* he's a boy—he has insights I might not."

"But—"

"I'll get some wine," Zenor said, rising from his chair and leaving quickly.

"Here," Nuella said, gesturing toward the baby sleeping in her arms, "help me put her in her crib."

Fiona found herself moving before she thought about it. With a sly grin, Nuella slid the baby into Fiona's arms before rising from her chair and beckoning to Fiona and Terin to follow her.

They went into the next room, one that had been recently hewn out of the rock to accommodate its newest inhabitant. The walls were finished with touches of wood and daubed with a pink coloring. The smell of new baby was stronger there.

"Bottom first, then slide your arms out from under her head," Nuella instructed as she nodded toward the crib.

"I know how," Fiona said with a touch of acerbity in her voice.

"But you've never done it before," Nuella replied, her tone of voice carrying two meanings.

With a tender glance at the beautiful child in her arms, Fiona slid Nalla into her crib.

"I'm not sure I'm ready," Fiona said, as she slid her arm slowly out from under Nalla's head.

"If you think you're not ready, you're not ready," Nuella assured her. "There's no reason to rush."

"I know that," Fiona replied, her tone just short of a snap. "It's just that . . ."

"I see," Nuella said after it was clear that Fiona had finished speaking. "Sometimes you'd like to, is that it?"

Fiona nodded before remembering that Nuella was mostly blind, then said, "Yes."

"And you're afraid that you might?" Nuella asked.

"I'm afraid of the consequences," Fiona said, nodding toward the sleeping baby. "Not just *that*, but also how it will affect the other riders."

"Worry about yourself," Nuella told her. "You can't control how the riders will feel, and besides, they will have feelings whether you do anything or not—you and Terin are the only two eligible women for them."

"There are trader girls, too," Terin piped up.

"Not eligible," Nuella said. "*They* won't be going back to your time in nine months."

"Nine months," Fiona repeated thoughtfully.

"That's not much time at all," Terin said.

"And then it will be more than seven Turns before I'll see either of you again," Nuella mused regretfully. She gestured toward her sleeping daughter. "She'll have over seven Turns then."

"I'll have almost fourteen," Terin said. She glanced at Fiona. "I'll be nearly the same age as you were when we came here."

They heard the sounds of Zenor returning in the other room and moved to join him.

"Wine," Zenor said as he placed a tray on their dining table, snaking glasses around to each in turn. He poured for Nuella first and carefully placed the glass in her outstretched hand. He waited until she'd tasted it and pronounced it "Wet" before he served the others.

"Are you trying to get us drunk?" Fiona asked as she eyed the large glass Zenor had filled to the brim in front of her.

"Of course!" Zenor agreed pleasantly. He filled his own glass and raised it. "To Fiona, Weyrwoman of Pern!"

"Fiona!" Terin and Nuella echoed enthusiastically. Fiona went bright red. Terin took a large gulp of her wine and giggled.

"To Nuella, Wherwoman of Pern!" Terin cried, raising her glass once more. Fiona sipped her cool wine only to find Zenor scowling at her.

"This is not Benden white, Weyrwoman," Zenor told her brusquely. "This wine is *meant* to be gulped!"

"It is?"

Zenor nodded emphatically. "I said to Silstra, 'Silstra, I've two very nervous weyrfolk who need to talk and laugh—what sort of drink would you recommend?'"

"You told Silstra?" Fiona cried, aghast.

"I did indeed," Zenor said, raising his glass again and gesturing that she should do the same. "And she said, 'Well, if it were the Weyrwoman, she'd have to have Benden white, but as I *know* it isn't, then you should have this instead. It doesn't cost much and they won't remember in the morning.'"

"And you believed her?" Terin demanded in surprise.

"I wasn't sure," Zenor confessed, refilling their glasses. "I imagine I'll find out in the morning."

What Fiona found out in the morning was that her head ached terribly, her mouth felt funny, and she was sure she'd said far more to Zenor about her worries than she'd ever imagined.

Somewhere between the third and the fourth bottle of wine— they seemed to appear from *between*—Fiona found herself pouring out all her worries and fears to Zenor. Nuella had quietly taken herself off to bed.

" . . . and I almost kissed him!" Fiona exclaimed as she summed up her encounter with F'jian.

"I'm glad you didn't," Terin murmured beside her, her eyes carefully fixed on her glass.

"He's cute but he's not my kind," Fiona admitted, dimly becoming aware that she was missing something from Terin's response.

"Tell me more about F'jian," Zenor said to Terin. She blushed but, under his gentle questioning, proceeded to regale them with tales about his kindness, his smile, his strong arms—

"I'll say!" Fiona agreed, earning a scowl from her friend. Again feeling that she was missing something, Fiona turned to Zenor appealingly, but the goldcrafter only cut his eyes toward Terin, indicating that she should keep listening.

"What does he think of you?" Zenor asked Terin softly.

"I don't think he knows I exist," Terin said morosely.

"He likes your cooking," Fiona told her, earning herself another glower from Terin.

"I think she's looking for more than that," Zenor told Fiona quietly.

"Oh," Fiona said, suddenly understanding. Her face split into a broad grin and she turned to Terin. "You fancy him!"

"He seems like a good choice to me," Zenor observed smoothly, smiling at Terin. He refilled Fiona's glass and nodded for her to have some more wine while he said to Terin, "And if he likes you, he'll show excellent sense."

"But I've not yet thirteen Turns!"

"Age has nothing to do with it," Zenor told her kindly. He smiled fondly as he continued, "Nuella hadn't more than twelve Turns when she first kissed me."

"What was it like?" Fiona asked in wonder.

Zenor blushed bright red. "It was marvelous."

Terin let out a deep sympathetic sigh and Fiona found herself following, although in her mind's eye it wasn't F'jian she thought of kissing—the person was a nebulous image, taller, older, but no one she could quite identify with certainty.

"Maybe you should just kiss him," Fiona suggested to Terin. "Like Nuella."

Terin's eyes grew huge at the notion and she shook her head in mute denial.

"From what I've heard," Zenor began, "from Fiona—" He nodded to the Weyrwoman. "—and T'mar and countless others, you're the sort of woman that any dragonrider would be proud to call his mate—"

"Ew!" Terin exclaimed, scrunching up her face. "I don't want to . . ." She trailed off uncomfortably.

"Well, you want to kiss him, don't you?" Fiona demanded matter-of-factly. Reluctantly Terin nodded, and Fiona's face took on a triumphant expression, but before she could speak, Zenor said, "Kissing is a good thing." Fiona glanced at him sharply, but he persisted, "A kiss is good enough by itself for most people I know."

Fiona closed her mouth, considering his words.

"And a kiss isn't such a big thing that it would of itself cause anyone to talk too much," Zenor continued, topping off Terin's glass and passing it to her. She sipped reflexively. Zenor turned the conversation to Fiona, asking, "And who would you kiss, Weyrwoman?"

It was Fiona's turn to blush then. Sometime later she felt the warmth of Terin's head resting on her shoulder and realized that the younger woman had fallen asleep.

Zenor seemed not to notice, as he was engaged in a lengthy account of Silstra's wedding and Kindan's part in it, a topic which Fiona found quite engaging.

"M'tal said that he's with Lorana now," Fiona broke in as Zenor paused to sip his wine.

"I don't know who that is," Zenor told her and raised a hand to stop her from telling him, saying, "And if she's from the future, I think it best if I know nothing more."

Fiona stopped, frustrated, until Zenor asked if she would share her memories of Kindan, which she gladly did. Somehow her memories reminded her of her flight to Fort Hold with T'mar and that got her talking about T'mar.

" . . . he's so demanding, always saying, 'Do it three times, then you'll know!'" she exclaimed, shaking her head and suddenly wishing she hadn't. The room started spinning. Zenor was instantly at her side, deftly removing the glass from her hand and steadying her, offering her a drink from a glass of water and talking soothingly all the while.

When she recovered, she shrugged off Zenor's suggestion that she get some rest. She had to tell him something, she was certain, but she couldn't think what. It took him a while to realize that something was troubling her but the moment he did, he peered directly into her eyes and asked her quietly, "Are you in love with him?"

"Kindan?" Fiona asked in response. "Or T'mar?"

"Or both?"

"A Lady Holder doesn't—" Fiona responded instantly, her face set in a frown.

"A Weyrwoman *can*," Zenor told her kindly.

"But he has Lorana!" Fiona objected.

"And you would never come between him and the one he loves," Zenor observed respectfully. "But you don't have to tear your heart apart to save his, no more than you have to avoid kissing T'mar."

"Why would I want to kiss T'mar?" Fiona had asked, suddenly feeling very tired and very confused.

"I wouldn't know," Zenor admitted with a slight shake of his head. He rubbed the back of his neck wearily. "Perhaps I was seeing things where they weren't." He gestured to Terin. "I think we should get her to a proper bed before she gets a crick in her neck."

Fiona turned to gaze down at her friend, stroking her dark hair fondly. "She is such a good one."

"She is at that," Zenor agreed, rising as he extended an arm toward Fiona. With some effort, she found her feet and helped Terin to hers, and somehow they found their bed and slipped into it.

It was no surprise to Fiona to find that she had slept in her clothes, nor that Terin's breath was foul. She suspected hers was just as bad and turned her head away to spare the young headwoman from it.

They returned to the Weyr much later than Fiona had expected, both somewhat relieved and somewhat subdued by their night's festivities, seen off by a weary Zenor and a warm and wakeful Nuella.

"Don't forget that you have a home here," Nuella said, hugging each of them in turn.

"Next time, we'll let you change the baby," Zenor added with a grin.

"Deal," Terin replied, rubbing her temples wearily, "as long as you don't serve us any wine."

"You might think now that you'll never drink again," Zenor warned her. "But I suspect you'll be wrong."

"Oh," Terin replied, "I might drink again. Just never that much."

Now, as Talenth was challenged by the watch dragon, Fiona felt a sense of relief to be back at Igen. Her questions and worries were not all resolved, but she felt certain that they would not overwhelm her.

T'mar greeted them with a mixture of relief and concern: glad to have them back but worried about their demeanor. "I take it you were not served Benden white."

"How did you guess?" Terin wondered.

"You wouldn't have such awful hangovers this late in the day," T'mar replied with a humorous snort.

"Silstra was told that she wasn't serving the Weyrwoman," Terin replied, glancing over to Fiona with a grin.

"I'm glad to hear that," T'mar said. "I'd hate to think that the Weyrwoman of Igen was being served second-class wine."

"The Weyrwoman of Igen is not sure she wants to be served *any* wine for a long time," Fiona told him.

"I understand," T'mar said with feeling. "All the same, I'm glad that you two had some time to yourselves, away from all this . . ." He gestured to the gathering riders, groping for the right word.

"Maleness?" Fiona suggested.

"I was going for exuberance," T'mar said, "but I think you've got the better word for it." He paused a moment before adding solicitously, "Is it a great strain for you two?"

"Being the only women who came from our time?" Fiona asked in clarification. At T'mar's reluctant nod, she continued, "Yes, it is. A strain and a temptation, too."

T'mar sighed. "I was afraid that it would come to that at some point."

"But do you think that you could have managed without us?"

T'mar pondered the question for only a moment before shaking his head resolutely. "No."

"So," Fiona continued, "that being the case, we shall just have to persevere, shan't we?"

"You're old enough, and Talenth is old enough, that you two could go back to Fort Weyr—"

"Oh, no!" Fiona cut across him. "I'm Igen's Weyrwoman, wingleader, and I will stay until we *all* go back!"

Wisely, T'mar said nothing in reply.

But if T'mar said nothing, he made up for it in his actions over the next several months. There wasn't a day when the dragonriders weren't drilling: flaming or practicing formations or practicing formations and flaming or practicing formations, flaming, and going *between* all at the same time. He drove everyone to exhaustion. Tempers flared, but no blows were exchanged until the beginning of the third month since Fiona's visit to the wherhold.

Fiona and Terin, for their part, had found themselves often at the Wherhold—one of them was there at least one night every sevenday. Terin and Fiona both had experience changing Nalla's diapers, feeding her, and wiping spittle and other bodily fluids off of her and themselves when things went wrong. Partly this was a consequence of Terin's insistence that they provide Nuella and Zenor with time to themselves. Privately, Fiona was pretty certain that Zenor and Nuella had no lack of volunteers from among the remaining holders—after all, for all their humility, they *were* the Lord and Lady of the wherhold, and even if they found it strange, the rest of the holders from Silstra on down felt it not only their duty but their honor to treat them with the respect and deference that would be given any Lord Holder.

Terin's services were more than simple repayment of a kindness: They were part of a trade she'd arranged with Zenor and Nuella—to help her find and fashion a suitable gold ring. Terin kept silent on her intent with the ring, but Fiona was willing to bet, in the silence of her mind at least, that the ring would be sized to fit a young man's hand—probably that of a certain bronze rider.

So it was a double shock when the riders returned that evening to land in the Weyr Bowl to see F'jian leap from his bronze Ladirth, race over to J'gerd's brown Winurth, and bodily drag the brown rider down to the ground.

"How dare you!" F'jian shouted as he slammed J'gerd to the ground.

From her seat on the queen's ledge beside Fiona, Terin let out a shriek.

"Hold!" Fiona cried, her voice echoing loudly around the Weyr, her power of command surging as she reached out to Talenth and, in an instant, stilled both riders and dragons as though they'd been frozen in the wastes.

T'mar raced over to the two as they stood grappled but unmoving, cast a mixed look of admiration and—fear?—toward Fiona, then gestured for her to release them.

Fiona did nothing of the sort, instead racing from her perch on her ledge to stand beside T'mar, gazing at the two riders as they stood breathing raggedly, fighting against her control.

Let them go, a voice urged her. Fiona glanced around in surprise for the source and found no one—all eyes were locked on the two riders. With a hiss, she released her hold on the two even as J'keran and J'nos reached for the two riders and drew them apart.

"What happened?" Fiona demanded, glancing from F'jian to J'gerd and then to T'mar. The wingleader shrugged.

"He accused me—" F'jian began hotly but broke off abruptly as he spotted Terin in the distance.

"You should know better—" T'mar began consolingly.

"Don't talk to me, wingleader!" F'jian snapped back. "You have no command over me."

"I do," Fiona told him softly.

"A Weyrwoman is a Weyrwoman when her dragon rises," F'jian retorted, the veins on his neck straining with his anger.

"No," Fiona replied, her voice steady and cold. "A Weyrwoman becomes senior Weyrwoman when her queen is the first to mate in a new weyr." She gestured around the Bowl. "Do you see any other queen dragons here?" F'jian swallowed and glanced away from her, and she continued, "So we know that if Talenth rises, I will be senior Weyrwoman."

"It won't happen here," F'jian said in a snarl.

"No, it won't," Fiona agreed. She leaned in toward him, her eyes narrowed dangerously. "And it doesn't matter. Because I *am* a Weyrwoman, here or at Fort Weyr in the future. And because I am, the dragons—and their riders—listen to me."

F'jian's eyes started in alarm, but he dropped his head, unwilling to meet her gaze.

Fiona felt herself in a strange place, in a moment in time where she knew that whatever she did was crucial, would alter not only her future but the future of everyone here—perhaps even all of Pern.

You can do it. The voice wasn't the strange one, it was an echo of Nuella's faith in her, of Tannaz's eyes, of Aleesa's confidence, of

Mother Karina's strength. Without looking, Fiona knew that the old trader woman was near, watching, unable and unwilling to interfere.

The moment was Fiona's alone.

She walked closer to the young bronze rider, raised a hand under his chin, and forced his head up so that his eyes met hers. "What should we do, bronze rider?"

F'jian met her look with a mixture of shame and horror.

"I can imagine what J'gerd said to you," Fiona told him calmly, ignoring the sudden shift of the brown rider beside her. "And I'm sure he regrets it."

"Bronze rider," J'gerd spoke slowly, miserably, "I apologize for insulting you and your intentions."

"Pretty lame," Fiona told him out of the corner of her mouth. "You've been teasing him unmercifully for at least a month, I'm sure."

J'gerd's reaction confirmed Fiona's suspicions and she berated herself for not acting sooner. T'mar might be the oldest bronze rider here, but his power over the now-grown weyrlings had been fading every day. And, as it faded, the responsibility for the Weyr fell more and more on Fiona's shoulders—shoulders that up until this moment she had felt too frail for the strain.

Now, as she felt Talenth's silent love, approval, and strength, and as she felt something even more—the unspoken fealty not only of dragons to their queen but of their riders to their queen's rider—now, Fiona knew she'd made a mistake. Risen or not, mated or not, Weyrwoman or not, hers was the responsibility and her shoulders—so much thinner than her father's—had all the strength of Fort Hold and Fort Weyr supporting them.

"T'mar," she ordered, "get the suits." She paused, glancing at J'gerd and F'jian. "These two are going to get their chance to knock the stuffing out of each other."

Fiona felt but did not see T'mar's nod and heard him as he turned and delegated a group of riders to bring out the thick stuffing suits.

As the riders set up an impromptu circle, Fiona caught sight of Mother Karina and nodded to her. The old woman took the glance for an invitation and joined her.

"What are they doing?"

"I thought you would have seen this earlier," Fiona said in surprise. Four riders struggled in, two each to the heavily padded suits that they carried between them. "If riders have a disagreement, we can't let them fight to the death—their dragons would be lost with them."

Karina nodded, then gestured to the suits. "And those . . . ?"

"They are heavily padded," Fiona told her, adding with a smile, "and very restricting."

The two riders were being helped to drag on the thick trousers and tunic, then were engulfed in fluffy helmets and huge, balled gloves.

"I've only seen one other fight myself," Fiona said, shaking her head. "There is something about being back in time, by the First Egg, that makes riders more irritable."

"Queen riders, too?" Karina asked softly.

Fiona nodded bleakly. "Queen riders, too."

"So who knocks the stuffing out of you when you need it?" Karina wondered.

"Usually, I do," Fiona admitted sourly.

"Hmm," Karina murmured, her expression neutral.

"They'll be exhausted before too long," Fiona predicted as the two riders stood opposite each other and began the formal salute.

"How long will you let them fight?" Terin demanded from behind. Fiona turned to the younger woman and pursed her lips before answering, "Until one of them can't fight anymore."

"Won't or can't?" Terin persisted.

"Can't," Fiona told her firmly.

F'jian delivered the first blow, rocking J'gerd back on his heels. The brown rider kept his hands at his sides.

"You wanted this fight!" Fiona shouted at J'gerd angrily. J'gerd looked at her entreatingly, but Fiona shook her head, her anger growing. "You fight, brown rider."

Reluctantly, J'gerd raised his hands to block F'jian's blows, but the wiry bronze rider ducked around him and started pummeling the brown rider on his side, harmlessly.

"If you don't fight now, J'gerd," Fiona called to him, "I'll have you fight again tomorrow and the next day until you do fight."

"Why are you forcing him?" Terin demanded in horror.

"So that he will never want to fight again."

"That's stupid!"

"Yes, it is," T'mar agreed as he crossed to Fiona's side. "But it is the only way to get them to stop."

F'jian landed a good blow on J'gerd's face, bloodying the brown rider's nose and suddenly J'gerd was fighting. He lunged into F'jian and landed one solid blow, but then the bronze rider dodged, slammed both gloved hands into J'gerd's back, and sent the brown rider stumbling away.

When J'gerd turned back, F'jian caught him another double-fisted blow in the face, sending J'gerd reeling backward until he stumbled and fell down.

"Enough." Fiona said the word quietly, but it traveled throughout the circle with a weight of its own. She rushed over to kneel beside J'gerd, eyeing his bruised face with muted sympathy before glancing up at F'jian. The bronze rider was breathing heavily and had a cut over his right eye, that Fiona judged painful but superficial.

"Is honor satisfied now, bronze rider?" she asked him in a tone that dictated the response.

"Yes, Weyrwoman," F'jian replied. Fiona nodded to the other riders, saying, "Get them out of the suits."

When F'jian was once more standing in front of her in his riding clothes, Fiona pointed to his cut. "I bet that stings."

"Not much," F'jian said cockily.

Before she could have any second thoughts, Fiona raised her hand, spun on her heel, and slapped him hard on the cheek.

"I'll bet *that* does," she growled as she turned back to face him, her hand raised for a repeat performance. In the distance, Talenth rumbled angrily, echoed by the distressed calls of the Weyr's dragons.

"Yes, it does, Weyrwoman," F'jian cried, his tough stance disintegrating into the bewildered look of a young man uncertain of his ground and standing.

"Good," Fiona growled, hating herself even as she said it. "Don't make it necessary for me to do that ever again."

As she turned away, Terin rushed past her, crying in sympathy for F'jian's injuries.

Fiona knew that Terin would be furious at her for days to come, but she also knew that she'd done exactly what was necessary to enforce the discipline of the Weyr. She did not turn back when Terin loudly commiserated with F'jian over his injuries and his hurt pride, but her lips curled upward when she heard Terin kiss him soundly. She had hoped that would happen.

T'mar stepped in front of her, one eyebrow raised questioningly as he glanced back over her shoulder.

"What now, Weyrwoman?"

"Well, they'll have to be punished," Fiona said with a sigh. "J'gerd will get extra duties for the next fortnight."

"And F'jian?"

"Bronze riders are not exempt from Weyr discipline," Fiona said. "I think I have a special duty for F'jian."

"And that would be?"

"I think that Talenth and I need to spend more time here," Fiona said. "And as Terin so often represents the Weyr with the Wher-hold, I believe that I shall require F'jian to provide her transport." Her lips turned upward as she added, "She is trading babysitting duties with Nuella and Zenor for some special trinket." She paused. "Let him change diapers for a while."

Beside her, T'mar chuckled evilly.

For the next several sevendays, Terin slept elsewhere than Fiona's weyr.

"You've only solved one problem, you know," Mother Karina said to Fiona late one evening as they tended the hearth together.

Fiona made an attempt to look quizzical, but the old woman was having none of it. With a sigh, Fiona nodded.

"It's difficult," she said.

"It always is," Karina agreed gently.

"I mean, I've got a queen and I'm Weyrwoman," Fiona objected.

Mother Karina smiled unsympathetically. "I'm an old woman and a trader."

Fiona fumed to herself at that response, and all the while Mother Karina simply waited patiently until Fiona recovered her composure and carefully examined Karina's words and compared them to her own. At which point her expression fell and she sighed again, her lips turned down ruefully, as she said, "So we've got the same problem, only different."

Karina nodded silently, her eyes gleaming in congratulation of Fiona's insight.

"But I'm scared!" Fiona blurted in a wail.

"Of course you are," Karina said, leaning forward to pat Fiona's hand reassuringly. "That's natural. You wouldn't be you if you weren't."

Fiona avoided her problem by plunging herself even deeper in Weyr matters, but as sevendays became months and they neared the time when the older dragonriders were due to reappear and the massed riders would return to their proper time at their proper Weyr, Fiona realized that time was forcing her hand.

Terin never quite apologized to Fiona for leaving her, but she did return, although she never spent quite as much time with Fiona after that, preferring to spend most of it in F'jian's company—that much of Fiona's plan had worked out so perfectly that she was not at all surprised to find that Terin had given F'jian her hard-earned gold ring as a Turn's End present. Judging from Terin's expression the next morning, F'jian's response had been everything that the young headwoman could desire. As Terin had celebrated her thirteenth Turn several sevendays beforehand— just twelve days after Fiona had herself turned sixteen—Fiona did not feel it necessary to comment to either headwoman or bronze rider on the new arrangement.

For her part, Fiona found herself growing misty-eyed as she caught the sunsets over Igen, the desert all hued with reds and purples in a cloudless sky, the stars suddenly appearing like brilliant jewels visible in an instant, the two moons with their stately progression, the Dawn Sisters waiting to greet her in the early morning or, more often, to find her greeting them in the strange double-day cycles that they had adopted so long ago to manage the unbearable midday heat.

Fiona had found the time to engage Terregar and Zenor in solving the problem of a flamethrower that didn't require the old firestone.

"The holders would pay plenty for it," had clinched the argument—she had so intrigued Zenor and Terregar with the difficulties of the project that they only needed the merest incentive for trade to commit themselves wholeheartedly to the project.

Trade flourished between Weyr and Wherhold. Azeez and Mother Karina shrewdly had established a major depot at the wherhold, allowing for a convenient meeting place for the Igen riders and a permanent basis for expansion in the whole central region of Pern.

When Terin was at the Wherhold, Fiona would spend time with Mother Karina and other traders interested in cooking, developing new recipes and perfecting old ones, all the while learning and engaging in the joys of gustatory arts.

But it was T'mar who engaged her attention the most. Since the fight between F'jian and J'gerd, the older bronze rider had treated her differently. Worse, his treatment of her seemed to change and morph almost daily. He would be obsequious one day, disdainful the next, reclusive, fearful, garrulous.

Almost in response, Talenth grew more willful and demanding. She insisted upon being ridden every day and often she would inveigle Fiona to take her for long flights or jumps *between* to far-off destinations. Her attitude toward the Weyr's remaining browns and bronzes alternated between standoffish and coquettish almost as frequently as T'mar's moods changed. Through it all, she was still respectful and adoring of her rider, but Fiona began to find herself fearing that she might wake one morning to a dragon inflamed with the mad bloodlust of a mating queen.

The brown and bronze riders all treated her differently, as did the blue and green riders. She could find none among the latter with whom she could bond as she had with F'dan—she missed him dearly—even if they were easier for her to be around than the sometimes overly sensitive bronzes and browns.

Of all of the riders, J'gerd's behavior toward her had changed the most. At first he had been fearful of her, but then he had sought her out, at first to apologize and later to confide. It had been his heartfelt loneliness—a loneliness with which Fiona found herself keenly sympathetic—that had decided Fiona to encourage the riders to spend more time mingling with the traders and the wherholders.

T'mar had been reluctant to permit the change until he discovered that it was not his decision to make. Fiona had been careful to limit the meetings so that no long-term relationships could form, only to have to be painfully broken when the dragonriders were forced to return to their time, but they had still left plenty of opportunity for dancing, singing, and an occasional heartfelt romance to blossom.

Resigned to her will, T'mar had enthusiastically joined in with the festivities, and Fiona was reasonably certain that there was at least one holder lass who would devoutly regret his leaving.

"We'll need to start clearing the unused weyrs," Fiona said to T'mar at their morning meeting. "The older riders will return in the next fortnight."

T'mar nodded. "I've spent some time with J'keran and F'jian discussing how we'll drill when they arrive." He paused before adding in correction, "And it's thirteen days, actually."

"We shouldn't linger here," Fiona cautioned him, accepting his correction with an irritated look.

"We think that we can get enough drill done in seventeen days."

"Is that enough?"

"It's all we can afford," T'mar told her simply.

Fiona narrowed her eyes at him suspiciously.

"Talenth will have three Turns then," he explained.

"What's that—oh," Fiona responded, breaking off in chagrin. "She'll be ready to rise."

"I thought you would want to have the largest choice possible," T'mar told her softly. "She deserves no less."

It was a moment before Fiona could find her voice. "Yes," she said quietly. "Yes, that's very considerate."

T'mar made a slight half-bow in his chair. "I try, Weyrwoman." He finished his *klah*, rose, and said to her, "And, with your permission, we will drill this morning and clean after midday."

"Yes, that seems good," Fiona agreed, also rising from the table. Karina, who had sat at the far side watching them in silence, glanced from one to the other and shook her head sadly. Fiona noticed and shot her a challenging look.

"You will be leaving in thirty days," Karina told her, pushing back her chair. "We must get ready."

Fiona grinned at her. "Last chance for ice!"

The cleaning, as Fiona had expected, was tiring and irritating. None of the riders were pleased with her as they sat for their evening meal, especially faced, as they were, with the knowledge that they would be repeating their efforts in other weyrs for the next sevenday at the least.

F'jian groaned as he stretched after dessert, glancing apologetically toward the Weyrwoman, but he was less out of sorts than many of the others who had not had to do such menial duties for the better part of a Turn.

"We need to leave the Weyr better than we found it," Fiona reminded, trying vainly to suppress a glower.

"I know Weyrwoman," F'jian replied apologetically. "It's just that my muscles forget."

"It'll be easier tomorrow," she assured him.

"Or the next day," J'keran muttered sardonically from his seat at the far end of the table.

"Or the next," Fiona agreed.

"They grumble but they're not upset." T'mar's voice coming from right beside her was startling; he had been silent throughout dinner. He seemed ready to say more but restrained himself.

"What?" Fiona prompted.

T'mar hesitated before replying, "I only wanted to say that I think you're doing a great job as Weyrwoman." He paused, again obviously weighing his words carefully, and seemed ready to remain silent until Fiona gave him a challenging look. "I hope you won't be angry at this, but I wonder how you will handle becoming *a* Weyrwoman when we return, and you are not *the* Weyrwoman."

"It'll be a relief," Fiona responded impulsively. T'mar raised an eyebrow at her questioningly, and Fiona reassessed her feelings. "I'll miss it, certainly, but I think I'm too young—"

"Once, maybe," T'mar interjected softly, shaking his head in firm denial. Fiona found herself meeting his soft brown eyes, really looking into them, and felt herself flush.

"Excuse me," she said hastily and rose from the table, moving as quickly as she could without attracting too much notice through the Dining Cavern and out into the still night of the Weyr Bowl.

She didn't know what she was doing; her feet moved instinctively until she found herself in Talenth's lair, her head leaning on the hinge of her beautiful gold's jaw, just in sight of her calmly whirling green eyes.

How long she stayed there, she couldn't say. It was only when she heard boots softly climbing up the queen's ledge and entering T'mar's weyr that she realized her purpose, and with a final caress of her beautiful queen, Fiona stepped out onto the queen's ledge and turned left, toward Zirenth's lair.

A noise, the sound of her shoe dislodging a rock, alerted him to her presence.

"Weyrwoman," T'mar said, coming from his bathroom, dressed in his sleeping tunic, "you startled me."

Fiona's eyes were wide, her breath rapid as she forced herself to cross the distance between them and looked up at him.

"Talenth will rise soon," she blurted, not saying the words she'd rehearsed before.

T'mar's eyes narrowed as he glanced toward the queen's weyr in alarm, then he looked back down at her. "Not today, surely."

"Soon," Fiona repeated. She raised a hand to stroke his cheek and was surprised at how smooth it felt. "I—I don't want her first time to be . . . my first time."

"I see," T'mar replied softly into the silence that stretched between them. He regarded her silently for a moment. "What about Kindan?"

Fiona shook her head soundlessly and buried her face against his chest, her arms loose around him.

T'mar drew back, raised a hand, and gently drew her chin up until she was looking into his eyes once more. And then he leaned down, draped one arm around her waist, and kissed her.

Much, much, much later, as T'mar lay breathing softly beside her, Fiona leaned over and twitched his chest sharply. T'mar's eyes flew open and met hers in surprise as she leaned over him, her hands moving toward places she had never been before. "You always say that to get it right, you must do it three times."

The bronze rider had only time for a startled smile before Igen's Weyrwoman leaned heavily into him for another kiss.

Drifting through euphoria and back to mere consciousness the words were said:

"I love you."

"I know."

But Fiona could never remember who said them, or if they were spoken simultaneously, or even uttered aloud.

TWENTY

Igen Weyr, Evening, AL 501.3.18

"I will miss you so much!" Fiona cried as she buried her head once more against Mother Karina's chest.

The last of the traders were gathered in their caravan, ready to return to their depots.

"It is likely you will never see me again," Karina told her softly, causing Fiona's tears to redouble in intensity. Fiona resisted as Karina pushed her away from her, forcing her to look her in the eyes as she said, "My life is richer for knowing you, child, and knowing that you will be there in the future to protect my children and their children."

"And theirs," Fiona vowed, her voice strong even through her sorrow.

"And theirs," Karina agreed, hugging Fiona tightly once more before parting again. "Do you know what a gift that is?"

Fiona shook her head and wiped her eyes free of the latest rain of tears.

"You will, one day," Karina foretold. She shoved Fiona toward her dragon and the assembled dragons and riders.

Fiona paused and turned back, pulling the heavy leather jacket off her shoulders.

"I almost forgot," she said, as she handed the Igen Weyr-woman's jacket to Azeez, who stood with an arm draped over his mother's shoulders. "Would you put this back in the Records Room for me? It belongs to the Igen Weyrwoman."

"I'll put it back for you," Azeez said, raising his eyebrows to add emphasis to his double meaning.

Fiona shook her head at him ruefully. "The next group will be from Benden Weyr. They'll probably trade with you, I've left a complete Record behind."

"They might trade," Azeez agreed, waving for her to join the waiting dragonriders. "We'll be certain to give them the chance, and we'll leave them goods to start with, as we agreed."

"Fair trade?"

"More than fair," Azeez said with a smile. "We are in your debt."

"If you get the chance, come visit us at Fort Weyr," Fiona begged.

"We will visit you," Azeez replied, his expression strangely smug. "Tenniz has seen it."

Fiona found her lips curving upward in the first happy expression she'd had in a sevenday. "I'll look forward to it!"

She gave him one final hug and turned away, racing toward Talenth.

At her orders, wing by wing, the healed dragons and riders of Fort Weyr rose and took their positions above the Star Stones, ready to return to their future, their duty, and their fate.

Fiona spared a moment for one final wave to the traders, then took a deep breath, squared her shoulders, and told her queen, *Let's go, Talenth!*

Above the Star Stones, the dragons blinked *between*, leaving only the wind and stars to guard the silent, empty Weyr.

EPILOGUE

Drummer, beat, piper, blow.
Harper, sing, and soldier, go.
Free the flame and sear the grasses,
Till the dawning Red Star passes.

Fort Weyr, AL 508.2.2

"We're here," Fiona said calmly to Terin perched in front of her as they burst into the skies above Fort Weyr. She signaled to T'mar and the bronze leader spread the word to the rest of the flight. Wing by wing the recovered convalescents of Fort Weyr and the now full-grown weyrlings wheeled and made a triumphant descent into the Weyr Bowl to be greeted by the startled and gleeful cries of their weyrmates. From the Kitchen Cavern a stream of riders and weyrfolk rushed out to greet them, their voices rising and carrying clearly from the Bowl into the air around Fiona.

She waited quietly as she watched K'lior rush to T'mar and grab him in a gleeful bear hug, saw the bronze wingleader give his report, saw K'lior's reaction as he noticed T'mar's bone-weariness, stifled a similar twinge of her own, and saw the riders and dragons disperse to their weyrs to rest up and recover from the strangeness of their three-Turn sojourn.

"There's Xhinna!" Terin called over her shoulder, pointing down to a forlorn figure coming from Fiona's weyr and scanning the skies above her anxiously. "Wait until she finds out I'm as old as she is!"

Fiona twitched at the words and the worries they aroused in her. Xhinna was a distant memory, a treasured friend buried in a mountain of moments they had not and would never share.

Fiona was suddenly aware that Terin had turned her head to face her. "What is it?"

Fiona shook her head slowly, unable to find the words. Somehow, Terin guessed; she looked into Fiona's eyes and told her, "No matter what the future, you will always be the Weyrwoman to me!"

Fiona smiled gratefully and, buoyed by those words, took Talenth down, back to her Weyr—and her home.

ACKNOWLEDGMENTS

I am very pleased once more to acknowledge Shelly Shapiro, ace editor at Del Rey, for her patience, encouragement, perseverance, and grit. I would also like to acknowledge, also once again, the marvelous Martha Trachtenberg for her brilliant copyediting. I would like to thank Judith Welsh, my editor at Transworld, for her keen insights and constant encouragement.

Donald Maass has been my literary agent since the very beginning, when he put me through a grueling two-hour phone interview when I first considered writing *Dragonsblood.* He continues to hold me to ever-higher standards.

Of course, none of this would be possible without Mum: Anne McCaffrey—love you!

Needless to say, any errors, omissions, or just strange ol' words are mine, all mine, and no one else's.